The Aurora Marelup Saga

5 Year Anniversary Edition

Serenity Rayne

Content Warning

Content warnings are an important element to any novel. I don't ever want to harm a reader. So for this reason, I will list the warnings here.

- 6 mates total

- med-fast burn

- Two of the guys fall madly in love

- m/m - m/m/m/m/m

- PNR Why Choose

- Blood, death, decapitation, gut garland

- Wolves, Dragons, bears, eagle

- **pregnancy books 3&5**

- **SHIFTED WOLF ON MATE** book 1&5

- True/fated mates

- Strong Female main character

- Twin Sandwich

- Bonus content and deleted scenes added

This is a paranormal why choose romance with poly elements. It's a journey of self-discovery and personal growth.

There are many situations included that are intended for MATURE audiences (18+)

Throughout this book, there are references/ instances that may trigger some individuals such as: **decapitation, murder, beheading, skull collecting, blood everywhere, attempted murder, group scenes, near death experiences, birth, ancient burial rites. Other woman drama.**

FMC is slightly unhinged and has no issues ripping her enemies to shreds to accomplish her goals.

Ultimate Skull Collector

Catherine E. Stull

Jennifer Bishop

Linnea Taylor-Sowders

If Dominik chased you...

Would you submit?

Author Ramblings:

Dear Readers,

It's been a hell of a ride since I started back in 2019. As I continue on my author journey, it's been a path of growth and constant learning. I feel in the last year my craft has grown from the savage and aggressive in your face FMC's to the ones that have depth and problems like the rest of us. As silly as it sounds, I call them more realistic fantasy female main characters. I feel like my girls have become more relatable over time and their worlds are more immersive than before.

Aurora has always had a special place in my heart. She was my first FMC I ever wrote, and she helped me heal a part of myself. Each of her mates that she gathered along the way had a quality that made them stand out. It's hard to write a single male main character that has all the qualities we wish to find. Reverse harem lets us have our cake and eat it too. I expanded this edition, giving Aurora and her men the much needed additional time they deserve. For those of you that loved her the first time around. I hope you get to fall in love with them all over again, reading it as a continuous story.

Blessed be.

Serenity

Inspiriational Playlist

Hail to the King - a7x
Welcome Home - Metallica
She-Wolf - Megadeth
Of Wolf and Man - Metallica
Crush'Em - Megadeth
Devil - Shinedown
Wish you were here- Pink Floyd
Nothing Else Matters- Metallica
Cemetery Gates - Pantera
Bulls on Parade- Rage Against the Machine
How Did You Love - Shinedown
Right Here Waiting - Richard Marx
Break Stuff- Limp Bizkit
Mission Impossible theme- Danny Elfman
Heathens- TwentyOne Pilots
The Blue Danube, Op.314 - Johann Strauss
Oh Tannenbaum- Sasha Cohn

PT. 1

INSPIRIATIONAL PLAYLIST

Pony- Ginuwine

November Rain- G-N-R

Feel Invincible- Skillet

Sail- AWOLNATION

Silent Lucidity- Queensryche

Architecture of Aggression- Megadeth

You Could be Mine- G-N-R

Popular Monster- Falling in Reverse

Take What You Want- Post Malone, Ozzy Osbourne

Look What You Made Me Do- Taylor Swift

The Chain (Gears of War 5)- Evanescence

I Am the Highway- Audioslave

I Am the Fire- Halestorm

Killer Wolf- Danzig

Outlaws & Outsiders- Cory Marks

The In-Between- In This Moment

PT. 2

PART TWO

Aurora's Family Tree

If you ever wondered how many children were born through this series or spinoffs, here's the list in its entirety.

You get to see and meet all the children in the Holiday Edition. If you haven't preordered it yet, here is the link.

The Aurora Marelup Holiday Edition

Aurora & Alaric

Tiamat

Mates: Draven & Khal

Children-Draven: Melione, Orion, Garyx

Children-Knox: Tria & Bethany

Ladon

Mate: Jade

Children: Crystal, Tyr

Aurora & Dimitri

Odette
Mate: Jackson

Children-Amber, Jackson Jr, Leia

Sage
Mate: Wyatt
Children: Wyatt Jr. Greer

Dimitri Jr.
Mate: Gasmy

Children: Dimitri 3rd, Jalen, Jonas

Aurora & Klaus

Keanu
Mate: Danica

Children-Seraphina, Angelica, Luke

Kirra

Mates: Takeo, Egon, Lance, Jakob

Children- Takeo: Khan

Children- Egon: Sapphire

Children- Lance: Denzel

Children- Jacob: Myra, Jaden

Aurora & Jayce

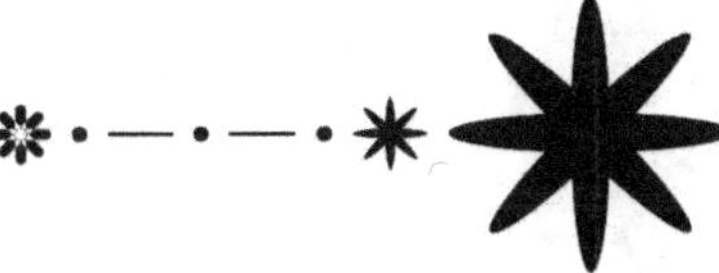

Luna
Mate: Marco
Children–Skaldi, Fenrir, Anca

Lucas
Mate: Zeta
Children– Lily, Lucas Jr

Aurora   &   Dominik

Noah
Mate: Gia
Children—Bryce, Belle

Isabella
Mate: Lara
Children— None

Aurora & Arnulf

Zephyr
Mate: Ember
Children–Mara, Kent

Lorelei
Mate: Boaz

Children– Hudson, Lyr, Emmi

CHAPTER 1

Prologue Ascend

OBERON

Royal Fae Court Winter 500AD

This morning I have received word that the other four fae kings have arrived for today's council meeting. The Drow have entirely broken with the beliefs of our race under the leadership of Lolth. They have fled to Illythirr in the Underverse to escape prosecution for their countless crimes. Hundreds have died because of the insurrection that Lolth started, trying to overthrow our once stable government.

The crystalline viewing room is made from varying quartz shades since it harmonizes well with our natural powers. For what I wish to do, I need the other four kings to touch the viewing pool at the same time to harness its full potential. The viewing pool I'm using today is made of pure lapis lazuli, meant to amplify astral travel and clairvoyance. I need to see into the future to ascertain precisely how much trouble the Drow will cause in the future.

Pacing within the viewing chambers, my anxiety has hit an all-time high. My heart hammers within my chest as I wait for the others to join me. First to arrive is King Arathorn Chaephyra of the Woodland Fae. Majestic, as always, he stands tall and proud. His skin a similar hue to the bark of a tree, and his long hair a smokey gray in color. In the tradition of his people, his crown is constructed of dragonroot and bloodstone.

"Blessings and health to you, Arathorn," I say with a flourished bow.

"Blessings and health to you, Oberon. I hope today is productive. The concerns you raised are rather troublesome if they come to fruition," Arathorn states before bowing to me in return. His lithe hands adjust his sand-colored robes before he moves to stand before the leaf carved in the edge of the viewing pool. Slightly I bow my head to him just as the door opens again.

King Arlen Trazana, the most flamboyant of all of us, enters next. He flutters his sliver-blue swallowtail-like wings before folding them behind him. Arlen has short, cropped blue hair, exceptionally on point today; he must have stopped and got a trim on the way here. Bowing deeply, he smiles, looking up at me. "Greetings and health to you and your home, Oberon." His voice hits tones that make mine pale in comparison. If I had to imagine what Gaia's voice sounded like, I would imagine it is similar to his.

Gracefully I return the bow and flourish my hand in the direction of the viewing pool. "Greetings and health to you and yours, Arlen. Please join Arathorn at the pool, if you would be so kind." A soft smile graces my lips as I stand back up again. Before Arlen moves past me, I adjust his flowing, shimmering baby-blue robes so that his folded wings wouldn't get tangled.

"Thank you, brother," Arlen says on his way to his place at the pool. He looks for his wind symbol and traces it with a single finger, smiling all the while. I catch him admiring his own reflection in the waters of the pool, looking over his perfect pale skin and gray, almost silver, eyes.

King Tanyth Parona of the Moon Fae and King Narbeth Quivaris of the Sun Fae arrive simultaneously, still bickering over which clan makes the best weapons. Rolling my eyes, I move forward to garner their attention. Once I possess both kings' attention, I bow deeply and flourish my hand in the direction of the viewing pool. "Greetings and health to you and yours," I say to both kings at the same time, showing no favoritism to either clan.

The stark contrast between the kings is evident in appearance, manners, and tone of voice. Tanyth responds in a soft musical tone. His bright blue eyes are mesmerizing, contrasted with his iridescent silver hair and pale skin. Narbeth, on the other hand, lacks the musical quality to his voice that most Fae possess. His flame-red hair and sunkissed golden-brown skin sing of the days he spends in the bright sunlight. They both respond with the traditional greeting and move to their places on the viewing table.

As the King of the High Fae, it is my place to keep order of all known species within the realms. Unfortunately, with Lolth breaking away from his kin and taking all of the Drow with him, this poses a significant safety issue within the realm. Once everyone is in position, I place my hand upon my mark and the pool's surface begins to ripple.

The initial vision moves to Skaldi Nyx Atriox, otherwise known as the Blood Queen. "Our first creation seems to be doing well, is she not?" Narbeth questions as the pool focuses on her rending the flesh from the Orcs that had invaded the southern part of her territory. The Orcs were released from the Underverse by the Drow; thankfully, Skaldi is strong enough to handle it.

"Yes, she is, but we need to see what the future holds if we don't interfere," I state, and the other kings agree with me. I move the visions forward twelve-hundred years, and Skaldi is in decline. Her Grandson, Nicodeamus Tepish, rises to power next and rules for almost three hundred years before the Drow rise-up. Battle after battle, the species of old are slowly slaughtered to extinction. Next, the Drow begin to march on the Strigoi as well as the human settlements. Each skirmish brings about a higher death toll until the human race has no paranormal defenders left to protect them. In the end, the humans are slaves, and our settlements are burned to ash.

Arlen, the most peaceful of us all, stands there with his hands in fists and his teeth gritted so hard his jaw trembles. "I implore you to allow us to interfere yet again. We must create a defender that no Drow will ever be able to destroy." His gray eyes flash wildly as he looks to each of us, hoping to sway the verdict.

"I second the motion; there are many powerful bloodlines that we can mix. Perhaps create a hybrid similar to our cousins, the Lythari, that helped create the Lycan and Dire Wolf races." Arathorn shrugs his shoulders as he passes a hand over the pool to the point in time where Anca Marelup is forced to take her mates. "What if we send Skaldi's grandson here, and he's a true mate of the last Marelup? We would have to send a special tincture to make sure the hybrid is created and survives gestation." Arathorn stands tall, knowing full well his plan so far is the most solid.

Leaning forward, waving my hand over the pool, the scene rewinds and then proceeds how Arathorn suggested. "Who shall we send with the tincture?" I question, looking directly at Arlen.

He rolls his eyes and huffs. "We can send my niece, Laurel, to deliver the tincture and make sure our plans are carried out to the letter." Arlen bows his head, having offered his niece's services for part of the plan.

"Excellent," is all I say before I wave my hand again, fast-forwarding through time. The Marelup Queen dies in labor, and our creation is born. Waving my hand again, moving time forward, we see our creation as a young child, shifting for the first time after being attacked by a cougar. She decimates her attacker and carries the head home. So far, so good. We leap through time again until she's about a hundred years old. Furrowing my brows, I study the tea the older woman keeps sending her. I rewind time to when the tea is packaged. Blood magic is at work, but to what end? Our creation's beast loves her protector's Bear; they're mates, but something in the tea is blocking the bond. "Should we interfere here and free their bond, so it flourishes?" I question the others.

"No," Tanyth states, then moves time forward and shows the importance of the stalled bond. We watch her battle time and time again, success after success. That is, until the Drow rise again. Hmm... She never took a dragon mate. Sebastian lives even after all of his deception.

"This blasphemy cannot be allowed to happen," Arlen says, then waves his hand over the water moving through time at a break-neck pace. He stops at a particular point and allows a Polar Bear to get involved. The course of history changes dramatically. Our creation takes an Ice Dragon – Gold Dragon hybrid as a mate. They birth twins, which is unheard of for Ice Dragons to do. The female has all the markers of Skaldi, plus the attributes of the Titanium and Silver dragons that had long since been extinct.

"Perfect," I say as I move time forward again, watching the hatchling mature and take her mate. Unexpectantly with the Drow's abduction, she ascends far younger than we had anticipated. The amount of power that child holds is staggering. Simultaneously we release our grips on the table and look at each other in shock. We may have just have figured out how to end the Drow once and for all. I stare down at the blank reflective surface of the pool in awe of what I had just seen. In my gut, I have a feeling this may be me signing my own death warrant. All of this interference isn't natural; then again, neither are the Drow. I can only hope the Goddess keeps me safe over the centuries to come. The other kings bow and leave quickly to carry out their part of this plan. At sunrise tomorrow, I shall set my part in motion. After that, it's all just a matter of time.

CHAPTER 2

Anca

My ancestral home resides at the top of one of the most treacherous mountains in the Moldivian range. Winding narrow cliffside roads are the only way to ascend the mountain to my castle. At the very peak, my family's castle sits. Tall, proud, white spires reach towards the heavens, getting lost within the cloud cover. The main gates are hand-forged wrought iron depicting a pair of wolves locked in battle. The roadway leading up to the castle doors are made of cobble stone; the clacking of the horses hooves can be heard where I sit. I seek refuge within the castle's library. So many centuries of knowledge are contained within these walls. The shelves are a myriad of colors on every subject you could imagine.

I'm stuck sitting here looking over the scrolls of the families whom have sons of proper age that make a good mate for me. The list feels never ending as I sort though the bloodlines, making sure no one is related to me. It's such tedious work, and my father wants a list of suitors I'm willing to meet. Gently I shake my head, looking over what seems like a mile-long list. Out of all the females of my family, I am the oldest to ascend. None of the healers know why it took over a hundred and fifty years for it to happen. All of the mystics my family consulted had no answers as to why. I honestly don't care; I don't want to face the trials to select my mates. Whatever happened to falling in love naturally? instead of being forcibly brought together and hoping they click. I furrow my brows as I ponder my soon to be sealed fate. Today, hopefully, will pass quickly and without incident.

The click of the latch for the door echoes in the library, forcing my eyes to raise and watch to see who has come to disturb me. The high priestess of the clan enters without knocking, carrying a jug and cups.

"Have you made a decision, Princess?" the priestess states, a sneer crosses her lips as she narrows her eyes.

"No," I state as tersely as possible. I don't want to have to deal with the priestess at this moment.

"The king expects a list from you by sundown today. Otherwise, he will send for the males I've selected for you to meet." The priestess tilts her head, looking at me, waiting for some sort of a reaction she can complain to my father about.

If she wasn't warming my father's bed, I would have slit her throat from ear to ear years ago. I roll my eyes, then I finally answer, resigning myself to my fate. "Fine, you and Father pick the males I'm supposed to meet. It's not like my choice makes any difference; you'll get your way in the end." I stand and grab the scrolls I was looking over and walk over to the fireplace. Before the priestess can react, I toss the lists into the fire, watching them turn to ash. I turn triumphantly, smiling, placing both hands on the tabletop, and staring at the priestess.

"You wonder why we make all the decisions for you, Princess; you're brash and impulsive," she says, flailing her hands in the air. "You'll never make any male a good mate with the way you are." The priestess waves her hand dismissively in my direction. "You need Alpha males to put you in your proper place and guide you to make the best decisions." She bares her canines at me as she looks back at the ornate pitcher she brought with her.

The priestess pours two cups of the scented tea she has brought with her. With a flourish and a smile, she places my favorite flower-covered teacup in front of me, filled to the brim. Suspiciously, I look at the cup before me, staring at the dark amber fluid within; then over to the priestess, studying her features. The priestess makes a big deal out of sipping at the tea before her. I scrutinize every movement of every muscle in her face and throat, trying to discern if she actually drank the tea or not.

I have never liked the priestess and her bossy ways; the trust has never been there, she always seems to have ulterior motives. The priestess is very close to Grigore and his family. Every waking moment she's encouraging me to take Vladimir as my mate. I ponder as I look down at my tea. It smells okay, and it would be rude not to drink it. Several moments pass before I raise the glass to my lips and drink the sweet tea. The priestess's expression changes, and a wicked smile plays upon her lips. Fuck, she tricked me. Deep in the recesses of my mind, my wolf begins to howl and rage. Something is wrong; my fight-or-flight instinct kicks in. I find out quite quickly that I can't summon my beast anymore. Suddenly, the fight drains out of me, and I just don't seem to care anymore.

The priestess moves to my side and walks me out of the library. In the hallway, she hands me off to my handmaiden. "Dress her appropriately; she's meeting the mates her father has selected for her tonight." The tone of her voice chills me to the bone, the lack of emotion is frighting. I move, not of my own volition, following the handmaiden. The further I walk, the less I seem to care about what's happening; I'm numb to everything.

THE Priestess-

The handmaiden nods and moves off with Anca, heading to her suite. After handling things with her, I head towards the west wing and into a secret passageway; one no one seems to know about. Looking left then right, I slide the secret door open and walk through. The door moves slowly and closes on its own with a soft whoosh, sealing me inside. Several twists and turns later, I enter a large room in an older part of the castle. The smell of mildew and mold hangs heavily in the air as I push open the large oak door.

The room used to be the original war room. The walls are still covered with maps of the kingdoms along our borders. A small weapons rack still sits close to the desk loaded with rapiers and dirks. Several suits of armor are placed between the bookcases from different points in our kingdom's history. The man standing at the head of the table is Grigore, captain of the king's guard. "Did you succeed?" Grigore stands tall, broad shoulders back as he puffs his chest out, looking down at me.

"Yes, she drank the tea and herbs. I have the handmaiden preparing her to meet the mates you picked out for her, M'lord." I make sure to bow deeply and gradually stand up to face him again.

"Good. Of my three sons, I only trust Vladimir to handle this unruly bitch." Grigore motions to Vladimir who's leaning against a bookcase not far from his father. His chiseled features scream predator and to run at the first chance you get. His eyes bore into you, hollow and filled with hatred. Grigore starts to speak again, snapping me out of my inner monologue. "If we didn't need an heir from her to ascend to the throne, I'd say kill them all. Let the gods sort the bodies out." Grigore looks to his left, where his sons Vladimir, Josef, and Jacob sit together.

Vladimir is smug and almost a spitting image of his father, hatred and all. Josef and Jacob are twins, though much smaller than Vladimir. I glance back over Grigore's three sons then back to him quickly.

"I must take my leave before anyone goes looking for me." Carefully I start to back up, attempting to cut this meeting as short as humanly possible. It's probably the smartest move that I have made today. Never give a predator your back; you never know when they may strike.

"Oh, I forgot to inform you: you'll be teaching my daughters blood magic. They may need it in the future." A twisted smile plays upon Grigore's weathered lips as his yellowed teeth are exposed in a creepy manner. "A father only wants what's best for his daughters; they need to be able to handle any situation that may come up." He looks over to his daughters, Elena and the elder dame. *Grigore must be a lot older than I had initially thought, I say to myself.*

I lightly bow my head to Grigore and his children, then exit the room swiftly. I run down the stairs heading towards the dungeons. Just past the primary cells off to the side sits my private study as well as laboratory. Several books are thrown onto the table, most on blood magic as well as transmogrification.

A gentle knock sounds at the door which catches me off guard. I look up from the book I am reading, startled to see Laurel standing there wringing her hands together.

"Priestess... has it begun?" The beautiful, young Elven woman stands there, several strands of her pink hair covering her eyes.

"Yes, my dear, it has." I finish writing on a scroll and hand it to Laurel.

"Take this directly to Oberon and then return." I stare down at the scroll as it leaves my hand. "I gave the unsuspecting mother the herbs mixed in with the blood magic I used. She will produce a hybrid at the cost of her own life." I try to show no remorse over my role in this event.

Laurel takes the scroll and holds it close to her chest. "I will deliver it straight away. Oberon will be most pleased with you." A quick bow of her head, and she is gone in a wisp of glimmering light.

"What have I done?" I lower my head into my hands; regret almost instantly begins to sink in. My stomach is in knots, knowing full well the magnitude of what I have done. Basically, I have assisted in assassinating the last pureblood Marelup. I'll be responsible for bringing an abomination into this world.

Later today, those two wicked daughters of Grigore will begin to learn blood magic. Tonight, poor Anca will be bound to four males undeserving of her. The last of a noble bloodline shall forever be tainted.

I STAND off to the side, watching the gala in full swing as dignitaries from all around begin to gather to watch Anca accept her mates. On the other hand, Anca sits upon her throne with a blank expression on her face, devoid of any emotion. The king is off speaking to Grigore before the presentation begins. Vladimir, Josef, and Jacob all approach the throne heading directly towards Anca. Her dead eyes lock with Vladimir.

Languidly she rises from her throne and moves to stand before him. Anca is easily five inches shorter than Vladimir and has to crane her neck to look up at him. They stand there, staring at each other for several minutes. There's zero emotion betrayed on Anca's face. A sigh escapes her lips before she leans her neck off to the side. Submission to Vladimir is given without contention, and quickly he moves and bites her shoulder, sinking his canines in deep. My stomach churns with bile watching this mockery of a mating ceremony taking place. No pain or pleasure registers on Anca's face as she stares off over the crowd with dead eyes. Vladimir releases her shoulder and grips her neck to bring her mouth to his shoulder. Several attempts are made before Anca bites his shoulder in return. Cheers go up throughout the hall. Boldly, Vladimir moves to the king's throne and sits down. He's already assuming the mantle of king.

Anca is just a shell of herself as she sits upon her throne. She watches the party with unseeing eyes. The leader of the Great Bear Clan, Mikhail, arrives; Vladimir stands and greets him. With Mikhail is Dimitri Kovac, now assigned to be the queen's personal guard. Dimitri doesn't look thrilled with how Anca is acting. His eyes narrow, studying her closely. Vladimir motions to Anca, and she stands only to move sluggishly to Vladimir's side. Vladimir passes Anca to Mikhail as if she holds no value to him. Her dead eyes look up to Mikhail, and Vladimir issues the order to submit once Dimitri has walked away. Gradually Anca tilts her head to the side and exposes her throat to Mikhail. He hesitates for a moment, then sinks his canines deep into her flesh. Anca shows no reaction to his bite, except a single tear that rolls down her cheek. Mikhail withdraws his canines and then presses Anca's mouth to his shoulder. Several seconds pass before Anca bites Mikhail's shoulder; she holds on for only a few moments before she heads back to her throne.

Even drugged, Anca's depression becomes evident. She's now bound to two males unworthy of her. The doors to the grand ballroom blow open, and with it the temperature begins to drop swiftly. Anca's head remains lowered as she stares at her wine glass, barely able to keep her thoughts straight. Frost on her glass catches her attention, and it's the first time this entire gala that her wolf has stirred. Gradually she raises her head, and sees the beautiful man standing before her. I'm finally excited for her. This time, she appears to have some semblance of control over herself. His eyes churn like liquid mercury around his Dragon slits. His hair is as white as freshly fallen snow, and his skin is as smooth as fine china. Anca moves for the first time tonight of her own volition.

Without warning, her Lycan forces her shift and raises its head to howl her summoning call. All the Lycans within the great hall break free of their human bonds at her call, my own beast included. All eight feet of heavily-muscled Lycan stalks forward, toward the beautiful man.

"*Mine,*" her wolf says through the pack bond, and that is all Anca needs to hear.

Quickly her beast strikes, sinking her canines deep within the unknown male's shoulder. I watch Anca react to his fingers threading through her rough fur in soothing circles. Carefully she withdraws her canines and licks his wounds clean. Her pure-silver orbs stare down at his draconic eyes, while the beautiful man removes his cloak and wraps it around her beast's shoulders.

Anca shifts back to her human form quickly and stares up at the hunk of a man. His shoulders are broad and heavily muscled. He gently kisses Anca's forehead, then nuzzles her cheek and she willingly moves her head to the side. He finds an unmarked spot close to her throat and bites her. Anca wraps her hand around the back of the man's neck, holding his head to her shoulder. For the first time tonight, I see that Anca is actually smiling; this man's powerful blood has erased whatever spell she was under before. He gently cleans his bite and looks Anca in the eyes. "My name is Nicodeamus Tepish, of the Ice Dragon court, firstborn prince. You, my beautiful, fierce Anca, are my mate. I will love you forever and a day." He reaches down and lifts her hand to his lips, and kisses her knuckles.

I watch Vladimir standing off to the side, fuming while watching the event transpire. Anca's shift marks her true mate's arrival, thus lowering his chances of fathering the first child with her. Suspiciously, he gathers those closest to him and begins to plot what to do next to secure his place on the throne. The representative from the Dire Wolves arrives tomorrow evening. All he has to do is drug Anca again and get her to accept the last fool to arrive. Her heat is due to start any day now, so in theory all he has to do is make sure he's the only one able to produce an heir.

CHAPTER 3

Dimitri

Moldavia, Romania

Night of the Wolf Celebration

November 30, 1791

Festivities are underway within the Lycan castle. Wolves and other shifters from surrounding clans are gathered for the celebrations. Queen Anca sits upon her gold and crimson dais, hand resting on her heavily pregnant belly. Her dark crimson gown hugs her generously. Within her womb is the heir to the Lycan Empire. Her gunmetal-gray eyes follow her mates' movements throughout the hall as they mingle with the various creatures gathered. I notice the mild contractions had begun almost a half-hour ago. It was still too soon to alert anyone to the impending birth. This child would be the first one born in about one hundred years. How fitting that the pup chose tonight to make its appearance.

I am a local Great Bear Shifter, tasked with the protection of the Queen and Heir. My hazel eyes lock onto the Queen's hands and her stomach; something has changed. My eyes churn, turning golden as my bear rises to the surface. Quickly I cut through the crowd and arrive at her side.

"My Queen, is it time?" I tilt my head to the side, eyes focused and muscles tensed, ready to spring into action. The Queen slowly turns her head to face me.

"Soon, my friend. Send Andre to gather the Elder Dame to my chambers. We will follow shortly." Anca's voice is strained as she tries to remain composed, watching the gala. I turn slowly and lock eyes with Andre; a simple short nod of the head sends him off to do his Queen's bidding. I then watch for the Queen's mates to look towards the dais; one by one, they are given the signal—only the Alpha King, Vladimir, approaches.

"Is it time, my love?" he speaks reverently to his mate. His tone, however, doesn't convey the affection his words suggest. He offers her his hand and helps her stand up. Anca nods her head slightly. Carefully and slowly, she stands. Vladimir and I flank her as we escort her to the birthing chambers. Several stops are made as the contractions increased in power. Poised and proper to a fault, Anca refuses to show pain or weakness. She clenches her jaw and lightly growls through the pain. Her eyes bleed to the liquid mercury of her she-wolf, both of them anxious to meet their pup. Once within the chambers, the Elder Dame leads her to the bed and prepares her for the birthing. Vladimir paces the rooms anxiously, waiting for the arrival of his firstborn child. I move and take my post just outside of the chamber, but remain close enough if I need to get back quickly. The Queen's agonizing screams during labor makes even my big bear cringe. The tones she hits sounds like she is being murdered within her chambers.

A sudden pounding on the door startles me, making me turn and rip the door open. In the hallway, I find the Queen's second mate, Mikhail. His face and clothes are covered in blackened blood. "The Strigoi are attacking; we must evacuate Anca and the pup, now!" As soon as his statement leaves his bloody lips, I whip my head around, looking back towards the birthing chambers. Anca's blood-curdling screams pierce the night.

"I'll see to it myself, M'lord. Send Andre. Worst case scenario, he can fly off with the pup while we move your mate." I hope my words are what Mikhail wanted to hear. A swift nod was all he gave before he retreats and takes off running down the hallway. I double bolt and barricade the door before running to update my charges. Andre's Golden Eagle sits on the windowsill before dropping into the room to join the evacuation.

Anca screams and thrashes on the bed with each contraction. Unable to shift, she grips onto the sheets for dear life. The Elder Dame keeps passing different herb mixtures to Anca, but nothing is helping. Without warning, the sheets start staining red with blood. Way too blood much for it to be from labor alone. The Elder Dame draws back the drenched sheet to find tiny white talons ripping through Anca's flesh. Anca screams, her voice growing horse from effort. Nicodeamus's dragon calls back to her in the distance.

Several moments pass, and the partially-shifted little baby has clawed its way free of her mother's womb. The blood-drenched, hairless Lycan pup paws at the flesh of its mother as it drags itself free of her womb. Vladimir orders for his daughter to be cleaned immediately and tended to. He shows no concern for the Queen as she lies dying, bleeding out in her own bed. Her dying words whispered, begging for her Seraphina to be protected. I watch Anca as the life drains from her body, desperately wanting to save her but not sure how to. The internal damage to Anca's body is too significant. The Queen expires silently, her lifeless gray eyes looking in the direction of her daughter. I turn, watching the Alpha pace back and forth next to the bed. Vlad is deep in thought as the Elder Dame slowly covers Anca's lifeless body, as he gently rocks the tiny package in his arms, humming softly.

The Elder Dame brings forth the family crest—the blackened brand that all Marelup descendants were marked with. Andre and I stand shoulder to shoulder, watching the little bundle get marked. A shrill scream comes from the pup as the silver burns her flesh. The sounds of battle drift to us as the fight draws ever closer to the birthing chambers. Swords clashing, and the shrieks of the Strigoi draw closer. His back suddenly straightens, and his presence becomes commanding. "Take my daughter, Aurora! Please, protect her with your lives!"

The Elder Dame comes forth with a magical potion and a very sharp dagger. "I must bind her to one of you; otherwise, without a pack she will be amongst the lost ones—insane from the lack of a pack." Her eyes dart between Andre and I then settle on me. "You're a predator like she is; a beast. You will be the best candidate! Give me your arm, Dimitri!" Such authority from a little old woman almost frightens me. I hold out my left arm to her. She dips the blade into the magical elixir, then makes a swift cut across my forearm. The wound stings then turns to a warm tingle as the flesh begins to knit back together.

Her amber eyes turn to the pup still in Vlad's arms, pulling out her tiny left arm and repeating the process. Instantly I feel her like she's a part of me. I feel such a sense of wonder as I am handed the pup. This tiny cherub looks like a mini version of her mother, right down to the gunmetal-gray eyes and ruby lips. Hands grip my shoulders and turn me, snapping me out of my inner thoughts. "You must go!" the Elder Dame shouts at me, then pulls out a gnarly, twisted stick from her robe and flourishes it in the air. Energy explodes into the room as a rip in the fabric of reality opens before us. "Go! My sister Elena will shelter you in the new world. Go now!" As soon as she finishes imploring us, a harsh pounding starts coming from the direction of the door. The cracking sound of the wooden door starting to give way dispels any hesitation we had. Without a second thought, Andre, the pup, and I venture into the unknown.

VLADIMIR-

Wood splinters fly everywhere as a dozen Strigoi break into the room, remnants of the door littering the floor. The metallic tang of blood and the scent of spilled birthing fluid mixed with magic lie heavily in the air. The Elder Dame and I remain in the room, looking without fear at the monsters beginning to fill it.

The Strigoi are a vile bunch; ashen skin, long, pointed, bat-like ears, and dozens of needle-like teeth fill their mouths. Their noses are the most disturbing part of them. They are a larger version of a bat's flared and rippled nose. On the tips of their long, boney fingers, sharp, hooked claws glisten with the blood of my people. These horrid creatures reek of sulfur death and decay and look as if they had freshly risen from the grave. They stand there as Tomas moves through the gathered horde to stand before myself and the Elder Dame.

"You shouldn't have tried to exile us forever, Vladimir, we are many." He flourishes his boney, clawed hand towards the door. "Your kind is dying off." I face off with the Strigoi Alpha showing no fear. Tomas's needle-like fangs glisten in the candlelight, fresh blood staining his chin and chest. "Once our pets, now our wardens... Wardens no more! Now you are food for the horde." Tomas steps forward. Slender, clawed hands flexing as he tries to bait me. "Your kin lay dead at the feet of my kind. Your allies run in fear and die before me. You are king no more." As he speaks, droplets of blood fall from his mouth and onto his chest. Tomas's black eyes drift to the sheet-covered body on the bed and smiles. "Shame, I wanted to dine on the blood of your pup."

That made my blood boil. That creature wanted my daughter, my only heir. We lost the pup's mother in childbirth. I would not let anything happen to alert the Strigoi that my daughter had survived. "You want the crown, come for it..." I know this fight could mean my death. My eyes drift to the Elder Dame, a slight nod tells me my precious cargo is safe. My last thoughts are of the daughter I would never get to know as I charge into what may be my final battle.

On the far side of the castle, I fall from the sky the moment my mate died. My chest feels as though the weight of a thousand worlds lay upon my heart, smashing it to dust. My dragon bellows his grief into the night; its mate is gone. Slowly, he releases his hold over me and allows me to return to my human form. By some miracle I feel the faint thread of life that is my child. Somehow, even though my mate had perished, she lived long enough to deliver our baby into this world. This small joy spurns me on to seek out what's left of my mate and my surviving child.

The battle wages on throughout the castle as I barrel through Strigoi and Dires alike. Reaching the demolished birthing chamber to find the Elder Dame in a magical sphere, where a lone Strigoi attempts to attack her. My hands shift into my taloned gauntlets, and without a second thought I cut the Strigoi's head free from his shoulders. A satisfying, wet thud resounds through the room when its body hits the floor.

My eyes drift to the blood-covered sheets before me. Slowly, walking to the edge of the bed, I lift the corner of the sheet. I have to see my Anca one last time. Her abdomen is shredded, a hole was created where it looked like something punched its way out. My eyes go wide, horrified at what's left of my beloved mate. Silent tears stream down my cheeks and drip onto the floor. My heart sinks further as I begin to mourn the death of not only my mate, but also my hatchling too. I turn slowly, looking at the destruction around me. The Elder Dame approaches and squeezes my shoulder. "I couldn't do anything for Anca, M'lord. The baby was partially shifted during the birth and ripped her way out of her mother." The Elder dame moves forward and motions to the hole in Anca's abdomen. "She's a powerful one, the strongest I've seen in generations."

The Elder Dame lowers her head and sighs. "I sent the baby to my sister, where she will be safe. The Strigoi have yet to cross the ocean, so she will have time to grow strong. They won't be able to find her until she ascends." She lifts her eyes to lock with mine, hoping to give me some comfort.

I turn back to look at Anca; carefully, I close her eyes and kiss her lips one last time. Slowly I pull the sheet back up and over Anca's body before turning to the Elder Dame. "Leave now. I will cremate my love and send her to the great beyond." I wait for the Elder Dame to leave before breathing my frost flames upon my love. I watch as the bed ignites and begins to burn as I back into the hall-way, watching the fire burn my beloved mate.

That was my fatal mistake; once outside the door, a broadsword comes down and lobs off my left arm. My remaining hand shoots up, burning white-hot to stop the bleeding and cauterize the wound. I whip around quickly to find the Dire's Beta, Lucian, holding the sword's point to my throat. "Surrender and live; fight, and I'll take your head where you stand." A sinister sneer crosses his thin lips as he stares at me. His cold, hazel-green eyes bore into me, challenging me to make a move against him.

For now, I have to bide my time and make sure to live long enough for my child to find me. Even though my dragon fights against my decision and wants to rage for what has been done. I must surrender so we could live to fight another day.

CHAPTER 4
Aurora

Heavy tones ring out from my amplifier as I jam out on my guitar. The main riffs from Avenged Sevenfold's "Hail to the King" fill my room and probably most of the house and yard. The tones make the glass in the windows vibrate with each cord I hit. The song speaks to me about things to come, about things that could have been. Playing music is how I work through the vast span of time that I've lived through. For the last **two hundred and twenty-eight years,** we've always been on the move. Never have I been able to call a house a home or a section of woods my territory.

My wolf grows restless as time goes on, feeling more like a listless rogue than the Alpha I am meant to become. My guardians keep me isolated from most of the world for my own safety because of who I was born to be. I am the last Lycan Princess destined to reclaim my mother's throne from the Strigoi. No pressure, right? Music has always helped me work through all the anger that has built up over the past decades. Why am I so angry? One may wonder. Well, let's see here. An ancient evil murdered my family, took over my kingdom, and because of that, I'm stuck in some fucked up witness protection program.

The last hundred years have been the most difficult. Not only do I have dreams of battles I've never fought in, but I've also started dreaming of a man that looks like a Viking, who has been teaching me how to fight in my dreams. The man in my dreams has long white hair as I do, and his eyes are the same steel-gray as mine. I believe him to be a relative or an ancestor of mine. His lessons are in images and actions; I never hear his voice, but instinctively I know what he's trying to convey. From the descriptions Dimitri has given me, I believe the man in my dreams is the lost Dragon King. But why would I be dreaming of him? The lessons I've learned are quite useful. Hell, I've used some of this new knowledge against Dimitri in some of our sparring sessions.

I stop playing as Andre drops off a new cup of tea from Elena. Something about this tea takes the edge off of everything. Sipping my tea slowly, I start thinking of Dimitri; I have a major crush on him. Like really bad. My wolf is convinced he's ours; though, I'm not so sure. Shouldn't I feel something towards him as well? I mean, I do love him, and that love has changed from father-figure to friend; and with the urging of my wolf, it's a little more than it used to be. If he were ours, he wouldn't go out to be intimate with other females. Maybe it's just a first love crush that eventually I'll forget ever happened. Then again, I admit it; I'm jealous. Angry even... Though honestly, I'm not sure if it's just the mystical bond that makes me think I love him. It's probably because I'm always so lonely. Sighing deeply, I switch songs to something a little sad to fit my heartache.

My fingers trace the length of the scar that, over time, seems to have stretched as I grew. I find myself staring at this mystical lo-jack. What male in his right mind would want to be bound to a baby? Dimitri is kind of stuck with me because of the Elder Dame's magic that binds us. Dimitri's and Andre's lives are directly tied to mine, thus extending their lifespans far beyond what it should have been. Andre, I had found out, was attached to Dimitri because of their jobs. So when Dimitri was bound to me, Andre had been roped in—to a lesser extent. How fucked up is that?

I wonder what will happen to them when I choose my first mate and the bond is broken. Will they instantly die? Or will they slowly age like ordinary people? Lost within a sea of emotions, I almost miss feeling Dimitri coming closer before I see him. He must be sensing the turmoil within me at the moment. Sometimes I can't stand to look him in the eyes. I know he sneaks into town to take care of his needs, I *feel* it—probably the cruelest part of this binding. He gets to share my lifespan, and I get the eternal pain of knowing when he gets laid.

Speaking of the bear, there he is in the doorway; looking at me, sipping his tea, and trying to discern my mood. "Aurora, are you okay, love? You feel like a maelstrom of emotions." He tilts his head to the left and studies me more. His eyes glow a gold-tone, signs that his bear is flaring to the surface. Honestly, lately, I've enjoyed the bear's company more than his. Dimitri is a rather large man in stature in comparison to Andre. Think of the guys from the strongman competitions, and that's D. His honey-brown hair and matching hazel eyes make him appear as if he's very approachable. His current expression betrays his concern because of my mood. The air shifts slightly, and a new scent is blown my way. Instantly my beast becomes a raging mess; it's another female in her territory. I sit my guitar down and stand up. Slowly, stalking towards him, sniffing the air. Panic streaks across his face; he knows what I smell, and a deep guttural growl escapes my curled lips.

My wolf makes her presence known as my canines lengthen while I assess him. I see Andre coming over his shoulder, running towards us before he skids to a stop halfway down the hallway. Slowly, turning my attention back to Dimitri. I find myself not even a foot away from him, my nostrils flaring.

"How dare you!" Baring my canines at him, "Entering my den smelling of some whore!" I growl. I am literally shaking, trying to keep from ripping him apart. My snow-white fur ripples up and down my arms as my beast demands retribution. "It's bad enough I fucking *feel* every time you get off. I don't need to smell her too," I seethed through clenched teeth. "My wolf wants her head and her blood on our talons. You may have signed that bitches death warrant just 'cause you wanted to get your dick wet," I snarl and feel my hands shift and lengthen into talons. Flexing my hands several times, my eyes are fixated on my talons' sharp planes, imagining them covered in blood. Raising my gaze slowly, I watch his face visibly pales as he takes several steps back with his hands up in a pacifying manner.

"I didn't know Aurora..." He gulps, eyes wide as saucers. "I didn't know you could feel that?" He looks honestly horrified and remorseful at his actions. Shaking his head slowly, a single tear breaks free from his left eye and rolls down his cheek. I've never seen a sign of weakness from the big guy. Hell, he's six foot five and over four hundred pounds of solid muscle. I've never seen him cry. Hell, I never in a million years thought I'd see him cry.

"I'd love to say it's fine, but it's not. I've been dealing with this for the last hundred years." I take a deep breath and push my wolf to the back of my mind as I turn and walk to the other side of my room. "Please, leave... go shower, burn those clothes... Fuck... just please leave... I can't deal with this right now." My voice breaks as I utter the last half of the statement. My heart feels as if it's in a vice being crushed.

Fuck, *I* was ready to cry. I hate fucking crying. I wipe my eyes, trying to hide my pain. How many times can my heart get broken before my damned wolf will give up on the bear that honestly doesn't want us? After a few moments, I hear a sniffled "sorry" and listen to Dimitri walk off. I remain standing rigid, trying to show no signs of weakness even though I feel my world come down around me. A softer set of footsteps enter my den and slowly approach. I know it's Andre, and I lower my head in defeat and relax my stance considerably. "Hi, Andre," escapes my lips far softer than I anticipated.

"Baby girl. I'm so sorry this is hurting you so badly." He hesitates as he starts to reach out to me, then stops himself. "Why didn't you say anything to him? Or to me?" He sighs softly. "I would have talked to him and let him know what you're going through." Andre was distraught; he's the best friend I could ever ask for. He slowly approaches me, his movements careful and calculated, making sure not to set my wolf off. His lithe hand gently rests on my shoulder and rubs softly, trying to comfort me.

"Why would I take away his freedom and his choice?" Raising my eyebrows, I open my eyes wide. "I'm the one that must wait for my first heat to come into my full power." My emotions are a mess as tears freely roll down my cheeks in frustration. "I'm the one who must wait until then to start choosing my mates and gaining power. No one needs to share my hell with me. No one needs to suffer as I do." Wrapping my arms tightly around my stomach, I slowly turn my head to look into his eyes; he seems just as sad as I feel.

"Baby girl, we are here for you. I am here for you," Andre says with so much conviction. "I'll talk to the big guy. Why don't you go hunting? You know that will make you feel better." Andre motions back to the kitchen. "Elena sent us another care package, I'll leave it for you to open later."

As usual, Andre is right. Hunting will clear my head, and I can take my aggression out on my dinner. "Okay, I'll be back by nightfall." Slowly, I turn fully and kiss him on his forehead. "You have been a wonderful father, Andre." I had to let him know how much I appreciate him. I smile weakly at him before moving off to get ready to hunt.

I start stripping off my clothes as I head out of my sliding glass door. As my feet hit the grass, the shift takes me quickly. My bones break and grow and shift alignment. My muscles stretch and gain in mass, my arms and legs elongate, and my knees break and bend backward. Thick, white fur covers my body as the final changes take place. Last to change are my fingernails that grow to look like long-hooked talons. Tiny, silver-white, scale-like growths surround them. It seems that with each shift I go through as I get older, more and more white scales appear. My muzzle is longer and broader than the average Lycan. The boney prominence on my muzzle is raised, unlike any wolf I have ever seen. My skull is broader and thicker, with long pointed ears. Almost all eight feet of Lycan stretches out before I start moving towards the woods. Unlike other wolves, I'm bipedal—like the werewolves of horror movies, but bigger and scarier. I'm a freak, and I know it. I kind of like being unique; it makes me feel special. I would almost say I was an albino, but I tan every summer, so that thought is out of the question.

I haven't ever seen another Lycan like me. Then again, I've only ever seen one other. Our friend Elena is also Lycan, but her fur is black as night. She says that's the natural color for our species coat. It makes me wonder if the Alpha, my mother's first mate, was my father or if one of the other males is my sire. The shit you think about to distract you from heartache. Logically, the Alpha couldn't be. I mean, his fur was black like my mother's.

I take a running start and leap up into the air to sink my talons into the cliff-face and start climbing. The cliff's face is a vertical climb and so worth the strain to get to the top. I've been climbing this cliff for the last few years—to be honest, it's gotten relatively easy. The area I want to hunt in is on the other side of this divide. Reaching the top, I haul myself over and creep on all fours to look down into the valley below. My liquid-mercury eyes lock onto a herd of deer in the distance, moving towards the lake. It's a good-sized herd for this time of year. There's a decent blend of old and young deer, which usually means the herd is healthy. Calculating the distance to the large oak tree, I take a running start and leap through the air flying towards my target.

Landing softly, my talons sink deeply into the tree's bark. I scan the perimeter and plan the next several jumps needed to be within striking distance. One last jump and I'm at a fork in the trail where the deer should cross. The wind is blowing from behind them into my face; the wind is perfect for my attack. A roar sounds in the distance, scaring the herd and sending them running. Okay, now I'm genuinely pissed off. There went my mother fucking hunt. Something is going to die, so help me.

I remain in the tree, talons digging into the bark, as I wait to see what just ruined my fun. Then it hits me; Dimitri, or should I say his bear. The big guy is upset with its human counterpart. Personally, I can't blame the furball. I'm not overjoyed with his human side at the moment either. Ever so slowly, the bear lumbers its way towards my hiding spot. His snout lifting slightly in the air as his nostrils flair, trying to catch my scent. By the looks of it, he has sensed me and starts looking around for me. Silly bear never looks up. When he's close enough, I release my grip and fall to the ground about ten feet in front of his nose.

Landing in a crouched position, I look up at Dimitri's bear, who is now standing on his hind legs. Quickly, I launch myself at him, my shoulder catching his bear right under his ribcage, knocking him off balance. My momentum causes him to fall backward, allowing me to pin him on his back. My canines lightly press into the bear's throat, and I let off a soft, non-threatening growl. The bear releases its control of their body, and before I realize it, I have Dimitri's smooth human throat in my massive maw. I could quickly kill him at this moment, crush his throat like a grape. His fingertips begin to run through my coarse fur. He's calm, too calm; he trusts me, but right now, I don't trust me. I'm hurt and angry. Quickly, I release my grip on him and scoot back to see what he does next.

"Aurora, please shift back so we can talk," he says. I grumble and shake my head, my tail thrashing wildly against the ground. "Okay, but please listen to me. I didn't know you felt what I was doing; you never hinted that anything was bothering you." His eyes stare at the ground; his guilt and anxiety coming off him in waves.

I almost feel sorry for him. I growl a little bit more and grumble. Deep down, I'm still debating on hunting the whore down. It's not like there are many towns close to here; it should be easy. My wolf is calling for her blood; she believes that Dimitri is hers alone, and no other should touch him. She's too smug, too demanding. I'm mildly concerned she may try something at some point. I snap back to the present. I'm feeling Dimitri's pain now; his heart almost feels like it's breaking. Sensing his emotions, my damn wolf betrays me and forces me back to my human form. Of course, because it's not planned, I fall flat on my ass.

"Son of a bitch!" I stand up and rub my ass. Real fucking graceful. "Listen, Dimitri..." I never call him by his full first name, and the visible wince is evidence enough that I've gotten his attention. "You've done as nature intends. Your instincts and drive can't be silenced because you've been sentenced as my eternal babysitter. I'm sure being forced to be bound to a baby for life really wasn't high on your list of shit to do." I begin to pace, running my hands aggressively through my hair.

"I'm doing my best over here. My wolf still wants to hunt that female, she's jealous and has a sick idea that you and your bear belong to us." I scoff and scrunch my nose as I turn and swipe at a tree. Just before impact, my talons extend and cut through the tree like a hot knife through butter. I get ready to swipe at another tree, but a firm hand wraps around my wrist and stops me.

"I'm sorry I hurt you, my bear is furious at me. He forced the shift and dragged me out here, knowing that this is your favorite hunting ground." He releases my wrist and starts wringing his hands together. "I'm not trapped as your babysitter. It was, and is, a great honor to protect you. Now, you quite honestly don't need my protection. I've half been waiting for you to tell me to move on, that you've outgrown wanting me around." His eyes are sincere, and yet there's fear behind them. He's afraid I'll do away with him.

"I haven't outgrown wanting you around, D. It's my damn wolf, she's got it in her thick skull that you and your bear are hers." I look down and away after admitting that. "I don't know what to think or do anymore. I should be ascending soon. I feel the change coming. My wolf is anxious and becoming more aggressive. We may need to sedate me, as Elena suggested." I didn't like that idea at all, but what was I to do? Risk hurting others? It wasn't worth it. I didn't give him a chance to speak his mind on the matter. Honestly, I didn't want the answer. I start walking back the way I came. "Come on, D, up the cliff face we go. Time to head home."

My shift comes quicker than usual, bones pop and realign to take on the form of my Lycan. She turns her head to look at Dimitri then motions for him to climb on. Dimitri isn't all that heavy to me in this form. His thick arms wrap around my beast's neck and his legs wrap around my waistline, holding on tightly. When I was absolutely sure he was secure, I leap up and sink my talons into the rock and clay of the cliff face and start my climb. The bear is afraid of heights, so part of me revels in the fact that he's worried. The climb that would typically be over swiftly, stretches out because I want to enjoy his suffering. When we reach the top, I give him a few moments to relax before I launch us off the top of the cliff. His screams fill my ears as we head towards a tree. I use my talons to grip the small tree and slide down, almost like a fireman's pole. Bark and tree-flesh litter the ground when we land. Dimitri quickly slides off my back and starts walking.

I don't bother shifting back to my human form, and he returns to his bear. It was going to be a very long night. My wolf is still tearing me apart mentally. She is going over the logistics of plotting out which possible towns Dimitri could have gone to. Every time he left, it was long after I had fallen asleep, which gives the woman an advantage at the moment. I know my wolf; she'll figure it out. I just hope I'm aware enough to stop her.

CHAPTER 5

Aurora's Wolf

I'm going to find that bitch. I'm going to kill her and rip her head from her body and leave it on the bear's bed. How dare she touch what's mine? I silently stalk through the fifth town, scenting the air from my hidden position in the shadows. It's been effortless to overpower Aurora lately. With her body changing, preparing for the ascension, her mind has been distracted because of the surges in hormones and the increased drive to hunt.

Five hundred feet ahead of me I scent the female, and yes, she's turning tricks in an alleyway—not a shocker. This will be an easy kill. The only question is, how long do I want to make her suffer? Hmm... minutes, possibly hours, or maybe even a few days of suffering would possibly please me. I will ponder this further while I wait for my opening. Once her date walks away, I strike. I stick to the shadows, moving silently towards her. My monstrous form looming over her from behind as I prepare to strike. With deft precision, I reach around her with my talons and sever her vocal cords, careful not to hit an artery. I just silenced the lamb and it was totally worth it. I throw her over my shoulder and run off into the night. Her blood is turning my white fur *vermillion, its warmth running in rivulets down my back. The iron tang in the air is almost driving me to the point of frenzy. I must keep my wits about me. I must do this the smart way so that the inhabitants are none the wiser to my mission.*

We make it to the woods about a thousand yards from the main house. I pause and close my eyes sensing where Dimitri and Andre are. Both are none the wiser to my escape and abduction. I drop the female on the ground, watching her sad attempts at begging for her life. Sliced vocal cords make it so much easier to ignore her pleas. She's crying, and from the smell of it has pissed herself from fear. My night just keeps getting better and better. I wonder if my human counterpart will be proud of what I've accomplished for her. I mean, revenge is a great gift to give, right? I know what I'll do, I'll leave the head for Aurora. Hmm... leave it on her bed? Or maybe on her table? Either way, at least she'll appreciate the trouble I've gone through.

My taloned hand shoots out and sinks into the human's soft flesh. Blood slowly runs down, coating my talons as my grip slowly tightens on her. Holding her down, I strike quickly, wrapping my maw around her throat and slowly increase the pressure on her soft flesh. Warmth starts to flood my mouth, the coppery tang of her blood soothing my soul. Soft sniffles fill my ears. I'm not entirely heartless, so I twist my head violently, severing her head from her shoulders, ending her life quickly. I proceed to rip her body limb from limb before heading back home with her head in my hands. I can't wait until tomorrow morning; Aurora will be so proud of me.

~**Aurora**~

It's been several days since the fight with Dimitri. Several days where I keep losing chunks of the evening and most of the night. I woke up this morning covered in blood. And it's definitely not animal blood; it has a different texture and scent. That means only one thing; it has to be human. My eyes widen as I take in what's before me, screaming as loud as I can, I look around my room. My once beautiful room now looks like an active crime scene. Two sets of feet come thundering down the hall and my door blasts open, almost coming off its hinges. Andre shoots past Dimitri, then stops short and turns pale.

"Aurora, what have you done?? This looks worse than most of the horror flicks you and I watch." Andre studies me, then looks at Dimitri.

He's pale, really fucking pale. Then it dawns on me; my wolf must have made good on her promise. I feel horrible thinking about what my wolf may have done. "Aurora? Talk to me, baby girl. You and Dimitri are scaring me." Andre walks around my room looking at the chaos around us and positions himself by my open window. His fight or flight instinct is kicking in big time... damn bird.

I raise my hands, staring at the sticky, half-dried blood. "I've been losing hours the last few days... like I can't remember most of yesterday. After dinner too, now it is blank. I don't remember going to bed or anything." I start sniffing at my hand that's coated with sticky, half-dried blood; then I move my blankets. A severed head rolls off the bed and stops right in front of Andre. Andre screams like one of the old-school scream-queens and it honestly has that blood-chilling quality to it.

Dimitri has gone so pale he looks like he's going to throw up. I slowly slide out of bed and look around the room. Bloody paw prints cover the wood floor, from the doors leading to the balcony and straight to my bed. My wolf kept her promise to hunt the human. She's all smug in the back of my head, sitting there proud of herself. Dimitri is beside himself. His horrified eyes slowly drift to lock with mine.

Part of me is sorry we did it. The other part, the part that is all wolf, is sorry too; just not that the woman is dead. She's sorry it took so long to find the fucker.

"I'm sorry, D. I'm a monster... She's stronger... She's never been able to take over completely before. I need to go find the rest of the remains." I release a slow breath and take my pillow out of its pillowcase.

"Watch out, Andre. I need to take the head with me." Reaching down, I scoop up the head. Blood drips from the exposed arteries as well as what is left of the neck. Tendons and part of the spinal cord dangle beneath the ribbons of blood-covered flesh. After examining what was left of the neck, I determined my wolf had bitten her head off—what a way to go. I sniff at the scalp and recognize the scent. It's the same one that set me off the other day. My wolf had hunted down the woman that Dimitri slept with.

Andre loses it, shifting into his golden eagle, he shoots out the window. Honestly, I can't blame him. He's more of a pacifist than Dimitri and me. I don't expect the boys to help me clean up my mess. I'm just wondering what else I have done in the last forty-eight hours where I'm missing time.

"Aurora?" Dimitri snaps me out of my inner monologue. "I'll help you search. I... I know you didn't do this." Shaking his head, he seems to reconsider his statement. "I mean, I know you wouldn't have done it if you were aware of what was going on." His strong thick arms encircle me as he squeezes me to his chest, holding me. I wonder which one of us he is trying to comfort, him or me? I can't help but cry when Dimitri embraces me. I feel like a monster, yet here he is holding me. Slowly he releases me from the hug, and we both look at the double doors leading to the patio. We open the door and walk out onto the deck—more dried bloody paw prints. We follow my tracks into the woods, and about a thousand yards from the house, we find the woman's remains.

She was absolutely shredded. Bone fragments littered the ground, as well as chunks of muscle and sinew haphazardly thrown about. It was as if my wolf had a hunk of meat in her mouth, and thrashed her head violently around sending pieces flying. Slivers of flesh and blood clots hung like tinsel off of the pine tree bark. The one small Douglas fir had her large and small intestines draped upon its boughs like a garland. What was left of the woman's clothing was ripped to shreds and hung like tinsel.

Further away on a small balsam fir tree, hands and feet hung off the boughs by their tendons. I'm guessing my wolf was feeling rather festive towards the end of her destruction. I stand there admiring her handy work, though maybe admiring is the wrong word for it. While I'm deep in thought, staring at the gut garland, Dimitri moves to stand next to me. I turn to look at him, and he's three shades of green and appears to be on the verge of wanting to puke. Gently I rub his shoulder, and he jumps back, startled by the contact. I let out a slow, sad sigh as I look around, taking in the full magnitude of what my wolf has done.

Scavengers were up in the trees, some with chunks in their talon's others just with bloody beaks. I shift and start digging a deep hole. My solution to the problem is to dig deep and bury everything. Dimitri realizes what I'm doing and shifts to help out. His bear is shoveling the dirt into a pile off to the side after I shoot it out of the hole I had made. Once the hole is deep enough, I shift back to my human form and begin throwing chunks into the hole. This is a forensic nightmare. It has become a fucked up scavenger hunt for all the missing pieces. I start singing "Dem Bones" to make sure I'm not missing any body parts.

"Really, Aurora? You think this is fucking funny?" Dimitri is pissed. He honestly thought I was making a mockery of what we were doing. To be frank, I was so busy I didn't notice when he had shifted back to his human form.

"No, D, I don't think this is funny. It's the only fucking song I know to remember all the fucking body parts," I say softly as I pull the gut garland off the tree.

Dimitri was so angry he shifted back to his bear and returned to what he was doing. His reaction was rather upsetting to me. As much as he says it's not my fault, I know deep down he blames me. I remove the last of the hanging body ornaments then shift back to my wolf to continue cleaning. I claw up chunks of bloody moss and scraps of bark. If it has blood on it, it is going into the hole. After about two hours, and several searches in circles as far out as eighty yards from ground zero, we began to fill the hole in. Thankfully it was a ton easier to fill the hole in than it was to dig the fucking thing.

I suddenly feel a surge of energy run through my body, and it brings me to my knees. The surge was so powerful, it forced my shift back to my human form. What is happening to me? I feel like my blood is on fire. It feels like my wolf is ripping my body apart from the inside. I use a young ash tree to stand, only to fall back to the ground. Screaming out in agony, my voice a mix of my human and wolf.

Dimitri rushes over and shifts back to human. His large hands rest on my narrow ribcage, gently rubbing the muscle. The entire length of my body is going in and out of spasms each time the wave of power passes over me. My wolf's fur ripples across my skin as each power surge hits me. Skin-to-skin contact seems to take some of the pain away, but not all of it. I can tell he is in pain too but is trying to hide it.

"It's time, Aurora... You're ascending, which means your heat is about to start. We need to get you home." All I could really do is nod and close my eyes tightly. I feel like I'm going to die. As the pain increases, I notice it's starting to affect Dimitri; he can't stand either. He's in my hell with me. I scoot, so my back leans against his body, seeking any kind of comfort. My eyes snap open when I hear a branch break. It's Andre, he is back in human form, and he's notably concerned. Dimitri quickly explains to Andre what's happening to both of us.

He approaches me and scoops me up into his arms. "Come on, baby girl, let's get you some of that special tea and get you settled into bed for a very long nap." I snuggle against his bare chest and plant my forehead against his neck. His arms band tightly around me as we walk. As he carries me home he's able to feel just how strongly the spasms are. Every time one hits, he stops and tightens his grip on me. The poor man doesn't know what to do for a few reasons. Firstly, I know for a fact he's not used to holding a naked woman. Secondly, I'm not sure if he's ever witnessed an ascension before.

I need something, anything, and a nap sounded wonderful compared to the pain I'm currently in. I close my eyes and trust Andre to take care of me. We make it back to the house and through my double doors. In our absence, Andre had already cleaned up my room and changed my bedding. He gently lays me down on my soft bed, just in the nick of time, before the next spasm rips through my body. I scream and arch my back, lifting off of the bed. My muscles tense and burn from the exertion. Sweat breaks out along my entire length and runs off of me in streams; my bedding is soaked.

I hear a heavy thud, and Dimitri cries out at about the same time my pain spikes. There is nothing I can do to help him or myself at this point. He must have been on the phone because Andre quickly takes it from him.

"Elena, it's Andre... Aurora is ascending, and it's affecting the big guy too. Can you make it here? Yeah, I have the tea, I'm brewing her some now. She lost something, like at least twelve hours yesterday, and her wolf went all homicidal." I can hear him pacing my room, and then he goes down the hallway.

Eventually, I feel the side of the bed dip and open my eyes to see Dimitri; he looks like shit. I feel like I've been put through a food processor, I can't imagine what he's feeling because of our bond. "I'm so sorry, D... If I could sever the bond so you wouldn't suffer, I would." Guilt was suddenly all I was feeling at the moment, a soft lull in the sea of pain I was in.

Dimitri raises his large hand and rests it on my sweaty cheek. "Don't worry, little one, we bears are tough. We can survive anything. As for the bond," he takes a deep breath and lets it out slowly. "That will only be severed when you choose your first mate. That's something we don't want you to rush... that bond is forever. I don't want to see what happened to your mother happen to you." He looks down and away before getting up to sit in the recliner near the bed.

"What do you mean, D? Are you saying my mother was forced?" I quickly sit up straight and stare at him, my wolf flares to the front at that thought. She doesn't like the idea of being forced to do anything.

"Yes, that's exactly what I'm saying happened. Vlad, her Lycan mate, forced their bond, so he was the first mate. Her second mate, Mikhail, wasn't met with any resistance, and he was a bear like me. Nicodeamus, your mother's third mate, was a true mate. Their animals loved each other. He was an Ice Dragon. Your mom's fourth mate, Liam, was a Dire Wolf, and he met with no resistance either." He stares at his hands as he explains my mother's history, and then it dawns on me.

"Wait! Only a true mate can produce offspring." My eyes were focused on my hand as I shifted it.

"Nico is the reason my fur is white, isn't it?" I look away from my hand to Dimitri, and he nods slowly. Shit, my father is a dragon. Who knows how fucking long I'll live now?

Footsteps sound down the hallway. I look up to see Andre with the tea in his hands. Soft scents of lavender, honey, and hibiscus drift to me. There are a few underlying scents mingled in that I can't identify. "Baby girl," Andre says as he gently caresses my cheek. "Elena said it's time to start drinking the tea she gave us. Without a mate, she says your temperament will be unpredictable." Andre looks down at the tea, his sadness tugging at my heartstrings. "She said she needs to make several phone calls, and in three days' time, at the end of your cycle, she'll be here with the last, single Lycan males she can find." Slowly, he extends his hand out to me, offering the tea.

I carefully take it and drink deeply. It honestly doesn't taste too bad—honey always makes everything better, in my opinion. "If that's what she thinks is best, then I shall sleep. I don't want D suffering because of me." I offer him a sad smile before looking back to Andre. "Question for you... if, in theory, a suitable mate was presented to me, how will I know?" I mean seriously, I have two very good-looking males in front of me—granted one is gay, the other straight but my wolf is drawn to one and not the other. It's an honest curiosity.

Dimitri decides to answer me. "Your mother said it was like seeing a rainbow for the first time—like breathing." Dimitri gets a dreamy looks in his eyes. "Everything just clicked. That's how she described meeting your father." He watches me carefully, trying to gauge my reaction.

"I understand. Thank you, D." Without warning, I start to yawn. My eyes drift to my glass before I raise the remaining tea to my lips and finish it off. I yawn again before lying back down and snuggling myself deep into my blankets. "Wake me when Elena arrives." I yawn once more before falling into a deep sleep. Over the next three days, I only wake for short periods of time to eat and use the restroom before being given another glass of tea.

CHAPTER 6
Aurora

Waking up on what I'm guessing is the fourth day, the smell of bacon and lilacs assault my nose. Although the lilacs smell wonderful, I'm all about the bacon. Cracking one eye open, there sits Elena in the recliner in the corner of the room with a plate of bacon. Gods, I love this woman. It's been over a hundred years since I had last seen her, and she's barely aged. Being almost five hundred looks damn good on her. At most, she seems like she's in her mid-thirties, black hair, blue eyes, and a rather light build for a Lycan female. "Morning Elena, is that bacon for me?" My voice is still scratchy and rough from lack of use. I stretch out my stiff body before accepting the plate of bacon from her.

"Princess, it's good to see you looking so well. You look so much like your mother." Gently Elena caresses my cheek. "She would be proud of the female you have become." She smiles softly as she watches me inhale the plate of food. "I have brought you the last, single Lycan males that I could find." She quirks her lip and tilts her head to look at me before raising a brow. "I've also brought to you my son. He isn't mated and about a hundred years older than you." She smiles confidently. "I believe you two may be a good match. I do have to warn you though, he has a female he's been considering." Elena rolls her eyes. "Her father has been in talks with us about a betrothal. In the meantime, Dimitri and Andre are getting the boys ready for your inspection."

Okay, now she has my undivided attention. I have males. Willing males wanting to be inspected? What the fuck was I supposed to be inspecting? "Okay, I need a shower before I go inspect hotties. Oh, and coffee, plenty of coffee..."

I hear Elena giggle on my way into the bathroom and take the world's fastest shower. I mean seriously, I think I was in there like fifteen minutes max. I waltz out of the bathroom to find Andre and Elena holding a robe and coffee. "Why the robe?" I question as I slip it on before taking the coffee. Downing half the mug in a few gulps, coffee was definitely needed.

Elena stifles a laugh. "Because more than likely, if you scent your mate, your wolf will make herself known at that exact moment. It won't happen with the second one, but the first it's like *bam!* here she is!" She claps her hands together loudly to emphasize what will happen.

My eyebrows shoot up at the explanation, as Andre is laughing his ass off. "Okay, how does this work?"

She moves and opens the double doors so we can look into the yard. "Each male is standing in a different part of the yard, so their scents don't mix. All you must do is walk up and sniff. Your wolf will do the rest." She says it so matter of factly that, yeah, okay, not a problem.

"Andre, put "Sanitarium" by Metallica on for me. It's kind of fitting." I listen for the first few notes to echo through the yard before I step out onto the deck. Which way to start? Well, the question is answered for me quickly as Elena pushes me to start on the right side of the yard.

I guess counterclockwise is the order for the day. Slowly, I move towards the first male. His body language screams anxious, and his scent screams fear, which doesn't make my she-wolf happy. She assesses him as a weak male, not worthy, even before I get close to him. I lean in and sniff at his neck, just under his ear. The acrid scent of urine fills the air. Seriously? I can't believe he actually pissed himself. A growl escapes my lips, and he scurries backward.

"Wuss." That was the first and last word spoken to the coward.

I snort a couple of times to clear the urine scent from my nostrils as I move towards the next male. He's standing stock still, his frame slightly muscular. Typical dark hair, dark eyes, and he's about an inch taller than me. So far, nothing exciting to write home about. I get closer and begin circling him. I want to see if I can throw him off his game. Nothing yet. Leaning in from behind him, in a very dominant move, I sniff at his neck and smell perfume on him mixed with his male musk. Apparently, he took this meeting very seriously... not. I grab him under his arms, sinking my now extended talons into his ribcage, and throw him away from me.

"Next time you visit a potential mate, don't smell like your last conquest." The words are growled out, my full Alpha power behind it. He visibly pales, then runs off into the woods. Two down, two to go. Hopefully, one of these two has balls and common sense. I swear what has happened to guys? They just don't make men anymore. My eyes seek out Elena, Dimitri, and Andre. The three amigos are up on the deck, laughing their asses off over this bullshit. I flip them the bird and stalk towards the next contestant, only the male is wrong. Poor thing, someone forgot to tell him he was male. He's built like a human male and shorter than me. What the fuck!

I mean, really, has the gene pool gotten so shallow that I'm built more substantially than these so-called males? I am so disgusted by what I see, I bypass him completely and start towards unlucky number four. I stop in my tracks when he looks up at me. His eyes are sky blue, his hair is black as pitch. He's muscled, but not over-done. His skin is a golden brown, and scars litter his body, marking him as a fighter. Finally, an actual male! We lock eyes, and he doesn't back down. My wolf makes her presence known, and I feel my eyes turn to liquid mercury.

He smirks, and his wolf surges forward; his eyes are almost a white-blue. His wolf's eyes are beautiful. He begins to move towards me, and I freeze in my tracks. This is starting to get inter-esting. I hear Elena gasp, and the guys hush her. I'm studying this bold male, and in the back of my mind, I'm hoping he's the one. We stand about a foot apart, his nose in the wind catching my scent, his nostrils flare and his wolf rips into existence. He's beau-tiful, thick black fur, white-blue eyes, and long talon-like claws. If I had to venture a guess, he has to be about nine feet tall and is thickly muscled.

Ever so slowly, he lowers his muzzle to me. I tilt my head to the side, granting him access to my throat. I just submitted to this male without even realizing what I was doing.

Once his nose touches my neck, I get a good whiff of his scent... he's *mine*. My wolf doesn't want to wait to shift; she tears free and begins to sniff at him, rubbing her muzzle along his neck and chest. Damn, my bitch is the happiest I've ever seen her. Clapping erupts behind us, snapping us out of our little bubble. Elena has tears in her eyes as she runs down the stairs and hugs us both.

"My baby has found his mate!" She wraps her arms around the male wolf, jumping up and down while holding onto him. Her eyes move to me before she pounces and hugs me too. "Princess, you chose my baby boy. You bring so much honor to my bloodline, thank you!"

Hold on. Back that fucking train up. I back away and shift again. Andre is ready with a pair of beach towels and hands me one. "What do you mean, Elena?" Puzzled, I look back and forth between her and this stud of an Alpha before me.

"Oh. Forgive me, Princess." Elena motions to the man with great pride, "this is my son, Sebastian Lupi. My first-born," Elena says as she introduces him. "He has trained for over two hundred years in the art of war and every known fighting style." She beams with pride telling me of her son's pedigree.

I nod as I move back towards him and wrap my arms around his taut, furred waistline. "Mind shifting back, big guy? I'd like to get to know your human side too." I smile, looking up into the wolf's eyes, he leans down and licks my cheek before I feel his body starting to break and shift back. Sebastian is easily six foot five and relatively easy on the eyes.

His arms tighten around me as he holds on. "I never thought you'd accept me." He speaks so softly, and with such reverence, tears threaten to break loose. "I've waited for what has felt like forever for you. I saw you as a baby in Dimitri's arms; you were so tiny and precious. Your scent called to my wolf and I wanted to protect you." He buries his face in my white hair, and I feel his warm breath upon my shoulder.

He's shaking slightly, overcome with emotion. I squeeze him tightly to me, holding on to him like I am afraid he will vanish. My protective instincts kick into overdrive because of his emotional state. "Did you know what I was to him?" I raise my eyes to look at Elena, watching her cry, "If you did, how could you keep him from me?" My own tears run down my cheeks, sensing my mate's pain. Wait... I was feeling Sebastian's emotions, not Dimitri's? My head whips up, and I stare at Dimitri, and he holds up his left arm. The scar... it's gone. I look down at my arm, my scar is gone as well. I run my fingers through Sebastian's hair in a soothing manner as I wait for Elena to answer me.

"Yes, child, I suspected, but you were far too young to have a male that was getting ready to ascend around you. His wolf would have demanded to complete the bond long before your body was ready." I nod slowly and nuzzle Sebastian as he scoops me up. Ever so carefully, he carries me up onto the porch and sits down, situating me on his lap. "I don't think he's going to let go for a while, child; you may have to get used to it."

I giggle and nuzzle his cheek. "That's okay; he can hold me for as long as he wants to." A muffled "*forever*" comes from Sebastian, and all I can do is smile like a lovesick puppy.

"We still have one matter to attend to, Princess, before you can complete the bond." There was a sadness in Elena's voice that made me raise my head to look at her.

Slowly, I nod and look at Sebastian, kissing his temple. "Let's get this over with. If I must battle, then I must battle." I stand and stretch, my bones pop and crack as I look back to Elena. "Set it up, have the witnesses ready, we do it the old way; wolf-on-wolf. Winner lives, and the loser dies." Everyone's jaws drop, shocked by how matter of fact I agree to battle.

Apparently, I stunned the group into silence. Quickly, I turn and start heading towards my bedroom door, when a large hand grabs my wrist. I look down and notice it's Dimitri's. "Say what you must, bear. You have prepared me well. I am battle-ready." My tone is nothing short of full-blown Alpha and bleeds dominance. "No bitch will take what's mine without a fight."

"Aurora, I do not doubt your training. Though, with so few Lycan females left, you may wish to fight to submission." Dimitri is wringing his hands, looking at his feet.

I know he didn't want to question my desires, but I understand where he's coming from. "I will consider it, D, as long as she's not some insolent wench." I bare my canines at him and then look back at the group.

"We leave in an hour." I watch as Sebastian battles his wolf to leave with his mother. I know he wishes to remain at my side, but until that other bitch dies or submits, honor states he's not entirely mine. I head in and pack only a day bag to take with me. The boys are quick to pack as well, thankfully. Honestly, the wait is killing me. I want to go. Within minutes we are heading to the battlegrounds.

CHAPTER 7
Sebastian

How could I be so dumb to accept the advances of Ravenna? I knew I had a mate, but a hundred years was a long time to wait. Now I've sentenced both females to battle to the death. My mother yells at Ravenna's father about protocol and traditions. He's insistent we sign the contract now before Aurora arrives so that it's binding. But you can't ignore a mating call; it's impossible. I've scented my mate, currently in her adult ascended form, and damn, she is powerful. I almost feel sorry for Ravenna —almost.

Here she is, strutting around the compound, in what she calls an outfit—that barely covers anything. From what I've been told, she's slept her way through the pack, trying to find a suitable mate. I look at my watch for the millionth time when I hear the tell-tale sound of a diesel motor coming up the road in the distance. My wolf surges forth, bouncing with anxiousness; he knows his mate approaches. To be perfectly honest, I've never been happier in my life. Once this battle is over, we can complete our mating bond and move on to find the others she requires for her harem. Dimitri and Andre hop out first as soon as they park and proceed to open the back passenger-side door. My mate looks stunning as she slips out of the truck. Her long, snow-white hair is braided down her back and on her muscular form, a blood-red Bodycon dress.

She turns to assess the crowd before starting to walk barefoot on our soil. Her eyes are swirling liquid pools of mercury. You can practically drown in the power that's coming off her in waves. Aurora lightly dips her head to me then locks eyes with Ravenna. Ravenna attempts to keep her eyes locked with Aurora but can't —she can't even look for more than a few seconds at a clip. You can tell Aurora is out for blood; the look on her face screams rage.

Aurora snorts before she looks to Elena. "I am ready to battle my elder." In a show of respect, Aurora drops to one knee and lowers her head to my mother.

Elena looks to Ravenna. "Are you also ready, child?" Mother is wearing her priestess robes for this occasion, a sign of her station within the pack.

A growl rips from Ravenna's lips. "There's no way she's Lycan! Look at her hair! She's an imposter! I demand my right to be mated to be honored!" She crosses her arms and smirks, thinking she has won.

Surprisingly, Aurora remains calm and stands slowly. "I am Aurora Marelup, daughter of Anca Marelup and Nicodeamus Tepish, dragon mate of my mother. I bare the royal brand." She turns her right arm, baring it so it can be seen. As clear as day, the black, raised seal of the house of Marelup is there on her flesh. Most of the pack drops to one knee, including me. My true mate *is* the lost Princess. She continues to stare down at Ravenna and cants her head to the right. "Get in the ring, bitch. Let's see who the real Lycan is."

Aurora turns, giving Ravenna her back, which is the ultimate insult. Without warning, Ravenna charges at Aurora. Just before impact Aurora turns, grips Ravenna by the throat, and throws her into the ring. A slow shake of her head is all that is offered before Aurora shifts. Her wolf has gained mass that almost rivals my wolf's size, and she is easily over eight-feet tall, and heavily muscled. Her claws look more like talons, and on her muzzle she has snow-white scales. Ah, the ascension must have gifted her access to some of her father's gifts. This should be interesting, to say the least. She stalks forward, growling continuously at Ravenna, who still hasn't shifted yet.

"Shift and fight!" was shouted by someone in the crowd. Aurora stands there—statue-still—waiting for her quarry to shift. Ravenna knows she can't beat Aurora wolf-on-wolf.

"I wish to fight as humans!" Ravenna shouts. Boos echo around the ring before her father, the pack's Alpha, steps forward.

"Daughter, you will fight as a wolf. You disgrace our proud blood-line. To think, I whelped a coward!" Angus is beside himself, looking at his chicken-shit daughter. First, she spoke ill of the princess, and now she is trying to change tradition. The pack starts to grow restless over her childish behavior. Aurora is clicking her talons together, waiting as patiently as an enraged she-wolf could be expected to wait. "You leave me no choice, Daughter." Angus forces Ravenna to lock eyes with him, and when she does, he forces her shift on her. She howls in pain, then lands on all fours. Her body contorted, breaking at odd angles because of the forced shift. She pants heavily, trying to regain some semblance of composure.

Her head whips up to see her father walking away, giving her his back. She's practically been disowned by her family for the disgrace she's brought upon them. You can tell when it clicked—when Ravenna felt she had nothing left to live for. Her wolf immediately takes over, having scented me on Aurora. Within moments, the smaller, black wolf is attacking the great, white wolf. It's kind of sad to say, but Aurora's wolf looks bored. She's playing with the smaller wolf, swatting at her and tossing her across the challenge circle.

Without warning, Aurora shifts back to her mostly human form. She only left her hands and feet changed to that of her wolf. Honestly, her shifted hands and fingers look more dragon than a wolf. Thick, rigid, white scales adorn her hands and fingers like armor. The talons at the ends of her armored hands look like velociraptor claws. Her tail still sways behind her, showing just how relaxed she truly is. There is a defiant smirk on her lips as she stares down the pissed off black she-wolf. With a flick of her hand, she signals for her to come at her.

As Ravenna charges, Aurora leaps up, right hand out and talons extended. She uses the momentum to send her over Ravenna's shoulder, sinking her claws into the she-wolf's throat. Aurora's left-hand shoots out and digs into the she-wolf's back. In one fluid move, she severs Ravenna's head and rips out her heart. Thick crimson fluid sprays the crowd as Aurora completes her finishing move. If I hadn't seen it with my own eyes, I never would have believed it.

Aurora lands gracefully, head in one hand, heart in the other, covered in her opponent's blood. She saunters towards me, shifting the rest of the way back to her human form. Her face is blank, nothing betraying her emotions at the moment. She dips her head in my direction, before heading towards my mother and her guardians.

She drops to one knee and holds up Ravenna's wolven head and her heart to my mother. "I have defeated the challenger set forth before me. I offer you her head and heart to honor your bloodline." My mother gently takes the offerings from her. "I wish to petition for the right to claim my true mate, Sebastian Lupi." Her head is dropped in submission, eyes closed, waiting for the judgment of all the elders present. Aurora fought for me—for us. I am so proud of her I could burst.

"Come forth, Sebastian." Elder Grayson was the one to call my name. I move swiftly and drop to my knees beside Aurora. I lower my head in submission, as she did, and close my eyes as well. I hate waiting, but for her, I'd wait forever if I had to.

"It has come to our attention that some dark dealings have come to pass within the pack. This business of the Alpha using his position almost to force a mating when you had a mate already." Elder Grayson began to circle Aurora and me before speaking again. "How old were you, Sebastian, when you first discovered Aurora was your mate?"

I drew in a deep breath before answering. "Barely one hundred, Elder. Aurora and her guardians lived with us for a few months, before going into hiding."

Elder Grayson stops moving beside me. "How did you know she was yours, for one so young?"

I dare not raise my head or look at him like I want to. My wolf isn't happy he is questioning us. "My wolf knew by scent. I got to hold her as a baby. She was and is everything to me."

Elder Grayson snorts. "If you knew, how could you agree to start the process with Ravenna?" He puts his hand under my chin and raises my gaze. "You sentenced that girl to death today."

Aurora's growl could be felt by those close enough to her. Her eyes narrow on Elder Grayson, and his hand on my jaw. "Release my mate," she growls. Her voice takes on the pure force of her wolf, along with eyes, and canines lengthened. I watch as the fur starts to ripple across her flesh. Her wolf is fighting for control; she wants the elder dead. I just know it.

I rest a hand on Aurora's shoulder in an attempt to calm her. It didn't ultimately work, her anger is palpable. Immediately the elder releases me and joins the others. Aurora lets the full magnitude of her Alpha powers be felt as she slowly stands. Lesser wolves cower and whine, backing up slowly. Most of the elders begin to shrink back. Everyone except my mother; she just smiles proudly.

"Come, Aurora, let's feed you and clean you up. We have a mating ceremony to perform tonight for you two." My mother opens her arms, and Aurora, without hesitation, slips right in and hugs her tightly. She gently nuzzles my mother's neck, enjoying the affection being shown to her. It's kind of scary how quickly the switch flips. Aurora goes from hellhound to snuggle puppy in seconds. I can't help but smile, watching the two of them interact; it is a thing of beauty.

Aurora pulls out of my mother's arms and looks at me, smiling. She wiggles her index finger at me as if to say come here. I rise to my full height and slowly remove my button-down shirt, offering it to her. Typical Aurora, she cants her head to the side and slowly slips my shirt on, buttoning up the front. She lifts the fabric of my shirt to her nose and sniffs. A slow, gentle sigh escapes her lips as she raises her eyes to look at me.

"Thank you, my love." Those four simple words falling from her lips in almost a whisper rocks my world completely, tilting it on its axis. Aurora's steps are cautious as she approaches me—I can tell she is a little unsure of herself. Her hand rests over my heart, and her eyes lock on where her hand rests. "I do not enjoy killing lesser beings. But I will burn the world to the ground to protect what is mine." She leans forward and kisses my chest over my heart before looking up into my eyes. Her eyes are human, a pale steel-grey, and I knew the woman had said what was in her heart, not the wolf.

"Aurora, my love, I feel like I've waited a lifetime for you. I will continue to wait until you are ready. I am yours, you are mine; we are one." I rest my hand over hers as I speak, a slight swirl of mercury surfaces in her eyes then vanishes. Both woman and wolf agree. We turn, hand in hand, heading to the main hut to catch up with my mother. I bet she's already counting how many grand pups she wants to have. I shake my head and laugh to myself as several females rush up and try to steal Aurora away. She's instantly a big, growling mess.

"Ladies, my mate isn't used to being handled. Just ask her to follow, I'm sure she would like to get cleaned up before the cere-mony." Aurora nods slowly, and hesitantly follows the females, stopping to look where I am. I almost want to laugh. This badass bitch just ripped her opponent's head off and ripped out her heart, but is concerned about following a bunch of females to a bath. A large hand lands on my shoulder, turning my head slightly to find Dimitri. He has that psycho Joker smile going, and it looks kind of disturbing. "What can I do for you, big guy?"

Dimitri's eyes bleed gold, then back to hazel. "Not much, future Prince. Our girl did good today, *Da*?" He crosses his arms over his chest—he's fucking huge, six feet tall and easily almost four hundred pounds of man-bear.

"Aurora was phenomenal. That finishing move, holy shit, it gave me chills. But seriously, I hate that part of the tradition. Usually, it's two males fighting, not females—there's so few fertile females left. To lose one is a hit to our species as a whole." I look out across the great hall watching everyone preparing for tonight's ceremony.

"There are even fewer great bears, if there's any left, besides me." He looks down at his beer stein and then takes a long pull of the amber fluid. "I knew that day, way back then, that Aurora was yours." He draws in a deep breath, getting lost in the memory. "Not many hundred-year-old males would want to fawn over a pup all day." I smile thinking about it. Those were the best three months of that year. "You were the only one that could get her to stop crying. I believe in my heart she knew you were hers back then too." Dimitri's eyes lift to meet mine. You can tell he is holding back laughter as he begins to speak. "I kept the shirt you gave to her to soothe her until your scent was gone. Man, did that little hellion have a fit to end all fits that day." He starts laughing hard. "She clawed the hell out of Andre and bit his nose when he leaned over to take the shirt away."

"That wasn't funny, Dimitri! That was so many shades of wrong!" Andre bellows from the other side of the hall. Damn eagle has excellent hearing and eyesight. I start laughing just as hard as Dimitri. Man, if only I could have seen baby Aurora go postal because my shirt was taken from her.

I was so distracted I didn't notice my mother emerging from the alcove. In my mother's hands, she is carrying a blood-red, crushed velvet tunic. A smirk crosses her lips as she hands it to me. Don't get me wrong, I love Aurora with everything that I am... but holy shit! I'm finally taking a mate, and she kind of scares me. I don't care that she's a princess, but fuck me, she's the last Lycan Princess and fucking lethal. Honestly, I'm more nervous that I will fuck this up and not make this perfect for her. Quickly I run over to my good buddy Pete, and give him instructions for what I need him to do for me. I'm hoping that Aurora likes camping and that my favorite spot pleases her. Otherwise, this is going to be a very long and miserable night, potentially.

CHAPTER 8

Elena

PRIESTESS

I KNEW WHEN MY SISTER HAD SENT THAT TINY, SNOW-WHITE HAIRED BABY to me she held great power. Dimitri had bestowed upon me the gift of knowing Aurora's true birth parents. To think the dragon was the true mate of Anca amazes me. I knew that Anca wasn't fond of the Lycan Alpha. It was a political mating more than one out of love. Now, to see the woman that Aurora has become makes my whole heart swell with joy.

My son was instantly taken by her when he met her. He held her every day and halfway into the night every night. I knew what she was to him. To watch him miss her and pine for her all this time has been torture. There's only so long a male can hold out on urges, and he impressed me, waiting fifty years before touching another female. I knew nothing would ever come of it. Then there's that psycho, Ravenna, who thought using her father would get her the prize she wanted. Sadly enough, it had almost worked—*almost*. Even if it had, if his true mate showed up, Ravenna would have been tossed aside like the trash she was.

My eyes drift towards the head and heart I had placed on the ceremonial table. At least the wicked bitch is dead and no longer an issue. Watching Sebastian interact with Aurora's guardians makes me so happy. The first leg of her journey is now complete, and the next is very difficult. My hands glide over my scrolls. I'm searching for the one on the dire bloodlines here in the states. Looks to be only one Alpha left here, and he's somewhere in the Grand Canyon.

He's been blessed with four sons; one set of twins, and two single births. Sadly, the jackass sends the females to battle the prisoners he's collected over the years. No female has survived the Wendigo or the Ice Dragon he's got. I suspect the Ice Dragon is Aurora's father. If I'm right, and she can survive long enough to battle him, he will know his bloodline by scent and not harm her.

Herbs are gathered by my acolytes and placed in their proper places upon the table. I arrange the dagger and the bowl, even though I know neither of them wants a hand binding; they will use their canines to mark their mate. Both are warriors and strong, stronger than most that live in these current times. Aurora will gain the strength of my son after they complete the mating tonight. Each mate will gift her a particular attribute unique to their species. The dires, there are so many possible gifts... wow, there are so many unique traits. She could gain shadowmancy, their toxic bite, a traditional wolf form, and the list goes on. A throat clearing makes me look up to see my beloved son waiting for permission to approach.

"Come in, please. After all, this is where you need to be." I smile at him and come out from behind the table to embrace my boy. It doesn't matter how old he gets, he'll always be my little boy.

"Mother, must we have Ravenna's head and heart present? It's kind of weird for a mating ceremony." He scrunches his nose like he always does when something is distasteful to him.

"Baby boy, I was honored by your mate with these gifts. They deserve to be in a place of honor. That, and to remind the others to not fuck with the two of you." Yup, I can be the evil priestess when I need to be. With all the bullshit concerning the Alpha, he needs to be reminded where the real power lies. That power is in a pure-white Lycan hybrid named Aurora, my future daughter-in-law. My son starts to laugh; he's learned to read when I have a wicked thought.

"Mother? You're trying to scare the Alpha, aren't you?" He tilts his head and looks at me, smirking. Damn, I'm busted. He freaking knows me too well. I raise one hand to my chest in the *who me* motion, and he laughs harder—yup, totally busted. Moments pass and the pack starts filtering into the hall, taking their seats.

The Alpha approaches me and glares. "So, how much damage did my daughter do before her demise?" He just smirks—almost laughing. *What an asshole!*

Before I can answer, Aurora makes her entrance. The doors bang against the wall making everyone jump, including the Alpha. "No damage. She wasn't strong enough, fast enough, or skilled enough to lay a single claw on me," Aurora practically growls out her sentence. "If you want Alpha... you can meet me in the ring in the morning, and you can see for yourself if it was just a fluke." Her eyes swirl between mercury and steel-grey—it's quite apparent she is fighting for control at the moment.

Thankfully, my son moves and touches her arm, drawing her attention to him. I let out a relieved breath and nod slowly, signaling for the lights to be lowered and the candles to be lit. I raise my hands slowly, drawing the pack's attention to the front of the room. Once everyone's eyes fall on me, I begin.

"We have gathered here tonight to bear witness to the mating ceremony of my son, Sebastian Lupi, and Princess Aurora Marelup. We bore witness to her strength and power today; we felt she was the true heir to the Lycan throne." I move and start to pour red wine into the chalice. In my right hand, I grab hold of Ravenna's heart and hold it up high. "As in ancient traditions, I was offered the heart of her enemy. I, in turn, offer the heart to the wolf Goddess Morrighan! May she smile upon this union." I take the heart and place it on the copper platter, then set it aflame. As it burns, the flames change colors several times until they turn white before the heart turns to ash. A smile crosses my lips, having witnessed the white flames; the Goddess has accepted our offering. I raise my hands again.

"Our Goddess has accepted our offering!" The crowd erupts in cheers; it truly is a blessed day. I turn my gaze back to the smiling couple before me. "As per tradition, I must ask if any in this hall objects to this union before we proceed." Silence greets us for several moments before the Alpha steps forward.

He has a wicked grin on his lips, I know he's up to no good. "I claim my right as Alpha to take the princess as my own!" A bold statement, but also a fact. He doesn't realize a true mating trumps his claim. Sebastian and Aurora begin to growl at him. Over half the villagers are growling at him as well. It's about to get really interesting.

Aurora's laughter rings out and fills the hall. She moves to stand before the Alpha. The full weight of her dominance ripples throughout the room. Her eyes are pools of liquid mercury as she stares at him. He's trying like hell to keep his eyes locked with hers. He squirms where he stands, and shortly after the staring contest begins, he turns his head and lowers it. Aurora shifts her right hand and places a talon under his jaw to raise his eyes to meet hers. "You are not worthy. You are a weak, pathetic excuse of a male." She scrunches her nose, giving him a look of disgust. "Look at yourself; you pissed your pants all because I stared at you, you pussy." Aurora turns and faces Sebastian, locking eyes with him. Wave upon wave of power come off both of them, but he doesn't submit. Aurora smiles and approaches him.

Her eyes close, and she touches her nose under his jaw in submission. She holds her position until he releases her. Steel-grey eyes meet Sebastian's white-blue, the eyes of his wolf. Ever so slowly, she bares her neck to him. Sebastian leans in with an open mouth and lightly bites her throat, holding her there. It's more for show, but it's a massive symbol of the trust between these two titans.

Once he releases her, he stares at the Alpha. "With all due respect, Alpha. She'll kill you in a heartbeat without question. That is if my wolf doesn't beat her to it." Sebastian's voice holds the growl and power of his wolf.

The Alpha lowers his head and backs away. He mumbles that he withdraws his claim as he runs out of the building. "Okay, so now *that*," I wave my hand in the direction of the departing Alpha, "bullshit is over, let's get back to the important part—the sharing of blood to start the bond. By scent and sight, your wolves have accepted each other. Now by blood, they become one. You have two choices: cut your palms, bleed into the wine, and drink; or, you can go traditional and bite each other. The choice is truly yours."

As one, they turn to look at each other. No words pass between them as they shift to their wolven forms. The unexpected shift makes many of the pack nervous, others sit there in wonder. A traditional bonding hasn't been done in public since my day.

Aurora chooses to submit first and bares her shoulder and throat to Sebastian's black wolf. He closes the distance between them and licks the area he intends to bite. A slight nod from Aurora and Sebastian opens his great maw and clamps down on the muscle between her neck and shoulder. He holds her like that for what seems like forever, her white fur stained red from her blood.

Carefully, he releases her and licks the wounds clean, healing them instantly, and leaving a black ring where her fur changed color from the bite. Aurora raises her head and nods slightly again, and he crouches down slightly for her. When Sebastian is ready, he rests his taloned hands on her wolven hips to stabilize himself before baring his throat to her. Aurora slowly lowers her muzzle to his shoulder and begins to clean the chosen area. Her eyes turn to watch Sebastian for a moment; he nods, letting her know he is ready.

Aurora draws in a deep breath and opens her maw to bite at the muscle between his neck and shoulder. Her taloned hands rest on his shoulders, careful not to slice him to ribbons. Sebastian's blood could be scented in the air but not seen. When she feels she held him long enough, she releases her grip on his shoulder. Gently, she cleans his wounds, sealing them instantly. A pure white ring of fur covers her mark upon his shoulder. Both wolves turn to face me.

"I bless this union. May their lives be filled with love and longevity… and many pups!" I had to throw that in. The look on both of their faces is priceless. In the corner, Aurora's guardians stand there like sentinels. Poor Andre is having a hard time with his little girl growing up. He's an emotional mess but still standing tall and proud, even with his puffy eyes. Aurora and Sebastian bow to me before they leave the hall out the back door. Now is the time for their hunt and the true mating to occur. At least some things are still kept private, thank the Gods. I move towards her guardians and shake both of their hands. "Gentlemen, we have succeeded in our missions. Aurora has ascended and found her first mate. I call that a win."

I watch Dimitri rubbing the spot where the binding mark once was. His eyes eventually find mine. "*Da*, we did. Now it's just a matter of time before time catches up to Andre and me. Don't get me wrong, we are grateful for the extra time, but now we know the end is near. We just hope we live long enough to help her ascend the throne and take her rightful place." Dimitri hugs Andre to him and holds the overly emotional bird to his great chest.

I study them closely, and the sands of time have begun the run. Delicate wrinkles now grace the creases of their eyes. A sprinkle of grey hair can be seen on their temples. A soft sigh escapes my lips as I watch them. I feel horrible about what's to come. My sister's magic gave them the extra time, and perhaps I can extend it again. I leave them to have their moment and walk back to my hut to start studying my sister's notes. Maybe I'll find a solution for them. I can only hope.

CHAPTER 9
Sebastian

Both wolves run through the woods far away from the village of my birth. The sun is starting to set as we come upon the place called Mirrored Lake. The water is so calm and still it's like looking at a mirror laid flat on the ground. The surrounding area has heavy timber as well as an apple tree grove that has fruit available. I come to a stop at the edge of the water before shifting back to my human form. Aurora cautiously approaches the water's edge then shifts back to her human form. She slowly tilts her head to the right and studies the area... it's absolutely breathtaking. You can tell she's watching the sun setting over the mountain tops. The sky is streaked with reds, blues, purples, several shades of oranges and yellows. I move and lightly place a hand on her lower back before gently kissing her cheek.

"I hope this is acceptable to you?" I was nervous about my choice of where to take her. This particular place held so much meaning for me; it's where I made my first kill and learned to shift and fight. Aurora smiles at me and moves in closer, resting her head on my chest.

"It's beautiful, Sebastian! Can we stay here for a while? I can't wait to see the moon upon the lake's surface." Her smile made the long run worth it. Gently I guide her to a small grove of apple trees. Under the oldest tree, I have camping gear and a cooler set up for us. Aurora begins to bounce up and down. Apparently, I have chosen wisely. "Awesome, I've never been camping before; this will be an adventure!" She bounds away from me to look around at all I have prepared for our first night together.

Suddenly she freezes and begins to growl. Her wolf bursts forth from her body and takes on a defensive stance as she begins to back up towards me. Seeing my mate shift so quickly, I decide to shift as well. My sizable black wolf moves to stand at her right flank, staring in the direction she is. A pale being reeking of death, decay, and sulfur begins to amble through the woods towards us. Its face looks like the being from the old black and white movie Nosferatu.

Aurora's eyes narrow; she knows what it is. It's a Strigoi—the same creature that had a hand in the destruction of her bloodline. Silent communication passes between us. I shift back to my human form and look for the phone I packed. Quickly I call Dimitri and tell him what is standing before us. It was Dimitri's worst fear. The Strigoi sensed when Aurora came into power and began to hunt her. I keep my eyes on Aurora as she circles the Strigoi, sizing it up. Dimitri gives me detailed instructions as to how to destroy it.

"Aurora, we must take its head! And don't let it bite you; it's poison!" I yell as loudly as I can. Quickly I shift back to my wolf as I spot a second creature approaching. I know this is going to be a fight to the death. Aurora's guardians are on their way to help us, just in case. Backup isn't far behind, now we need to dispatch these two before it gets too dangerous.

Aurora charges at the Strigoi, making sure to stay out of range of its swiping distance. Her talons sever its left arm from its body—blackened blood pulses out of the artery poking out of the remnant of the creature's arm. The second Strigoi starts going nuts, smelling the blood from its companion. Its dark eyes, burning red like blood, have taken on an unearthly glow before it lunges at me. I dodge, barely getting out of the way of the crazed creature.

My taloned hand reaches out and catches the back of the Strigoi as it passes me, ripping its flesh to ribbons. Blood pours down its back, and its movements are slowed from the strike I delivered. Both Strigoi are moving slower from blood loss. The one Aurora is fighting now has a massive chunk of his thigh missing and can barely remain standing.

Dimitri's bear is seen breaking over the top of the ridge. Damn, that male is freaking huge; he makes a Kodiak look small. He charges forward and into battle, knocking Aurora's Strigoi to the ground and ripping its head off. While Dimitri is busy with the first one, Aurora joins me with the second one. Both of us now circle the lone Strigoi, it screams—calling for help—but no one answers.

The last Strigoi doesn't stand a chance being trapped between Aurora and me. Her eyes flair to life, and the liquid mercury of her eyes seems to glow brighter for a mere moment. Suddenly she lunges forward, her taloned hand extended with her fingers splayed wide as she aims for the Strigoi's throat. With a flick of her wrist, the Strigoi's head is severed from its body. Blackened blood sprays in an arc, painting the once green grass onyx. The body falls with a thud at her feet, blackened blood oozes from the severed arteries, coating the ground. The thump of the severed head landing near draws our attention away for a moment, before our eyes refocus upon the remains in front of us. The threat is now over, and the Strigoi bodies turn to ash and blow away with the wind.

Dimitri shifts back first and walks over to us. "You both did well. Congratulations on your first Strigoi kills." He claps his hands briefly. "It's been over two hundred and twenty-nine years since I've seen these fuckers. It's only going to get worse from here." His eyes move skyward, watching Andre's Golden Eagle circle overhead. He is doing lazy circles in the air, keeping watch for any more surprise visitors.

Aurora, still in wolf form, walks away from the group heading towards the water. Her normally snow-white fur is now spotted like a dalmatian from the Strigoi's blood. Once in the water, she shifts back to her human form and begins to wash away the blood from the battle. I watch her, hypnotized, my eyes transfixed on everywhere her hands touch.

"Sebastian?" Dimitri says, trying to draw my attention back to him. "Shift back, we need to talk." Dimitri is all business all the time, and the look on his face at the moment proved that this is about to get serious.

Quickly I resume my human form and move my hands over my erection, trying to cover it—I'm failing miserably. "Thanks for getting here so quickly. How the fuck did those things find us so fast? I thought we had time." My voice held concern as I look between Aurora in the water and Dimitri before me. I'm not panicking, just shocked that the Strigoi arrived so quickly.

"Andre and I will stay within howling distance tonight. You must complete the bond. She will gain power from you and you from her." Dimitri's eyes drift to Aurora and linger there longer than I think would be decent. My own heated gaze caresses every single visible inch of my mate's curvy form.

"Each mate she adds, she will gain a gift from them, and thus it spreads to the others as well. Your mother told us where the local Dire Wolf pack is." Dimitri tilts his head, making a very stern face at me. "So, when you two get your act together, that's where we're heading next. They are somewhere in the Grand Canyon in some old Indian dwelling." Shortly after Dimitri finishes speaking, Andre lands.

All you can see is Andre shaking his head and throwing his arms about. "Wait! We have to play hide and go fucking seek to find her mates? Do I look like the dude from *Pickers*?" Andre has a *what the fuck* face on as he looks between Dimitri and me. We both crack up over the frazzled look that Andre gives us.

The laughter carries to the water, and Aurora's head snaps up as she stares at us. Slowly she walks out of the water. Rivulets of water caress her curves in a hypnotizing manner. Each droplet catches my attention, my eyes follow their path hungrily. Aurora smirks, looking at my state of being—my poor penis is rock solid, the head is turning purple and leaking. Aurora raises an eyebrow looking at it, then up to me. "That looks painful. What'd you do? Slam it in the cooler lid, or did one of those things hit it?" And there you have it—her innocence on display. Dimitri's and Andre's jaws drop. I honestly don't know what to say. Aurora just smiles at me then moves to grab a towel.

"As for the others. We'll find them, and I'll take what's mine." She raises her hand and taps a finger on her plump lips. "Speaking of which, Dimitri and Andre, you need to leave." She waves her hands, making a shooing motion. "I have a mate to claim, and I refuse to do it in your presence." She crosses her arms over her chest, staring at them. Dimitri and Andre almost fall over each other trying to leave. Andre takes to the skies, and Dimitri shifts back to his bear and lumbers into the woods.

"So, Sebastian, how do we do this?" The look on my face must be priceless. Aurora flat out asked me what we needed to do to complete the bond. Dimitri and Andre are long gone, so there was no one to use as a distraction.

"Well, Aurora, I was hoping to ease into this to make it special for your first time." My eyes drop to the ground at my feet. I've had sex so many times I've lost count, but this time means something. My eyes meet hers for a brief moment before looking down and away again. This is my mate, the one I'd be spending the rest of my life with. Aurora's hand gently caresses my jaw, raising my gaze to meet hers.

"I won't lie to you, Bash; I'm nervous. Instinctually I know what I need to do. But instincts and practical application are two different things." I watch her shift her weight nervously. "But I trust you. You're my mate, my forever, and I know it's insanely soon... but I feel like I love you already." She leans in and gently kisses my lips. "Don't tell the guys I'm a big softie; they'll never let me live it down." She smiles and winks at me before moving to sit on the picnic blanket.

A gentle pat was given to the spot next to her for me to join her. I laugh and move quickly to be at her side. Aurora opens the basket and starts spreading out the food I brought for us. There are several types of meats and cheeses, two kinds of wine, and water. For dessert, there is a homemade apple pie. The amount of thought I put into this moment pleases Aurora and her wolf.

Ever so carefully, Aurora dishes out food onto plates for the two of us. With a deep cleansing breath, she lifts the plate for me and offers me my food first. Her eyes remain locked on me until I begin to eat. Once the first morsel is swallowed, Aurora begins to eat.

"Why did you serve me and wait? We are equals." I am puzzled by Aurora's actions, so why not ask?

"Well, Dimitri and Andre both said tradition dictates I should serve my first mate before myself." She shrugs her shoulders. "It's the way things were done back when my mother ruled and her mother before her." Her eyes drop to her lap, where her hands are tightly clasped. "I'm sorry if I didn't do it correctly. The guys did their best trying to teach me, but I'm stubborn and willful, and honestly, don't give a shit half the time." She raises an eyebrow and looks up at me to find me smiling and trying not to laugh. My smile must be contagious because soon, Aurora begins to laugh. "What's so funny?" She cants her head to the side.

I reach out and pull Aurora onto my lap. "Fuck tradition! We'll make our own as we go along!" I nibble on her throat and make her giggle. I reach out and grab a piece of meat, then offer it to her. Ever so gently, Aurora takes the offered meat and eats it. Her own hand reaches out and grabs a piece of meat to offer it to me, and I take it in my mouth and eat it. An hour passes as we take turns feeding each other. We are so relaxed with each other, it is just what we need to settle our nerves.

I pick Aurora up, making her squeal. I have her now straddling my lap, facing me. Her eyes move over my body, then back up to my face. I lean forward and capture her lips, kissing her slowly, savoring the moment. Breaths between us begin to deepen as the kiss grows in intensity. Aurora starts to paw at my shoulders, leaving fingernail tracks from my spine to my biceps. She doesn't understand what she wants, but instinctively she knows what she needs. A deep approving rumble reverberates deep in my chest.

Aurora's scent thickens with her arousal as she starts to become more aggressive.

I can't hold back anymore, and my wolf demands I take our mate now. My erection is throbbing, thick and hard as steel, pulsing in time with my heartbeat. I grab hold of Aurora and flip her onto her back and come to lay down over her. I'm not about to give in completely to my wolf. I refuse to be rough and set a punishing pace her first time. No, the man was in control, no matter how much my wolf howled in the background. My lips come to rest against Aurora's.

"Baby, this may hurt, I'm not a small man." I kiss her again, looking into her eyes for some sort of acknowledgment. Slowly she nods and nips my jaw. "I'm going to go slow. Stop me if you need to." I'm worried about her comfort; I love her too much even to cause the slightest bit of pain. My hand slides between her thighs to position myself at her entrance. Aurora is soaked, absolutely beyond wet. I slide myself through her moist lips, coating my length before starting to enter her.

Aurora inhales quickly as she adjusts to my girth. Her eyes lock with mine, and she nods again, showing she is okay. I stop when I meet with resistance. Hesitating, I know this is the part that is going to hurt her. My mouth drops to her shoulder over my mating mark, I sink my teeth in hard as I slam forward, breaking the barrier. Aurora grips me tightly, wiggling from the pleasure my bite is bringing her. Slowly I begin to move, setting the pace for our mating. The slapping of skin, pants, and moans can be heard in the distance. Aurora is whining, sounding more wolf than woman as she approaches her climax. When she finally cums, her screams morph to a long haunting howl. My own howl soon joins hers as I, too, reach my peak.

We lay there cuddled up, tangled within each other's arms for what seems like hours. We consummate our mating many times throughout the night, deepening our connection and strengthening our bond. In the morning, it will be time to begin the hunt for the dires and whatever may come after that.

CHAPTER 10

Aurora

I CLOSE MY EYES AS I SIT AT THE LAKE'S EDGE. I CAN FEEL PRECISEL
where Sebastian is, and if I concentrate hard enough, I can almos
see what he's seeing. A gentle breeze blows and shifts, and in th
winds I smell Dimitri and Andre approaching. Thankfully th
Strigoi that attacked had only been scouts. Although by tonight
they will know that their scouts were killed and that I was now a
threat. Heh, they don't know the half of it. I'm sitting here, with
my head thrown back, enjoying the breeze with my eyes close. I'm
still trying to figure out what gift I received from Sebastian wher
Dimitri decides to interrupt my thoughts.

"Princess, we should get moving. The Strigoi won't attack during
the day so we can move quickly, and the village won't ge
attacked." He spoke with truth and logic—he's learned not to fluf
things with me. After all, they raised me to be a no-nonsense kind
of girl. Give it to me straight, and I'll respect you more for it.

"Fine, D." I roll my eyes. "Have Andre fly ahead and tell Elen
what happened with the Strigoi. Also, tell her I'm going to need

that map she said she had." Standing up, I stretch and crack my back. Faint pink lines cross my ribs like tiger stripes from Sebastian's grip on me last night, and I can feel D studying them. "Don't stare, D, it's creepy." I smirk, looking at him as I head towards Sebastian to help him finish packing up the site.

The sneaky male has a golf cart hidden nearby, so we load up everything in it. My eyes drift back to Dimitri. "D, please drive the cart back. I wish to stretch my legs before getting trapped in the truck with three stinky boys." I playfully pinch my nose before turning back to look at Sebastian.

"Race ya!" I shout as I run and shift in motion. My great, white Lycan glides swiftly and soundlessly through the woods heading back to the village. To my surprise, Sebastian is on my heels. Guess I gifted him with my speed. That may come in handy in the future. We weave in and out of the trees, almost playing tag as we approach the edge of the forest.

Suddenly stopping, I look about... hmm, something isn't right. The scent, it's wrong. Raising my muzzle in the air, there's a scent of blood carried in the breeze. In the distance, I stop and prick up my ears to listen closely and discern what I hear around me when suddenly I hear Andre screaming for help. We run towards him without a thought. The village center looks like a scene from a horror flick. Several wolves lay dead, and there are just as many ash piles. Sebastian takes off looking for his mother as I prowl the village. I catch the scent of a single surviving Strigoi hiding out in the meeting hall.

Without a second thought, I leap onto the roof and let loose a warning howl, so no others will approach. Sadly, it has the opposite effect, and the surviving wolves begin to gather. We listen to the screeches of the trapped Strigoi. The sun will destroy it if it comes out, so I think the smartest thing to do is let the sun in. My talons begin to rip at the metal roof, opening it up like a can of tuna. Light begins to flood the hall. I stick my head down into the hole I created and see where it's hiding. It's blocked in a corner, trapped by the beams of light I let in. Now was the time to fry it. Quickly, I leap to the other side and rip off the roof directly over its head and watch its body burst into flames. The Strigoi's screams fill the air until its body is frozen in mid-scream with no more sound coming out.

Satisfied that I ended the threat, I leap down and the villagers drop to one knee before me. All except the Alpha, that dumb ass decides to walk up to me. "How dare you bring this threat to my people! Many have died because of you!" he snarls at me, pointing a finger. "I hope they rend the flesh from your bones and drink your blood like wine." He stands there all cocky, thinking his title will protect him. Over his shoulder, I see Sebastian, Dimitri, and Elena. I didn't want to do this, but I cannot let him poison my people anymore.

I shift back and stand before him, my eyes that of my wolf. "It's amazing how you have short periods of time that you have balls —no brains, but balls. I'd almost respect that if I didn't scent the terror oozing off of you." I narrow my eyes at him. "Not one of the Strigoi fell by your claws. No, you hid in your cellar waiting for the sun to come up so you could claim the glory to the survivors." I shake my head and circle him. "You forget your place in the hierarchy. You forget that Alphas have no power while a Royal still lives." I smirk at him then point a finger in his direction. "You are a leader with a handed down title from a weak bloodline." Jabbing a finger in Sebastian's direction, I continue. "My mate's bloodline is older than yours, from the old country where our kind comes from." I circle him with my eyes narrowed. "You, you're a thin-blooded, American Lycan no history, no lineage. I'm ending your rule today," I say, baring my canines at him. "Step down and submit... or die. Your choice." I give him my back and close my eyes. Sebastian feels what I am doing, and he locks onto the Alpha, watching his movements closely. I see every move through Sebastian's eyes without having to turn.

"Like my daughter said, she's not pure Lycan She's part dragon and unfit to rule!" He charges at me, and just before impact, I regain my Lycan's form and sink my talons into his chest straight to his spine. I hold him there, feeling his heart beating against my forearm. Blood pulses out and around the hole in his chest and down to my elbow. He's in such a state of shock that he just stares into my pure mercury orbs. With one quick flick of my wrist, I end him, ripping out his spine in one fluid move.

I shift back, his spine still in my hand. My arm bloody to my elbow as I turn to face the gathered crowd. "You are my pack, my people. I will fight for you and protect you. All I ask is that you train hard in the old ways." I raise my clean hand and wave at Elena to come forward. "Elena and her family have faithfully served my family for countless generations. I ask her to serve me now. Watch over our people; guide them in the old ways. Her word is my law. Those that stand against her will die by my talons." I address the survivors who all nod and bow their heads, showing I've gained their respect and loyalty.

I turn to Elena, "Train them well in the battle skills. War is coming, and I'll need every strong Lycan at my side for the final battle." I pace back and forth. "Gather the rogues and the ones the old Alpha exiled, bring them back into the pack and give them purpose." I kiss the top of Elena's head before moving towards my shocked mate. I hold out my hand and offer him the spine of the old Alpha. "For you, my love. Do with it what you will." I walk off towards his hut, listening to his mother comfort the survivors. I've chosen well, she knows these people, and she'll do right by them. In the meantime, I need to clean up and pack. We have a road trip ahead of us.

I DRAG out the guitar and amp I found in Sebastian's room and sit on the front porch to tune it. Usually I like playing Ax7, but today is a little different. Instead, I start playing Megadeth's "She-wolf," letting the notes carry through the compound. My head is down, my eyes closed, and I'm lost to the music. In my head, I'm singing the song. But somewhere around the first chorus, I hear several voices join in singing the lyrics.

I smile as I look up to see it's Sebastian and several other young males. One joins in with his guitar, playing the backup rhythms for the song. We jam out, and I bask in the glory of how my mate and his wolf are staring at me while he sings. I stand up and start walking around playing the song, and eventually, it turns into a full-out performance for the pack. The young male playing back up approaches as we bounce back and forth toward the end of the song, taking turns playing the lead rhythm. It's a thing of beauty when you can be in sync with another. I see Elena approaching, and she smirks at me. I look to my new buddy and change it up. I hit the opening riff of "Of Wolf and Man" from Metallica. Peter—I find out his name—is grinning from ear to ear as the pack sings the lyrics as we play.

Elena stands there enjoying the pack's flow; they are alive and acting as one, as a pack should. I breathe new life into them. Slowly I move toward Elena, still playing along with Peter. "Can I help you, pack master?" I smile at her as I thrash through the cords, and everyone begins to howl along with this part of the song.

"Princess, you have performed many miracles for your people." She smiles. "You freed them, and gave them a purpose. We are blessed to have you." She pats my shoulder as I hand the guitar off to my mate, who starts up an early 90's tune. "I stuck a new author's book in your bag. The female main character reminds me of you." Okay, that got my attention.

"Oh, is she a wolven badass like me?" My smile spreads wide like the Cheshire cat—or is it the cat that swallowed the canary? Either way, it isn't an innocent look.

"Definitely not. It's a mob book. She shoots this girl..." She waves her hand in front of her, then adds, "just wait 'til you read it. With the way you handled the last two threats, she's right up your alley." Elena has that innocent as fuck look going on, so I know she's up to something. Now I really need to read that book.

I shelve that thought at the moment and turn to look at my people. *My people...* I never thought I'd be saying that. I was kept separate, raised off-grid for over two hundred years, all because of my bloodline. Now I have a pack, a mate, and other mates I must still find. I feel like I'm playing an advanced game of manhunt, well, a literal manhunt.

I stand here watching everything unfold and ponder what my parents would think of me at this moment. Am I too brutal? I mean, my death toll is rising, and I haven't traveled more than four hundred miles in the last week. I'm mildly concerned as to how high it will reach before the final battle. I've killed a woman, an Alpha's daughter, and the Alpha. So only three in the last week... not horrible, maybe. Dimitri once told me I was going to need an army to take back the castle. A pack's loyalty is to its Alpha. So, unless I'm sure of the Alpha's fealty, he cannot live. I must ascend to take over the pack. Many cogs in the machine, so many pieces to the puzzle, but I clearly understand how they fit together.

Then it dawns on me. Sebastian's gift is battle strategy. I never had the ability to plan things out to this level previously. This is freaking amazing. Speaking of that hunk of a Lycan, he walks straight towards me. "You look deep in thought, love. Everything okay?" He smiles and sits next to me, taking my hand in his.

"Just a lot to process. I've done so much, yet it's just the tip of the iceberg." I rest my head on his broad shoulder and take comfort in his presence. "Oh, and I figured out that I gained your gift of battle strategy. That is a most excellent gift to receive." I smile, and he starts laughing.

"Great, I made the perfect weapon even more dangerous!" he says, still laughing and smiling, so I know he's just teasing me. "But on a serious note, good decision on killing the Alpha. He would have promised backup for the war then left us to drown. He's always been a self-serving asshole." Fan-fucking-tastic. I didn't read him wrong. I'm not sure if I'm more happy or relieved at this point.

"That's exactly what I was pondering. You know I'm going to have to challenge and kill the Dire Alpha to secure his pack for the war." My face is dead-serious, not even a slight sign of joking in my tone. Sebastian's face drops, the joking smile falling from his lips.

"I know, love. If I could bear the weight of all this death for you, I would." He kisses my cheek and hugs me. Giving me the love and support I need. It's not his fault he hasn't yet realized I'm not some Disney Princess that needs saving. I'm like Selene from

Underworld... but a wolf instead of a leech. I'm a trained killer; it's all I've learned since I could walk.

"Killing doesn't bother me, love. I know in a sense it should, but it doesn't," I say, shrugging my shoulders. "It's a means to an end. I don't know how many of the Strigoi still enslave any of our people." Slowly I stand and start pacing back and forth. "I fully intend to do everything within my power to free our people and take back my mother's castle. If I have to slaughter every Alpha between here and there to get the army I need... then so be it." I stop right in front of him and look him in the eyes. "They are either on my side or in my way." The last line is accented by my Lycan, making her presence known.

Dimitri and Elena walk up halfway through my little tirade. Elena wears a look of concern, while Dimitri just looks smug. "Now there's that fire I've been waiting for! You are ready, Princess. You are ready to become a mother fucking Queen." Dimitri picks me up, hugging me tightly. "That fire will spread in the hearts of your pack-mates; our strength will become theirs. It's both a blessing and a curse, how a pack works." He releases me and backs away. "One strong Alpha can influence the whole pack either to great-ness or to ruin. I know, little one, you will inspire greatness, just like your mother did with the entire nation." Dimitri cups my cheek and smiles. "If any of the old-timers live, they will see your mother in you and follow you without question." He bows slightly and backs away. "Say your goodbyes, it's time to go. We have a long trip to our next destination. Only twelve hundred miles to go." He smirks and walks off, heading to the truck where Andre is throwing what looks like mine and Sebastian's bags under the cover in the bed of the truck.

I look back at Sebastian, and he seems like he's in a bit of a shock. "Are you okay, love?"

He double-blinks and then locks eyes with me. "Most of your plan is solid. But are you sure killing off Alphas and dominating packs is the way to win the war?" he asks, puzzled. Then adds, "I mean, the Dire pack alone is like four to five hundred strong. If they revolt, we have one hell of a battle ahead of us." He makes a valid point.

"I look at it this way: the Dire Alpha has four sons, odds are at least one will be *the* one. Worst case, I take two of them as mine. They will stand with their mate. Thus, it's in their father's best interest to play nice, or he dies. It's really pretty black and white..." I start cracking up because of the unintentional fur color reference. Thankfully Sebastian gets it and starts laughing.

"Please try not to kill everyone off, hmm?" Sebastian's request is filed in the maybe pile.

I'll divert him with boobies later since they seem to distract him. My plans are solid, well, for the most part. Then again, I like flying by the seat of my pants. I like to change it up on the fly, so my enemies have no clue what the fuck hit them. I wink at Sebastian and take off running towards the truck. "Shotgun!"

I am so excited about the gifts that Elena has given me. There are several books in the bag, all of them some form of reverse harem romance. She chose mostly new authors because she liked giving people a chance. She had strongly suggested that I read the mafia book first. Granted is only MF but she said the female is one to learn from. Elena said her main character was like me, a badass bitch that takes no shit. I've got to respect that.

She also said the books would give me a good idea of how to handle multiple mates and what may happen once I find them all. It's kind of starting to feel like a horrible episode of Pokémon... Gotta catch 'em all. Gotta hunt them all down? I mean, really.

What happened to the days of the males pursuing the females? Wait, I know what happened. I'm supposed to be fucking dead or not even exist. But those mother fucking Strigoi found me. Do I have some fucked up magical lo-jack on my ass or something? I open up and start reading the first few pages of the book and damn, this will get good; I can just tell.

CHAPTER 11
Sebastian

I CAN'T BELIEVE SHE JUST YELLED *SHOTGUN* AND TOOK OFF LIKE THAT. She's taking this hunting for her mates thing better than the rest of us. Mostly I'm concerned about her safety, especially after the first attack of the Strigoi. Mother has trained me well for the last two hundred years to be ready for what was ahead of us. Underneath it all, I believe that mom has an ulterior motive behind all this.

I know Aurora's guardians have trained her well because she's fucking lethal. Like scary brutal, like *I'm concerned for the rest of the world* deadly. So far, I've witnessed her kill my suitor and the Alpha without breaking a sweat. Not to mention the one-night stand Dimitri had that she killed. Yup... better make sure I keep my mate super happy, so she doesn't go all homicidal on us.

My mother stops me halfway to the truck. "My boy, here's all the information I have on the pack you're looking for." She hands me a thick envelope. Inside it has a map, a family tree, and a breakdown of all the key players in the pack. The Alpha has four sons, three mates, and a love of barbaric gladiator games. Mom grabs my jaw to make me face her. "Don't let the bear and bird enter the den. They don't trust anyone other than other wolves," she says, concerned with trying to educate me. "There's a rumor the Alpha may have Aurora's father and a Wendigo. The Wendigo will lose its magic if its antlers are broken off. Remember what I tell you." She grips my jaw tighter to make sure her point was heard.

I nod slowly. "I hear you, Mom. I will tell Aurora about the Wendigo, but I'm not sure saying anything about her dad possibly being there will help keep the peace."

Mother releases me and kisses my cheek. "I will see you soon, my boy. By the time Aurora summons us, the pack will be whole again and the exiled returned." Mom smiles at me and walks back towards the village.

She's up to something; I can feel it. The question is, what did she do? Changing my focus, I make my way to the truck. Aurora apparently is playing DJ for this road trip because I can hear the music from here. What does she have in her hand? Hmm... it looks like books. Oh, shit, what did mother give her? Looking closer, I can make out a a couple in a heated embrace. She seems the most excited about that one. Just the cover art has me concerned. Just what Aurora needs: more inspiration to rip people's heads off. I climb into the back seat, sliding mother's care package out of the way and get comfortable. "What are you reading, Aurora?" My interest is piqued. She is so engrossed in the book, it takes her several moments before she answers.

"I'm reading a new female powered mafia book. According to the back, it's full of sex, blood, hot guys, and a mob war." She smirks and then winks at me. "It sounds right up my alley. I'm at war, I have a hot mate, and about to collect others." She shrugs her shoulders. "So far, there's been plenty of bloodshed with more to come. I wonder if she rips someone's heart out like I did." Aurora smiles sweetly at me and grips my hand. "I love you, Bash. And I'll kill anyone who stands against you." As comforting as her declaration is, it's just as scary.

She looks at me so innocently. Deep down, I know she's dead fucking serious when she said she would kill for me. She's already done it twice. I can feel through the mate bond she's calm and at peace, so her words are from the heart.

I squeeze her hand back and smile at her. Ever so slowly, I raise her hand to my lips and kiss her knuckles gently. "I would burn the world to ash for you. I love you so fucking much." My words please her, I can tell. Deep down, something does and doesn't sit well with me making that declaration. Brushing that confusing feeling aside, I refocus on my beautiful mate before me.

Slowly she nods her head and lays her head against the headrest to watch me. At the moment, I have her full and undivided attention; her book temporarily forgotten. "Mom gave me directions to the Dire's lair and instructions on how to gain passage." Both guardians have climbed into the truck and made themselves comfortable. Dimitri gives me a nod, so I proceed.

"Andre, the ascent is vertical, so Aurora and I need you to scout it out before we start our climb. Once you determine it's safe, we'll shift and use our talons to make the climb." Shifting my gaze left, I look at Dimitri, "Dimitri, you need to make sure we have our packs secure and keep the getaway vehicle ready to go." This is the exact moment his bear makes itself known, and a soft rumble escapes his lips.

"I'm going with you. I'm Aurora's guardian! No pup will keep me from my duty." He is deadly serious, but Aurora's growl—because he raised his voice—silences the entire truck. Her liquid mercury eyes are locked on him; he is now the target of her budding rage. "Aurora, you must understand, it's dangerous. You are the only family that Andre and I have left in this world. It would kill me if anything happened to you on our watch." I look between Dimitri and Andre; the poor bird has tears in his eyes. Dimitri's words struck a chord with him.

Aurora takes a deep breath and her beast retreats. Her eyes move between Dimitri and Andre, trying to gauge their emotional state. "I love you both. You are the only family I ever got to have, the only ones I've ever known." She reaches out and gently touches them both. "We are preparing to enter a den of wolves that with one bite can be lethal. There's a very good chance that Bash and I are immune because of our bloodlines," Aurora says, tilting her head.

"There is little to no chance that you and Andre are immune, Dimitri. I couldn't live with myself if you two died because I couldn't protect you. My heart would break into a thousand pieces if I lost the two of you." She sighs softly, trying to keep it together. "I'm treating this like we're walking into an ambush. I'd rather be over-prepared than not prepared at all." Aurora speaks with a wisdom far beyond her years. None of us can argue with her logic; it is solid.

To break away from the heavy emotional topic, I start again with my mom's information. "I have intel on the den and the ruling family. Apparently there are four heirs involved, two single births and a set of twins." Aurora's eyebrows shoot up at the mention of the twins. Oh, dear Gods, what did my mother tell my mate? If she were shifted, her freaking tail would be wagging right now. I know that look—mental note, give her plenty of dick before we storm the castle. "Okay, so back to the important stuff. The Alpha holds gladiator type fights between prisoners. It wouldn't shock me that one of us will have to battle to prove our intentions to him." That thought makes the boys feel uneasy. Aurora looks bored; I know she loves to battle, so the idea of a fight is like second nature to her.

"Okay, let's get this show on the road. There's blood to spill and naughty books to read!" Aurora ends the meeting quickly. "Come on, D, fire up that diesel, and let's get rolling. Twelve hundred miles isn't getting any shorter just sitting here." She nudges the grumpy bear, and he turns the key—bringing Aurora's beast she had named Black Betty—to life. I never thought I'd see the day a female would give her truck a female's name. Aurora fiddles with the radio until she finds a station she likes, and it's a bit odd when she puts on a pop radio station. Dimitri visibly cringes when some female pop singer begins to sing about a dark horse. The smirk that plays on my mate's lips makes me want to kiss it off her face. She's so damn adorable it almost makes you forget the beast within. I continue to flip through the papers my mother gave me, learning all that I can on the long drive to Nowhere, Colorado.

Twelve hundred miles is going to take forever with as slow as Dimitri drives. I know bears are slow, but damn, at least go five miles over the limit. We're going to die because he's over-cautious. "Hey, Dimitri, I know this diesel is quick; I can see the tuner head from here. Can we bump the speed up a bit?"

Dimitri's eyes dart to mine, then down at the dash. "What's a tuner head, and where is it?"

Aurora's head whips around to give me a death glare. I just fucked up big time. "Sebastian is seeing things, D, just use the gas pedal more; it's the long vertical one on the right side. It makes the truck go Vroom Vroom." Aurora is in a wise-ass mood, as well as pissed off—longest road trip ever. Her eyes lock on me again. Yup, I'm in trouble. "So, Sebastian. As the first Lycan to need glasses, how the hell are you?" She's used my full first name twice now. Definitely in the doghouse. Dimitri and Andre both laugh at me.

"Well, love, since your beauty is so blinding, it's not shocking that I need glasses. To look at you for a long period of time is like staring at the sun. All I can see is you, and nothing else matters." Aurora narrows her eyes again at me; I just can't win. Then she shakes her head and turns back around to read her book. I may be safe.

"Andre, take the file from Sebastian and tell me about the four sons. I'm curious," Aurora says with a playful tone to her voice. I fold the sheets up and stick them between my thighs, thinking they were safe. Nope! Andre reaches down, brushing the back of his hand against my cock and balls, and grabs the papers. The look on my face has to be priceless. I mean, I am more in shock that he had the stones to go near my balls. Aurora snorts as she watches Andre's antics. My mate just let another male touch my balls! What the fuck! I look from my crotch to Andre.

The bird just smirks. "I can see why baby girl is smiling. You, my boy, are stacked!" He smiles sweetly at me, then looks back to Aurora. "Hmm, looks like the firstborn is named Johan. He's four hundred and thirty-five years old, six foot six, and about two-hundred and thirty pounds. He's a politician in the pack serving as beta to his father. Johan is unmated but does have an arranged mating coming up this winter." Andre twirls his finger in the air as if to say *whoop de doo*. I can tell he's not impressed by the pack's beta. "The second eldest son is Alexander. Hmm, he's on my team, so that's a no go for you, sweetie." Andre pauses to read the next part and grins at Aurora before reading the next line.

"Now, the twins are interesting. Jayceon and Dominik are two hundred and eighty-seven years old. Dominik is the pack enforcer, standing at six feet three and two hundred and fifty pounds." Andre waggles an eyebrow at Aurora before continuing. "He has served this country as a ghost, whatever that means. Jayceon, or Jayce, as he prefers to be called, is a historian and organizer. He's currently dating a pack mate, Sinclair, and was previously involved with a Chrystina. I'm guessing he doesn't care what gender he dates." Dramatically, Andre pauses and raises both eyebrows looking at Aurora, watching for her reaction. Aurora purses her ruby red lips listening to Andre, carefully waiting for him to continue. "Jayce is six foot one and two hundred and ten pounds, more brains than brawn from what it says here. Elena has footnotes that she believes the twins will be the best match for Aurora." Andre passes the papers forward to Aurora, and she starts looking at the pictures and bios, weighing the pros and cons of all the males listed.

Aurora turns around and looks right at me. Her eyes flicker between her's and her Lycan's; they appear to be formulating a question. "What's your opinion of the males listed, love? You are my first mate and I value your opinion. Because if none of them is a true mate like you are, who do you think would be the best fit for the political alliance?" Slowly she turns to be able to look at me, studying my facial expressions.

I'm glad to see that my gift of strategy is serving her well already. She isn't just looking at the pretty faces and all the muscles... she is being tactical. That line of thought will serve her well with all we have to do before us. "The beta wouldn't be bad, but I'm not sure having another potential Alpha in the pack would be a great idea. There would be fights for dominance and possession constantly. The second born being gay wouldn't help at all there;

the bond at best would be weak." I draw in a deep breath. As much as I hate admitting it, the twins look to be her best option. She's smiling, looking at me; she knows her assessment is solid and is just looking for confirmation. "The twins look to be the front runners for this pack. Sadly, there are very few Dire Wolf packs left, so the selection is meager." Aurora nods slowly before turning back around.

"Fucking Strigoi," she mutters before picking her book back up.

I look over the remaining sheets in the file my mother had given us. Surprisingly she had a geographical survey of the Nankoweap Ruins. There must be hidden tunnels leading into the den from the ruins that humans haven't found yet. Andre has scoots closely, looking over my shoulder at the diagrams.

"If I fly up here," he points to the eastern edge of the ruins, "I can catch and ride the thermals across the face of the site to get a look inside. With it carved into the cliff face, I won't be able to glide silently in and out. I'd have to fly around, which means they'll hear my wings." Andre is thinking like a military man. It makes me start to question what they had done before I came to know them.

"I have a question for you, two guardians. I remember the night you arrived. It was dark and storming. Both of you were wearing armor with crests on them. What was your position before becoming bound to Aurora?" I needed to know who was with us and what they can do to help in the final battle.

Dimitri's eyes find mine in the rearview mirror. "I was the queen's sword, her personal guard, and her enforcer. I had my room right off her chambers when she became pregnant with Aurora." He looks down briefly. "We lived in a time that King Vlad had caused a lot of civil unrest because of his treatment of the

Strigoi. Lycans were originally their daytime guardians. Pets, if you will." He shakes his head slowly. "The Lycan's began to rise in power as they discovered the females took on their mates' powers. It's why Aurora now thinks strategically... it's because of you." He motions to me. "That was one of the gifts you've given her. Nothing else new has manifested yet, but who knows what other gifts she'll gain from you as the bond grows." He shrugs slightly.

"Andre, back there was the spymaster of the castle. Since Golden Eagle shifters are so rare, he could sit in his shifted form anywhere in the castle and no one gave him a second thought, thinking he was just a trained pet." Andre smirks at Dimitri's comment. "Shortly after Anca started taking mates, she had Andre and me bonded. It's similar to a mate bond, but its purpose is more strategic than anything else." He waves his hand slightly. "It's why when I was bound to Aurora, Andre's life was also extended. I've been teaching Aurora different fighting styles since she was able to run." He smiles fondly.

"As new forms became available, I'd join the classes, learn new skills, then come back and train Aurora. It's not that I didn't think she could handle the outside world; I didn't think the outside world could handle her." Dimitri's eyes remain on the road. I watch his face morph throughout the conversation. He's taken his job very seriously over the last two hundred years. Something deep down tells me at some point, it stopped being a job for him and it became a passion. Through all of his hard work and effort, Aurora is as efficient and lethal as they come.

Out of nowhere, Aurora starts laughing hysterically. Like out of control, belly laughing, to the point the noise stops, but the open mouth laughter continues. "What's so funny, love?" The look she gives me makes me think I'm going to regret the answer.

"Well, the main character... she's betrothed to a mafia prince." Aurora does the air quotes when she says prince. "She goes to visit him and he's caught in what looks like a compromising position." Her eyes drop to the page, then looks back up again. "So, he's standing there, this chick has him backed into a corner, her hands sliding down his body. So, she pulls out her gun and aims it at the female's head." Aurora makes a gun with her fingers. "Soon as the girl turns and sees her, Luci shoots her in the head. Blood and brain matter everywhere, the guy is left in a state of shock. Totally something I would do." She nods. "Then again, I prefer my talons. I'm more of an up-close and personal kind of girl." She just fucking smiles! Smiles and laughs about a chick getting her brains blown all over the place.

I'm concerned. Dimitri clears his throat. "Aurora, your Lycan bit the head off of my one-night stand just because I forgot to shower before seeing you." He glances at her, and she is still smiling and nodding before he looks at me in the rearview. "Good luck!" He fucking smirks at me. What in the nine hells have I gotten myself into? Poor Andre is fucking pale, and Aurora is still laughing when she holds her hand up.

"Remember how we had to play manhunt for the missing body parts after we found the severed head in my bed? My Lycan must've been really pissed at you, Dimitri!" She's still laughing. I would almost think my mate has become unhinged, but unmated she-wolves can be quite unpredictable at times.

"How is finding a severed head in your bed funny, Aurora?" I had to ask, though I think I should have kept that question to myself.

"Okay, so Andre and I have a movie night at least once to twice a week. I think it was the week before that we had a Godfather movie marathon." Aurora turns to sit sideways with her back against the door so she could look at me. "In one movie, the boss wakes up with a horse head in his bed. I guess my Lycan decided to bring her prize to bed with us." Aurora exaggeratedly shrugs her shoulders after explaining, then goes back to reading her book like nothing fucking happened.

We continue to drive through the night, switching off every six hours so we can sleep in shifts of two. I honestly don't think anyone slept when Aurora was driving. She has a lead foot and a love of that tuner mod that makes that diesel of hers fly like a bat out of hell. At this rate, we should reach our destination in two days tops. Perhaps not sane, maybe not in one piece... but we'll get there sooner rather than later.

CHAPTER 12
Lucian

I received an email today from Elena of the Lycan pack to the north. The old Alpha has finally fallen. To my surprise, the lost princess had done it and taken over the pack. Per protocol, Elena informed me that Aurora was on her way to meet my sons. Now I can finally have my revenge on her parents for the slaughter of my old pack at the hands of the Strigoi.

Slowly I move to my desk and look over the prisoner list. Nicodeamus is still alive. *How fucking long do damn dragons live?* I'll set him as the last opponent, as usual. I still have the Wendigo and several Dire's will save me time from killing them if they die. I am almost salivating, thinking about the bloodshed to come. Maybe I'll let the Princess live and take her as my mate and increase my power. I'll use her to take back her mother's throne then murder her in her sleep. That would give me the Lycan pack and keep my pack under my control.

Now to plan the battle... who should I have her fight first? Hmm... I'm going to start it off easy for her and let her warm up with several Dire prisoners. A knock sounds at my office door while I'm deep in thought.

"Enter!" I shout and don't bother looking up. By scent I know it's one of the twins. "I need you to prepare some prisoners for battle." I raise my eyes up, briefly looking at Dominik, then back down to the prisoner list. "Pick three of our best Dire fighters, The Wendigo and the dragon. Make sure they are fed and in top shape for Friday. Drawing up to my full height, I cross my arms over my chest to look directly at my son to gauge his reaction.

"We have a visitor coming. She's supposedly the missing Marelup princess. As far as I know, that child died with the queen. Regardless, if she's anything less than the heir to the throne, she'll die swiftly in the early battles." Waving my hand dismissively because, in the end, her life won't matter for long, no matter what her bloodline.

Dominik steps forward to look at the prisoner list. "Alpha Lucian, are you sure this is necessary for one female? I mean, they are in such short supply as it is. To lose one is the loss of several potential pups." Dominik regards his father's cold, calculating assessment of the list. It's clear he's already signed this female's death warrant.

"If I may be so bold to ask, why is she coming here?" Dominik furrows his brows, looking at me quite curiously, studying me like I had taught him to do to assess a possible threat.

I draw in a deep, irritated breath. "The old order of things requires the she-wolf princess to take mates from all four clans as a political alliance." I hold up my right hand with four fingers up. "Do the math boy... that's four mates—three other dicks to try to race to knock her up first." I huff irritatedly. "The Shaman from the Lycan pack didn't state if she has a mate yet. Part of me blames the old Alpha for the deaths of thousands of our pack mates." I narrow my eyes as I look up to my son. "I want his seed to die. Then again, if she's not his spawn, perhaps letting her seek a mate here would be to my benefit." I go deep into thought again and turn away from my son. Before leaving, Dominik takes the list and the printed letter with him out the door to do my bidding.

~DOMINIK~

Once out of my father's sight, I race to the suite I share with my brother, Jayce. The door almost comes off its hinges with as hard as I hit it. Jayce just about falls off his stool from the shock of my arrival. "Shit, Dom, what the fuck's going on? Where's the fire?" Jayce stands up and moves towards me, resting his hands on my shoulders, his eyes search mine for answers. I smile briefly before starting to explain.

"Remember the Dragon, Nico? How he used to beg to be set free to find his hatchling?" I raise both thick, black eyebrows hoping my brother will remember.

"Yeah, he was babbling about the hatchling again about two weeks ago. Something about an ascension and full access to power." Jayce throws his hands up in the air. "You still haven't told me what the actual fuck is going on." Jayce is a little pissed off and puzzled by my actions.

"Jayce, if she's who I think she is, we are going to have one pissed off dragon on our hands. The Princess isn't lost anymore." I pace back and forth anxiously. "She's coming here to look for a mate." I motion out the balcony doors, to the desert beyond them. "Father wants her to battle the prisoners before getting to meet any of us." Gripping my hair, I'm stressing the fuck out; no female should have to battle for a mate.

"Okay, so if you're right and she's the princess and the dragon's daughter, Father is going to be in deep shit." Jayce taps his chin in thought. "Especially since dragons and dragon kin share power when they are close to each other. If she can wield her father's ice, we are going to be ice skating in the middle of the desert." Jayce is pacing now, his nerves getting the better of him too.

"Calm down, brother. I'll protect you as I've always done, don't worry about a thing." I step in front of Jayce, attempting to get him to relax. "I kind of hope she's related to the dragon. Father has gone further down the rabbit hole and is losing what's left of his mind." I raise my hands several times in frustration, then point down in the dungeon's general direction. "We have a Wendigo here! Those things are the most fucked up abominations I've ever seen." Roughly I run my fingers through my hair again. "If she's the dragon's daughter, she'll win." I half-smile. "Her father will sense she's his kin, and then they will turn on our father. Then his reign of terror will be over." I say it and partially regret it—kind of. Lucian has been nothing but cruel to our brother, who's gay, and Jayce for being bi.

I do my best as a brother to protect them. Now I have a chance to free all of us from the hell we're in. "Get some rest, Jayce, and lay low… Father is in a mood. I leave our suite and head down towards the dungeon. I pass the guards on duty, and they leave the area thinking I'm just as cruel as my father. A misconception that I have had to foster in order to survive. My eyes survey the

Dires and the Wendigo that the princess must fight. They are quite sturdy but shouldn't be too much of a challenge.

As I approach the Ice Dragon's cell, there's an immediate drop in temperature. Icicles hang from the ceiling. "Nico? I have news for you." I see his glowing, silver eyes regard me.

"What is it?" Slowly the massive male moves towards the bars, his left arm missing from the Strigoi war. His good hand grips the bar. There's a tinge of hope in his eyes. A healthy dose of fear throttles through my system as the much larger predator regards me. There's a tiny part of me that hopes he accepts the information I bring him in a positive way and does not go into a rage ahead of time.

"It's not all good news, Nico. There is to be a battle here tomorrow night. You are the last fighter, like always." His eyes drop for a moment, the years of being a slave in the gladiator pit weighing heavily upon his weary soul. "I believe your daughter is on her way here. She is coming to claim her Dire mate, but my father wants her to battle for the right," I say and back up, slightly prepared for anything.

His head whips up quickly, and the slits of his dragon bleeds through his silver orbs. "I was right. I've been feeling her all these years." His gaze drops just before he begins to pace. His bare feet slap upon the stone as he moves back and forth. "She has ascended; I felt her touch my power." He opens and closes his hand several times. There's a subtle shift in his mood as the ramifications of the news I've delivered him hits home. "Your prisoners do not stand a chance against her. You are a good, strong male with a good heart; I hope she chooses you."

Nico winks at me then smiles. "As for my battle with her, we will not fight. Our animals will not permit it. She is dragon kin. Just by entering your den and being close to me," he smirks, "she will be able to use my powers." An evil grin crosses his lips as his hand moves to rub where his arm once was. "I will finally get my revenge against the traitor." Nico slowly turns and paces around the cell. "I need to eat and regain my strength. My daughter will need me." His eyes, now back to human, lock on mine. "I feel her; she's already taken her first mate and has gained gifts from him." Lightly he strokes his beard before he looks back at me. "Prepare yourself as well as your brothers that they may do right by her. I will speak to her once she's within the den and will share my knowledge with her." Nico goes and sits down on the edge of his bed, watching me.

"I'll send more food to you, and drink. I swear on my life I will do all that I can to protect the princess and reunite you two." My eyes turn golden as my wolf surges to the surface; he agrees that it's time to stage the coup. I bow slightly to the dragon king, my fist to my chest over my heart. He returns the gesture before I head back upstairs. I walk back towards my suite and move towards the balcony. Pushing the doors open, my eyes search the vast desert before me. Night has fallen, and the temperatures are steadily dropping.

Slowly I raise my binoculars from the table to scan the desert. I see a flickering light far out in the desert. Quickly I switch to the telescope and try to focus on that flickering light. It's definitely a campfire and a large black truck. Figures are moving about the fire, and they appear to be large bodies. So far, I'm not seeing anything that would make me think the princess is with them. Just as I am about to walk away, a large white Lycan comes into view. In its maw, a pronghorn hangs limply, obviously dead. "Holy fuck!" I accidentally say out loud.

Quickly I look around to make sure no one has heard me. When I am sure the coast is clear, I find myself watching the campsite, hoping to see the princess again. At about one in the morning, all the motion around the fire ceases—bedtime for them and me. Tomorrow is going to be rather interesting indeed.

Morning comes too quickly for me today. My nerves are on edge as I know what is going to happen. I don't want to fight my brothers, but I will if I have to. Our father has poisoned my eldest brother for years, and he's the only one I have to worry about standing against me. I promised the dragon king that I'd protect the princess.

Last night I got to see her beast with my own eyes; she's definitely dragon kin. Today's battles will be a walk in the park for her. I dress quickly and make my way into Jayce's room. "Wake up, Jayce! There's a lot we must do today!" He's curled up with his current boyfriend—limbs all tangled together.

"Go away, Dom!" Jayce waves his hand in the air, trying to shoo me away. I use his pool cue and poke him several times until he growls at me. "Damn it to hell, Dom, go the fuck away! Don't you see I'm not alone!" He buries his face against the male's back, between his shoulder blades.

"Jayce, we have a very important visitor today, and we need to talk before they arrive." That gets his attention. His head pops up, and his eyes focus on me finally. I hold out his robe to him. "Go shower. I'll explain as you get cleaned up." Jayce's face becomes solemn as he leans over and whispers into his boyfriend's ear; it is time for him to leave. The man rises and doesn't bother to dress when he walks out of the suite and into the main den. I turn to look at Jayce. "Having fun pissing Father off with your latest conquest?" I say this half-joking, half-serious as well. He knows how Father treats our gay brother. Why he wants to bring torture on himself is beyond me.

"You know I love making him uncomfortable. Especially with how shitty he treats our mother most of the time." I can't disagree with him on that count; Father treats our mother like shit. Dire's don't need a true mate to breed, just a female in heat. It's sad, really, and it's the only reason our numbers are so high. Jayce finally gets in the shower and starts to bathe.

"What if I told you the dragon is right? His child lives. I have it on good authority that she's on her way here to find her mate." Jayce's head pops out of the shower to look at me, shocked.

"Are you fucking kidding me? Like, are you serious? She lives? Father said the queen died before the baby could be brought into this world." Obviously, Father didn't know the whole truth... Nico did, and up until two weeks ago, he hadn't mentioned the child in years.

"Jayce, we must be ready. If Nico is right, the winds of change are blowing. Our only decision is: do we help the princess or let Father kill a female Lycan?" I hate the idea of Father killing a female... any female. There are so few females left and even fewer that are fertile. To lose even one more life is a crime.

Jayce's answer is simple. "We save the princess. It's the right thing to do." There is a finality to his words, and all I can do is nod. He may not be the strongest of us, but his heart is always in the right place. For an omega to take such a strong stance is a rarity.

"Father said to be in the viewing room behind the tinted glass by ten in the morning. I'm going to make sure our brothers are all ready." With that, I search for the others, anxious to see what kind of female the dragon's daughter is.

CHAPTER 13

Aurora

Camping in the desert isn't as fun as I thought it would be. We can see the ruins from where we have set up camp. At one point, there is a single spot of light that flickers for a moment on the cliff face. I watch the area for a while before I finish my hunt and return to camp with the pronghorn I killed for dinner. My Lycan is getting restless. There's a strange energy I'm feeling; it's making my blood hum. I can't explain it, but I feel like a part of me that has been missing is so close that I can almost grab it. I walk the outskirts of the camp for most of the night before Sebastian makes me follow him back and go to bed.

We're on the move again early this morning, the adrenaline pumping through my veins in anticipation of what's to come. We could be walking into a trap. Then again, a trap could be fun at this point. It's been five days since I killed the last Alpha, I'm about due for some carnage. The boys go over the hypothetical plan while I stand over here like, let's do this.

After a short drive, we arrive at the ground below the ruins. There are plaques and various other tourist crap for those that will never see the ruins up close. While the boys chat, I move to the rear of the truck and grab my go-bag for the ascent. I double check the contents while Andre flies around, assessing the ruins. Sebastian moves up alongside me and rests a hand on my lower back.

"Ready, love?" He's got one of those megawatt smiles that usually melts my insides, but today his smile seems forced. Those eyes of his are as blue as the bluest sky; I can get lost just staring up at him. I can tell he's worried about this being a setup. I'm ninety percent sure that this whole thing *is* a setup. Something is off. I mean, there's no security, no sentries; at this point, I'm not feeling super safe.

I just smile and nod, looking at him. "Let's go. The cliff won't climb itself." I shrug out of the summer dress and shove it in my pack. The shift comes easier than usual; my blood is singing to me. I swear I feel like my strength has been amplified. Half of me wants to ask Sebastian if he feels it also, but I don't think he does. He's not acting any differently than usual; it's just me. I feel like I chugged a half dozen energy drinks and some espresso.

Once Sebastian's Lycan is beside mine, Dimitri helps us strap on our go bags for the climb. My usually growly bear looks nervous about us going without him. I lightly nuzzle his cheek, and he smiles at me.

"Be safe, princess. Not all wolves favor the ruling family." He sighs before looking up. "If I'm correct, this alpha was the son of the current alpha before the attack. Their pack was almost wiped out because of the Strigoi." He raises an eyebrow at me. "So, don't expect a warm welcome." Sebastian and I nod our heads then look up at the vertical climb before us.

Andre approaches from behind. "I didn't notice anything out of the ordinary. Though one building looks like it's got fancy double doors recessed out of the line of sight." Slowly, Sebastian and I nod, then leap for the wall. Our sharp talons sink into the stone as we make our climb. Thankfully it doesn't take us long to make it to the ledge of the ruins.

Sebastian is the first to scout the area as I shift back and get dressed. He returns to me and shifts back too. "There seems to be an entrance in the far-back, right corner. I think we should start there." My eyes follow the path that he points out and we start walking in that direction. As I approach the door, the humming in my blood seems to increase. I carefully reach out to grip the handle on the wooden door, and frost begins to spread across the wood.

Sebastian and I both stare at the frost and the door. We are both puzzled as all fucking hell as to what's going on now. "Maybe it's because of who my father is? I mean, you did say my Lycan has gained white scales on my muzzle." I shrug my shoulders, confused. "I also noticed I have dragon scale gauntlets that go all the way to my talons. I wonder if I can blow ice fire. I mean, is it frost flames?" I raise an eyebrow curiously. "Okay, whatever it is, an Ice Dragon freezes things with."

Ugh, it's so frustrating not knowing what the hell I am becoming and not knowing what kind of gifts—besides scales and frost touch—I've gotten from my father. Sebastian's shoulder delivers a light hit to the door, and it splinters and falls to the ground in a wintry mess. We glance at each other and enter the hallway. Sebastian takes the lead, and I follow behind him, just in case. Besides, he would never let me go first. He is dead set on protecting me. We make it to a foyer, and several males are standing about, looking right at us.

Sebastian speaks first. "The alpha is expecting us. Elena sent word a week ago to him." Two of the guys disappear down the hallway before returning with a man in a suit. He isn't muscular in the least, and he looks to be in his decline.

"Ah, welcome, esteemed guests! Come this way so we can speak." He turns and heads back down the hallway. The question is, do we follow? Yeah, why the hell not? I move forward, and Sebastian is close on my heels. We enter a room with a one-way mirror and a balcony overlooking the gladiator pit. I move towards the mirror and stare at it.

My Lycan surges forth, her liquid mercury eyes studying the glass. I can see heat signatures behind the mirror. Two appear to be the same height; one is built heavier than the other, one tall and thin, and the last tall and muscular. The two males of the same height move closer to the glass; I can almost feel them. I cant my head to the side then straight again.

"What do you want, Lucian? You have your sons behind the mirror watching us. To what end? I'm not exactly sure. My gut tells me you're going to add conditions to meet your sons. So? What are they?" I cross my arms over my chest as I watch the myriad of emotions flicker over the alpha's face. Apparently, I've read him too well, and he's not used to it.

"You're very wise, princess. I do want something, and I do have conditions." He moves to lean his back against the mirror. "I'll give you two options. The first is that you forget my sons and accept me. Your other option is to fight in the pit, and if you live, you get to meet my sons." He smiles in a way that would make the Cheshire cat jealous. He is definitely off his rocker if he thinks he would ever get his grubby paws on me.

I walk over and lean my back against Sebastian's chest. Immediately his arm wraps around my shoulder. "I'll take option B. I'll fight in your pit." I start to laugh. "I have to battle before I meet your sons... the dick better be worth it!" Sebastian laughs behind me as he tightens his grip.

"Say the word, my love, and we leave." His head lowers as he moves my sundress to the side to show his mating mark upon my shoulder. His mouth comes to grip the same place, making me squirm slightly.

"I came to fight, my love. Apparently, Lucian wants to see if I'm worthy of his sons." I look up into Sebastian's eyes before kissing him chastely. I turn back to look at the alpha. "At least let me see who I'm fighting for. After all, if by some fluke I die in the ring, I want to see the four males that had the chance to see me." I move forward, slowly placing my palms flat on the table, staring at the glass. What I didn't expect was for the frost to spread from my hands across the table.

"As you wish, princess. Though I do have to warn you, I have one dud of a son. One who can't make up his mind what team he's on, one that's betrothed, and the last one that is in love only with his armory. So, good luck." He flicks the switch, and the reflection disappears from the mirror. I can see the twins and the other two males clearly.

It is the twins who catch my attention through the glass. I watch as the males regard me. The two older ones don't even appear to be interested at all. The twins, though, their wolves are making themselves known. Dire's know their mate on sight, Lycan's need to see and scent their mate. I would definitely have something else to fight for. I *need* to win. I *need* to kill all my opponents and then the alpha to free my mates from under his rule. But my question is, will the other sons side with daddy dearest or their brothers?

"Gentlemen, let the games begin, shall we? Give me my first opponent, and I'll give you their head." The twins begin to hit the glass trying to break through; their drive to protect is admirable. I return to Sebastian. "Protect the twins."

My eyes lock with his, and he gives me a quick nod. That's all I need to be able to enter the ring. As I'm led out of the room, I get close to the glass. The twins are still pounding on it, trying to break free. I press a kiss to the glass, leaving blood-red lipstick behind. The lighter built twin is beside himself, and the stocky twin looks pissed. Good, one has a temper—they'll be just fine. I follow the alpha down a series of hallways that lead down deeper into the den. I scent so many bodies and species down here that my senses are on overload. Then there's that hum that's getting stronger.

Daughter?

I hear the words in my head. Cautiously, I look around to see if anyone else heard the voice. I listen to it several more times before I think of a response.

Dad?

I mean, I never met the man, and as far as I knew, he was over two hundred years dead. I feel a wave of relief wash over me. Wait, dragons can communicate telepathically?

Nicodeamus? My mother's dragon mate?

Part of me wants to cry. I still have family left. I not entirely without my bloodline. Tears threaten to break free. I have to make myself mad to not alert the alpha to what was going on.

Yes, little one. We don't have much time. Lucian plans to kill you in the ring. Use my gifts, my strength. When we come face to face, we will burn this place to the ground.

His voice holds such confidence and authority, I can't help but smile. Now I know where I get my *don't fuck with me* attitude from. I walk with more confidence and bounce in my step.

In my mind's eye, my father shares years of information: our history, our family, and the night of the attack. The alpha is the one that helped the Strigoi breach the castle's defenses. For that, he will pay dearly.

"Are you ready, princess?" The sarcasm is strong with this one. I give him two thumbs up and turn my back to him.

"Yup, let's get it done." I crack my knuckles and my neck, getting my limbs loose. I'm as ready as I'm going to be. The great doors open, and I hear the roar of the crowd. Closing my eyes, I start hearing the Megadeth song "Crush 'em" in my head. The opening line fits so well, and I start singing the first lines out loud.

Poor Sebastian must think I've lost my mind, entering the ring singing. I need to focus, and one of my favorite training songs makes me feel like my mentor is right beside me. Opening my eyes, scanning the arena, they fall on Sebastian and the twins. This is the first time they will see me shift. It should be worth seeing the look on their faces. Especially now that my father taught me how to use the frost in the shift; it should add a whole new element to my theatrics.

I breathe in deeply and let out the deepest, most haunting howl I can muster as the shift takes me. Frost seeps from my every pore as my body takes on its new shape. I embrace my father's magic and let it bond with my Lycan. By the time I am done, the arena is dead silent. Not a single sound besides my breathing can be heard.

"Hell yeah, babe!" I hear Sebastian shout. He knew through the bond about the influx of power I have gained. My mercury eyes seek out the twins. Their eyes glow golden like their wolves'. *Yes, we are one.* Bring on my opponent!

The door across from me slams open, and a rather large Dire Wolf comes charging out and skids to a stop. I don't think this poor bastard was expecting me. I roar at him, my voice a mix of wolf and dragon. His scent screams he's frightened; that's good. Two more Dire's come out behind him; this is about to get interesting. I raise my right arm before twitching my finger at them, signaling for them to attack. All at once, they charge.

Now the fun really begins.

CHAPTER 14
Dominik

Holy fuck, what a day. Aurora is the princess, our mate, *and* part dragon. *Can today get any more fucked up?* My brother Jayce and I race to the balcony with Sebastian close on our heels. He's trying to reassure us that she'll be fine. But damn, every female we know can barely hunt for herself. We just found our mate and we aren't ready for her to die yet. Halfway into the suite, Sebastian's knees buckle, sending him to the floor. He's panting heavily through whatever is happening to him. He appears to be in immense pain the way his face is contorted and his jaw clenched tight.

"Shit, that hurt. I hope Aurora knows what she's doing." He looks up to me. "She's tapping into her father's power. They are close enough for her to do it now. Fuck did that pack a punch." His eyes are swirling between an almost white-blue to his regular sky blue.

If the mating bond can do this, I'm almost afraid of the power she's wielding at the moment. I go and help Sebastian to his feet and we make it to the balcony to see her enter the ring. I can't believe my ears; she's singing while entering the ring. Sebastian laughs, saying how the pack is in trouble now.

Her gaze finds us, and she smiles just before tilting her head back, allowing her long white tresses to flow down her back. Her crimson lips twist up in a mischievous smile before letting out the most bone-chilling howl I've ever heard in my life. Fur ripples over my arms as my wolf fights me for control. My bones and tendons tighten as her howl echoes through the pit, calling forth my wolf. He wants nothing more than to be at his mate's side when she battles. I agree with him, but it's not our place at the moment. Looking to my right, I can see Sebastian and Jayce having the same problem.

We look at each other briefly before watching Aurora shift. Her body bends and breaks, reforming to that of her great, white Lycan beast. Every inch of her body is covered in frost as the change takes hold of her. Her beast grows larger by the second, far larger than any female Lycan in recent history. Unlike your average Lycan, her's has white dragon scales along the length of her muzzle as well as armored gauntlets with talons. Holy shit, she has dragon talons instead of the normal Lycan claws. Aurora flexes her hands several times, looking over her weaponry before looking around the arena briefly. She appears to be bored with the way her long, white tail sways slowly behind her. A couple of quick stretches later, and the double doors in front of her are thrown open.

One Dire wolf comes running into the arena. Aurora looks bored with only a single wolf arriving. The roar that comes out of her mouth is the thing that nightmares are made of. A chill runs down my spine hearing the tone that comes out of her mouth. The male in the ring is terrified, his body shaking; that is until two more join him. Aurora raises her right arm and bears the royal seal.

Fuck, she *is* the lost princess. To attack royalty is an immediate death sentence. The Dires move as one towards her, and her fingers spread, exposing her talons. They aren't even claws; they are fucking talons—long, curved, and lethal.

In one fluid motion, she flicks her hands out, catching the two leaping in the air at her, and rakes her talons across their throats, severing their heads from their bodies. Blood sprays everywhere as the decapitated corpses hit the ground. Her snow-white fur stains vermillion as she stares down the last remaining wolf.

Her rage is palpable in the air. Energy crackles around the arena as if a thunderstorm is approaching. As the final wolf charges and leaps, Aurora catches it in midair. Her talons sinking deeply into the ribcage of the Dire. Blood oozes freely from the wounds she has dealt him as his feet dangle off the floor. The poor wolf whines, whimpers, and squirms, trying to free itself from her vice-like grip. Her eyes lock onto my father as she rips the Dire in half; bloody entrails dangle from the two halves in her talons. She throws the upper half of what is left of the Dire at my father's balcony. Blood splattering all over the white marble and some of it manages to land on my father's face. The hind end in her talons falls to the ground as I swear her beast smirks at my father's reaction. He isn't happy that she threw the body at him, his lip still curled up in a snarl. *Personally, I find it funny.*

The carnage in the ring is unlike anything I've ever seen in all my years of watching these battles. Aurora turns and looks back up at us, trying to gauge our reaction to her brutality. I bow my head and raise my fist to my heart. I witnessed my brother and Sebastian repeat what I have done out of the corner of my eye. Aurora lightly dips her head to us and raises her taloned fist over her heart in return.

My only question is, how far is my father going to take this farce? He's up to something; I'm just not sure what. The door to the right opens, and the energy in the air changes. The air becomes thick and humid. Fog begins to roll into the arena, making Aurora adjust her stance to face her new foe. I know what it is: the Wendigo. It stands almost equal in height to Aurora's Lycan. But where Aurora has bulk, the Wendigo is gaunt with bones protruding out of its half-rotted flesh. Its face looks like the skull of a bear with terrifying teeth and a blue tongue that can be seen tasting the air. Upon its head are great horns like that of a stag. Its eyes are deep-set, glowing red orbs like that of the demon that it is. Its arms are long and at the tips of the boney digits, sit razor-sharp claws.

The two titans begin to circle each other. One more terrifying than the other. Height wise, they appear to be equally matched. Both have white fur matted with blood. Aurora takes a quick swipe at the Wendigo's chest, ripping a layer of flesh off it. The creature doesn't even seem phased by it. But the look on Aurora's face tells me she noticed something we can't see from where we are sitting.

I turn to Sebastian. "Is she okay? I mean, I know you can feel her." His eyes never leave her in the ring.

"She's fine. My mother told her about the Wendigo and how to kill it. She's just making sure what my mother knew is accurate before she goes on the attack." His tone doesn't sound concerned; instead, it almost sounds detached and bored. In my opinion, his reaction isn't appropriate for what happening currently. I'll file this tidbit of information away to process later. My eyes return to watch Aurora move about the ring, testing the creature.

"It's better to test than to be sorry. Aurora's very wise." I walk over to Jayce, who's still beside himself, and I wrap an arm around his shoulders. "She'll be fine, you'll see!" I have to have faith in our future mate. I refuse to have any negative thoughts about the female my wolf has chosen. The Wendigo suddenly roars and charges at Aurora. She jumps to the side, barely getting out of the way in time.

Unfortunately, the Wendigo's claws catch Aurora's ribs, slicing thin lines along her right side. The scent of Aurora's blood has put the creature into a frenzy. It's not thinking straight, and Aurora takes full advantage of it and charges. Quickly she drops down and sweeps the legs out from under the creature, causing it to land flat on its back. Her talons come down swiftly, severing the horns from the Wendigo's head. The creature's high-pitched scream fills the arena, blackened blood oozes from where the horns once were. Aurora grabs the horns and drives them down into the Wendigo's arms, pinning them to the earth below it.

Aurora's taloned hands take on an unearthly glow as frost begins to gather in her hands. She drives her talons into the creature's chest and rips up quickly. Within the now hollowed rib cage lay a human curled up in a fetal position. It is the man the Wendigo possessed to enter this world. Aurora's Lycan studies him before ripping him free of the creature's remains. Once the human is free, the Wendigo's corpse ignites, burning blue in the center of the ring. The man is covered in a black, viscous material, almost like a cocoon. Aurora cants her head left and right several times, studying the man before ripping his head free of his shoulders and throwing the severed head onto my father's balcony.

She roars again, looking around the arena, calling for her next challenger. The massive doors on the far side of the stadium opens—a deep bellow echoes throughout the arena, followed by a blast of blue flames. The temperature in the arena drops quickly as frost and ice begin to coat the available surfaces. An Ice Dragon lumbers into the arena; his head mere feet from the roof. His white scales are thick and armor-like—with each scale having a thick raised ridge with a sharp spiked tip. Not only would the scales protect him, but they would also slice his attacker to ribbons.

It is quite scary to see such a battle-hardened warrior lumber in on three legs and missing a wing. His scales tell the tale of his years of battle, not only here but in his past. His silver serpentine eyes search the arena then lock on Aurora. He raises his head high and blows his flames down upon her. Wave upon wave of blue-white flame encapsulates Aurora. The fire itself seems to roar and crackle as they fall from the dragon's great maw. Aurora doesn't even try to evade the dragon fire. We can't see her as the flames begin to coat the arena floor.

My eyes shoot to Sebastian, and he is calm as all hell. How the fuck can he be calm when our mate is getting burned to a crisp? The fucker just smiles. Sebastian exudes an unearthly air of confidence that is a bit unnerving. Slowly, his eyes turn to me. "They are showing how powerful Aurora is. She's immune to his dragon fire because she's his daughter."

Well, now that makes more sense. The crowd is quiet as the flames recede. Aurora stands there, her fur cleaned of blood and her wounds healed. She begins to walk towards the dragon and shifts back to her human form. The dragon lowers its great horned head to her, and Aurora places a hand to his cheek and kisses his muzzle. She turns to face the crowd, choosing this time to shift partially. Her hands look like white armored gauntlets all the way down to her white talons. Her legs break backward and are that of her Lycan—a light dusting of fur-covers her most intimate of parts. Aurora walks to the middle of the arena and locks eyes with our father. Her rage is evident by the trail of frost she left in her wake.

"How dare you imprison my father! Your lost dragon king! You have betrayed the royal family! You have betrayed your people, Lucian!" Aurora calls out our father, the alpha.

He claps his hands and starts laughing. "What does a little bitch like you think you can do to me? I have five hundred Dire Wolves at my command." He raises his arms as if to gather his forces, but none move. Not one single being except my eldest brother—his beta—moves to his side. All the others begin to move to the far side of the arena, behind Aurora and her father.

Aurora looks over at her father's dragon. He's missing his front, left leg and wing on that side. She begins to growl low in the back of her throat. "You want to see what I can do? So be it." She rips her eyes away from her father to gaze upon the gathered wolves within the arena. "My people, I'm going to apologize now for what I'm about to do." She shifts the rest of the way rapidly and howls... ripping the wolves from all of us. None of us have control when her Lycan calls to ours. My body breaks and reshapes to that of my Dire Wolf far faster than I've ever shifted before. I look to my right to see Sebastian and Jayce both have shifted just as quickly.

She summons all of our animals, and only a true alpha could force the shift of an entire pack at once. We leap down from our balcony to flank Aurora, moving in sync to stand at her side. Her father stands like a great sentinel behind us. The rest of the pack fills the arena, slowly closing in on my father. Do I feel bad for Father? Not one bit. The way he treated my brothers because of whom they love... he deserves everything he is about to receive.

Aurora breaks free of the pack and bolts towards my father's balcony. Her father's wing shoots out about midway between her and the balcony. Aurora leaps up and grabs onto her father's wingtip and uses it to launch herself up and into my father's suite. Next thing you know, my father is flying through the air with a tremendous, white Lycan hot on his heels; they land within seconds of each other. Aurora monopolizes on her momentum and pins him to the ground. Her head lifts to lock eyes with her father.

He shifts back to human and approaches Aurora and my father. "You killed my family. You allowed the Strigoi passage into the castle. You took my arm, and in my grief, you made me a slave in your games." He nods to Aurora, only to have her grip my father by the back of his neck to lift him off the ground. "My daughter was swept far away to be raised without me, because of you." He extends a single finger and touches my father's stomach. The flesh turns to ice spreading slowly over his body.

"The time for me to show mercy is long over, Lucian. Now you will know my pain. But know this, the Strigoi will die, and my daughter will be queen in her castle. You," Nicodeamus smiles sadistically, "on the other hand, will just be a memory. A blip in time to be easily forgotten in years to come." Ice covers my father's body completely. He is frozen solid—kind of like Han Solo in carbonite. Nico takes my father's frozen body from Aurora and throws him to the ground, smashing him to bits. Johan comes out of nowhere, sailing through the air with Father's rapier in his hands. He heads towards Nico and closes the gap quickly.

Before he can get close enough, Sebastian's Lycan slams Johan to the ground. The force of Sebastian's impact knocks the rapier from Johan's hand and the air from his lungs. Aurora is way too calm for what is going on. Her eyes lock with her father's, and they stare at each other for a moment. I'm guessing they have an in-depth conversation in the middle of a foiled assassination attempt. Nico makes a graceful sweeping motion towards Johan, and Aurora walks over to where Sebastian has him pinned. With every step, Aurora returns slowly to her human form until she stands beside her Lycan mate.

She threads her fingers through the fur on the back of Sebastian's head. A single hand raises up, caressing his ear as she leans down to stare at Johan. She speaks to him in the most condescending tone she can muster. "Poor, little beta thinks he's wolf enough to attack my father." She keeps tilting her head from side to side, assessing him. "You have been weighed and measured. You simply aren't wolf enough to breathe the same air as me."

Her gaze falls on Jayce, and me next. "Please forgive me for what I must do next. We will not be safe if he's allowed to live. Your father's will has poisoned his heart and mind." Her eyes remain bouncing between mine and my brother's as her fingers glide through Sebastian's thick, black fur.

This dominant-as-fuck female before us is asking for our forgiveness. My brother and I choose this moment to shift back to our human forms. We glance at each other quickly and nod our heads at her. Jayce makes a heart with his hands—being the softy that he is. That little gesture earns him a smile from Aurora before she moves before Johan again.

"I sentence you to death for the attempted assassination of my father, the dragon king." She raises her hand and shifts it, allowing her talons to catch the light in the arena. The talon on her index finger touches the artery on the right side of Johan's neck. And ever so slowly, she applies pressure. We watch the skin flex and bend before finally granting passage of the sharp tip of her talon.

Every beat of his heart, a little more blood pumps out and runs down his chest. Aurora almost seems fascinated watching the blood flow. Carefully she removes the talon from the artery and moves to the other side to repeat the process. Now two streams of blood flow slowly down my brother's chest. With surgical precision, Aurora pierces the brachial artery in his right arm, causing yet another stream of blood. She's bleeding him out slowly. For some reason, she skips the other arm and goes straight to his femoral artery, and slices it open just above his left knee. Now that one really pumps the blood out. His face grows pale, and yet he doesn't utter a word. Johan doesn't beg for his life or even to be spared.

Not that I think Aurora would have spared him at this point. She finally got her father back, and Johan has tried to kill him. I understand she needs to make him suffer, but to what end? Her head tilts one last time and moves forward.

"It's nothing personal, but you tried to kill my father after your father tried to kill me. It's only fair." Just before he loses consciousness, she uses her talons to rip his heart out. Her eyes lock on the final twitching of Johan's heart before she offers it to her father. Nico takes it with a smile before she walks off toward my father's remains. Her talons gain purchase on his frozen skull as she lifts it off the ground.

Carefully measured steps carry her back to where her father stands. She drops to one knee and holds up my father's head to him. He takes the offering then pulls Aurora up into a hug. It is probably the most surreal thing I have ever seen.

He holds his daughter with his only arm while my father's hair is wrapped around his fingers, and my brother's heart dangles off of his pinky. "My baby... My beautiful, powerful baby. I never gave up hope I would see you again!" Nico nuzzles the top of her head softly, crying into her blood-soaked mane. Aurora starts crying as well, holding her father tightly, afraid she will lose him again. Nico shakes his hand, freeing him of his presents to grip her better. Aurora looks like she has a Kung Fu Ninja death grip on him. Lord, help the being that tries to end this hug-fest. I think there would be another body hitting the floor quickly.

CHAPTER 15
Dominik

Sebastian moves up slowly and cautiously. "Aurora, love? We should appoint someone to watch over the pack until we need them. And don't forget we have Dimitri and Andre waiting outside for us. You know how Andre gets; he's like an old mother hen." Aurora's head lifts, and she nods slowly. Her eyes find her smiling father looking down at her.

"Daughter? Do Dimitri and Andre still live? How can this be?" Nico looks puzzled because, by all rights, those two should have been long dead by time alone. Both types of shifters are not very long-lived by shifter standards.

"Yes, Father, they live. The elder dame bound them to me until I found my first mate, Sebastian. I fear now they may not have much time left." She turns to face Jayce and me. "Can we trust Alexander? Will he lead in our stead while we are gone?"

My brother and I think long and hard about it. "Yes, we believe he would. Father always mistreated him because he's gay. Trust me, he will be thankful and most faithful to you for freeing him from our father." I say with great finality, truth rings with every syllable that passes my lips.

Out of the corner of my eye I notice Sinclair, my brother's lover. Jayce stands stock still watching him approach, afraid of what Aurora may do to the competition. Jayce's fear is palpable in the air as he watches his lover approach. Without a second thought, Sinclair closes the distance and hugs onto Jayce for dear life. I am prepared to intervene if needed, but what could I do? It is my mate and my twin—possibly having to choose between them is breaking my heart.

Aurora shocks me as she moves slowly and touches Jayce's shoulder. "If this is where your heart truly lies, I can and will release you from this fragile bond." Her eyes are the pure mercury of her Lycan. She is anxious, and you can scent her sadness in the air. Aurora is trying to do what is right for my brother. My older brother Alex hears the whole exchange and waits to see what Jayce chooses.

Jayce takes in a deep breath and kisses Sinclair hard on the lips. "I'm sorry. My wolf and I want her as our mate. I never thought I'd find my mate; I thought we had forever." He glances back to Aurora, who has tears streaming down her face. She's ready to release him if that's what he wants, even if it causes her pain.

Aurora shifts quickly and runs across the arena. She leaps high into the air and lands a good twenty feet off the ground. Her talons sink into the wood and mortar as she climbs higher and higher until she reaches the alcove just below the roof. It was the first time Sebastian witnessed his mate run from anything. He just stands there in a state of shock. His eyes swirl between his normal sky blue and that of his wolf. It appears that they are battling each other for control.

"Sebastian!" I yell at him to knock him from the trance he appears to be in. Slowly he looks at me, then back in the direction Aurora had fled. Everyone, now watching the alcove. "Why did she run?"

Sebastian draws in a deep breath, grabbing everyone's attention. "She's not good with handling anything outside of rage, desire, or apathy. The possibility of losing a mate before really having him fucked her world all up." His eyes find Jayce's. "Choose whatever will make you the happiest. She wouldn't have offered you an out if she didn't mean it. Besides, I think you've figured out that she doesn't hold back when something pisses her off or gets in her way."

Jayce nods and looks towards the alcove then back to me. "Dom, please go talk to her. I need to talk with Sinclair a bit, and I'll bring Alex up to speed while you try to make Aurora happy."

I smile at my brother and bring him in for a quick hug before heading to the side of the arena. A hand grips my shoulder, turning my head slightly; it's Nico, and he is smiling. It's kind of terrifying that he's smiling at me right now. "Son, she's hurting and volatile. Tread softly and talk with your heart. Her beast isn't going to listen to reason right now." He spoke from a place of years of wisdom, his connection to his daughter giving us insight into her emotional state...

"Is it safe to approach her? I mean, we're not bonded yet, and she's wedged in a small area." I wasn't afraid of being attacked. I was more fearful of setting her off on a rampage.

"Soon as she can scent you, you'll be safe. Be patient with her. Perhaps the company of your wolf will help her once you get up there." He smirks at me because there is no visible way for me to get up there.

I stare at where she is hiding, then look back at Nico. "Mind giving me a lift? My wolf isn't like hers, and I can't climb walls like she can."

Nico starts laughing and walks away from everyone before he shifts back to his dragon. He looks from me to the alcove and back again before opening his huge taloned hand, waiting for me to walk into his grip. Well, here goes nothing. I walk towards him— poor Jayce is in panic mode, and Sebastian has to hug him to keep him from chasing after me. Once I am in the dragon's grip, he rears up on his hind legs and stretches out his arm, and places me on the ledge of the alcove.

Glowing mercury orbs find me swiftly. She is curled up against the back wall, hugging her knees to her chest. I slowly shift into my wolf and belly crawl over to her, whimpering the entire distance. The great white Lycan in question lies down and curls up around my wolf. Never in my existence have I felt like a small wolf until now. Slowly she starts licking the back of my head, grooming me as if I am the one that needs comfort. When she moves to get a better angle, I can start grooming her.

After a while, she stops and shifts back to her human form. "Your wolf is beautiful, Dom." Her fingers thread through my thick, obsidian fur as she examines the path her fingers blaze. "Father must like you to lift you up here. I'm sorry I took off as I did." Her voice quivers with emotion. "I was afraid of Jayce's rejection. I was afraid that my Lycan would kill his lover in retaliation." She lowers herself to lay her head on my ribcage, curling into me for comfort. "I'm glad you're here, Dom. I don't think I could take Sebastian coddling me."

Her fingers continue their exploration of my wolf's body. Her fingertips are getting dangerously close to my sheath. I can feel my body responding to her proximity. Her own scent is starting to change as she scents the change in mine.

I turn my head and nip at her exposed shoulder. I didn't expect that she would move her head to the side to expose her neck to me. My wolf is ready to claim her right here, right now. He isn't giving me control anytime soon. We nudge her with our muzzle, and she moves onto all fours. Apparently, our princess is a bit of a freak behind closed doors. My wolf is in the driver's seat as he moves behind her—his long broad tongue laps from her clit through her soaking wet folds to her engorged entrance. Her moan makes our fur stand on end. We lick her like an ice cream cone, enjoying her sticky sweet taste on our tongue.

"Please, Dom," is all she says as she looks back over her shoulder at us. Who am I to deny my mate what she is begging for?

I hesitate, knowing my wolf won't be gentle, nor will he go slow. She shakes her ass at us one last time, and he surges forward, mounting her quickly. Quickly we thrust forward, burying ourselves to the hilt. Aurora moans at her sudden fullness and draws in a deep breath as she wiggles again. Her movement spurs my wolf to bite her shoulder hard to hold her in place as he decides to fuck her as hard as he can. Our dew claws dig into the tender skin near her hips so we don't lose our grip of her as we pound her relentlessly.

The sloppy wet sound of our cock sliding in and out of her is music to our ears. Her voice changes as her orgasm grips her. Her muscles grip us tightly, rhythmically pulsating while milking our cock. We won't last much longer; our balls draw uptight as our mating knot forms just before filling her with our seed. Soon after we orgasm, my wolf releases his hold on our body and allows me to shift back to being just a man. The mating knot is still in place as I kiss at the bite my wolf gave her.

Aurora turns her head to look over her shoulder at me and just smiles. "Totally worth it." She starts giggling to herself, and then I feel it. I feel another presence beside myself. It's a somewhat confusing feeling, half elated and at peace, the other part angry. The mixed emotions have me baffled. Aurora looks to be quite happy and content at the moment. The second emotion is definitely puzzling me. As we lay here together, my mating knot finally releases so I can pull free from Aurora's welcoming depths.

"What am I feeling? Better yet, who am I feeling?" I pull her onto my lap, waiting for her answer. I know I feel her, but is that also Sebastian I am feeling? She snuggles into my lap, and without warning, she bites my shoulder near my neck. Everything I was feeling becomes clearer. I'm feeling Sebastian, and well, he is none too pleased my wolf took part in the claiming.

"He'll get over it," Aurora says rather matter of factly after she cleans my mating mark that she just made. "Let's go. I'll have to shift and carry you back down."

Slowly she stands and stretches by the entrance. I watch my seed drip freely from her pussy before she shifts back into her Lycan. She gives me a short bark as if to say *get over here.* I climb onto her back, lock my arms around her neck, and use my thighs to hold onto her rib cage. This most certainly is a strange turn of events. I'm holding onto my mate for dear life as she takes a running leap off the ledge towards the wall that seems miles away. Sadly, I must admit I think I saw part of my life flash before my eyes as we sail through the air. The landing leaves a lot to be desired; it is jarring and sudden. Through the bond, I feel her joy at my dismay, and I can feel Sebastian's state of panic over what she had just done. Aurora is definitely enjoying this way too much because about halfway down, she launches us backward. All I can think is, *this is it; I'm going to die because my mate is insane.*

A large, taloned hand shoots up out of nowhere and snatches us out of the air. Nicodeamus has decided to join in on her fun and my panic. Thank the gods I have such great control over my bowels; otherwise, there'd be a mess I'd have to clean up later. Nico places us on the ground, where I promptly slide off her back and move away slowly. I thought I was in the clear until Sebastian's fist meets my jaw, stunning me for a moment.

"What the fuck! You took advantage of her emotional state, you fucking heartless bastard." Just as he gets ready to strike again, a large, white maw comes between us and starts growling at Sebastian. Aurora makes him back away and rethink his course of action.

Her shift comes quickly as she moves to get in Sebastian's face. "I love you, Bash, and I appreciate what you're trying to do. But if you ever hit another mate for doing what I wanted, you and I will be brawling," she growls out. "I touched his wolf's sheath." She jabs her hand in the direction of my cock. "I waved my ass and soaked pussy in his face. I taunted them 'til they gave me what I wanted!" Her hands clenched into fists. "I needed to feel something other than death and sadness. I needed to feel like something other than the monster I become when I'm forced to kill." She begins to pace between the two of us. Her hands coming up to run through her hair, almost violently, over and over again.

I can see what he meant when he said she doesn't deal with emotions well. I choose, at this point, to back away slowly. This part of the fight is between them, not me. My gaze finds my two brothers and Sinclair huddled over by the exit.

I move slowly over towards the group. "Hey, guys, what's going on?" They all appear to be happy to see me, so that's a good start. "I'm going to accept the title of pack master until Aurora calls for us." Alex is his usual get-to-the-point self. His eyes fall to his nails before he speaks again. "It will be nice to get the pack back to the way it was before Father lost his marbles." I nod slowly and look around. The pack is moving slowly, interacting like I haven't seen them do in the last fifty years.

"That's great to hear, Alex. I'm sure you'll bring about much-needed changes here that have been long overdue. You're one of the most compassionate and understanding people I know. You'll make a great leader." I embrace Alex then look at Jayce and Sinclair. Sinclair seems to be in disbelief over what's happening, and Jayce is getting frustrated. "How are you two doing?" I figured I'd ask in case my twin needs backup. Sinclair was always a very needy bitch when it came to their relationship. Jayce's wolf is showing, and Sinclair looks like he is on the verge of tears.

"What could she possibly do that I can't do, Jayce?! I've been with you for almost fifty years!" Sinclair huffs, completely in touch with his inner bitch.

Jayce shakes his head and draws in a slow, measured breath. "For one, she can give me pups. Two, she's not a needy bitch like you are. Three, she's my fucking mate! That won't change, no matter how much you beg!" Jayce flails his arms.

Jayce's screaming gets Aurora's attention, and she sprints over to stand behind Jayce. She is still human for now, but who knows how long that will last. Her face comes alongside his, and she speaks softly next to his ear. "Are you alright, sweetheart?" Her arms wrap around his shoulders as she stands on her tippy toes to rest her head on his shoulder.

"I'm fine, your royal hotness, just trying to get Sinclair to understand that it's over and that I choose you." He made probably his smartest move of the night, leaning his head against hers and placing his hands on her arms. Not only do his words please her, but he also immobilizes her in case she wishes to attack. Because after all, if she moves wrong, she'd end up hurting him too, and she wouldn't ever do that.

Sinclair starts to move towards them, and he appears angry. Aurora isn't having any of it. Her eyes burn molten mercury, and scales ripple over her forearms as she growls at Sinclair. "Choose wisely, male. Jayce has chosen; his word is final. He is my mate, which places him on my level. To move against him or me is to move against the throne." She releases Jayce and moves him behind her. Sinclair slowly lowers his head looking down.

Aurora isn't budging at all, and she has made her stand. Once Sinclair moves off, Aurora turns and kisses Jayce. "I'm sorry you had to go through that." Her eyes return to human grey as she moves to embrace Jayce. They hug for a very long time before they break apart.

Aurora steps away and moves close to Alex. "I heard you accepted the position." She holds her hand out to him, her royal brand facing Alex.

"I do, my queen." He bows his head to her, already proclaiming her queen. "I will be fair and just and treat everyone better than my father had treated me." He grasps her hand tightly and shakes it. He lifts his head, and they smile at each other.

"Thank you, Alexander. Please prep your people for war. Free the prisoners that were unjustly imprisoned. If any wants to fight alongside us, they are welcome. The guilty prisoners execute them. There is no sense in being imprisoned for life." Alex nods along, taking notes on his phone. He is the organizer of the sons, so he is perfect for this role. "Oh, and Alex, I need the Dire's with the toxic bite to be trained for assault." That gets his attention.

"For assault, my queen... like assassins?" Alex is quite curious about where her thought process is going. I nod along, sensing where Aurora wants the team to be.

"Yes, Alex. We send them in, almost like scouts, to weaken the forces already in place." Aurora starts drawing in the sand. Nico moves up alongside her and starts adding to the drawing. She draws a place that she's never been to. Somehow she knows the layout of the castle grounds.

Nico takes over drawing at this point. "If the Strigoi didn't completely destroy the castle, they will hole up in the bottom chambers in the center during the day." He points to the structure in question. "A daytime assault will be the best bet. If we can gather other Ice Dragons, we can freeze them in their tracks and behead them."

It's kind of scary to think that Aurora was raised without her father, and their thought processes are perfectly in line. She looks at her father's drawing, pointing at parts of it, and you can see the gears turning. "Father, what if we use the tunnels to the south and send the Dire's in through there?" She has a puzzled look on her face, mostly because she's unsure how she knows these things.

Nico starts to laugh, which draws Sebastian to the group. "I'm so glad to see that you remember all that I've shown you in your dreams over the years. I wasn't sure what you learned in your sleep." He hugs Aurora tightly as he gazes upon us. "Come, all is settled here. Let's head back to your guardians, Aurora."

My brother and I return to our suite to pack. It's time to go and plan our next moves as a pack. Jayce still seems off, but his spirits are much higher than they were earlier. I think Aurora verbally claiming him made the difference in his mood. I guess we shall see. After all, we are about to meet the two men who raised her for the last two hundred plus years.

CHAPTER 16
Nicodeamus

After all these years, I finally have my little girl. She is everything I have dreamed of and more. Though I must admit, she took after me so much. She has my white hair and silvery eyes, but her face and build are all her mother's. And her Lycan has some distinct dragon qualities to it—for example, her talons and the white scales. Her Lycan's muzzle is far longer and broader than your run of the mill Lycan. It killed me to have to sit back and feel her battle without me. Even though I knew she would defeat the challengers without an issue. The draw on my power had been intense, and she's far more potent than I could have ever imagined possible. When I walked out and saw her Lycan standing there without fear, it made me beam with pride. She trusted me completely even though she didn't know me, per se. We stood against the alpha together, and it warmed my heart that she was there with me.

Now we move slowly through the tunnels to come out somewhere near where Aurora's truck and guardians are waiting for us. Aurora is ahead of me between Sebastian and Dominik, with Dom in the lead. The other twin, Jayce, is still with the brother we left in charge of making sure the transfer of power went smoothly. I think I'm more anxious about being free after all this time. I haven't seen the skies in over two hundred years.

We approach the sealed passageway, and Aurora looks back at me, sensing my unease. She breaks loose of her mates and comes to my left side to wrap her arms around my waist. "I've got you, Daddy... no worries, I'll protect you." Her smile is infectious and warms my soul. I'm *Daddy* to this grown woman. It brings tears to my eyes, hearing her call me that.

"Thank you, little one. I love you, baby girl. I always have and always will." I kiss the top of her head and nod to Dom to open the passageway. I squint my eyes as the first rays of light flickers through the opening. It feels like forever since I've seen the sun or smelled the fresh air. I move slowly with Aurora, looking outside, amazed by how little this area has changed since my imprisonment.

Dimitri and Andre come rushing over, seeing Sebastian exit first. They immediately start asking about Aurora. She steps out next while I remain in the shadows for a few moments, just taking it all in. She is smiling and laughing as Dimitri hugs her and spins her around in a circle. The next moment he's shaking a finger at her as she tells him about the new body count. His head whips to the opening, then back to her quickly as he processes what she's told him. *I still live.* Andre and Dimitri come running over to the passageway and drop to their knees before me.

"M'lord," they say in unison, still looking at the ground waiting for me to speak.

"Rise, my friends. You've done a glorious job with raising Aurora. I am forever in your debt." They both look up at me, astonished. It's now that they finally notice I'm missing my left arm. Andre looks like he's ready to cry, and Dimitri isn't sure what expression is appropriate at the moment. "I lost my arm the night of the invasion. The now-dead alpha was the one that took it. With the help of my daughter, I got to take his life tonight. It's been a very good day." I smile at them, and they look between Aurora and me several times. I guess my daughter is more like me than I realized.

Aurora moves to my side and snuggles in close. She was choosing me over her three mates; it truly soothes my soul. In all the years I dreamed of my child, I never pictured the strong female before me. When I would dream walk to teach her in her sleep, her animal never revealed their gender or even their fur color. It was very protective of her even in her slumber. Perhaps her Lycan is more dragon than I first suspected.

Dimitri is the first to approach and kneels before me. His bear surfaces as he looks up to my daughter and I. "M'lord, if I had known you were captured, we would have come for you sooner." His head lowers, and he looks to the ground. I guess, in a way, he blames himself for not knowing.

"Dimitri, do not blame yourself. You carried precious cargo; my daughter, last of her name. You performed a great service to our people and me. I am forever in your debt." I gently place my hand on his shoulder. "Rise, old friend." Aurora moves off to the side and into Sebastian's waiting arms. Dimitri slowly stands, and I can see clearly now that he is starting to age.

Whatever magic that has extended his life is fading slowly. I move forward and hug Dimitri, bringing the big old bear in close. I missed having my trusted guardian at my side. Few from the past still live, yet those that should not be here are still alive. My eyes find Andre; he is another that has outlived his species lifespan. "If there is anything I can do for you and Dimitri, name it and it shall be yours."

Dimitri backs up and hugs onto Andre. His eyes dart to where Aurora is standing with her three mates. Slowly his eyes return to me, and I can see a sadness deep within their depths. "I fear we will not be able to serve in the final battle as we are now." Andre begins to sniffle and hides his face against Dimitri's chest; he fears death. Dimitri looks down at his faithful companion and sighs. Perhaps there is something this old dragon could do.

"We can try something; it's old magic and might not even work for long." I look down, staring at my hand as I shift it, looking at my snow-white scales and long, white talons. Even after all these years, it is odd to only have one arm. My dragon's eyes lock onto Dimitri before I look up and over to Aurora. "Daughter, I need your assistance." Aurora and her mates look plenty puzzled by my request before they come running over without question.

"Yes, Father?" She cants her head to the right looking up at me. Her Lycan surges to the surface, sensing my dragon's urgency. Her eyes fall to my shifted hand and arm, then back up to my eyes.

Our animals are in deep conversation that even I'm not privy to. Aurora's hands shift quickly, and then plucks two scales off of my wrist. She turns and promptly plunges her talon into Dimitri's chest and sinks the bleeding side of my scale into his skin. She repeats the process even faster, with Andre knowing how sensitive the bird is. Once her task is complete, her hands begin to glow with frost. Her eyes lock onto the scales, and she presses both frozen palms over the scale transplants, cementing them to their new hosts. She draws in a deep panting breath then collapses from the exertion. Dominik is the one to catch her before she hits the floor. He cradles his greatest treasure against his chest, rocking her gently.

"I'm not sure how much more time my scales and Aurora's frost will grant you. But for now, it will slow the process that has already begun." I speak truly; I'm honestly not sure how long it will give them. For Aurora's sake, something is better than nothing; she will need their guidance and wisdom to train the troops. They both look down at their chests then over to Aurora, who is still sleeping. "We need to get moving. Dominik, do you or your brother have transportation? As we are not all going to fit in that." Motioning to the black truck that isn't far from where we are standing.

"Yeah, we have a couple of vehicles we can take. Where are we headed?" Jayce is the one who answers and now looks to Sebastian—apparently, he is being recognized as alpha while Aurora is incapacitated.

Sebastian moves forward and sniffs the crown of Aurora's head, then kisses it before turning to me. "We'll head to my birth pack. My mother will be most pleased to see that you live, my king." He bows slightly to me. Too alpha to fully submit, yet smart enough to show ample respect where it's due.

"Sounds like a solid plan. Let's depart as soon as possible. It will be nice to have a bath and sleep in a real bed again." I turn to Dimitri and smile. "I'll ride with you, old friend. We have a lot of catching up to do." Dimitri nods and starts heading towards the giant black monstrosity that they call Aurora's baby. Baby? An odd thing to call a structure of metal—it doesn't live or breathe. Nor does it resemble my daughter in stature or scent. Andre notices my puzzlement and moves closer.

"Aurora calls the truck her baby because she loves it. It's her most prized possession, besides her guitar." Ah, she has placed a term of endearment and possession on a lifeless object. So much has changed since my capture. Like I'm supposed to ride in this metal beast. Dimitri hops behind what looks like a wheel and does something that makes it roar to life.

Black smoke billows from the beast, and in that moment, I feel at home. Perhaps it is part dragon? I decided to pace around the loud metal beast. I touch it, and its scales are more rigid than my own. I sense no life from it, yet it makes noise. What other wonders will I find now in my newfound freedom? After my second lap around the smoking beast, Andre opens it up. I peer around what he is calling its *door* and see two rows of what appear to be soft seating. It's like a carriage, but there is music playing in it, and the wind blows out of holes in the front.

"Have you captured tiny musicians and frost sprites to have music and cold air?" I stare into the slotted holes, looking for the beating of the sprite's wings. I hear muffled laughter from Dimitri, and Andre is holding his breath, trying not to laugh. "I demand to know what's so funny!" I turn and stare at them both in turn. "Has my daughter wrongly imprisoned sprites and tiny musicians?" I attempt to cross my arm over my chest and wait for a sound explanation. "Oh, and the dragon whose smoke comes from this metal beast, how dare you let her capture and imprison her kin!"

Dimitri is the first to compose himself and turn to face me. "M'lord, a lot has changed since the last time you walked free. We are sitting in what is called a truck. It does not live; other than us, there is nothing alive in it." He motions to each object as he names it. "The air blows cold because of an invention called an air conditioner. This right here is a radio, and it allows us to find all different types of music. No one is needed to be awake or present to hear the music." I nod along slowly as he explains the wonders I am witnessing.

Never in my wildest dreams did I imagine any of these things before me. I still stare, puzzled at the knobs and buttons that are before me. Each one does something... what will they think of next? Dimitri pushes buttons on the thing he calls a radio, and soon, the sound of an orchestra fills the vehicle.

I smile; it reminds me of the last time I was happy and free. "Thank you, old friend, this is a gift." I reach over and pat Dimitri on the shoulder before leaning back to listen to the music. A rumbling that you can feel in your chest destroys my peace. A sleek-black, metal beast comes straight for us super-fast. I was getting worried, but Dimitri starts laughing when the car suddenly turns and covers us with dust.

Aurora jumps out of the left side of the vehicle and walks over to Dimitri's door. "Hmm, I cut it a tad bit too close. I got my baby dirty. We're gonna head back to Sebastian's pack, so try and keep up!" Before I can get a word out, she hops in through Dimitri's window and flips down a panel, hits a few buttons, and the sound of the vehicle changes. "There, just woke up a few extra ponies so the beast can keep up with the harlot. Hi, Daddy!" She smiles at me before popping back out the window and running back over to the car.

"Is she always like this?" I watch my daughter jump back into what Dimitri called a *HellCat* and take off, leaving a cloud of dust in her wake. The beast is far away, and we can still hear it clearly. It makes me remember the days when dragons flew free and were the lords of the skies. My eyes lock on a metal bird overhead—what I wouldn't give to go back to when it was simpler.

"Yes, she's always like that. Free as a bird and reckless, with an obsession with speed and power." Dimitri's eyes lock on the switch box Aurora had fiddled with, then shakes his head, dismissing it.

When his foot hits the pedal, he quickly figures out what she had meant. The truck launches itself forward much faster than any of us had anticipated. "Holy shit!" he screams as his knuckles turn white, holding onto the steering wheel. I watch the numbers in the middle of the dash get higher and higher, and we gain ground on Aurora at breakneck speed.

I lower the window and stick my hand out, feeling the wind rush over and around my fingers. It feels like I am flying again. Without a second thought, I stick my head out the window to feel the wind in my face. I was robbed of flight, so this would have to do for now. I hear Andre yelling at me to get my head back in as he panics over my safety. At least some things didn't change; he's still a worrywart. I resume sitting in my seat when Andre leans forward and ties me to the chair with a strap. "What is the meaning of this, Andre? You dare to restrain your king?" My dragon makes his presence known as his slits burn through my silver eyes.

"It's called a seat belt, M'lord. It's to keep you safe in case of an accident." He looks quite sheepish, having to explain it to me. I look down at the offensive belt, then back to Andre.

"Fine, it can remain for now. Next time, warn me before you decide to restrain me for my own good." I breathe out sharply, and a frosty mist escapes my nostrils. I wasn't thrilled, but he did have my best interest in mind, so I couldn't stay completely mad at him.

I drum my fingers on the windowsill as I watch the miles fly by me. We've been on the road for several hours already, and they said we still have a few hours to go. Being terrestrial is the worst fate ever. I could have already been at our destination if I still had both of my wings. I could have carried everyone. It was a lifetime ago when I last had the wind in my face. There's an odd ringing noise in the truck, and the music stops playing, and I see my daughter's image on the screen in the dash. "How is my daughter in the truck?" I point at her picture and inadvertently, unbeknownst to me, answer the phone call.

Her image is now gone, but I can hear her. "Hey, guys, time to stop for food. We're at the diner about five clicks north of your position." I tilt my head to the side and stare at the screen.

"Aurora, baby how are you in the truck and the diner? What witchcraft is this?" I look frantically between the screen and Dimitri; who, by the way, is laughing at me again.

"Daddy, it's called a telephone. Dimitri's phone was answered when someone touched my picture on the truck's screen. It's safer than taking your eyes off the road to fiddle with the phone. I'm sitting on the hood of Dom's car talking to you at the diner." She was so helpful. I look around the truck and see her picture on the rectangle object in the cupholder.

"I think I found that thing you call a phone. It has your picture on it. Did a witch make this?" Aurora and Dimitri start laughing at me now. I'm starting to get mad about being laughed at. "Why must you laugh at me? I swear I'm ready to set things on fire if this continues." Soon as the words leave my mouth, everyone goes silent. I look around and see the diner in the distance.

"Well, we know where I get my lovely temperament from!" Aurora giggles before the line clicks and the music returns.

I look at Dimitri. "What did she mean by that?" I was honestly puzzled by my daughter's statement. I feel I was relatively calm. I used to burn things and then question the survivors. I fully believe that my temperament has improved quite a bit. I guess I came off a bit smug, evidenced by Dimitri's eye roll.

We pull up next to the Hellcat, and the truck stops and becomes quiet. Hmm, that little black thing makes it move and makes it stop. I'll have to question my daughter later about what it is. Andre comes and opens my door; I go to exit and am suddenly stopped. The evil belt he put on me is still in place. How do the others tolerate this horrid thing? It most certainly gets in the way, but I see its possible uses. My daughter is surrounded on three sides by her mates. Sebastian is being incredibly dominant and possessive of Aurora. Out of the three, only two have been fully claimed by her, but Sebastian seems to have problems sharing.

"Everything okay?" I look at each one of them in the eyes. Sebastian and Dominik can maintain eye contact for a decent amount of time, whereas Jayce can barely raise his eyes. Hmm, two potential alphas and one omega. This is definitely going to lead to problems down the road.

"I believe so, M'lord," Sebastian answers me first. "Dominik just needs to learn what being chosen as the first mate means in our family." Sebastian's wolf flairs to the surface and emphasizes his point. Ah, now I understand what's going on. A soft growl escapes Dominik's lips at the end of Sebastian's statement.

"I see…" I state plainly. My eyes find Aurora's; she's mildly distressed by all of this posturing these young pups are doing. "The first mate's role is to help their queen make levelheaded decisions. It's not to rule or dictate the direction of the pack. The last king that did that ended up losing his kingdom and his mate and pair bonds." My eyes churn liquid mercury to accentuate my point. "I've already seen a first mate destroy a pack. I will not let it happen with my daughter." I motion for Aurora to join me.

Swiftly she untangles herself from the guys and snuggles into my side. When she looks up at me, I see her mother's eyes so clear and pure. It makes my heart ache to see those eyes again. I have to remind myself this is our daughter and all I have left of my beloved Anca.

"Thank you, Daddy." She squeezes me tightly again as she begins to move us towards the diner's entrance.

At the door, a woman stands dressed like one of the serving girls we had in the castle. She asks how many in our party, which thankfully, Aurora answers her with seven. "Why was she asking about a party when we are just passing through?" I furrow my brows because to be quite honest, I am puzzled. Aurora just shakes her head and guides me to the table, pushing me to the side closest to the wall. Ah, I see what she did; she's protecting my left side. Something here has her on edge, and I can feel her animal bristling near the surface.

Jayce slides in next to Aurora and begins to rub the back of her neck. Slowly she begins to settle down. I wonder what set her off. "Let's get some food in you, sweetie. You'll feel better with a full tummy." Jayce speaks to her so lovingly, and she instantly responds to it and rests her head on his shoulder. Her beast settles as well, once the other males join us finally. Jayce continues to pamper Aurora throughout the meal, distracting her from the petty, childish bullshit that Dominik and Sebastian are portraying.

At this point, I am quite thankful that at least one of her mates has his priorities straight. Aurora's eyes find Dimitri, and he kindly orders for the table. I have a feeling this is going to be one very long and exhausting journey.

CHAPTER 17

Jayce

What in the world have I gotten myself into? Not only has my ex gone totally mental, blowing my phone up to the point of lunacy. Sinclair is never going to understand the pull of the mating bond because he only likes men. He'll never feel the way your blood sings the minute you see your mate for the first time. He'll never experience that first kiss that sets your whole world on its axis.

I get to sit behind Aurora as she drives after the diner debacle. I can't believe that Dom and Sebastian can be so petty. Aurora chose to sit next to her father, and I decided to shield her from their shit. I mean, come on, get over it! Then it became a pissing contest as to who was going to pay the bill. Dear lord, guys, just whip them out and measure them already. My brother is across from me, checking in on the pack while it's Sebastian's turn to sit up front with Aurora.

I can tell she's aggravated as she's dead silent, not a single peep out of her. My eyes glance towards Sebastian, and his thumbs are flying over his keyboard, texting someone. "Mother has the alpha's house ready for us when we arrive," he states flatly. "I've already texted Andre to let them know what's going on," Sebastian says, his tone flat and authoritative.

Aurora just nods then tells her phone to pair to the car. The familiar ping that the connection was made is heard. She grabs her phone for a moment and scrolls through songs on her phone. She searches out the song "Devil" from Shinedown and looks into the rearview. Her eyes are that of her beast's as she looks at everyone in turn.

Oh yeah, the silent ultimatum is read loud and clear. Well, at least by me, it was. Dom's eyes shift for a moment, and he nods briefly. He goes back to texting our other brother, whom we left in charge of the pack. Everything on that front, at least, is calm and quiet.

Her eyes fall on Sebastian, who doesn't even look up at her at all. Oh, you can see she is getting angry; the corner of her right eye starts to twitch. She has so many subtle facial cues, like how she's gritting her teeth and the tenseness in her jaw. Her eyes keep shifting back and forth between human and liquid mercury. The temperature in the car starts dropping quickly. It is only when Sebastian begins to see his breath does he bother to look over at her. Her canines are visible, and her knuckles are white with how tightly she is gripping the steering wheel. The muscles of her right bicep twitch and flex as she white knuckles the wheel.

"I hope you accomplished something great while you ignored me." Her tone is all beast; it is growled out and accented with a frost after bite. He sighs and turns to face her. I don't know if that was his smartest or dumbest move to date, but I'm thankful I'm back here.

"A half dozen rogues have returned to the pack. Some are semi-feral, most are okay. Mom has the feral wolves sedated until your return. She figures either they will live or die by your talons depending on their actions." He draws in a deep breath and lets it out slowly. "I just hate that the weight of the world is on your shoulders. I can handle some of this responsibility for you, and Dom can help as well." He shrugs his shoulders and rolls his eyes. "I don't think killing everyone who doesn't agree with you is the best course of action," he says just before crossing his arms over his chest, trying to drive his point home.

Aurora cuts the wheel hard and puts us into a spin. She doesn't care, she is at her breaking point, and Sebastian has finally pushed her last button. Once she stops us from spinning, she slams the car into park, gets out, and starts pacing.

"Who the actual fuck do you think you are?" Her eyes flair and begin to glow the liquid mercury orbs pulse with untold power.

"Telling me what I should and shouldn't do!" She is partially shifted and quite terrifying. Dom and I stand back as she faces off with Sebastian.

Dimitri and the guys finally catch up and stop dead in their tracks. Aurora is so worked up, she is between forms and freezing the ground around her. "Can you do anything?" I look to Nico, and he shrugs his shoulders then shakes his head *no*. Fantastic, we have an Lycan-dragon hybrid, pissed off beyond all recognition, and not even the dragon can stop her. My eyes fall on Dom next. "Brother, can you do anything?"

Dom just starts laughing. "And have her get mad at me too? No way, brother; he buried himself. I'd like to see him claw his way out of this one." Some help my brother is. I begin to pace and watch the fight. Sebastian isn't fighting back, and Aurora is mostly yelling at him, so it isn't Defcon one; we are maybe a three or a two-ish. Not total nuclear war, but definitely not at peace.

Then I have my most brilliant thought. I strip out of my clothing and shift to my wolf. I begin to belly crawl to her, whimpering. That gets her attention. Her head snaps up as she turns to look at me fully, checking me for wounds. She immediately shifts back to human and kneels beside me, her fingers thread through my thick, obsidian fur as she checks my body over for injuries. I roll over, giving her my belly. Aurora smiles when she figures out that I'm in one piece and begins to rub my stomach. *Success!* I got her out of rage mode, and now it's cute snuggly Aurora. She starts to laugh as I lick her face and paw at her several times. I get up quickly and shake out my fur and play-pounce her, knocking her onto her ass. Now she's hysterically laughing, and officially, we are back to Defcon five. I move closer and let her use my shoulders to pull herself back up to standing. Am I feeling a bit smug? *Yes, yes, I am.* I freaking prance past Sebastian and my brother to get to my clothes.

Nicodeamus pats me on my shoulder and tells me I did well. Now that's worth every slightly degrading moment, and her father appreciated what I just did. Quickly I return to my human form and dress, not wanting to hold the group up if they're going to get rolling again.

Dimitri is the first to approach me once I am fully dressed. "You did good, son. You read her correctly, and you were exactly what she needed at the moment. You bring balance to your brother's brashness." The Great Bear pats me on the shoulder then starts walking back to the truck. He's truly a man of few words.

Carefully, I move between Aurora and Sebastian and look between them. "Are we okay now?" Being the omega at times has its advantages. Like now, I'm not even remotely considered a threat. I'm not even a contender for the crown. To be honest, I don't want it.

Aurora and Sebastian nod and move towards the car. Aurora suddenly stops and turns to me. "Care to drive, Jayce? Or would you rather Dom drive? Either way, I'm climbing in the back and taking a nap." She smiles softly at me and tilts her head towards the car.

I look to Dom, and he makes the key in the ignition motion to me, signaling he'll drive. "Dom can drive; after all, it is his baby. I'll climb in back with you, and you can use me as a pillow." There's the smile I was looking for. Aurora's smile can light up the darkest night. She walks past Sebastian and kisses his cheek before moving to me and taking my hand. There's that tingle that only she can give me; goosebumps move up my arm, and the flutters start in my belly. The humans call it butterflies, which is the giddy feeling you get from the person you love. I draw in a slow, deep breath and smile. We stop in front of Dom, and she kisses his cheek as well and whispers a quiet, heartfelt *thank you* to him. My normally stoic brother cracks a smile and caresses the back of Aurora's neck before drawing her close to kiss her temple before releasing her.

We walk in silence to the car; it is nice just to be able to be in this moment with her. When we reach the car's passenger side, I open the door and let her slide in first. Carefully I slide myself in place behind the passenger seat, press my back against the window ledge and prop a leg up on the seat. Aurora watches me with rapt attention until I signal for her to lie down on me. The back seat isn't huge, nor is it all that comfortable, but at least if I can keep her comfortable and safe, then I've succeeded. Aurora moves slowly, like the calculating apex predator she is, her eyes roaming over my body and the way I have positioned myself.

"Jayce, are you sure you're going to be okay? I mean, the hard plastic against your back can't be comfortable." Aurora's concern for me warms my heart and eases some of the pain I feel after breaking up with my long-term boyfriend.

"I'll be fine, sweetheart. I'm more concerned about you. You've had a rough couple of weeks, and I'd like to be able to take care of you for a while." My choice of words must have set her mind at ease. She leans forward and kisses me lightly on my lips, lingering there for a moment, looking into my eyes. Slowly her eyes swirl mercury, then back to grey. She and her beast are in agreement; they completely accept my wolf and me. My wolf stirs for a moment, just long enough to see Aurora smile at having seen him. A soft yawn escapes her lips before she snuggles against me—her hip against my groin and the bridge of her nose against my adam's apple. Gently her forehead comes to rest against my neck. I wrap my arms around her, holding her firmly to my chest. I must admit that this is one of the best moments of my life.

My brother and Sebastian get in the car and break me out of the bubble I was in when they both turn to look at us. I'm not good at reading alpha-types well. I mean, they both continuously look pissed. Seriously, if men could have a resting bitch face, these two have perfected it. I smile, what could they possibly do that wouldn't send Aurora into a rage for disturbing her? For once, I feel I possess the ultimate power by having the nuclear bomb we call our mate, sleeping on me. The rumble of the Hellcat comes to life, causing Aurora to stir slightly. I simply tighten my grip and inch us down in the seat a tad to make both of us a bit more comfortable. She's out cold in my arms, and I'm the luckiest wolf alive. It doesn't take long for the engine's rumble and Aurora's soft breathing to lull me to sleep as well.

CHAPTER 18

Jayce

Who knows how long we slept for, but before we know it, we are at our destination, Some woman is asking for Aurora. My eyes crack open first, and slowly, I look around to get my bearings. I notice Sebastian opening the driver's side door up and sliding the seat forward. He leans in slowly and smiles, seeing our precious cargo still sleeping so soundly. His head tilts to the side, studying her and her positioning on me. The fingers of her left hand have a death grip on my shirt, and her right-hand grips my forearm.

Sebastian starts laughing. "I guess Dom's driving scared her in her sleep. At least she didn't see what I had to see on the way here." He widens his eyes in mock horror and smiles before he starts rubbing her hip. "Wake up, beautiful. Mom is getting impatient about seeing you, you know how she gets. She has to make sure you're in one piece after your journey," Sebastian says, his voice and facial expression don't match yet again. His tone versus the look on his face is saying two different things.

Aurora shifts slightly, causing my cock to stiffen instantly. It's been years since a woman has had such an effect on me. Quite honestly, I am fucking amazed and impressed at the same time. I watch her eyes blink rapidly then finally open. She stretches and yawns, opening her mouth wide. Sebastian and I are both shocked to see her canines have dropped. Was it a moment of aggression, or was she scenting my arousal? Her beast is present when she turns those pure mercury orbs on me. Her smile is completely predatory, her pearly white teeth on full display. I do believe she would take what she wanted to whether I was ready for that step or not. Well, my cock is a traitor, and fuck, he'd sell our soul to the devil to get lost in her for a few hours, days, years… In moments like this, being omega sucks. I lower my eyes and submit to her. My mate is a dominant alpha, and there is no way I'd be able to hold my own against her.

Lithe hands swiftly cup my cheeks and pull my head up so that my eyes meet hers. They are human again and look quite concerned. Tears threaten to break free from her eyes as she looks me over quickly. "I'm so sorry, Jayce. She got away from me a bit. I'm not that type of alpha. All my mates are equals in my heart. I hold none over the others." Gently she kisses my lips when I nod, acknowledging her statement. I know deep down she said it more to remind Sebastian of his place and help me accept mine.

I am equal to three alphas; that thought is very foreign to me. Sebastian mentions the others are waiting, trying to tear her away from me. Aurora's eyes drift back to Sebastian, and she lets out a soft growl, baring her canines at him. Our girl doesn't like being told what to do. That was a very simple lesson to learn, but the muscle-bound male hasn't figured that out yet—easy points for me. Eventually, she extends her hand to Sebastian, and he helps her slide out of the car.

This little wisp of a woman wraps Aurora up in a hug and snuggles into her so tightly. Aurora looks almost panicked as the woman continues to hold on. To me, it is absolutely the most adorable thing I've ever seen. I take this moment to extract myself from the car and join the others. My eyes flitter between Sebastian and this little woman, then it dawns on me, she's his mother.

Dom moves over to bump into me and starts to snicker. "I don't think our girl is overly comfortable with physical contact." It was true, Aurora didn't look overly thrilled, but she also didn't look like she was going to harm the little woman. Her eyes find mine, and she extracts herself from the woman's grip and starts to drag her to us.

"Elena, I must introduce you to the twins!" Aurora has that mischievous look to her, and I just knew she was up to something. Elena looks between Dom and me and just smiles, then pulls Aurora down to her height and whispers in her ear. Aurora's cheeks turn bright pink. Quickly she pulls back up to her full height, looking back and forth between my brother and me, then back to Elena and blushes more. *Oh, dear Gods, what did that sprite tell her?*

Aurora clears her throat, then places her hand on Dom's shoulder. "Elena, this is Dominik. He was his pack's enforcer, and now he's mine." A gentle kiss is placed on Dom's cheek, and he nods lightly to Elena. Aurora then comes over to me and straightens out the collar on my button-down. "This sharply dressed hunk is Jayce. He was an advisor and historian to the alpha. Now he shall be my voice of reason." She snuggles into my side for a moment then kisses my cheek. Sometimes there's an advantage to being an omega.

"Elena, you won't believe who we found!" Aurora is squealing and bouncing up and down like an excited child. Apparently, none of us have ever seen Aurora like this because we're all fucking puzzled.

"Daddy!" She screams at the top of her lungs then sprints over to her truck to try to drag him out into the open.

Elena looks at Sebastian. "Daddy?" Her brows are furrowed, and her confusion is quite evident. All the screaming and squealing has started to draw a crowd. It appears the entire pack is now in the central courtyard.

Sebastian simply nods his head as Dimitri and Andre approach. "Apparently, the Dire Alpha took the Dragon King hostage during the Strigoi attack. He also cut off the King's arm." Elena and Sebastian both look towards the truck where Aurora is in a heated discussion with her father. Heated is a relatively poor choice of words since the ground and the truck are now covered by a thick layer of frost.

I start shaking my head as I move towards the truck—my brother and the others yelling at me not to go, that it would be my funeral, and so on. My hand slowly grips Aurora's shoulder and rubs her neck gently. "M'lord, what seems to be the problem?" Addressing the dragon directly was scary as fuck. Then again, so is the nuclear winter they were plunging us into.

His dragon eyes lift and regard me. "I am not the king I once was. The focus should be on you and her other mates with her, not me." He gently rubs the socket where his arm used to be. His sadness is palatable, and yet there is a hint of fear with it as well.

"M'lord, your presence and wisdom will be a great asset to your daughter and her mates for the upcoming war. You know these creatures, their habits, and what their weaknesses are. Your involvement can be the deciding factor for our victory." I appeal to his honor and sense of duty. Most importantly, I am appealing to his desire to protect his daughter. I can feel the shift in his mood almost immediately, and a smile graces his lips.

"Daughter, you have chosen well. You have a wise and reasonable mate." Nicodeamus slides out of the truck at this point and wraps me up in a one-armed hug. "Let's go see the pack, shall we?" I remain tucked into Nicodeamus's side as we head back to the others.

Everyone—including the other mates—all kneel before the dragon king. He smiles gently at everyone and keeps me tight to his side as we move to the alpha house. Aurora opens the door for us, and once everyone is in, she turns to the pack. "Prepare a feast! We shall welcome my new mates and father properly." The pack erupts in cheers and begins to scramble to prepare for tonight. Aurora presses her back against the door and slides down it laughing. "Well, that went better than I expected!"

Sebastian moves and crouches down in front of her and shakes his head at her. "For being the alpha of this ragtag bunch, you can be so silly at times." He leans forward and kisses her lips, and caresses her cheek. "Good thing you're cute even when you're homicidal."

Aurora smirks and looks around the living room. A Lycan skull and vertebral column are hanging on the wall. A huge smile graces her lips as she jumps up to look at the bones on the wall. Moving swiftly towards her trophies, she almost knocks Sebastian flat on his ass in passing. "Aw, Elena, you shouldn't have! I love it, and the little plaques are absolutely precious!" Aurora's fingertips trace the edges of the plaques as she reads each one.

Out of the corner of my eye, I catch Sebastian facepalm and shake his head. "Really, mom?" His eyes are an ice blue, almost white, as he stares at his mom. Elena is laughing so hard at him.

"Oh, come on, you know she loves it! Why wouldn't you want her prizes on the wall of your home?" Elena comes up beside Aurora with a Swiffer and begins to dust the bones.

"It's disconcerting, Mother." Sebastian states flatly.

Dimitri looks like the cat that swallowed the canary. In his hand is a cooler that I overlooked before. My eyes find my brother, and he rolls his eyes. He quickly points at Aurora, cutting the head off move, signals seven, and then points to the cooler. Holy shit, she has my father's and brother's heads and the others in the cooler. I'm feeling a little ill at the moment when Aurora looks at me. *Shit, she knows I figured it out.*

"Elena, Mother... I have seven more for you to prepare to go onto the wall. Maybe over there." She points to the wall space to the right of the head and spine. She's actually fucking serious about wanting to put their skulls up. What the actual fuck am I witnessing? I start to back up and run into a hard, warm body.

Large hands grip my hips. "Where are you going, little omega?" Sebastian whispers in my ear. Lightly he nips my earlobe as he watches Aurora interact with his mother. "Disapprove of our mate's collection? Honestly, it disturbed me in the beginning as well. The Lycan's head is the female I was betrothed to, and the spine belonged to the alpha." Sebastian cants his head with that sexy smirk on his lips. He's just as out there as Aurora is; apparently, keeping parts of your enemies is a Lycan thing. His deep breathy, baritone voice makes my cock stir. I feel it heat and swell to life, pulsing in time with my heartbeat.

Why does he have to be so fucking sexy? He kind of looks like that vampire Damon. Sebastian is the full package: dark, brooding, and oozes sex appeal. I could easily lick him for hours. I wonder how Aurora would feel about her mates having sex with each other?

Speaking of that crazy female, she's dancing around with the heads in her hands, spinning in circles. Sebastian turns me around in his arms, so my hands land flat on his taunt muscular chest. His eyes shift to that of his wolf, and our hard cocks are side by side, pressed against each other. Time has officially stopped; the rest of the room falls away, and all I see is Sebastian leaning down to kiss me. His lips are smooth as silk when they first touch mine. His kiss intensifies and becomes hard and demanding; our teeth hit just before he bites my bottom lip and draws blood. I can't help but moan into his mouth as I feel my cock pulse. It was one of those intense kisses that makes your cock leak with antici-pation. My fingertips grip his shoulders tightly as we grind against each other. Out of nowhere, there's a flash of light and then another.

Aurora is standing on a chair not far from us, taking pictures with her cellphone. Her eyes are pure mercury, and I can smell her arousal. So apparently, our girl likes to watch. "Okay, guys, that was hot!" She jumps down off of the chair, walks over, and sticks her hand between us, gripping our cocks and wet pants. "Ooh, someone was having a good time." The way she's biting her bottom lip ramps up my desire.

I really want Sebastian to make me his bitch, and yet I really wish to have Aurora dominate me as well. She slowly brings her wet hand to her lips and licks our essence off of her skin. That thick, wet muscle of hers coils around her fingertip as she laves up every single drop. I'm so close to coming it's not even funny anymore.

Sebastian looks like he's in the same personal hell I'm in. As quickly as she fucked my world up, she moves away towards Dom. That motherfucker has the nerve to smile at me right now. I have the absolute worst case of blue balls in the history of blue balls, and he's smiling. He leans slowly to nip at Aurora's neck; without warning, she sweeps his legs and puts him to the ground.

"It's not nice to taunt your brother!" She stands over him, her eyes churning liquid mercury as she stares down at him. "He's still fragile over his breakup, and if he can find comfort with Sebastian, then so fucking be it! If I catch you giving him a difficult time, I'll beat your ass myself." Holy fucking hell, that was even hotter than the kiss that Sebastian just gave me. She stood up for me. I look to the others, and they are slowly clearing the room to get ready for later.

My eyes land on Sebastian, who can't stop smiling at me. "She loves you, Jayce. She's protective of what's hers. She'll wait until you're ready to be with her, with no pressure. In the meantime, you know where to find me." He smacks my ass so hard it's still stinging. My cock starts to twitch to life again; apparently, I have a new kink. Time to go shower and rub one out before dinner. My life just got very interesting.

CHAPTER 19

Andre

I NEVER THOUGHT I'D LIVE TO SEE THE DAY MY LITTLE GIRL WOULD FIND her mates—and two being bi-sexual. When I was young, if you even showed interest in someone of the same gender you were put to death. So being a gay Golden Eagle was a touch depressing. I just got to witness the most open display of attraction I've ever seen in my life. To be quite honest, it was hot as all hell. I felt my nether regions twitch to life for a few moments. Over my shoulder, I hear a young lad clear his throat. Slowly I turn to look at him, and he smiles at me. Hmm, today may be getting interesting, after all. My eyes fall back on Aurora; it warms my heart with her level of acceptance of her mate's and my choices. I draw in a deep breath as tears threaten to break loose, I feel the love in the room, and it's the most beautiful thing ever.

Dimitri chooses that moment to come over and give me a side hug. "You okay, old friend?" He looks down at me with that smile he gets on a rare occasion when he's feeling sappy.

"Aye, just remembering our baby girl when I used to get the chance to mother the hell out of her. I know I'm not a mom. Hell, my bollocks prove I'm not a mom. But out of the two of us, I've always been the gentle one." I look at my soft hands and my wrist where Aurora's bracelet she made me so very long ago still rests. "I wonder how long we have left." My eyes well up further, and the tears break free rolling down my cheeks in streams. I blubber like a bloody idiot, but I can't help it. I can't see myself or Dimitri without Aurora in our lives. My hand absently moves to touch the scale the dragon king gave us. Who knows how much magic is in it or how long it will sustain us? My heart hurts thinking about leaving her when she needs us the most. She's only gathered mates from two of the clans, and there are two left. I turn and embrace Dimitri, burying my face in his strong shoulder.

A small, warm hand lightly touches my shoulder. Turning my head to find Aurora with Nicodeamus at her side. Her eyes hold unshed tears as she looks between Dimitri and me. "Father told me what's happening; I don't know what to say or do. I don't want to lose you two." Tears pour down her cheeks at her confession. She quickly snuggles herself between Dimitri and me, and the three of us start balling our eyes out. Aurora's lithe body shakes as she sobs uncontrollably; Dimitri and I try to hold her and comfort her. Deep down, I'm afraid of what will come when Dimitri and I pass to the great beyond. Aurora's inability to process emotions is a concern as she cries in our arms.

The double doors to the alpha's house fly open and slam against the wall. Sebastian and Dominik are both completely shifted, looking for danger. Jayce comes walking from the other side of the hall to stand before them. "Nothing to worry about guys; they're having an emotional family moment." Both males shift back to their human forms and move closer to us; both males lay a single hand on Aurora. She seems to calm almost immediately. Her head slowly raises to look at each mate in turn. Wordlessly she shimmies out of her guardian sandwich and moves to her mates. All three surround her and hold on until she stops crying.

"We're going to take her to our room and comfort our mate," Sebastian states calmly and with the authority of an alpha.

Dominik bends and scoops Aurora up into his arms, cradling his precious cargo tightly to his chest. Jayce, who is the most in touch with his emotions, kisses the crown of her head. "I'll draw a hot bath for you, Aurora, and I'll give you a massage while you tell us what you need from us." He gives the other mates a look—probably the most dominant look I've ever seen from him. The other guys just nod and smile as they croon softly to Aurora.

Watching them move as a unit makes me smile; I know in my heart of hearts that she will be taken care of no matter what. My eyes find Nicodeamus and he's smiling. "You two have made wonderful parents for my Aurora. I am forever in your debt." He sighs softly as his eyes move between Dimitri and me. "I can see she's become more than an assignment to you. She's the child you two never got to have. For that, I am sorry that your lives were put on hold for her. I am grateful, however, that she's known love her whole life. For that, she is blessed." He bows at his waist to us. A king is bowing to us; it's going to take some time for that sink in.

"We are the ones that are blessed with the gift of time we have had as your daughter's family. We have been blessed with the countless extra years her life has given us. We only wish to live to see her ascend the throne—like her mother hoped she would. God's willing, we will be granted long enough to do just that." I sigh deeply as I slowly bow to the king. Dimitri follows suit, bowing as well. We all turn to look at the door as Jayce closes it behind him. "I don't know who's taking this harder, Aurora or us. I hate seeing her cry; it's actually quite scary to see." My eyes widen, and I start to laugh, thinking about the past. "Remember Dimitri, that time Aurora got hurt and started crying? Then she shifted, and her Lycan destroyed half the house and part of the forest."

Dimitri starts laughing and shakes his head. "Yeah, or the time her Lycan forced the shift and at least a half dozen trees were taken down because her wolf couldn't handle the tears."

Nicodeamus smiles gently and nods slowly. "It seems like my daughter acted more like a dragon than a wolf. Hatchlings tend to be confused by emotions. Sadness turns to anger. Fear turns to anger. Pretty much everything turns to anger until they get older." Nicodeamus starts laughing. "I'm sorry, it's quite dangerous to raise a baby dragon or dragon hybrid without a dragon to temper its emotions. I was just thinking about all the craziness my daughter must have caused in her first hundred years." He's still laughing his ass off as he finds a place to sit down nearby.

"First hundred? Try two hundred plus, and we're still waiting for her to mellow out." I look to Dimitri and then over to Nico, who just nods along until he cants his head to the side.

"Hmm, must be because she's a hybrid. I'll have to ponder this further." Nicodeamus rises up to his full height and walks away. I sit here wondering how many centuries that male has lived to know everything he does. I draw in a steadying breath as I turn to go for a walk.

Elena stops me and pulls me around the corner with her. "Shhhh... don't alert the others." She's going all James Bond and shit on me and has us sneaking around the compound. It's gotta be a Lycan trait to be bat shit crazy. She leads me to a shed outback. Not creepy at all... no, not at all. I roll my eyes, following behind her towards the creepy shed.

I'm half expecting this to turn into a slasher movie where heads and body parts will be hanging from the ceiling. Nope, it's much worse! The two heads Aurora brought back are being boiled in a large cauldron in the middle of the room. I feel sick to my stomach seeing the Dire Alpha's head and his beta son bobbing around, floating and sinking in the cauldron's water. Random eyeballs float around in the cauldron, giving it a Halloween feel. Unfortunately, it's all real and not for Halloween. Clearly, Elena isn't fazed by what Aurora has done, but she can tell I'm disturbed by it.

"Death is but a doorway, Andre. Do not fear what cannot be controlled." She comes out carrying herbs and some bottles of an unknown liquid and dumps them in. She starts mixing it until it is boiling without a fire. Okay, now I'm getting concerned. She leans forward and plucks several hairs from my head, and throws them into the mix. Okay, either I am about to be cursed, killed, or turned into a zombie. Maybe I shouldn't have watched all those horror movies with Aurora when she was growing up. Oh, shit, am I the reason she's the way she is? My eyes shoot to the only escape route, then back to Elena. Can I make it out in time before she turns me into a zombie? "What are you so afraid of, Andre? I'm trying to figure out the magic my sister used to bind the two of you to Aurora."

Apparently, I've been panicking for nothing, but you must admit, it hadn't looked good for me. "Dimitri may be the better one to test. He was the one that the blade sliced. I'm bound to him by blood because of our jobs in the castle. My gift is an echo of what he got." Echo, side effect, a happy accident... however you want to call it. It's really disheartening to think my extended life span was a mistake or an accident. I look down at the ground when Elena comes over and hugs me. She knows this whole thing is breaking me. I love that homicidal wolf like my own child. To leave her now, I can't bear to think about it. A single tear rolls down my cheek thinking about the possibility of passing away.

"I will do everything within my power to help you and Dimitri." She kisses my cheek gently and moves back towards her cauldrons. "The best I can figure out is that my sister used blood magic combined with black magic. I'll need Dimitri's hair to determine how far down the rabbit hole my sister went." Her eyes lock with mine, and I can see the faint glow of her wolf backing up her claims. They genuinely believe they can help us. I give her a slight bow and back out of the shack.

Aurora's mate Jayce is walking around with his head down and kicking a rock around. "Something bothering you, son?" His head snaps up and his wolf blazes to the surface, then fades slowly; he gives me a soft nod and motions towards the swings. I follow him, watching his body language. He looks dejected. I wonder why? Aurora isn't the type to ignore anyone for any reason. We reach the swings, and we choose the two right next to each other. Side-by-side, we begin to swing. "You gonna talk, or did ya just need someone to hang out with?" I ask playfully with a slight chuckle.

He laughs softly, then turns to look at me. "Sorry, I'm still dealing with leaving a man I've been with for the better half of fifty years for a female. Don't get me wrong, I'm thankful and blessed that I've found my mate." Jayce sighs deeply and draws in a slow, measured breath just before a single tear falls. "Part of me, I feel like I'm betraying what I had before. The other part can't wait to start my forever with Aurora." He rubs at his eyes then looks back at me. "I thought Aurora was going to murder me for kissing Sebastian back the way I did. I swear to the gods I saw my life flash before my eyes, and I pictured her ripping my head off or my spine out. That female is fucking lethal and then cool as a cucumber like nothing happened afterward." His eyes are wide, as if he is still in shock over it all.

I start laughing and honestly can't contain it. "I'm sorry, Jayce, I'd love to say you'll get used to Aurora's antics, but two hundred plus years later, I'm still not immune to her. She literally can go from serial killer to snuggle bunny in like point five seconds." I widen my eyes in mock horror then smirk. "It scares the bloody hell out of me half the time. Gods help you if someone fucks with anyone she's claimed as hers, that's an instant death sentence." Mentally I'm ticking off the last ten deaths at her talons; sadly, I see her point in all of it. I finally hear Jayce laugh a little bit.

"Yeah, she's intense, to say the least. I need to sit and talk to her later." Jayce stops swinging and folds his hands in his lap. "I don't want her to think I don't care; I'm just trying to get my head straight before I get intimate with her." Slowly he shakes his head left to right. "The last thing we all need is for me to say the wrong thing at the wrong time, and heads start rolling, literally." He looks up at me, double-checking his logic.

Smart man, he's figured out our girl quite early on. "I have to ask you a personal question. I know Aurora only says what she means, but do you think she regrets accepting me?" He shrugs his shoulders. "I mean, I've spent more time in relationships with males than females." On a loud exhale, his shoulders lower and curl as if defeated. "To be honest, Sebastian is fucking hot as all hell. I mean, I hope to get to ride that pony at some point. But will she kill one or both of us for being intimate?" Jayce slowly looks back up at me, his brows furrowed, hopeful I have the answer he's looking for.

I double blink as the crux of his problem just became blatantly apparent. He's obviously more attracted to males than females. "Okay, umm... she's used to being around a gay male." I point both index fingers at my face, wiggling them around. "She's always been very accepting of my lifestyle and choices over the years. I tried dating, but I couldn't bring myself to be away from her for too long. What can I say? I'm an old mother-hen when it comes to her." I smile warmly, thinking about how blessed I've been over the years with her. "She loves all of her mates equally. None is above the others no matter what they think." I cough out "Sebastian," and Jayce starts to laugh again. "All Aurora is going to care about is that everyone is happy and safe and that no one fucks with her wine and dark chocolate." Jayce raises an eyebrow when I mention her kryptonite to him. A slow, knowing nod is given, and I smile in reply to him. I just gave him the ultimate insider information that will win him instant brownie points with our alpha.

He bounces up from his swing and hugs the hell out of me, and kisses my forehead. "Oh, my gods, Andre, thank you so much!!! I'm going shopping. Don't wait up for me!" When motivated, a bitch power walks.

He takes off like someone set his tight ass on fire. Perhaps I just gave him something that the other guys can't give her. It's sad that I just lost his company, but a delight to watch him leave. My eyes roam the town square, and that male from earlier is watching me again. I wave to him, and he waves back. Hmm, perhaps I'm getting somewhere? He slowly starts to move towards me, and I feel my heart rate pick up. I'm trying my damnedest to fight my fight-or-flight instincts. He's probably the hottest guy I've seen in years. His eyes are forest green, and his hair looks charcoal black. The best part, he's got muscles for days. "Hi." Oh, my fucking gods, I am so freaking lame. What the actual fuck am I thinking? I know what I'm thinking. I'm thinking with my dick. You know, the thing in my pants I haven't used in forever.

The hunk smiles. "Hi to you too. I'm Darren." He extends his hand to me, and for a moment, my dumb ass just stares at it before placing my hand in his to give him a firm shake.

"Andre. The pleasure is all mine." I stand before him, and we're almost the same height—my tall, lithe frame to his I'll-end-your-fucking-world muscular build. I rest a hand on his firm shoulder and look deep into his eyes. Mine are boring compared to his, but I can easily get lost in his. Just as he leans in to kiss me, I hear catcalls coming from behind him. Damn it to all hell; the gods must hate me. Aurora and her other two mates are approaching.

She's smiling from ear to ear and has to rub it in that in the last two weeks, she's gotten more dick than I've gotten in the previous hundred years. "Hey, Dre! Darren, I see you've met Dre!" She's way too fucking chipper; it's scary to witness this side of her.

"I thought we would have lost you for the better half of the after-noon with these two young studs." I quirk a brow and look between the two of them. Immediately they both start posturing and puffing out their chests, trying to look all badass. Aurora smacks them both and starts laughing.

"Oh, trust me, they can handle me. I was more concerned where mate number three disappeared off to." Her eyes shift to that of her beast as she scans the area. Her nose twitches for a moment, and I know she picked up his scent. A soft smile crosses her lips briefly before continuing. "He's so... I don't know how to explain it." A sigh escapes her lips as her steel-gray eyes stare at the ground. "It's almost like he has a hard time adapting away from his boyfriend. I gave him the option to stay with him. I don't want him unhappy." Both of the boys' wolves surge to the surface, making their eyes glow as they sense and, perhaps, feel her distress. Aurora is sandwiched between the two of them within moments, and she visibly starts to calm down. She sighs gently and rests her head on Dominik's chest. "I just don't want him unhappy, Andre. Please talk to him for me. I honestly don't know how to broach the subject."

"I talked to him a little today already... he sought me out." That gets her attention, and she pries herself away from her mates. She grasps both of my hands to drag me to the picnic bench to sit. "You're partially correct. He is having a hard time adapting, but I think it's mainly because he's mostly dated males." Gently I kiss her cheek and rub my thumbs over the backs of her hands. "He loves you, and he's grateful he's found his mate. From personal experience, it takes time to get over a breakup. He appreciates that you gave him a choice." Smiling confidently, I squeeze her hands tightly, trying to reassure her. "Jayce knows in his heart he made the right decision. His mind just needs time to catch up with what his heart wants." I draw in a deep breath and watch Aurora. I can tell she's in a deep conversation with her Lycan and just nods slowly.

"I understand, Andre. Thank you for being the best momma bird a pup could ask for." She leans forward and kisses my cheek, hugging me tightly. Her mates slowly move off to give us time and space. "I hope he understands I accept him fully. I don't mind him kissing or having sex with any of my other mates." Sebastian's head shoots up with that, and his eyes glow faintly. "There are things only another male could give him. I know I'm strong, and I can be rough at times. But let's face facts, I don't have a schlong, and I'm not about to put a strap-on on to rail my mate from behind." Every male within hearing distance coughs, and their eyes bug out of their heads.

I cough and clear my throat, attempting to look as serious as possible. "Aurora, love, that was quite the visual you painted." She smiles and nods, proud of herself. "Trust me, we fully understand the differences in the mechanics between the genders." Stifling my laughter, I shake my head at Aurora. I swear you never know what's going to come flying out of that girl's mouth. "You're absolutely right; there are things a male can do to another male that a female could never do on her own. But that would never replace your part of this whole bond." I can't help but smile at how far my baby girl has come. "You are the glue that holds these boys together. It's fortunate for all of you so far that they have been all true matings. Trust me when I say that when a bond is forced, it's never the same or as strong as a true mate." Sebastian winces at my statement; I study him closely as he regains his composure. "Your poor mother, gods, rest her soul. Her only true mate was Nicodeamus. She had to force the bond with the other three males to make the political alliances."

I grit my teeth. "That fucking Lycan Alpha chose her other mates for her. She didn't have the choice as to who was in her bond." I release Aurora's hands abruptly and make fists trying to contain my anger over what happened. "I was so thankful when I saw her Lycan reveal itself to Nicodeamus. The Lycan Alpha was furious, and it's why shortly after that, he forced the other males to be castrated—including Nicodeamus. He wanted to be the only male capable of being able to father children." I start to laugh. "Little did he know that during one of his meetings, I snuck Nicodeamus in to be with your mom before the Shamans arrived to perform the castrations." I look down, thinking about those dark times, and I feel a hand land on my shoulder. The dragon king is standing right behind me. My eyes widen in fear because I didn't know if he had wanted Aurora to know the whole story, and I just blabbed everything.

"Relax, old friend. I've been dreading having to tell Aurora that story since we've been reunited. You have once again done me a great service." He gives me a gentle side hug and moves forward to stand before Aurora. "Jayce is a smart man. He has a lot to sort out in his mind. Moving and relocating isn't easy for everyone." Nico walks over to his daughter and hugs her. He holds her as only a father can. "Little one, he loves you so very much, never doubt that. Before your mom... I also had a male that I was considering bonding myself to." Nico slowly lowers his head on top of Aurora's and sighs softly. "He was the most beautiful male I had ever seen; he and his dragon were lean and sleek and brilliant." Nico closes his eyes as he remembers the past. "My brother, the alpha of our clan, called for me one day and told me I was being sent to the Lycan fortress. I argued with my brother as I had no interest in an arranged mating. After all, I already had someone I loved right at home with me." Nico opens his eyes and pins a returning Jayce with his stare, rooting him to his spot.

"I arrived at the Lycan Fortress and was escorted to the main hall. Your mom was already so defeated after her first couple of mates were forced matings. She was so sad she wouldn't even meet my eyes when I first entered. My dragon had other plans. He dropped the temperature in the room so swiftly that frost began to gather on the wine glass your mother was holding." Nico closes his eyes again and nuzzles the top of Aurora's head. "Anca's eyes opened wide as the frost spread across her glass. That's the moment she looked up at me. She actually saw me. Her Lycan in all of its glory burst forth and made her presence known and ran to stand before me."

He sighs wistfully. "I only allowed my eyes to shift to that of my dragon, for the hall we were in wasn't large enough for me to fully shift in safely. I touched her face, and she nuzzled my cheek. I knew at that moment that she was mine." Nico hugs Aurora and kisses the top of her head, and backs away so she can look him in the eyes. "It took a while before your mother, and I slept together and completed our bond. It took Andre running to tell us about the alpha's plans to castrate all the mates, other than Vladimir, to force my hand. Mentally I was ready; I knew what she was to me. Emotionally, that was a whole other demon to deal with. Emotionally I felt like I was betraying the male I had loved for many years." There was a hollowness to Nicodeamus's haunted gaze.

You can see the gears turning in Aurora's head as she takes in Nico's story. "So, what you're saying, Dad, is that just because he's not trying to bone the hell out of me doesn't mean that he doesn't love me. It just means that he has a few things to work through first." Aurora bites her bottom lip and searches her father's features.

"*Da*! That's exactly what I am saying. Give the lad some time. I'm sure when he's ready, he will make the first move. In the meantime, be supportive of him, love him, and show him affection." Nico smiles. "Make quality time just for him because out of your mates, he's the most emotionally sensitive. With two potential alphas in your bond already, you need someone that isn't always trying to prove themselves." He smiles a smile that tells you of the years of wisdom he is speaking from. Nicodeamus gently hugs Aurora again and then pats me on the shoulder. He heads straight to Jayce, and they both walk off towards the main house.

I look between Aurora and her two mates as they move to join her. Her eyes search mine for a bit, then look between her two mates.

"You guys know I'm all good with ya'll being together, right?" Sebastian and Dom nod and look at each other, then back to Aurora. "Sebastian, I'm counting on you to make sure Jayce feels secure and comfortable. Dom, you're his brother and know him best. Any advice you can offer would be wonderful. I know it may be months before he's ready to mate with me, and I'm fine with that." Her eyes turn to me.

"Andre, take flight and find that stubborn bear of ours. We will not go in search of the next mate until my bond with Jayce is in place. We cannot venture forth without being able to sense everyone in the bond." Her hand rubs over her heart as she closes her eyes, clearly concentrating. "I feel him faintly, just barely a whisper. That's not strong enough to be venturing into new territory."

The guys nod, and so do I. We had our orders, and now it's time to put them into motion. My first mission: seek out the bear. Secondly, watch over all my new pups and make sure they all play nice. I start to walk away from the love fest behind me and strip as I go. Before my new admirer knows it, I shift into my eagle and begin my bear hunt.

CHAPTER 20

Dominik

I'VE ALWAYS BEEN MY BROTHER'S KEEPER; IT'S NOT A TASK I TAKE LIGHTLY. Jayce has always been the sensitive one between us. I was schooled in combat, where he was schooled in the art of negotiating and politics. For being twins, we're polar opposites. I'm a brute; I'm bulky and have a horrible temper, whereas Jayce has a toned, athletic build and is calm as all hell. I mean, seriously, it takes a lot to rattle his cage. Our faces are almost identical, except I have more green in my hazel eyes, and he has more gold. I always thought it was unfair because it seems like his wolf is showing more often than not.

I stand here listening to Aurora talking to Andre about Jayce, and my chest hurts thinking about how this is hurting her. The level of understanding she has for what he's going through is mind-blowing. I wish Jayce could hear what she's saying. Then I remember I have my cell phone, so I start recording the conversation. He needs to know that she's seeking help to understand. Listening to her makes me love her more. How could you not? She defended my brother against me, of all people, when she first met us. Put me flat on my back, and sadly, she was right I... was being a dick.

Andre is a saint of a male having raised her; it couldn't have been comfortable with as jumpy as he always seems to be. Nico, her father, has arrived, and shit, I didn't know he is bi also. Am I the only one that hasn't fucked or been fucked by another male?

I'm kind of feeling like the odd man out here. Sebastian kissed my brother, and the way Aurora confirmed what I smelled... shit, it was hot. I didn't think two dudes kissing would ever be seen as hot by me, but it was. I almost was able to imagine myself in Jayce's place. What the fuck am I thinking? Am I bisexual? Do I want to fuck my bond mates? I mean, anyone other than my brother because that would just be fucking weird. I know it's common among our culture for the dominant wolves to fuck the weaker ones to establish dominance. Hmm, I wonder if I could dominate Sebastian by fucking him stupid, then I will be viewed as an equal to him instead of a threat.

I start to turn to walk away and spot my brother reappearing with a brown paper bag in hand, looking suspicious. Nicodeamus roots Jayce to the spot with a glance as he tells his sad tale. I watch the emotions flitter over my brother's features, and he seems more at peace with the way Aurora responds to her dad. Nico moves to join Jayce, and they walk off together. What the actual fuck just happened? Did I miss a secret meeting or something? I must have. I return to Aurora's side, and she snuggles in closely and kisses my cheek.

"What can I do to help your brother? I mean, I don't want him to feel pressured, but I also don't want him to feel ignored or isolated." Her beautiful brows furrow as she ponders her predicament.

"The best thing I can suggest is to spend time with him. He likes to cook and bake, so maybe hang out in the kitchen with him. Tell him which foods are your favorite, and he'll be thrilled to cook for you." I beam with pride. I am always so very proud of how good of a cook my brother is. And if his cooking could bring them closer together, then that would be awesome.

Sebastian and I could definitely use the help. There have been times where we have come damn close to tapping out. Aurora is a beast in the bedroom, with an appetite that we're having problems keeping up with. I hope my brother gets with the program soon as I don't know how much longer Sebastian and I can last. She's got the drive to handle three mates, and when only two are in the game, it gets exhausting.

As I step into his line of sight, my brother's surprised expression speaks volumes, his eyes widening in shock at my unexpected arrival. But any tension that lingers in the air is quickly dispelled by the warm smile that spreads across my face as I approach him.

"It's all good, brother," I reassure him, my tone gentle and reassuring. "Let me help you." I move to join him at the picnic table, taking in the array of chocolates and the carefully arranged basket before us.

As Jayce's gaze meets mine, I can sense the weight of his uncertainty, the doubt that lingers in his heart as he grapples with the complexities of courting Aurora. And yet, beneath his uncertainty, there's a determination, a fierce desire to show her how much she means to him.

"I hope it helps," he confesses, his voice tinged with vulnerability. "I mean, I don't want Aurora to think I don't care for her. I want her to know that she's special, and I'm only hers." His words resonate with sincerity, a heartfelt confession of his deepest desires.

With a soft smile, I reach out to place a reassuring hand on his shoulder, offering a silent gesture of support and understanding. "You're doing great, brother," I assure him, my voice filled with encouragement. "And I'm sure Aurora will appreciate the effort you've put into this."

But as he continues to stuff the fluffy stuffing into the basket, a shadow of doubt crosses his features, his uncertainty laid bare for all to see. "I'm not sure how to date a female anymore," he admits, his eyes searching mine for reassurance. And in that moment, I realize the depth of his vulnerability, the fear of rejection that lingers just beneath the surface.

With a gentle squeeze of his shoulder, I meet his gaze with unwavering confidence. "You'll figure it out, Jayce," I assure him, my voice filled with conviction. "Just be yourself, and let your heart guide you. That's all anyone can ask for."

And as we continue to prepare the surprise for Aurora, I can't help but feel a swell of pride for my brother, his determination to show her how much she means to him a testament to the depth of his love. For in this moment of uncertainty and vulnerability, I know that he'll find his way, guided by the unshakeable bond that binds us together as family.

"Okay, not a problem; that's an easy one, and I'll do what I can to help. You know how you like being held and snuggled?" He nods emphatically. "Well, Aurora loves touch, especially her neck. It's super sensitive, and she'll soak her jeans if you kiss her just right. If you're looking to build up to sex but not have it, then offer to give her a massage, but don't touch her neck." I can tell he's taking mental notes, and his eyes are pulsing between human and wolf. "Maybe go hunt with her. She loves a good hunt, and it would be a good base layer for you two."

He raises his right eyebrow and tilts his head to the left. "Seriously, Dom! You know I'm not a great hunter. I don't want to look like a complete ass in front of her. You know it would be my luck Sebastian shows up and makes me look like a worthless pup." He already looks defeated, and he hasn't even tried yet.

"I'll get Dimitri to keep Sebastian busy so you can have some quality time with our girl. I promise it will be okay." I walk over and give my brother a heartfelt hug and kiss to his temple. "Your present looks fantastic, now let's go find our queen so you can give it to her. I'll be right there with you, I promise." He smiles and nods, then starts to head towards Aurora's favorite tree on the property.

There she is, our future queen, hanging upside down from the lowest limb on the tree, just swinging back and forth. Her hair is so long the tips are touching the grass blades. "Keep that up, love, and your beautiful white hair will be stained green." Her eyes pop open, and she smiles at Jayce and me.

Curiosity is getting the better of her, so she drops down out of the tree. "Whatcha got there, cutie?" Slowly she moves towards us, like the apex predator she is—her steps, silent and deadly as she approaches Jayce and kisses the corner of his mouth.

Gently she snuggles into him, trying not to spook my poor brother. Jayce bands a single arm around her waist and touches his nose under her chin in submission. "I brought you a present, love. I hope you like it." He carefully backs up and offers her the present. Up to this point, I believe my brother is the first of us to get her one. Aurora's eyes light up, and she bounces up and down before dragging Jayce over to a picnic table. Ever so gently, she sets the package down, afraid to break its contents. I've never watched her do anything so carefully in my time with her. Nico and Andre are on the hill to our left, watching with rapt attention.

Slowly the bow is untied, and the ribbon is laid out flat on the table. The first layer of the iridescent paper is gently pulled away and folded neatly. It's placed reverently next to the ribbon. Watching her closely, I see tears forming in Aurora's eyes; this single action has touched her heart so deeply. The following layers are peeled away in the same careful manner and placed on top of the first. Now she's down to the fluffy stuffing. Aurora looks completely baffled as to how to remove it without damaging anything. Her steel-grey eyes plead with Jayce for help, and he swoops in quickly to assist her. "Close your eyes, love."

Aurora obeys Jayce immediately. Everyone gathered is completely shocked, watching her immediate obedience to the omega of the pack. Jayce removes the fluff and sets it down beside the basket. Now all the different chocolates are exposed. "Open your eyes, love."

Aurora can't open her eyes fast enough. Those same eyes open so very wide in shock. It appears he's the first to render her speech-less. Her eyes dart between him and the chocolates, then back again. "They're all for me?" Aurora's tone is so innocent you could almost forget the carnage she caused less than a week ago. Jayce gives her a single nod, and she leaps into his arms, burying her face into his neck, sobbing and thanking him repeatedly. Poor Jayce doesn't know what to do. Honestly, he kind of looks fright-ened. I catch his attention and motion for him to hug her and hold her tight.

Instantly he bands his arms tightly around her middle, holding her. Aurora slowly lifts her head, and it's the happiest I've ever seen her. Her eyes search his face, questioning if he's okay. Jayce smiles like the big idiot he is and kisses her cheek gently. Aurora buries her face between his neck and shoulder again. He turns in my direction and locks eyes with me, mouthing *thank you.*

I give him a thumbs up and walk off towards Andre and Nico. As I approach, they hand out high fives all around at my arrival. "I thought that would never happen." I breathe a sigh of relief. I was starting to get frightened that he was going to be stuck in a holding pattern forever. Apparently, I wasn't the only one—Andre and Nico nod.

We watch my poor brother fumble through the gift exchange. He's finally hit by a stroke of genius, or should I say a text message. Andre shoots him a text suggesting he feeds Aurora some of the chocolate. He glances our way just briefly, and by the look on his face, my brother thankfully takes the hint. He sits on the tabletop, and Aurora lays her head in his lap as he feeds her piece by piece.

Possible disaster averted by our covert team of matchmakers. Now, if we can get Sebastian to stop being a fucktard, we'd all be in a better place. Speaking of the fucktard, I better have a talk with him so he doesn't piss in Jayce's cheerios.

CHAPTER 21
Dominik

I HEAD OUT IN SEARCH OF THE FUCKTARD, AND AS USUAL, HE'S IN THE outdoor gym pumping iron as his mother talks to him about pack politics. "Got a minute Sebastian?" He puts the weights down and flexes a bit before walking over to me. I never realized how sexy muscles covered in sweat look. Now I understand why Aurora likes watching us work out. Sebastian is now in my personal space and way too fucking close just for a conversation.

I lock eyes with him and tilt my head to the side. "Like what you see?" Challenging him? Absolutely. Why the fuck not? I want to see what kind of wannabe alpha he is. I look over his shoulder, and his mom is long gone. Thankfully there is no one else around.

Without warning, he reaches down and cups my balls, and gives them a gentle squeeze. "What if I do? Are you wolf enough to stop me?" He puts a finger under my chin to keep my gaze locked with his. Slowly his eyes turn the ice-blue of his wolf, and his fingertip turns into a claw.

Its sharp point lightly digs into the soft skin under my jaw. I'm not about to show discomfort or fear. I reach down and cup his balls. His cock is hard as steel and pulsing under my hand. Obviously Sebastian likes being challenged. I back up a step and raise my chin in defiance. "Maybe I am, maybe I'm not. There's only one way to find out, isn't there?" I'm very curious as to where this new desire to fuck or be fucked by Sebastian is coming from. In all actuality, the strongest bonds come from all the mates being mated to each other. I turn and start walking back towards the alpha house. Sebastian hot on my heels. He takes the bait: hook, line, and sinker. I don't need to turn around to know he is right there. I head into my room and begin to remove my shirt.

I start thinking of the way Aurora would strip slowly out of my button-downs. I stop in the middle of the room and turn around, locking Sebastian's eyes and start undoing the top button. His wolf surges to the forefront, watching me undress with rapt attention. Each button slowly reveals my muscular chest hidden beneath the soft fabric. I bite my lower lip hard, drawing blood—it's something that affects us males, and any blood play makes us rock fucking hard.

Sebastian's gasp is audible as my blood drips slowly onto my exposed chest. I reach the last button and ease the shirt off my shoulders, letting it fall to the floor at my feet. My hands go to my favorite black jeans. Claws burst free of my fingertips as I pop the belt buckle open. Sebastian strips down at a record pace, trying to get ahead of my agonizingly slow progress. His massive, veiny cock springs free of his once restrictive briefs. He's already dripping precum down his thick, pulsing shaft. This is getting more and more interesting by the minute. My jeans hit the floor, and I'm bare before him.

What he has in length, I have in girth. I do not lack in any sense; I'm just thick and throbbing at the thought of being able to dominate Sebastian. But the look in his eyes tells me he has other ideas.

"Turn around, Dominik. Hands on the mattress and feet by the posts," Sebastian growls out his commands, and fuck, my cock is leaking a small river thinking about what he may do. I slowly obey. After all, I don't want to make it too easy on him. A loud crack is heard, and my left ass cheek is burning from his hand's impact on my flesh. It's moments like this that I'm thankful I love pain. I don't turn to look at Sebastian as I hear him freeing a belt from the discarded pants, and then the sound of a second belt is freed. Smart male using the leather belts to bind my ankles to the bedposts.

I feel his sharp claws run up the backs of both of my thighs as I stand there, curious as to what he has in store for me. His clawed hands grip the meat of my ass hard, probably drawing blood. His lips are so close to my neck; I feel his hot breath caressing me.

"Someone's just as turned on as I am. I can smell your need, Dom." Sebastian's hands slide around my waist and down my V until he grips my rock-hard cock. He gives me a few firm tugs as he thrusts his wet cock between my ass cheeks. I can't help the moan that escapes my lips. I'm trying to fuck his hand as he's thrusting from behind. Suddenly he pulls away quickly, and instantly I miss his heat and his hands upon me. I look over my shoulder to him, and he's grabbed a tube of lube from god knows were. That shit is going to be fucking ice cold. "Lean on your forearms on the mattress Dom. I'm going to get you ready for me because I can't promise I'll be gentle once I'm in you."

I do as he commands and slowly lower down onto my forearms. I'm so fucking close to orgasming; it's not even funny at this point. I understand entirely why Aurora fully submits to Sebastian... the man is a sex god, and he fucking knows it. I feel his lube covered fingers slowly rubbing around the tight pucker of my asshole. The tingles he's producing causes my cock to jump against the mattress. "Grab your cock, Dom. I want to know you're stroking yourself while I play with your ass."

I apparently don't move fast enough for him because he chooses that moment to bite my ass cheek. I hiss from the sting of it and rise up higher on one forearm to grip my cock with my right hand. I angle myself so he can watch my hand gliding over my length in the mirror on the wall. A grumbling growl of appreciation escapes him as he presses his first finger past my sphincter. My hips thrust forward of their own accord in response to his invasion.

"Damn, that feels good. Give me more." I'm breathy like Aurora gets when you tease her too much; I can't help it. I'm stroking my cock painstakingly slow, making sure to give Sebastian a good show. My moans are becoming deeper and longer. I feel that familiar tingle at the base of my spine, and my balls draw up tight.

Sebastian stands once he's satisfied that I'm loose enough. I feel the cold squirt of lube on my asshole again; this time, there's the pressure of the head of his cock pressing down on me. I breathe in slowly and push back against him until he pops past the muscular barrier. Sebastian gives me a few shallow thrusts before he buries himself to the hilt deep within me. I'm so full, almost to the point of bursting.

The burn hurts, yet feels so fucking good. His hand comes up and grips my throat tightly, and pulls my body back against his. I now know precisely how our girl feels at this moment. The adrenaline high is so fucking worth it. Sebastian pulls almost all the way out before he slams back home as hard as he can. I'm not going to fucking last long. He must sense how close I am because he starts to fuck me as hard and as fast as he can. The echoes of our slapping flesh bounce off the walls. Our grunts and moans echo off the walls... I stroke my cock in time with his thrusts keeping up with his punishing pace. I scream out my orgasm as ribbons of my seed shoot out over my comforter. Sebastian's movements become erratic as he gets close too.

I arch my back, changing his penetration, and that does it for him; he howls deeply as he cums. Without warning, he sinks his canines into my shoulder, biting hard and deep, marking me as his. I feel the feather-light tether snap into place as he slowly releases my shoulder. He licks my wounds clean then frees me from his grasp and the bed.

I stretch my body out before walking to the bathroom to retrieve two wet towels to clean ourselves up with. We sit on the bed side by side in silence. It's not awkward or anything; we know what needs to happen next. It's his turn, and I'm looking forward to it. My cock starts to swell again, so soon after that killer orgasm, so I reach over to stroke Sebastian's soft cock. Wouldn't you know, that's the moment my brother decides to walk in. My shoulder is still bleeding, and Sebastian and I are both naked in different states of arousal. The look of shock on my brother's face is priceless. His tears, though, gut me. "Jayce? What's wrong?" I stand slowly, walking over to him, and place my hand on his shoulder.

Jayce's bottom lip quivers, and he smiles at me. "I love you, Dom. I don't know what to say. I never thought I'd see the day you would ever let another male touch you." His eyes drink in Sebastian's prone hard form sprawled out on the bed. "So, how are we finishing the bond?" His innocent eyes bounce between Sebastian and me.

"That's easy," Sebastian says as he moves off the bed and stands before me. His index finger rests under my chin and raises my head so I can look in his eyes. "I take your brother right here, where I had you moments ago. You take me while I take your brother. That's two matings done, and only one left." He removes his finger, then moves to Jayce and kisses him deeply. His hands roam all over my brother's body. He is much gentler than he was with me. I'm honestly fascinated watching him move and position my brother on his back on the bed. Carefully I squeeze the lube in Sebastian's outstretched hand. And gently, he prepares my brother for his intrusion. My hand grips my thick cock, and I stroke it slowly, coating it with the lube before I move to start grinding myself against Sebastian's tight ass. The baritone rumble coming from Sebastian makes my cock leak. My index finger begins to massage his tight sphincter trying to get it to relax. Ever so slowly, I press my index finger and middle finger in as deep as I could go. Rhythmically I begin to scissor my fingers to loosen up his rectum. Jayce gasps the minute Sebastian enters him, and he remains still. Now's my chance.

Without warning, I press the head of my thick cock into him. Watching his muscles tense and his head bow backward. I've got him now. I do a few short thrusts letting him adjust to me before I drive it home. Sebastian's claws tear through the comforter as he moans deeply. My thrusts are slow and controlled, drawing out every inch before pushing it back in deep. We find our rhythm, thrusting and drawing back. One almost out while the other is seated deep in the other. Our fucking seems to last forever.

Jayce is the lucky one; he fucking came at least twice already. Me, I'm holding off as long as I can, enjoying this level of control over Sebastian. I start to lick and nip Sebastian's shoulder, and his thrusts start to become erratic. Swiftly he lunges forward and bites Jayce on the shoulder, completing the first half of their bond. Soon as Sebastian stands up, I start pounding the hell out of him, driving my cock as hard and as deep into him as I can. I show no mercy, just like he did to me earlier. I feel the tightening of my testicles and that telltale sign of my impending release. My hand shoots forward, and I tightly grip Sebastian's throat and pull him back against me. My other arm wraps around his straining abdomen while he whimpers from my erratic thrusts. One final thrust and I'm buried deep within him as my mouth latches onto his shoulder, biting deep into his flesh as my seed fills his ass.

Several flashes of light slowly disrupt my post-orgasmic bliss. Slowly I release Sebastian and lick his wound clean as more flashes of light go off, and I hear Jayce giggle on the other side of Sebastian. Okay, that has my attention. I turn and look towards the door to find our mate with several wet towels in one hand and her phone in the other. "Really, love?"

Her smile is so broad and bright; I can almost forgive the incriminating evidence she now has on her phone. "Okay, I thought Sebastian kissing Jayce was hot... This will fucking inspire so many damn wet dreams, it's not even funny!" Aurora passes out the wet towels as we withdraw from each other. Sebastian looks about as uncomfortable as I feel right now, and well, Jayce honestly is fucking glowing. Aurora climbs onto the bed and lays her head on Jayce's shoulder, and snuggles in close. "Hey, baby." Aurora kisses Jayce's chest and watches Sebastian, and I clean up. "So? This is a thing now?" She asks while smiling like the cat that swallowed the fucking canary.

Sebastian stops wiping his flaccid cock off and stares at Aurora. "You ever want to be the wolf in the middle... pick your two, and I'm game, doll." And just like that, cocky Sebastian is back in full effect. I shake my head at him, then move to the other side of the bed and sit next to my brother.

"Elena suggested that all three of us should be mated to each other as well. It will provide the strongest bond and give each other immunity for the war ahead." Aurora nods, taking in all that Sebastian is telling her. Carefully he leans forward and kisses her, then Jayce. He turns towards me next. And roughly grips the back of my neck, kissing me deeply. I can't help the soft grumble that escapes my lips. Sebastian saunters off, clothes in hand, buck naked.

My gaze then falls on Aurora and Jayce, who are snuggled up tightly on the bed. Perhaps my brother is finally making progress. "I'm going to hit the shower. You two are more than welcome to stay here tonight if you like." Aurora smiles and keeps stroking Jayce's abs tracing every bump and line. I can see her wolf swirling to the surface, then her struggle to suppress her. Traveling my gaze to Jayce, his wolf is also on the surface. Who knows, maybe he'll take the next step with her soon. I mean, it's killing me knowing my brother is struggling with this.

My shower time sets a new world record for speed in every division. Returning to my bedroom, I find Aurora in the middle of the California king bed and Jayce on her other side. Both of them are snuggled under the covers, giggling at the rom-com they've decided to watch. I honestly couldn't care less what is on the t.v. at the moment, two of the most influential people in my life are in my bed. The bed looks so inviting, but first, I have a plan. I gently kiss both Aurora and Jayce on the forehead and head down to the kitchen. What movie night doesn't have popcorn, right? After making the massive bowl of extra cheesy popcorn, I return to my room. You would think I discovered cold fusion the way Aurora and Jayce are acting. They hoot, holler, and bounce all over the bed, demanding the bowl of popcorn. Reluctantly I give Aurora the bowl and wink at my brother. He is consciously putting forth the effort to spend quality time with our mate and it is paying off. He is more relaxed, and most importantly, Aurora looks very happy with her current situation. Once we all get settled in bed, we watch several movies until Aurora falls asleep between us. Leaning back in bed, looking down at our sleeping Aurora, I sigh. This is a good night for all of us.

CHAPTER 22
Sebastian

WHAT A NIGHT! TWO OUT OF THREE COMPLETE MATINGS ARE DONE WITH the guys. At some point today, I have to catch up with Jayce and finish my mating with him. I'm not looking forward to letting the omega fuck me. Still, I'll do anything for Aurora—especially to secure her safety and my place in the pack. I lay here in my bed, staring at the ceiling.

We've made progress on all fronts. Under the threat of a painful death at the hand of the dragon king, I was ordered to leave Jayce alone if he's near Aurora. We need him to complete his bond with her for so many reasons. The main one is the strength of the pack bond. The second one, I honestly think my dick may fall off eventually. Aurora has a sex drive strong enough to handle three virile mates.

Unfortunately, there are only two of us in the game while the third tries to dislodge his head from his ass. I'm guessing Aurora spent the night with Dom since she's not in bed with me. Reluctantly I get out of bed and dress for the day. Slow steps carry me down the hallway past Dom's door. A few moments later, Dom steps out and silently attempts to close his door. "What's up, Dom?" I motion towards his door.

Quickly he moves towards me and drags me down the hallway. "Shh, Aurora, and Jayce are still sleeping. I'm hoping they fuck when they wake up." Decent idea, letting nature take its course without interruption.

"Brilliant idea, hopefully her pheromones override his reluctance." I give him a brotherly slap on his shoulder as we move downstairs for breakfast. From the smell of it, Nina, my mother's friend, is already making breakfast for us. I honestly don't think I'll ever get used to others doing things for me. But here we are… we have servants now all because Aurora is the lost princess.

Nico is sitting at the head of the table, drawing on parchment. This can't be a good way to start the day. Coffee and battle plans are apparently how he rolls, though. "Sit, boys, we have much to discuss." He motions to the chairs near him. It isn't a request; it's an order. We take our seats next to the king and fill our cups with coffee. "I hate to be the bearer of bad news, but I have reports of Strigoi attacking not far from here. I believe they will attack tonight." On the parchment before him, he has the town drawn out. He's even got individual buildings marked.

"What are the x's on the map for?" Dom beats me to it, damn it. He already seems to be more in favor than I am because of his prior relationship with Nico.

"The **X**'s are buildings with bomb shelters in the basements. If we send the females, children, and the mated males down there, it will be safer. The five of us, as well as Dimitri, will take a stand in the center of town." I lean over to get a better look at his map.

"Where will Andre be?" I assume he will be the early warning device, but I can't swear to it. "Are we using him as an advanced warning system?"

Nico finally smiles at me and pats my shoulder. "Exactly my thoughts, son. Eagles have the best eyesight of all the shifters. He can watch for the attack and call out when he spots them. We all nod in acknowledgment of the plan. Several hours are spent with some of the pack elders going over evacuation routes to the buildings. Once the courses are planned, a pack meeting is called in the great hall.

Aurora and I stand before the masses, getting ready to address them. The twins are off to the side but up here with us. Aurora winks at me, then closes her eyes, and her voice booms in my mind, calling the pack to order.

Damn, now that's an impressive alpha power to have. I spot Nico and her guardians at the back of the hall. Nico, the proud father, gives her an approving nod. I guess she tapped into his ability for the force she used.

My people! We are about to be attacked by the Strigoi! Everyone here has a copy of the piece of the plan which they are a part of. Please initiate the plan the moment you hear Andre's screech from above. That will be our only warning. Run, hide, follow the plan. We need everyone to survive this attack. I have a team set up for defense. Do not come out until you hear Sebastian or me in your head. She moves to the edge of the platform and looks out over the crowd.

I have to admit, my mate is powerful and commanding. I'm sure her mother would be proud. Nico wipes a stray tear from his cheek. Aww, a proud daddy moment, indeed. Andre's eyes keep darting out the door, watching the sun. His head turns to Dimitri, and in a blink, Andre shifts to his eagle and is resting on the glove on Dimitri's right hand.

Aurora catches Andre's shift and draws in a deep breath. Her eyes lock with mine, then the twins.

Her command echoes in our minds for us alone. A single, short nod is given to Dimitri and Andre, and out the door they go. I remain at Aurora's side for a moment longer. "It's time; go get ready, the sun is starting to set. We don't want to be caught unprepared." She looks at Nicodeamus. "Father, the town square is yours. Four of the five safe houses are there. I will join you shortly. After all, they are coming for me." Aurora fucking smirks; she's actually enjoying the idea of the impending battle. Wow, do we have our hands full with this one. I step outside with the twins. We're heading towards the one building set back and away from the town center. Our theory is because Aurora is staying in the center of town, the Strigoi will focus their attack there. As the plan stands now, I'm supposed to be on top of the building between the center of town and the twins.

The sun is slowly setting on the horizon—the sky burning bright with shades of yellow-orange fading to a pinkish-purple. The wind has shifted, blowing in from the southwest. The faint hint of death lingers in the air. If I were a betting man, I would bet the Strigoi are holed up in the caverns about two miles from here. I text the group about what I'm scenting, and they agree with me that it is more than likely where they are hiding.

Andre starts his lazy circles in that direction, trying not to look conspicuous. Aurora climbs up to stand on the rooftop with me as she keeps her eyes locked on Andre. "He sees movement in the cave. You're right, Bash. They are in there. Odds are they have a second hiding place we aren't aware of."

I move back a bit and update the others and watch the horizon. "Aurora, tell Andre to check out the knoll over there to the east where that one lone cedar is. I think I saw movement over there, I'm just not positive." Aurora gives me a nod and looks back to Andre, and he changes course quickly as it's getting way too close to full sunset for him to delay. Andre's screech fills the air as he raises the alarm. Aurora shifts almost immediately and howls, sending all the wolves into action. Her father's dragon takes up most of the town square as he starts coating the ground with ice to slow the invasion.

Aurora takes a running leap as the last person enters the building the twins are guarding. Her talons grip the wood as she starts to freeze the building. Nico sees what his daughter is doing and starts coating his safe houses in a thick layer of ice as well. In the distance, the mob can be spotted moving steadily towards the town. My eyes narrow as I search in both directions. The dead heads have planned a smart two-front attack. Aurora finishes icing her building and looks towards where her father is. Two quick, well-timed leaps, and she's on the ground again, pacing by her father's side, waiting for the fight to begin. She's not fun to be around when she's made to wait for too long. I watch her flexing her taloned fingers, already itching to rip something apart.

It doesn't take too long for the first wave of the assault to blow past the twins and head right for Aurora, as we predicted. Now that we are one hundred percent sure they are only after her, we all convene in the center of town. Aurora and Nico's fighting prowess is on full display as they weave in and out, dancing around each other. You would think they have fought together for the last hundred years. The fluid movements executed by the two of them are almost hypnotizing. Then you remember you're in the middle of a battle, and there's Strigoi to kill. I'd love to say we made short work of them, but that would be a lie.

Each wave seems to be followed by another and yet another after that one. Nico and Aurora show no signs of stopping, but the twins are starting to fatigue. Three hours straight we have been fighting, ripping off heads and limbs as we go. Aurora, I've just noticed, has a pile of fucking skulls again! What is her obsession with collecting heads? One of the twins falters and falls before Aurora. She lets loose such a deathly bellow it's frightening. Nico sees the Dire Wolf down and unmoving, his taloned hand reaches out, scoops him up, and tucks him under his wing. Aurora nods to her father and begins again, ripping heads off.

Out of what seems to be thin air, an arrow shoots Aurora in the shoulder. She growls and falls to one knee while Nico starts covering everything with ice. I've never seen him this angry before. I rush over to Aurora and sniff the arrow. A wolf shifter shot her... what the actual fuck?

She's starting to lose consciousness. Whatever is on this arrow is either killing her or sedating her. I grip the shaft as close to her skin as I can and rip it out quickly. It's now as I hold my mate in her human form that I wonder why the attack stopped. I look up to find Dimitri and the remaining twin standing in front of us. Nico turned the town into a winter wonderland.

Sliding down one of the ice walls comes my cousin, Michael. Oddly, he's here. I haven't seen him in years, and yet on the night of the attack, he decides to show up? Something doesn't add up. I see my mother stepping out of her home, and I give her a quick shake of my head to stop her. Thankfully she obeys and remains on the porch. I shift back to my human form, so do Dimitri and Jayce. One mystery solved, Dom is the wolf under Nico's wing. I hand Aurora over to Jayce and motion to my mother. He and Dimitri move quickly with her away from us. "Long time no see, Mike. What brings you back?"

I'm already suspicious of him as something seems very off with the way he's watching Jayce walk away with Aurora. "You know, cuz, a little bit of this, a little bit of that." He won't make eye contact with me for long, so I reach back and place a hand on Nico. *Can you hear me?* I wait, hoping he can; otherwise, this is going to suck.

I can, young prince. Oh, thank the gods...

I think my cousin shot Aurora. Please take Dom and guard my mother's home. I'll handle Michael. Nico's head comes down even with my shoulder, and he snorts frost.

Consider it done. Bring Aurora his head and heart. With that said, he lumbers over to my mother's cabin and wraps his body most of the way around it, watching Michael and me.

"That was freaky. I mean, that Ice Dragon walking around the place." Michael looks nervous, his eyes continuously looking back to see where Nico has gone.

"So, Mike, did you ever get that ink on your arm finished? I see some color poking out of the sleeve." I'm hoping I'm wrong, but Mike was always getting string slapped when he would shoot. I pray that telltale welt isn't on his arm; otherwise, I will have no choice but to take my cousin's head.

"Hell yeah, it's done!" He unbuttons his sleeve and rolls it up. He turns his arm so I can see the back of his forearm, not the soft inside. I grip his forearm and turn his arm over. There, sitting plain as day, is the welt, the mother fucking welt. My eyes lock with his, and he knows that I know what he's done. "I can explain. Honest, I can."

He backs away quickly and bumps into the solid mass of Dimitri's chest. Mike knows he's in deep shit now. Dimitri grabs him by the back of his neck and lifts him off the ground. "What do you want me to do with him, Sebastian? Break his neck? Rip his head off? Or torture him for the next month... slowly." Dimitri's bear is making its presence known. Fur is rippling over his arms and face. He is very unstable and furious.

"I'll handle it, big guy. Go protect our girl." I watch Dimitri come back to his senses, and he drops Mike on his ass. My wolf is demanding blood. This fucker hurt our mate—possibly killed her —he will not walk out of here. "What the fuck were you thinking? What was worth betraying your own kind for!" My words are growled out and barely human as my body starts shifting on its own accord.

"I was paid to kill the white-haired female because she's a threat to our kind. Tomas said he would keep attacking the pack until she's dead. She must die! I can't let my mom and sisters die because of one female," he growls. His wolf isn't an alpha, he isn't even wolf enough to be considered a beta.

My Lycan looms over him as he pisses himself out of fear. His begging for his life falls on deaf ears. Mike makes the fatal mistake of running from me. Oh yeah, my wolf is quite happy he fucked up to that level. We chase him and play wolf and fawn with him. We track him for the better half of an hour. Finally, he shifts and turns to face me. His Lycan isn't even half the size of mine. His hand raises, and his claws flex as he swings for me. I strike. My claws dig deep and rip into his chest and grip his heart. I can feel the rhythmic contractions of the smooth muscle in my grip. I close my clawed hand a little tighter, and his eyes bulge out of his head. The blood vessels in his eyes begin to rupture as my grip increases. His arms drop. He knows death is imminent for him, and I am the angel who will send his ass to hell.

With a quick flick of my wrist, I sever all the arteries that hold his heart in place. I have his quivering, bleeding heart in my hand right in front of his face. Several seconds pass before his body drops like a ton of bricks before me. I now understand the feeling of holding the final moments of someone's life in my hands. I know why my love, my mate, said she needs to feel something other than being a monster. I look at my cousin's heart in my hand and then back to his blood-covered corpse. Nico steps up to me and scares the fuck out of me. I shift back to my human form and stare at him. "Seriously?"

"Yes, you were deep in thought, my child. You did well; I am proud of you." Nico gives me that fatherly smile, and for once, I'm not freaked the fuck out by him.

My eyes fall next to the literal silver platter he is holding. Okay then. I place the heart on the platter then proceed to cut my cousin's head free from his body. Once I finish, I put the head next to the heart and arrange them to be aesthetically pleasing. Gently I take the platter from Nico and begin to head back to the house. My mother is famous for her rose bushes, and thankfully they are in full bloom. Carefully I place the platter on the deck and pick a half dozen roses to decorate my offering. I stare at my handiwork and start questioning my sanity.

What the actual fuck am I doing?

I'm bringing my injured mate a severed head and a heart on a platter lined with roses. I look from my presentation then back to

Nico. The fucking dragon just gives me a single thumbs up with his only hand. Daddy dearest is just as fucked in the head as the rest of us.

CHAPTER 23

Sebastian

Fear grips my heart as I ascend the stairs. The house is quiet; this can't be good. I run through the lists of gods and goddesses that favor the wolves, begging them to make sure Aurora is okay. I make it back to the guest room, and my heart almost fucking stops.

She's so fucking pale it looks almost as if all the blood has drained from her body. Her ruby lips shine so brightly against her now alabaster skin. Tears break free and roll down my cheeks. I can't breathe; I'm gasping for air and having a borderline panic attack. Dimitri comes up to me and takes the tray away.

"Mom! Please, tell me she's okay?" I blubber like an idiot looking at my ghostly-white mate. Jayce is snuggled up so tightly against her, and his eyes are bloodshot from crying.

"Sit down, boy. Nicodeamus, I need your blood to help Aurora." Mom is like a brigadier general ordering us around like peons. She is calm and commanding as she begins setting up a makeshift hospital in her home. Alexis had arrived at some point and is setting up for the transfusion. Thank fuck we have a nurse in the pack; otherwise, I think my beloved would be doomed.

Nicodeamus sits in the chair as directed and stretches his arm out. "Take it all if you have to. You must save my baby!" Even Nicodeamus is crying, looking at his near lifeless daughter. Alexis moves quickly, setting up to take at least three pints of blood from him. She has a pole set up next to him with saline to help replace the blood volume he is about to lose.

"Mom? What's wrong with Aurora?" My heart is in my throat as I lean on the counter next to Nico. I rest my hand on his shoulder as we both look at my mother for answers.

"It's quite simple; they tried to poison her. The arrowhead is made of silver, and the toxin it's coated with is a blend of aconite and nightshade. They didn't know of Aurora's true sire; otherwise, they would have known this combination wouldn't kill her." Elena moves to adjust the saline drip for Aurora, making sure to hydrate her to help flush out the toxin. "I'm going to flood Aurora's system with her father's blood to try to reverse what damage the toxins did to her body. I'm positive it's the quickest way to heal her safely." Elena doesn't look up to regard anyone as she prepares everything for the tricky transfusion she will attempt.

I watch how carefully Alexis moves towards my mother with the first pint of blood. Together they hook Aurora up and start the drip. Jayce won't move for anything. He is far too frightened to leave her side. At this point, I'm too afraid to close my eyes or even go to relieve myself. "How long before we know if it's helping her, Mom?" My voice quivers like a scared, tear-filled child. The love of my life is before me, fighting for her life, and I can't do a fucking thing to help her. I'm so fucking grateful that her father lived and is with us. Without him, she'd be dead.

"Have faith, son. Alexis is a nurse and specializes in hematology. The first signs of a positive response will be the return of color. While this pint infuses, we need to drain a pint, which will make her body start to produce more red blood cells and platelets." She sighs softly. "It's pretty much going to be a rinse and repeat the process with the three pints. Tomorrow if we need to, we'll take two pints from you, Sebastian, to help wake up her wolf. Then the tough part will be that you are going to have to force her shift, so her wolf finishes healing her." *Say what?* I stand there, blinking as Dominik comes flying through the door.

Dom immediately drops to his knees when he sees the state our mate is in. His tear-filled eyes seek out my eyes and then his brother's. My mother pulls him out of the room to catch him up quickly. When he returns, he thanks Nico for protecting his fallen body and hugs it out with him. Jayce calls Dom over and switches out with him, and runs out of the room. I watch Jayce leave, then look at Dom. "Bathroom run." Ah, that explains the swift departure.

I swear to the gods above, Jayce just broke the land speed record for taking a piss. He rushes back into the room and tugs on Dom's arm to get him out of bed. Dom reluctantly leaves Aurora's side and walks over to me. "Makes me want to cry. It takes Aurora almost dying for my brother to get over his shit." Dom bites his bottom lip and sighs; a single tear rolls down his cheek, and I draw him in for a tight hug. Honestly, I don't know if I'm hugging him to comfort him or to comfort myself. "I feel so fucking power-less, Bash. I'd trade places with her if I could."

Nico's head whips up at that exact moment. His eyes burn liquid mercury as he stares at Dom. "Did you not hear what was done? You would be dead, leaving that poor girl behind without her mate. A severed bond feels like you died right along with them."

Nicodeamus's voice cracks with emotion. "I fell from the fucking sky when her mother died. I didn't want to live without her. If it weren't for the fact that I felt my child's life, I probably would have mourned myself to death." Nico looks away at that moment; the pain from the loss of his mate still evident on his face. Over two hundred years later, and it looks like it was just yesterday to him.

Seeing the depth of Nico's loss really puts how lucky we truly are into perspective. I kiss Dom's temple, then lean down, and side-hug Nico and kiss the top of his head. We are all suffering together. Unfortunately, Nico is in hell all over again. My eyes remain locked on the pint, and Aurora's color is slowly improving, so that is a blessing. I exhale a bit louder than I thought, and everyone looks at me. "Her color is coming back." Everyone's eyes shoot to Aurora, and tentative smiles break out across the room.

My mother enters the room, passing out food and drinks. "Eat! She'll kick your collective asses if you don't take care of yourselves. That means you too, M'lord." She winks at Nico and hands him a burger as well. Only Jayce doesn't budge; he is still too frightened to move. When I finish my food, I move over to him and sit on the edge of the bed. "Please eat. She needs us all strong for her. I'll lay with her until you're done eating, okay?"

Jayce slowly sits up and nods. He's so broken up he's practically gone mute. Ever so carefully, he slides out of bed. He reaches over and readjusts Aurora's pillow and her blankets before he motions for me to slide in where he was. Once I am situated, he adjusts my pillow and pulls the covers up. "She needs to stay warm. Keep her warm for me." He whispers when he speaks—his voice quivering with emotion. Tears well up, threatening to overflow as his eyes turn bloodshot again. Jayce's cheeks flush as he attempts to hold back the feelings that threaten to break free. Out of the males, he is the one most in touch with his emotions.

To see him fight against his nature hurts my heart. "I will guard her 'til my dying breath and then some. I swear to you I will keep her warm and safe." I allow a few rogue tears to flow down my cheeks, and Jayce smiles at me. He then leans in, kissing my lips softly, whispering his thanks before walking over and hugging his brother. As soon as he is in Dom's arms, the dam breaks, and all the tears and sorrow flow freely.

My heart starts aching for him, and that's when I feel it. Aurora's arm moves slightly. "Guys!! I think she just moved!" Everyone crowds around the bed, watching Aurora. She's midway through the second pint of her father's blood when she starts to twitch a little. Anyway, you look at it; it is a step in the right direction. Any positive is a bonus at this point. Jayce moves closer to the side where the transfusion is running and slips two fingers into her hand. Without warning, her hand snaps shut, gripping him tightly. His eyes widen, and a moment later, he starts bawling like a baby, saying she had just grabbed his fingers. I decide to expose her hand on my side and try it myself. Gently placing two fingers in her cupped hand, moments pass when she slowly closes her fingers around mine. Greatest moment ever! We look to Dom, and he moves to her ankle and places his hand there. Within moments she wiggles her toes on that foot.

"Okay, boys, back the fuck off and let me check her!" Holy fuck, my mom can still be scary even at her old age. Jayce and I hold up our hands that were being gripped by Aurora, and my mother smiles. She leans over and forces Aurora's eye open, and shines a light to test pupil reaction. My mother is shocked to find the silver orbs of Aurora's wolf looking back at her. Aurora's pupils react very sluggishly, but at least they respond this time. "She's improving. We need to keep round the clock watch on her. One in the bed, one awake. Switch out every four hours to give each other a break. So, to spell it out for her mates, one awake, two asleep. If you all need a break, get Nico or me."

Mom leaves quickly after that, and we all look at each other. "Jayce, why don't you sleep beside her first? I'll take the first watch. We can switch about midnight and so on if that's okay?" I look between Dom and Jayce, and they both nod. It takes several attempts for Jayce and me to get our fingers free. Once free, he scoots in where I was, and I make sure that he and Aurora are comfortable.

The first watch isn't bad at all. I discover that both twins snore quite loudly. I also discovered that Dom laughs if he farts in his sleep. When it is my turn to slide in, I defer to Dom since he hasn't had the chance to lay next to her yet. It kills me to give up my chance, but to be a good alpha means putting others before your-self. I move to the recliner and lie back. I keep my eyes on them for as long as I can.

The warmth of the morning sun is on my face when I wake up. Fuck, I slept through my watch. I wake up with a start, ready to launch out of the chair, when a firm hand lands on my shoulder. I look back and see Nico. "Shhh, all is well, son. The twins weren't handling her being ill very well, so I took over for the last eight hours to let them both sleep beside her. You wouldn't wake up when it was your turn." Well, that explains that. I nod slowly and examine Aurora. Her color has fully returned, but she still isn't waking up.

"Sebastian, get in the chair; it's time to draw blood from you." My mom is way too fucking happy about stabbing me this early in the morning. Dimitri, my savior, comes in carrying a mug and a pot of coffee.

"Thank the gods that Dimitri brought coffee. I don't think I can handle getting stabbed without it." Mother allows me long enough to get my coffee made before she sticks my happy ass in the chair to start draining me dry. I watch my lifeblood drain into the bag and hope and pray that this finally wakes sleeping beauty up. It's been two days since she fell in battle, and it feels like forever. We are starting to look worse for wear as the days tick on. Hell, I sound like it's been a month instead of two days.

Jayce won't leave Aurora's side for anything, except maybe for a bathroom break. I guess since he can't feel her through the bond, he's twice as leery as the rest of us that can feel her. I can almost bet that once this is over, that bond gets put in place the moment Aurora is able. I watch him as he sits there, brushing her hair, talking to her as if she's awake. Then again, no one knows for sure how much someone who's in a sleep-like state actually hears. Bag one gets taken away, and bag two gets hooked up.

"Ow, what the fuck!" My eyes dart to Alexis as she starts the I.V in what is my free arm. She mouths *sorry* but continues to do her job. I can see her looking me over from head to toe. Her arousal is palatable in the air. Something makes my wolf stir for a moment. Just as quickly as it happens, it passes, and I refocus on what's going on. Lord fucking help Alexis if Aurora wakes up right now. "You know I'm a mated wolf, right, Alexis?" That catches her off guard and gets my mother's attention. Mom comes over and takes one sniff of Alexis and boots her ass out of the room immediately.

"Fucking vultures," Elena grumbles as she walks back into the room. Dom and Dimitri both spit their coffee and look at me. All I can do is shrug. Mom approaches me, leans down, placing a kiss on my temple. "You know Aurora is more than likely going to hunt her ass down and kill her?" Slowly I nod, then turn to stare at my mate.

"I hope she wakes up soon. I don't know how much more we can take, Mom." Jayce is still in his own little world, giving Aurora a sponge bath in bed. Me? I feel so fucking helpless. I've put myself on self-imposed guard duty. Every night Dimitri and I take turns standing guard while the twins keep Aurora warm at night. It's not that I don't want to sleep next to her; my wolf would do better in close quarters.

Aurora's color is improving more with the first bag of my blood, and I can see how happy Jayce is looking. He gently leans over and kisses her lips like a prince from a fairy tale. Aurora's left-hand shoots up, gripping the back of Jayce's head, holding him in place. The rumble of her wolf echoes throughout the room. We all gasp and stop what we are doing. It's eerily quiet. We all practically hold our breath, waiting. Just as quickly as her hand rose, it falls, and she is silent again. She's fighting, and that's the most impor-tant thing.

CHAPTER 24

Jayce

I feel so guilty. I fought hard but not hard enough. Aurora ended up shot and fell in battle, and I blame myself because I'm the weakest link. As much as Dom, Sebastian, and the others try to convince me it's not my fault, I still blame myself. I'm over-analyzing every move made around Aurora. I won't let her be harmed again. I wish I were more dominant—being an omega fucking sucks. I'm not as strong as my brother, who's a potential alpha. I'm not even in the same orbit as Aurora or Sebastian. It does get quite interesting to watch when Sebastian would get too full of himself and Aurora would knock him down a peg.

Aurora's dad, Nico, has been fabulous with me. He worries about if I'm taking care of myself while I tend to his daughter. That's what a father is supposed to be like. Not like the monster Dom and I had for a father. I was so happy when Aurora and Nico killed him. Dare I say best day ever? For the first time in years, I saw Alex smile, like really smile. There was a noticeable weight lifted off of Dom's shoulders as well. After all, he was next in line for the polit-ical mating. Ugh, the bitch he was supposed to get was a hag. I hope my brother realizes just how blessed we are. Sadly, it took my mate almost dying for me to see how truly wonderful she is.

When Aurora wakes up, everything is going to change. No more being a chicken shit and hiding. Instead, I'm going to face my feelings. I love her with all that I am. I will lay beside her all day and all night for as long as I can. The guys have been incredible, letting me stay and not enforcing the rotation rule with me.

At the end of day one—yesterday—her father's blood had brought back a lot of color to her skin. We are so thankful that Elena knows what she's doing when it comes to poisons. Pint after pint, her color has improved, and at one point, her hands moved. I keep talking to her, and the guys look at me like I'm nuts.

Elena gives me that motherly smile and touches my shoulder. "Don't worry, prince, she'll wake up." She gently runs her fingers through my hair in a soothing manner. "Keep talking to her; she needs to know you're waiting for her. Right now, her wolf is in protection mode, making sure she heals right." Elena leans over and kisses my temple, and hugs me. "I'll get you dry shampoo and a brush for her hair. And I'll show you how to use it, so she wakes up not feeling gross."

Elena makes a final check of everything and leaves to go procure the goods. I wave for Sebastian to trade out with me; I need to stretch my legs and hit the men's room. I don't think I've ever pissed so fast in my life as I had since last night. My chest fucking hurts being away from Aurora for too long. My wolf feels like he's trying to rip free of my body to get back to her. I can't blame him; I feel exactly the same way. It's never easy for an omega to deal with the alpha being injured. We tend to go into nurture mode and mother the hell out of them until they recover.

Elena returns with all the hair care and skin care products she could find. The boys and I all watch as she explains what each is for and how to use it. We all want to help with her care; some of us are just more in tune with our nurturing side than the others. I can see how uncomfortable Sebastian is with everything, and I snicker out loud. The boys only really hung around for the bed-bath portion of the care instructions. Figures, right? I smile and copy everything that Elena showed me. I feel like I'm really making a difference in how Aurora feels.

We slept peacefully last night, and I wasn't bothered. Sebastian and Dimitri were like sentries watching over us as we slept. Kind of creepy, but with everything that's happened, it's a necessary evil at this point. I wake up to them prepping Sebastian for his donation and fresh coffee. I sit up and start fussing with Aurora's hair and cleaning up her face, making sure she is ready for the day. I made sure I explained to her what was going on with Sebastian.

My hands shoot to cover Aurora's nose when I smell Alexis's arousal. Thankfully Sebastian and Elena handled it before I said something. Slowly I begin Aurora's bed bath, making sure every inch of her body is cleaned and dried. The first bag of Sebastian's blood is hooked to her IV and is flowing into her. I can already see tiny differences in her color and skin texture. I can't help myself. I cover her up and lightly touch her face before I lean over and kiss her gently. *I miss her so much.*

Without any warning, her hand grips the back of my head, holding my lips firmly to hers. The rumble from her wolf makes me hard in a second as she holds me in place. I surrender to her completely in this very moment. My heart is pounding in my chest; I feel as if this kiss has gone on forever. She manages to nip my bottom lip, drawing blood. I feel her suck at my bleeding lip, and flick her tongue over the wound before her hand and teeth release me. I'm panting from the intensity and the passion I felt. I can't bring myself to look at the others just yet. I know in my heart this was her way of telling me that she's going to be okay, and I just have to be patient.

Slowly I turn and look at the guys. I can't help the lovesick puppy look I have on my face—the single most significant moment of my life. I return to giving her the sponge bath and whistle while I work. Sebastian comes to sit next to her once all three pints are taken from him.

"Love, I found and killed the person that shot you. I took their head and heart to give to you as a gift." Sebastian's eyes drop to Aurora's hand, and he picks it up, holding it. "If you can hear me, baby, please squeeze my hand. I beg you." I feel so much sympathy for Sebastian. He's an alpha without his mate. Alphas usually don't do well when they are separated from their mate for any reason. I can see Aurora's fingers twitch in his hand then close slowly. Part of me is pleased as punch that she reacted stronger to me.

But on the other hand, I feel horrible that he's not receiving just as strong of a reaction from her. There are no words of comfort in moments like this. We tend to beat ourselves up when bad things happen.

An audible sigh escapes Aurora's lips, and she moves her entire body, adjusting her position. Dimitri runs off, yelling down the hallway for Elena. Aurora is fighting so hard to wake up. Her eyelids flutter, and her eyes move rapidly. "Come on, baby, you can do it. Please open your eyes." I can't help but prompt her. I can't resist urging her to return to us.

One eye pops open first, then the other. She blinks them rapidly and yawns. "Did we win?" she croaks, her voice scratchy from lack of use. Of course, Aurora worries about victory at a moment like this.

"Yes, love, we won. You were shot by a poisoned arrow. If it wasn't for Mom taking pints of blood from your dad and me, I don't think you would have lived." Sebastian's voice cracks, mentioning her near-death experience. His eyes well up with tears, and he lets them run down his face.

Dom and I share the same side of the bed as we observe Aurora. Her eyes lock with each of us in turn until she gets to me. "Thank you, Jayce, for keeping me clean and telling me about the day. Thank you for keeping me warm at night." She reaches out and grabs my hand. "Thank you for remembering to treat me like I was awake and here." Tears roll down her cheeks as she smiles at me. She truly appreciates all that I have done for her.

"Anytime, my love, anything for you... anything you want, it's yours." I mean every word. I lift her hand and kiss the back of it, looking into her eyes as I do.

"Jayce, when I'm stronger, I want you in my bed, just the two of us. We need to finish our bond. I love you so very much." She makes the motion with her lips like she wants a kiss. Who am I to deny her? I lean forward and let her control the kiss. It starts sweet and tender until she bites my lip again and licks my wound. I can't help but smile. I am the happiest wolf on the planet at this point.

I reluctantly move out of the way for the others and let everyone in to show our girl some love. I feel so relieved and scared at the same time. I am scared because as soon as she heals, it's going down! Or should I say I'm going down? Crap, most incredible, and worst day ever. Performance anxiety? Absolutely. My eyes catch the movement of Sebastian leaving the room quickly. I wonder what the cheeky bastard is up to.

Sebastian returns, carrying something with a towel over the top of it. Nico strolls in right beside him with his hand on the edge of the towel. "My love, I present to you the head and heart of the man that attempted to kill you." Sebastian drops to one knee next to the bed and holds the covered platter out to Aurora. Nico removes the towel with a practiced flourish. The smile that creeps across Aurora's face is worth witnessing this disturbing scene. Who in their right fucking mind gives a head and heart as a present?

It fucking must be a Lycan and dragon thing because Aurora is elated. Nico beams with pride and Sebastian is smiling. Meanwhile, Dom and I are looking at each other like *what the fuck just happened*? We're confused as all hell by this display, but it makes Aurora happy, so it's worth it.

"Elena? Mom?" Aurora calling Elena *Mom* brings tears to the old lady's eyes. She moves forward and sits on the opposite side of the bed as her son.

"Yes, sweetheart?" Aurora rests her hand on Elena's. "Can you please prepare the skull to hang with the others? It deserves a place of honor in our home." Elena nods and motions for a Lycan male to enter the room and take the tray from Sebastian.

"Aurora, I took the liberty of taking your skull pile and sent them to be cleaned as well," Elena states plainly. Well fuck… The look all three of us give Elena and Aurora is one of shock. *Has Sebastian's mom finally wholly lost her shit?* How is it that this skull hoarding is now a thing?

Nico clears his throat. "It's a dragon thing to horde the skulls of your enemies. The more skulls, the stronger the dragon. I didn't think my baby would have that instinct." He sniffles and wipes his eyes with a handkerchief. "I'm so proud right now, I can't handle it. Please excuse me."

Aurora waves everyone off, and her father comes to sit before her; she holds him tightly as they both cry together. Perhaps her odd behavior isn't so odd after all. She's merely following the instinct of her dragon side. That explains a lot. Well, maybe not, but it makes a little more sense. "Daddy, will you show me how to make a menacing display of my trophies?" *Seriously? I must be in the twilight zone.* Nico nods and smiles before getting up and leaving the room.

"Guys, I'm famished. Can I have steak and pasta and something cold to drink?" Everyone scrambles about while I move and sit beside Aurora again. I'm not letting this girl out of my sight until the bond is dead solid. I pull Aurora into my lap and nuzzle her neck. Fucking instincts, of all the times for them to kick in, now isn't it. Aurora giggles and snuggles in closer, holding on for dear life. "You're a good fighter, Jayce. You held off a lot of Strigoi after your brother had fallen. I'm very proud of you." She kisses my cheek gently and rests her head on my shoulder.

Everything is right in the world other than my mate collecting skulls. It's something I'm going to have to adapt to and overcome. Gently I run my fingers through her hair and carefully massage her scalp. A soft sigh escapes her lips as she relaxes into the massage. With a giggle and a flop, she ends up with her head in my lap, looking up at me. Those stormy grey eyes shine with love and happiness. Deftly I seek out the knots in her hair and remove them with my fingers. Gently I move my fingers and start massaging her temples and forehead. The sounds she's making—lord save me—go straight to my cock.

I'm praying she won't notice my erection, but let's face it, she is right there, inches from it. Her eyebrow raises, and she looks right at it. "Someone's happy to see me."

That devilish smile has Dom stopping in his tracks in the doorway and raising his eyebrow at me. I wave at him to enter, which may or may not have been my brightest idea. I would sit here suffering from the boner from hell until I knew she was fed and strong enough. Fucking bastard has a mind of his own at times. After helping Aurora sit up, Dom and I set up the table for her and watch her eat. I never in a million years thought I would take pleasure in watching someone else eat. But here I am, watching our mate eat like it is the most beautiful sight.

Dom elbows me, and I follow him out the door. "Sebastian and I are going to patrol the grounds tonight. Dimitri is going to remain as his bear on the porch and Andre on the roof. You'll have the house to yourself." Dom grips my shoulders tight then pulls me in for a hug to end all hugs. "She knows you love her. It's time to show her how much. Let her in Jayce, let her love you back." He raises a knowing eyebrow at me. "And don't give me that *I'm an omega* bullshit. You're a great warrior when you have to be. You're a far better man than I am; you can understand emotions. That's a gift I wish I had." Dom smiles at me, and in his way, I received a pep talk. Now, if someone had a roadmap to a woman's G-Spot, that would be awesome. One last snicker from Dom before he starts to turn and walks off. "Don't worry about what to do. Aurora is dominant; she'll submit when she wants to, but most times, it's hold on for the ride of your life." Dom gives me his usual wise-ass two-finger salute before heading off down the hallway.

What the actual fuck have I gotten myself into? I run down the hall to my room, take a quick shower and trim my mustache and beard. Once I am pleased with my appearance, I pick out a nice silk shirt and my favorite slacks. My suit jacket is perfectly tailored to me. I stand before the mirror and do a last-minute check; I fucking love the way this suit looks on me. Reaching into the top drawer of my dresser, I retrieve the necklace I had bought Aurora while I was in town. Carefully I pull it out of its satchel and stare at it. The pendant is an exact copy of the paw print Dom and I have tattooed on our wrists. One can only hope she appreciates it. Gently I place it in my right coat pocket before I head back to see my mate.

Lightly I knock on her door and wait. Man, I've never been this nervous in my entire life. The clicking of the knob turning draws me out of my inner monologue quite quickly. Aurora stands there, hair in a messy bun with a nightshirt that aptly says *Fuck off*. I smile and lean in to kiss her gently, but the princess has other plans. Aurora grabs onto my lapels and drags me into the room, and locks the door behind her.

Mercury orbs gaze back at me, and in this moment, I know what a rabbit feels like when we hunt them. Slowly her gaze moves over my body inch by inch; I swear to the gods that I can feel her eyes caress me. A gentle smile graces her lips as she moves in closer. Ever so lightly, her fingertips glide over the soft material of my jacket. Her hands stop at my waistline before she steps back and makes the turn around motion with her finger. I'm quick to comply with her silent command. I'd do anything for my mate, absolutely anything.

Her smile lights up the room and puts my soul at ease. "You look very handsome, Jayce. A well-cut suit on a man is like a tiny lace thong on a woman. Very much appreciated." Her eyes bounce back and forth between human and wolf; apparently, I have the attention of both. "Allow me," she says softly as she reaches forward and slowly unbuttons my suit jacket. I gently toe off my dress shoes because fuck if I'm going to be fumbling with them later.

Slowly she exhales and reaches up, placing her hands on my shoulders and slides my jacket off. I don't know who's getting more turned on here, me because I'm being stripped, or her. It's quite evident she's getting worked up. The scent of her arousal is filling the room and engulfing me in her scent, almost strangling me. Her hands gently hold my jacket as she moves to lay it over the arm of the chair. When she returns, her eyes remain locked with mine as she undoes my tie.

Fuck, this is the single hottest thing I have ever witnessed or been apart of. I'm literally terrified to speak; I don't want to break the spell. She slips my tie off and lays it on top of my jacket before she returns and works on my silk shirt buttons. She stands on her tippy toes and lightly presses her lips against mine, and whispers, "do not move a muscle." I feel my cock harden and pulsate, straining against my boxer briefs. For the first time in history, I'm afraid of blowing my load too early. After what seems like an eternity, she has my shirt open, and with feather-light touches she caresses my skin.

Aurora keeps her eyes locked with mine as her fingers roam over my chest and abs. Holy fuck, she's tracing every single cut and ripple of muscle I have. Silently I thank my brother for forcing me to work out with him. Every pain-filled workout is now made worth it seeing the appreciation in her eyes. Aurora moves behind me and grips the collar of my shirt, and pulls it off. Again, I feel her soft touches moving over every bump and ridge of corded muscle. My eyes close of their own volition. I can't help the shuddering breath that escapes my lips when she kisses my left peck right over my heart. "Can I call this mine?" She speaks so softly; her breath tickles my skin.

I open my eyes to see this dominant female looking so unsure of herself. I can't have that. I reach down and take her hand in mine and place it over my heart. "It's always been waiting for you, my love. It was yours long before I knew your name. I just hope to be wolf enough to deserve yours in return." Tears threaten to break loose from my eyes as I finally speak my heart to her.

Aurora's eyes well up with tears, and she begins to softly cry. I bend down and gently kiss away her tears. Lingering on the last one, I press my forehead against hers. "You've always been wolf enough for me, Jayce. I love you for you. You are the kindest, most thoughtful mate a female could ask for. I am grateful I was blessed with you."

Her hands come to grip my belt, and it comes off super-fast. That confidence she lacked just a moment ago is now back in full force. I can't help but laugh at her antics as my pants hit the floor.

She steps back and cocks her head to the side, and smiles. "I've found a huge difference between you and Dom. *Yours* is definitely bigger." She bites her bottom lip as she grabs hold of my boxer briefs. One finger shifts, and her talon slices through the cotton like a hot knife through butter. Mercury orbs lock on the sight of my rigid leaking cock.

Just for good measure, I give my cock a slow, measured stroke. Her eyes follow my hand as it glides up and down my length. Now I've got her. I reach forward and use my claws to slice the nightshirt free from her. She looks a little shocked, but it's worth it. There it is, the fabled black lace thong she favors. I drop to my knees before her and grip the lace with my teeth. My hands rest on my thighs as I slowly begin to pull the thong down.

CHAPTER 25

Epilogue Ascend

TOMAS

Moldavia, Romania

I PACE back and forth within the castle walls. The calls and emails I've been receiving are quite disturbing and concern me immensely. Apparently, I failed in killing off the Marelup line. To make matters worse, it's a female child that was born. I summon Bane Kraus, the alpha of the Ice Dragons, and Ellis, the Polar Bear clan's beta. In theory, if that Marelup bitch is following tradition, these are the last two clan's she'll need a mate from.

Lucian from the Dire Wolf clan called me a week ago about the missive he received from the shaman's sister. The fucking bitches hid the last heir to the fucking throne from me. I throw my chalice of blood and watch it smash against the wall. The white marble is painted red as I watch the life essence run down the length of the wall. Shaking my head, me and my fucking temper, that was a good tasting AB positive. My eyes scan through the last several messages from Johan the beta. He is frightened by the Marelup bitch. Somehow, she was able to kill a Wendigo—whatever the fuck that is. Damn new world abominations. In his last text, he said he and his father would kill her if she survived the battles she had left. The arrogance of Vlad was the downfall of his people, and now his child will be tortured.

Honestly, I can't wait to sink my fangs into her neck and drain her dry over a series of days. Her stupid father secured his breeding right by neutering the other mates. Heh, I had to laugh to myself. A purebred Lycan female was weak and frail, so this should be easy. Perhaps the other shifters in the new world are more vulnerable as well. I walk out onto the balcony of what used to be the north tower. Slowly I look over what remains of the castle. Most of it is in ruins from the attack over two hundred years ago. Some sections, like this one, I've made my slaves repair. What's left of the Lycan forces, as well as the Dire forces that enslaved my people are now my slaves. I felt it was only fitting. They started as slaves and are now slaves once more.

Bane enters my domain, and I see his white dragon making slow, lazy loops in the air before he lands in the courtyard. I'm still waiting on Ellis to arrive. Fucking bears are slow as molasses in winter. Returning to my desk, I roll out the area's map, extending into Bane's territory and over into the Polar Bears'. There is only one path for the bitch to take, and that's to cross the land bridge. I sit here calculating the distance from the Lycan compound in North America to the land bridge. Unless she flies, it will take the better half of a week to two weeks, depending on the weather.

In mid-thought, Bane bursts through my doors and enters my office—the fucker didn't even knock. Maybe I should put dragons back on the menu because of his insolence. "Glad you could make it," I mutter under my breath. *It took you long enough,* I say to myself. I force a smile, though I know my grin is one you see in nightmares. Unlike Vlad the Impaler, we Strigoi don't have retractable fangs. Instead, it's rows of needle-like teeth that leave hundreds of puncture wounds; the better to bleed you with.

"Why am I here, leach?" Dragons are always so fucking dramatic. He seems put out by being summoned. His boots clop on the floor as he moves towards my desk. Every little thing about him irritates the fucking hell out of me.

I make a graceful sweep across the map. Each of the three territories are marked clearly, including the Dire Wolf and the Lycan's compound. "What the fuck, man? I thought the last of the wolves were here, under your control?" He moves quickly away from the table to the balcony. He glares at me, and I can see that fabled dragon temper flaring. Blackened slits bleed through the green of his eyes, making his dragon's presence evident.

"It gets worse. Anca's daughter survived that night. She's now collecting mates. There's no answer from Lucian or Johan, so I'm figuring they were killed off or failed and are hiding. Either way, it doesn't bode well for anyone involved." I lean over the map, watching the dragon alpha process the information given to him. He pulls his phone out and starts typing out a message.

"I just alerted my son to be watching for any communication from the Lycan's about a visit. He said nothing yet. So perhaps the problem sorted itself out, and no one survived the battle in the Dire compound." He shrugs his shoulder like this is one big fucking joke.

"So that's your answer to this problem? Just wait for the message stating she's on the way?" I am getting more and more irritated with the giant fucking lizard. I swear to the nine hells that he is so fucking stupid even a rock would know better than him.

"Yes, that's my fucking answer. Are you daft? Think of it this way; if she follows protocol, she'll reach out to me to meet my sons. Then we know exactly when she's on her way. No wasted resources. We can set the trap when we can estimate her travel time to the land bridge." He takes my ruler and starts measuring mileage. "Depending on how fast she drives and what route she takes, she should get to the ice shelf in eight days. Once she hits the ice shelf, it's on foot from there. Besides, how hard is it going to be to spot a pack of black wolves on snow?"

He has a point, and I hate admitting he's right. I'm stressing over nothing. "Okay, so now we wait for her to reach out. Ellis, the beta from the Polar Bear clan, should be here in a few moments. They'll lead the initial attack on the ice bridge. Your people will be the last line of defense." I draw a line from Wales, Alaska, to Diomede Island over to Naukan, Siberia. Next, I draw a diagonal line from Uelen, Siberia to Naukan, Siberia, and put a pewter dragon on the line I drew. I make my lines as Bane watches and nods along.

Ellis chooses this time to knock on the door frame. I wave my hand at him to enter, not wanting to lose my concentration. "Just in time, Ellis. I need you and your bears on Diomede Island when I call you. You'll be waiting to ambush a pack of black wolves and Lycan's trying to cross the land bridge. There will be a single female with them. Bring her to me alive, everyone else you can do with as you please."

Ellis nods slowly before adjusting his hat. "So basically, the bears are doing all the heavy lifting while you two sit up in your ivory tower?" He crosses his muscular arms over his chest as his eyes lock with mine. Have to hand it to the bear; he's got more balls than brains. He kind of looks like the bald guy from that police show—chiseled features, chocolate skin, and well-defined muscles. I always found it odd how a white bear had black skin, but hey, how can I judge when I'm a walking nightmare creature?

"No, not exactly. Lycans and Dire Wolves aren't built for the conditions. I think mother nature will do most of the damage for you. I mainly need you to recover the female." I smile—just this once, I do so without showing any teeth. I don't want to frighten the help too severely now.

"What's so important about this female? I mean, Polar Bear females are small and weak. Unless you're looking to breed her, I can't see the value. Just saying." Ellis shrugs his shoulders because, quite honestly, he doesn't give a fuck what the bloodsuckers want. Little does Bane know that his son is working against him behind the scenes, and Ellis was doing the same behind the back of his alpha. Neither alpha deserved the title, mostly since they sold out to this reject from the old movie Nosferatu.

I twitch when Ellis speaks back to me. I know I need the Polar Bears because they could stay out on the ice for weeks without any problem. Dragons could only hold that position for a short time, and well, the Strigoi would freeze solid if on the tundra for too long.

So, there is only one solid tactical choice... the Polar Bears. "Gather your forces, and let me know what supplies you'll need to pull your mission off." I move behind my desk and pull out two burner phones. I toss one to Ellis and the other to Bane. "These will only ring if it's me. No one else has these numbers. They also have GPS trackers implanted in them in case you fall in battle."

Ellis and Bane nod their understanding. Then in typical Bane manner, he runs and leaps off the balcony and takes flight, heading home. Ellis shakes his head and walks out of the office.

I reach into my pocket and turn on the mapping program on my phone. This was not only a bullshit meeting; it was a recon mission for the resistance. I took a significant risk attempting to map and double-cross the Strigoi, but it was worth it. When I finally reach outside the castle gates, I hop on my dirt bike and take off.

Riding as fast as I can to put as much distance between the Strigoi and me. I get about a hundred miles outside of dragon territory when I pull over and wait near what used to be a factory. The steel skeleton of the factory remains—the brick and mortar long since fallen. Mother Russia can be a real bitch when it comes to weather. Only the strong survive. After what seems like forever, the outline of Alaric's dragon can be seen on the horizon. "It's about bloody time."

Alaric shifts and pulls a cloak from the bag his dragon carried. "Ellis, my man, how did the meeting go?" We exchange a proper bro hug—complete with the typical manly side hug and the exaggerated claps on the back.

"Bro, this situation is so beyond fucked up, it's not even funny." I start pacing back and forth. "Your dad was there planning on attacking the lost Lycan Princess when she crosses the land bridge. That's wrong on so many levels." I grab a stick and begin to draw the sketch that the Strigoi had drawn in the snow to give Alaric a clue as to what's going down.

"Hmm, looks like the leach put some thought into this. Then again, Tomas has had over two hundred years to plan his defenses. Don't worry, I'll post my team on the front line. We'll protect her and her pack when they come across." Alaric grabs a metal rod and points to the spot he intends to hold. "You and your team can bring up the rear. We'll attack those loyal to my father together." Alaric has a coldness to him beyond that of being the son of the Ice Dragon alpha. You can tell that he has hit the point where he is tired of the injustice.

"You think we can take them? I mean, I know dragons are fucking tough, but it's dragon versus dragon, man. We bears can't take a direct hit from your ice blast." I watch Alaric closely as he paces when he then suddenly stops.

"Rumors are floating about that the princess is a hybrid; dragon and Lycan, first of her kind. If that's true, the ice blast won't phase her." He stops and looks up at me for a moment before continuing. "Also, if it's true, she will make a perfect political alliance to have. I know a non-true mating won't yield children, but having the last Marelup heir as my mate would be impressive." Alaric seriously ponders the implications of this pairing, nodding slowly as if deciding for himself.

I shake my head in disagreement. "Not cool, bro. I know she needs a dragon mate, but you have brothers that may be a true mate to her. At least give her a chance to have a true mate. I know she also needs a bear; she can check out my entire clan for all I care as long as she's happy in the end." I cross my thick arms over my barrel chest and puff myself up a bit. I know head-to-head I wouldn't be able to beat Alaric, but fuck, I'm not some chicken shit. I believe in being fair and not being a selfish fuck like the prince before me. "Seriously, bro, everyone deserves to be happy. Not all of us get forced into mating because of a passed down title."

Alaric's eyes flare to life at the mention of his title. He fucking hates being the damn Prince. "Yeah, it's a shit ton of fun while my father sucks Strigoi dick to keep his dirty dealings hidden. Yeah, it's fucking awesome that my people have no faith in the monarchy because of my father's shit. My father is a fucking puppet for the Strigoi" Alaric roars into the frozen wasteland before him. His rage is tangible in the air. Surprisingly, there is a slight edge of pain to the scent. His eyes turn to mine. "We need to make this right. We need to take down the Strigoi, my father, and any other leader tainted by their poison. I know by now, your alpha was informed of the mission. Choose as many as you can that you trust." Alaric rests his hands on my shoulders and presses his forehead to mine. "Don't die."

I smirk and draw Alaric in for a tight hug. "Yo, you go from plotting domination to getting emotional and shit on me. Shit, I think I have whiplash. But seriously, be careful on your side of this shitting mess. It is far more dangerous than mine."

Alaric can't help but laugh. "Yeah, I know I'm all over the fucking place, man. There's so much to do and not enough time." Alaric's phone starts to ring. His eyes fall to the caller ID. It's Alexander from the Dire Wolf compound. "Hey man, what's up?" Alaric puts the phone on speaker. "I've got Ellis here with me; speak freely."

"You sure it's safe to talk? What I have to tell you is super important." Alexander sounds more nervous than usual. There's a quiver to his voice that speaks volumes of what he is dealing with.

"What happened, Alex? Talk to me. Did your father kill your boyfriend like he's been threatening the last hundred years?" Alaric is getting agitated; he hates that Lucian treats his son like shit because he is gay.

"No, he's dead. Aurora and Nicodeamus killed him after Aurora survived the gladiator pit. That's why I was calling. We're preparing for war here." He swallows hard. "She's building an army. A horde, so to speak. She's going to be heading your way the minute the twins complete their mating to her. She's fucking terrifying. Her wolf is bigger than any Lycan I've ever seen." Alaric and I stare at each other, jaws dropped in shock and total awe.

Once I can compose myself enough to piece together a complete thought, I'm the first to ask, "Hold up. How many rounds did she fight through before she got to Lucian?"

"Technically three. Though the last round really didn't count as it was her father she went up against. He bathed her in his blue-white flame and healed her. She was covered in fucking fire!" he practically screams. "She walked out and kissed her father's maw, and then they proceeded to fuck shit up. It was the scariest and most exciting thing ever to happen here." He dramatically pauses for a few moments then starts up again. "Then she left me as pack master to train a team of assassins. Seriously, what the fuck happened? I still don't get it. She came through here like a force of nature," Alex states.

Alaric begins to pace with the phone. "The dragon king lives, which means my father's claim to the throne is shit. You say she survived two rounds before her father and then his flames? Those flames he used were no joke. I'm curious, what color is her fur?" His eyes lock with mine at that exact moment. If his suspicions are correct, her fur definitely won't be black.

"We've been calling her Snow White. Her hair and fur are as white as freshly fallen snow. Her eyes are pools of mercury like her father's. She has the shifted form of a Lycan, with some dragon scales on her arms, like gauntlets near her talons, muzzle, and around her eyes. She's also got a disturbing obsession with collecting skulls. Just a heads up."

Alaric starts cracking up and pointing to himself after the skull comment.

I shake my head at Alaric's antics. "Apparently, Romeo over here has a skull collection too. It must be a dragon thing; skulls are fucking creepy. It's not Día De Los Muertos up in this mother-fucker. Crazy ass fucking dragons. Either way, thanks for the heads up, man. If you know when they are heading out, shoot us a text with a smiley face emoji and nothing else, so we'll know what's up."

I shake my head at Alaric, laughing hard enough to have tears in his eyes. "This is what I have to deal with. Peace out, Alex, keep in touch, and stay safe." I hang up the phone and stare at Alaric, waiting for him to compose himself. "Time to move, lover boy, we've got to set our plans in motion."

"Stay safe, brother. See you soon." Alaric turns then runs and leaps into the air shifting into his dragon. Great white wings carry him higher and faster; now he's even more inspired to fight, knowing that now there is a chance at victory. I return to my dirt bike and start it up. The ride home will be a long journey, but at least I will have something worth thinking about—an unknown princess and an impending war. Life was about to get real inter-esting real fast.

CHAPTER 26
Prologue Hunt
ALARIC KRAUS

Ice Dragon Fortress

I sit at my crystalline desk reviewing the maps available for the Bering Land Bridge between Siberia and Alaska. According to what Ellis told me previously, Tomas has the Polar Bears wait for Aurora and her troops on the island in the ice bridge center. The Diomede Islands, located in the dead center of the soon-to-be land bridge, seem to be where the attack will occur.

I quickly take out my cell phone and text Alex what I have discovered, so hopefully, he can relay the information to Aurora and her people. Almost immediately, my phone dings, and it's a text back from Alex. He's been in contact with his brothers, who happen to be two of Aurora's mates. They are currently training with Lycans as well as the old Ice Dragon King. Within Alex's compound, he's presently training his people to be ready to join Aurora in her final fight.

I look back through messages I've been exchanging with Alex, and I finally find what I'm looking for. The video in question shows Aurora shifting for the first time in the middle of the arena. I replay the part where her fur and body are blanketed in frost. I watch as the frost crystals form on her coat and on the ground around her. It's truly a vision to behold. The uniqueness of her existence brings a whole new level of wonder to her theatrical display. Aurora appears to be a very proud and dominant female with how she handles herself in the arena. To be quite honest, I've watched this video of her far too many times for it to be considered research anymore. My dragon is beyond obsessed with her and her shifted form. He wants to feel her talons rake across his scales. My dragon wants to bathe her in his frost fire. If I'm to be honest with myself, I want all those things too.

I sigh and close the video, returning my gaze to the maps before me. I have to calculate the distance from the Lycan camp in Ferdig, Montana, to Wales, Alaska. It's approximately twenty-three hundred miles on land. I already know that most of the trip through Alaska will be on foot for them. If they are able to drive or fly, they are looking at about a fifty hour trip just to get to Wales. Sadly, most of the flights will be grounded when they are attempting to travel due to unpredictable weather.

I quickly look through my resources to see if I can somehow send aid to her. My dragon's instinct is pushing me to help and protect her. He wants her for himself. I pause when that revelation is made. *Shit...* my dragon has chosen... I breathe deeply before getting up to walk to my balcony. Pushing open the double doors, I step out into the blizzard. Without hesitation, I leap off of my balcony, shift, and take flight. I need to investigate the islands for myself and then meet up with Ellis.

The miles melt away quickly with every beat of my wings. Hundreds of miles of ice and snow separate me from Ellis. I scan the ground and sky around me to make sure I'm not being followed. A couple of hours pass before the Polar Bear Camp becomes visible. Carefully, I land about twenty miles away from the camp and head to the cavern Ellis and I use for our meetings. I shift back to my human form and enter the cave. Quickly, I move to the far back towards my hidden crate and remove spare clothes and my cloned phone. I power up the phone and text Ellis, alerting him of my arrival. Slowly, the clone phone catches up to where my other phone is.

I'm experiencing an emotion I've never dealt with before. It's rather disturbing to think I'm currently feeling anxious. My right hand raises and starts to rub my sternum. Anxiety is something I don't know how to deal with. I am an Ice Dragon Prince—I'm battle proven with many victories under my belt, but I fear failure for once.

Shit. I'm actually afraid of something.

I ponder this thought for several moments. Eventually, I arrive at the conclusion that I'm not scared of something, but for Aurora. I don't want to lose the princess before I've even met her. I start kicking rocks and ice chunks around the cavern because I can't deal with what I'm feeling. I wouldn't say we hit the end-of-the-world danger level, but inside I feel like my world is in danger of ending. While I have my moment, Ellis arrives and bears witness to my mini flip out.

"Whoa, bro, settle down! What's wrong?" Ellis crosses his thickly muscled arms over his chest, appraising my temperament.

"I'm fine, Ellis, just dealing with some heavy shit." I reach up and run my fingers through my long, blonde hair. After settling myself down, I decide to speak again. "I started calculating the time and distance for the princess to travel. It's a minimum of fifty hours if they can drive and fly to Wales." I begin to draw the map out for Ellis in the snow between us using a stick I found. "We both know in the next couple of days all flights will be grounded until the spring thaw." I look up at Ellis, and I know he can fucking read me like a book. I'm deflecting hardcore, trying not to deal with what I'm feeling at the moment.

"The plan is solid, man, but what's eating at you? You never throw a temper tantrum like you did when I walked in." Ellis cocks his head to the side. He's staring at me with that knowing look. *Fucking hell.* Maybe I should have just texted him. I begin to pace. *Fuck.* Dead giveaway that something's bothering me. Quickly, I turn to face Ellis. My eyes are the silver-gold color of my dragon.

"My dragon has chosen." I drop my gaze quickly. Finding a mate is so very rare for a dragon—those picky bastards. I should be elated, be shouting it from the mountain tops. Instead, I feel like a child who got caught with his hand in the cookie jar. Honestly, I feel like a thief because no one else even had the chance to meet the princess, and my dragon has called dibs. Ellis looks frozen in his state of shock. His mouth hangs open and his eyes are wide as he stares at me.

"Hold up! Back that mother fucking train up! Your dragon has chosen? Seriously?" Ellis moves quickly and wraps me up in a tight bro-hug. "Horrible timing, but excellent news, man! I'm so happy for you! Let me guess, the Fire Princess? It's gotta be her, she's got curves for days!" Shaking my head, I place both hands on Ellis's shoulders to get his attention.

"It's none of the females my father has been parading around the castle." I reach over and grab hold of his cell and find the message from Alex, then I fast forward to where Aurora shifts. Understanding flitters across Ellis's face. He watches the full shifting sequence before looking up at me.

"Oh? Oh boy... You can't be serious. For real, bro?" He throws his arms up in the air dramatically. "I mean, she's hot, but she's not a dragon. Your father will have a fucking cow if he finds out! It's bad enough he wants her dead." Ellis stands there shaking his head and even starts pacing. "How loyal are your boys to you?" His eyes lock with mine, searching my face for answers.

"Very loyal. I was planning on tonight's training flight to detour away from our normal route and tell them of my recent development." I walk to the back of the cave to retrieve a skull I had hidden there. It's a skull from a Tizheruk, the snake-like sea creatures that hunt the village fishermen. I stare at my prized possession, then offer it to Ellis. "Please send this to Aurora for me." Ellis takes the skull from me with an odd look on his face.

I shift my left arm to that of my dragon gauntlet, pluck off a single armored scale, and place it on the line where the skull plates meet. "It is of utmost importance that the scale remains with the skull. She'll understand it, trust me," I plead with Ellis for understanding. I hope against all hope that she accepts my prized skull and knows the value of the scale I send her. It's a promise of forever and a far deeper bond than a mate bite could ever create. Scale exchanges between dragons mean forever; this life, and into the great beyond. Ellis's facial expressions clearly convey his dislike of my gift.

"You dragons are fucked up with your customs. What happened to sending girls flowers? Instead, you send her rare ass skulls? No

worries, bro, I got you! I'll box this bad boy up and ship it off."
Ellis sets the skull down, then takes his phone and texts Alex for
the address. A few moments later the reply is received. Ellis
fucking smirks at me and screenshots the address. The next thing
I know, my phone goes off and it's the screenshot. I nod slowly
and stick the message in my hidden folder in my phone. I also
move her video and any other photos of her there and delete all
my text messages.

"Just let me know if you hear anything. I have a shit ton of
arrangements to make." When Ellis's phone goes off again, he
bursts out laughing, causing me to look over at him and tilt my
head at his reaction.

"Man, you two are perfect together. Sick fucks." Ellis holds up his
phone as the video starts playing. Aurora is looking at the bones of
her enemies displayed on the walls of her home. She's smiling and
laughing—excited, happy, and proud. Apparently she has a lot of
dragon tendencies. I must have that love-sick puppy look on my
face because Ellis is shaking his head at me. "You've got it bad.
Damn, I never thought I'd live long enough to see this day come to
pass. I'm gonna jet and get this mailed to your girl. I'll let you
know if she sends anything back." One brief bro-hug, and he's off
on probably one of the most critical missions I've trusted him
with to date.

I turn to leave and stand at the mouth of the cavern. The snow is
just starting to fall here, and it's a beautiful sight. I wait long
enough for the snow to begin falling harder before I prepare to
leave. I shut my spare phone off and leave it and my clothing
hidden in the cavern. The snow is cool upon my skin as I walk out
far enough to shift back to the form of my dragon. I take flight and
decide to follow Ellis for a bit, making sure he's safe. He's heading
to the nearest town with a UPS store in it. I can only imagine the

look on the poor attendant's face. I circle several times before heading back to my home. There's going to be lonely days and nights ahead of me. My dragon won't let me touch anyone else now; he's chosen, and his word is final. The most frightening part is, I'm actually okay with that.

CHAPTER 27

Sebastian

Going against my wolf's insistence to stay with Aurora, I slowly walk outside. Mentally, I know Jayce needs his time with Aurora to complete the bond. But fuck, we almost lost her, and all I want to do is hold onto her for dear life and never let her out of my sight again. I stand on the porch and look out across the compound. Dom slowly approaches me from behind and places a hand on my right shoulder.

"Scariest three days of my life. I don't know what any of us would have done if Aurora died," Dom says in a low, relieved tone. He looks around the central part of the compound, then back to me. "Which direction do you want to start the patrol?" Dom, a potential alpha, waits for my command. It's a nice change for once.

"I mostly want to stay close to the main part of the community. If there will be another attack, they will focus on Aurora again. We can't afford to be too far away with her in such a weakened state." I honestly half expected a fight over my decision, but Dom nods in agreement.

"I figure we'll start at the furthest house and walk clockwise around the perimeter." I step off the porch and head in the direction I just indicated. Dom catches up to me and begins fiddling with his phone. Apparently, it was shut off for the last few days.

"Hmm, Alex sent several texts. Apparently, we have informants in the Ice Dragon and Polar Bear Compounds. Tomas is plotting to attack us as we cross the Bering Land Bridge on the two islands in the middle." Dom's eyes lift to meet mine, then shift back down to his phone as more texts come through. "Apparently, the Dragon Prince and one of the Polar Bears are part of the resistance. We are assured assistance, protection, and shelter along our journey." More messages come through, and Dom reads through them quickly. "The prince has shipped a package to Aurora, but Alex has no clue what it contains." Dom goes back to texting back and forth with Alex, informing him of the recent attack and Aurora's near-death experience. Dom felt that the prince and the bear needed that information. "Alex said he'll pass the news along once he hears from them again."

"Shit. Well, we should start planning for the battle on the ice then." I pull out my phone and bring up my mapping program and search for the Bering Land Bridge. It's not fully intact yet, but it should be when we are ready to cross. I see the islands in question and show them to Dom. "If your brother's information is correct, here's the attack zone." I don't doubt Alex's integrity, but I don't know the other males involved to fully trust them yet. As we stop in the middle of the road, we draw the attention of Aurora's father, Nico. Silent fucker almost scared my wolf white with the way he seemed to materialize before me.

"Holy fuck, Dad. You just scared the hell out of me!" I pause, my skin becoming paler. I just called Aurora's father *Dad*. Nico smirks at me—like father like daughter.

"It happens, son. What has drawn your attention to the phone? Is that the correct name for the magic information box?" His brows are furrowed in concentration, much like his daughter when she's in deep thought. I retake my chances.

"Yes, Father, it's a phone, and we've received intel from Alex about where Tomas is setting up to ambush us." Dom takes this moment to show Nico the islands' map and shows him the text messages from Alex. Nico starts to smile and lets out a slow breath.

"Wonderful news!" Nico says in probably one of the most jovial tones I've heard him use since seeing his daughter. "Alaric was just a hatchling when I last saw him. He was such a good boy. His mother is a Golden Dragon. They are known for their sense of justice." His eyes light up as he reads further. He glances between Dom and me, then back to the message. "Can you find out when and why the prince is sending Aurora the present?" Nico's dragon is so close to the surface that scales randomly ripple along his flesh. Dom looks up at the king, a little spooked by his behavior.

"Of course, Father. I'll question my brother immediately." Dom takes the phone back from Nico and fires off several questions to Alex, then begins pacing, waiting for the answer. I'm not used to seeing Dom rattled, but you can feel the anxiety coming off him in waves. Several pings of incoming messages fire off in quick succession. Dom's face goes pale as he passes the phone to Nico. Dom locks eyes with me, and the look he has on his face makes me worried. On the other hand, Nico has that Cheshire Cat smile on his face, making him look like a deranged serial killer.

"Alex heard from the bear that it's a Tizheruk skull with one of the prince's scales." Nico hands the phone off to Dom, then grips my left shoulder tightly. "Do you know what this means?" He gives me several shakes. Nicodeamus's excitement level is turning frightening at an alarming rate. What kind of a shit storm is about to hit the fan for us?

"No, Father, I don't. Remember, I'm not a dragon, and we're all trying to get used to and learn dragon customs." Okay, now I'm genuinely getting concerned. Either the news is really good or really bad. I'm going to safely assume it's okay because he's still smiling.

"Forgive me, boys. I forget you have no clue. A male dragon bestows his prized skull to a female he swears fidelity to. In short, it's a promise of protection and an offer to become mates." He quickly snatches me up in a one-armed hug before turning and doing the same to Dom.

Nico takes off shouting for Dimitri and pretty much anyone else who will listen to him. Dom and I stare at each other, absolutely gobsmacked at the information relayed to us. Game changer, yes. On the positive side, we possibly have a legion of dragons on our side. However, we have a Dragon Prince—another alpha—to contend with. *Fuck...* Dom finally comes back to his senses and looks at his phone, then back to me.

"Okay... um, back to planning for the attack. We should probably find Dimitri and speak to him. Maybe he can shed some light on how the Polar Bears think and operate." At least Dom isn't shaken by the revelation that the prince is now involved.

"That's probably a good idea, Dom. Let's go back toward the center of town." We start heading back, and as we approach the Alpha House, what do we find? My mother and Nico jumping up and down, hugging each other like they won the fucking lottery.

Both Dimitri and Andre look just as gobsmacked as Dom and I did at the news. We both pause to take in the scene before us. I personally feel like I'm in the middle of a shitty episode of *The Twilight Zone*. We start to walk toward the group again, and we can hear my mother and Nico discussing where and how to place Aurora's skull collection so it may impress the prince. I facepalm, and my mother looks up after hearing my hand hit my forehead. Before I can react, my mother plows right into me and attempts to hug me to death.

"Isn't it wonderful news! A Dragon Prince on our side for the battle!" She quickly releases me, then proceeds to take Dom hostage next. "Nico and I decided we're going to build Aurora a Throne of Skulls. Imagine it: walking into the Alpha House, and next to the fireplace is Aurora sitting on her Throne of Skulls. Her hands are shifted to her hybrid's with the dragon scales, talons gripping the Strigoi skulls." Mom has that dreamy look in her eyes, pleased with her idea even though it's creepy as fuck.

With the way my warped mother describes the scene, I could easily visualize it; my beautiful mate, her eyes pools of mercury. The dominance pouring off her in almost oppressive waves, forcing the weak to be subjugated before her. Her dragon scales coating her forearms and hands in their partially shifted state to look like armored gauntlets. Her long, white, hooked talons digging into the skulls of the Strigoi. Yet, she's a vision of beauty in her blood-red gown, legs crossed at her ankles. Dom and Jayce, in their wolven forms, are sitting on either side of her throne. Their large, heavily muscled black Dire Wolves ready to attack at her command. As for myself, I stand at her right as her first mate, prepared to advise her or quell her rage. I blink my eyes rapidly, then look at Nico. The fucker is smiling at me.

"Did you just share that vision with me?" He starts laughing.

"Yes, I did. I also shared it with Dominik. With both of you fully bonded to Aurora, I had to test my theory. Soon, you will all be able to share visions as well as talk without sound. It's a dragon thing. You'll get used to it." He smirks. "She is a vision of beauty on that throne, wasn't she?" Dom and I nod our heads, and I turn to my mother.

"So, what do we need to do to make that vision a reality?" My mother looks to Nico, then goes up on her tippy toes and kisses his lips before leaving the room. What the fuck just happened? When the fuck did this happen? I fucking quit. I drop my head and follow my mother. Dom chooses to remain behind to catch Dimitri and Andre up on what's been transpiring behind the scenes.

I follow my mother back to her workshop. Apparently, she has already abducted every able-bodied male she could find. Mom is standing by the men, directing them as they carefully stack the skulls in crates. Another group is picking up the containers and carrying them through the back door of the house.

"Mom?" Slowly, my mother turns to face me. By the look on her face, she knows the question I was about to ask.

"Don't look at me like that, baby boy. You look at me as if I am wrong to have any kind of relationship with anyone besides your dead father. I've been alone for the last hundred and ten years. I deserve to be happy too." Unshed tears finally break free and silently roll down her cheeks. Okay, I absolutely feel like shit for making my mother cry. I move quickly and wrap my arms around her and hug her tightly. Gently, I press a kiss to the crown of her head.

"I'm sorry, Mom, I was just shocked. I'm glad you're happy." I smile as I look down at her. Hopefully, she can see that I'm sincere. Mom's eyes eventually find mine, and she smiles at me.

"I had a crush on Nico when I was a young woman. He was such a brave and selfless warrior." Her eyes glaze over, and I can tell she is lost in a memory. "My sister and I were sent as emissaries between the clans. We were the ones versed in the most customs. On one visit, I had the chance to watch Nico sword fight a Red Dragon Prince," she sighed softly. I look up and see Nico approaching, and I motion with my hand to halt him. "That was probably one of the most epic battles I had ever seen. Unbeknownst to the Red Dragon Prince, Nico was equally dangerous fighting with the sword in either hand. In probably one of the most unforgettable moves I've witnessed, he dropped the sword from his right hand to his left. He thrust it into his opponent's chest, ending the battle." Mom giggled like a schoolgirl at the memory.

"I was instantly smitten with him. It's amazing how quickly a crush is forgotten when your mate stands before you. The sun rose and set according to your dad. No one will ever take his place, but I can care for another." Mom kisses my cheek, then walks into the house. Nico's face is priceless. Apparently, he had no clue mom ever had a crush on him. I take a page out of his playbook and smirk at him before moving to grab a crate.

CHAPTER 28

Sebastian

I MOVE THROUGH THE ALPHA HOUSE, CARRYING THE CRATE OF SKULLS AND come to an abrupt halt. Apparently, the throne idea didn't just happen. By the looks of it, they are halfway done with their little project. Now that I look at it, the throne seems kind of wicked. I place my crate close to where the guys are working before walking around the throne to study it. My mom honestly had a brilliant idea, and I know Aurora will love it. Dimitri enters through the front door with Dom following closely behind. They both stop dead in their tracks and stare at the half-way done skull throne.

"It's a brilliant gift for Aurora, isn't it?" Maybe I'm becoming just as daft as the others, but I'm starting to see the need for the throne. Dom looks to Dimitri, then back to me.

"Um, yeah. It's a great idea, and I'm sure our mate will love it, but don't you think planning our strategy is more important than home decor?" Dom and Dimitri assume the same stance, crossing their thick arms over their chests. I look at the two of them and realize they are fucking dead serious, so I text several more young pack mates to come assist with the project. I pull myself away and head toward the office off of the main chamber. Dimitri and Dom follow me, then close the door behind them.

"Here's a map of the area we'll have to cross." I pull the map out of the tube, which arrived this morning. Carefully, I spread it out on the large meeting table and use the crystal paperweights to hold it down flat. I move back to the desk and take little pewter wolf-shaped figurines out of the drawer. After, I open two small boxes on the corner of the desk. One holds little bear figurines, and the other has dragon figurines. I start placing the figures in the proper places near the Bering Land Bridge.

"Okay, this is what we're looking at; according to intel, the dragons will be waiting on the Siberia side, the Polar Bears on the islands, and we're here in Alaska." I slowly push our wolves and Dimitri's bear toward the Polar Bears on the island. "I'm not one hundred percent sure when the prince will make his presence known, but I'm assured of his intentions." I raise my eyes and notice that Nico let himself into the room and is now approaching the table.

"Very nice, young prince. Only one problem: where's my dragon on our side? I will be in attendance." He's quite firm in his declaration. Dom reaches across the table without skipping a beat, grabs a dragon, snaps off the wing and front left leg, and then places it next to our wolves. Nico praises Dom's work and gives him a nod of approval. Fucking picky ass dragon. Nico studies the map and figure placement, and you could almost hear the gears turning.

"It's times like this when I wish I still had both wings." His right hand comes up to absently rub where his left arm used to be. "We need eyes on that island, or at least over it. I'm not sure how well Andre's eagle will handle that type of cold—all things considered." It's nice to think Nico is taking into consideration Andre's aging problem.

"Other than dragons, I'm not sure how many other flight shifters can handle that kind of cold." Dom wears a look of complete concentration as he studies the map. "If we really bundle Andre and he rides on Dimitri's back for warmth, maybe he can fly long enough to identify what we are getting into." Dom's eyes search mine, then Dimitri's and Nico's.

"That's a question only Andre can answer. I, for one, am not willing to risk his life for a peek." Dimitri wins the prize for the best resting bitch face of the night. He is deadly serious and unwilling to budge and sacrifice Andre, and I can't say I blame him. Other than the Dire Wolves, other species really can't handle that kind of cold.

"I propose we send the Lycan forces as well as Andre overseas by plane. There's a rogue faction of Lycans in Germany that my mother has been friendly with over the years. According to her, they will house our troops and aid in the battle. Andre can fly from there and do recon on the castle itself." I return to the closet and pull out the map of Europe. "The Lycan pack is located just outside Wegscheid, Germany. It's almost a straight flight to The Carpathian Mountains section in Moldavia, Romania." I measure the distance between the two locations and write it down. "It will take approximately sixteen hours by vehicle to reach the mountain. Then, who knows how long to scale it to get to the castle." To my surprise, Dimitri pulls out his phone, opens a satellite image app, and shows me precisely where the castle is located on the mountain. I study his program and spin it around, finding the main road that leads to the castle. Nope, we won't be going that way.

"There are the old tunnels the Strigoi used to invade the castle down over here." Dimitri pans and zooms the image to the stream that runs through the mountain. "It's an underwater access. Not many alive now would know where it's at. I suggest sending someone to scout the entrance to see if it was closed off in the last two hundred years." My eyes fall back to the stream on the map before I look up at Dimitri.

"I'll have my mother call the other Lycan alpha and see what she can arrange for us." As soon as the words are out of my mouth, that devilish sprite of a woman enters.

"What are you having me do, boy?" Elena's eyes become the white-blue of her wolf as she stares at me, her hands on her hips. Fuck, I'm in trouble now. Yup, I'm going to be killed by my mother.

"Mother, Dimitri relayed information about a hidden escape tunnel that we can use to gain entrance to the castle undetected." I press my finger on the spot on the map where the entrance should be in theory. "We were merely suggesting to get one of the Lycans from the pack in Germany to scout it. We need to make sure it's still viable before we plan to use it." I watch the anger slowly bleed away from her expression as she ponders the information.

She reaches into her pocket and pulls out her phone. I watch her scroll through the contacts and hit send. "*Hallo, Gustav. Es ist Elena. Sie müssen einen ihrer besten späher auf mission schicken. Ich werde ihnen die Einzelheiten schreiben sobald sie fertig sind. Danke, alter freund.*" Mom looks between us and shrugs her shoulders.

"They'll go in the morning and look. No worries, as you kids say. I have a throne to build. Have fun storming the castle, kids." Mom waves over her shoulder as she departs the room. What the actual fuck just happened? And since when can mom speak German? I look at Dimitri and Nico. Both guys shrug their shoulders at me.

"We both speak multiple languages. It's like traveling between states here, over there. Except every time you cross a border, you're speaking a different language," Dimitri says like it's no big deal. I guess to them, it really isn't a big deal. They were raised that way.

"Okay, so the tunnel exploration problem is being handled. We're flying the Lycan team to the other Lycan pack. What else do we need to plan for, Dad?" I look to Nico for guidance because he's had the most direct contact with our enemy out of all of us. Nico moves slowly around the map, studying it, then heads over to the whiteboard on the wall.

"First thing we need to do is educate your pack and the dire pack about the Strigoi. Then, we can train both packs on how to kill them. The European packs have been dealing with them for generations. We will employ the same tactics here for training purposes." Nico begins to list the strengths and weaknesses of the Strigoi on the board. It's kind of frightening to think they have far more strengths than weaknesses.

"Question: will the Dire Wolves' toxic bite have any effect on the Strigoi? It works by rupturing platelets and degrading the cellular integrity of muscle fibers." I look at the notes on my phone that Alex sent me this morning. Making sure I don't miss any important questions, I raise my eyes again to Nico, watching him closely. I see several different emotions flitter across his face before he smiles.

"I believe their bite would be most effective. Dominik, do you or Jayce possess this toxic bite that Sebastian speaks of?" Dom snaps out of whatever little bubble he's in and looks up.

"Jayce does. He took after our mother in that sense. He possesses one of the strongest toxins in the entire pack." Dom's eyes widen in realization of what he just said. Panicking, he looks between us and then the door. "Aurora... Oh God's no.." Tears well up in his eyes as he bolts for the door. Nico, one-handed, stops him in his tracks.

"Fear not, son. You already bonded with her. She will be safe from your brother's toxins. Besides, if my daughter is like me, she will bite him first," he says with a cocky smirk. Dom and I look at each other, knowing we both bit her first. In unison, we close our eyes and concentrate on the bond, reaching out to sense our mate. So far, she's good, real good.

Dom reaches out to her gently. *Bite Jayce first. His bite is toxic.* His voice echoes in my head; it's a pleading tone. We both hope she listens to him.

I know! Go away! she answers back, booting us both from the connection. Nico is still smirking at us. Nico shakes his head slightly.

"She does pack a punch, doesn't she?" He laughs at his own statement before looking to the whiteboard again. "What special combat gifts do Lycans have?" Nico turns and looks at me. I move to stand next to Nico and start writing on the board.

"The two advantages I feel stand out the most are bi-pedal and able to grip things. We each have different gifts; some have speed, strength, agility, the list goes on. We can easily separate the pack according to abilities." Sebastian's eyes move between the three of us, then come to rest finally on Nico. Dimitri and Nico are both nodding slowly as they absorb the information I just gave them. Dimitri is the first to speak up.

"I believe that would be a wise move, young prince. Let's set up a pack meeting for tomorrow night and address this idea." Dom moves forward and pulls out a small notepad from his back pocket. He flips it open and turns the pages until he finds what he's looking for.

"There's still the matter of the ferals and rogues to be dealt with." Dom looks back to his notes again. "With both groups being pack-less for so long, there's no telling where their loyalties lie. There's no definitive answer if they will fight with us." Dom's concerns are valid. If the two groups join us, that adds another twenty to thirty fighters to our cause.

"We agreed to let Aurora sort the bodies out. It's better if she plays judge, jury, and executioner than any of us. Who knows, she may be able to save all of them." My eyes drift to Dom, then Dimitri, and finally Nico.

"Or we're going to end up with a huge pile of skulls that Elena will have to prepare for Aurora." Nico's spot-on assessment of his daughter's all or nothing mentality is kind of frightening. Dimitri chooses this time to speak up.

"What can we expect from the Ice Dragons? Are there any weaknesses we can exploit?" You can tell that Dimitri's question rattled Nico because his eyes flicker to that of his dragon, then human again.

"Very few, old friend." Nico looks down, almost sad to relay that information. "Dragon versus dragon would be best. I can't fly, so I'm a target, but I can help with the ground troops." He looks back at the whiteboard again. "When we get Jayce's venom, we can test it on dragon blood to see if the cells explode under the microscope." Nico draws in a deep breath before speaking again. "If that works, then we need to get ahold of some sniper rifles with armor-piercing rounds that are hollow points. We can turn the toxins into a gel and fill the hollow points." Nico sighs then turns back to face us. "It's my only suggestion. Unless the prince helps, it will be lambs to the slaughter." Well, that revelation just shot the meeting straight to hell.

"Dimitri, what can you tell us about the Polar Bears?" Dimitri moves to the whiteboard and doesn't bother writing on it.

"They will be smaller than I am. So, we train the wolves to fight me. If they can defeat me, they are ready for the Polar Bears." I move slowly and place my hands on Dimitri's shoulders.

"Are you sure you want to do this?" There are more wrinkles around his eyes and more grey hair dusting his temples. Granted, time isn't catching up as fast as it was, but it's still progressing quickly.

"It's for Aurora. I swore my dying breath to her. If I die training troops to protect her, then it was worth it." I can see the tears he's fighting to restrain. I give him a curt nod and a brief bro-hug and move back. Nico full-on hugs Dimitri, both of them blubbering like babies. Nico keeps thanking Dimitri for all he's done for his daughter.

I look over at Dom, and he has silent tears rolling down his cheeks. Slowly, I move to his side, wrap my arm around his shoulders and remove him from the room. We move to sit in the kitchen. I grab two beers and pop the tops. Dom takes his and downs half of it in one gulp. His emotional state hasn't improved, but it hasn't gotten worse.

"Wanna talk about it, Dom?" He shakes his head but starts talking anyway.

"His love for our mate knows no bounds. She's not just a job to him." Tears hit the tabletop as he keeps his head hung low. Slowly, he raises his head. His eyes are bloodshot and that of his wolf. "You know, if it's anything other than time that kills him, Aurora is going to be a force to be reckoned with. Her thirst for vengeance will know no bounds. Her pain will turn to rage that will burn brighter than a thousand suns." When Dom puts it that way, I'm terrified of Dimitri and Andre's death. I honestly don't think the world will survive our mate's pain.

"Mother plans to sit and talk to Aurora about it. Mom thinks, all things considered, they may live another year at most. It could be a lot less with strain and exertion." I gently rub Dom's shoulders, and I look up to see my mother watching us. She, too, is grieving right alongside us.

"There's only so much that can be done, boys. We have done all that we can. Time is a bitch." Mom goes to the fridge and pulls out three beers, and opens them before passing them around. "Nico feels horrible that his scale isn't helping. If my sister was still alive, I could find out what spell she used and bind them to Nico. Her journals may still be in her room in the castle, if we can find them before it's too late." Mom's look is pensive as she studies the beer bottle as if searching for answers. "I don't know what else to do for them." She downs her beer quickly before abruptly standing and leaving the room. Everyone in the room is in some semblance of pain this afternoon. We just have to hope and pray our fearless leader has a better plan in mind.

CHAPTER 29

Jayce

I REACH FORWARD AND USE MY CLAWS TO SLICE THE NIGHTSHIRT FREE from her. She looks a little shocked, but it's totally worth it. There it is, the fabled black lace thong she favors. I drop to my knees before her and grip the lace with my teeth. My hands rest on my thighs as I slowly begin to pull the thong down. I slowly move it down over her bare mound, my hot breath caressing her flesh as I move. I get to her knees and release my hold on the thong, letting it fall to the floor at her feet. Her hands rest carefully on my shoulders for balance as she steps out of the thong. I remain on my knees before her, staring up at her for a moment before I place a feather-soft kiss right above her clit. Her sharp intake of breath tells me I'm on the right track.

I run my hands slowly up her calves to rest on her thighs. Gently, I urge her thighs apart so I can have an unobstructed view of her glistening wet pussy. The scent of her arousal is driving my wolf and me insane. Lightly, I lick the tip of her clit, teasing her. Aurora's fingertips dig into my shoulders before one hand moves up to grip the back of my head.

"Jayce, please... please, my love... I need you." Her breathy pleas almost cause me to cave. Aurora attempts to move her mound closer to my mouth, wanting to grind upon my face. I sit back on my heels and look up at her. I'm not dominant by any means, but for fuck's sake, a man has to take a stand at some point.

"Be patient, my love. I'll make you cum so hard you'll be begging me to stop." Without warning, I stand and scoop her up in my arms to toss her onto the bed. Aurora squeals upon impact then goes into a giggle fit. I move as slowly as I can toward her. She's my prey today, not the other way around. Sadly, that idea doesn't last long. By the time I have one knee on the bed, she flips me onto my back and sits on my chest, looking down at me. Aurora's eyes flicker back and forth between the steel-grey and molten mercury of her wolf.

I now know what a deer feels like when it's stared at by an apex predator like her. My best bet is to give the lady what she wants. I hook my arms under her knees and move her, so her dripping wet folds are over my waiting mouth. I start to tongue fuck her pussy while both my hands begin to tweak and pinch her nipples. Aurora starts to ride my tongue with reckless abandonment. I know I got her when the first orgasm rips through her, as she pulses and throbs around my tongue. I remove my right hand from her breast and coat it in her slick, sticky juices. As she's coming down, my index and middle finger start exploring her tight rosette. Based on her gasp and sudden bucking, I know I'm doing something she likes very much. I wet my fingers again as I begin the assault on her clit with my tongue. She's back to grinding down hard on my face, so I apply pressure to her rosette and gain entrance. I'm easily two knuckles deep in her ass as I begin to time my thrusts with her rhythm.

I swear to the gods I feel her squirt all over my face when she comes. Aurora curls forward, bracing herself on her forearms and using the headboard for support. Slowly, I withdraw my fingers from her backdoor and wipe them on the covers. I caress her ass and slide her down my body, leaving a snail trail in her wake.

We're finally face to face when I notice her eyes are back to human. Apparently, the wolf has been appeased for now. I watch Aurora slam her eyes shut for a moment, a low growl escapes her lips before she opens her eyes again.

"Your brother just warned me about your bite." She leans down to kiss my lips as she wiggles her hips, attempting to line my cock up with her entrance. "I'm going to bite you and make you mine, Jayce. Now and forever together." I take the hint and scoot up the bed a bit, using pillows to support me. When I scoot up, my cock finds what it's looking for, and I sink deeply into her welcoming embrace. Aurora sits up straight and smiles at me. Apparently, she's quite pleased with what she's feeling.

I stay as still as I can even though my balls are begging for release. Aurora begins to move ever so slowly, and it's the single most exquisite feeling I have ever felt in my entire life. Every wet slap of skin on skin, every slip and slide, magnifies as the bond begins to slip into place. Aurora's muscles start to twitch and spasm around my thick cock, and I know she's getting close.

Aurora lowers her head and begins to kiss my neck and shoulder. Without warning, her canines pierce my shoulder muscle and her pussy begins to milk my cock for all that it's worth. I'm not going to last much longer. I start meeting her thrusts, driving up into her harder and harder. I feel my mating knot form, locking me in place as my seed erupts into her. Quickly, I lunge forward and sink my canines into her shoulder, opposite of where Sebastian and Dom claimed her. I feel the final bands of the bond snap into place as I taste the coppery tang of her blood in my mouth. We remain locked, both of us still biting each other.

A content sigh eventually escapes Aurora's lips. Carefully, she withdraws her canines and proceeds to clean the wound. I follow suit, being extra careful that I don't accidentally release my toxins into her. Slowly, I tend to her wounds and make sure I promote her healing. Eventually, I lay back and look up at my beloved mate.

"Are you okay, my love? I didn't hurt you, did I?" I search her features for any sign of pain or discomfort, and I see none. Aurora smiles at me and gently kisses my lips.

"Everything is perfect, Jayce. I feel you in here." Aurora brings her hand up and touches over her heart. I can completely relate to what she's saying. I feel her in every fiber of my being. I also feel the relief from my brother and Sebastian that the bond is fully intact, and we are truly bonded. I pull Aurora down to lay beside me as my mating knot releases, and I make sure she's comfortable before extracting myself from the bed.

"Stay here. I'm going to get you some food and drink." I'm very anxious to please her in every sense of the word. I walk into the ensuite bathroom and retrieve a washcloth and a dry towel. Carefully, I clean Aurora's nether regions, staying mindful of the fact she may be tender. I pat her dry, then look up to see her smiling at me. I can't help but blush at the look of affection on her face. I smile back as I finish cleaning her up. Slowly, I lean forward and kiss her lips before I head downstairs to gather some food and a drink for her. As I make it into the kitchen, I find the full crew passing around drinks and having a freaking party without Aurora and me.

The world seems to stop for a moment as they all notice that I've seen them. The high fives and bro-hugs ensue for what feels like forever. I get passed around from Dom to Sebastian, then over to Dimitri and even Andre. Finally, right when I thought I was safe, I end up in front of Nico. Just what I fucking need. I look up into his eyes and attempt to smile. Nico reaches up and pulls my collar to the side to inspect Aurora's bite mark. He smiles and gives me a brief hug.

"Get her food and go back to her now." Dimitri shoves a platter with food on it into my hands. He turns me and smacks my ass, sending me on my way. I don't even have the chance to say a damn thing to anyone.

I head back upstairs with a bounty of food to find Aurora curled up on her bed, asleep. I set the platter down on the small table next to the window. Carefully, I lay out all the food, trying to set the perfect spread for her. Once I'm absolutely sure it's as perfect as it's going to get, I return to the bed and sit beside Aurora. My hands slowly massage Aurora's back, trying to wake her up gently. Her eyes flutter open and, initially, they are pure mercury before they fade to her human steel-grey.

"Hey, baby, do I smell bacon?" Aurora asks with a sleepy, raspy tone to her voice. She smiles as she looks at me. I choose to just wink at her, answering her question.

I lean down and kiss her forehead, then offer her a nice, soft terry robe. Aurora gently takes the robe from my hands and slips it on. I offer her my hand and walk with her to her lunch spread. The look on her face is thanks enough. You would think that no one had ever taken the time out of their day to do something so simple. Aurora devours the meal that I set before her, but halfway through, she stops and moves to sit on my lap.

She gently begins to feed me the food I brought up for her. I've never been pampered in my entire life, and yet here is my alpha —my mate—feeding me her food. Aurora is so happy; she's softly singing to me as she feeds me. This gentle side is almost as frightening as when she's in a full-blown rage. My phone dings, and it's a text from Sebastian. Apparently, a package is downstairs and it's imperative that Aurora comes downstairs to open it. I show Aurora the message, and the look of puzzlement on her face is worth it. Aurora goes over to the walk-in closet and slips into a blood-red bodycon dress that drapes to the floor.

"Let's go, love. I'm super curious what was sent to me." Quickly, she grabs my hand and drags me down the stairs behind her. I am really starting to fear what she's going to be like come Christmas time. We make it to the kitchen, where everyone seems to gather. When I say everyone, I mean our entire bond, extended family, and some of our closest pack mates. On the preparation island in the middle of the kitchen sits the box in question. Aurora pads slowly across the floor silently as she cautiously approaches the box. It's not like the damn thing will bite her, but her wolf makes her investigate everything before proceeding. Once she and her wolf are satisfied that the box isn't a threat, she looks closer at the labels.

"Do we know anyone in Wales, Alaska?" Most of us shake our heads no—all except Dom and Sebastian.

"Alex's contact sends intel from Wales when he's able to get into town." Sebastian approaches the box and studies the label. "It's from the same man. I think his name is Ellis. You can trust him, love." Sebastian kisses the top of Aurora's head before backing away.

Aurora looks to her father, who gives her a single nod to proceed. Without a second thought, Aurora shifts one finger and extends a talon to cut down the sides of the box. She then cuts the top off, and the sides fall flat to the table. Packing popcorn goes every-where and exposes its precious cargo. It appears to be a giant snake skull at first glance, that is until you really look at it closely. The skull plates are heavily armored and its jaw is thick, heavy, and hinged like all snakes. There are a few significant differences, though. Not only does it have fangs, but it also has rows of razor-sharp teeth like a shark.

Aurora gently brushes the last of the popcorn off and suddenly stops. Scales ripple up her forearms as well as the fur across the rest of her body. It's almost as if she is fighting for control over her body. Her pure mercury orbs are locked on the top center of the skull. I move closer to see what caused such a reaction from her, and then I see it: a heavily armored, silver and gold scale placed in the center of the skull.

"Nico, you may want to look at this... I don't understand what it means, and Aurora won't budge." I look up to see my brother recording Aurora's reaction, no doubt a request from the sender. Nico approaches and sniffs at the scale, and a low growl escapes Aurora's lips at her father's intrusion. Her lips curl up defensively, exposing her descended canines.

"It's as I suspected. It's a mating offering from the Ice Dragon Prince. His prized possession, along with one of his scales. By the looks of it, Aurora's animal accepts the gift." No sooner do the words leave his mouth than Aurora reaches out and takes possession of the skull and scale. Aurora turns to leave, heading toward the main hall to look for a good place to display her new prize. We quickly follow behind to find Aurora sitting on her skull throne while petting the giant snake skull.

"Dimitri, do we have anything left from the Wendigo?" Her eyes haven't left the scale on top of the skull. Dimitri moves forward and drops to one knee before her.

"We do. We have its skull and both horns." She nods, slowly running her fingertips over the bony plates of the skull. I move to rest beside her, leaning on the arm of the throne to look at her new prize.

"Please bring me the skull. I feel compelled to send a skull back to him." Her eyes raise, and she looks at Nico. "Is that the correct protocol, Father? I don't understand why my animal is pushing me to do it." Nico moves forward and looks at the offering, then back to Aurora.

"The dragon half of your nature accepts the offering. It wishes to send something of equal value to the sender. Even if this only ends up as a political marriage, at least he did it the proper way and offered your animal a prize." Nico leans forward and kisses the top of Aurora's head before heading out the front door. Shortly after Nico leaves the room briefly then comes back. Dimitri returns with the skull and a box to ship it in.

Aurora slowly stands and places her prize on her seat before moving over to the Wendigo skull. Gently, she picks up the skull and hands it to me. I start to worry that I might fuck this whole thing up for her, so I remain perfectly still. Before my very eyes, she shifts her left hand, and it's covered in armored scales. Her eyes search for the perfect scale to pluck. After several times of flipping her hand back and forth, she finally removes one. Carefully, she places the scale on the center of the Wendigo skull—in the exact same spot as the male's scale on her prize. She does something a bit different, though.

She reaches up into her hair, finds one of her small braids, and cuts it close to her skull. Andre offers her a small rubber band to tie the end off with. Aurora takes the braid and sticks one end into each eye socket, so the braid rests on the nose plate. Dimitri stands stock still, holding the box out to her. Gently, Aurora lowers the skull in. Andre comes from behind her to refill it with the packing popcorn.

Meanwhile, Dom texts his contact in Wales and asks for a return address, then writes it on a label. Dimitri leaves the Alpha House with Andre in tow, heading out to send Aurora's offering to Alaska. Aurora moves back to her prize and removes the scale from the top.

"What do I do with his scale, Father?" She turns the scale several times over in her hand as she inspects it. The flesh on the back still looks relatively fresh. Damn, freaky dragons and their crazy-ass shit. Nico moves forward to remove the scale from Aurora's grip.

"Your animal accepted the gift. Proper protocol would be to place the scale above your heart. Either Sebastian or I will cut your flesh and insert the flesh on his scale into the wound. If it takes and lives, it's a good match." Aurora slowly nods her head and moves the skull off her throne and into Dom's waiting hands. Aurora then guides me to sit on her throne. Yeah, I'm so not comfortable in this position of power. Aurora climbs up and sits upon my lap without warning, then turns sideways so her head is on one arm and her legs hang over the other.

"Sebastian, I'm ready to see if you can place the scale." Her hands rest on her stomach, and I can't help it, I have to hold one of her hands through the procedure. Aurora calls Sebastian's name, drawing his attention away from his phone and back to what is going on.

"Are you sure about this? I don't wish to hurt you," Sebastian says as he leans down to gently kiss our mate's lips and stare deeply into her eyes. A single nod is all she gives him before looking at me. A soft smile crosses her lips before she winks, then she closes her eyes and waits.

Sebastian approaches with the scale in his right hand, which is partially shifted. Now, his own claws look more similar to Aurora's talons. He takes a few moments, staring at them, before moving into position. His talon moves swiftly, cutting deep into our mate's chest. Blood oozes out of the wound and pools between her ample breasts. Quickly, Sebastian shoves the fleshy side of the scale into the cut he just made, and almost instantly, the area begins to frost over and the wound starts to knit shut. Once Aurora senses that Sebastian is done, she sits up and remains in my lap. I gently lick the blood from her chest and in between her breasts. A sharp intake of breath catches my attention. I turn to see Dom, who looks quite shocked.

"What?" I ask, confused. He immediately holds his hand up and turns away. I guess he didn't expect me to be so openly affectionate with our mate. I examine the scale closely; it appears to be healthy and vibrant. It most definitely survived the transplant.

"Sebastian, do you think we ought to send a close-up picture of the scale on our mate's chest?" Gently, I run the back of my finger past where the scale is implanted, accentuating my point. "I mean, so the prince knows we're allies and all?" I'm honestly not sure what the correct thing to do is at this point. Aurora looks between Sebastian and me before readjusting her top, so the scale is evident. Aurora then decides to shift both hands, so they are covered in her armored scales, and her long white talons are on display. She angles her left arm, so the spot where she removed her own scale is visible.

"Jayce, pull my top down. I'm going to use my scales to cover my chest." As soon as her tube-top pools around her waist, she brings her right arm up to cover and support her breasts. With the way she is posed, the prince's scale is on full display. Her eyes bleed liquid mercury as she stares at Sebastian. "Take the picture before you come in your pants." Sebastian snaps several pictures, with Aurora making several minor adjustments.

When she is sure that Sebastian has at least one good shot, she shifts her arms back and pulls her tube top back into place. Quickly, she snags the phone out of Sebastian's hands and starts going through the pictures he took of her. She is angled in such a manner that I can see all the images on the screen. When Aurora notices me looking, she turns so I can look along with her.

Out of about fifteen pictures, we narrow it down to three. I send all three to me and then to Dom. Within seconds, there is a crash in the kitchen, and Dom comes running out into the main room. The look of disappointment on his face is totally worth it. He looks back at the images and forwards to his favorite. Without a word, he turns to leave, visibly adjusting his cock in his pants. Aurora gives a single nod, and I send the image and the video off to Alex, so he can forward it to the prince. After handing Sebastian his phone, I return to mine and set Aurora as my new wallpaper. Aurora couldn't help but giggle before she grabs her phone as well.

"Take a picture of us," she says it so softly, it sends butterflies straight to my stomach. I immediately obey, and I go into her camera to set up selfie mode. Aurora presses her lips to my cheek and I snap the picture. I don't think I've ever had such a genuine smile in my entire life. I'm finally happy. I'm truly loved and in love for the first time in my life.

Best day ever.

CHAPTER 30

Aurora

Everything's right in my world at the moment. I just spent a full thirty-six hours in and out of bed with Jayce. I definitely understand why his ex was fighting so hard to keep him. Hot damn, can that man move! And the things he can do with his tongue, *holy fuck...*

Now, there are several things on my agenda that I have to investigate. First on my list is the rumor that Alexis tried hitting on Sebastian while I was at death's door. To find out the truth, I decide to hunt down my most reliable source of information in the pack.

I approach Elena's house, and there's an argument going on. I don't like people going against the chain of command. Her word is my law and to go against her is to challenge me directly. I don't even bother knocking. I walk right in the front door and stand behind the female who's yelling at Elena.

I'm easily a head taller than this little firecracker, and I'm definitely built for war. Elena looks up at me and smirks. Apparently, I arrived just in time. I shift my hands into my taloned gauntlets and tap the wall next to the female's head. The scent of fear instantly fills the air as she stares at my talons. I don't budge, nor do I say anything. She whips around and tries to stand behind Elena. I don't recognize this female, and that's a problem. I narrow my eyes as I feel my beast surge to the surface.

"Who do you fucking think you are, yelling at an Elder One? She is the Pack master," I growl out while I stare the female down. Suddenly through the bond, I can feel the guys closing in fast to my position. She bows slightly and then extends a hand out to me. About the same time, the guys barrel into the room.

"I'm Alexis. I'm the nurse that helped save your life." Recognition barrels through the bond, and I knew in that instant that the rumors were true. I stare at her hand, refusing to accept it. At that moment, she realizes I know what she did. "I thought you were going to die, I swear it." She's panicking now and searching for a way out. I'm having a hard time restraining my wolf, and the boys know it.

They move as one and attempt to restrain me. Elena yells for the girl to run. Yeah, that wasn't going to save her and Elena knew it. Reason four thousand, eight hundred and seventy-two of why I love my mother-in-law. She knows my Lycan loves the thrill of the chase. Once Alexis is clear of the house, the guys relax, which is a huge mistake. The second I know I won't harm any of them, I bolt out of the kitchen and run through the house. *The hunt is on.* I shift fully to my Lycan and give chase. I can feel the guys hot on my trail, but they won't be able to save her.

Father, stop my mates. I'm hunting the bitch that hit on Sebastian while I was ill. I continue running, knowing my father will aid me in my quest for revenge. Nico reaches back out to me as I hear the roar of his dragon.

Consider it done, is all daddy dearest has to say. I know he's probably putting them in an ice bowl to stop them.

Once I realize her scent is weaker, I slow down. Hmm, she's hiding somewhere nearby. I take in the scenery around me; there's a pond and a muddy bog, both of which can hide someone's scent quite easily. Out of the boys, only Sebastian's Lycan catches up to me. Apparently, our bond gifted him my talons.

Aurora, nothing happened. She desired me and I rejected her in front of everyone. Mother removed her from the house. I look at Sebastian as his words attempt to quell my rage. Then, it dawns on me: she's hiding in the bog somewhere. I turn to face Sebastian and start backing up toward the marsh. Oh yes, I'm going to turn Alexis into a bitch-cicle.

So, you expect me to forgive her trespass? To forget she tried to take what's mine when I was unable to fight? How would you feel if a lesser pack mate attempted to take me from you while you healed? I allow Sebastian to feel the pain and anguish I was in over the fact that a pack mate who knew we were mated attempted to take what was mine. I don't hold back; no, not this time. They all need to know just how much I love them and the lengths I will go to defend my claim. Through our bond, I feel understanding, acceptance, and a flood of love from Dom and Jayce. From Sebastian, I feel instant rage pulse through the bond at the idea of another male trying to take me from him. I have him now. His great, black wolven head lowers slightly.

Do what you must, love. I wouldn't let the fucker live if someone tried to take you from us. I dip my head slightly to him before I sink my talons into the mud at the edge of the bog.

I watch as the ice spreads rapidly across the mud and water. Eventually, Alexis flushes from her hiding spot, the look of absolute terror on her face adding to the excitement. My father and the twins eventually catch up to us as the ice begins to blanket everything. Frost clings to my fur and, in spots, small icicles hang off of me. Elsa, eat your fucking heart out!

It's quite entertaining, watching Alexis jump as she tries to escape the ice that's chasing her. When she's finally herded into the deepest part of the bog, I begin to walk out across the ice after her, each step freezing the ice thicker as I approach. I simply crouch down, staring at her before I lunge at her. I open my great wolven maw wide, taking her head into my mouth and crushing her small, human skull like a cantaloupe. I howl my death song into the wind, alerting the pack that justice has been served.

As I return to my mates, the ice slowly recedes behind me. In a sense, I feel better, one less internal threat to worry about. For now, everything is in the clear. Tonight, we feast and celebrate the return of my father. But before anything, I really need a shower and a toothbrush.

We walk in relative silence back to the central part of the compound. I refuse to shift back to my human form. There are still things to be done. As we approach Elena's house, she comes out of her front door and stands on the porch. She smiles gently, noting that my snow-white fur is splattered with the blood of my enemy.

"The ferals need your attention first, Aurora. For everyone's safety, I fear some may need to be put to death. They may be too far lost to their animals." Elena walks with a single hand on my heavily scaled forearm like it is perfectly normal. For us, it is the status quo.

"Mother! She can't go around killing every time things don't immediately fall into place!" Sebastian has no trouble walking around the compound with his dick swinging in the breeze. He also has no sense of self-preservation either.

I stop dead in my tracks, feeling the frost creep across my flesh. I'm already shifted, armored, and in a rather foul mood. Is he seriously going there right now? Elena releases my arm and moves far away from what may end up being an impact zone. I turn my head slowly, a deep guttural growl escaping my lips as I stare at my Lycan mate. He's really trying my patience today. He feels my eyes on him and freezes in place. For once, he actually looks scared as he assesses the situation.

Bad mood? *Check.*

Already shifted? *Check.*

Talons clicking on scaled forearms? *Check.*

The look of actual terror on your alpha mate's face? *Priceless.*

I stand locked in a staring contest with him for what feels like forever. Eventually, he makes a smart move and averts his gaze and lowers his head, then exposes his throat to me. I huff out a large puff of frost before turning and heading to where the ferals are being held. Personally, I think I handled that well. I didn't harm my mate, and I didn't lose my temper. I'll chalk that up as a win.

After some walking, we arrive at the feral's pen. I call it a pen because it's a ten-foot-tall, electrified fence that keeps the ferals isolated from the rest of the pack. Elena moves alongside me and looks over the last fifteen that haven't shifted back to their human form independently. I begin to pace back and forth along the front thirty or so feet of fencing. Let's be honest here, it's not easy to miss an almost nine-foot-tall, snow-white Lycan with dragon scales on its arms and muzzle. The ferals begin to gather, curiosity getting the better of them.

Most of the rogues are smaller than I am and quickly break eye contact. Like always, there's one mother fucker that has to be complicated. He's a rather large male, about the same size as Sebastian's Lycan. The fact that he's feral makes me extra wary about allowing him to continue to live. As soon as I shift back to my human form, he attacks the fence and is hit with ten thousand volts. He flies backward and lands on his ass before getting up to charge again. The stubborn son of a bitch doesn't learn after getting shocked the first time. I stand there, watching him charge at me over and over again until I eventually have enough.

"Let me in there... He's either going to submit or die." My voice is gravelly with the aggressive tones of my wolf.

Reluctantly, Elena opens the gate. Dom and Jayce restrain Sebastian from coming after me. My father uses his ice to hold the male back so I can enter safely. As I walk into the pen, my shift comes quickly; bones and tendons break and realign at an alarming rate. In all these years, I can't remember a transformation as fluid as this one. The male now notices I'm inside the pen and charges, so I evade him and slice his side with my talons. Honestly, I'd prefer to force him to submit rather than to kill him. He's an extraordinarily resilient male, and to lose him would be a detriment to the Lycan kind.

I evade several of his attacks, slicing at his flesh as he goes past me. His blood is making his fur slick and lay flat against his sides, and the scent makes my beast want to go for the kill. At this point, it's becoming more difficult for me to resist the urge to kill him. One last charge and I grip him tightly by the throat, sweep his legs out from under him, then slam him to the ground. Quickly, I kneel on his left arm and grip the right to restrain him. Blood loss has tired him out enough that there's not much fight left in him. Lowering my muzzle, I growl into his face with my canines bared at him.

He's fighting a losing battle for control, and he has a hard time keeping his eyes locked with mine. I press harder on his throat, still growling and snapping at his muzzle. Eventually, I say fuck it and quickly move my taloned hand up his jaw, turning his head to the side just before I sink my canines into his soft flesh. My growls rumble against his delicate throat as the crushing pressure reminds him of the dire situation he's in. Suddenly, he shifts back to his human form and cries and begs me not to kill him. He begins to thank me for saving him from his animal between sobs, explaining he had been trapped as his beast for years. I snort a plume of frost before I release him and stand at my full height.

My eyes lock on the remaining fourteen Lycan ferals in the cage. I stalk forward in full attack mode, growling and baring my canines at them. I'm hoping self-preservation will free their human from the hell they are in. One by one, they drop to one knee and shift back to their human forms. I assess all of them, noting they are all malnourished and worn out. However, after suffering for so long, the packless are finally home. I look back, and Jayce holds out a robe for me to put on. I motion for him to approach, and he moves to my side and flings the robe over my shoulders. I turn away from the ferals to shift back to my human form, my gaze once again falls on the ferals.

"Pledge your life to me and I will fight for you and beside you. We will return to our ancestral home and return it to the glory it once knew in my parent's time." I raise my right arm and show them my brand. My father, who's right behind me, also raises his arm to show off his brand. All at once, they say they swear their lives to me.

Fifteen lives are spared, all because I can show mercy. Hmm… perhaps Sebastian may be right. I ponder this odd occurrence for a bit. I step out of the pen, and each of my mates check me over, making sure I'm okay. I smirk while looking at Sebastian.

"You were right this time, love. Please, don't ever mess with my train of thought before a potential battle again. It may cost me my life one of these times. Doubt is a killer." I stand on my tippy toes and kiss his forehead, and he hugs me tightly to him, whispering he's sorry. We snuggle tightly for several moments before we're joined by my other two mates. I look over at my father and he's smiling at me. I'm happy that he's proud of me and how I was able to handle the ferals. Gently, I break away from my guys and move to hug Elena. "Please find them a place to stay and make sure they are fed." Before taking her phone out to call down to the main camp, Elena nods and kisses my cheek. I turn back to the cage and look at the men standing there.

"Welcome home, my brothers. Please, follow Elena back to the compound and she'll make sure you're fed and clothed." In a sweeping motion, I point at Elena and she waves at the men. "You'll be housed in the meeting hall until the dorm is completed. Take your time to get settled today, and sleep well tonight. Perhaps tomorrow you can help with the construction. You will find a purpose again." I smile after seeing how excited these men are with the prospect of starting over. This is definitely the differ-ence between a tyrant and a benevolent leader. You can tell by the change in their stance that they have never been treated as if they have value. I'll be damned if any of my people ever feel worthless on my watch. My father approaches me once the crowd thins out and my mates are escorting the new pack members home to make sure they are accepted.

CHAPTER 31

Aurora

"You did well today, daughter. You chose to rule with your heart and mind and not just your talons." Nico gives me a hug before we start heading back to the compound behind the others. We walk in relative silence as I'm tucked up under his arm, much like you would do with a child. It's fitting, really; I am his only child. To be quite honest, I'm actually enjoying having one of my birth parents around. Andre and Dimitri are great, but they're not part dragon or Lycan. They did the best they could for me, and I'm forever in their debt. My right hand absently comes up to rub at the implanted scale on my chest.

Nico catches the movement and stops walking. "May I see it? I wish to make sure it took properly." Nico tilts his head as he moves to stand before me.

Slowly, I move my robe to the side so he can examine the scale over my heart. Nico shifts one finger so he can touch the scale with his talon. I watch in wonder as frost coats the tip as soon as he makes contact. Nico smiles, then shifts his finger back to human and touches the scale again. This time, no frost, just pressure where my father is touching. "Very good! Your body has accepted his scale." Nico lets out a short laugh. "I honestly don't remember the last time the scale trading tradition was done. It's been several hundred years, at least. I believe I was only a young boy back then. My own parents didn't share scales since their marriage was political." I'm quite puzzled by what my father tells me.

"Why wouldn't your parents share scales?" I had to ask—there's only so much he's able to teach me while I sleep. He whispers in my mind so the others wouldn't hear. *Scales only live on true mates.* Nico smiles at me, and everything starts to click. My eyes widen, and my mouth drops open from shock. Ladies and gentlemen, I have officially been rendered speechless.

The guys must have sensed my inner turmoil because they all stop dead and look back at me. I keep looking from the scale, then back to my father. Jayce, who was sent back to investigate what's happening, looks at my scale, then over to Nico. Realization dawns on him and, slowly, a smile creeps across those perfectly plump lips of his. Ever so gently, Jayce kisses my lips then looks deeply into my eyes.

"I'll love him like I love you. The others will just have to get over themselves." Jayce winks and kisses me again. He's the perfect mate. Then again, I think he secretly wants another hot male to ogle over. I couldn't help but smile at Jayce. He's definitely the most light-hearted one out of my mates and brings balance to my rage. Without warning him, I run behind him and jump onto his back for a piggyback ride.

"I wish to get a cold drink and rest. Take me home, love! Giddy up!" I reach down and slap his ass, which makes him squeal and laugh.

My omega mate would move Heaven and Earth to make me happy, and my two potential alpha mates would rain fire and brimstone upon the Earth to protect me. One protects my heart, the other two, my body and my life. I wonder what role my dragon mate will play. Sometimes I believe that I see him in my dreams; it's so faint, so distant, I'm not sure it's even real. I lay my head down on my arm as Jayce carries me home. I have a lot to think about over the next few weeks. So much to do, so many Strigoi to kill. What's a girl to do?

We return to the Alpha House, and Jayce makes me comfortable on the porch swing. While I watch Dom and Sebastian supervise the ferals' care and the dorm's construction, Jayce disappears into the house. Housing here on the compound was insufficient, considering the size of the pack we're building.

Sebastian, make sure the dorm has a central kitchen and individual bedrooms with bathrooms for the single males. Sebastian makes eye contact with me as he listens to what I have to say. Like most packs, the male to female ratio is completely screwed. Not many males are willing to share their females, but from what I can see, there are more and more menage pairings than before. Perhaps my guys and I are setting a positive example and breaking enough barriers that others will follow in.

Way ahead of you, love. I'm putting a gathering place with a large TV in the central kitchen, so no one feels isolated. I smile and nod while listening to Sebastian. His idea will be a tremendous help as we integrate new members into the pack. These were his people long before they became mine, so he knows what they need far better than I do.

Jayce appears at my side with a tray of drinks and hands me my pomegranate juice with vodka—he knows me too well. I watch my gentle mate go and offer our other two mates cold drinks before he comes back to sit with me. He sits on the far side of the swing and pats his lap, offering it to me. I quickly finish my drink and move to lay my head on his lap. Jayce gently runs his fingers through my hair, working out the knots. Perhaps a nap will do me some good. After all, I've had quite a busy day today.

I don't know how long I napped for, but I wake up feeling refreshed and with my head still in Jayce's lap. I slowly roll over on my side so I'm facing Jayce, and I notice that he's asleep, leaning his head against the back of the swing. He looks so peaceful; his face is so angelic and innocent. Slowly, I rise from his lap and move so I can appreciate the handsome man before me. Yeah, it looks a bit creepy to an outsider, but my pack knows that I watch over my mates closely. They are my greatest treasure. For some reason that word resonates with me. I brush the thought aside before going into the house to retrieve my favorite blanket, which I use to gently cover Jayce.

Once more I go into the house and pull out my guitar and amp. I sit down next to Jayce and begin to play Pink Floyd's "Wish You Were Here." Technically, it should be an acoustic set, but I'm a bit too metal for that. Dimitri used to play a lot of Pink Floyd for me when I couldn't sleep, so I guess you can say I get my love of music from him.

Slowly, the pack begins to gather once they hear the melody coming from my guitar. I know there are dark days ahead of us, and I know the days of peace are limited now, so I do my best to enjoy every second. Just as Sebastian and Dom approach, Jayce wakes up. I switch it up a bit and start playing Metallica's

"Nothing Else Matters." Although I sing it for the pack to enjoy, it's more so meant for my mates.

I make sure to hold eye contact with each one of them. I'm not like Jayce who wears his heart on his sleeve; I keep my feelings in, tight and protected. However, before this battle from Hell, my men need to know and feel what I'm feeling. I play the song in its entirety, all six minutes and twenty-something seconds of it. At the conclusion of the song, the guys swarm me. I feel the love they have for me, and I revel in it. I also fear for them with the battle to come.

In the distance, I spot Elena and my dad walking hand in hand toward the lake. It's about time both of them find happiness. Jayce is the first to notice that I'm staring at the hillside. He smiles and lets a soft *aw* escape his lips. Unfortunately, his cute reaction draws both Dom's and Sebastian's attention. Dom simply shrugs his shoulders and heads back to work, while Sebastian looks like he's beside himself.

He motions toward the hill and shouts, "Our parents! What the actual fuck!" He drags his hand down his face, then looks to me to do something. I can't help but start laughing. I'm not bothered by them being together, but apparently my big, bad—almost—alpha mate can't handle it. I give Sebastian a quick hug and pat his back.

"Don't worry, Bash. Dad's castrated, so there's no fear of any pups being born." I kiss Sebastian's cheek, then bound down the stairs and go for a walk to check out the new dorm the guys have been working on. I turn back briefly and the look of shock on Sebastian's face is really worth it. Dom bounds down the stairs and jogs to catch up with me. He gently takes my hand as we enter the building. He takes the time to explain the upgrades and little, special features it has. It's everything I could have wanted for the single males and more: private quarters for sleeping, a large living room, and an open kitchen design.

"I'm so proud of you guys! Everyone has done a wonderful job." I kiss Dom on the cheek as we finish the tour. Since Dires are apparently quite well off, Dom and Jayce had extra funds to go into the project, and all of the planning fell on Dom.

We continue our walk back to the Alpha House. My throne has become the focal point of the main hall and today, I find flowers left on the table to the right of it. I can tell it's the pack children because there is a single flower from each child—about nine or ten flowers left for me. It brings a smile to my face, thinking about how thoughtful these little ones are. We run into one of the housekeepers, Anna, and her new baby, Lia, in her arms. I've never seen a baby before, so I'm quite curious. Dom looks at me, puzzled.

"Babe, you act like you've never seen a baby before." I remain staring at the little one, then I turn to him.

"I've only ever seen them on TV. They never look this tiny." I lean down to sniff at the baby , and its eyes open. I pull my head back quickly because I wasn't prepared for the baby to look at me.

"Would you like to hold her, My Queen?" Anna asks, offering her precious child to me. I look at Anna then back to Dom, tears threatening to fall.

I don't know what to do. I don't want to break it, I say to Dom through our bond. Understanding flitters across his features as he guides me to sit on my throne. Gently, Dom takes the baby from Anna, then comes to me next. I watch in amazement at how he looks so perfect holding the baby.

"Hold your arms like I am. Trust me, you'll be fine." I mimic the position that Dom's arms are in and he gently rests the child in my arms. I'm honestly frightened I'm going to accidentally hurt the baby. My other mates arrive quickly, sensing my anxiety and fear. They suddenly stop, watching me nuzzle the baby I am holding.

Lia grips a lock of my hair and pulls hard. I can't help but smile at this little being's strength; she dares to pull the alpha's hair. I nuzzle her again and make a low, comforting rumble at her. I look up to my mates, my wolf and I in agreement.

"I want one." I immediately drop my eyes back down to Lia when I hear the thud of a body hitting the floor. Sebastian passed the fuck out. I guess he can't handle the day today; way too many changes in such a short amount of time. The twins take this opportunity to approach and stare at the child together.

"Soon as the war is over you can have as many as you want," Dom proclaims. Deep down, I know that's the smartest course of action. I keep sniffing and nuzzling the baby; she's such a precious gift. Fertility is becoming rare among the Lycans; to birth a daughter is nothing short of a miracle. I carefully shift my arm under Lia and pluck a single scale before shifting back. I look at Anna and hold the scale out to her.

"Give this to Lia when she's old enough to understand the boon I have given her. I will come for her no matter where or when. That is my promise to this baby." I lean down and kiss Lia's forehead before offering her to her mother. "She is the first daughter born in a long time. She has my protection." Anna, practically in tears, looks from me to her baby. I have a gut feeling that she will be pivotal to the pack one day. I look up to see my father and mother-in-law have returned. Apparently, they witnessed the whole exchange.

"Child, are you okay?" My father asks softly. I know why he's asking; I feel the power of my beast pulsing. She tapped into some part of the dragon's ability that she can't access alone. I snuggle into my father's embrace and look up to him.

"I held the baby and felt that she has a part in the pack's future. I know it sounds strange, but my beast just knows." I search my father's features for answers. A slow smile creeps over his lips, and he nods slowly. Gently, my father kisses my forehead, then walks me back over to my mates.

"The first time I met Dominik, I knew he would play a role in your future. Our dragon side is very intuitive like that. I suspect once you mate with the prince, your dragon side will become better balanced with your Lycan side." My father briefly hugs me before letting go. I walk over to a prone Sebastian and decide to sit on his chest and stare down at him.

"Hey, Bash!" Quickly, I poke his chest several times before I receive a response. He's still kind of pale, definitely looking off-kilter a bit. "What happened to you?" Dom helps me off Sebastian, then passes me over to Jayce so he can help Sebastian stand up again. A quick look over and Sebastian is back to normal.

"Ever experience déjà vu? I mean, really experience it. I saw you, Aurora, with a baby nursing on each breast. One with white hair and one with black; one boy and one girl. It was really fucking surreal." I blink several times, looking at Sebastian, then back to my father. Nico walks closer to the group.

"I see Aurora's dragon side is gifting everyone with visions. It's a rather unique situation." The weight of my father's words hit me like a freight train. My hand flies up to the prince's scale on my chest. Gently, I rub the scale, tracing the unique shape of it against my soft flesh. I have been feeling slightly different since it was implanted on me; a little stronger, a little faster. But the most significant change I've noticed is that I'm not as quick to go straight to murder anymore. My gaze lands on my father, and he's smiling at me. He raises his finger and taps on his temple. Apparently, I've come to the same conclusion as he has. My eyes roam over my other mates, slowly assessing them one by one. Other than Sebastian, no one else has had any noticeable changes. I'll have to keep a very close eye on them. I love them too much to make them worry.

CHAPTER 32

Dominik

Watching Aurora with the baby and seeing the look of wonder on her face made my heart melt. I feel her desire for a family through the bond, along with another entity entirely. It's faint, but it's there. Just like her father pointed out, I believe it's the prince as well.

Sebastian and I have been working on training the Lycan troops day and night. We run drills and shift to fight against each other so they can see the difference in the species' approach in battle. Dimitri, against Aurora's wishes, has been fighting with the groups, so we are prepared for the Polar Bears. In order for him to train the Dires before they head to Siberia with us, I'll need to sneak him out of the compound later today and put him on a plane to head to my brother. I don't know how anyone thinks going against Aurora's wishes is a good thing though. I mean, seriously? Do we all have a freaking death wish?

I never thought I'd say this, but the ferals are a godsend. Their animals are so primal that they can outlast the regular Lycans. It's definitely something to study for the future. I text my brother, Alex, to catch him up on all that's been going on here. I send him the videos of Aurora opening the present and the placement of the scale. My phone immediately blew up since I'm now apparently in a group chat with my brother and some guy named Ellis. Ellis is beyond excited and can't wait to tell his friend the news. They are supposed to meet up before the attack and plan out what they can do to help. I remind Alex about sending Dimitri down later today. He, too, is concerned for Dimitri's health and doesn't want to face Aurora's wrath. Honestly, no one wants to face Aurora when she's in rage mode. I text over the supply request that Dimitri has for training.

What used to be the arena is now a full-blown training ground. Alex is trying to erase the years of fear the arena held by turning it into a positive place for our people. One of the most significant moves my brother pulled off, with the help of a video from Aurora, was the ending of the forced matings. It freed so many females from matings they didn't want anything to do with. The females were moved into a protected wing of the den and guarded twenty-four-seven. Several males have been locked up and await Aurora's sentences. Think of it as death row, where the death isn't a threat; it's a promise.

Apparently, my pacing has drawn my mate's attention. I look up to see Aurora, standing there and holding Lia again. I wonder to myself if Anna knows Aurora has her baby. "Hello, love." I gently kiss her cheek. "Does Anna know you have Lia?" Aurora smirks at me, then kisses the baby's forehead.

"Yes, she said she needed to ride the pony. It's been a while… whatever that means." Aurora shrugs and continues to rock the baby in her arms.

"Um, babe? It means she went to go fuck her mate." Aurora makes the *oh* face, then laughs. "Anyway, I've been talking to my brother. We are doing well with preparations for the journey. Alex feels the Dires would benefit from seeing Dimitri's bear and learning how one moves." Aurora stops rocking Lia and stares at me, her eyes churning liquid mercury. Oh god, I pissed her off. Not good. Aurora cracks her neck and takes a deep breath.

"I understand where you're coming from, Dom. I really do. But I worry about Dimitri's health and what the extra strain may do to him. I know he's willing to die for me." Tears break and roll down her cheek. I see Sebastian and Jayce come out of the dorm. I raise my hand to stop them, and thankfully, they listen. "Is this what he truly wants, Dom?" As Aurora looks up at me, Dimitri walks up behind her and kisses the top of her head.

"Aurora, I'll be fine. I've always done what's best for the defense of the family, haven't I?" Aurora nods slowly, with that innocent little girl look going on. "I'll be fine, sweetheart. Besides, now that you've ascended, I think you can kick my ass." Dimitri smirks at her and gently caresses her cheek, forcing her to look deep into his eyes. Aurora whines softly as her eyes flicker between human and liquid mercury. Heartache echoes through the bond, almost like she's already in mourning for Dimitri.

"Be safe, old man. I love you!" She turns her head briefly and kisses the palm of his hand before backing away. "Train the Dires well. I don't want any losses on our side if we can help it." Lightly she taps her chin as she ponders what to say next. "Remember, there will also be dragons. Perhaps, you can take my father with you so he can work with the Dires as well." I could practically see the gears turning in Aurora's mind as she sorts out what needs to be done.

"Make sure you and father leave Sebastian and Dom a list of what needs to be worked on in your absence. In about three weeks, we'll be flying the Lycans to Germany and the Dires here. The second dorm will be completed before their arrival." Aurora's eyes turn toward me, and she notices I'm recording her directions. She gives me a curt nod. "Did I miss anything, Dom?"

I answer her from behind the phone. "No, love. I believe everything is sorted. I'll send this video to Alex and arrange transport for everyone." Aurora shakes her head no at me. I couldn't help but raise an eyebrow at her.

"No offense, love, but Jayce does much better at arranging these kinds of things. You get back to training the others, and if you're a good boy, I'll give you a massage later." Aurora places a hand on my forearm and kisses my cheek before walking away with Lia.

"Shit, that went better than I expected." I look over to Dimitri. Damn, that bear is a fucking huge man. "Well, we have our marching orders straight from the princess herself. We better hop to it before she hands that baby back to Anna." Dimitri shakes his head at me and I see sadness briefly cross his features. I know the future isn't certain for anyone, but they are living on borrowed time for him and Andre.

Slowly, I move through the compound, watching all the citizens move about without a care in the world. I kind of miss those days, to be honest, but back in those days, I didn't have Aurora. So yeah, I wouldn't change it for anything, as much as I miss the simple life. In my wandering, I find Aurora leaning over Jayce's shoulder as he works on his laptop. It's nice to finally see my brother happy for once in his life.

Time seems to move in slow motion as I watch the events unfold before me. Sinclair comes out of nowhere, dagger in hand and heading toward Aurora. I start to scream when Aurora's sixth sense seems to kick in. She shifts rapidly to her beast, so fast it's terrifying. The blade hits the armored scales on her forearms and glances off, causing no damage. Aurora's taloned hand instinctually grips Sinclair by his throat and lifts him off the ground. He's kicking and thrashing, trying to pry her hand from around his throat. Aurora's Lycan beast walks forward with Sinclair dangling in the air like it's nothing.

Everyone starts gathering as soon as Jayce starts screaming at the top of his lungs, cursing at his ex-lover. I've never seen my brother so angry. Yellow-green toxin drips from his canines as he screams at Sinclair. Fuck, Jayce is partially shifted, flailing his arms around. Wow, Hell has officially frozen over—Jayce is in a rage. All it took was him to find his mate and for her life to be threatened. Aurora throws Sinclair into the practice ring and stares him down. Jayce prepares to charge in, but Aurora grabs him and shakes her massive head no. Jayce only nods and steps back.

"Still doing the mix-breed bitch's bidding? She's going to bring death to all of you. Kill her now, and the Strigoi will forget this camp exists!" There's the reason for his boldness. Apparently, Tomas found the weakest link in the Dire camp and it's Sinclair. He hasn't realized he just signed his death warrant, and no one here will stand against Aurora.

Sinclair, in a move of absolute stupidity, shifts, and charges at Aurora—our mate looks positively bored until he moves. Sinclair leaps into the air, his mouth wide open and toxin dripping from his mouth. He latches onto Aurora's armored forearm, attempting to bite through the dragon scale. You can see the look of *you've got to be fucking kidding me* on Aurora's wolf's face as she watches Sinclair attempt to harm her. Suddenly she whips her arm up, then drops to one knee as she brings the arm with Sinclair on it down hard and fast. The thud of his body and the audible crunch of bones breaking sends shivers down my spine—Sinclair's smoke-gray wolf whines, its body broken on the ground and unable to stand or move.

Aurora shifts back to her human form and stands over Sinclair, her head tilting from left to right. Her eyes lift to Jayce as if waiting for his judgment. Before he's even at Aurora's side, Jayce shifts into his enormous black Dire Wolf.

She threads her fingers through his thick fur and says, "I can end him for you, love. You don't have to do this." Shockingly, Jayce growls and snaps at Aurora, making her jump back a bit. Her eyes widen in shock staring at her gentle mate.

Jayce suddenly lunges at Sinclair and bites into his throat, starting to thrash his head violently from side to side. The sound of flesh tearing and tendons popping is almost sickening; chunks of flesh and blood spray out from Sinclair's throat. Eventually, Jayce severs Sinclair's head from his body, tendons and blood vessels twitch as if still alive as they dangle freely beneath his skull. He bites into Sinclair's fur one last time to lift his head up and carry it to Aurora. He drops the bloody mass at her feet, then stares up at her. Aurora touches the offered head, then wraps her arms around Jayce's thick neck, hugging his wolf tightly. I've never seen my brother so violent, but then again, he's never had someone he's loved so much to fight for. Aurora slowly stands and grips the fur of Sinclair's head to pick it up.

"I'm going to go take care of Jayce. He needs me." Aurora's tone rings with sorrow and heartbreak. Watching her sweet, innocent Jayce kill someone he once loved must have hurt something in her. I'll talk to her about this later to see where she's at emotionally. I know my brother isn't in a good place either, having to kill an old love to save his mate. It's a sight to see: Aurora holding Sinclair's head in one hand and her other hand on Jayce's back. It's confusing to feel Jayce's anger and Aurora's sorrow. It's very odd for the roles to be reversed with them. I move over to where Sebastian and Dimitri are standing. We're still shocked over what we just witnessed.

"Dom, what got into Jayce? That was way out of character for him." Dimitri says. I know Sebastian feels what I am, but Dimitri can't.

"I'm guessing watching Aurora with Lia made something snap in him. He's always loved and wanted children of his own. I guess the threat to Aurora's life and the possibility of him losing the chance at pups pushed him over the edge." I shrug my shoulders. After all, I'm only speculating at the moment.

"I can see that," Dimitri says, not missing a beat. "He constantly worries he's not strong enough to protect his mate. He completely forgets he has the toxic bite that, by itself, makes him lethal." The matter-of-fact way Dimitri says it is kind of frightening.

"Sebastian, can you do me a solid and drive Nico and Dimitri to the airport? I really need to make sure Jayce is okay with everything that just happened." Sebastian nods and claps Dimitri on the back. They head toward Elena's house to collect Nico. I head back to the Alpha House and go straight to Jayce's room, and I'm not particularly shocked to find it empty. I arrive at Aurora's room, where I find candles lit and soft music playing. Then I hear the water running in the shower. I decide not to waste any time and strip before I enter.

Slowly, I push the door open to find Aurora washing my brother under the hot water from the twin shower heads. Jayce has his forearms on the tile, letting the water run down his back in streams. Aurora is gently washing every inch of his body, and it's probably the sexiest thing I've ever witnessed. Aurora slides down between Jayce and the wall before leaning forward to lick his cock from base to tip. My own cock is rigid and pulsing as I watch our mate lick my brother's. The soft, pleased rumbles of her beast echo off the tiles, calling to the more primal side of me.

Jayce lowers his left hand to grip Aurora's hair as she sucks his cock into her mouth. I watch her head bob slowly as Jayce gently thrusts his hips forward, fucking her mouth. I feel my balls draw up tight from listening to the moans escaping my brother's mouth. When Jayce finally comes, he roars out his release while Aurora slurps down every drop greedily.

Without skipping a beat, Jayce lifts Aurora up, quickly hooking his arm under her left leg and holds it up before he thrusts his cock into her. I gasp at the force he drives his cock into Aurora and watch as my brother fucks our mate hard against the tiles. The wet, slapping skin mixed with their moans... I'm damn near ready to blow my load without being touched. Aurora screams out Jayce's name as she comes hard, and Jayce's first instinct is to bite her shoulder, marking her as his again. His bite causes Aurora to come once again, only this time, she bites him back. I honestly can't help it; I blow my load like a randy teenager. I moan through my orgasm as strings of cum coat the nearby wall. Jayce and Aurora slowly turn to look at me, smiling.

"Um, hi? I just wanted to, um, make sure you're okay and stuff." Gods, I sound like a bloody idiot. Jayce slowly lowers Aurora to the floor and waits for her to regain balance.

"Learn anything, Dom?" Jayce says without missing a beat. He walks over and grabs a towel for Aurora and one for himself.

"When the hell did you get aggressive, Jayce?" I was kind of speechless at the moment. My usually soft-spoken brother has developed a set of brass balls. Aurora decides to answer as she walks toward me.

"You should know by now, Dom. I love it when you guys get all dominant with me. I don't always like being in control." She stands on her tippy toes and kisses my cheek. "To be perfectly honest, I kind of want a twin sammich before bed. That is, if you two are up for it?" Aurora runs her hand over my abs as she passes me, heading back to her bedroom. Jayce simply starts laughing and follows after her.

"You heard our woman, she wants a twin sammich. Let's give it to her!" Jayce briefly grips my shoulder as he moves past me. I swear to the gods, I'm in the fucking Twilight Zone.

I walk into the bedroom to find Aurora already sliding Jayce's cock back into her waiting pussy. How the actual fuck does he still have an erection? I move onto the bed behind Aurora, and she sits up to lean back against my chest. She holds out a bottle of lube.

"You do know what you're doing, right, Dom?" I blink at Aurora as I take the lube from her.

I place a hand between her shoulder blades and push her down onto my brother. Then I lube up her rosette and work the tight muscles until they loosen up. Jayce does his part by distracting her while I stretch her to fit me. I slowly insert one, then two fingers into her tight ass. Oh, my gods, she is going to feel amazing when I finally get there. Several minutes pass before I lube my cock up real good. I squirt an extra glob of lube right onto her rosette. Slowly, I push the head of my cock past that tight muscular ring. I pause for a few moments and rub Aurora's lower back to get her to relax more. Jayce reaches forward and grips

Aurora's ass cheeks, spreading her wide for me. I push forward steadily, until I'm fully seated in our mate's tight ass. It feels like fucking heaven.

She's so tight and full, especially feeling my brother's cock in her pussy. We all release a sigh before Aurora starts trying to move.

"If someone doesn't fucking move soon, I'm going to get pissed off." I can't tell if she is joking, so I pull back first. When I seat myself deep within her, Jayce pulls out. It takes several moments before Jayce and I find our rhythm. Aurora seems to let out one constant moan as she nips at Jayce's chest and my forearms. I lean forward and bite her shoulder blade and release a low growl. Aurora quickly stops her biting nonsense, allowing Jayce and I to pick up the pace a bit. We're thrusting in and out as fast as we can until Aurora's orgasm rips through her. Her muscles milk our cocks hard in a rhythmic, pulsating motion. It takes all the willpower I could muster to not cum with her, and I see my brother is fighting the same battle.

I decide to switch it up and pull Aurora up to me and off Jayce, then I lay down with her back flush with my chest. Jayce rises up on his knees and thrusts back into our mate's soaking wet pussy. I wrap an arm above and below Aurora's chest, holding her tight to me as I thrust up into her ass. Jayce and I find our rhythm again, but this time much harder than before. My balls are drawn up tight, and I feel my mating knot starting to form. I look up to see Jayce's wolf present in his eyes, and his thrusts are getting as erratic as mine. Aurora cries out as her orgasm crashes over, and like a chain reaction, Jayce and I cum within seconds of each other. Both of us bite Aurora on her shoulders again, sending her into a second orgasm.

Several moments passed before Jayce and I release Aurora. We lick her wounds clean before moving her so she's more comfortable. Jayce gets up to grab wet washcloths for us while I merely stare in wonder at our beautiful mate. Aurora is such a powerful, unique being, yet she submits here in private. It's a thing of beauty to think she trusts us enough to release control, if even for a little while. Gently, I run my fingers through Aurora's hair, untangling the knots we made tonight. This was the first time I have ever shared anyone with my brother, and I get the feeling tonight will not be the last. Jayce returns with some washcloths, and we clean ourselves up first before we consider waking Aurora.

"I think we should do what we can without waking her. I'd like to keep my balls attached to my body," Jayce says with a smirk. Aurora has been a significant influence on Jayce, she's really brought him out of his shell.

"That would be our safest move. I think she's going to be asleep for a while," I say, nodding slowly. We take turns lifting Aurora's limbs while we clean her. It kind of reminds me of that game, Minesweeper, we used to play as kids—one wrong move and we'll have one pissed off she-wolf on our hands. To be honest though, I think a minefield would be safer than our sleeping mate. Once I'm sure Aurora is adequately taken care of, I motion for Jayce to follow me out of the room.

CHAPTER 33
Dominik

We head to the study across the hall from Aurora's room, that way we're close enough in case she wakes up early. I move to where the maps are spread out behind the desk and consider what lies ahead of us.

"There's going to be a lot of casualties going across the Bering Land Bridge," I state very matter-of-fact. I can't candy-coat this at all. It's going to get ugly real quick, and not much can be done to stop it.

Jayce looks up to me as he speaks. "Have we heard more about this prince? I feel a faint presence, but I can't put my finger on it." So, I'm not the only one sensing the new entity. I release a measured breath before texting Sebastian to join us.

"I know what you mean, Jayce. I just messaged Sebastian to join us. He's been bonded to Aurora the longest, so he would know better than me." Speak of the devil, that smirking, arrogant asshole is now standing in the doorway with his arms crossed over his chest.

"Ask, and ye shall receive. What's the secret meeting for?" Sebastian closes the door behind him, then flops into the chair behind the desk and hangs his legs over the arm.

"Have you been feeling another presence beside us?" I get straight to the point. If Aurora didn't love this fucker and have that "no hitting the other mates" rule, I'd love to beat his ass. The arrogant fuck acts like he's in charge when Aurora isn't present. I can't wait until the day someone bigger and worse than him knocks him down a peg or two. Sebastian quickly sits up and looks between Jayce and me.

"Yeah, it's different than when she acknowledged you two. This feels stronger, almost more primal." He shakes his head, looking at his hands. "Whatever it is, it's fucking strong." Sebastian looks worried, which is a first.

Nico's voice fills the hall after apparently hearing part of our conversation. "The *it* in question is an Ice and Gold Dragon mix. Alaric's mother is a Golden Dragon, and his father is an Ice Dragon, both of which are very powerful in their own rights." Nico breathes in deeply before continuing. "One sides with justice, the other with his horde and power. I, being an Ice Dragon, know the temptation of treasure. Treasure, when it's physical, can corrupt—in this case, Alaric's father." Nico strides into the room and shoos Sebastian from the office chair to sit behind the desk.

"If you three are starting to feel the prince, imagine what Aurora is feeling." He tilts his head to the side, looking at each of us in turn. "She has his scale implanted in her flesh." Nicodeamus taps the area over his heart. "He will always know where she is and how to find her, no matter the distance. Until they are mated, it will be faint, almost ghost-like—a whisper in the back of her mind, and his." A sly smirk creeps across Nicodeamus's lips as he looks at us.

"Be prepared for a battle of wills between Aurora and the prince, as they are both true-born alphas, unlike you three." His smirk turns into a sadistic grin as his eyes lock with Sebastian to drive his next point home. "Sebastian, you and Dominik are maybe betas in the pack; you'll never achieve full alpha because your animal will put survival over dominance." His almost feral look softens as his gaze turns to my twin. "Jayce, you already know you're an omega, and you're fine with your role. You are the safest of the three when it comes to the prince's arrival." Nico, with his ancient wisdom, literally told us that Sebastian and I may be fucked. We will not stand a chance against the prince in a physical battle. Kind of a bummer to hear, but at least Nico put Sebastian in his fucking place. I start to pace the room a bit, pondering everything that Nico said.

"So, if I understand this correctly, if Aurora's in a very high-stress situation, she may act like a homing beacon for the prince during the battle? Similar to how the guys and I sense Aurora's distress?" I stop my pacing to look at Nico. I've put a lot of thought into this, and I want to make sure my theory is sound.

"It's similar, but not the same. A dragon's bond is blood deep— spiritual, in a sense. It transcends time and space; distance means nothing to a dragon's bond." Nicodeamus sighs softly before stroking his beard a moment. "As Aurora grew and her beast became stronger, the easier it was for me to dream walk and teach her things in her sleep. I believe in time, the prince may be able to reach out to Aurora." My body tenses, and Nico holds up his hand to stop me from speaking. "However, we won't know how powerful he truly is until he attaches her scale to himself." Nico taps his index finger on his chin, then comes up with an idea. He rises up from the chair and goes to the lamp, shifting his index finger and using the talon to cut through half the electric cord. He bends the halves apart, so the power never passes through.

"Okay, so to make it simple, here's an example: the solid wire is Aurora, having attached the prince's scale to herself. The broken wire represents the prince on one side and Aurora's scale on the other side. Until he implants the scale, the connection is half-assed. Once he implants the scale..." Nico pushes the halves together and the light blazes to life. Across all our faces, realization dawns. Their connection may be the strongest out of all of ours. Sebastian seems to be taking this the hardest as he begins to pace the room, stress pouring off him. Besides, when we almost lost Aurora, I've never seen Sebastian look so terrified.

Suddenly, the door explodes, sending splinters and chunks of oak flying everywhere. Aurora, in all her hybrid glory, is ready for battle. A low growl rumbles in her chest as frost coats her fur and yellow-green toxin drips from her canines. Her beast looks around the room, talons clicking together as her mercury orbs search for the threat. Apparently, Sebastian's stress triggered Aurora's shift and attack mode.

"My love, it's okay, there's no threat. We're sorry Sebastian's anxiety woke you up like that." Jayce approaches Aurora with his hands held in a placating manner, trying to soothe her enough to shift back. Aurora shakes her massive wolven head, snarling before slowly regaining her human form. Jayce quickly removes his T-shirt and gives it to Aurora. Reluctantly, Aurora pulls the T-shirt over her head and stares Sebastian down.

"What the fuck are you drama queening about now? I was sleep-ing, fucking sleeping soundly until your dramatic pansy-ass woke me the fuck up. What's got your man panties in a bunch?" Jayce and I give each other the *oh shit* look before watching the train wreck that's about to happen. Don't get me wrong, I love Sebastian like only a bond-mate could, but he's an entitled, royal pain in the ass.

"Drama queening? What the fuck, Aurora! You're not about to be usurped by an unknown male who's not even here yet!" Sebastian flails his arms like a girl on the flag squad at a football game. Nico is trying like hell not to laugh out loud, but it's challenging, to be honest. Sebastian is being ridiculous.

"Usurped? Who the fuck do you think you are, the fucking king? The only king in this pack, is my father. Goddess fucking help me, if you ever try to usurp him—mate or not—I'll kill you myself." She growls and freezes the ground around her as she stares Sebastian down. Now is not the time to interject, but of course, Jayce does.

"Love? I think Sebastian is trying to say that we feel the Dragon Prince, even though he's not here, and we know you must too." He raises his eyebrows and smiles, putting his dimples she loves so much on full display. "We're just concerned since all of our bonds are so new. Some of us suck at expressing our feelings though." Jayce took that moment to smirk at Sebastian as Aurora steps up and snuggles into his side. She holds onto Jayce tightly and kisses his throat before looking at Sebastian and me.

"Guys, I love you, even when some of you drive me bloody mad with your insecurities. I feel the prince, but he's like a whisper in the back of my mind. I feel his anxiety, like something is going on behind the scenes." Aurora raises her hand to rub the prince's scale lightly. "Jayce, Dom, has Alex said anything new? Something's up. I just know it." Her eyes turn liquid mercury as she looks between all of us, and I watch Nico's eyes also change to that of his dragon. I'm not sure what's going on, but it has their animals on edge. While I text our brother, Jayce gently runs his fingers through Aurora's hair.

Motherfucker, something is up. My phone blows up with messages from Alex as he fills me in on everything that's going on. I hand the phone over to Nico so he can catch up. I watch his eyes fly over the messages, then he hands the phone over to Aurora and leaves. Aurora nods along as her eyes pass over the screen, then she hits call and starts pacing.

"Alex, it's Aurora... Yeah, I'm good. I see we need to adjust our tactics. My father and Dimitri will be there tonight. Yeah, I saw that. Hopefully the prince receives the skull sooner than later. I may need to summon him when the battle starts." Aurora goes silent as she switches to video call to show Alex the map. Her fingers glide over the map as she explains her plan for the attack. Her brows knit tightly together. "Yes, I know there's going to be dragons! I'll handle them, and you train the Dires to evade them. I'll bring the fuckers down." She sighs softly.

Through the bond, I can feel the idea of killing possible kin is tearing her apart. "I will do what I have to, to keep our people safe. Get a hold of Ellis; he needs to get to Alaric and secure a dragon force. The bears may or may not be enough." Aurora looks exhausted—more emotionally and mentally than physically.

Possibly as his smartest move, Sebastian goes over to hold her. Aurora rests her head on his chest and sighs again, still listening to my brother. "I get that, Alex. We are going to be fucking lambs to slaughter if Alaric doesn't bring reinforcements with him. My father can't fucking fly, and he's going to be a fucking sitting duck. If you think I'm going to lose him now, you're sadly mistaken!" Aurora hands the phone over to me and starts crying on Sebastian's chest. Okay, this now ranks in the top five scariest Aurora moments on record. Aurora plus emotions usually equals rage and destruction.

"Jayce, can you please take Dimitri and Nico to the airport? I'm currently being held hostage by a potential nuke." Sebastian kisses the crown of Aurora's head and holds her tightly. He's correct in thinking this can go bad really quick. I watch Jayce nod and kiss Aurora on the cheek before leaving on his mission. I motion for Sebastian to follow me. He carefully scoops Aurora up and carries her bridal style down to the kitchen. I decide that pouring her a glass of wine and giving her ice cream is probably an excellent idea to help calm her down.

Aurora won't release Sebastian for anything, like he's her own personal woobie. Watching him try to maneuver so he can sit with her on the stool is comical. However, I'm not used to seeing our mate in this state. She is by no means defenseless. Sebastian picks up the spoon and starts feeding Aurora the ice cream. Hesitantly, Aurora takes the ice cream from the spoon, and her eyes slowly fade back to their normal steel grey. Softly, she smiles at us and starts feeding herself instead.

"I'm sorry I lost it, guys. I don't want anyone to die because of me. I just got all of you, and I'm not even remotely close to consider being ready to lose any of you." Aurora sighs softly, then looks between the two of us.

"I'm almost thinking a small force will be easier to hide than a large mass of black bodies moving across the tundra. Number wise, it puts us at a disadvantage, but it may give us the element of surprise." Aurora taps the spoon to her plump lips, pondering what move to make next.

"Dom, get your brother to put together a group of the absolute best fighters in the pack. We're going to go in hard and fast. We'll break into alpha and bravo teams and converge on the Polar Bears. I'll run straight up the middle since my white fur will cloak me the longest. I'll head straight for the leader and rip his head off," Aurora says, so matter-of-fact it's almost scary.

Sometimes, her gaining Sebastian's battle strategy is a blessing and a curse all in the same breath. I don't like the idea of her charging alone into battle while we attack from different sides. The Polar Bears also have the white fur advantage as well.

I began to pace as I notice Sebastian grab the notepad on the island and draw a mini version of the large map we have upstairs. Aurora looks as well, making small adjustments to his drawing. "Her plan is solid, Dom. The only problem I see is that the Polar Bears and Ice Dragons are also white. It will be tough for us to spot them in time."

"Gee, ya think?" I say under my breath. Captain Obvious strikes again. I roll my eyes. Seriously, does Sebastian think we're stupid? With the way he speaks to everyone, he must think we are at times. Aurora spots the faces I'm making while Sebastian is busy. Aurora rolls her eyes at me, then slides off Sebastian's lap. He's so engrossed in what he's doing, it barely registers that she moved. Aurora goes behind Sebastian and starts making some of the silliest faces I've ever seen her make.

Sebastian must sense something is up because he turns to catch Aurora sticking her tongue out at him. He quickly grabs her tongue between his index and middle finger and growls at her. Aurora simply smirks at him. I look down to see she has shifted her hand, and her talons are millimeters away from his cock and balls. Realizing his family jewels are endangered, he quickly releases her tongue and backs away. Aurora clicks her talons together and looks them over before shifting her hand back to normal.

"Just remember, love, you may be my first mate, but I am still alpha." She pats his cheek and smiles at him. Aurora winks at me, then grabs her empty bowl and dumps it in the sink. I could tell she has a lot on her mind by the way she stared at Sebastian's drawing. Just about any way we slice this mission, there's going to be a high body count.

"Sebastian, I want to go swimming at the lake. Mind taking me?" Aurora smiles when Sebastian agrees. Slowly, she stands before me and gives me a soft kiss—one that could set your loins ablaze.

Gently, she rests her forehead against mine and says softly through our bond, *Don't fear, my love. Call your brother. Make the arrangements. All will work out.*" Her terse sentences don't fill me with comfort. They do, however, give me something to do while they are off swimming.

CHAPTER 34

Elena

Jayce is the one who comes to gather up Dimitri and Nico. I give Jayce a questioning look and he only laughs. "Aurora had a mini-meltdown, and Sebastian volunteered to remain at ground zero if she loses her temper." He shrugs and goes back to loading the luggage into the car's trunk. "Come to think of it, Elena, he's been pissing her off more often than not lately. Do you know why he's pushing her buttons?"

It's times like this when I wish the boys thought more with their heads than with their hearts. I know Jayce means well, but if looks could kill, Sebastian would be dead. To be honest, I'm not sure which of her two father figures would do it first.

"I believe, Jayce, it's because he's afraid of losing Aurora, be it in the war or because of this new male. His dad wasn't exactly the best example of how to be a good mate and father." I lower my head for a moment and give it a brief shake. Nico is by my side in a second, lending me his strength. His arm bands around me, tightly holding me to him. I smile up at him to let him know I'm ok.

"Let's just say I wasn't sad when he lost the alpha fight to Angus. Sebastian believes it's his birthright to be alpha. My son isn't alpha material. He doesn't have the same commanding presence that Aurora has. In a sense, I believe he's jealous of his mate. Correct me if I'm wrong, Nico, but First Mate's title is just that: a title. He may think it gives him dominion over the others. Aurora would be wise to set him in his place," I say as Jayce nods slowly, taking in all that I've told him.

"Aurora has put Sebastian in his place many times. If he keeps his nonsense up, I fear for his safety that she may tear him apart one of these days. He likes trying to keep her for himself, and it's not right," Jayce says, looking down sadly. You can tell he's trying to keep his emotions under control. I fear the damage my son is doing to his bond mates, especially this gentle one. I wiggle out of Nico's grip and go to embrace Jayce. He snuggles into me tightly, needing the emotional security. I run my fingers through his hair in an attempt to soothe him. The guys continue loading the car while I take care of Jayce.

"Son, don't worry about Sebastian. It may do him some good if Aurora kicks his ass and makes him submit. He might actually get the silly notion he's an alpha out of his head." I smile at him as he stares at me in disbelief. I kiss his temple before patting his bottom in a motherly move, sending him on his way.

"You need to get going. You don't want to miss your flight. May the Goddess watch over you and keep you safe." I hug Dimitri next and thank him for what he's doing. My heart breaks for Aurora every time I look at Dimitri and Andre. Time is catching up to them far too fast for my liking. Nico steps up to me next and kisses me passionately. He stirs the fire deep within me, making me wish he wasn't leaving. Reluctantly, I pull back and look up at him.

"Elena, I will make sure the forces are prepared properly. We have too much at stake to accept anything less than perfection. Only the strongest will run beside our children. We shall not fail you." The strength of conviction in Nico's voice soothes my nerves. I stand on my tippy toes and kiss him once more. I back away, watching the guys get into the car. I trust in Nico's judgment completely, but as a mother, I still worry.

I approach the training ring in measured steps, where Dominik is sparring with the other pack members, honing their skills for the battle ahead. However, something makes me stop and start looking around. Something isn't right. My eyes scan the area quickly, trying to find what's causing this uneasy feeling.

"Dominik, get Aurora and Sebastian back here! Wolves, prepare for battle! Something's coming!" It's been ages since I last shifted and even longer since I actually had to fight as my wolf. The familiar snapping and cracking of bones is almost music to my ears. My body slowly shifts forms as my bones, muscles, and sinew shift alignment and grow in size. It's been years since the pack has seen me like this. I tilt my head back and howl, calling all the wolves that can hear me. Dominik's dire joins in, our blended tones carrying far and wide. In the distance, I hear Aurora's bone-chilling howl soon joined by Sebastian's. I know whatever is coming doesn't stand a chance. I raise my eyes skyward to find Andre circling, calling out, and flying toward whatever he sees. Now that we know the direction of the attack, we adjust accordingly.

The first Strigoi breaks through the trees, followed closely by a Black Bear. Damn, now the local bear dens are involved in this mess. Strigoi and bears clash with our wolves. The once white gravel of our town center is painted crimson and black in a matter of moments.

One of the bears comes straight for me. I quickly dodge to the left and sink my claws into his side, rending flesh from bone. He turns, now favoring that side, and charges again. I never repeat a move, so instead, I leap up and land on his back. My canines sink deeply into the back of his neck as my claws rip out his throat.

Aurora bursts through the tree line, leaving a trail of frost in her wake. The air around her is supercharged with her rage. I've never seen her Lycan look this angry and aggressive. She charges into the fray, swiping left and right, ripping throats out, and severing heads as she goes. Her growl is so deep, almost demonic , you can feel it as if she's standing right next to you.

Sebastian finally makes it to the party and stops next to me. We watch in wonder as she goes on a rampage. Sebastian leaves my side to assist Dominik, who happens to be surrounded by five bears. He makes quick work of the first bear by ripping his head clean off. The rest of the pack is doing quite well holding their own against the Strigoi and bears. I'm watching them work as a well-oiled machine. Everyone is looking out for each other, making sure to fight in pairs like we trained.

Suddenly, Aurora leaps up on top of a building and closes her eyes. She shakes her head several times before jumping back into the fight. I wonder what that was all about? She looks a little shaken by what happened. Her rage lessens as she finishes off the last few Strigoi.

One large Black Bear moves toward me and shifts back to his human form; it's the leader of the bear's den. He drops to his knees before me and says, "Please, stop the slaughter. Tomas lied to us, told us that we had to kill you to save ourselves. Please, call them off. Bears! Stop! Submit and live!" the leader yells, and all the bears immediately obey him.

Aurora stops and shifts back to her human form. Dominik and Sebastian flank her side. Anna runs out of the Alpha House with Aurora's robe and quickly assists her with putting it on, then scurries off. Aurora raises a single hand and, through the pack bond, she sends everyone home. Her eyes fade to that of her human.

"You beg for mercy after attacking my people because a leach said so?" She tilts her head to the side, assessing the leader of the bears. He's not that big of a man, but he's slightly bigger than your average human male. Aurora's fingers run through Dominik's thick, coarse, black fur. Her eyes dart to Sebastian, and he moves back toward the Alpha House. Slowly, Aurora reverts her attention back to the scared man before her.

"They took my daughter. If we didn't attack, they would kill her." His head hangs low as he begins to cry. I watch emotions flicker across Aurora's face, then vanish almost as quickly as they came. Her eyes narrow on the man before her as she turns her right forearm out to face him. Once he sees her family brand, his eyes widen. As soon as recognition hits him, Aurora turns and heads back to the Alpha House.

"Follow me," she says without turning around.

Inside the house, Sebastian helps her get cleaned up and dressed in her blood-red, floor-length gown. By the time the leader of the bears and I enter the house, she is perched on her Throne of Skulls. In her left hand is a glass of red wine, Dominik's wolf sits at her right side, and Sebastian—dressed—stands to her left. Aurora looks majestic as she sits there, and quite frightening, to be honest.

The bear leader drops to his knees before Aurora, and Dominik growls in warning, not liking how close the man is. Aurora's right-hand goes to rest on his head to calm him. "How long ago did the Strigoi kidnap your daughter?" Slowly, Aurora raises the glass to her lips and takes a sip of her wine.

"Two nights ago, My Liege." He keeps his eyes lowered. I'm guessing he realizes how badly he fucked up today.

"Sebastian?" Aurora turns her head to regard my son. "Take a team and scout the area around the bear's den. The weather is in our favor. Now, bring back his daughter." Sebastian leans forward and kisses Aurora's lips before heading out. "Go with my mate. He will find your daughter. In repayment for this boon, I require your people to guard my people in my absence when we go to war. There shouldn't be any attacks. The Strigoi are after me, and with me gone, there's no reason for them to even think about coming here. Do we have a deal?" Aurora's eyes churn liquid mercury as she watches the leader of the bears. Her hand is extended to him, waiting for him to accept. The man quickly moves forward and takes her hand without a second thought. He shakes her hand firmly, then kisses her knuckles.

"I swear to you, on the last beat of my heart, I will not fail you. We will fight beside you and guard your people as you command." Aurora nods and looks at me.

"Elena, we seal this the old way: a blood oath." Aurora's canines elongate, and her hands partially shift to talons. I bring her a wine glass and hold it out to her, then she quickly cuts her left wrist and drips blood into the glass. Aurora's tongue darts out and licks her wound, sealing it instantly. She grabs the man's arm and slits his wrist over the glass. I watch his blood mix with hers. Aurora grabs her other glass and pours some wine into the blood mix, then stands up, holding the glass high.

"I hold my blood and the blood of the bear's leader in my glass. On this blood, I swear we—the Lycan clan—will help find your missing child." Aurora takes a sip of the blood wine, then holds the glass out to the bear leader. He takes the glass and raises it up before those gathered.

"I swear on my blood and on the last beat of my heart to serve the last Lycan Queen and to protect her people in times of war without question." He too, drinks the blood wine, then hands the glass to me. Aurora gives him a nod, and he proceeds to follow Sebastian.

She returns to her throne and runs her fingers through Dominik's fur. "I heard the prince mid-battle today. He's placed my scale, and the bond is slowly growing. Dom, shift back, love. I'd like to talk with you." She smiles softly, caressing his muzzle, and kisses his wolven lips. She shows such reverence to all of her mates. I have yet to see her favor one male over the others. Dominik seems to be her voice of reason. Jayce is the peacemaker and the one that helps her deal with emotions. My son, Sebastian, seems to be her sword and shield, her guardian and protector. I reach back and grab the spare robe I keep near the throne, just in case. I hand it to Aurora, who takes it and waits for her mate to shift. She offers him the robe and he slips it on.

"You can hear him? It must be the dragon bond the scales have forged." Dominik begins to pace, but Aurora grips his forearm, stopping him in his tracks. She backs him up until he's sitting on her throne. She smiles, admiring him sitting on her throne. Aurora's gaze meets mine, and I smile and nod at her. Slowly, she looks back to Dominik.

"You do look rather handsome on my throne, like a conqueror." I watch Dominik sit up a little straighter, a little prouder, at his mate's assessment of him. "Each of you have a strength and a weakness. Dom, I have to say your thought process is the most similar to mine: use force only when needed but destroy my target utterly." Aurora is walking around the throne, watching Dominik. She is studying him closely. His pride isn't getting in the way, and he just smiles and nods at her words.

"My love, I will be whatever you need me to be. I wish only to be at your side and to be seen as an equal." His eyes flash to that of his wolf, then back to his human hazel. Aurora smiles, then sits on Dominik's lap. Her fingers thread through his thick, black hair while her eyes are searching, studying him up close.

"Elena, I wish for you to announce to the pack that we have dragons on our side." Her eyes close quickly, and she pauses her breathing. Dominik tightens his grip on her, studying her features for any signs of distress. Her eyes suddenly open, and they are the liquid mercury of her wolf. "He has eighteen loyal only to him. Do not mention the numbers. He's in flight to the court of his mother's birth to petition the Gold Dragons for help as well." Dominik kisses Aurora's cheek and nuzzles her jawline. Unlike my son, when the dragons are mentioned, I don't sense any anxiety from him. He's calm and measured in his thoughts and actions.

"That's fantastic news, love! The prince seems to be very generous and concerned for your safety. That means the world to Jayce and I. I'm not too sure if we should fill Sebastian in on how strong the bond is yet. Elena, he's your son. What do you suggest?" Dominik and Aurora turn as one to face me.

"I believe your assessment is correct. I don't think my son can handle the idea of the bond growing stronger. We'll have to break it to him slowly when it gets closer to the start of the war." Sadly, I feel the need to hide things from my son, especially the role I play in this scenario. Honestly, he's a bit immature with this whole situation. He knew from the start that Aurora was destined to have a harem. I know he secretly dreamed of his mate as only his. But if he keeps fucking up and pissing her off, Aurora just might add his skull to her collection—mate or not. I sigh softly. My poor son always feels like he's on shaky ground with Aurora. He doesn't realize she treats them all equally, that no one is favored over the other.

My cell phone pings, alerting me to a message. I look down to find a text from Nico saying they are at the airport. He felt a shift with Aurora and is wondering if she's okay. I text him back, filling him in on what has transpired. He sends back a heart and a thumbs-up emoji. I guess he's almost caught up with everyone else.

"The guys have made it to the airport. Jayce is on his way back." Aurora nods slowly and turns to look at Dominik; her eyes bleed liquid mercury as their gaze locks. His eyes are now the gold of his wolf. I'm not sure what I'm witnessing, but it's impressive as all hell to watch.

"Jayce is stopping at the store to get me more ice cream. He says everything went fine at the airport. It took him almost twenty minutes to explain to my dad what a plane is though." Aurora shakes her head and rolls her eyes, laughing softly to herself. "My dad wants to know what enchantments are on the metal beasts to make them fly. Since they can't use their phones on the plane, I told him I'll watch a video about it in a bit so he can watch too."

"Wait a second, you can speak to your father as well as your mates?" This is exciting news to me. I've heard of dragons dream walking, but communication on this level is scary. Scary, but useful.

Aurora shrugs her shoulders, but Dominik says, "It freaked me out in the beginning as well. It comforts Aurora's wolf in stressful moments when her father's dragon can reach out and soothe her." Dominik smiles and brushes a lock of Aurora's hair behind her ear. "The communication thing is definitely a dragon gift. For years, her father was dream walking to train her before seeing each other for the first time. As mates, if Aurora concentrates hard enough, we can see through each other's eyes." Aurora's smile turns gentle just before she kisses both of Dominik's cheeks.

"We were talking to Jayce together and planning dinner. He wanted our opinion of a cut of beef, so we took a look," Dominik says like it's the most natural thing in the world. I guess for them, it has become that way. I never experienced that with Sebastian's father. Ours was a true mating, but not a fated mating. Only the animals loved each other; the humans, well, we barely tolerated each other. Deep down, I have to admit I'm a bit jealous of Aurora. She knows and feels precisely what her mates are feeling. In her lifetime, she will never have to question where she stands with them. Honestly, it's a thing of beauty.

I look outside, and the sun is beginning to set, painting the sky in so many vivid colors. Tonight is the first night of the Hunter's Moon. It's a beautiful, crisp October evening, and soon the moon will rise high in the sky and illuminate the ground. The Hunter's Moon is typically when the pack goes to hunt elk on the ridge. I watch as families gather and prepare for the hunt. Young ones, finally into their teens, prepare for their first hunt with the pack.

Aurora and Dominik walk onto the front porch to send off the hunters tonight. It is tradition that the stag head is returned to the alpha in offering. This kind of ritual is right up Aurora's alley, especially with her impressive skull collection. Aurora and Dominik share a look, then lean their heads back and howl, signaling the start of the hunt. The pack splits into three teams and runs off in different directions. Both of them watch as the last of the pack members disappear from sight. Aurora stops moving rather suddenly and looks at Dominik. In the distance, the sound of a car crash can be heard. Smoke rises up into the sky, marking the area of the impact.

"Jayce!" Aurora screams before shifting to her beast to run toward the accident.

CHAPTER 35

Aurora

THE SUDDEN BURST OF ADRENALINE THAT SETS MY BLOOD ON FIRE IS unlike anything I have ever felt before. One minute I get to appreciate the beautiful sunset with Dom, the next, I'm running as fast as my wolven form can carry me. My shift came so quickly, the fear for my mate overtook any sense of self-preservation I had. Anger begins to flood my thoughts. The fucking bears, they had to have set this up as a last-ditch effort to please the Strigoi.

As I get closer, I see the Strigoi and bears circling Jayce. Oh yes, all those fuckers are going to die. Quickly, I break through their ranks, using my talons to rend flesh from their bones as I pass. Blackened blood and fur from the bear's pelts fly through the air as I battle my way through their ranks to get to Jayce. I am of a singular focus, destroy anything that comes between Jayce and me.

Dom, Elena, and several other Lycans are in the distance. I lay a taloned hand on Jayce's side before I start freezing the ground around us. Jayce leaps up onto the hood of the car as the ice spreads, rooting some of the Strigoi in place. Through the bond, I warn Dom not to get too close. He obeys and steers Elena and the other Lycans to fight on the edge of the group. After I make sure Jayce is safe, I systematically shred and rip the heads off the Strigoi closest to me. I'm in a rage, betrayed by the bear clan after swearing a blood bond. There would be no bears left standing after tonight. This I swear on the blood of my mother. I know Jayce is injured from the accident; his jerky movements are a dead giveaway.

With most of the Strigoi dead, I move on to the bears. The largest Black Bear charges at me—a fatal mistake on his part. I know this particular one is the leader, but if he's here, where is Sebastian? When the leader gets close enough, I sink my talons into his pelt and encase him in ice. I need him alive for now. Once he's neutral-ized, I move on to the next bear. He charges as well, yet another idiot in the group. I show no mercy and sink my talons deep into his chest and wrap my fingers around his beating heart. The bear is clawing at me, fighting for his life as I stare into his eyes. Slowly, I tighten my grip on his heart, making it harder for the muscle to beat. Blood pumps out around my arm and down to my elbow before dropping onto the ground. The light in his eyes slowly fades away as the blood pumps out of the hole in his chest. Violently, I rip the still-beating heart from his chest and drop it to the ground.

Several bears still live, but not for long. Jayce is off the car now and fighting a bear with his brother, Dom. It's interesting to watch the two of them fight together. A second bear joins their fight, and now I see the change in Jayce: toxin drips yellow-green from his canines as he charges the bear. Because I'm distracted from watching the twins, I get blindsided by another bear. This fucker is going to die.

I roll onto my feet and remain low with my hands flat on the ground. The bear attempts to circle me, but I mirror his movements easily. I watch how he favors his one foreleg, and I realize he has a weakness on his right side. He goes to charge, and I leap out of the way only to land on his back. I sink my talons deep into his pelt until I feel his ribs. One by one, I start snapping them. I feel no remorse as it becomes harder for him to breathe. My wolven muzzle comes down and clamps onto the back of the bear's neck, applying as much pressure as I can. I listen to the tendons snap, and bones crack under the pressure I'm exerting. A quick twist of my head snaps the bear's neck. I call it a mercy killing.

My eyes turn back to the leader, who—in his only smart move—has shifted back to his human form. Jayce, Dom, and Elena have him surrounded. I shift back to my human form with every step in his direction. I leave only my hands and forearms shifted, so my gauntlets and talons are at my disposal.

"Where is Sebastian?" I practically growl in his face as I press the tip of my talon into the soft flesh under his chin.

"He's safe, I swear! I have him knocked out and tied up in a cave near our den." The leader of the bears looks at me, fear radiating off of him like a bad cologne. I tilt my head left and right, studying him. I know my silence is only frightening him more.

"You swear? That's fucking funny. You swore a blood oath, yet here we are!" I dramatically throw my arms out to encompass the remnants of the battle. "You attack two of my mates and one you actually tried to kill. If Sebastian is dead…" I laugh; it's a borderline unhinged kind of laugh. Am I crazy? Maybe just a touch. "If Sebastian is dead, you will know exactly what Hell on Earth is. You will be begging for me to take your life by the time I am done with you." I pull my hand toward me, slicing my talons through the soft flesh under his chin. His ice prison starts melting around him.

"Start walking. If there's even the slightest hint of a trap, you die. And know this: at the end of tonight, none of your clan will be left alive. I cannot take the chance of them betraying me again." The color drains from his face as he finally realizes he just caused the extinction of his people. I'm not joking, nor am I one to play games or make empty threats. Betrayal isn't something to be overlooked. It's not something to be forgotten or forgiven.

The walk through the woods is in relative silence. I had shifted back to my Lycan form before we entered the forest. I don't want to be vulnerable, just in case this is a trap. Jayce and Dom flank my sides as we move deeper into unfamiliar territory. Part of me wants to call my Lycan pack to join in the hunt for Sebastian. The other part doesn't want the pack to watch what I feel I need to do.

In the distance, the cave in question comes into view. Elena prepares to bolt toward the cave, but Dom and Jayce move to block her path at my command. I give her a short growl to warn her of the possible danger that lies within the cave. As we get closer, the first scent I pick up is blood and Sebastian. A menacing growl escapes my lips, and my hackles stand on end as I stare at the bear's leader. My lips are curled back, exposing my long canines and sharp teeth. I motion for the guys to investigate the cavern since Dire Wolves can see in the dark better than Lycans.

Dom's voice appears in my head through the bond. *He's ok. He's bound and gagged, and it seems like he's been drugged. The blood isn't his; he must have killed the three bears in here before the drugs kicked in. Jayce and I will get him out of here.* I'm relieved that Sebastian is safe and sound. I am, however, still royally pissed off at the bear's leader. He knows he's in deep shit.

I shift back to my human form to address my mother-in-law. "Elena, I need you and Jayce to take Sebastian home and make sure he's really okay. Dom and I have matters that need attending to." My voice is as cold as ice and as harsh as a hurricane. There will be no mercy; only women and children will survive this. Any threat to my people is a direct threat to the throne, and I must deal with it as such.

Dom and Jayce walk out with Sebastian in their arms. I quickly create an ice prison for the bear's leader before I look Sebastian over. Slowly, I walk around the guys, looking at every inch of him. There's barely a bruise on his body; in that sense, I'm pleased.

"Lay him down and elevate his head." Carefully, Dom and Jayce lay Sebastian down with his head on Jayce's lap. My beast is out for blood after seeing her mate defenseless. "Tilt his head back and open his mouth." I watch as Jayce does as I've instructed. When Sebastian is positioned correctly, I bite my forearm, allowing my canines to elongate and pierce my own flesh and muscle. Rich, sanguine fluid drops slowly into Sebastian's mouth. My theory is since I heal faster than the guys, perhaps my blood will help remove the sedative from Sebastian's system.

I watch the rivulets of blood slowly drip onto my mate's tongue, turning it vermillion. I observe as he slowly swallows the first gulp of my blood. My hand tightens its grip on the other to squeeze more blood out and into his mouth. Sebastian's color slowly improves, and eventually, his eyes open. He reaches up with shaky hands and grips my bleeding arm. He gently licks my self-inflicted wounds, healing me. A soft *thank you* echoes in my head from Sebastian. I kiss his lips softly and lock eyes with Jayce.

"Get him and Elena home safely. Your word is my law. Anyone questions it, fucking bite them and let the toxins take them." Jayce simply nods; no words are needed at this point. My eyes move to Dom, he knows what I have planned, and he's completely on board. Without warning, I partially shift my arms. Thick, sharp, white dragon scales create gauntlets on my forearms and down my fingers to the long, hooked talons on my fingertips. I look over my weapons as I defrost the ice prison that's holding the bear's leader. He's begging for his life, begging for mercy. His pleas are falling on deaf ears, and I'm past the point of accepting any sorry from him.

I stand directly in front of him, my eyes turning the liquid mercury of my beast. My left-hand grips his throat, and both of his hands fly up, trying to loosen my hold on him. What he doesn't notice is that my right hand is aimed at his upper stomach. I slowly press my talons to his flesh about five inches above his navel. The skin bends and flexes only so much before my talons pierce through his flesh, then through the thick muscle layer of his abdomen. His eyes lock with mine, shock starting to set in. I continue to press deeper, feeling his intestines slide along the back of my hand. I sense Sebastian shuffling behind me. I keep pushing until my talons touch the muscle of his diaphragm. His blood is slowly running down my forearm, leaving streaks of crimson along my scales.

I pause in my forward movement to watch the blood trickle along the various scale plates. It's almost a work of art. Then again, death can be beautiful if done properly. I look over my shoulder at Sebastian and smile at him. I'm happy to see him standing up. His hand grips my right forearm as he presses his chest to my back. Quickly, he thrusts my right arm up and through the diaphragm. I literally have the man's heart in my hand. Sebastian places his left hand lightly around my throat and brings his full lips to my ear. His voice is low and sultry; it drips of raw, sexual power, hitting a tone that sets my blood on fire. Sebastian utters four words, and I honestly can't help myself. "I want his heart."

I comply immediately. The man's eyes go wide as I suddenly grip his heart tight and rip down. The wet, sucking noise fills the air as my arm comes free of his body. The bear's leader drops like a ton of bricks on the forest floor before me. Slowly, I turn and offer the heart to Sebastian. He kisses me softly and takes my offering, giving me that cocky smirk of his. If he wasn't so panty-melting hot, I'd probably be pissed at him. Jayce comes up alongside Sebastian, and they begin to walk home. My gaze lands on Elena next. She looks at the man's body and begins removing his skull to add to my collection. She knows me too well. Dom places his hand on my lower back and tilts his head to the side, silently questioning what was next.

"The bear's main camp is to the north over this ridge. We shift and go in hot. Only sow's with children live." I may be heartless at times, but I refuse to kill children or leave them as orphans. We shift and take off in the direction of the bear's compound.

It's not as big as I initially thought it would be. We see Strigoi moving about the compound, but no bears out in the open. Part of what the leader said was true. He didn't, however, admit to the Strigoi using his compound as a base. I motion for Dom and I to retreat. We need to plan this as a team, and a night-time strike is not the smartest move for us to make.

CHAPTER 36

Aurora

We return to the Lycan compound, and I send Dom off to gather the others. I call Dimitri and tell him we need my father's wisdom. The guys all gather around, as well as some of our strongest fighters. My phone rings, and it's Dimitri and my father on the other end. Dom goes through his observations from the attack and the hunt for Sebastian. Then Sebastian fills everyone in on what he overheard before he was sedated. I notice Jayce is writing everything down in bullet points on the whiteboard, making it easier to track where the conversation is going.

"Okay, so I'm going out on a limb here." I stand in front of the whiteboard to look over the notes. "What if the bears have been involved since the beginning? For a group that recently arrived, the Strigoi have too much knowledge to hunt my ass down. At some point, we need to make sure there are no other moles in our ranks. For now, we need to plan the attack for the morning. Put the compound on lockdown. No one goes in or out until tomorrow night." My eyes search those that are gathered; none flinch from what I just said.

My father's voice cuts through my thoughts. "Good idea, daughter. Only one problem: more than likely, the Strigoi will have prisoners in the basements. How do you plan on handling that?" My father raises an interesting point. I ponder the idea further, then I slowly turn to Sebastian.

He steps forward and bows his head to me, presenting his idea. "We need to evacuate as many bears as possible and burn the main buildings the Strigoi are in. From what we have seen, they tend to bunch up, so I assume they do the same for sleep." Sebastian turns on the smart TV in the office and hooks up his phone to it. I grab my phone and switch the call to video. I turn the camera to face the TV as Sebastian pulls up his map program to show the bear's camp.

"Not every house will have a basement, so we can eliminate those houses first. I suggest we wait until the sun is high in the sky before we move in. Aurora and I can rip the roof off the houses we suspect have Strigoi in the basement. Worst case scenario, after that, we can rip up the floorboards as well." Sebastian keeps his back turned from the group as he explains his idea. I mean, most of it has merit.

"Okay, so let me get this straight: I'm supposed to use precious energy to rip a house apart when we're not even sure the Strigoi are there? Logistically, it doesn't make any sense to me at all. Dad, is there any way to track the Strigoi that would make pinpointing them easier?" Who knows how old my father is? Maybe, in all his years, someone had a stroke of brilliance and figured it out. It's a long shot, but worth asking. I watch my father pace while Dimitri rolls his eyes. I see now where my flair for the dramatic comes from.

"Nope, no easy way to find them other than the distinct scent of sulfur and rot," my father says like it's nothing. Has he been hanging out with Andre too much? Everyone in the room turns to Jayce and Dom. The Dires have the best nose out of all of us. Compared to the rest of us—especially me—they are the closest to pure wolves. Jayce and Dom look at each other, then back to me.

Dom is the first to speak. "We've got this. Dimitri, have Alex send two enforcers and two wolves with toxic bite as soon as he can. We need more help here in the future." Dimitri gives a short reply, then he ends the call. "Let's get some sleep; tomorrow is going to be a long day." Dom immediately offers me his hand and I sigh softly, giving him a gentle kiss before hugging him tightly.

"I need to spend time with Sebastian. He may be an ass and an arrogant fuck at times, but he's still our mate, and I've been spending more time with you and Jayce than him. I don't favor anyone, and I don't want anyone to feel as if they don't matter as much as the others. Besides, if anyone is going to kick his ass first, it's going to be me." Dom and I share a good laugh over that before I turn and leave him behind.

Upstairs, I find Sebastian sitting on the edge of his bed with his head in his hands. I feel the emotional rollercoaster he's on, and it's partially my fault. I walk past Sebastian and into his bathroom. I decide to fill his oversized tub, and I add in different oils and herbs as the hot water begins to rise. Curiosity must have gotten the better of him because, eventually, he joins me in the bathroom. After I shut the water off, I turn to him and put a finger to his lips, asking for silence. He gives me a slow nod. Tonight is about him, not me.

Deep down, I feel like I've been neglecting Sebastian. He brought some of it on himself, taunting the other mates. Sebastian always had the bad habit of trying to place himself above the others. This made me distance myself from him, mostly because I was continually trying to reassure the other mates of their place. After thinking I lost him, I know I need to set things right tonight and spend quality time with him. My hands grip the hem of his Henley, and I slowly lift it above his head. I drop his shirt to the floor and lightly run my fingers over his taut muscles. I almost forgot what it's like to appreciate what's before me with all that's happened lately. I reign in my desire for now. I must remember to stay on task.

I motion for Sebastian to sit on the edge of the tub. Carefully, I remove his shoes and socks, then go for his belt. Sebastian stands to help with his pants. Adonis has nothing on Sebastian's physique. He is pure, sculpted perfection; the definition of man-candy. Fuck, I got lucky in the mate department. I motion for him to get in the tub, and he gives me that look. You know, the one that makes you want to lick every inch of the person. The look that makes your insides melt and your lady bits weep with joy. Sebastian steps into the hot water and lowers himself into the tub. His moan of appreciation makes my insides clench. I try to ignore my pussy, but the bitch is screaming at me. I grab the softest washcloth I can find and load it with the body soap I keep hidden in his bathroom.

I spend the next half hour washing every square inch of his body. My fingers trace every bump and ridge of Sebastian's muscles, his baby blue eyes locked on mine as I bathe him. I'd be lying if I said I wasn't turned on. Other females would kill to be where I am right now.

"My love, you don't have to bathe me, you know? I appreciate how thorough you're being. I'm okay, honest, Aurora." I move so I'm now straddling Sebastian's lap. My fingers roam over the rock hard muscles of his chest.

"Sebastian, I feel like I haven't been a good mate to you. When I thought you might have died..." My words fail me as tears slowly roll down my cheeks. Sebastian's hands come up and cup my face, using the pad of his thumbs to wipe away my tears.

"Shh, love. You haven't been a bad mate. Jayce needed a lot more attention than me. I'll always be right here waiting for you." He punctuates his statement by gently kissing my lips. "As much as I want to bury myself deep in you and fuck you until dawn, we need sleep. And to be honest, I'm still feeling off." He's making sense, like always.

I look closely at Sebastian. Why didn't I notice how tired he looks? I'm so fucking selfish sometimes. Carefully, I remove myself from Sebastian's lap, then out of the tub. I quickly grab our towels and offer one to Sebastian. I can't help but stare at my sexy mate. Sebastian has a well-defined athletic build. His shoulders are thickly muscled, and his waistline is tapered in. My eyes roam hungrily over his chest, down to his defined abs. You know that *V* everyone talks about? The one at a man's hips that trails down to his groin? Sebastian blows that expectation out of the water.

"Aurora?" I snap out of my inner monologue to look up at Sebastian. "Your wolf is showing," he says. He gives me that cocky grin that infuriates me, and turns me on more in times like this. Evil, evil mate. If he keeps looking at me like that, we won't be sleeping.

I grumble on my way back to the bedroom. I need to reign in my desire and put Sebastian's health first. My towel falls to the floor before I climb into bed, snuggling myself in and watching Sebastian move about his room. Honestly, I'm starting to get sleepy. I didn't realize how much the day has stressed me out. Sebastian climbs into bed behind me and pulls me flush against his chest. I fall asleep quickly. For once, no dreams disturb my slumber.

Sebastian and I are awakened by Jayce jumping on the bed. Have I mentioned I'm not a morning person? I grumble and growl at Jayce and try to hide under my pillow. The next thing I know, I see Jayce's face looking at me under my pillow.

"Love? Reinforcements arrived very early this morning. Alex sent us six Dire Wolves: three enforcers and three with the toxic bite. We need direction from our leader." He smiles before leaning forward to kiss me. Jayce extracts himself from my hiding place, and I toss the pillow to the floor. I turn to find Sebastian and Jayce lip locked. So, I do what any red-blooded mate would do: I grab my cell phone and turn off the flash to take several pictures of them kissing.

Ever so carefully, I extract myself from the bed to get changed in my room. I search through my clothing for something that says *I'm not going to take anyone's shit.* I find my black leather pants and a blood-red bodice. It's kind of a steampunk meets dominatrix look. After searching for what seems like forever, I finally find my knee-high boots.

I head down the stairs and into the main hall. The Dires stand immediately, then bow before me. I stroll toward my throne and take a seat. My eyes assess the Dires before me until, one by one, they slowly look up at me.

"Welcome to my home. Please, make yourselves comfortable. We'll have breakfast first, then off we go to take back the bear camp." Dom comes up to my right side and offers me his hand. He guides me to the table and begins introductions for the reinforcements. All six of them are in agreement; the Dire compound has become a much better place ever since the alpha was killed. I sit and listen to them telling stories and cracking jokes at each other. Dom remains on my right side as I watch everyone eat.

My beast is a bit on edge, and I can't place what's setting her off. *Dom, something isn't right. Colin, the enforcer, watch his body language. He's nervous. His scent is acidic from fear. An enforcer shouldn't be afraid.* Dom gives me a very terse nod and squeezes my hand. Sebastian and Jayce finally make it downstairs, and Dom gets up quickly to pull Sebastian aside and fill him in. Jayce comes to sit on my left and takes my hand. He knows something is off by how rigid I'm sitting in my chair and the fact I haven't touched my bacon yet.

"Aurora, my love?" Jayce says in such a soft tone. The reverence in his voice warms my black heart. I slowly reach up and brush his cheek with my hand. I know, in that moment, my eyes shift and swirl liquid mercury. He feels the power flow through me, and his wolf's eyes glow in response to my agitation. Dom and Sebastian stand behind me, each placing a hand on my shoulder in an attempt to calm me. I give the signal to my personal guards, and they leave the room, locking the doors from the outside. The sound of the locks clicking into place sets the Dires on high alert.

"I'm truly blessed to receive help so quickly. But it's come to my attention that there's a traitor in our ranks." Five out of six Dires are calm and looking directly at me. Number six—that fucker—is fidgeting and restless. I feel a little different, and I have a very bitter taste in my mouth. My eyes search Jayce's as I part my lips slightly and run my tongue over my canines. His eyes widen at the sight, thinking it's sexual in nature. Realization hits him, and he stares at my canines closer. My sweet, innocent mate smirks at me, then winks. I stand and walk soundlessly around the table, stalking my prey.

My fingertips lightly run over each of the guys' shoulders as I pass them. When I reach Colin, both of my hands come to rest on his shoulders. I lean down and nuzzle his cheek, freezing him in fear. I can hear his heart pounding in his chest, racing a mile a minute. My guys are standing on the opposite side of the table, watching with rapt attention. My tongue darts out and licks his throat, tasting the fear and salt in his sweat.

Without warning, I strike. My canines sink deep into this throat. The snaps and crunches of tendons and sinew breaking can be heard clearly—the sharp, metallic tang of his life fluid coats my tongue, spurring my beast on. I can taste the taint of the Strigoi in his blood. Through the bond, I share my knowledge with the guys. Their growls fill the air, but it doesn't distract me from my task at hand. Colin starts to thrash and tries to throw me off of him. I sink my talons into his shoulders to strengthen my grip as I start pumping the toxin into his bloodstream. I've gained enough knowledge from his blood. The Strigoi taint has touched the Dire compound far worse than I had initially suspected. I jump off Colin's back and watch him stumble before he falls to his knees.

"How many more, Colin? Tell me, and I'll end it quickly." I'm on all fours in front of him on the floor, staring him down and trying to will him to answer me. Alpha powers, don't fail me now.

Colin shakes his head several times before spitting blood. Fuck, I wrecked his vocal cords. He uses his blood to draw the number three. His breathing is labored, and he's having a hard time keeping his eyes open. In one final push, he writes the names of the tainted. His green eyes plead with me for mercy. My resting bitch face game must be on point today because he looks panicked right before I slam my taloned hand into his chest and rip out his heart. His body falls to the floor with a wet splat into a pool of his own blood. Within seconds, Sebastian is at my side, offering me his hand to help me up. I rise to my feet, still holding Colin's heart. I turn my attention to Dom.

"There are tainted ones within your pack. Call the other enforcers. Have these three dispatched and their heads sent to me." My voice has a wolven growl to it as I fight to enunciate the words. I'm so close to losing the battle with my beast when Jayce's hand slips under the back of my bodice. The simple act of him pressing his hand to my skin seems to soothe my beast. I draw in a slow, deep breath and then kiss his temple. Through the pack bond, I have the guards open the doors to the room again. You know it's pretty bad when they don't even blink after seeing a dead body or a puddle of blood in the house anymore.

Elena comes running into the room, chattering away with a phone stuck to her head. Suddenly, she stops dead in her tracks as she took in the scene before her. "Yeah, Nico, Aurora killed someone in the house. No, no, no, she's okay. She's got a heart in her hand again." Sebastian facepalms, listening to the way his mother describes the situation to my dad on the phone. I shake my head and start walking out of the room. I step over Colin's body and make my way out into the main hall. About another thirty minutes and it's go time. The Strigoi won't know what hit them.

CHAPTER 37

Jayce

It frightens me to think my pack mates would turn against Aurora. The way she decided to handle the traitor was something my father would have done. However, there is one huge difference: he wouldn't have shown mercy and ended it quickly.

I'm not sure how the mate bond thing is supposed to work. Is Aurora supposed to gain a unique ability—a gift—from each of us or just each species? Personally, I know I've gotten stronger and faster since we've mated.

My phone dings, and it's a text from Alex. He's just as upset as I am over the betrayal. The three in question will get beheaded tonight. Alex also tells me the prince received Aurora's gifts, and he asks me to gather the others before he sends the video over to her. It will be the first time she gets to see him. Part of me is scared. I'm not afraid of losing my place in the pack, but I'm so frightened of having a pure-blooded dragon in the bond. What if he has a bad temper? What if his bad temper makes Aurora's worse? So many questions bounce around in my head as I enter the main sitting room to find my other bond mates.

"Aurora, love, Alex has forwarded a video for you." Aurora scrunches her nose and tilts her head to the side as she studies me.

"Please cast it to the smart TV, Jayce," Aurora says. Sebastian turns the TV on and sets it up to receive. I send the video to the TV, and we watch as it pans from the vast white of the tundra to the mouth of a cavern. A blonde man is standing inside; if I didn't know any better, I'd swear he was a Viking. He's easily three hundred to three hundred and fifty pounds of solid muscle. His hair is a light, golden blonde and hangs down past his shoulders. His face is rather rugged, complete with a full beard and mustache. Aurora is so focused on the video she barely notices Sebastian picking her up to sit on his lap.

Dom and I share a look and watch as Alaric receives Aurora's box. You can clearly feel the anxiety through the bond when he starts cutting the top open. Alaric slowly removes the popcorn and stops dead, looking at the box's contents. He reaches in and pulls out the braid of hair she had stuffed in there. Sebastian turns to me and mouths, *When did she do that?* I shake my head at him. If he had been paying attention to our mate and not his phone, he would know when she did it.

Alaric brings the braid to his nose and sniffs it. His eyes become the gold of his dragon, slit and all. I know the look of recognition, and that was it. Aurora has gotten quite antsy in Sebastian's lap as she waits to see what Alaric thinks of the skull. A black man—I believe his name is Ellis—steps into the frame and reaches into the box. He pulls out the Wendigo skull and holds it out to Alaric. I can tell the moment Aurora starts to hold her breath. Her heart rate picks up, and her scales begin to ripple up and down her arms.

Alaric's eyes lock on the skull, then the silver-white scale that Aurora placed on top. Alaric rubs the back of his hands across his eyes, wiping away tears. Ever so gently, he takes the scale from the skull and sniffs it. His right hand comes up quickly, and he cuts into his own flesh. Ellis freaks out and runs back behind the camera. Alaric pushes the fleshy side of Aurora's scale into his wound, and Ellis zooms in on how quickly the flesh knits around the scale.

Alaric gasps and whispers, "I can feel her."

As soon as he says he can feel her, Aurora's hand moves to touch his scale in time with him touching hers. It's times like this I wish Nico was here to explain exactly what the hell is going on. We watch the remainder of the video in silence. Alaric turns to the camera and smiles.

"My princess," he places his hand flat on Aurora's scale over his heart, "I am yours to command. I have gathered forces beyond my father's reach. We will take back what is rightfully yours. By my blood, I swear this to you." He draws in a deep breath as his eyes flicker between human and dragon. "To the first mates of our princess, we will be brothers in arms. We will fight for her and protect her together." His flattened palm turns into a fist against his chest, signifying the difference in his promises. "Dream of me? Aurora?" Alaric smiles one last time and winks at the camera before the video cuts off. All eyes are locked on Aurora, waiting to see her reaction to his video.

"Holy shit, he's hot!" comes from behind us. All of our heads whip around to find Sebastian's mother, Elena, fanning herself in the doorway. "Hot damn, baby girl, that's a mountain of a man that's pledged himself to you. A dragon's word is worth its weight in gold. Don't forget his mate bond and offered scale. He's yours for life." Elena casually walks into the room and flops into the recliner opposite Aurora and Sebastian. Aurora's cheeks are cherry red, and Sebastian looks like he wants to kill something.

"Elena? I have questions. The wolf's mate bond seems to be much different than the dragon's." I figured I'd ask since I believe I'm the only one not threatened by Alaric's arrival on the scene.

"Jayce, to be honest, there's not a lot that's different between the two species when it comes to choosing a mate. It's exactly the same by sight and scent. To a dragon, its mate is its greatest treasure. A dragon's hoard means nothing to them once they find their mate." Elena draws in a deep breath before beginning again. "Unlike wolves, there is no bite needed to forge the bond. Dragons offer a scale, a piece of themselves to their mate. That, and a skull, of course." Elena looks down to her phone, briefly types on it, then looks back up.

"Unlike wolves, dragons cannot live without their mate, except if there's a hatchling. The remaining mate lives only for that hatchling. Like wolves, dragons only get one shot at a true mate." Elena's phone pings again, and we watch her eyes scan the message. Her fingers fly over the screen before she looks up. "Nico needs to explain a bit of history to everyone. We need to cast his video up on the big screen TV."I take the phone from Elena and pair it with the TV. Carefully, I balance the phone under the TV so Nico can see us. I hit dial and connect the call.

"What do you mean it's on video, you giant furball! All of them won't fit on this tiny screen." Watching how animated Nico can get is quite comical. In the background, you can hear Dimitri tell Nico to look at his phone. "Oh! Hi! Umm, okay, so congratulations,

Aurora, on gaining your dragon mate. Sebastian, stop being a grumpy ass! I see the faces you're making behind my daughter!" As soon as the words leave Nico's mouth, Elena gets up and slaps Sebastian on the back of his head. The growl that comes from Elena is enough to straighten him out quickly.

"Thanks, love," Nico says before clearing his voice to continue. "You probably have a ton of questions. I've been answering them the best I can by messaging Elena. The past was a dark time—a lot of magic and mystery. The alpha Vladimir was an evil, evil man." Nico looks down as he gathers his thoughts.

"He possessed blood mages and kept the Strigoi on a leash. He used blood magic to subdue your mother's mates to have us all castrated. If it wasn't for Andre's spy network and Dimitri's quick thinking, you wouldn't be here." Nico reaches up to wipe a stray tear from his eye. "Rumors spread a while back that Vladimir still lives. I'll be honest, I didn't check his body before I set your mother's body on fire. I also didn't get to watch the whole thing burn to ash." He ponders that thought for a few minutes, then looks back to the phone again.

"Elena, use your contacts with the European Lycans and see what they can find out. We need to be prepared for everything." Elena nods and leaves the room, heading off to make her phone calls.

"Anything else we need to know, Nico?" I ask as I watch my brother and Sebastian take notes. Only Aurora seems disturbed by the information.

Nico watches Aurora closely before speaking. "My beautiful, powerful daughter. Elena was correct when she said a dragon cannot live without its mate. You die, so will Alaric. Your wolven mates will be left behind to wish for death. You are a special case, and I'm not sure what will happen to you if one of your mates die." Nico's sadness is apparent as he speaks to Aurora. All I can do is move to Aurora's side and run my fingers through her hair. I feel my eyes turn wolven as I stare at Sebastian. He's not even trying to comfort Aurora.

"What the fuck is your problem, man! Can't you see our mate is in pain! Can you get over yourself for five fucking minutes?" I reach down to take Aurora from Sebastian and pass her off to Dom. It's interesting to see my larger twin shocked by my actions. I'm not a fighter, nor am I even a beta, but our mate needs us, and Sebastian is being a self-absorbed jerk. Sebastian stands and goes toe to toe with me, looking down at me like I'm nothing.

"What the fuck do you think you're going to do to me, omega? You're weak and soft and can't fight your way out of a paper bag." Sebastian's sky blue eyes turn the white-blue of his wolf. I know I'm in trouble, but I won't back down. He's trying to use his power to dominate me. For once, it doesn't feel oppressive like it usually would. I hear Nico in the background start to laugh.

"It's about bloody time Jayce stood up for himself. Good for you, lad, good for you!" Nico is proud of me? Wow.

While I'm distracted, Sebastian takes this opportunity to strike. He grabs me by my shoulders and attempts to throw me. I squat down like Dimitri taught me and grab hold of Sebastian's forearms and use his momentum against him. I pivot and whip my body to the side, sending Sebastian off balance and onto the floor. I shift quickly and grab him by the throat. I hold him there, growling until I feel Aurora's fingers threading through my fur.

"Sebastian, love, what have I told you about picking on the other mates?" Aurora's power is oppressive as she speaks. Sebastian is squirming under me, trying to escape. "Jayce, love, please release Sebastian. I believe you made your point that he cannot pick on you anymore." I release Sebastian as asked. When I look up, I see Elena in the doorway with tears streaming down her cheeks. Her son's actions disappoint and hurt her. I let out a huff of a breath and stand next to my twin. I don't bother shifting back. I don't want to talk to anyone at the moment.

"When did he get so fucking strong?" Sebastian is pissed off that I put him down. You know what? I can't wait for the dragon to get here and beat his bully ass. Aurora slaps Sebastian across the face to get him to stop.

"What the actual fuck did I tell you about fighting with the other mates? I'm really disappointed in you, Sebastian. You're starting to act like my mother's Lycan mate. I swear to the gods, you even start going down that road, and I will fucking rip your throat out my fucking self!" Aurora is screaming and crying at the same time. This really isn't a safe state for her to be in. I look back at Nico on the screen, and he shoos me toward her. I place my muzzle under her hand and lift up, so her hand rests on my head. I gently place the weight of my wolven body against her hip, trying to comfort her.

Nico's voice booms through the speakers. "You have a village to liberate. Get your heads out of your collective asses and go free the remaining bears." We turn as one and nod. Nico is right; we got off task and forgot what had to be done.

CHAPTER 38

Jayce

As I turn to walk out of the room, a sense of purpose propels me forward, my steps steady and determined as I make my way toward the front door. Behind me, I can sense the presence of my brother, Aurora, and Sebastian, their energy palpable as they follow close on my heels.

As we reach the front of the Alpha House, we are joined by the five Dire Wolves from our pack, their forms shifting seamlessly as they fall into step beside us. Together, we form a formidable group, united in our shared mission as we prepare to venture into the depths of the forest.

With a silent nod of acknowledgement, we set off into the woods, the rustling of leaves and the crunch of twigs beneath our feet the only sounds that break the stillness of the morning. The air is alive with anticipation, the scent of pine and earth mingling with the primal energy that surrounds us.

After crossing a few small streams and navigating the winding paths of the forest, we begin to ascend a steep hill, our muscles burning with exertion as we climb higher and higher toward our destination. At last, we reach the cliff's edge, the village below spread out before us like a patchwork quilt.

As we take in the breathtaking vista, Aurora is the first to shift back into her human form, her eyes scanning the horizon with a sense of purpose. And as she turns to look at each of us in turn, a silent understanding passes between us, a shared determination to see our mission through to the end.

"The center house is the only one with a basement of any size. From what my father told me about Strigoi, they tend to nest together and sleep in a pile during the day. The leader will be in the center of the pile. We will systematically search all the outlying houses first before we converge on the center house." We descend upon the town like phantoms, moving silently through the remaining shadows along the edge of the town.

Aurora moves directly to the center house and begins to freeze the wood, making it brittle. Dom and I search several houses, finding nothing of interest in any of them. Seven Dire Wolves and Sebastian join Aurora at the center house, which now looks like a giant ice castle. I cannot sense nor find any signs of life anywhere in the compound. As far as we know, the Strigoi have eaten all the bears.

Aurora and Sebastian start moving as one, using their talons to rip the boards off the house. Sometimes, I think it must be nice to be a Lycan and be able to do shit like that. Several moments pass until they have all the walls ripped off the house. The stench of rot and sulfur fill my nose, causing me to sneeze. The Strigoi are definitely down there. Sebastian leaps onto the roof and begins to rip the wood off of the house.

Aurora watches closely as Sebastian starts to remove the rooftop. Movement can be heard below the floorboards. Aurora's beast smirks and raises an eyebrow as she cocks her head to listen to the movement. A few of the Dires shift back to human and start to remove the furniture from the house. Dom and I move to flank Aurora's great white Lycan beast as we wait for the last of the roof and furniture to be removed.

Eventually, Sebastian leaps down and lands right next to us. I turn my face to the sun, which is directly overhead. Now is the time to rip up the floorboards. Aurora and Sebastian move as one and begin at the room's outer edges, ripping up the floor. Shrieks and screams can be heard down below as the Strigoi start to panic and try to hide from the sun. The other seven Dire Wolves move into position around the house's perimeter, making sure none try to escape through tunnels. Aurora suddenly stops and tilts her head, listening to something I can't hear.

There might be a child left down there." Aurora is beside herself, thinking about the defenseless little one that could possibly be down there. She also knows it could be a trap to lure her down. Her growls rattle the floorboards as her talons sink back into the wood. Her drive to destroy this house is fueled by her need to find the possible child below. Sebastian joins her in the destruction, and soon, only a three-foot-wide section is left. The scent of ash is thick in the air from the Strigoi, who couldn't get to cover. We all peer down into the basement. About a dozen are left, but no signs of the child.

Plank by plank, Aurora and Sebastian rip up the floor. Off to the side, I notice a small tunnel by the bookshelf. I don't think it's big enough for a Strigoi, but who knows, a small one could possibly make it in there. The last of the planks are removed, and the Strigoi are reduced to ash and bone. I leap down into the basement and approach the tunnel. In the far back is a small bear cub —the last survivor of the bear clan. I whimper at the cub, and it slowly waddles its way out of the tunnel to me. I gently pick it up by the scruff of its neck and leap out of the remains of the basement. Aurora quickly comes to my side, sniffing at the cub. Her shift comes quickly, and my mate takes the cub from me. The little cub rolls onto its back, giving Aurora its belly. She smiles and starts walking.

"Our job is done here. Let's go home." Aurora doesn't even turn to look at us; she continues to walk, carrying her precious cargo. We walk in silence back to the compound following Aurora. We arrive, and Sebastian's mother runs up to Aurora, looking at the cub in her arms. I didn't know cubs could shift that young, to be honest. I know Dire Wolves don't shift until we're at least five years old. Elena attempts to take the cub from Aurora, and she growls at her. I shift back and slowly approach the two of them.

"The cub may be hungry. We should probably take it to the kitchen and feed it." Aurora's mercury orbs land on me, and she gives me a gentle smile. A slight nod of her head sends me into the house before her, opening the doors en route to the kitchen. Before raiding the fridge, I set Aurora and the cub up in her favorite window seat. I make bacon, eggs, and ham for them. I also thin slice some brown trout filet's I found in the bottom of the fridge from Dom's fishing trip yesterday. I carefully arrange the platter and bring it over to Aurora and the cub. I can't help but laugh; Aurora is still naked from her shift and holding a bear cub against her chest, softly singing to it. Definitely not typical Aurora behavior.

Speak of the devil, Dom comes strolling in with a pair of shorts and a T-shirt for me and one of our T-shirts for Aurora. He stops dead, watching her with the cub. I can bet that he and I have the same thought; we can't wait to see Aurora with one of our pups. Dom slides in close to the window seat and offers to hold the cub so Aurora can put the shirt on. She reluctantly hands the cub over and quickly puts the shirt on. Her eyes lock on the tray of food in my hands, and she waves me over. I wiggle a strip of crispy bacon at Aurora, and she lunges forward, biting the bacon strip in half. In the back of my mind, I fear for my cock's safety when she does shit like that. Dom gives me the same look. Yeah, we thought the same thing.

Aurora tears through the platter of food like there's no tomorrow; the only thing left behind is the ham and the fish strips. Aurora makes the *give me* motion with her hands, and Dom hands the cub back to her. I bring the fish closer, and you can see the cub's nose sniffing the air. He starts making a distress call and tries to scramble toward the food. Aurora makes a soft growl to correct the cub, and it immediately obeys and settles back down on her lap. Strip by strip, Aurora feeds the cub while Dom and I watch.

As I look around the kitchen, something dawns on me. Where is Sebastian? He never detaches himself from Aurora for too long. My eyes scan the area outside the window that overlooks the backyard. Sebastian isn't there either.

I lock eyes with my brother and speak only to him. *Where's his royal ass-ness?* I know it's not nice to call names, but Sebastian is a royal pain in the ass. Dom looks away for a moment, scanning the room and outside the nearby window.

Not sure. He's been acting rather suspicious lately, Jayce. Ever since he implanted the scale on Aurora, he's been off—even more so than usual. Dom furrows his brows and shrugs his shoulders lightly. I catch the change in Aurora's eye color before she speaks, and I know we're busted.

"Guys, it's not nice to have private conversations in front of others. You know I don't like it." Her eyes lock with ours only for a moment before looking back to the cub in her lap.

"We're just concerned. Sebastian has been acting odd lately—*even* more so than usual." I keep my eyes downcast. I don't want to challenge my love. Dom stays quiet as well, waiting for Aurora to speak again. The cub has fallen asleep on her lap as her fingers gently move through the baby's fur.

"I went to bed naked with him last night, and he didn't even try anything. Something is eating at him, and I don't think it's just the prince. I sent Andre off to investigate Sebastian's bloodline further." Aurora's eyes flicker between mercury and steel-grey. I can tell the subject is bothering her, but at least I wasn't the only one sensing it.

Before I get the chance to continue the conversation, Sebastian decides to stroll into the kitchen like nothing's wrong. He gives Aurora his usual megawatt smile and offers her a single flower. She regards the flower, then gently takes it.

"The baby just fell asleep. You missed all the fun, Bash." He just smirks at Aurora in typical Sebastian fashion before heading to the fridge to grab a beer.

"I bet," is all he says before returning his gaze to his phone and typing away on it. I hear the low grumble from Aurora. I honestly believe, one of these days, she's going to shove that phone so far up his ass the proctologist will call it a lost cause.

"Sebastian? I want dick," Aurora says, so matter-of-fact. His eyes never leave his phone. He mutters something incoherent, sounding almost like "we'll get it at the store" or something along those lines. Aurora shakes her head, scoops up the cub, and walks out the back door.

I can feel her aggravation clear as day through the bond. I'd love to find out what's so fucking important on that phone that would cause Sebastian to start ignoring Aurora. Motioning for Dom to follow me, I step outside into the cool morning air, the familiar sounds of the compound fading into the distance behind us. There's a sense of urgency gnawing at the edges of my consciousness, a feeling that something isn't quite right, but I push it aside for now, focusing instead on the task at hand.

As we walk deeper into the woods, the silence between us hangs heavy in the air, broken only by the rustle of leaves and the distant calls of birds. With each step, the weight of the situation settles upon us, a tangled web of emotions and unanswered questions swirling around in our minds.

But as we continue to navigate the forest in silence, a sense of determination begins to take root within me, a resolve to find out the truth and set things right. For Aurora's sake, and for the sake of our pack, we cannot afford to let this situation spiral out of control.

CHAPTER 39
Dominik

My brother and I walk into the woods to clear our heads. I really want to believe our issue with Sebastian is just him trying to keep Aurora for himself. Now that his behavior has changed, I'm blaming it on the idea that a real alpha joining our ranks has him on edge.

"Jayce, did you notice how attached Aurora is to the cub already? I think her next heat is coming soon." I raise an eyebrow and wiggle it at Jayce. He shoves me and shakes his head.

"Really, Dom? Though, you're probably right. You saw how she was with Lia. I'm concerned about Aurora and this battle. I know she's powerful, but none of us are immortal. I mean, she's going to protect her father, which may put her in more danger." Jayce brings up a valid point. We need Nico with us since his dragon's sight is far better than any other creatures on the battlefield—besides, maybe, Aurora's.

"He's going to be a sitting duck for the dragons. If we can keep the ground troops away from him, he should be able to defend himself enough." We keep walking, discussing little things here and there about how we should approach this battle. Our major concerns are to keep Aurora alive and to keep Nico from getting killed.

After what feels like an eternity of walking, we finally arrive at the lake Aurora mentioned, its tranquil surface stretching out before us like a vast expanse of liquid glass. The scene before us reminds me of that eerie lake from the movie where the giant alligator lurks beneath the surface, ready to strike at any moment. Yet, despite the comparison, there's a serene beauty to this place that captivates me.

The water is perfectly still, reflecting the surrounding trees and sky with crystal clarity. It's as if the lake itself is a mirror, offering a glimpse into another world hidden beneath its surface. The air hangs heavy with the scent of pine and earth, mingling with the sweet fragrance of wildflowers that dance along the water's edge.

All around us, the forest comes alive with the sounds of nature, the chirping of birds and the rustling of leaves blending together in a symphony of life. It's a stark contrast to the chaos and turmoil that often consumes our lives, a reminder of the simple beauty that exists in the world around us.

As Jayce and I settle onto the soft sand, we take in the scene before us, watching as birds flit and flutter on the other side of the lake. There's a sense of peace and tranquility here that soothes the soul, a welcome respite from the tumultuous events that have brought us to this place.

We remain at the lake for a few hours, catching up on different things. Hell, we even had time to call Alec who broke the news of his wedding next summer. Something positive finally happened for Alec. We're so happy for him.

As we get up to leave, we hear an eagle's cry that is cut off halfway through. Jayce and I look at each other before we head in the direction the noise came from. We find several golden-brown feathers on the forest floor mixed in with the moss when we reach the area. Tiny droplets of blood are splattered on random leaves here and there. We follow this weak blood trail until we find a crossbow bolt covered in blood and feathers.

Who would shoot a bird with a crossbow? That doesn't make any sense. There's what looks like a drag mark along the forest floor, and the blood trail is heavier here. It looks like someone took a paintbrush, dipped it in blood, and painted the moss. We follow the blood to its end, and over the edge of the rock face, we see what made the trail. An eagle lays prone in the valley below us. Jayce was the first to be able to form words.

"No!" He leaps over rocks and scales down to the valley below. I'm frozen in my vantage point, watching everything as if it were happening in slow motion. Every step, every noise is slower and drawn out as one of my worst nightmares came to life. If that's Andre down there, we would have to tell Aurora. Jayce looks up to me as he kneels by the body. His wolf rips free of his body, exploding into existence and howling its grief into the wind. It's as I had feared: Andre has been murdered.

I feel Jayce's pain and anguish through the bond, and Aurora's haunting tone soon fills the air. One by one, pack members join Aurora in her eerie howl. We know it's only a matter of minutes before the pack starts making its way here. Jayce anxiously paces the valley, whining and whimpering. His anxiety is understand-able; our beloved mate is going to be on the warpath.

The sound of paws thundering through the forest can be heard long before the pack can be seen. My eyes focus on the pebbles near me as they vibrate from the paws' staccato rhythm hitting the ground. Aurora lets out a location howl, which Jayce promptly answers to give her proper bearings. Soon enough, that great, white beast of a Lycan hybrid comes into view. She's clawing and shredding everything that gets in her way. Sebastian is right behind her, with his mother trailing close behind. The rest of the pack brings up the rear.

Aurora whips past me, launching herself across the divide to the other side. She repeats the leap back and forth until she reaches the bottom. Aurora's shift comes quickly as her human form falls to its knees, her wails and cries echoing through the valley. Her hand shakes as she hesitates to touch Andre's prone form. Aurora withdraws her hand several times before she finally rests it on his feathers. Jayce shifts back to his human form and rests a hand on Aurora's shoulder. No one else dares to go down there with her. Aurora doesn't handle emotions well, and to interfere now would more than likely end in a death sentence. Sebastian comes to stand beside me and rests his hand on my shoulder.

"She's going to need all of us after this. Her thirst for vengeance is going to burn brighter than the sun. No more macho male bull-shit, right guys?" Hopefully, we have a truce until we get this shit storm settled. Sebastian moves to the edge and looks down at Aurora and Jayce. I'm not noticing any signs of remorse or sympathy for what Aurora is going through. Yup, I still don't like Sebastian. Aurora takes the shredded remains of Jayce's shirt and wraps Andre up like a bird mummy. Now, Jayce chooses to embrace her and hold her tightly. Thankfully, Aurora accepts his affection before she tells him what she's planning on doing.

"Oh, this ought to be interesting," Sebastian states flatly. I guess my brother will see what it's like to get a piggyback ride from a half-crazed, grieving Lycan hybrid. Aurora shifts back to her beast's form and places the hoop of fabric in her mouth so she can carry Andre. Her eyes lock on Jayce and motion for him to climb on. Reluctantly, he climbs onto her back and wraps his legs around her waist. Aurora launches herself at the rock wall, sinking her talons into the sandstone to gain purchase on the almost vertical ascent. Foot by foot, she climbs steadily with Jayce on her back and Andre's death shroud in her mouth. Unlike my descent, she's not launching herself back and forth. I've never witnessed her move so cautiously before in all the time I've known her.

Before she reaches the top, Sebastian and I reach down to help them over the edge. I back up for a few moments to give Aurora and Jayce some time to breathe. Cautiously I move forward and hold out my hands, waiting for Aurora to either drop Andre into my hands or refuse. I watch Aurora look between me and Elena, who gives her a somber nod. Aurora lowers her head and releases Andre's body into my hands. I'm almost overcome with emotion from holding our good friend's body. Gently, I cradle Andre against me and watch my mate as she shifts back to her human form.

"How'd it happen? Did you see it?" Aurora's voice quivers as tears roll down her face. Her eyes are locked on the death shroud in my arms. They shift between human and beast faster than I can keep track of. Jayce steps forward and lays a hand on Andre.

"We heard an eagle cry. The second time it called out, it was cut short. Dom and I started walking in the direction we last heard the cry come from. First, we found feathers, then blood. Eventually, we found a bloody crossbow bolt with feathers on it." Sighing softly, I have to swallow hard, attempting to keep my voice from breaking. Aurora needs me to be strong for her right now.

"Further in, we found blood marks where we suspect the eagle dragged itself. When we got here, I looked over the edge and prayed it wasn't Andre. I didn't hesitate and got to the bottom as fast as I could. His body was cold when I got there." Jayce looks up, the raw pain evident in his eyes as he looks at Aurora. Not only was he feeling hers, but his own pain runs bone-deep. My brother is so comfortable with his emotions that his tears roll freely down his cheeks. Aurora grabs ahold of Jayce and squeezes him tightly. Her eyes are practically glowing with the raw power she's struggling to contain.

"We need to call my father and Dimitri home and gather the Dire Wolves. To strike at someone close to me is an act of war. There will be no survivors. I swear on my blood that he will be avenged, and the murderer will know pain like no other." Aurora closes her eyes for several minutes, then draws in a deep breath. "Father and the prince know what happened. I've been advised on what to do. Let's go home. We need to build a funeral pyre for Andre in the customs of his people. Dad and the team will be here by nightfall. At midnight, we perform the ceremony." Aurora releases Jayce and kisses his forehead.

"Please, carry us back. Shift for me, my love." Aurora's eyes are all human, tears welling up and threatening to break free as she turns to take Andre from me. Jayce nods at our mate and shifts back to his wolf. Sebastian and I move to assist Aurora onto Jayce's back. Slowly, Jayce leads with his precious cargo. Sebastian and I shift next, following close behind Aurora and Jayce. The pack moves in sync as we head back to the compound.

When we reach the Alpha House, Jayce lays down so Aurora can get off his back easily. Our mate has one hell of a resting bitch face because I can't read what the fuck she's thinking or feeling at the moment. Our immediate family group is the only one that enters the house. We lock the doors behind us as we follow Aurora into the office. She grabs two pillows and lays Andre's body on them. Her eyes raise up and lock on to each of us in turn, sending a chill right to our bones.

"It goes without saying: I want vengeance." She slowly unwraps Andre's body to look upon his fallen form. Her fingers come up to close his golden eyes. "I need linen, sage, arrowroot, and barberry. Sebastian, your mother should have these in her workshop. Please get them for me." Her eyes are haunting—almost dead looking— without her normal inner light. She's running on autopilot at this point, numb from the loss of a parental figure. Sebastian moves forward and kisses Aurora's temple before leaving the room on his mission. Aurora watches Sebastian leave, then looks at the two of us. The gears are turning in her head, and I'm not sure we're going to like where she's going.

CHAPTER 40

Dominik

Aurora exhales loudly, "When your pack arrives, catch them up on *everything*." We nod and remain quiet as she looks over Andre's body. She takes notes of the entrance and exit wound, her canines visibly pressing into her bottom lip as she does so. I can't tell if she realizes that she's doing it or if she's just so lost in her thoughts. I watch her eyes flicker between human and her liquid mercury. She's in conversation with someone.

"Aurora? Is there anything we can do to assist you?" I'm concerned about her bottling up her feelings over this. I watch her emotions flicker over her face, as well as a wave of scales and fur. She breathes in deeply, composing herself, before looking up to me.

"Don't leave me. I'm barely holding myself together." Aurora looks between Jayce and me. I can clearly see how distraught she is. I will strike down anyone who brings this level of pain on her.

"I know I speak for the both of us when I say we won't leave you. I will be your sword, and Jayce your shield. Stay with us tonight, and let us watch over you in your sleep." I move behind Aurora and wrap my arms around her waistline, trying to lend her my strength. I kiss the back of her head as she continues her work. I can feel through the bond that she's struggling to remain strong for everyone.

Sebastian returns with the ingredients Aurora asked for and sets them on the table before her. He looks at my positioning and then over at Jayce. "I've made arrangements for everyone at the airport. They should be here within the hour. Mom said the pyre is almost ready." Sebastian looks concerned for Aurora, which is nice for a change. Aurora smiles at him and nods before returning to what she was doing. Sebastian takes a seat by the door, watching Aurora work on Andre's remains.

I watch closely over Aurora's shoulder as she mixes the herbs and then starts tearing the linen. Everything is set for when the others arrive. I sit down in the office chair behind Aurora and pull her into my lap. She's trying to remain strong for everyone. Aurora slowly turns her head to look at me. I do my best to smile and be the strength she needs.

"Thanks, Dom." She sighs softly before stopping her work. "I think I'll take you up on your offer. It's probably not smart for me to be alone while this upset. Ask Dimitri what happened the last time." Aurora raises both eyebrows and rolls her eyes. I remember Dimitri retelling the story. We definitely don't have time to clean up a mess like that.

The crunching of rocks from tires in the driveway catches everyone's attention. Aurora looks at Sebastian, and he goes to retrieve Dimitri and Nico. Aurora slowly extracts herself from my lap and goes to stand in front of the desk. Eventually the knob turns, and Dimitri sticks his head in. His normally bright hazel eyes are bloodshot, and his cheeks are stained with tears. Nico shoves past Dimitri and bands his arm tightly around Aurora. Her arms fly up and around his neck. Dimitri moves slowly toward the desk and stands there, staring at his fallen friend. He stays statue still for what seems like forever. Aurora comes up alongside him to wrap her arms around his waist. They stand there in silence before Aurora breaks away to start the binding process with the linens. Elena eventually enters and clings onto Nico, resting her head on his chest.

She whispers softly. "How does she know how to do this? She's not old enough to have seen it done." Nico smirks and kisses the top of Elena's head.

"I taught her while I was flying back here. Her dragon side is quite strong for being a hybrid." He rests his head on top of Elena's and continues to watch Aurora work. Sebastian returns and remains in the doorway.

"We are ready when you are," Sebastian raises his hand and offers it for Aurora to take. Ever so carefully, Aurora picks up Andre's body and holds it tight to her chest. She cradles his body like a mother would a baby as she approaches Sebastian. Her head turns quickly, first locking on the table, then on me.

"Dom, please grab the remaining herbs to bring with us." I nod in agreement, and her eyes land on Nico. "Father, I need your fire." Nico audibly swallows, then nods to Aurora. Only when she felt everything was in place did she allow Sebastian to lead her out.

We walk to what would typically be the training circle. The sandpit will contain the embers and stop them from spreading. The heat alone will possibly turn some of the sand into glass. The entire Lycan and newly arrived Dire pack gather to witness a ceremony that hasn't been performed in centuries.

Elena runs up to where Aurora positioned herself at the top of the pyre. Carefully, Elena lays out the blood-red cloth with the embroidered Marelup crest as well as the symbol for the Golden Eagles. Aurora reverently places Andre's wrapped body on the fabric. She folds three of the four corners to cover him, leaving only his wrapped head exposed. We watch her layout the spices as well as crystals that Elena must have given her. Aurora draws in a deep breath and raises her hands above her. As she does so, we watch her arms shift and become covered in thick, white, armored dragon scales. Her snow-white talons appear even more menacing by torchlight. Everyone falls silent and kneels before her and the great pyre.

"My people!" We hear and feel Aurora's words and power through the pack bond. "One of our own was murdered right here on our land." Her eyes scan the gathered wolves, searching for any sign of the betrayer. "He was sent on a mission for me that only he could complete. He died on his way back to me, to us." She keeps a close watch over everyone present.

"Andre and Dimitri were tasked with my protection from the moment I drew my first breath upon this Earth. For over two hundred years, they were the closest things to parents that I've known." Aurora's voice gains the familiar growl of her beast. "A small piece of me died with him today." Her eyes move from Dimitri to Nico and gives him the signal to shift.

Nico moves behind the pyre and shifts to his Ice Dragon, his head adorned with a crown of horns—denoting his age and lineage. His great head is raised above Aurora, waiting for her next signal.

"I..." Aurora hesitates for a moment, overwhelmed with emotion as tears stream down her cheeks. It's then I notice the scale on her chest glows faintly. Her right hand rests over it, and she calms almost instantly, her mercury eyes returning to steel-grey. "Today, I lay to rest a man I am proud to call a father figure. I lay to rest a man that has put his life on the line time and time again for my mother and me. Today, I lay to rest my best friend." Aurora shifts her right hand back to human and slits her palm over Andre's body. She lays her bleeding hand upon him. "With my blood, I swear to seek out Andre's killer and rip his heart from his chest. I will not rest until it's done." Aurora holds her bleeding hand up to the crowd. She turns her head to look at her father and nods.

You can hear the clicks of the dragon's ignitor firing up before the roar of flames fills the arena. Most watch in horror as Nico bathes not only the pyre in flames, but Aurora too. We see her stand there, watching over Andre as he burns. Out of the corner of my eye, I catch Jayce on the phone. I can read his lips; he's reassuring whoever is on the other end that everything is okay. I return to watching the flames and the pyre burn brightly in the night.

A miracle happens: a smoke wisp shaped like an eagle takes flight straight up into the night sky from the flames. Gasps are heard around the fire. Apparently, that's what we were hoping and waiting for. Jayce switches his phone call to video just before Aurora walks out of what's left of the burning pyre. Neither a scratch on her nor a hair out of place. Sebastian quickly offers Aurora his fleece button-down, which she gladly accepts. Aurora smiles brightly at us and looks up into the night sky.

"Did you see? I freed Andre's soul and sent him off to be with his ancestors." She's beaming proudly at her accomplishment. I only heard stories of events like this when I was a child. I honestly didn't think things like this were possible. Then again, a Dragon-Lycan hybrid shouldn't be possible either.

Jayce comes over, back to talking on the phone. I can tell by the changes in his tone that more than one person is on the line. I tilt my head to the side, looking at my brother. Jayce holds up one finger, then ends the call.

"The connection is stronger than we thought. Alaric called Alex directly when he felt Aurora's distress. He was ready to fly here, which would have destroyed everything we've been working for." Jayce's eyes focus on Aurora and reach out to touch Alaric's scale. He smiles sweetly at her before looking back at the rest of us. "I need to get everyone settled. If you need me, call please." His eyes are glassy from unshed tears; he's trying to be strong for Aurora. I know he's going to find a private place to cry. I turn to look at Sebastian, and the fucker is back on his phone again. What the actual fuck could be so important that he never puts that fucking thing down?

"Hey, Sebastian! Got a minute?" He slowly looks up from his phone and nods. He continues to type on his phone for several moments before he finally walks over.

"What's up, Dom?" Sebastian says with that almost bored tone of his. If only Aurora didn't have that *no hitting the other mates* rule; I'd love to deck him with something hard. I have to admit, Sebastian has that swagger that makes him attractive. But his attitude? Shit, I can't wait for the dragon to get here and knock him down a peg.

"Sebastian, I need your help organizing the clean up as well as the training for the Dires who just arrived. Right now, I believe it's best for Aurora to take it easy and heal from her loss." The Lycans are his people, and now we're almost on equal footing with both of our species here together. Sebastian's sky blue eyes change to the white-blue of his wolf before he smirks at me.

"Finally accepted your place in the family, I see. It's about fucking time. I'll organize my people, you handle yours. Training starts tomorrow. As for the mess, give me ten of your people, and I'll get ten of mine to return the training grounds back to normal." His look is one of challenge, and to be honest, I can't fucking take it anymore. My Dire Wolf rips free of my body, pissed off to all hell. I feel different; my vision is different. Most of my vision shows shades of colors that outline the beings before me like a light is cast behind them. My night vision has evolved. I watch the blood pump through the bodies before me. I hear voices around me, and even Sebastian looks stunned.

"Dude, your eyes are mercury like Aurora's! Fuck!" That explains it. I see the fear in Sebastian's eyes as I stare at him. I stalk forward, growling at him. As I get ready to lunge, I feel Aurora's hand on my back. I immediately abandon my original plan to attack Sebastian. Carefully, I turn to look up at Aurora, her liquid mercury eyes looking back at me. The look of wonder on her face is worth all the aggravation that Sebastian caused. I would give anything to remain in this moment forever.

"I see you have my vision, Dom. Use it wisely; it takes a bit to get used to." Aurora leads me away from Sebastian and sits down on a nearby bench. I shift back to my human form and take a seat next to her. I turn my body so I'm facing her, gently taking her hands in mine. "Dom, my love, I know things are tense between you and Sebastian. I get it. It's a constant measuring contest between you two. I know Sebastian can get on your nerves. Hell, he constantly gets on mine." Aurora grips my hands tightly as she looks at me. I know deep down she's in Hell, but right now, she's more worried about me than herself. I look down to our joined hands, then back up to her. I can feel the moment my eyes go back to my human hazel; no more outlines and shining silhouettes.

"Thanks, Aurora. I'm not concerned about Sebastian at the moment; I'm more worried about you. Sebastian can go to fucking Hell for all I care. I want to make sure you're okay emotionally, mentally, and physically. Death of a loved one is never easy to deal with." Slowly, I lean forward and gently kiss her lips. Aurora lets out a pleased sigh and smiles at me. Then she cups my cheek and rests her forehead against mine. Through direct contact of the bond, I feel everything: her love for me, the pain she's hiding, and the fear of losing one of us in the war.

Please be patient, Dom. All will work out in the end. Aurora's voice is a breathy whisper in my mind. Her words embrace me and strengthen my resolve. We'll be okay. I know we will. I lightly place my hands over hers and remain still, enjoying the connection.

"Kids, I hate to break up this love fest, but we need to plan to train and then to depart." Like all parents, Nico has the absolute worst timing. Aurora rolls her eyes at her father before she pulls away from me. She stands abruptly and salutes Nico, then walks off in a modified march. I shrug my shoulders at Nico before I stand.

"I'll go grab some pants and make sure everyone is settled in properly for tomorrow's training push." I also decide to salute Nico, which inflates the Dragon King's ego even further. Thankfully, he doesn't realize we're being complete wise asses and that it wasn't done out of respect but sarcasm.

CHAPTER 41

Aurora

The next morning, I wake up alone in Dom's room. He and Jayce must have woken up early to get everyone started on their tasks. Silently, I return to my room and pull on a pair of leggings and a Bad Wolves T-shirt from my closet. My guitar amp is by the door, offering me solace from the pain I'm in. Yeah, I need to play something straight from the heart this morning. Pete is standing in the meeting hall, dusting my throne.

"Hey, Pete!" He jumps at the sudden noise. After realizing it's me, he smiles and approaches me.

"Morning, My Queen. What can I do for you today?" Pete is ever so eager to please me. It helps that he's an omega, and their drive to please their alpha is all-consuming at times.

"I need you to grab your bass and grab our drummer. I need to play this morning." My eyes well up with tears that threaten to break. Pete looks panicked, then runs off to do my bidding. I walk around the main hall to open all the windows and set up my amp by my throne. I start to tune my guitar, preparing to play a song that embodies my feelings right now. Footsteps fill the hall, and I look up to see Pete and the usual crew ready to play together. To achieve the perfect acoustics, we turn our amps to face the halls. The guys look at me expectantly as I move to take my spot in the middle of the room.

"*Cemetery Gates* from Pantera. Pete, be prepared to take over vocals if I falter during the song." Pete gives me a nod before I start the opening riff of the song. I climb onto my throne and keep the tone going. When it comes to the lyrics, they flow from me, dripping with the pain I'm feeling. My voice is almost raw with emotion. I swallow hard as I go into the riffs between lyrics, pouring my heart and soul into nailing this song and making it perfect.

Out of the corner of my eye, I watch the guys move around as they play along. My guys and several others file into the hall as I sing. My eyes close as I tilt my head to the ceiling, tears escaping out of the corner of my eyes rolling freely down my cheeks. I hear Dimitri enter and sniffle. My eyes open and I slide off my throne then begin to walk toward him. My eyes shift to that of my beast, and I feel scales ripple up my arms then recede. When I pronounce the word *gates* before the big solo, the word is growled out with the voice of my beast—its fierceness coming through strongly. At the end of the song, I practically howl out the word *gates*. My guitar cries, holding the final tone until I finally release it. I feel a little better after playing that song. It happened to be one of Andre's favorites.

Next, I decided to do another favorite of his. I choose to play *Bulls on Parade* by Rage Against the Machine. I have to say, it's hard to play this song as well as the great Tom Morello does, but I give it my all. I end up jumping around the room and jamming out as Pete tries to scream the lyrics like they should be. The song changes the room's feel from the gloom that my first song invoked to a bouncing, playful tone. It doesn't last as long as I'd like it to. Unfortunately, now I have adulting to do—damn responsibilities.

"Thanks, everyone, for coming and watching us perform! You know me by now; I needed to vent through my music." I walk over and hug Dimitri tightly. His partner for the last who knows how many hundreds of years died yesterday. I know the pain of his loss has to be hitting him harder than it's hitting me. We remain in each other's arms, silently crying.

"D..." I nuzzle his cheek like I did as a pup. I can't help but look at him through tear-filled eyes. He's trying to be strong for me and hide his pain, but I see right through that big, grumpy bear. I kiss his cheek and attempt to smile at him. "We have a murderer to hunt, D. We will hang whomever it is by his entrails and beat him like a piñata." I get half a laugh out of Dimitri.

"Baby girl, you make me very proud of you. For once, I will not temper your rage. Release the beast and let it shred anything in its wake. We will dance on the bones of our enemies!" Dimitri's Russian accent is very thick when he speaks. He's not hiding who he is anymore.

I felt my beast stir when Dimitri called for it. To be honest, I want nothing more than to hunt the fucker that killed Andre. I want to kill everyone and everything that had a hand in his death—my prime suspects at the moment: several high ranking Lycans and Sebastian. Andre went off to gather information on a total of five beings and died before he was able to relay what he found. I'm now positive there is a traitor in our midst somewhere. I will carry on as usual, as not to show my hand yet.

"Back to work, everyone! The war won't win itself!" Everyone scatters, and all that's left are my mates, father, and Dimitri. I can tell by how my father is looking at me that he knows something is on my mind. "Guys—dad, Dimitri, and I need to go talk about the old days. I want to learn more about my mother and the castle." Jayce is the first to smile. He runs up to hug and kiss me. Dom takes his time and picks me up, kissing me passionately before setting me down. Sebastian comes to stand before me, attempting to lock eyes with me—almost in challenge. My beast isn't having it and makes him turn his eyes away. I lightly grip his jaw and turn his head to face me.

"Please don't test me." Sebastian smirks and kisses me, nipping at my bottom lip for good measure. Forever the wise ass. My father approaches and offers his hand to me. The minute I take his hand, I hear his voice in my head.

I know something is plaguing you, daughter. Is this the reason for the walk? My eyes turn to my father briefly, and I barely nod my head. He squeezes my hand to let me know he saw my answer.

"Come on, D. Lets go!" I extend my hand to Dimitri, wiggling my fingers at him. He half laughs and takes my hand. I almost got him to smile.

Okay, guys, I don't know if trying to talk to both of you at the same time is going to work, but here I go. We have a traitor somewhere here in the compound. I'm not sure who it is, so don't ask. I had Andre investigate four elders and Sebastian's family." My eyes drift between my father and Dimitri as we walk out the door and head toward the stream at the property's southern edge. I know they heard me by how tense their bodies have become. As soon as we get out of range, I stop and stare at both of them. I let out a slow breath, looking at them expectantly. I can see the gears turning between the two of them.

"What made you come to these conclusions, Aurora?" Dimitri is the first to question me. All I can do is breathe in deeply.

"Some of the older Lycans questioned my bloodline, and I overheard them mention Vladimir. They were speaking as if he's still around. It kind of makes me wonder.." I look between the two of them, and I see both of their animals surge to the surface. We stand there in silence. There were suspicions that the old alpha was possibly still alive. We still don't have confirmation, and Andre would have had that answer.

"Andre was bringing me his findings. I never got the answers I was looking for." I lower my eyes to look at the ground. I miss Andre so much. He was my confidant and a mother figure. My father nods slowly, taking in all that I've said.

"The Elders could be old enough to remember the old alpha. The question is, where do their loyalties lie? Sebastian is a mate, so I seriously doubt he would plot against you; but it could be possible." Nico rests his hand on my shoulder and gives it a squeeze. I force a smile as I look up at my father.

"I was hoping you would say that, Dad. So, we agree to focus on the Elders and try to figure out which of the four houses has it out for me." My eyes lock on Dimitri, and I watch him straighten up, his shoulders pushed back and chest puffed up. "D, I need you to watch and listen to the ones who are training. Someone might slip and say something. You know how pups talk." I've never seen Dimitri with such a stern look on his face. He's actually quite menacing looking.

"I will do it gladly, baby girl. Anything for you." He wraps his thick arms around me and hugs me tightly to him. My arms band around his neck and I squeeze him back. I love my mates, but these are the only two that I can completely trust with behind-the-scenes things. I hate having to be suspicious of my people, but something doesn't add up. Reluctantly, I let go of Dimitri and motion for us to head back to the camp.

"Dad, I have a question for you." I turn to face him and tilt my head to the side, thinking about how to phrase the question. "Before the ascension, why was my wolf insanely jealous of Dimitri having a sexual relationship with anyone? She pretty much claimed him as hers but didn't physically claim him." I watch Dimitri's cheeks burn flame-red from embarrassment. He wasn't the only one embarrassed, but I needed answers. After all, my animal's possessiveness of Dimitri ended the minute she smelled Sebastian. Nico simply laughs. He laughs so hard he's bent at the waist with his hand on his thigh.

"Sorry, daughter... That's a very dragon trait. You were magically bound to Dimitri, so your young animal confused it for the mating bond. It's an honest mistake. In truth, without that bond, you probably would have gone insane and took me with you." Nico slowly stands up and regains his composure, still smirking at Dimitri. "I know the stories you told me, old friend, and I'm sorry it happened. If I was able to be with my daughter from the beginning, that bond never would have existed." Nico looks down after the words leave his mouth. He realizes what he said was a tad insensitive. "I am grateful for all you've done for us. I am sorry if my words were cruel." Nico furrows his brows. I'm betting my father isn't used to apologizing when he messes up. Dimitri lets the comment roll off his back. It doesn't even look like it phased him. He moves closer to my father then gives him one of those side bro-hug things with the exaggerated back-patting and everything.

"We're good. We better get back before the others get suspicious."

I roll my eyes and start walking back, ahead of the guys. I listen to the sounds of battle going on in the training grounds. Yup, that's where I'm headed. Why not? I mean, seriously, I have three smoking hot mates who could potentially be shirtless. Shirtless and sweaty with beads of sweat rolling down their well-defined abdomens... Damn, I need to get laid.

I creep through the shadows, observing all the guys in their half-naked glory. Dom and Pete are sparing, using bow staves. Dom's muscles elongating and flexing then tightening has me mesmerized. I am so lost in my own little wet dream, I don't even notice when Elena comes up beside me. When I do notice, I scream like a little girl and claw half-way up the tree. I'm hanging from the tree by my talons when I look down and notice it's only Elena. She's legit laughing her ass off at me. Dom is now also under the tree, trying not to laugh, along with several others. Just to be an ass, I let go of the tree and fall, so Dom has to catch me. What a crying shame! He's half-naked and holding me. What's a girl to do? Dom lets out a heartfelt laugh then kisses my cheek.

"Crazy wolf! Are you trying to give me a heart attack?" He smiles and kisses my cheek again. His lips find my neck, and he nips me gently. Then Dom lets out a primal growl and starts to walk away with me. Our forward momentum is suddenly halted by Dimitri, who steps in front of us, and my father places his hand on Dom's shoulder.

"I know that growl, lad. I can't let you follow your instincts. We need Aurora at full strength for this journey and the battles ahead." Nico isn't budging until I'm released from Dom's grasp. My feet hit the floor, and I look between my father and Dom. Then it dawns on me; that was a short two months. I step away from the guys, disappointed that I was denied dick. But my father is right; I will slow everyone down if I am heavily pregnant.

"Elena, I need the tea again. Dad, Dimitri, can you two watch over me?" They both smile and nod. Dimitri grabs my hand and starts leading me to his small cabin set off away from everyone. I didn't know the shack he chose was so little. He deserves better. I make a mental note to improve his living conditions when this is all over.

CHAPTER 42

Aurora

Dimitri leads me into a room off the main one and I freeze in my tracks. It was Andre's room. I walk in slowly. There are so many pictures of us over the years that I didn't know existed. I stare in wonder, watching myself grow up in the photographs—birthdays, holidays; they are all here. I quickly look back to Dimitri, who's in tears like I am.

"He kept a photo album of you growing up. I know he would have wanted you to have it." Dimitri reaches into a drawer, pulls out the album, and sets it on the table beside the bed. Elena's in the doorway, listening to our exchange with tears freely flowing down her cheeks. She can't bring herself to speak and offers me a cup of special tea. I look down at the contents and sniff it. Something's different. My beast surges to the surface, and I shove the tea at her.

"You drink it!" I stare at her, my instincts on high alert. Something isn't sitting right. Elena takes the cup from me and sniffs it, and all the color drains from her face.

"Princess, no! I didn't do this! Someone must have tampered with my herbs." Dimitri's bear makes his presence known as fur ripples down his arms and recedes just as quickly. My father comes up behind him and placed his hand on his shoulder.

"Old friend, we will just have to keep Aurora isolated, that's all. I will try to put her into a frost slumber. It's a state of torpor that some Ice Dragons use to leapfrog through time. If it doesn't work, I'll turn this house into one huge ice cube." My father shrugs his shoulders like it is no big deal. Then again, to him, it probably isn't a big deal.

"Before I sleep, Father, I want to try something for Dimitri." I look to Dimitri and he nods, moving closer to me. "Please sit, D. My blood healed Sebastian quickly. I'm wondering if it would do the same for you. Perhaps slow the progression of time." I watch the idea process quickly behind my father's eyes. His dragon surges forward just before he runs out of the room. Either I had a stroke of genius, or he doesn't want to witness what I'm going to do. When my father returns, he's holding a goblet, a bottle of vodka, and a spoon. Okay, I'm really puzzled now.

"My brilliant daughter, I completely forgot about the blood bonding. Dimitri, we can bond you to the two of us. It should stop the aging process and possibly reverse it some." Nico pours about four shots of vodka into the goblet, bites his own wrist, and bleeds into the goblet. He licks his wound, sealing it before he looks at me. I bite my right wrist deeply and hold it over the goblet, making sure the majority of the blood makes it in. Carefully, I pick up the goblet and hold it out to Dimitri. He bites his wrist and bleeds into it—about the same amount as my father did. Nico looks between Dimitri and me then decides to explain.

"I know you're wondering, why the vodka? It keeps the blood from clotting, and it makes the blood taste better." His eyes turn to Elena. "Knowledge of this does not leave this room, am I clear?" Elena nods slowly. She's obviously still frightened and sad that she almost assisted in killing me. Since I'm still holding the goblet, I drink about a third of the contents. I immediately feel the power of my father's blood in my body. Carefully, I pass the goblet to my father, and he drinks half of what's left.

Finally, Dimitri gets the remaining blood. He smiles at me quickly before drinking the rest of it. The surge of power that goes through him knocks him to his knees, and I rush over to keep him steady. I feel his muscles tense under my fingertips as they become thick and solid. Almost twenty minutes pass before he lifts his head and looks at me. It's as if I dunked Dimitri in the fountain of youth. He's absolutely handsome. I never noticed how beautiful of a man he was until just now.

"Aurora, please don't look at me like that," Dimitri says softly. He stands to his full height and stretches his heavily muscled body. He's a mountain of a man. I know part of it has to do with his bear, but damn. Maybe my wolf isn't fucking delusional for thinking of Dimitri as hers. Perhaps it's my heat talking, perhaps not. I would have to revisit this subject once my heat passes.

I laugh softly to myself and turn away from Dimitri to look around Andre's old room. He held onto so many little things that I brought him over the years. All the small animal skulls litter the shelves in his room. Looking at them, I start cracking up. My father comes to stand beside me in front of the shelves of skulls. He starts chuckling to himself.

"I guess you took after me more than I thought. I'm guessing, by the size of these skulls, you were a little one when you started this collection." He tilts his head to look at me, the liquid mercury of his dragon's eyes focused on mine. I nod slowly and look back at my collection.

"At first, it freaked Andre out that I was bringing him my trophies. After a while, he began to look forward to seeing what I would bring him that day." I pick up a cougar's skull and hold it in my hand. "I was ten when I killed the cougar. The guys were out hunting when it came into our yard. I had chores to get done, so I was in the garden when it attacked me. I guess it didn't or couldn't smell what I was. I felt its teeth sinking into the back of my neck as its claws dug into my ribs. Something came over me and my body went into its first full shift. Before that day, most times, I was only able to shift my hands and canines. It released me and tried to escape, but it didn't get far before I caught up to it and ripped it to shreds." I start laughing as I look over to Dimitri, who's definitely having a proud moment.

"Poor Andre had to deal with not only a freshly shifted she-wolf but cougar parts all over the yard. You know how jumpy Andre could be. He tried so hard to fight his instinct to run. In the end, Dimitri had to watch over me until I shifted back." Dimitri laughs for several moments before regaining his composure.

"She was stuck as her wolf for almost four days. That little white hellion was like a force of nature, hell-bent on testing out her talons and her newfound strength and speed. Hell, Andre was the only one fast enough to keep up with her when she went hunting." My father beams with pride as he listens to our story. He begins to walk around Andre's room, picking up different pictures —basically catching up on the last two hundred some odd years.

Nico holds up a picture that I hadn't noticed. I walk over to my father and lean over his shoulder to look at it with him. It's a picture of Sebastian holding me as a baby. I wonder how long Andre hid this picture from me. Sebastian looks so enamored with me, like the sun rose and set with every breath I took. I take out my phone and send my baby picture to Sebastian. I manipulate the photo to have a heart frame with the caption awe. Within a matter of seconds, he sends me several heart emojis and asks where I am. I tell him I'm in Andre's room and I'm being quarantined until my heat is over. He sends me several sad faces. I shake my head and put my phone away.

My father is now on the bed, sitting next to Elena, and they're both looking through the album. She tells him about the night of my arrival and the three months we spent with her and Sebastian. My dad thanked her profusely for caring for me and providing us shelter when we needed it most. I watch the exchange for several minutes until my phone goes off again. It's Jayce, and this time he wants to video chat. I walk to the corner of the room and sit in Andre's rocking chair.

"Hi, love," I say when I see his smiling face. The video changes; he must have cast it to the smart screen in the office. "Hi, everyone! I'm currently grounded because of my heat." The guys nod, and all start speaking at once. "Whoa! Settle down. First off, I need to let you know someone tampered with Elena's herbs. I was almost poisoned today." The guys start yelling back and forth, threatening to rip the compound apart. "We don't need to go that crazy. There is a traitor here, and we've been aware of that for quite some time. I want you to spread the rumor that I'm very ill, and you're not sure if I'm going to survive." I watch the guys ponder what I just said.

Sebastian speaks first. "Are you sure that's wise? I mean, they could attack, and we aren't there to protect you."

"Positive. I have protection, don't worry about that aspect. Besides, I'm in heat, not fucking dead, Bash. Give a girl some credit here." Dimitri prepares to step forward, and I raise my hand to stop him. I don't need my secret weapon revealed quite yet. I look back at the guys. "Any questions?" The twins look at each other then back to the screen.

"We'll patrol outside to keep appearances up. We need to keep this as legit-looking as possible for it to work." I agree with them and nod slowly.

"Do you want me or your father to make the announcement to the packs?" Sebastian is the next to speak. I bite my bottom lip, pondering what he said. There are very few who know about the tea's existence, and he's one of them.

"I think it's best if you and my father make the announcement together. The king and the first mate standing together makes for a stronger, united front. Say very little about what happened, just that I was somehow poisoned, and your mother is working around the clock and trying everything she can to save me." Sebastian nods then smirks.

"I'll keep the pack and the boys in line until you're able to return." He looks over at the twins and gives them a look I really don't like.

"No need, love," I state flatly. "It would be far better if my father oversees everything. After all, he is the Dragon King. Who in their right mind would oppose him?" I watch Sebastian's face contort a dozen ways before he reigns in his emotions.

"As you wish, princess," Sebastian says with a mild inflection of a venomous tone. I keep my eyes steady on him until he leaves the room the twins are in. I signal the twins to watch each other's backs. I carry on with casual conversation as I start writing messages to hold up to them.

CHAPTER 43

Aurora

I'm not sure how far away Sebastian is, and I'm concerned for the twins' safety. I end the video chat and stare at Elena. "What family do you have left in Romania? Who was your sire?" Gut instinct tells me she's related to Lycan Alpha Vladimir. My heart hopes I'm wrong. Elena's bottom lip quivers as she looks at me. She starts shifting from foot to foot, showing her nervousness. I can scent the fear in the air—it's rather acrid. Dimitri blocks the door behind her as I wait patiently for her answer. Well, as patiently as I can.

Elena finally speaks. "We are first cousins with Vladimir. I swear, we are only loyal to you." Elena drops to her hands and knees, exposing her throat to me. My eyes narrow as I stare at her, and my hand lands on my father's arm.

I think this is the news that got Andre killed. If I'm correct, either one of the Lupi's—Elena or Sebastian—ordered the hit, or the real puppet master did. I don't bother turning to look at my father. I feel the rage building within him. It's quite interesting that her herbs are tainted, she's dating my father, and I'm mated to her son. My eyes move to Dimitri, and he notices they have swirled to liquid mercury. He gives me a nod of understanding. He knows I'm talking to my father and that he will be filled in eventually.

I openly pose a question. "Can a mating bond be faked or forced with herbs and magic?" Elena's head whips up, and her face turns as white as snow.

"Yes, daughter, it can. It's how the alpha tricked your mother into being his mate. The elder dame made the drink and cast the spell." Dimitri's and my animal begin to growl. I want to destroy, and I don't care about the repercussions. My eyes land on Elena next. Her life hangs in the balance at this point.

"Was the tea you had given Andre for me laced with anything besides the sleeping tonic? Choose your words wisely." I can hear the guys yelling for me to stop, *don't do it*! I'm not a pawn or a plaything. Elena is sobbing loudly, her tears falling to the floor. Her cries don't move me or stir any kind of emotion from me.

The door behind Dimitri flies open, and the guys scream for me to listen to them. My arms and hands shift to armored gauntlets as I stare down at the woman I once called mother. "Did you force the bond between Sebastian and I?" I practically roar out the sentence. My heart is aching with the knowledge that perhaps what we have isn't real. The guys all freeze as what I said dawns on them; Sebastian is the only one who is let past Dimitri. He's hesitant as he kneels next to his mother. He wraps his arms around her then looks up to me. The pain in his eyes almost cracks my resolve.

"They have my brother. We thought if I was mated to you..." He's frustrated and hurting, but how can I forgive this betrayal? "If I knew then what I know now, I would have asked for help." My eyes remain narrowed on Sebastian. His mother is crying, and he's showing the appropriate emotions. He's trying to console her as he looks up at me, hoping for forgiveness.

"Dimitri, was there a brother when you took care of me as a baby?" I can tell when Dimitri begins searching his memory because he starts to bite his lower lip. Damn this fucking heat; I love and hate when he does that.

"I remember a wee little one running around, but I'm not sure if he was introduced as Sebastian's brother or not." Dimitri tilts his head to the side after he finishes speaking, letting me pass judgment.

My eyes fall on my father. He's clearly upset by this new information. If he's anything like me, he feels used. Slowly, my father moves closer to me and rests his hand on the back of my neck. *Daughter, I don't know what to tell you to do. If you suspect them, don't let on that you do. We can use your leniency to our advantage in the long run. They are related to the old alpha. Who knows if they believe as he did.* I take his words into consideration before I look back to Elena and Sebastian. I step away from my father and glance at the twins. I know they will stand by me no matter my decision. My eyes fall to Dimitri, who nods and brings his fist over his heart.

"I have come to a decision." Heeding my father's words, I calm myself down and shift my hands and arms back to human. "For the sake of appearances, Sebastian, you can remain in the Alpha House. You are stripped of the title of First Mate. By rights, it's now Dom's proper title." I watch as Sebastian's beast flairs up in his eyes, turning them the white-blue of his wolf. "Go ahead, Sebastian, challenge me! Your wolf is pissed, and rightfully so. Though, he should be pissed at you for forging a false bond."

Sebastian's eyes return to his normal baby blue. "I'm hurt, I won't lie about that. I never would have thought the two of you would sink so low. I have a lot to sort through mentally and emotionally." I feel the prince's scale warm up on my chest, and my hand absently reaches up to touch it. My eyes return to Sebastian, and they flicker between human and the mercury of my beast. "You robbed me of the possibility of a true Lycan mate." I shake my head at him and move toward Dimitri, letting him hold me as I start to cry. My father chose this time to shove everyone out of the house, except the twins. I feel both their hands on my back as they try to soothe my pain away. I lift my head up and turn in Dimitri's arms to look at them.

"Thanks, guys, I appreciate it. I'm just very lost at the moment. I mean, my true mate is out there somewhere, and because of Sebastian, I'll never meet him." I sigh softly and lower my head. Dom reaches up, gently grips my chin, and raises my head until he can look me in the eye.

"Princess, we love you and will support you in whatever you desire to do. As for your true Lycan mate, who knows? He might be able to break the magic placed over you. Honestly, I don't know how that shit works. I hope, for your sake, we can break it." As Dom kisses my lips, Jayce's phone starts ringing. Dom and I both look at Jayce, and he starts laughing.

"The prince is threatening to fly down here and burn the village to the ground. Nico, would you mind speaking to him?" My father takes the phone from Jayce and walks out of the room.

"As much as I hate to kick you out, I'm having problems keeping my urges under control." Quickly, I kiss both boys on the lips, and Dimitri ushers them out of the room. Once the guys clear the front door, I walk over to my father while he video chats with the prince

—I just can't help myself. I walk around the table to stand behind my father and rest my forearms on his shoulders to see Alaric myself. Dare I say, he's a beautiful man. He's rugged and handsome, and his beard definitely works with that Viking look he's got going on. I lower my head to be even with my father's and stare at Alaric. He blushes for a moment then clears his throat. I watch his almost golden eyes look back and forth between my father and me.

"I assume your beauty comes from your mother, princess?" He smiles and starts to laugh with my father.

"Yeah, I guess so. I never had the pleasure of meeting my mother. Apparently, I was the reason she died." I quickly drop my eyes, and my father leans the phone against the napkin holder to embrace me. Alaric, realizing his folly, clears his throat again. Smoke rings come out his nostrils. This catches my attention, and I raise my head up, watching him intently.

"My mother is a Gold Dragon. I have her fire as well as my father's resistance to ice and cold." Alaric feels compelled to explain what happened. "As for your mom, I met her several times. She was magnificent and brilliant. She was a very fair leader, unlike most of the Lycans at the time." Alaric looks down then back up at me. "I just needed to know you were okay. I mean, I feel the turmoil." He opens his shirt to reveal my scale. He rubs it gently, and it feels like he's touching me. I look down at his scale and watch it change from golden- white to white. I smile, realizing the connection. I lightly touch his scale and rub it in return. His smile broadens when he feels my touch. My father starts laughing his ass off.

"Silly kids, wait until after you mate! You think that feeling is intense? It gets stronger! Only downside: Aurora's dragon half may get stronger than her wolven half." Nico looks between the two of us then stands to leave. "I'll let you two talk for a bit. I'll be on the porch if you need me, baby girl." With that, my father leaves. My father's antics make me laugh. In the background, I hear Alaric say, "breathtaking."

"What? You act as if you've never witnessed a woman laugh before." He smiles and shakes his head at me, refusing to speak. "I get it, it's the mate attraction. I honestly can't wait to see your dragon in all his glory. If he's anything like his human half, he must be magnificent." As soon as I call his dragon magnificent, he flares to the surface. Alaric's eyes turn the silver-gold of his dragon. "Ah, there you are. Hello, handsome. Will you take me flying?" The slits in Alaric's eyes dilate several times. "I guess I pleased him." I can't help but smile at the thought. I pleased a Dragon Prince, and I haven't even touched him yet.

"I was concerned that perhaps my dragon would frighten you. I'm so happy you wish to meet him and go for a flight. A mating flight is a dragon tradition, you know?" Alaric states it as a question, and I shake my head no at him. He sits back, looking shocked for a moment. "Oh! Well, um, that's a conversation for when we can sit side by side. This isn't the proper way to discuss such a serious conversation. I should go, my love. Rest well. Tomorrow will be another day that we're closer together." He kisses his fingertips and presses it to my scale. I sigh at the warmth I feel.

"Sleep well, my prince. Dream of me?" I tear up a little at the thought. I smile before I kiss my fingertips and press them to his scale. I watch him smile as he mouths, *always,* before ending the call. I hate to admit I stare at the blank phone screen longer than I should have. Slowly, I stand up and walk outside to return the phone to my father.

"Please return this to Jayce for me. I'm going to try to sleep." I kiss the top of my father's head and wave to Dimitri as he returns. I head back to Andre's room and curl up in his bed. This is going to be the longest three days ever.

CHAPTER 44
Nicodeamus

The revelations that have been made in the last twenty-four hours are borderline insane. First, we discover that Sebastian tricked Aurora into a mating. Elena more than likely doesn't love me, and she's been faking it all this time. Plus, we managed to solve Dimitri's aging problem. That, in itself, is a miracle.

I manage to get the alpha of the German Lycan pack's number from Elena. I call him and request that he sends me six of his strongest warriors that he trusts the most with guarding Aurora's life. I hope this will help cut down the possible threats to my daughter's life in the future. Who knows, with any luck, one of the six that he sends to us might be her real mate, and we can get rid of this Sebastian bastard. I can't believe, in all these years, someone of her kind would stoop so low as to force a mating, just like old Alpha Vladimir. You better bet that I'm going to do every-thing within my power, with the last dying breath I hold in my chest, to take care of and protect my daughter. I wait for confir-mation of the tickets that will send the Lycans here straight from Germany. I now have to entrust the pickup of these young men to

Dominik, since he and Jayce seem to be the only real mates that my daughter has.

The fate of our world as we know it is hanging in the balance. People we thought we could trust are now held as suspects in the back of my mind. Days like today make me regret my decision to trust the old alpha. We allowed him to live past the night he decided to curse us all and perform blood magic on us. Here we are, almost two hundred and thirty years later, and the repercussions of his poor choices are still felt today.

Now, I watch the American Lycan pack move amongst each other. Each one, in my mind, could be a possible threat to my child. I am fully prepared to turn this entire compound into nothing but a sea of ice. Hell hath no fury like a Dragon King scorned. I watch Dimitri approach slowly, his great, hulking forum exuding nothing but the primal confidence of his bear. It's nice to see my old friend back in his prime, ready to go to battle and destroy the enemies before him. As Dimitri gets closer, I see that he's smiling. I wonder what the old bear's been up while we were separated. "Dimitri, old friend, where did you manage to get yourself off to?"

"Nico, I was checking on the training. Dominik and Jayce have really stepped up. Those two are really trying to pick up the slack Sebastian's absence has caused." He smirks and looks between the alpha house and his own cabin where Aurora is. "I'm sure if Sebastian is up to something, we should know shortly. I can't see him sitting there on his hands waiting for Aurora to pass judgment on whether he lives or dies." Dimitri's observation is concrete. I just hope he isn't right.

"That's fine with me. Let Sebastian stew. I'm not concerned at all about this whelp, who would have been king." I tap my fingers on the arm of the rocking chair. I'm still watching out over the compound, ever vigilant for any signs of deception. Aurora still slumbers, though her sleep has not been peaceful at all. She woke up several times last night, crying in her sleep, upset over Sebastian's betrayal. The deception he carried on for all this time has been eating at her something horrible. One of two things will happen: either her wolf is going to lash out and destroy everything in its path. Or hopefully, if the dragon side of her nature is stronger, she'll bide her time and exact her revenge.

I rise from the rocking chair and lean on the rail of the porch, still keeping my eyes on the training circle as Dominik man-handles the American Lycans. Nothing is more enjoyable than watching a Dire Wolf fighting to prove his position within the pack. He's proving that he's the real first mate of the princess, my daughter. Jayce is off to the side, doing what he does best: keeping records. He observes everybody's movements and interactions, taking note of anything that may or may not be significant. He is the one who's organizing the flights for the Lycans when they arrive from Germany. I can't wait until they get here. "Dimitri, what do you think we should do with Sebastian and his mother? I mean, honestly, I don't think we can trust them any further."

"I'm not sure, Nicodeamus, but I believe our best course of action is to wait for Aurora's heat to end then have her come out and pass judgment." He crosses his thick arms over his barrel chest, looking like a mountain of muscle. I can understand now why the Great Bears of the past invoke such stories of fear when they were angry. The sheer size of him is quite imposing.

"You're right, old friend. I know I shouldn't be trying to make all these decisions for Aurora. After all, he is technically still her mate, and they are still bound until a real, true mate is found or until he dies." I give Dimitri a Cheshire Cat grin that I've become so famous for. Yes, in the back of my mind, I definitely want to rip that boy apart for the pain he's causing my daughter. But, in one sense, I almost hope his feelings for her are real and that the bond actually did some good and forged a genuine relationship for the two of them.

I remember looking at the picture of Sebastian holding Aurora as a wee baby—something I didn't get the chance to do. At that point, the look of amazement and infatuation on his face didn't seem forced. Perhaps, his wolf had fallen in love with her but may not have been a true mate like the stories they initially told. Maybe his wolf was more in love with the idea of having a pup around versus thinking of her as a potential mate. There are too many factors involved for me to make a logical decision on the topic of Aurora and Sebastian. The whole thing is too fucking frustrating for me at this point.

I let out a soft growl and grip the railing a little too tightly—the wood beneath my hand splinters and cracks. A gentle touch is laid upon my shoulder. Slowly, I turn and see Aurora smiling at me.

"Daddy, you worry too much." Aurora looks past me to the training ring; I watch her eyes churn liquid mercury. "I can't wait until the day death and betrayal doesn't hang over our heads." She sighs softly, then caresses the scale on her chest. Her connection to Alaric seems to have gotten stronger. In times of stress, she reaches out to him the only way she can.

"Little one, do you feel better today? I mean emotionally." I gently wrap my arm around Aurora, offering her the comfort only a father can provide. Aurora snuggles in close and rests her head on my chest. I feel her body relax as she holds onto me.

"Physically, yes. Emotionally, I feel gutted. How could he be so cruel? A true mate is a blessing, a gift. He betrayed that sacred covenant. How can I ever trust him again, Dad?" Aurora looks up at me, her sadness evident on her face. My powerful daughter is suffering from heartbreak.

"Little one, if Dimitri or I could bear this pain for you, we would do it gladly." Dimitri moves closer to us when I mention his name and rests his hand on her shoulder, rubbing it gently.

"Baby girl, all will be well. I will do everything possible to make sure all your dreams come true." Dimitri leans down and kisses Aurora's cheek, then rests his forehead against her temple for several moments before moving away. "I'm sorry, my king. I should remain outside from now on." His eyes change to the brilliant gold of his bear, then back to his normal hazel. Hmm, interesting. My daughter's heat calls to him. Perhaps, her wolf wasn't off base with Dimitri. Aurora pulls away from me and heads back to the cabin door.

"Prepare the troops. Once my heat is over, we leave for Alaska. No more waiting, no more stalling. If, by accident, several traitors don't make it, oh well. Not my circus, not my monkeys." Aurora's animal surges to the surface, and the wave of power that comes off her is impressive. The fighting stops in the ring, and everyone turns to face the cabin. Aurora shifts quickly and lets out her death howl, its tone haunting and summoning. Every wolven being within earshot of her was forced to shift by the power of her will alone. She stands there for several seconds before shifting back and walking into the house. My eyes pass over all the wolves now as they prowl the compound. I'm not sure what's more frightening: the power my daughter wields or the fact she can wield it.

Dominik returns to the compound with the six Lycan warriors from the German pack. These men are stout, unlike the American Lycans who still do physical work. Dimitri is the first to greet them and catches them up on what has been going on. Then I notice the alpha's sons, Klaus and Kaden. Another set of twins have arrived. It would be comical as fuck if my daughter started a collection of twins.

Klaus is the first to approach me. Instinctively, I hold out my right forearm to show him the brand of the royal house. Klaus, in turn, shows me the brand of his father's pack. Once our identities are confirmed, we embrace briefly then head toward the cabin Aurora's staying in. Risky, yes, but I need to have them meet so he sees who his people are fighting for.

We arrive at the cabin's door, and I mentally reach out to Aurora. Several seconds later, she opens the door and her jaw drops and nostrils flair, inhaling his scent deeply into her lungs once she sees Klaus. She blinks several times before she moves out of the way to allow us to enter. I've never seen my daughter speechless before, so this is quite impressive. Aurora's eyes churn liquid mercury, and I feel her reaching into my memories.

Aurora clears her throat and speaks to him in German. "Thank you for making the long journey here. Please forgive my appearance. I haven't been myself lately." She motions to the couch and waits for both of us to sit before going into the kitchen. She returns with three beers. Aurora sets the beer bottles on the table, then shifts her right hand into her armored gauntlet and uses her talons to open all three bottles. Carefully, Aurora picks up the first beer, and we watch the frost move across the glass before she offers it to Klaus. His eyes go wide, looking between Aurora and me. Apparently, stories of her ability haven't reached his pack yet.

Aurora continues to speak in German. "I am sorry if my grasp of your language is lacking. I recently learned it." She hands me my beer then sits down in Dimitri's favorite recliner in front of us. Klaus looks completely gobsmacked as he stares at her. Neither of us expected her to conduct business in his native tongue. As if it just dawned on her, she shifts her right arm back and shows her royal brand to Klaus. Klaus immediately drops to his knees before her and rests his forehead on her knees.

"You are the last true ruler of my people. We serve only you from now until death and beyond." His German flows like the Rhine River, smooth and sure. Klaus looks up to Aurora, his eyes golden like that of his wolf. I watch him try to stare her down and fail. "Forgive me, princess. I had to make sure you were the one." Aurora reaches down and threads her fingers through his thick, medium-brown hair. She seems very interested in him, which could be a death sentence for Sebastian. Quickly, Aurora pulls her hand away like it touched fire.

She draws in a shaky breath, still speaking to Klaus in German. "I forgive you. If you wish to call your men inside, I shall shift for you; let you see what exactly you're dealing with. No secrets." Aurora climbs over the back of the couch and begins to shove furniture out of the way. Klaus goes to the door and shouts for his men to come in. Aurora's eyes fall on me and, in the back of my mind, she says to stop her if I need to. She's not sure how her beast will react to strangers in her temporary den.

I place myself in front of Aurora, who decides to stand in the house's dining area. She's wearing a simple robe that will tear easily. I listen to Klaus explain to his people that she's the true heir. Aurora raises her right arm and shows the guys her mark before she begins her shift.

She does it slower than usual, allowing them to watch each bone break and reform as her thick, white fur slowly blankets her muscular Lycan form. Frost begins to coat her fur just before her white dragon scales ripple up her fingertips to her elbows. Scales slowly form on her muzzle and around her eyes. Her wolven head is broader and longer than the average Lycan's. I can actually see some of my dragon's features in her animal. For instance, her eyes are almond-shaped, and she has a boney ridge up her muzzle like my dragon. Aurora's beast has grown in size as well. She easily stands nine feet tall. Klaus and his men stare in amazement, looking at Aurora's impressive beast.

"Gentlemen? Do we have your allegiance?" I state. All six men fall to their knees before Aurora. I watch her study them for a few moments before she turns and walks to the back of the house.

"Now that's settled, I have an announcement to make to the pack. I need you guys to stand with me. The pack hierarchy has been shifted, and we must settle the masses. I know you've been briefed on what's going on here, so let's make haste." I lead Klaus and his team of men toward the porch of the Alpha House. Sebastian stands there with his arms crossed over his chest like the self-important fool he is. Klaus moves forward, lets out a low growl, and locks eyes with Sebastian. Both are alpha's sons, but there's one huge difference: Sebastian's title was handed down. At the same time, Klaus's was earned through repeated battles over the centuries. I look between the two males; Sebastian, even though he's built heavy for the Americans, is considerably smaller than Klaus. Is it wrong that I hope they fight? Eventually, Sebastian backs down, and whispers move through the pack because of how quickly he submitted to the new male.

Without warning, the temperature plummets and frost begins to race along the ground. Aurora emerges from the cabin, the unease of the pack bringing her out of her self-imposed isolation. Her alpha power blankets the pack and drives the weak to their knees. The only ones left standing are the Dires, the German Lycans, Dimitri, and myself. The entire American pack is on their knees, whining from the pressure of her influence. Sebastian is also on the ground. From what I was told, he was once able to withstand Aurora. Now, he's on the ground like the rest of his birth pack. Oh, how the mighty have fallen. With a flourish of her right hand, she cuts the oppressive power that blankets the compound.

"Dom, summon your pack to the meeting point I gave you earlier. The North American Lycans shall remain here. It will be lambs to the slaughter if we bring them with us." Aurora's voice is commanding, leaving no room for questioning her authority. Sebastian moves to approach Aurora. She quickly shifts her hand and points her talons at her once first mate, she bares her canines at him. Her yellow-green toxin starts to drip from her exposed canines as she stares at Sebastian.

"You forced a mating by magic. It's going to take a long time to regain my trust. You cost me the chance at a true Lycan mate. For all I know, he could be right here," she motions at Klaus and his pack mates, "and I wouldn't know because of your betrayal." Her words are growled out, her body shakes with the effort to restrain her beast. I rest my hand on her shoulder, trying to stay her hand.

"Baby girl? Daughter? Consider this: he can fight alongside us and earn his place back at your side through battle. Or he can die trying?" I'm trying to appeal to my daughter's logical dragon side. It must have worked because she lowers her arm and shifts it back to human.

"You owe my father your heart, Sebastian. He just saved your life," Aurora says, devoid of any emotion. Then her eyes flicker to Klaus and Dimitri. She speaks in German for Klaus and his men. "We leave in an hour; be ready. Klaus, you and the twins are with me. Dimitri, take the other truck with father and Klaus's men. Dom, give your men the keys to the other four-by-fours so we can fuel up and depart. I'm done waiting." Aurora finishes with her instructions, flipping back and forth between English and German depending on who she's speaking to. She shoves past Sebastian, heading into the Alpha House to go pack. Klaus and I look at each other, then to Dimitri. The big guy is trying so hard not to laugh his ass off over Aurora's latest antics. We turn and start heading toward Aurora's truck.

"Guys! Wait up!" Sebastian is yelling and trying to catch up to us. Right now, I wish I had both wings. I'd be gone. Then I'd fly over him and shit right on his head; just cover the bastard in molten dragon shit. I must have what he perceives as a friendly smile on my face.

"Thanks for waiting up! Where are we going, and who do I ride with?" Sebastian says hopefully. I raise an eyebrow at Sebastian. Can this fucker be serious?

"I suggest you wait for Aurora and ask her. This is, how do you say it? Her rodeo?" I'm not sure if I'm using the phrase right. I glance at Dimitri, and he gives me the thumbs up, so I change my expression to a serious one and stare the whelp down. Sebastian double blinks and looks back at the Alpha House. He visibly pales, thinking about dealing with Aurora in her angered state.

"Um, okay? I mean, you are still King Nicodeamus. I'm sure you can tell me where I should be going." In my mind, I'm screaming, *go to hell and rot."* Or, better yet, *go visit your ancestors and not come back."*

"Yes, I am still king. My daughter out-ranks me by birthright. So, yes, I know where you should go. It's Aurora's job to make sure you get there." I smirk at him. Cocky mother fucker has finally been knocked down a peg. Sebastian heads back to the house and enters. We can hear Aurora clear as day when she yells that he better find his own ride because he wasn't riding with her. Dimitri and I can't help but laugh; they sound like an old married couple. Sebastian comes running out and heads toward his Jeep. Once inside, he pulls up to where the other vehicles are waiting.

Aurora steps out of the Alpha House with a duffle bag over her shoulder. She takes her time heading to her truck, where the twins and Klaus are waiting for her. I watch my daughter climb into the bed of her truck and look out over all the gathered vehicles.

"Roll out!" she yells before jumping down and firing up Black Betty. Plumes of black soot shoot from the diesel stacks as she begins to roll. We fall in line behind Aurora and so on down the line. Sebastian chooses the rear. I start to laugh; this isn't a regular wolf pack where the alpha leads from the back. My daughter is the soon to be mother fucking queen when she takes back the throne. Strigoi, beware: you have one pissed off hybrid coming for you.

CHAPTER 45

Jayce

The last forty-eight hours have been hell on my nerves. We discovered Elena and Sebastian manipulated the most sacred of bonds for their own ambitions, and Aurora accepted a Dragon Prince before even meeting him. Now, she seems more powerful than ever. Andre, my best friend, was murdered because he must have found something important.

The American pack was deemed unfit to fight once Aurora saw the German Lycans. I have to admit, they are huge in comparison to the American pack. Personally, I understand why she left them behind; they can all turn on us in a second. Strategically, it's brilliant and dumb. I mean, we would have had higher numbers for the battle. On the other hand, if they turned on us, our odds would be far worse.

"Klaus? Can you tell us what you know about the fortress?" I watch Klaus turn his heavily muscled frame so he can face all of us when he speaks.

"It's heavily fortified but has developed flaws over the years, which we plan to exploit." He studies Aurora's side profile while she drives. I notice he seems appreciative of what he sees. "The flaws have to deal with the lower levels. They are flooded, which means the Strigoi are somewhere on the first level." Klaus looks between the three of us. His English isn't bad, which is a pleasant surprise. Aurora receives word that some of the smaller vehicles need to refuel, so we pull up to the diesel pump to top off the tank. Aurora turns to look at all of us.

"If your information is correct, that means they are more than likely in the throne room." Aurora's grey eyes slowly examine Klaus. He has medium-brown hair that's longer on the top, and his eyes are grey like Aurora's. They seem to stare at each other forever before Sebastian breaks the spell by knocking on Aurora's window. I've never seen her go from zero to demon bitch so fast. She's snapping and growling at Sebastian.

Gently, I touch Aurora's shoulder in an attempt to calm her. She turns to look at me, and I notice her beast is close to the surface. Dragon scales line her eyes like eyeliner. The silver shimmer makes the grey of her eyes look ethereal. Her head tilts left then right as she studies me. My wolf chooses now to come to the surface. Through my wolf's eyes, I see Aurora with a bright light behind her. My vision has never been like this before. The world is in tones of grey and black with lights behind the objects to outline them.

"Aurora? Is this how you see when you shift?" I look around in wonder; everything is so sharp. If I really concentrate, I can see the blood flowing through my brother's veins. Aurora starts laughing.

"Apparently, both you and Dom got the same gift from me. Yes, I can tell by your eye color you gained my vision. It's most helpful when a species can use glamours. Now, you can see right through them," she says so matter-of-factly, like it's no big deal. To me, it's a total game-changer. I smile broadly and start examining the world around me. I hear Aurora lower the driver's side window. "Yes, Mister Lupi? What can I do for you?" Oh shit, he's really redefining being in the dog house. My vision goes back to normal, and I watch Sebastian cringe at Aurora's tone.

"Aurora, please, love… can we talk?" Sebastian says in a pathetic tone. Hell has officially frozen over. Sebastian I-don't-give-a-fuck-about-anyone Lupi is begging. I start videoing it. I'm positive Dimitri and Nico would love to see this.

"LOVE? LOVE! You don't even understand the meaning of the word!" Aurora screams at the top of her lungs. We barely made it into Canada, and I think she's going to kill him. Out of nowhere, Dimitri's hulking form rises up behind Sebastian.

"I suggest you leave, boy. She's not interested in talking to you right now." Sebastian doesn't even attempt to argue with Dimitri; he just turns and leaves. Dimitri faces Aurora and kisses her forehead. "Anything for you, baby girl. Anything." He gently caresses her cheek then heads back to the truck he was in.

Aurora shakes her head then fires the truck up again, getting the caravan back on the road. Klaus is pondering talking to Aurora. Part of me wants to warn him; the other part wants to watch the explosion. Klaus gently rests his hand on her arm. I watch Aurora glance at him but doesn't swipe his hand away.

"I was filled in on what happened. On behalf of the German Lycans, we are sorry." He furrows his brows and removes his hand from her arm. "We still treasure and honor the idea and dream of finding a true mate." I watch Klaus interlace his fingers as he stares at his hands in his lap. Aurora reaches over and rests her hand on his knee.

"Thank you, Klaus. It hurts so bad to be betrayed and to realize my true mate is out there somewhere waiting for me." I watch a single tear roll down her cheek. "He's out there somewhere, praying to the Morrighan to find me, and I'm here..." Aurora's voice cracks as she's overcome with emotions. Dom and I both lay a hand on her to soothe her. "I'm here with a false bond, all because Sebastian and his mother are self-serving assholes."

Through the bond, my brother and I push our love for our mate the best we can. Aurora rests her cheek on Dom's hand and then reaches up to touch mine. She keeps her eyes on the road and sighs softly. My eyes turn to Klaus; so many emotions flicker across his face. I can't tell if he's empathetic or he knows what she's going through.

I lean forward and kiss Aurora's hand before I speak. "Love, we are here for you. Your father and Dimitri are here for you. From what I can tell, you have the full power of the German Lycans and the Dire Wolves behind you. You do not walk alone." I see Klaus hesitate before resting his hand on Aurora's thigh. I watch her look down briefly, then back up to the road ahead.

I can tell Aurora is deep in thought. She sits up straighter and removes her hand from mine. Aurora hits a button on her steering wheel. "Betty, play my playlist," she says, her voice wavers and almost cracks as she utters the simple command.

A few seconds later, the truck responds by saying, "Playing playlist." The opening notes to Shinedown's *How Did You Love?* starts filling the truck. Aurora begins singing along with the song. I watch her lips move almost hypnotically until I notice her canines have descended. Klaus gives me a look of concern, poor man has no clue what the fuck he got himself into.

Gently I tap Klaus's shoulder to get his attention. "She's like a force of nature unleashed upon the world." Dom nods along with my words. His phone goes off and it's the prince. Quickly, Dom brings the prince up to speed. I look back over at Klaus. "Right now, we're sitting in the eye of the hurricane. Her rage and pain aren't focused on us. She's battling between her logical side and her beast's desire to royally fuck up what's hurting her." I lower my eyes briefly before looking back up at Klaus. "Aurora works through her pain with music. We've almost figured out when she's going to explode by the songs she picks."

Dom decides to cut in at this point. "What Jayce is trying to say is this: if we say run, do it. It's not going to be pretty when she finally loses the battle with her beast's instincts." Dom rubs the center of his chest, indicating the pain we are both feeling from Aurora. We all watch her; she's so focused on singing it's like we're not even here.

I turn away from my brother and watch the scenery outside my window. The miles blow by like dust in the wind. Aurora shows no sign of fatigue after driving for the last nine hours. We pull into a rest stop somewhere in the middle of Canada to refuel. Aurora sits on the tailgate of her truck once it's fueled. Dimitri approaches her cautiously while Klaus and I watch them from a safe distance. Dimitri holds out a bag of food and shakes it to break Aurora from her trance. She takes the food and pats the tail-gate beside her, Dimitri joins her. I can't decide if that's the bravest or dumbest thing I've ever witnessed.

Klaus returns to his pack mates and brother to update them. I spot

Dom over by Nico, so I decide to join them. As I approach, I notice Sebastian with his head in his mother's lap, looking distraught.

"What's going on over there?" I motion toward Elena and Sebastian. Nico wins for best resting bitch face today. He looks at Elena and Sebastian, then back to me.

"Old laws dictate death for betraying the ruling family. Forging a false bond is grounds for execution." Nico raises his right hand to rub where his left arm used to be. "Their lives are in Aurora's talons—literally." He turns to watch Klaus with his pack mates and motions toward them. "Their pack is the last of the true Lycans. I had and still hope Aurora's mate is there in their pack somewhere. A true mate can break the false bond." Nico looks almost sad as he turns to Aurora and Dimitri. "I just have to wonder, was there magic cast to keep those two apart?"

I watch Aurora and Dimitri interact. They do act like a mated couple; they're perfectly attuned to each other. Is their comfort level due to the fact he raised her, or is Nico correct in saying she's his? Nico then yells for Dimitri and Aurora to join us. They meander over; Aurora hugs and kisses her father, then snuggles into me, suppressing a yawn.

"Something wrong, Dad?" Aurora asks before yawning into my side again. Dom moves to my side and kisses Aurora on the top of her head. She looks up and smiles at Dom, then snuggles into his side.

"Nothing is wrong, sweetheart. I just have a few questions." This catches Dimitri's attention, and he looks around to see if anyone is within earshot of us. When he's sure it's clear, he gives Nico the all-clear. "The question is actually for you, old friend. Did Elena send you and Andre regular care packages?" Dimitri looks puzzled by the question then looks between Elena and Nico.

"*Da*, why?" Dimitri answers quite tersely. Nico taps his finger on his chin for several moments, then looks to Dom.

"Aurora looks exhausted. We'll stop here for the night. Secure enough rooms for everyone." Dom nods then leads Aurora off. Once they are out of range, he places his hand on Dimitri's shoulder. "What if I told you I think you're a victim of Elena's tea as well?" Nico backs up and looks at me, then back to Dimitri, waiting for it to dawn on the Great Bear.

Several moments passed before you can tell when it hit him. Dimitri falls to his knees, and his hands fly up to cover his eyes. Is the big guy crying? Holy hell, he is crying. The atmosphere changes radically and, in an instant, Dimitri shifts to his bear, and that hulking beast is out for blood. His bear stands on its hind legs and roars its pain and anger into the night, shaking the very ground we stand on. Those golden orbs lock onto Sebastian and his mother.

Over a half-ton of enraged Great Bear thunders across the field between the rest stop and the motel. Sebastian's and Elena's faces visibly pale as they watch their death approach. With his full force, Dimitri hits their Jeep, sending it flying through the air. The metal of the Jeep is twisted upon impact, and we all watch the attack in horror.

Nico raises his hand, halting anyone from interfering. Dimitri launches the Jeep once more before a blur of white and frost stands before him. Aurora's hybrid beast roars at the Great Bear. He slowly lowers his head and swings it from side to side. Aurora's beast looks back at the Jeep in time to watch Elena and Sebastian crawl out of the wreckage. They look like they barely survived the attack. Aurora's beast moves forward and presses her forehead to Dimitri's bear's forehead. They stand like that for what seemed like forever before they turn and head our way. The whole event played out like an action movie crossed with horror. It was very surreal; I still can't wrap my head around it.

As they walk side by side, Aurora's beast has its taloned hand resting on Dimitri's neck. Usually, it's her animal that needs to be reined in. This is fucking backward as all hell. She stops several feet in front of us and shifts back to her human form. Quickly, I remove my flannel shirt and help her slip it on. Aurora doesn't move far from Dimitri, her fingers running through his thick fur.

"I don't know what was said to Dimitri, but whatever set him off... I almost wasn't able to stop him." Aurora looks at the three of us. Nico waves off the approaching crowd.

"I wouldn't," he cautions the group. Once everyone leaves, Nico looks back to Aurora. "I have reason to believe that it's possible you and Dimitri may be mates. But something Elena put in her care packages blocked it." Nico studies Aurora's reaction.

You can watch as the rage moves over her face. Scales erupt then recede just as quickly. She takes off my shirt, shifts back into her beast's form, and howls her rage into the night. Dimitri's bear bellows right along with her. I move quickly and place my hands on Aurora's chest, trying to stop her. Aurora drops her muzzle until she's at eye level with me. She rests her forehead against mine and does the happy growl she likes to do. I feel the moment her body shifts back, and Dom helps her slip my shirt back on.

"They have a lot to answer for tomorrow," Aurora states, then grabs my hand and heads toward the motel. "I need a shower and sleep." I turn Aurora to face me and kiss her on the lips.

"Go with Dom. I'm going to help your dad sort things out." Aurora nods and follows my brother inside. Nico approaches me with Dimitri in tow.

"It's obvious that Elena lied about knowing the old magics. The real question is, what else did she do?" Nico turns to look at the remnants of Sebastian's Jeep. We stare at the crumpled, twisted remains. How in the world did they walk away from that wreck? Dimitri eventually shifts back to his human form and looks between Nico and me.

"I regret losing my temper, but I do not regret attacking them." Dimitri crosses his thick arms over his chest, looking at us. Apparently, he doesn't care about his dick swinging in the wind either.

"I'm impressed that Aurora was able to stop you," Nico states, studying Dimitri. Dimitri looks down, his brows furrowed.

"I would never hurt Aurora." He looks up and at us each in turn. "However, you fuckers wouldn't make out so well." Dimitri flips us all off then walks toward his room at the motel.

"Jayce?" Nico says as he watches Dimitri walk off.

"Yeah?" I tilt my head to the side, looking at Nico. He moves closer to me and puts his arm over my shoulder.

"We should go see what Elena and Sebastian are up to." He's got that mischievous look in his eye. It's almost like he's saying, *let's just kill them now and surprise Aurora with the heads.* I raise my eyebrows, looking at him after reading between the lines.

"Let's go get'er done." I might not be as bulky as my brother, Dom, but one bite from me and it's a death sentence. That knowledge makes me smile as I follow Nico into the night. We creep around the motel exterior, trying to catch their scent. Two laps around the building and nothing.

I text Dom and ask for their room number. He responds quickly and says it's room thirty-five—the one right in front of us. Nico places his hand on the door and freezes it solid. He makes a fist, busts the frozen knob off, and pushes the door open. There's no evidence they were ever here. Nico growls, and his dragon's eyes are visible.

"They're on the run." Nico darts to the parking lot and starts counting cars. No vehicles are missing, which means one of two things: either they ran off into the night or they were picked up somewhere. We stare at each other for several moments.

"Use your phone and tell everyone what happened. Alert Ellis as well; we need to change our route and plans. I will not give them an opportunity to ambush us!" Nico storms off to points unknown. Well, this trip just got more interesting.

CHAPTER 46

Dominik

It's sometime after midnight my phone dings, letting me know I received a message. It's from my brother, Jayce, who alerts me on what has occurred while Aurora and I slumbered. Apparently, shit went down after we went in to relax. Now, Sebastian and Elena are on the run and missing, henceforth proving they were the rats.

According to my brother, we have to amend our original travel plans and change our course of action. Aurora's father is looking over the maps and plotting which roads we should take and which ones we should avoid in case of an ambush. It's quite suspicious that they left without any kind of vehicle. They were apparently prepared in case of discovery.

Now, I wonder exactly how much information they've already passed on to the other side. Nico is handling all the planning from this point on, only allowing us knowledge of it within moments of his adjustments to the course. He's trying to eliminate any possible threats or leakage of information between here and our destination in the northernmost part of Alaska.

I sit up in bed to shoot a message off to my brother, letting him know I understand the necessity for all these extra preparations. My eyes slide over the sleeping form of my mate, and I watch her in her restless sleep. Aurora's skin occasionally ripples with fur or scales —depending on where the ripple occurs. I know her subconscious mind is working overtime, wanting to plot how to kill and destroy all those that stand against her. The betrayal of her mate runs deep, and it cuts her so profoundly that our hearts ache with her. Going forward now is going to be like walking around with a ticking nuclear bomb, never knowing exactly when she's going to explode.

I text my brother again to let him know about Aurora's rippling scales and her skin shifting in her sleep. I warn him that we have to be on guard. He replies quickly, saying her father knows of a way to help her sleep without dreaming. He'll figure out something within the next day to help us, so we don't have to worry about her disappearing in the middle of the night.

I know previously, long before us, her beast took advantage of her deep sleep. Somehow, it put her human thoughts to the back of her mind, allowing her to run on instinct alone. This knowledge causes me great concern, and it's why I don't sleep soundly tonight. I heard the stories of what happened before her awakening, how her beast had hunted a woman down just because Dimitri came home smelling like her.

I listen to the doorknob turn, and a little ray of light comes into the room. Slowly, my brother pokes his head in and looks around. As silently as possible, Jayce closes the door and locks it, then comes into bed and crawls on Aurora's opposite side. At least this way, we could possibly sleep in shifts to make sure both of us get some semblance of sleep. I nod to Jayce and allow him to curl up and slumber first. I feel a bit stalkerish watching them. Let's face it, taking these kinds of precautions isn't normal. But then again, our situation is anything but typical.

Dawn breaks over the horizon, painting the sky in blues and purples. As the morning progresses, the colors change to hues of oranges and reds until finally, the sun nears its apex and changes the sky to blue. I leave the room early and grab breakfast for the three of us. Nico and Dimitri are organizing our caravan and letting them know what transpired last night.

I return to our room to find Aurora and Jayce screaming from their climaxes. Well, at least someone is having a great morning. I wiggle the bag full of breakfast sandwiches. The first to turn around is Aurora, and she's off Jayce before he even has a chance to look at me. Aurora takes the bag from me and pulls out what she wants, then sits at the table to eat.

Jayce is the first to speak as he grabs his breakfast. "What's the plan?" I hop up to sit on the tabletop and look between Aurora and Jayce.

"That's a great question. Unfortunately, I don't know. After yesterday's debacle with Sebastian and his mother, Nico isn't telling anyone shit. He's going to take point when the caravan gets rolling. Nico is concerned that there might still be spies." I shrug my shoulders and dig into my breakfast sandwich. There's almost an uncomfortable silence that I have to break.

"All I know is they bailed after Dimitri launched them last night." I ponder that for several minutes. "Now I know why Great Bears are beasts of legend. Fuck, remind me to never piss Dimitri off." My brother and I nod in agreement, and Aurora shrugs her shoulders. She lowers her head and sets her sandwich down. I've never seen Aurora look so broken. I don't know what changed in her internal monologue, but I notice the minute that fire sparks back to life within her.

"I'm going to fucking destroy them all. I will tear them limb from limb and put their heads on spikes in my yard." Her voice is mostly the growl of her beast. Her mercury eyes have an eerie glow, and her hair is blanketed in frost. We can feel her rage building. Quickly, she jumps off the bed and runs out the front door. Nico meets her halfway in the middle of the parking lot.

"Father," Aurora says in a rather hollow tone. "They have stolen so much from me." Aurora's hands shift into armored scales, her long white talons lightly dusted with frost. "They will die by my hands. I will make their entire bloodline extinct." She bares her canines at everyone who gathered. Aurora is so enraged that she's not calming down for anything.

My phone rings, and it's an unknown number. I stare at it for several seconds before I answer it. It's Ellis, and apparently, Aurora's mood is sending Alaric's dragon off the deep end. Ellis instructs me to go near Aurora and put it on speaker.

I do as instructed, then I shout, "Okay, NOW!" Alaric's dragon bellows and forces Aurora's shift. Her beast whines and whimpers before she shifts back to her human form. I give Aurora my hoodie, and then she snatches my phone from me and goes to sit in her truck. I look back at Nico; the cocky fucker is just smiling. Nico looks at the truck then back to us.

"Alaric's dragon just forced Aurora's beast to submit." He shrugs his shoulders like it was nothing.

"How in the Nine Hells is that possible?" Dimitri's Russian accent is definitely more pronounced when he's angry. Nico huffs like we just asked him to perform a miracle.

"Male dragons only choose powerful females. Aurora is probably the most powerful female born in generations. His dragon basically said, *if I am worthy, you will stop*. Her shift and whining was her beast's way of telling him he was." Dimitri, Jayce, and I look between each other. Something is definitely missing in translation. It looked more painful than a romantic conversation. Nico huffs again. "Load up! We need to get rolling; we're burning daylight." My brother and I head back to Aurora's truck, and Klaus is right behind us.

When we get back to her truck, we find her in the backseat with her headphones on, still talking to Alaric. Jayce grabs the keys off of the center console and fires up Black Betty. Nico reaches over in front of Dimitri and honks the horn. Off we go again. This time, I sit in the back with Aurora and position her so her head lays in my lap. I've always hated road trips because my wolf hates being trapped in a vehicle. Every five to six hours we stop and refuel, switch drivers, then move on. We've been traveling like this for almost a week already. Our food is passed around while we continue our journey.

Something must have happened that spooked Nico because we suddenly take a hard right. We all snap to attention as we watch what unfolds around us. A truck comes out of nowhere and side-swipes the truck behind us, the one holding all of Klaus's men. Two more come from opposite directions as they try to box us in. Klaus cuts the wheel hard and turns our vehicle around. The rest of our caravan stops to assist. We are within one hundred yards of the impact zone when we all jump out. The shift takes us all quickly as we move as a single unit.

Klaus's Lycan is definitely heavier built than Sebastian's. His fur is grey and black, and he looks like the devil himself. He roars into the night and charges toward his pack's truck. A van speeds into the scene out of nowhere and twenty unknown Lycans pour out of the back. They head straight for the other truck and begin their attack. Klaus springs into action, clawing the back of their necks and severing their heads.

A great, white mass leaps into the fray, joining in on the action. Aurora's beast is larger and faster than Klaus, and her rage is palpable in the air. More Lycans file out of the trucks, but we outnumber them two to one. In the back of my mind, I realize this is a setup.

We fight valiantly and obliterate the opposing forces. Nico stands on the tailgate of his truck like a brigadier general. I can see him scanning the horizon for any more enemies. After we all shift back to our human forms and get dressed, we head back to Nico. He looks at all of us as we gather around. Not a single loss on our side and every one of our attackers have been killed.

"They are testing us, trying to find a weakness." Nico begins to pace before speaking again, "Check all the trucks and look for anything that may give away our position." Dimitri taps Nico on the calf, and he bends down to listen to what Dimitri has to say. "Dimitri says it's called a tracker or a GPS thing. Find it and destroy it."

We return to Aurora's truck and Jayce, who already shifted back to his wolf, walks beside Aurora as she inspects her vehicle. Jayce stops by the left side of her bumper. Quickly, Aurora slips under the vehicle and we hear something snap. She slides out and holds up a small, black box. Nico and Dimitri come over with three other trackers in their hands.

"We need to send a decoy with the trackers in it," Dimitri says in a very calm tone. I pull out my phone and look at the map program I have. There's a rather large truck stop up ahead. I show Klaus and Aurora, and she nods before taking my phone from me.

"Dad, Dom found a truck stop about fifteen miles ahead. We can hide the trackers on trucks preparing to leave to send them in different directions." Aurora shows her dad what she's talking about, and he smiles.

Nico approaches me and gives me a hug. "I am proud to call you one of my daughter's mates." He gives me a brief nod before he turns to address the others. "Roll out! We stop at the next rest area!"

Jayce, Klaus, Aurora, and I look at each other before running back to the truck. Aurora grabs a pair of leggings and a sweatshirt, then hops into the driver's seat. Several moments later, we arrive at the rest stop. Nico sends everyone out in different directions to look for trucks that seem to be ready to depart. Everyone moves quickly, hiding the little black boxes on unsuspecting tractor-trailers. Aurora sits on the roof of her truck's cab, eating a smorgasbord of tacos. Her mercury orbs scan the surrounding area, watching everything that comes and goes from the yard. It's moments like this where I feel the loss of Andre the most. Usually, he would be the one on the lookout, but it looks like Aurora tasked herself with remaining vigilant.

Nico and Dimitri are having a heated debate as they lean over a map that's spread out over the tailgate of Dimitri's truck. Neither one is speaking English, and I can only assume it's Romanian. Earlier this week, I learned that Dimitri's people were one of the proud Romani tribes of Gypsies. I clear my throat so as not to startle either of them.

"Ah, son, perhaps you can settle this for us. I want to take this route, which is about fifty miles longer. Dimitri wants to take this one because he's concerned about snow. Which do you think is better?" Shit on a shingle. Now I'm being pitted between my father-in-law and Aurora's possible new mate. I'm so fucked, and not in the good sense. Lucky for me, mother nature makes the decision easier because large snowflakes begin to fall. I look up to the sky and silently thank the wolf goddess for saving my tail.

"In light of the most recent developments, I believe the shorter route will be to our benefit. We're over three-quarters of the way to our port. We need to get as close to that land bridge as we can before we have to shift and travel by foot." Dimitri and Nico both look up at the sky. I want to tell them staring at the snow isn't going to stop it.

"He's right, my king, we may not have that much time left. We've been traveling for what seems like forever. Only four hundred miles to go and we are at the Wales port." Dimitri is trying his hardest to get the king to see reason. Our animals are getting restless from being caged in the trucks. I can only imagine what his dragon is feeling. Nico shakes his head and smirks.

"Ok, the snow wins; we take the short route. Get everyone loaded and ready to roll in twenty minutes. We don't stop until we hit the port." Nico heads back to the passenger side of the truck and gets in to wait. Dimitri and I shake our heads before heading off in different directions. I make it back to the truck to find Aurora asleep and curled up in a little ball. I furrow my brow and look at Klaus, who is standing watch over her and the truck.

"She crawled in the back, grabbed your sweatshirt, then went to sleep. She grumbled something about Ellis meeting us at some port." Hmmm, makes sense. I guess he's going to introduce us to his group. That way, we can catch their scent to prevent us from accidentally attacking them.

"Alright, we need to load up. We're driving straight through to the port. No more stops between here and there. Grab extra provisions and whatever you need to eat before we remain shifted until after whatever ambush we're walking into." The look of surprise on Klaus's face is entirely worth it. I look over and see my brother, Jayce, coming back from a different store. It looks like he bought every protein bar they had in stock.

"I've got enough to sustain the shift and then some. Aurora's going to need a lot, so we need to keep her fed." Jayce is funny when he goes all mother hen on us. I grab two of the bags from him and watch as the others walk out with similar bags in their hands—time to gorge ourselves. While we cross over to Siberia, our animals will burn more calories from trying to keep us warm through the blizzard-like conditions. With one of the bags of protein bars, Jayce slides in the back and lightly rocks Aurora. "Love, we need to start eating. We're not far from the port. You need to start storing the carbs for the crossing." Aurora pops one eye open, revealing the liquid mercury of her beast.

Slowly, Aurora sits up and rubs her eyes before rooting through the bag to grab what she wants to eat. Klaus climbs in the driver's seat and fires up Black Betty. While he is distracted, I watch Aurora's hand slide forward and snatch the cheesecake flavored bar that Klaus left on the center console. He acts like he didn't see her do it and just laughs to himself, watching her eat it in the back seat.

"About five hours before we make it to the port. Make sure you eat." Klaus's accent is heavy as he addresses us. He pulls out behind Dimitri and we're off again. I text Ellis and let him know our approximate ETA. He warns us about the storm and says its whiteout conditions at the port. I forward the message to Klaus's brother, who's in the truck with Dimitri and Nico, to let everyone else know what happened.

CHAPTER 47

Dominik

The next three hours are the longest hours of my life. It gets to the point where we have to stop at a town about fifty miles from the port. Ellis and his group are en route to the village before heading back out to the islands. We found an abandoned farm on the outskirts of the town and set up camp inside the barn. Several pack mates scouted the town beforehand. Apparently, the townspeople head further inland this time of year. Every building and store is devoid of people. Our scouts return with boxes of pasta and rice; you know, the heavy carbs we need for the remaining part of our journey.

A knock sounds at the barn door, and we all fall silent. Dimitri and I move toward the door and open it slightly. Ellis stands at the entrance with about twelve other men behind him. Dimitri gets out of their way, and they all file in, dragging a caribou behind them. Aurora remains in the shadows and watches as the strangers enter the barn. Ellis has another small box in his hand and refuses to hand it to anyone.

"I have a present for the princess from her future mate!" Ellis projects his voice, knowing full well he is being watched.

Klaus keeps his eyes on Aurora as she moves across the barn's rafters above Ellis. She drops down silently behind him, and her eyes are pools of liquid mercury as she stares at him. Aurora lightly taps his shoulder and holds her hand out to him. Ellis almost jumps out of his skin when she touches him. He spins around and leaps back, terror evident on his face.

Once he realizes it's Aurora, he holds the box out for her to take. Aurora gently takes the box from him then leaps back up to the platform—which is about twelve feet off the ground. All eyes are on Aurora as she opens the box. Inside is a hunk of meat and a large canine tooth. I watch Aurora smirk then devour the offered meat.

Aurora steps back out of sight and strips herself of her clothing. She shifts into her beast's form and leaps back down from the platform. The Polar Bear clan quickly backs up after seeing that monster of a Lycan hybrid move toward them. Jayce brings a frightened Ellis up to speed as Aurora examines the caribou. The upper lip of her beast curls up for a moment just before she sinks her canines into the rump of the caribou and uses her talons to cut a hunk off. She drops the chunk of meat into the box and pushes it to Ellis.

"You dragons are fucking freaky. Damn, what happened to chocolates and flowers? But no, y'all send dead things and hunks of flesh. Fuck man... Now, I have to bring this back." Ellis visibly shivers then freezes when Aurora gets in his face. She breathes frost on him—just a light coating—before walking off.

Nico steps forward and says, "I suggest you return her offering to the prince before she gets mad." He looks up to the platform where Aurora sits, still shifted, watching everyone moving around below her. Aurora backs into the shadows, and the glow from her eyes can still be seen. Then suddenly, it disappears.

"That's just fucking freaky." Ellis grabs the box, and he and his men disappear quickly out the barn door. Aurora moves from the shadow, shifts back to her human form, and fully dresses. She looks around and then jumps back down to join the rest of us.

"Silly bears." She shakes her head and giggles, looking back at Dimitri. "You can easily beat their fuzzy asses." We watch Dimitri closely, and his eyes glow the golden hue of his bear, then fade back to his human amber.

Slowly, he nods and smiles broadly at Aurora. She dips her head lightly to him, then moves back to the caribou and rips off a chunk of flesh. According to Ellis, the caribou is a gift from the prince. The fat content of this animal will help sustain our energy. Someone in the back asks what he sent Aurora. "The prince sent me a hunk of walrus. He figured I'd need the extra energy to power my gifts." A soft smile graces her crimson lips, thinking about the thoughtful gift she had received.

Aurora moves around the barn, watching everyone interact and eat. I'm honestly not sure what she's looking for, but something is apparently off to her and she wants to check it out. She stops at another food dump, grabs several protein bars, and starts eating as she moves about.

I look around quickly and—well, I'll be damned—Nico is doing the same damn thing. It's got to be a dragon trait to prowl around and make people uncomfortable. Aurora stops and tilts her head to listen, and Nico does the same thing before moving to the door. Aurora moves to follow, but he raises his hand to stop her. A frustrated growl can be heard from her as she stares at the door, waiting for her father to return. I move forward cautiously and hug her from behind. Aurora sighs softly and leans back against me.

"A dragon landed. I feel that it's the prince. Father doesn't want me out there for some reason." Aurora sighs again and leans a bit more against me. Her heat has just about passed, but that delicious scent still lingers on her flesh. "We need to organize our people. We will depart early in the morning. It's going to be a long, cold walk." Aurora moves away from me and starts to break the groups up. She encourages them to sleep as their animals to keep warm tonight.

Dimitri's Great Bear comes up alongside Aurora and begins to herd her toward the food, encouraging her to eat more. She shakes her head and laughs before jumping on Dimitri's back and riding him around the barn like a horse. I haven't heard her laugh that hard as he starts to swing his head, making his whole body rock.

The barn door pops open and a Viking-looking man stands in the doorway. Nico moves in front of him to stop him from going much further. Aurora is still playing with Dimitri and doesn't notice the prince enter. Aurora leaps off Dimitri's back, and shifts before her paws hit the ground. She charges Dimitri as he rears up and tosses her. Aurora lands on all fours, tail whipping back and forth before her talons dig into the dirt. She launches herself at Dimitri again, but this time her beast rolls his bear and sends him flying. Aurora just threw over a half-ton bear. I watch the prince's jaw drop, and Nico smiles broadly like a proud peacock.

The prince whispers, *"Holy fuck,"* which catches Aurora's attention. She growls as she turns her head to see who spoke. Instantly, her demeanor changes.

Aurora's beast tilts her head left then right, studying the prince from a distance. Dimitri moves alongside her and offers her a robe to wear. She looks down at the offered robe then looks at her talons and whines. She knows her talons will shred the material. Jayce moves forward and takes the robe with him, leading her into one of the stalls so she can shift and get dressed in private. I walk over and introduce myself to Alaric and wait nearby just in case.

Hesitantly, Aurora steps out of the stall with Jayce. I can tell he helped her brush her hair and made her look presentable. As she approaches, her eyes flicker between steel-grey and the liquid mercury of her beast. The prince isn't doing much better as he shifts his weight from one foot to the other. When Aurora is about five feet away, she lets loose all the power she could manage to test him. Her alpha power magnified significantly since the last time she unleashed it. Everyone is driven to their knees, including Jayce and me. Only three remain standing: Aurora, Nico, and Alaric. She had to test him and had to test us too, I guess.

Aurora releases her grip on the room and stares at Alaric. He smiles broadly. It's apparent he sees her like we do, like the sun rises and sets because of her. He starts to laugh and moves his hair aside. Weaved into one of his braids is her stark, white braid. Aurora closes the distance, looks up into his eyes, and then reaches slowly up into his hair to touch her braid. I can tell from where I'm standing she is holding her breath, waiting for rejection.

"You, princess, are more than I could have ever dreamed of. I can only hope to be the mate you deserve." He gently takes her hand from his hair, kisses her knuckles, then drops to his knees before her. "I am yours to command. My army is your army; my dragon is yours." He holds her hand as he looks up to her. There's nothing but love there for her. I know in my heart that my brother and I approve.

Aurora first looks to Nico, and he gives her a nod of approval. Then her eyes find both Jayce and me. We smile at her and do matching, sweeping bows. Aurora giggles as she watches our antics. Lastly, her eyes find Dimitri; his opinion means so much to her. He bows his head and raises his fist over his heart. Aurora mimics Dimitri's move, placing her fist over her heart. Out of character for Aurora, she lowers her head to Dimitri then looks up to him. Although shocked, the big guy gives her a shy smile, embarrassed by the level of respect she has just shown him.

Aurora turns slowly and looks down at the prince, who is still kneeling before her. Her slender fingers gently cup his bearded cheeks, threading through the coarse hair. Ever so slowly, she leans down and tenderly kisses his full lips. As she kisses him, the rumble of approval from his dragon makes her smile. They open their eyes simultaneously, and their beasts can look at each other up close.

It is said that when our beasts surface, they can see each other's true form. We are technically one entity, but it's almost an out of body experience when mates meet. The world around them does not exist, and time stands still.

Aurora and Alaric continue to look deeply into each other's eyes. Eventually, Nico decides to move forward and lightly touch Aurora's shoulder. She growls at her father for interrupting her. Aurora's eyes widen in horror at her actions, and she backs away quickly.

"I'm sorry, Alaric. I got lost for a moment." Aurora's eyes dart to her father then back to Alaric. "Will we be safe crossing? Our numbers are few due to the betrayal of the American Lycans."

Aurora looks back at the fifty that we brought with us. According to the last message I received, the other two hundred from my birth pack will be arriving in the morning.

"My love, two hundred Dire Wolves will be here by sunrise as requested. We will march with two hundred and fifty at your command." I raise my fist over my heart and bow my head to look at Alaric. "Any suggestions, M'Lord, would be most helpful and appreciated." Alaric looks at the force we travel with and then back to Aurora.

"My mother's people are with us. I am in command of fifty Gold Dragons and another twenty Ice Dragons that are loyal only to me. Ellis has about twenty Polar Bears loyal only to him on the ground." Alaric moves forward and offers his hand to me. "Brothers in arms and bond mates to Aurora, you and your family have my protection." I shake his hand firmly and watch him shake Jayce's hand as well.

"I speak for my birth pack when I say we are grateful for your help and protection." I look to my brother, Jayce, and he's smiling like a fool while looking at the prince. Well, I know who's going to be ogling the new mate together.

Alaric moves forward and hugs Aurora once more, then goes to shake Nico's hand before heading to the door. He pauses in the doorway and looks back at us. "Ellis will let me know when you arrive in the danger zone. My team and I will keep the dragons off of you. Destroy anything that isn't a part of your or Ellis's group. There's a pack of Lycans on the move to the islands. Be careful." He stares at Aurora when he speaks his final words. Surprisingly, she nods and waves at him. As soon as Alaric was out the door, Aurora runs as fast as she can after him. If I know Aurora, she wants to see his dragon. However, Nico blocks Aurora's path.

"No, daughter, not right now. He needs to focus on tomorrow, not you running out into the snow." Aurora growls at her father and walks away, pouting. It's going to be a long night.

We slept in shifts last night just in case of a surprise attack. I wake up the next morning and I can't find Aurora, and I realize that Nico is also missing. Shit, what the fuck did I miss? Jayce is by the fire making the last of the rice and pasta for all of us to eat. I walk over to the barn doors and shove one of them open. About a foot of snow fell last night, which blankets the ground for as far as I can see.

We are now in whiteout conditions. I concentrate and shift my eyes to be like Aurora's. After doing so, I'm able to make out the outline of Nico's dragon and Aurora's animal together. She is standing on top of her father's head, watching the countryside. I turn my attention to where she's looking, and I can make out the outlines of my pack mates on the horizon as they come up from the south. Good, we will be able to leave as planned. I return to the barn and rally the troops. Everyone eats quickly as they wait for the Dire Wolf pack to arrive.

CHAPTER 48
Dimitri

GREAT GODDESS CALLISTO, HELP ME. FIRST, I SPEND YEARS FIGHTING MY feelings for Aurora. Then, her wolf kills a female because she believes I'm hers. Then all of a sudden, I don't rank, and my feelings for her are squashed. Bloody hell, Nicodeamus is right! We were drugged so our bond wouldn't grow—a thousand curses upon the Lupi family and their heirs. By my Romani blood, I will have vengeance for what they have stolen from me.

Mate after mate, I watch Aurora gain in power. The theory that Nicodeamus presented seems valid, but the real question is, what can I do to break the spell? I watch Aurora assemble the troops in preparation for departure. The way she rallies everyone reminds me of her mother on the battlefield.

Nicodeamus's dragon roars and begins walking toward the Bering Land Bridge. My bear lumbers along toward the back of the pack. What I lack in speed, I more than make up for in strength. We know we're walking into an ambush, so it's just a question of when. We walk for miles, following the path that Nicodeamus's dragon blazes for us. We walk in this endless sea of white, not able to see more than a couple of feet in front of our faces. If it wasn't for the strong scent of Nicodeamus's dragon, our sense of direction would be thrown off by the lack of landmarks. However, I can faintly make out the glow of Aurora's eyes as she sits on her father's back. I pick up my pace to get closer to his dragon so I can see exactly what's going on.

Aurora sits statue-still on her father's back, watching the pack behind him. Her eyes slowly scan the horizon, watching for any signs of the impending attack. The Dire Wolves and I are having no trouble whatsoever moving through this heavy snowfall. Our only disadvantage is that, unlike Aurora and her father, we cannot see much further ahead of ourselves than maybe a couple of feet.

Howls erupt in the distance, coming from multiple directions ahead of and alongside us. Here it is the moment of truth. This is precisely what we've all been preparing and training for. Now we get to see how good Nicodeamus and my training is as the Dire Wolves aid us in battle. Aurora issues several short barks, and the pack splits into three equal units. These units end up splitting off: one going left, one going right, and the third still lagging behind Nicodeamus.

Aurora leaps off her father's back and comes up alongside me. Her eyes focus on the Lycans walking with us, and she issues several more barks at them, sending them off in their own direction. The wind shifts, and several different scents hit our noses. I pick up the first scent from the Polar Bears, the second scent—that bastard Sebastian. Aurora begins to growl deep in her throat. With that tone, you know someone is going to die. She separates from her father and starts walking about seventy yards to my left. Nicodeamus then goes another sixty yards to my right. Divide and conquer is the order for today, apparently. To keep everyone safe, I just hope we switched up the training enough after Sebastian left.

Nicodeamus roars loudly as the crunching of the snow becomes louder. I see Aurora's glowing eyes look back at me briefly before she takes off toward the masses. The spray of blood is a stark contrast against the bright, white snow. The scent of copper and blood fills the air as bellows of pain and anguish echo all around us.

A pair of Polar Bears charge at me. Finally, I get a chance to prove myself. I don't think they were expecting to see a bear of my size in existence. When they get close enough, I swipe at them with my long, hooked claws. His white fur is painted crimson, and the snow is littered with droplets of blood.

The second Polar Bear pisses himself when my next swipe rips the head right off his companion. Another skull for Aurora's collection. Too bad we're on the ice; it won't be here in the spring. Without a second thought, I charge the second bear and roll him onto his back. Quickly, my massive maw snaps down around his throat, and I shake my head violently until every tendon and blood vessel is severed.

It's a great time to be alive; I live for moments like this. With each Polar Bear that I dispatch, I feel more like my old self. Briefly, I look up and see Aurora running toward me. She sails through the air over me to take out a Lycan who had snuck up behind me. His head goes flying past me and hits a Polar Bear's face, knocking him out cold. I casually walk up and use my claws to rip his throat open. By the time I look back to where Aurora was, she's long gone.

How many fucking Polar Bears live out here? Damn. I mean, seriously, it seems like a never-ending supply. On a more positive note, they can't fight for shit.

I see the blue glow of Nicodeamus's fire raining down on the mass of bodies in front of him in the distance. I watch in horror as Aurora launches herself off her father's head, through his flames, and into the fray below. I did not teach that girl to fight like that!

I make a newbie mistake and stop paying attention to what is going on around me. I feel the pressing of a sharp blade against my left rib cage, too close to my heart for comfort. Slowly, I turn my head to find Sebastian holding the knife.

"Shift back and live, remain as a bear and die," Sebastian says in an ice-cold tone. I shift back to my human form. He still has the tip of the blade pressed to my chest.

"Coward," is all I say to him. He doesn't fight with honor. For all I know, that female, Ravenna, was his real mate and he had forsaken her for power. If I remember correctly, he only gained Aurora's speed and talons and nothing else. I look down at the blade again; it's tinted green, which means Dire Wolf venom. I can't survive that, so I decide to play along and see where this rat bastard takes it. He starts pushing me toward Nicodeamus and Aurora.

I walk with my hands up in the air to show there's an issue. One minute I see Aurora's eyes; the next, I don't. She just went all ghost on us. This is about to get seriously interesting. Suddenly, Sebastian's left arm is severed at the elbow. He screams in pain as he backs up, trying to escape. Aurora manifests out of what seems like thin air, and she stands there in her human form. Her hands and forearms are shifted, her heavily armored gauntlets covered in blood.

"Betrayer! False mate! Coward!" Aurora continues to call him names as she stalks closer to him, herding him back toward the edge of the ice.

The beating of wings can be heard, but Aurora is too focused on moving in for the kill. Flames rain down from the sky between Aurora and Sebastian. I leap into the air and tackle Aurora to the ground before she is burned to a crisp. The ice chunk Sebastian is on starts to float off to sea. A large, Red Dragon swoops down to grab Sebastian off the ice and flies off with him. My body tenses, prepared for another attack, but nothing comes. It's almost eerily silent except for the giggling I hear under me.

"D? I think you can get up now." Wait, shit... I look down, and I still have Aurora pinned under me. She's laughing almost hysterically, and tears are rolling down her cheeks from how hard she's laughing. I remove myself carefully from her then realize I have the boner to end all boners. How embarrassing. I try to cover myself with both hands. I feel my cheeks flush as Aurora just keeps staring at my cock. FUCK! Nicodeamus—thank the gods—comes up behind Aurora and slaps his hand over her eyes.

"Dimitri, get yourself under control. You can kill someone with that thing." Nicodeamus is half-joking, I think. Jayce is in a state of shock, staring at me in all my aroused glory. Fucking cock has a damn mind of its freaking own. Death and destruction litters the field around me, and here I am with a rock-hard, throbbing boner. Just fucking wonderful. Now is the perfect time to go for a swim. I jump into the arctic water and instantly regret my decision; it's much colder than I was anticipating. I crawl back out of the water, and thankfully, my cock calmed down. I shift to my bear and decide to remain in this form until after catching up with Ellis.

Everyone returns to their animal form and begins to walk toward the first of the islands, which we can now see. Ellis comes out onto the ice to greet us and lead us back to headquarters. There's a single cavern visible on the island, so we follow Ellis underground. He starts passing out blankets and clothing as everyone shifts back to their human form.

Aurora waits until Dom secures her something to wear before she allows him to lead her into an alcove to shift and get dressed. Once she's done, she emerges from the alcove wearing a full-length gown. It's a pale, powder-blue and fits her like a glove. It must have been left there for her by Alaric. I wrap a blanket around me like a toga before approaching the group. They are already in an in-depth discussion about what happened and what's yet to come.

Nothing new has been discussed since our last meeting before the mission. However, we gain further information from Ellis when he tells us that fire dragons, otherwise known as Red Dragons, have joined the fight. When we go for the second half of this journey, the Gold and Ice Dragons will await our signal to join in on the attack.

Now, Aurora sits next to her father as he looks over the maps with Ellis and Klaus. The battle strategy is being amended since we now know Sebastian is on the field. He knows way too much and can make this battle way too dangerous for us, so the original formation has been changed. Ellis is dividing his bears up into four groups to match our four groups of troops.

Everyone's mulling around the cavern, eating, drinking, and generally getting to know each other so in the heat of battle, we can recognize who is friend and who is foe. Ellis is about to make a phone call to Alaric when Nicodeamus stops him. He is concerned about Alaric's phone going off and giving away his position. We ponder his suggestion for a moment and then agree that he's probably correct. It's not safe with how close we are to the enemy.

I can tell Aurora is quite stressed. Even with her sitting on Dom's lap, scales still ripple up and down her forearms. I understand her distress level; a male she once considered her mate is now trying to attack and kill us. Jayce reappears, bringing Aurora a tray of meat and some sort of spicy drink with it. Usually food and drink is an excellent way to cheer Aurora up, but she doesn't appear to be hungry at the moment. Nicodeamus has the look of a concerned father as he watches his poor child deal with all the revelations that have happened in such a short time.

CHAPTER 49

Dimitri

I KNOW THE LEVEL OF BETRAYAL THAT SHE AND NICODEAMUS FEELS RUNS bone-deep. I don't know if there's anything I can do to help her deal with everything. As a young pup, when she would get stressed, I used to give her rides on my bear and purposely toss her and roll around with her. I start to laugh a little as I think about that memory. Aurora gives me a strange look because I'm almost laughing my balls off in the middle of a serious discussion.

"Aurora, do you remember when you were a little girl, and you would get upset or stressed out over what was going on around you? What would I do?" Aurora slowly stands up, looks around the room, and then snatches a drumstick off Jayce's plate and begins to pace. I can tell she's now searching her memory for all the crazy, little things I used to do just to make her smile. I can also tell the moment she figures out the answer to my question. Her smile slowly broadens, her eyes light up, and she looks almost ethereal.

"That's an easy one, D. You used to sit there and tickle the hell out of me. When that didn't work, you would shift to your bear and roll around on the floor with me, tossing me in the air with your paws." A melodic giggle escapes her lips as she looks deeply into my eyes, reliving the memory. "Or you'd lay down so I could climb onto your back and grab onto your fur, and we would go running through the forest while Andre would scream at us to slow down." Aurora is almost laughing hysterically. Slowly, she turns to look over at Nicodeamus. She smiles and sits down next to her dad, snuggling into his left side, still very protective of him.

"Dad, Dimitri deserves, like, national honors for dealing with me. My mood swings alone deserve hazard pay. I was stubborn and pig-headed and probably a royal pain in his ass." I try not to laugh as Aurora perfectly sums up her childhood for her father. "I definitely didn't make their lives easy, nor did I even attempt to. I had all this speed, strength, and agility, and I just wanted to go. Poor Andre. I'm surprised he still had hair when you saw him last. That poor man would be terrified and frantically searching for me while I clawed halfway up a tree, staring down at him and trying not to laugh."

Aurora's gaze lands on me as she smiles and points at me. "Damn, Dimitri and his sneaky bear with his sense of smell would find me every flipping time. I know one thing, between those two, I learned how to hide, I learned how to evade, and I learned that you cannot trick a bear's nose for anything." The way she is smiling at me makes me feel like the king of the world—like the sun rose and set around me for once in my life.

It's moments like this when I hope and pray that Nicodeamus is right and she's really mine. She has me so elevated upon a pedestal, it's like I can do no wrong. I've loved that girl since she was born, and I love her still, though it's changed. The rest of the guys are watching me as I smile like a lovesick pup.

Of course, while we're all jovial and laughing, remembering the past, Ellis gets a text message. The message is from Alaric, who informs us the German Lycan pack was attacked. Everyone survived except for the alpha. Klaus and his brother Kaden are so distraught that both of them want to go back to their birth pack to keep everything under control. Shortly after Alaric's text message, Klaus's phone starts ringing. He answers quickly and receives a report from his younger brother about the attack. Klaus gives detailed directions to his younger brother as to what to do. He decides to video chat with his brother, so it's projected for his entire pack to see. He reassures them that all will be well and he is on a mission of utmost importance to return the last living Lycan heir to the throne.

Aurora chooses this time to stand up and take the phone from Klaus, and she looks down at the phone itself. Aurora slowly raises her right arm to show his pack that she bears the royal house's mark. You can hear the chatter erupting on the other side with shouts of joy and excitement. They all begin to rally behind her, pledging their undying loyalty to her and to the remaining people of her house. Aurora stands perfectly straight, shoulders back, looking like the future queen she is. She addresses the pack in their native tongue, reassuring them she has the drive and ability to regain her mother's throne.

She looks up and scans those who are assembled before her. Aurora gives them a nod and acknowledges her forces before addressing the Lycan pack. She tells them she will be returning to the throne, she will remain in the castle after the war is over, and she will reunite all the packs and call them home. Then she issues an open-ended invitation to anybody who wishes to challenge her upon her arrival on Romanian soil.

No one dares to speak. Aurora watches the Lycans drop to their knees and lower their heads, submitting to her. Aurora lets them know she's going to hand the phone back to Klaus, and she allows him to handle the daily duties in her place. Slowly, Aurora walks back over to Klaus and hands him the phone. Aurora gives him a kiss on the cheek and tells him she's sorry for his loss. She creeps back over to where Dom and Jayce are, and she sits between them and starts to eat.

Her drive for vengeance has been stoked, and the fire is burning much brighter than it was before. Hell hath no fury like a woman scorned. And I am damn sure Aurora is going to rain hell on Earth upon those who stand against her.

Nicodeamus chooses this time to speak with Aurora about the weaknesses of each dragon species. We all listen carefully, making mental notes of where would do the most damage—with hits that we may or may not be able to rain down on them. Let's face it, dragons are a hundred times larger than any of us, except for maybe Nicodeamus.

I can see the gears turning behind Aurora's eyes as she starts to contemplate what her father's telling her. She tilts her head to the left then back to the right again. She scoots closer to her father and stares him right in his eyes, grabbing his hand with both of hers. Both of their eyes become that of their beasts. We can tell they're having a deep conversation, privy only to them. The way they are sitting stock still, barely even blinking, we can tell whatever is passing between them is of vital importance. The tension in the air starts to increase as the moments tick by. Nicodeamus is the first to break off.

"I am not a fan of this idea, baby girl. But if the opportunity presents itself, I will be more than happy to assist you in making it happen." Nicodeamus, like Aurora, does tilt his head left then right after he finishes speaking to assess whether his answer was enough. I decide to question them since his response makes no sense to me.

"M'Lord, what do you mean? What opportunity are you speaking of?" You know that look somebody gets when they are absolutely up to no good? Well, right now, Nicodeamus looks like the cat that swallowed the canary. That's usually the look he gets when something really reckless is about to happen.

"Well, I'm kind of happy you asked because it'll be much easier to explain it now than during battle. My crazy-ass daughter wants me to launch her into the air using my wing. That way she can sink her talons into a dragon flying overhead and rip out its throat. Honestly, from a logical standpoint, it should work perfectly. My only concern is the landing." I'm really starting to hate how Nicodeamus says everything so matter-of-fact when it has to deal with life or death.

Thankfully, Dom speaks up next and takes the words right out of my mouth. "Hold up, you mean to say you're going to send Aurora flying through the air to sink her talons into a dragon's hide? Then, we have to be concerned about her getting to the ground safely after she kills the dragon? Just fucking wonderful!" Dom throws his hands up into the air and begins to pace.

I look over at his brother, Jayce, and he is a ball of nerves. He's definitely very anxious about the possibility of his mate getting injured. Ellis is going back and forth, shaking his head no while saying, "Aww hell no, that bitch is crazy," under his breath.

I've decided that I'm in the middle of some sort of crazy rom-com that's gone horribly wrong. Aurora has lost her mind, and her father's not far behind her. Her two Dire Wolf mates are the only ones making any sense. The poor Polar Bear is beside himself. And I'm sitting over here, thinking what the actual fuck just happened?

I know Aurora can be reckless at times, but this absolutely takes the bloody cake. How does she expect to get to the ground without killing herself? I mean, seriously, these dragons are what, ten to twenty thousand feet in the air when they're flying? Even if she gets lucky and one swoops down close enough for her to launch at it, Who's to say he's not going to gain altitude to try to shake her off?

Between Aurora and her father, once they have their mind set on something, it's virtually impossible to get them to change their course. Tomorrow is going to be a shitshow. If we make it out of this in one fucking piece, I will be absolutely amazed. For now, I have to try to figure out a way to talk some sense into that girl before she ends up becoming a dirt torpedo.

Klaus walks over, listening to Aurora and her father discussing ideas for her to become a Lycan projectile. Poor Klaus ends up face-palming and starts shaking his head in disbelief at the lunacy he's listening to. I really can't blame him right now. I'm still pondering how the fuck I got myself into this shit. I've lived almost two hundred years—past what my species should have lived. And now I'm probably going to die because the princess lost her mind.

Aurora runs over to the fire pit, grabs a few charcoal pieces that have cooled, and then heads over to the cavern wall. She starts drawing pictures of flying dragons, her father on the ground, little circles and stick figures that are supposed to be us, and then a giant smiley face flying up toward the dragon. I thought her homicidal tendencies were kind of frightening, but this absolutely takes the cake. She explains that when the timing is right she's going to run toward her father, he's going to lower his wing, she's going to stand on his wingtip, and he's going to launch her into the air like a frisbee. I really can't see this working; no way, no how.

But if I start thinking a little bit left field with this, I can almost see it working. Shit, just like that, I'm beginning to see the brilliance in her insanity. Both of her mates are attempting to talk her out of her hair-brained scheme, but it ain't going to happen. We'll just have to wait and see what happens tomorrow. Hopefully, she stays in one piece, and we can all go home happy little campers.

CHAPTER 50

Aurora

I have no bloody clue what time I went to bed last night. But shit, if I could get about three more hours of sleep and a giant pot of coffee, I'd be golden. I look at the assembled group in front of me; we are well-rested and fed. None of us really know what we're walking into today.

What I do know is that Alaric is quite anxious this morning. I raise my hand and start rubbing his scale, trying to soothe him like he's done for me so many times already. I feel him relax, and I honestly think, somehow, he knows what I'm planning to do. It really doesn't matter though. It needs to be done. Without air support during the attack, we're sitting ducks.

I know my strengths and weaknesses. I don't think the boys understand entirely how strong I truly am. And I don't mean physical strength, I mean strength of will, drive, and integrity. After everything, my father has shown me about attacking the dragons. I know their weak spot is their neck—especially if I can get up close to the head just under its jaw and sink my talons in there. The scales there are so tiny and spread out that it'll be easy for the tip of my talons to get in and start ripping. I just have to figure out how to land the fucker. *I wonder if I can make dragon surfing a sport?*

I better not say anything about that to the guys because they'll really start to panic. It's bad enough I slept in a twin taco last night, neither one of them wanting to let me move. I really do understand their level of concern, but if I have the opportunity, why not take it?

Through my dreams last night, when Alaric visited me, he said he wouldn't be far away. I'm counting on it. But again, if more dragons than what he's expecting shows up, then dang, I guess I'm going flying. Either my father's going to have to launch me into the air, or Alaric will have to carry me. That way I'll only have to dive-bomb off Alaric and onto the dragons below him. Either way, I fully intend to get the job done.

That fucking rat bastard Sebastian... I swear to the gods if I see him, I am ripping his fucking head off. His head is going on my goddamn wall right beside his fucking mother's. Between the two of them, they have stolen way to goddamn much from me, and I will never forgive them for that. They better hope and pray I'm not the one who finds them first because unlike the others, I'm going to make it fucking painful. I growl as I work through my inner monologue, and everybody's head whips to look at me and see what exactly is going on. I smile and wave and start to laugh. Yeah, I just had a Harley Quinn moment. Oops.

I find my twins standing together and talking by the fire. Gently, I touch Jayce's shoulder and get him to turn to me. I kiss him deeply and passionately, making him growl. His fingertips dig into the meat of my ass as he lifts me off the ground.

I smile against his lips and whisper, "I love you." He returns the passionate kiss and tells me he loves me too. Slowly, Jayce lowers me to the floor. I don't even have both feet on the ground before Dom twirls me around and aggressively kisses me. Damn, I love when he tries to get all dominant with me. I growl and bite his lip before I start giggling. I whisper against his lips, "I love you." In no way am I saying goodbye. In my mind, I'm just making sure they know they are loved. Hesitantly, Dom lowers me to the ground.

I smile at both of my mates before I head off to find my father. When I find him, he's in an in-depth discussion with Dimitri and Klaus. I run my fingers up Klaus's back as I pass him on my way to my father. Klaus makes a soft growl in the back of his throat. I stop and turn to look at him. His wolf's eyes are beautiful; they're gold in color. I break eye contact and move to my father and hug him tightly. I'm not sure who needed it more, him or me. Gently, I place a kiss on my father's cheek and tell him I love him. In turn, my father kisses my forehead and tells me he's proud of me and loves me.

Just to fuck with Dimitri, I go to Klaus next to hug him and kiss his cheek. I thank him for coming to our aid and being there for me. He smiles at me then gently kisses my cheek. Klaus's hand slides through my long, snow-white hair, his smile radiating affection. *Does he wish for more than just my allegiance?* It doesn't really matter right now; Sebastian's false bond won't let me find my real mate. I break away from Klaus and move toward Dimitri.

Dimitri appears nervous, which isn't like him. I move slowly toward him and circle around him, looking him over. He's definitely a handsome man. His shoulders are so broad and thick, and I can't help but run my fingers over them. Dimitri's frame tenses the minute my fingers make contact with his shoulders. It's not fear that makes him tense, so what could it be?

When I move to stand before Dimitri, he's not looking at me like he usually does. That fatherly look of adoration is gone. Now, his hazel eyes move over my frame, almost caressing my flesh. Quickly, my eyes dart to my father, and he just smiles at me. I seek out the twins, and they're smiling too.

What the fuck is going on around here? I start to back up, and Dimitri wraps his large hands around my elbows to stop me. I stare at his hands and notice how gently they grip my arms. I draw in a deep breath then look up to meet his eyes. Dimitri slowly raises his left hand to cup my right cheek, and I lean into his touch.

"Aurora," he says in his deep husky voice. I can't help but feel like my insides are on fire with how he's looking at me. "Your father and I suspect that Elena cast a spell to keep us apart. We believe she used blood magic to stop our bond from forming." Dimitri gently rubs my cheek as his eyes beg me to understand. I stop breathing the moment everything Dimitri says clicks. Frost begins to spread from the spot I'm standing and starts to coat the entire cavern.

"I wasn't crazy? My wolf was right?" I start crying; I can't help it. The tears flow freely down my cheeks, and all I can do is stare up into Dimitri's eyes. I have loved this man before me for the better half of a hundred years. All that time, I thought I was insane, that my wolf was wrong and tricked by the binding. Dimitri quickly pulls me flush with his chest and holds me tightly. I feel the rumble of his bear in his chest, trying to soothe me like he used to. I push back lightly so I can look back up at Dimitri again.

"I swear you will have Elena's head. I will give it to you." I feel my canines descend, and my eyes churn to liquid mercury. Dimitri chuckles just before he kisses me on the lips for the first time ever. I can sense Jayce and Dom approach, but they don't interfere. My hands slowly slide up Dimitri's broad chest, and I rest my palms on his cheeks and hold him to me. I can feel him smiling mid-kiss, then I slowly pull back to look at him.

"Kill the witch, break the spell. Easy enough. Then, off to storm the castle!" Poor Dom facepalms again and complains it's not going to be that easy. I tilt my head to the right then give Dom the middle finger.

I start to turn away from Dimitri before I make my announcement. "I am the Poke-master! I have collected them *all*!" I scream *all* because Dimitri slapped my ass, hard. Quickly, I spin to face him as I rub my poor ass cheeks.

"Remember, princess, you collected the others. I've been right here waiting for you." Dimitri's dominant attitude is kind of a turn on, and I start laughing as I look at him. He went all cheesy on me by quoting one of my favorite eighties songs: the Richard Marx song about the guy waiting for his love to return. Damn emotional wolf; fucking tears start rolling down my cheeks. *What the fuck?* I'm starting to turn into a freaking wuss. I roughly wipe the tears away, then look to the pack, who's trying to act like they didn't see anything.

"We leave in ten minutes, so be fucking ready!" I head off to my part of the cavern. I can still hear the guys congratulating Dimitri. I slowly turn around to look at him, and he has a giant grin on his face. I haven't seen him smile so much in so long. He deserves to be happy. Several moments pass and I decide it's time to shift.

Quickly, I consume the last of the rations I hoarded away for myself before I head to the gathering point.

We have our marching orders from Nico, and we break off in our assigned groups to head toward Siberia. The larger one of the two Diomede Islands separates our forces. I feel Alaric's anxiety spike just as our groups pass the second island. I clamber up my father's back and start to watch behind us, keeping an eye out for any enemies. Knowing those sneaky scum bags, they'll attack from behind. Through the pack link, I order the group to converge and form a circle. Once everyone is in place, we have eyes in all directions.

What we didn't account for was a Red Wyvern swooping down to snatch me off my father's back. Stupid move grabbing me. The wyvern continues gaining altitude; I'm guessing it's planning on dropping me. Without warning, I reach up and cut the tendons on one foot. Once it loses its grip on me, I reach up and grasp onto the remaining foot. With my free hand, I slash at its exposed abdomen. The wyvern screams in pain as I continue to disembowel it. Blood and intestinal contents coat my scales as I continue to rip. In the distance, I sense Alaric gaining ground. He should reach me once I start to fall.

Now, I grip both legs of the wyvern and hold on tight. It's only a matter of time before it bleeds out. In my head, I start singing Limp Bizkit's *Break Stuff*. It seems entirely appropriate right about now. Suddenly, the wyvern begins to fall from the sky. I use my talons to climb up onto its back and hold its wings open to slow our descent.

I feel Alaric before I see him. His giant, taloned dragon hand comes down and gently grips me, and I release my hold on the wyvern's corpse. I gently rub my muzzle on Alaric's scales as he carries me. Then I notice he has a group of dragons flying with him in formation. Once the wyvern corpse reaches the ground, we watch it take out some of the enemies' Lycan forces. Yes! Two for one! Alaric's nest mates break off to fight the remaining wyverns.

We gain speed as we approach a Black Dragon. This thing is fucking huge—it dwarfs Alaric's dragon. I pat his hand to get him to drop me onto the monster's back, but his dragon only shakes his head *no* at my idea. Through the bond, I push my plan to him. Hopefully he sees it's the only way to take out that acid breathing monster. I can hear him huff before he changes course. Honestly, I can't believe I won that discussion.

He aligns himself over the center of the Black Dragon's back. While a small Gold Dragon keeps him occupied.

I do the unthinkable, I drop down from twenty feet above him and land on his back. Time to get to work.

CHAPTER 51

Aurora

The Black Dragon keeps circling the battle below, yet he's not interfering. Ever so carefully, I walk along the spines on his back, making sure to remain on his armored plates.

In the back of my mind, I start humming the *Mission Impossible* theme song. This dragon is much larger than I was anticipating. I begin to get concerned until I notice missing scales at the base of his skull. Mentally, I reach out to my father, and he confirms what I'm thinking: dig quickly and sever the spinal cord. Alaric and his group are close, making sure no one gets close to me.

When I feel the time is right, I sink my talons into the exposed flesh. The Black Dragon roars and starts to whip his head from side to side, trying to shake me off. I hold on for dear life and sink my talons into his skin as I wedge myself between his spines. He stops whipping his head around, so I go back on the attack. I rip out several more large chunks before he starts thrashing his head around again. My once white fur is now covered in blood and flesh chunks from the Black Dragon. This is getting irritating; every time I start getting somewhere, he starts thrashing.

The good news is I can see two decent-sized blood vessels and vertebrae. As the thrashing slows down, I lunge quickly and easily slice through one of the blood vessels. Blood goes everywhere. It covers me as well as the dragon's scales. His blood is coagulating almost the second it hits his scales and me. I'm a big, gloppy, blood-covered mess. The only bonus to this gory mess is that he's slowly losing altitude. The dragon's roars are getting weaker, and he's not thrashing as hard.

Seizing the opportunity, I sever the second blood vessel. I feel as though I am swimming in a sea of blood. I have to sink my talons deep into his flesh just to keep from sliding off. I carefully move to stand after I notice the ground is approaching fast. Thankfully, he's headed right toward his own reinforcements. I grab on to the crown of horns that adorn his head and brace for impact. Just as I sense the impending crash, I jump up to lessen the blow to my body. The Black Dragon's body slides for several hundred feet before stopping.

I jump off the dragon's corpse quickly. Alaric's dragon lands close by and observes me. I'm cold, wet, and feeling gross. The blood in my fur is coagulating and freezing at the same time. I can't shift to my human form, or else I will turn into an ice cube. Alaric lowers his massive head to my level and starts blowing his hot breath on me. I'm just thankful he has enough sense not to try his flames on me. One great wing comes forward and shelters me from the wind.

There's a war going on about two thousand feet from us, but Alaric's only concern is my health and well-being. After about his fifth or sixth heated breaths, I'm defrosted, and the blood chunks have started falling away. I rub my muzzle against his dragon's nose, and then I lick it affectionately. Alaric forgets his strength when he tries to nuzzle me back. I end up on my ass in the snow, shaking my head at him. If a dragon could look sorry, he was doing it. I dust myself off and start walking back to the battle. Apparently, I'm not allowed to walk anymore because Alaric's dragon scoops me up, flies me over to my father, and drops me on his back. With my arrival after the Black Dragon crashed, the remaining forces retreat quickly.

Without a second thought, I leap off my father's back and give chase. My mates come up alongside me as well as the rest of the Dire Wolves. One by one, we hunt down and slaughter the remaining Polar Bears and Lycans.

The only unanswered question I have: where the fuck is Sebastian? I stand there and watch as the last of my enemies fall around me. All this bloodshed and for what? The Polar Bears didn't need to die; they were lied to and misled. The Lycans that fought, I wonder which pack they were from? I stand here in the middle of the tundra, surrounded by corpses, and all I can think about are the pups back in America.

My father's dragon comes up behind me and bathes me in his blue flames. All the dirt and grime from the day is gone. I nod my wolven head at my father before I start walking.

Alaric's dragon lands before me and opens his taloned hand, revealing a wooden box. I tilt my head left then right, studying it. Carefully, I use my talons and open the box. Within it is clothing; a heavy coat and boots. I look up at Alaric and motion to his wing. Taking the hint, he drops both of his wings to block me from the cold winds. I shift and get dressed quickly in the clothes provided. My gloved hand lightly touches Alaric's wing, and he lifts it. The clothing he picked out for me fits beautifully, and I step out looking like a princess for the first time in my life. The twins and Dimitri come to stand before me. I gently rub my face along their muzzles.

"Alaric and I are going to fly to his summer chalet." I look over to my father, and his dragon is smiling—well, he's showing his teeth, so I assume he's smiling. "I know you remember where the chalet is. Please lead our forces there." Nico nods his great dragon head and roars, assembling the troops. They turn and start heading south as they follow behind him.

I look back to Alaric's dragon, he lays down in the snow and extends his wing. Carefully, I step on the scaled bone of his wing and begin climbing toward his back. Once on Alaric's back, I remove my glove and press it to his scales.

"Where should I sit?" I look around his dragon's back, puzzled.

I'll lower my head. Sit directly behind the ridge of horns. It should protect you from the wind. I look toward Alaric's head where he indicated. He turns his body so his head is close to his back. I carefully climb onto his neck then move to sit behind the ridge of horns. It's a perfect fit for me, and I feel safe and secure where I'm at. I pat Alaric's neck, and we take off.

It's interesting sitting here with a dragon's eye view of the world around me. I shift my eyes to that of my beast, and I get to see the world how Alaric sees it. Everything looks so amazing up here above the clouds. It looks like we are flying over a field of cotton balls. Through the bond, I can feel that my joy from flying with him pleases him and his dragon. Carefully, I reach down and start scratching at his scales under the horn ridge. It seems like there's a build-up of dead skin in some spots, so I carefully remove it. I keep working on his scales while I'm back here. Soft rumbles can be felt from his dragon as I preen his scales. I know I love the feel of my father's fire through my fur, so I assume Alaric is enjoying the attention.

In the distance, a castle on a cliff face comes into view. It looks like it stepped right out of a fairy tale story. Without warning, two Gold Dragons flank us. I shift my arms and hands quickly, ready to fight.

Through the bond, I hear Alaric's voice. *Settle, my love. It's my mother and sister escorting us home.* His words offer me a little comfort and reassure me that we're safe for the moment. However, I have trust issues now, and it's hard to relax when I'm surrounded by strangers. *Love, my life is tied to yours directly. I would never put our lives at risk. I have too much to live for now.*

Without a second thought, I shift my hands back and rub his scales. I attempt to relax and enjoy the remainder of our flight to his castle.

The castle is one that you would expect to hear about in a fairy tale novel. Tall spires adorn the four corners, and a tall wall surrounds the main structure. We fly in lazy circles, gliding on the thermals around the castle grounds so I can get a good look at his home. I can tell he and his dragon are very concerned if I approve of their nest because his anxiety is spiking. I gently rub his scales.

"Your nest is beautiful. Can we land so I can get a better look at you and your home?" No sooner do the words leave my mouth than his dragon banks and lands softly in the courtyard. Alaric lowers his head, allowing me to slowly slide off his neck to land on his foreleg. My hand rests on his dragon's cheek as I step down. Once I'm safely on the ground, he sits up and spreads his wings, and roars. My inner beast stirs at his call, and I feel compelled to howl along with him. We roar and howl several times until my human throat is sore from the effort. I smile up at him and shake my head as I laugh. His large dragon head lowers to my level.

When I'm this close, I notice the blues mixed in with the white. His scales also slightly change color depending on the angle I look from. Alaric stands perfectly still as I continue to touch his scales and look at his dragon form. His large golden serpentine eye follows my movements.

Out of the corner of my eye, I noticed movement off to my right. I quickly duck under Alaric's lowered wing. I remain firmly pressed against his body, slowly working on climbing up his leg to get my feet off the ground. Alaric's dragon huffs, and I guess he's laughing for some reason. I remain perched on his leg directly under where his wing attaches to his body. If he chose to stand up now, I would surely fall. A woman's voice reaches my ears and I start to growl, not happy another female is near what's mine. Slowly, Alaric lifts his wing and turns his head to face me. I stare into his dragon's eyes, my own churning liquid mercury; every move I make, Alaric mimic's.

My love, Mother wishes to meet you. That's the female you heard speaking. No threat, I promise. Alaric's voice echoes in my head. I gradually calm down and nod to him. I slip carefully back to the ground and straighten my hair back out. I draw in a deep, measured breath and make sure my eyes are back to normal. I adjust my stance to how Dimitri told me I should carry myself at court. My hand rests on Alaric's side just before I step out from under his wing.

His mother is a vision of beauty. Her hair is long like mine but is the color of spun gold. Her skin is the most perfect of porcelain, with lips the color of blood. She rushes forward and embraces me tightly. My look of apparent panic causes Alaric to make a rumbling noise, which gets his mother to back off.

"I'm sorry, my dear. I never thought my boy would find a mate. When he said it was you, I just couldn't contain myself. Oh, where are my manners? My name is Katherine. I guess you can say I'm Queen of the Ice Dragon Court." She smiles while looking at me and slightly bows her head. Two men come forth, one carrying clothing and the other with a dressing blind. The men start to herd Alaric's dragon to an alcove close by. I watch the men for a moment, then turn my attention back to Katherine. I move the ripped sleeve of my coat and show her the royal mark on my forearm.

"I'm Princess Aurora Marelup, last of my name, first of my kind—future queen of the Lycan packs." I curtsey to the queen and she returns the gesture. Her hand gently comes out to touch mine.

"I knew your mother. She was such a kind and caring soul. But gods help you, if you crossed her, she was downright ruthless." Katherine smiles as she speaks about my mother. It warms my heart to know someone besides my father and Dimitri is left alive that knew my mother. I smile and laugh a bit.

"I have a lot of my mother's tendencies and my father's black or white view of the world. Though, thankfully, I have a much better grasp of technology than he does." I watch his mother's visage pale considerably when I mention my father in the present tense. I straighten up my stance a bit more, my resolve as hard as steel.

"I rescued my father from the Dire Wolf camp in the Nankoweap Ruins. Apparently, their alpha—who was the beta in my mother's time—chopped off his left arm and took him hostage." I tilt my head left then right, assessing her reaction. Before I can speak again, Alaric wraps his arms around my waist and kisses my cheek.

"My father should be here tomorrow with the rest of my troops. That's not going to be a problem, is it?" I watch my scales ripple across my hands then recede just as fast. My eyes lock on Alaric's mother's eyes—there's a definite fear there. Katherine begins to pace in front of us before she turns and looks at her son.

"Alaric, you know what this means for all of us?" Tears are threatening to break free from her eyes. Katherine's flesh flushes from the effort of trying not to cry. Alaric kisses my cheek then locks eyes with his mother.

"I do. It means dad isn't the rightful king, and we no longer hold any title. Nicodeamus was next in line for the throne, but with him not wed to another dragon or dragon kind, he cannot sit upon the capital's throne. Aurora, however, can and will sit upon the throne—she is dragon-kin and my mate. If Aurora allows it, I wish to wed her before we dethrone father." I watch Alaric talk to his mother. It feels very surreal, like I'm watching some reality TV show. I have a prince, who's really not a prince, who wishes to be my husband and mate. I turn in Alaric's arms and look up into his grey eyes.

"Make the preparations. As far as my father is concerned, he will see the value of having not only our mating but our marriage to solidify the alliance between the Lycans and Dragon houses." I stand on my tippy toes and kiss his lips. "Besides, I think you'll look pretty damn fine in dress clothes." I feel my father reach out to me mentally, and I bring him up to speed. Alaric's grip on me tightens as I widen the connection, allowing both of them in on the conversation. I personally suspect anyone who gained power after my mother's house fell. Both my father and Alaric agree. I look at Alaric's mother over my shoulder, and my mercury orbs frighten her some.

"Father says hi, and the wedding will happen tomorrow at dusk. The Dragon Star is at its apex tomorrow, and he wants it to bless our union. Plus, it's my birthday." His mother's fear is clearly visible. She's shaking, which proves to me that she knows something about the attack. "Alaric, love, please show me to our chambers. I wish to freshen up." Alaric studies his mother's reaction to what I said before he leads me off.

CHAPTER 52
Alaric

Today has to be the absolute best day of my life. My mate flew with me, and she tended to the scales my dragon can't reach. Aurora even sought shelter under my wing when my mother approached. I feel like I'm king of the world right now.

Now, I'm only concerned about my mother's reaction when Aurora said her father is still living. She seemed to get very nervous after that. Maybe there was betrayal on my father's side? I'll ponder this later, but for now, I'm supervising the construction of my bride's wedding dress—nothing but the best for Aurora. I don't care if I don't have a title. I don't care if we have to walk through the fires of Hell to secure her birthright to her mother's throne.

I stand back and watch the seamstress work on Aurora's dress. Honestly, I don't think any fabric will ever be good enough for her. It's my own opinion, not how she feels. She doesn't care about finery or any of the usual court bullshit.

I receive news that Nicodeamus was spotted on the horizon with the rest of the packs. He's way ahead of schedule. Good, it gives me time to get them all settled, bathed, and fed before tomorrow. I tell the one manservant to prepare enough robes for their arrival. He bows and leaves to complete his task.

The second seamstress shows me the suit she's preparing for me. It's a beautiful compliment to the dress I commissioned for Aurora. I can't believe she agreed to marry me on such short notice. Our bond is different than that of her wolf mates. Our bond is bone-deep; no bite is required or even a mating. We were matched on the most primal and genetic level. If we were not a match, our scales would have died the moment they were implanted. I gently rub Aurora's scale on my chest, and I can instantly feel her joy. I wonder why my parents never swapped scales. Perhaps I'll ask my mother later.

"Alaric?" Speaking of the devil, here's my mother now.

"Hard at work, I see," Katherine says in a bored tone as she looks over the suit. She plays with the lapel, examining the stitch work closely.

"What do you need, Mother?" I tilt my head to the side and examine her body language, looking for a clue as to what her motivation is.

"I don't need anything. Why would I need anything? I'm the queen, after all." She looks at me and tries to hold my gaze. She couldn't do it for long. My mother starts fiddling with the hem of her sleeves instead of looking at me. I slowly cross my arms over my chest and lean against the wall, watching her.

"Let me guess, either you're bothered by the fact that Nicodeamus is still alive or the fact that his daughter is my mate," I smirk as I watch her eyebrow twitch, a dead giveaway that I hit the nail on the head. My mother bites her bottom lip and continues to stare at the hem of her sleeve. Katherine begins to walk around the room until she reaches the window.

"Your father knew about the attack before it came. That's why we didn't attend that night. He admitted to the knowledge a few months ago. He said those horrible Strigoi were sent in search of the last true heir. A puppet master is pulling their strings. Tomas is not the true leader; someone else is giving the orders." My mother looks frightened. I slowly move to embrace her.

"Mother, we will protect you. Aurora is quite strong; she took down Nexus all by herself." I smile broadly after seeing my mother's shock at the news. "Besides, I believe we can take back the throne, usurp my father, and assemble the nest to take back the main castle. Aurora is alpha enough to force every wolven creature to shift. I've seen the video that proves her power. Hell, I've felt her power for myself." I release my mother, and she breaks away to spin around and face me.

"Are you absolutely sure, Alaric? You know your father is a powerful male. I don't want to see my oldest son die." Katherine is practically in tears as she thinks about the possibility of me dying. A knock at the door makes both of us look at the sliding bolt lock. A single long, hooked, white talon makes its way between the doors then slices down, cutting the beam in half. A thud is heard as the door flies open. Aurora stands on the other side, partially shifted. She must have sensed my inner turmoil. Her eyes are fathomless orbs, the churning mercury not giving away where she's looking.

"My love, I know the mid-shift is exhausting. Why don't you take your full form?" I smile, looking at Aurora as she smirks then fully shifts. Her great, white hybrid beast looks down at us. I can feel my mother's body trembling beside me. "Mother, I told you she can defend herself." I smile as I look at Aurora's hybrid up close for the first time.

I slowly approach her and caress the heavy scale-like armor on her forearms. I raise her arm to look at how her scales form into gauntlets to protect her. Where the wolven claws should be, long, white, curved dragon talons exist. Aurora remains still as I touch her beast's form. I guess it's only fair; she did examine my dragon closely before.

My mother's eyes widen as she watches me manipulate Aurora's talons. My eyes move to Aurora's head; it's a unique mix of Lycan and dragon features. Her muzzle is broader with a ridge up the nose plate like a dragon. Tiny scales adorn her eyelids, almost like eyeliner. For a moment, as I stare at her mercury orbs, I can see a slightly darker shade of grey in the center of her eyes—the darker area in the shape of a dragon's slit. I simply smile at her and stroke her muzzle.

"I can see your eye slits," I say in a teasing tone as I look up at her. Aurora's ears flicker before she tilts her head to look at me, then rolls her eyes. Her long, white tail whips from side to side in irritation. I'm guessing I'm right; I can see where she's focusing her gaze.

"Are you sure that's safe, Alaric? She could be unpredictable," Katherine states from her spot near the window. She looks like she's ready to jump at any moment.

Aurora growls and begins to freeze the room. Her alpha power is unleashed, driving my mother and the seamstresses to the ground. In the distance, we can hear Nicodeamus's dragon's roar.

Aurora answers back in a mixed sound that can only be explained as a howling roar.

Then she approaches my mother and shifts back to her human form. "What do you know about the night my mother died?" I can see a fine line of scales ripple down Aurora's spine all the way down to her tailbone. This happens several times before my mother speaks.

"My husband knew and kept us here. He knew about the attack and didn't let our clan attend or even think about leaving the nest." Katherine lowers her eyes and puts her hands over her face as she begins to cry. Aurora looks back at me. I can see she's struggling for control.

I unbutton my dress shirt and wrap it around her. Her oppressive alpha power slowly diminishes, and everyone else can start moving about again. Aurora looks up at me with tears in her eyes. I can't tell if they're rage or pain tears. She slowly lowers her eyes, just staring at my chest. I gently kiss her forehead and hold her. What else could I do? I mean, the twins were right; she's quite scary when she's dealing with an emotion outside of rage. For all I know, she could lose her shit and take out everyone in this room in a few seconds. My mother seizes this moment to escape out of the room as quickly as possible.

Aurora, completely uncharacteristic, speaks in a soft voice. "You know I'm going to kill him, right?" She doesn't bother to look up at me. I rest my head on top of hers and just smile.

"Consider my father's head a wedding present." Aurora backs up and looks at me, my shirt barely staying on her shoulders. Her smile rivals the sun. I haven't seen her this happy since she went flying for the first time. Aurora's smile turns mischievous as she tilts her head to the left.

"Do you really mean it, Alaric?" Her hands slide down my chest to rest on the edge of my pants. Her fingertips slowly slip under the waistband and slide back and forth, touching my lower stomach. I can feel my cock come to life, quickly becoming almost painfully hard. Her scent has changed. In the back of my mind, I know her heat recently should have ended, but there's always that slight chance she's still fertile.

"Aurora, we should be careful. It's still so close to when your heat ended." I'm trying to be responsible. I don't have condoms here, and I don't want her to regret our first time together.

Aurora's fingers make short work of my belt, my button, and then my zipper. My trousers fall to the floor, leaving me bare for her inspection. Aurora's eyes slowly roam over every inch of my body. Her mischievous grin turns into one of appreciation. I'm now very thankful for all the extra training sessions I did every single week. Aurora shrugs my dress shirt off and tries to herd me to the desk behind me. She's got another thing coming if she thinks I'm going to allow myself to be dominated by my mate.

When we get close to the desk, I grab her by her waist and spin her around. Aurora's palms slap down hard on the desktop. I wrap her thick, white hair around my left fist and pull back so her neck is exposed and her back is arched. I press my body flush with hers, and my cock rests between her plump ass cheeks. My right hand comes up to lightly grip her throat as I growl softly. "We do this my way, love. I can't promise to be gentle. Your scent is driving me insane."

Through our bond, she responds, *Anything, my love, I need to feel you.* Aurora's breathless voice echoes in my head, making my cock leak with anticipation.

I slowly move my hips back and feel my cock slide down her ass crack to her dripping folds. Once I'm lined up, I thrust into her roughly. Each stroke out is agonizingly slow, but my thrust back into her is fast and hard. Aurora's moans are music to my ears. The soaking wet slaps of flesh on flesh drives me to start fucking her harder. I tighten my grip on her throat as my thrusts start to become erratic. All of a sudden, Aurora's powerful cock-crushing orgasm rips through her. My balls begin to tighten, begging for release.

A fresh gush of Aurora's cum spurts out of her pussy, drenching my cock and balls. I'm too close to my own orgasm to hold back any longer. I use Aurora's hair to move her head to the left. I roar as my orgasm rips through me, and my canines descend just before I sink them into the muscle of Aurora's shoulder. I feel my seed pulse in waves into her womb, every shockwave rippling through me. Instinctually, I know what's happening. I keep making small thrusts, milking every last drop of seed I have into her. I carefully withdraw my teeth from her flesh and lick the wounds clean. I release my grip on her throat and hair and start kissing her skin. "I love you so much. I hope I wasn't too rough?"

Aurora lays her chest on the desk and stretches. "Fuck no! That was phenomenal!" She turns her head to look at me over her shoulder. I withdraw from her slowly then slide her whole body onto the desk. I crawl onto the desk beside her as she rolls onto her back. Aurora bends her knees and places her feet flat on the desk. I lightly run my fingers over her soft abdomen.

"I have to say it's a first for me to have fucked here. I'm just glad everyone had enough sense to leave." I chuckle softly as I watch Aurora look around.

"You know I need to return the favor." Her fingertips trace where I bit her. She raises a single eyebrow and looks at me before she covers her mouth to yawn. I carefully extract myself from the desk. Aurora seems so happy and peaceful when she sleeps. I gently scoop her up in my arms and carry her to my room. Lucky for me, a maid is cleaning up in there.

She looks up, startled by my arrival. A knowing smile graces her lips, and she turns down the bed so I can tuck Aurora in. Once she's settled, I go and take a quick shower. When I'm done, I leave my room and make arrangements for Aurora's dress and appropriate jewelry to be left for her to choose from. I handpick attendants to help her dress for the wedding.

The castle herald announces the arrival of Nicodeamus and his army. I run downstairs as fast as I can to greet everyone. "Welcome home, everyone!" I approach Nicodeamus first and embrace him. In a whispered tone, I speak to him. "We need to talk. Gather the twins and Dimitri; we'll meet in the library." Nicodeamus nods then moves off into the crowd. I finish greeting everyone, then make arrangements with the servants to get the troops fed and food and drink to be brought to the library.

I wait for the guys to arrive in the library. My hand rests on the decanter for a moment before I lift it to pour a few glasses of well-aged bourbon. Once the guys arrive, and everyone is inside, I lock the doors, pass out the drinks, and turn on some music to prevent anyone from listening in.

"I have news," I blurt out the first thing that comes to mind. "Apparently, my father knew about the attack, and that's why there were no dragons present at the festivities. The second bit of news is Aurora and I are getting married tonight, so her claim to the dragon throne is stronger." The guys start talking among themselves then Dominik speaks.

"Aurora agreed to go along with this? She doesn't believe in putting one mate above the others." Dominik looks pissed, and so does his brother. Thankfully, our angel makes her appearance.

"You're right, Dom; no mate is above the other. The very public wedding tonight is part of a two-fold plan." Aurora holds up one finger. "It appears to be a political marriage since mates don't need a wedding. Our enemies will believe I haven't gained power from him. Without a true dragon mate, they will believe me to be weak and a target." A sadistic grin creeps across her vermillion lips as she holds up the second finger. "Then, I will kill them all and add their skulls to my throne." The way Aurora says it so matter-of-fact is kind of scary. I'm starting to understand why Nicodeamus said her dragon side is quite strong.

"Daughter, what would you have me do? I'm supposed to be dead." Nicodeamus smirks, then looks to me and bows his head for a second.

"That's easy, Father. You're walking me down the aisle. Let those fuckers gawk all they want. The first to raise a hand will die by my talons." The minute the word *talon* leaves her lips, she shifts both arms, displaying her weapons. I notice her scales have changed. The ridges are more prominent and now have sharp edges. Nicodeamus is the first to take notice as he reaches for Aurora's hand.

"What's the word? Upgrade?" He carefully twists Aurora's gauntlet in his hand, admiring the change. "I see you two had time to work on your bond." Nicodeamus smirks as Aurora looks between me and the twins, then finally Dimitri. Her eyes fall to her own arms, looking at how the scales changed. Her eyes light up and churn liquid mercury, except they're now adorned with dragonic slits. I'm guessing her vision is also altered by the way she's studying things.

"Are you okay, my love?" I move closer and shift my arms like hers. My scales are just as rough looking. They have shades of mostly blues and whites with the occasional fleck of gold. I lightly touch my talons to hers to get her to look at mine. Aurora has a look of wonder as she lines one of her arms up with mine. Almost identical in every way, except color.

"Wow. I guess I know what gift I got from you, Alaric." Her father almost chokes on his bourbon. I can see the guys' noses working as they catch her scent. The change in it is subtle, but it's there. I watch Nicodeamus huddle the twins together and bring them up to speed. Shock isn't even the word to describe the look on the twins' faces. Poor Dimitri just shakes his head and throws his arms up in the air. It's too soon to alert Aurora of the possible cargo she may be carrying. We'll know more in a month if it's taken root.

"What the actual fuck is wrong with you four? This is cool as shit, and y'all are over there measuring your dicks in the corner. Where's the damn food? I'm starving!" Aurora practically growls out. Dimitri and Jayce bolt out of the room to get more food while Dominik, Nicodeamus, and I deal with a heavily armored, hungry hybrid.

Lucky bastards made it out.

I'm almost jealous.

CHAPTER 53

Epilogue Hunt

ALARIC

THE LOCAL ELITE from surrounding clans have all gathered for the social event of the winter. A full string orchestra is playing in the foyer, and drinks are being passed to arriving guests. I stand on the balcony overlooking the festivities below in my full royal regalia. Tonight's wedding is two-fold. First, it's the Night of the Wolf, which is also Aurora's birthday. Second, we are luring all of the traitors to one location to completely clean the house.

Queen Katherine, my mother, moves gracefully through the crowd, greeting all of the dignitaries. My father, King Bane, his arrival is met with full fanfare. The king's eyes lock on mine as he motions toward the library to speak to me in private. Once inside, I lock the door and put music on to hide our voices.

Bane speaks first. "You know, Alaric, I disapprove of this marriage. Our benefactors will not be pleased with this move." I pour two bourbons and pass one to my father.

"I believe it to be a brilliant move. If indeed Aurora is the only heir to the Lycan throne, then marrying her secures us two provinces and three wolf packs. The smartest way to build an army is to conquer it—that's what you taught me." I slowly raise the bourbon to my lips and sip it. Bane starts to stroke his thick white beard, contemplating what I just said to him.

"Brilliant strategy, Alaric. You're a chip off the 'ole block. Perhaps after she gives you an heir or two, we'll attempt to oust the Strigoi. Then we will have a true winter retreat." Bane briefly embraces Alaric before heading to the door. "Do you need me to walk your bride down the aisle?" Alaric smiles and sets his glass on the desk.

"No, Father, we have it all under control. I believe the bear, Dimitri, is escorting her down the aisle." I move to the full-length mirror in the corner of the library and adjust my medals and ribbons. "I'm just waiting for the steward to tell me it's time to take my place and get this show on the road."

"Very well, son. I'll do my kingly duty and walk in the procession with your mother. The only thing that wench did right was produce a strong son." Bane practically snarls the last part out. Gritting my teeth, I make sure my poker face is perfect; not a single indication of the rage that boils below the surface is given.

"Thank you, Father, for this boon. I'm sure the princess will produce strong sons for me. After all, there were no stronger Lycans than Anca and Vladimir." I smile at my father, watching his reaction closely. Bane looks back at me and smiles.

"Yes, they were the strongest of their kind. I'll make arrangements to introduce Vladimir to his daughter very soon. Rumor has it that her hair is white, and she is dragon-kin." Bane studies me, both of us posturing for each other.

"Rumors..." I pull out my phone and show my father an image of Aurora with long, black hair. "She's almost an exact replica of Anca; gods rest her soul." Bane takes my phone from me and sends the photo to himself. He scrolls through my pictures, but every single one shows Aurora with black hair.

"I wonder why rumors of a white Lycan would surface," Bane says as he hands me my phone back. "All the mates other than Vlad were castrated before Anca went into heat. Which reminds me, I have the herbs for you to make your mate obedient. Even if she's the last Marelup heir, we can't allow her to gain in power." I accept the satchel and tuck it into my inner coat pocket. My dragon is roaring, wanting to roast my father to ash for speaking about his mate in such a way.

I smirk as I refill my glass, attempting to remain calm. "You know how the peasants are. They need a savior to believe in." I laugh to myself, thinking about my mate rending the flesh from her enemies. "A white Lycan, how absurd. It's like saying your scales are Easter egg color." We both enjoy a hearty laugh before exiting the room.

~On the other side of the castle~

Aurora-

I stand before the mirror, my black wig pinned in place with a dainty tiara in the middle of my curls. Nicodeamus moves up behind me to look at us in the mirror.

"You look exactly like your mother with this wig on," Nicodeamus says softly as his fingers lightly touch the curls. Dimitri watches from the bench near the window.

"*Da*, except Aurora is a wee bit taller and has more muscle tone." Dimitri's tone is almost reverent as he compares Aurora to Anca.

"I still hate that Vladimir named you, though the name does fit you. You are a beacon of light and hope, with so many facets to who you are." Nicodeamus smiles at me and kisses my cheek before he moves away. Dominik comes walking into the suite with a scroll. Jayce follows closely behind, carrying a tray of food.

"Alaric sends food before the ceremony. He said to only eat this tonight because he's not sure if anyone will try to poison us," Dominik says calmly as Jayce sets the tray down. "I have the processional line up. Traditionally, we all wear hooded cloaks until we arrive at the pulpit. Once we're up there, the friar will instruct us to lower our hoods. Aurora is the only one not required to wear a hood." Dominik turns and starts passing out cloaks to everyone. I touch my own face as I look in the mirror. *So this is what my mother looked like,* I say softly to myself as I examine my features over.

"Let's get this over with. It's all bullshit anyway. It just sucks that this stunning dress is going to get ruined." I move around the room, adjusting the guys' cloaks and hoods to make sure their faces are completely covered.

I look down at the flair of the sleeves of my gown. Alaric made sure I would be able to shift my arms without destroying the gown. The sleeves are long enough that no one will see until it's too late when I do shift my arms. The gown itself has a sweetheart top, which purposely exposes Alaric's scale on my ample chest. For strategic purposes, I move several locks of black hair over Alaric's scale to hide it for now. Three handmaidens approach me, fastening the train into the back of my gown as well as the embroidered veil. I roll my eyes, absolutely hating being handled this much. The handmaidens finally leave, and I finally get to look at my family.

"Our forces outnumber those in attendance three to one, so I'm not overly concerned. I still want to move in formation. Jayce, you and Dom enter first, then Dad and I. Dimitri, you watch our backs." Nicodeamus and Dimitri start laughing at the same time. Aurora can't help but growl at them.

"I'm sorry, daughter, you set the procession the same way your mother did when she married Vladimir. We found it funny. It will cause flashbacks for those who were present for your mother's wedding." Aurora smiles, canines bared, and her eyes are the liquid mercury of her beast. "When did you gain the dragon slits in your eyes?" Nicodeamus says. Aurora moves back in front of the mirror to look at her eyes.

"Hmm, nice upgrade. I look really freaky now!" Purposely I do that maniacal Joker laugh as I look at the guys. At least I'm in a good mood, which means the bloodshed shouldn't start too early.

A knock sounds at the door and I go on high alert. That was a five-minute warning. Everyone settles down and double-checks their appearance. I have the most glorious last-second idea and pull out my favorite lip stain. Untwisting the top, I stare at the rich, deep-red color of the stain that I have chosen. Carefully I paint my full lips making sure to accentuate my perfectly pronounced cupids bow. As the stain dries, it takes on the appearance of dried blood, and I feel it's the most fitting color for tonight's festivities.

"Time to reign in blood, boys." I start humming the song *Heathens* by Twenty One Pilots. Oddly enough, my song choice is quite fitting as I start walking in the line-up's third position.

My group moves as a single unit down the hallway, passing Ellis and his bears. I maintain my resting bitch face as I move. My steps are silent and calculated; the only sound from me is the soft humming of my chosen song en route to the pulpit. My group arrives at the double doors of the throne room. The steward is waiting to receive word that it's time to send us in. It's so quiet that you can hear the opening prayer in the throne room. We hear three knocks, and the steward opens the double doors. *It's show time*, I say through the bond to those who can hear me just before our group enters, walking in time with the music.

Whispers erupt throughout the throne room. Most are commenting on how much I look like Anca or that the Lycan Queen still lives. King Bane is the most shocked at my appearance —the blood-red lipstick was apparently my mother's signature color.

Once we're at the pulpit, I gracefully curtsey to King Bane and Queen Katherine. Next, I turn to Alaric and lower my head submissively to him, playing the role I'm in perfectly. Alaric reaches out and places his hand under my chin, allowing me to raise my gaze.

King Bane's ego gets the better of him as he moves to inspect me. He grips my jaw tightly and examines my eyes and then my teeth like I'm some sort of broodmare. Bane quickly raises the right sleeve of my gown to reveal my royal brand. Bane raises my arm for the entire throne room to see.

"Aurora is Anca's heir!" Bane shouts to the gathered dignitaries. My mates can easily feel the aggravation through the bond.

Alaric does the only thing he knows to calm me and rubs my scale, acting like his shirt is bothering him. That thoughtful action soothes me, and I calm down, remaining in Bane's grip. "My son has chosen wisely for this political alliance. This bitch will birth powerful sons," Bane speaks with such detachment, it's unbelievable. It's getting harder for the guys to maintain their silence as the king practically bashes and degrades me in front of them. I flood the bond with how much I love them trying to ease their concern. Bane finally releases me into Alaric's hands, and I instantly calm down. Now, the friar raises his hands and begins the ceremony.

"Lords and Ladies, we have before us tonight, on the Night of the Wolf, two powerful bloodlines. Though it is a political marriage, we pray for their love to eventually grow. We ask the Elder Gods for strength and fertility. That Anca's heir produces strong sons, who will be able to ascend the Ice Dragon and Marelup Throne." The friar takes out a piece of red silk and lightly binds Alaric's and my hands together.

"This sash represents the blood that shall be shared between bloodlines when the first heir is born." Next, a silver sash is wrapped around our hands. "The silver represents the prince's dragon's sight. May he always see the best solutions in the future." The friar places his hand on top of mine and Alaric's hands. "If anyone present has any reason these two should not be bound, speak now or forever hold your peace." The friar looks around the hall at all the attendants. He didn't, however, look to his left at my witnesses.

The guys move as one and rip off their cloaks and flinging them aside. Before their cloaks hit the floor, I reach up and rip off my black wig; my long, snow-white hair cascades down my back. In an instant, Alaric and I shift our arms, so our gauntlets and talons are at the ready. Nicodeamus steps forward with Dimitri at his side.

"I am Nicodeamus, mate to Anca Marelup and the true Ice Dragon King!" My group and I stand at the ready for the battle ahead.

CHAPTER 54

Prologue Fight

AURORA

Ice Dragon Chalet

Night of the Wolf

November 30, 2019

The guys move as one and rip off their cloaks, flinging them aside. Before their cloaks hit the floor, I reach up and rip off the black wig I'm wearing; my long, snow-white hair cascades down my back. In an instant, Alaric and I shift our arms so that our gauntlets and talons are at the ready. Nicodeamus steps forward with Dimitri at his side.

"I am Nicodeamus, mate to Anca Marelup and the true Ice Dragon King!" Chaos erupts after Nicodeamus's declaration.

Some begin to run, trying to escape, while others drop to their knees. Alaric and I turn as one to face Bane. Carefully, I point to

Alaric's scale upon my chest. An arrogant smirk plays upon my lips as I lock eyes with Bane.

"False King," I growl as my eyes churn liquid mercury. The dragonic slits slowly expand and contract as I stare him down. The eerie sound of Alaric and I clicking our talons together silences the hall. Our movements are mirror images of each other as we circle Bane, isolating him from the others.

"I had nothing to do with the death of your mother!" Bane shouts as his back hits the wall. A look of panic crosses his features when he realizes he can't call upon his animal.

"Nasty little thing, Dire Wolf venom is. Mixed with a second toxin, it suppresses the ability to shift." Alaric smirks, looking at his father. "Funny thing happened before the ball. Aurora and I consummated our bond. I tasted her blood and marked her as mine. Thankfully for me, her mate Jayce gave her immunity to the toxin." Alaric's temper is legendary, and now everyone is witnessing it firsthand. "I find it funny that the man who said we must protect our own left his king unguarded. Treason really doesn't look good on you, Father." Alaric shakes his head side to side before he moves to stand beside me; he kisses the crown of my head as we stare his father down.

Bane still searches the room for an ally, but none will stand with him. Bane grits his teeth then spits towards Nicodeamus. "Vladimir suspected you fucked that bitch of a mate of his. The blood magic could only do so much. It was good that Anca died because of that abomination!" He jabs his finger in my direction, and I can't help but laugh at him. "The half-breed finds it funny she killed her mother! Wait till her mate informs his uncle about you living, Nicodeamus. He will hunt you down!"

Alaric rips his father away from the wall and holds his arms firmly behind him as Nicodeamus moves forward. "I had a feeling that bastard lived. Why else would I be kept barely alive in a dungeon, held prisoner by Lucian?" I move to my father's left side, protecting it.

"The pieces are all falling into place now. The Elder dame and Elena were both sisters to Vladimir." Nicodeamus strokes his chin as he connects the dots. "Aurora's animal, though quite young, imprinted on Sebastian's scent, making it easy for the magic to work. After all, he was one of the first wolves she had come in contact with. Imprinting is a dragon trait, so it was a gamble if it would work." Nicodeamus's eyes fall upon me and then over to my mate, Alaric. "Daughter, I need your talons and your rage. If my people were with me the night of the attack, there would have been a better chance that your mother would have lived."

Nicodeamus's grief is almost all-consuming until I shift to the form of my beast. The entire room falls silent as I loom over Bane, baring my canines as I look at him. The thick yellow-green venom drips from my upper canines as I lean forward and roar in Bane's face.

"I promised my father's head and heart would be yours, my love. Take them as a gift," Alaric states coldly, his voice devoid of any emotion. With a single twist of his body, he hurls his father out and into the crowd. Apparently, Alaric has been paying attention; my beast likes the thrill of the hunt more than just fighting.

"Alaric, no!" Bane shouts as he flies through the air. His body hits the marble floor hard as he rolls to a stop. Bane panics: he can't summon his dragon to help save his ass. Stories are already being whispered by my pack about how I took down Nexus by myself.

Bane looks now to Katherine, tears freely flowing down her cheeks as she looks to her husband on the floor.

"Katherine! Save me! Shift and burn them to the ground!" Bane's last attempt at being rescued falls on deaf ears. Katherine shakes her head as I loom over Bane.

"Husband, you knowingly allowed our king to face the horde alone. His mate died because of you and your poor choices. How can I be a loyal servant of the crown and allow your deeds to go unpunished?" Katherine looks at her husband, the sadness visible behind her eyes. Slowly, Katherine moves to my side and lightly touches my beast's back. "Do what you must, child. Vengeance is yours." Katherine bows to me and leaves the grand ballroom swiftly.

I lower my massive head to his level and begin to growl, threatening Bane's very existence. I'm enjoying seeing him afraid. Bane slowly stands and dusts himself off, and he looks at me smugly. "You won't attack me like this." He motions to my beast's form. "I can't shift. It would be in poor form to kill a defenseless man."

I tilt my head to the side, pondering what he just said, then I look over at Dimitri. Dimitri then looks to Nicodeamus, who leans in and says something for his ears only. Dimitri reaches to his belt and pulls out a short sword, which he slides across the floor to Bane. When the blade hits his foot, I back up, giving him room to pick it up. Thus, in one single motion, I have given him a weapon, and he becomes fair game the minute he picks the sword up.

Bane grabs the sword quickly and dives for me, trying to catch me off guard. Bane aims the sword at my stomach. Quickly, I drop my gauntleted hand down and grab the sword before impact. I feel my eyes begin to glow a ghostly white as frost coats the sword. A quick twist of my wrist and the sword shatters in my hand. Several different clanging tones echo in the silent hall as the broken sword pieces hit the tile. Being the sarcastic bitch that I am, I attempt to make my beast curl its lips in a smirk as I stare at the now-terrified Bane.

I shift back to my human form, leaving only my arms shifted. Bane is so distracted by my nudity he doesn't realize what I'm about to do before it's too late. With one quick swipe with frost-covered talons, I sever Bane's left arm from his body. My talons, covered in permafrost cauterize the wound on contact. Bane screams out in pain and falls to his knees, holding his shoulder where his arm used to be. Dominik comes over to me and offers me his button-down shirt and assists with slipping it on. While we are distracted, Bane grabs what is left of the sword and lunges right at me.

Alaric sees what his father is planning and he's already in motion before Bane gets anywhere near me. Alaric's taloned hand punches through Bane's back and out the front, emerging with Bane's heart in his hand. Blood spray covers Dominik and me.

Me being me, I immediately start laughing as Alaric pulls his arm back out of his father's chest. With a quick swipe of my talons, Bane's head is severed from his body, sending more blood flying. The guests present are shocked at the scene that has just played out before them.

I watch Alaric's moves with rapt attention as he bends down and picks up his father's head with his free hand. When he stands directly before me, he drops to one knee and holds up his father's head and heart. It's such a romantic gesture. Slowly, I bend down and kiss Alaric gently on the lips before accepting my prizes.

"Friar, the wedding will go as planned in about twenty minutes. I need to go get cleaned up."

My eyes move to my other mates and close team; they nod and smile at me, accepting my choice. Nicodeamus and two hand-maidens escort me out of the grand ballroom and back to my bedroom to clean up. Squires arrive before I leave, carrying clean shirts and slacks for the men.

~Alaric~

Approximately thirty minutes later Nicodeamus shuffles us back into proper position. The band starts playing again and everyone turns their gaze to the double doors. Looking at the hall now, no one would be any the wiser that there was a killing in this very room so recently...

The double doors open, and the first person to appear is Dimitri in a tuxedo. Hell has officially frozen over—the big guy is in a fancy tux. You know that is Aurora's doing. Dimitri steps aside and reveals Aurora in a new gown: a replica of the one her mother had worn on her wedding day, blood red with gold embellishments. Seeing my mate as the bride she was meant to be earlier is breathtaking.

Aurora holds her head high and walks with fluid grace. Her steps fall in time with the music, as if she has done this a hundred times. Aurora arrives at the altar and bows to her father and then to each mate in turn. Her eyes finally fall on me, and she lowers her head and remains in a curtsy before me. I cannot allow her to lower herself before me. Quickly, I step down the three steps to arrive before Aurora. For appearance's sake, I lightly touch under Aurora's chin and allow her to rise. Traditions suck. Especially this one. Fucking old school bullshit. Aurora joins me before the Friar yet again.

The Friar begins the ceremony again, this time with Nicodeamus at his side overseeing the whole thing. "Ladies and Gentlemen, I stand before you a corrected and humbled man. The pair before me... not only are they fated and true mates, they have also done the ancient scale ritual. The ritual itself dates back to the first dragons that walked this earth. A prized skull is sent along with an offered scale." On the monitor behind the Friar, Aurora's video of her receiving the skull and scale from Alaric plays. "If accepted, the scale is cut into the female's flesh, and they wait to see if it heals."

The Friar motions for Aurora to show the crowd my scale on her chest. Once she does, he returns to the ceremony. "Alaric's scale lives on Aurora's chest. In turn, Aurora picked out a skull and a scale and sent it back to Alaric." The video changes to Ellis videoing Alaric receiving Aurora's scale and skull. I then unbutton my dress shirt to show the audience that Aurora's scale lives on me. We turn to the Friar as he repeats the sash ritual as before.

At the end of the ritual, Nicodeamus steps forward with a ceremonial dagger. He offers the blade to me, then holds his hand out. Quickly, I cut Nicodeamus's palm, and he allows his wound to bleed over our joined hands. "With my blood, this I swear." Nicodeamus places his bloody hand on top of Aurora's and mine for a few moments, then removes his hand.

Nicodeamus takes the dagger back from me and slashes my palm. My free hand bleeds over mine and Aurora's hands, then I lay my palm over our joined hands. "With my blood, this I swear." I lean forward and kiss Aurora's lips after speaking my part of the vow.

Aurora smiles radiantly at me and offers her father her free hand. Nicodeamus hesitates a moment before slashing Aurora's palm. Aurora bleeds over the bindings and then on my hand. "With my blood, this I swear." She smiles and places her hand on top of mine after completing her part of the vow. The blood itself is the vow; it's a promise to always be there. It's a promise to be loyal forever; to fail the vow is to accept death.

Nicodeamus moves and places his bloody palm over the top of mine and Aurora's hands again. The Friar looks at the completed ceremony, then back to the crowd. "I am honored to announce your new king and queen, King Alaric Kraus and Queen Aurora Kraus! They will jointly rule the Ice Dragon clan as well as the Lycan clans. Long live the king and queen!"

The Friar completes his part of the ceremony then departs through the side door. The cheering lasts for almost an hour straight before the crowd settles down enough that we can finally hear each other over the noise.

The celebration carries on well into the early hours of the morning. All the guests come and swear allegiance to Aurora and me in turn. Aurora makes it a point to introduce all of her mates to the dignitaries as they approach. None are above the others in her eyes, and she will maintain it that way. Every song, she finds herself in a different mate's arms. It warms my heart to see how loving and devoted my mate is to all of us within her bond. Unlike the Lycan rulers of the past, she actually puts others before herself.

Towards the end of the night, Dimitri finally gets the balls to ask Aurora for a dance. Dimitri leads her out on the dance floor and the lights are dimmed. Dimitri has picked "The Blue Danube"to be played for their dance. It's a lovely, spirited waltz that holds meaning for the two of them.

Aurora tears up slightly at the thoughtful gesture. It happens to be the first song he taught her to dance to. They spin and waltz around the entire dance floor alone. No one else dares to interrupt the fluid beauty of their movements. The poise and grace these two apex predators display is impressive. Aurora looks like a sprite dancing next to Dimitri's hulking form. Both are smiling like school children as they move in time with the music, not a care in the world.

The song changes to another, more modern slow song, and they remain together on the dance floor. Aurora moves and rests her head on Dimitri's chest, like a scene out of a romance movie. Dimitri's large hand spans the width of Aurora's lower back as he holds her tightly to him. Their movements are perfectly timed and slow beautifully with the current song. A man attempts to cut in, and Aurora damn near kills him. Dominik and Jayce move the gentleman away from Aurora and Dimitri. It's been a long time coming, those two getting together.

Four slow songs later, and Dimitri and Aurora call it quits, finally. Nicodeamus and I have been fielding questions about the unlikely pair spending so much time together. I decide to jump into the current conversation and tell the dignitary that Dimitri is a mate of Aurora's yet to be bound to her. The Dignitary bows his head and accepts my statement as gospel. Aurora moves to Jayce's side and whispers in his ear that she's tired. Dominik approaches Nicodeamus and me to let us know that Aurora needs to rest as we watch Jayce escort her out of the room.

The party comes to an end around dawn, the last of the guests are ushered out the door. There is a lot to be discussed once everyone has slept. There are massive changes on the horizon, and plans have to be made to accommodate them.

Nicodeamus ushers the guys into the large room that they share with Aurora. The main room is a sitting room and several bedrooms branch off the main room. Everyone separates and heads off to sleep.

CHAPTER 55

Aurora

December -

I rise out of bed and stretch slowly. I slept, but I'm still fucking tired. I swear, nothing I do seems to alleviate it. I head to the kitchen in my fuzzy sleep pants and Dominik's sweatshirt that I stole from his bag yesterday. I move silently, walking barefoot through the marble halls heading towards the kitchen. I must be radiating my aggravation due to my exhaustion because everyone clears the halls when I pass them.

Upon reaching the kitchen, I find Klaus teaching the chef some of the dishes of his clan. I guess I had a great idea when I chose to have heritage food nights to sample all the different foods out there. Dominik, Jayce, and Alaric are at the table having giant, fluffy waffles. My stomach begins to growl, and everyone turns to face me. I roll my eyes and take my seat at the table. Dominik smirks and pulls at his sweatshirt I'm wearing, letting me know he knows I took it. I shrug my shoulders, looking at him, then over to the chef. He comes running over with my steak smothered in salsa, fried peppers and onions, and homemade burrito wraps.

Nicodeamus enters the kitchen and starts laughing at my antics. "Seriously? What the fuck, Dad? Can't I enjoy what I want to eat without it being amusing?" I practically growl out my words as I feel my beast make herself known.

Nicodeamus raises his hand, trying to show he meant no harm. "I'm sorry, daughter. I'm just a little concerned for you. With everything that needs to come to pass, we have a guest among us, I believe." My father's eyes are those of his dragon, and my eyes shift to those of my beast as we stare at each other.

I'm cranky, tired, and really not in the mood for his games. I start shoveling my breakfast into my mouth. Tired, hungry... yeah, I'm a fucking ray of sunshine over here. The royal physician decides to come into the room and begins to approach me. A wave of frost shoots out in all directions from me as I stand to face him head-on. "Leave us alone!" My voice is not my own: its tone is that of my beast. My arms and hands shift rapidly. I am on the defensive, and I'm not sure why. I'm feeling my beast fight me for control. She hasn't done that since the time Dimitri smelled of the other woman.

Alaric waves the terrified physician off and comes to hold me, trying to soothe me. The soft rumble of his dragon puts my beast at ease. Alaric moves me to his side of the table, and I climb onto his lap and press my forehead to his throat.

Nicodeamus clears his throat. "Aurora, I believe we need to have a talk, sweetheart." Nicodeamus pulls up a chair close to Alaric and waits for me to lift my head.

"I don't want to. I don't feel good, and I'm fucking tired." I yawn promptly after speaking, then place my forehead back against Alaric's throat. One of the guys must have ordered hard-boiled eggs, and the smell makes my stomach instantly protest. I leap off Alaric's lap and run out onto the balcony where I vomit my breakfast over the railing. Jayce is at my side, holding my hair back so I won't get puke in it. Eventually, all my mates and my father come outside with me.

Great. I look and feel like shit, and now everyone wants to be all Kumbaya up in this mother. I'd start growling at them, but quite frankly, I don't have the energy right now. My father holds out a glass of ginger tea to me and I sip it slowly. I'm stressed the fuck out, and everyone is staring at me like, hell, I don't even know right now.

"Aurora, daughter, you're carrying the next heir. One of these geniuses got you pregnant while you were in heat." Nicodeamus gives the boys each a sharp glare before looking at me tenderly. "Depending on which male is the father, you could possibly deliver in as soon as three months or as long as seven months. Your mother carried you to term at five months because of your hybrid status." I'm hearing the words coming out of his mouth, but it isn't registering just yet.

I hand my father back the glass and walk away from the group. Dimitri always used to hold me when I didn't feel good, so he is the one I logically seek out. Dimitri, however, is still in bed, sleeping. He looks so peaceful, all stretched out on his huge bed. I approach slowly from the far side of the bed and snuggle into his side. He reflexively turns and kisses my forehead, mumbling something about how's his cub.

I flat out tell him, "I puked, I'm tired, and my dad is talking crazy talk." Dimitri turns and curls his large form around me and buries his nose in my hair like he always does. I almost fall asleep instantly in one of the safest places I know.

I know my mates seek me out at some point, but I am too tired and snuggled to care. Some poor male servant enters Dimitri's room, I'm guessing to wake him up like usual. Dimitri's shift happens instantly. His bear leaps off the bed and rises up onto its hind legs, roaring at the man. My mates and father come as quickly as they can.

Nicodeamus attempts to talk Dimitri down from his rage, not having seen me in his bed. I yawn and slowly slide out of bed to come up to Dimitri's side. I look up to his angry bear and wrap my arms around his middle the best I can. Slowly I feel his bear settle within my grasp, and I back away, allowing him to land on all fours. Dimitri's bear sniffs me from toes to nose, making sure I'm okay. Three times his bear presses its nose to my lower stomach then looks up to me.

I don't understand what he's getting at. Carefully, I climb onto Dimitri's back and lie down. At least with me up here, he won't do anything rash. My father ushers the frightened servant away before closing and locking the door behind him. Dimitri brings me back to what's left of his bed; I slide off and make myself comfortable.

Dimitri's bear meanders over to the ensuite bathroom, where he chooses to resume his human form. Dimitri comes back out in sleep pants and a bathrobe. "Aurora, I could have killed that man. If you're going to climb in bed with me, lock the door. My instinct to protect you and your child is too strong." Dimitri's eyes beg me to understand him, that he's not mad at me: he's worried for the rest of the population.

I sit there staring at Dimitri and think back over the last two, almost three weeks of being here. My eyes widen as all the pieces of the puzzle snap together. I look between the twins and Alaric, then over to my father. My hand lands on the small swell of my stomach, and I lightly rub the small dome.

"Holy fuck!"

Yeah, not exactly the most eloquent way of announcing a pregnancy, but hey, it's me, right? I'm about as subtle as a freight train. I start crying. I can't fucking help it. I'm scared more than anything. Me? A mom? Whose fucking brilliant idea was that? I have severe anger issues. The guys are honestly not sure what to do with and for me right now. Dimitri kneels before me and lays his head on my lap and hugs my legs. Out of reflex, I start to run my fingers through his thick brown hair. I slowly begin to calm down and relax again. I begin to hum the old Romanian lullaby he used to sing to me as a child.

Nicodeamus ushers the boys out of Dimitri's room, then comes to sit beside us. "You two share a bond that spans more years than anyone here. It's hard to go from guardian to lover. The bond is there; I see how you two seek each other out for comfort." Dad tilts his head as he studies Dimitri and me.

"For example, what happened here today. Aurora wasn't feeling well, so who did she seek out? Dimitri, you bring her a different kind of safety and security that her bonded mates can't. Aurora, Dimitri has been your rock since you were itty bitty. You both have a mental block that's preventing this bond from blazing to life after that witch's brew." Nicodeamus slowly rises and leaves the room.

Dimitri slowly climbs onto his bed with me and lays his head entirely in my lap so he can look up at me. I can see the turmoil behind his brilliant amber eyes. I know he loves me, and I know it's more than just as a guardian. I can't and won't push him; he needs to come to this conclusion on his own. I'm just glad I'm not nuts. My wolf was right; he is ours. I lean down slowly and gently place a kiss on his full, pouting lips.

My hands caress his beard-covered cheeks as my fingers thread through his facial hair. I always had a thing for the big guy, so I honestly can't help myself. Kissing Dimitri feels like coming home, where I'm always safe and protected. Dimitri breaks the kiss and sits up, kneeling on the bed with his ass resting on his heels. He carefully lifts me up to straddle his lap, which I do willingly. I wrap my arms around his neck and look deep into his eyes. He's fighting his instincts; I can see it. Part of me is upset he doesn't want me, and the other part wants to rip Elena's head from her shoulders.

"We don't have to do anything, D. I don't want you to feel pressured." I smile at him and lightly kiss his lips, trying to reassure him.

Without hesitation, Dimitri launches forward and pins me beneath him on the bed. He captures my lips with a renewed passion that he's never shown before. I can't help but sink into his embrace and follow his lead. Dimitri's hands roam all over my body, caressing every curve. Every new sensation is driving me nuts. I have to have him. My beast demands it. I break the kiss and begin to nip and suck at his throat. His moans are music to my ears. I feel his rather large erection press against my lower stomach as he begins to grind against me.

I take a chance and bite his collarbone hard, drawing a small amount of blood. In an instant, I can feel Dimitri's hands shift as he begins to shred the offending clothing off my body. It takes Dimitri mere moments to have me bare before him. We've been naked before each other many times in the past, but this time is different. Dimitri's gaze isn't passive like it has been for most of my life. His gaze burns with an inner fire that I never thought I'd see from him. He's staring down at me, looking like he's ready to devour me. Suddenly, he shakes his head as if clearing a fog and looks embarrassed. I feel the evidence of his excitement roll down my side and onto the bed. Dimitri was so excited he experienced premature ejaculation.

"I'm so sorry, I didn't mean to," Dimitri says in a hushed tone, low enough for only me to hear. He leaves the bed quickly, only to return a few moments later with a washcloth and a towel to clean me up.

Once I'm clean, I kiss him again before moving to his closet to find something to wear. I find Dimitri's fuzzy sweatshirt that I've always loved. I slip it on over my head, and it goes down to my knees. I have a woman's version of blue balls.

CHAPTER 56
Aurora

I exit Dimitri's room, and in the sitting room stand all my guys. I roll my eyes at them, then duck into my room. I shower quickly and dress in leggings and Dimitri's sweatshirt. Just before I leave my room, I can hear my father and Dimitri talking about what happened. My father sits there, giving him words of encouragement, and advises him to jerk off before he tries again. I stifle a laugh, picturing the look on Dimitri's face after my father says that. I can't help but shake my head at my father's logic. I turn and go out on my balcony and look around outside. On the terrace next to me stands Klaus, looking out over the frozen landscape.

"Penny for your thoughts?" I figure I'll break the ice.

"Just a bit homesick, princess." Klaus shrugs his shoulders, then turns to face me fully. He looks a lot like the guy that played the most recent version of Superman. Thick, broad shoulders, a strong jawline and thick, dark-brown almost black hair. He's now the leader of the German Lycan pack due to the death of his father at the Strigoi's claws. "A lot has changed in a short period of time, and it's a lot to adjust to," he says with a sigh before raising his eyes to meet mine. I don't take it as a challenge, so I don't push my Alpha power on him.

"Yeah, tell me about it…" I say as I rest my hand on my stomach for a moment. "Tell me about your pack, Klaus. What's your home like?" I lean on the marble railing, looking over at Klaus as he studies me. Snow is gently falling between us, giving the moment a very fairy tale feel.

Klaus smiles at me, then looks out over the frozen landscape, getting a dreamy look as he thinks about home. "I believe you would love it, my Queen. My family and pack are from the Swartzwald, otherwise known as the Black Forest. There are roe deer to hunt and plenty of wild boar. The forest seems to go on forever. I love being in the woods with my pack. You have to hunt with us before we attack the Strigoi." Klaus turns and looks at me with so much joy and excitement.

It makes my heart melt the way he's looking at me right now. My wolf softly makes her content sound in the back of my mind and gently says, "*Mine?*"

Her voice uttering those words makes me step back. I shake my head for a moment, and that movement causes Klaus to become concerned. He jumps the distance between our balconies to be at my side in an instant. He envelops me in his strong arms to support my weight. The boys all come charging in, feeling the change in me. All of them are concerned for my health and that of my pup.

Alaric swoops in and scoops me up. He carries me to the bed and lays me down. The royal physician checks me over and suspects my blood sugar must have dropped from getting sick this morning. Jayce grabs Klaus and they run out of the room to get me food and drinks. I shake my head and look at my father.

"Guys? Can I have a few moments alone with my father?" I look between Dominik, Alaric, and Dimitri, and they all nod slowly and reluctantly leave the room.

Nicodeamus comes to sit beside me on the bed and kisses my temple. "What is it, daughter? Are you not well? What do you need of me? Name it, and it's yours." My father gently rests his hand on my stomach, attempting to sense the baby. He smiles at what he's feeling, then looks to me, waiting for my response.

"I need your counsel more than anything, Father. My wolf asked me if Klaus was mine just before I got lightheaded. Is it possible that he's the mate I should have had before those assholes did what they did?" Nicodeamus comes to sit beside me, and I lean my head on my father's shoulder. I'm hungry, tired, and still aggravated at Sebastian's and Elena's betrayal.

Nicodeamus adjusts himself on the bed, then taps his fingertip on his chin, pondering my question. He gently kisses my forehead then begins to speak. "He's not a bad choice as a mate. I'm glad your wolf chose him over his brother. They did send a nice group to the original base, and I'm glad they were there with us during the attack on the road." My father hugs me the best he can, then gets up off the bed. "I'd better let all the boys in so they can see you. We shouldn't allow them to worry too much." Nicodeamus makes it to the door and turns to smile at me once more before letting the guys back in.

Jayce and Klaus have enough food to feed an army. I find out that everyone is staying with me to have brunch. Everyone finds a spot on my king-sized bed and begins to eat. I feel much better having all of the guys this close to me. Alaric apparently has something on his mind and clears his throat before beginning to speak.

"Not to ruin the calm atmosphere we have going on here, but we need to consider heading to the palace post-haste, to fully claim the throne. We have a large enough contingent of dragons to fly there in about two hours or less, as long as the winds are favorable. Aurora and Nicodeamus would be with me, if that's ok with you, sir?" Alaric bows his head to Nicodeamus as he steps back into the room. He knows that his offer could be taken as an insult because Nicodeamus is also a dragon.

Nicodeamus stands and moves to the same side of the bed as Alaric and places his hand on Alaric's shoulder. "I would be honored to be able to fly with you and my daughter." Alaric stands, and he and Nicodeamus embrace.

I'm guessing it had to be a big deal. How the fuck should I know? I'm sitting over here stuffing my face with all kinds of food, honestly not giving a fuck about too much. A knock sounds at my door, and the boys all go on high alert. I'm guessing their animals are even more protective now that I'm pregnant. I watch the door as Alaric goes to answer it. It's his mother, Katherine, come to visit.

"Arrangements are all made. We have enough dragons as well as flight cars for the troops to be carried in. We will be accompanied by our people as well as some of the Red and Black Dragons. Apparently, your father, Alaric, was not as liked as we were led to believe. After the display you and Aurora put on at the first wedding, you have gained a ton of supporters." Katherine moves past her son to come over to my side. I'm still leery as fuck when it comes to her, and to be honest, I really don't trust anyone outside of my core group. "Aurora, I had clothing specially made for you for the flight as well for your arrival at court." Katherine removes the large velvet pouch from under her cloak and offers it to me.

My eyes move to Klaus and he accepts the pouch and opens it for me. Within the pouch sits a beautiful crown cut from a single piece of ruby. I look it over, then lower my head to Klaus, who places it upon my head. Surprisingly, it is a perfect fit. I hear a gasp and look over to my father who looks like he's seen a ghost.

"What is it, father?" I shoot myself to the edge of the bed then move quickly to his side.

Nicodeamus kisses my temple and smiles as he gently removes the crown from my head. "This once belonged to the Blood Queen. She was your great-grandmother on my side. You want to talk about a woman who ruled by her talons and frost? That was her." Nicodeamus laughs a bit. "It's truly fitting that you now wear her crown; it will make a bold statement when we arrive at the palace. There's going to be a point you won't be able to shift, so we must make our point while you can." Nicodeamus gently places the crown back on my head, then kneels before me and kisses my stomach. "Never fear, little one, you will always be protected. Wait till you're old enough for story time. The stories we will tell you about your mother will impress you immensely." Nicodeamus kisses my stomach once more, then stands and kisses my forehead.

Katherine looks gobsmacked by the information she just witnessed and heard. "You're pregnant? When did this happen? Who is the father?" She looks frantically between all of the guys, and I just start laughing, one of those Joker laughs that are quite unnerving.

"Does it truly matter? I am queen; my blood runs through this baby's veins." I fully unleash my Alpha powers on the room. I am borderline in a rage over Katherine's line of questioning. My bonded mates do not bow or break under my power, and my father remains standing as well. Klaus resists much longer than Dimitri does, and poor Katherine hits the floor the minute I had to urge to subjugate her.

"My mates shall be referred to as Their Royal Highnesses from now on, Katherine. If I even think you are the slightest bit of a threat to what's mine… your head will go on my throne." I walk away from Katherine and sit next to my father. I am waiting for her to challenge my authority.

Alaric comes up behind me and wraps his thick arms around my body. His large hands rest on the small swell of my stomach. "Mother, you have gone too far this time. You need to respect Aurora's mates the same way you respect me. They are my brothers in arms, my bond mates. I am king, and so are they as far as Aurora and I are concerned." A rumbling growl from his dragon echoes in the room, showing his displeasure.

"If this is a problem, I will not allow you near our child. I say 'our' because no matter who sires the children, they will all be ours at the end of the day." Alaric's words make me tear up as I look at the other males gathered. They each raise their fists over their hearts in a sign of solidarity. Alaric bows his head to each male in turn. "My love, please release everyone. We need to get going." I nod slightly and rein my power in.

Carefully, I turn in Alaric's arms and kiss him. In turn, he passes me off to Dominik, who kisses me passionately before passing me off to Jayce. Jayce is such a show-off, sweeping me into a dip and kissing me enthusiastically. I'm giggling when he finally stands me up and passes me off to Dimitri. I look up to the big guy, and he suddenly looks bashful. He knows he's not a bonded mate, but

Alaric's mom doesn't. I grip his cheeks with both hands and pull him down to me for a nice, gentle, longing kiss. I feel his shaft harden between us, and I smile. *Mission accomplished.*

Dimitri reluctantly passes me off to Klaus. Klaus and I look shocked that we have ended up together. I watch his wolf's amber eyes flare to the surface, and I smile at his bold move. My beast isn't thrilled with the challenge, so she makes her presence known.

Without warning, my beast urges me to bite him. My canines elongate as I feel scales rippling up and down my arms and spine. I hear the guys as if I'm underwater. My vision blurs for a moment, then the next thing I know, I taste blood in my mouth. I struggle with my beast for control, and eventually, she backs down. I find myself with Klaus's shoulder in my mouth, my canines sunk deeply in his flesh. I'm almost to the point of panic when I feel the burning, stinging pain of him biting my shoulder in return. Klaus just so happened to bite me over Sebastian's original mark. The bond snaps into place, and the ghost of Sebastian is just about gone. I no longer feel him the way I use to. I release Klaus's shoulder and lick the wound clean, and he does the same to mine. The room is so silent you can hear a pin drop. What potentially could have been a dangerous situation has become a thing of beauty. Klaus's right-hand grips the back of my neck, and he presses his forehead to mine.

He whispers ever so softly, "I'm glad you never stopped looking for me, my angel." He kisses my nose before releasing me into my father's care.

Nicodeamus and I sit back and watch the guys hug it out and do their guy things. I just shake my head at their antics, and I look longingly at Dimitri. "Will he ever come around, Father?" My eyes turn to gaze up at my father, hoping for him to impart some great wisdom to me.

"In time, daughter. The big guy has been through so much. He will probably feel better back on his home turf, in Romania. I plan to seek out his clan, if any live, for him to have some form of closure." Nicodeamus kisses my forehead and ushers me through to my dressing room.

CHAPTER 57

Aurora

DECEMBER-

Formalities suck. I look down, and the slight dome of my stomach is visible, and ornate gemstones emphasize its presence. I roll my eyes, thinking that Alaric has done this on purpose. Next, the handmaids help me slip into the thick, caribou, floor-length coat. I notice hand sewn wolves and dragons adorn the length of the baby-soft leather. The fur on the inside is super soft and very warm. The handmaids then give me riding gloves and special fur-lined boots. A small satchel is handed to me, containing my dress shoes for when we arrive. I return my crown back into its velvet pouch and slip it in with my shoes. An arctic fox hat is given to me, and I clip the chin strap in place. Once I am fully dressed for the journey, the handmaids lead me outside to a great field filled with dragons as far as the eye can see.

I don't need any assistance spotting my mate among the other dragons. His horns reach high above his head. I gently reach inside my coat and rub his scale. The minute I touch it, his great head whips around to look at me. I remain where I am, not wanting to venture out into the snow and the ice in my human form for fear of injury. I spot my father sitting in front of Alaric's wings in a notch between his spines. Nicodeamus looks almost as excited as I do about this flight.

Alaric's great dragon stops before me and lays down flat on the ground. Dimitri and Dominik rush over to my side to help me get onto Alaric's back. I'm not that far along, I don't think, but then again, I'm not sure when I got pregnant. With the aid of Alaric's wing and the steadying hands of Dominik and Dimitri, I take my place behind Alaric's crown of horns. I look back and wave at my father before patting Alaric's neck. I reach out to him through our bond. *I'm ready, my love. Let's fly!*

His response through the bond is almost immediate. *As you wish!* Alaric says, filled with love and his own excitement. My silly mate is quoting one of my favorite movies of all time. I giggle softly and grip the horn closest to me as I feel his dragon rock a bit as he stands. Once standing, he roars, sending the Black Dragons into the air first as our guards. When he feels the moment is safe enough, he leaps up, launching us into the sky. I hear my father, Nicodeamus, screaming his excitement and joy into the afternoon sky.

Your father seems to be quite pleased, my love. Are you happy as well? Is the baby ok? Alaric asks, happy yet concerned for our well-being.

We are well, love. No nausea and no discomfort. As for my father, you've given him the gift of flight again. I laugh a bit through the bond. *You do realize you are going to be his favorite after this?* I state as I try not to laugh. Poor Alaric doesn't know how badly my father yearned to be sky-bound again. I can feel his dragon jiggle a bit as if laughing to himself.

I look at all the other dragons flying around us in formation. It's truly a beautiful sight to behold. I watch a myriad of colors move around us as we fly. We have a good tailwind, and the dragons get to glide on the thermals more often than not so as not to expend excessive energy. We fly over small villages and mountain ranges. It's amazing how far one can see from up here. I try not to move too much so I don't distract Alaric. His dragon occasionally makes noises, and the four Black Dragons with us turn in unison so Alaric can show me the sights he wants me to see on our trip.

The palace's spires can be seen in the distance, nestled in the cliff face of one of the tallest mountains. There is no access except if you can fly or be carried up there by the looks of it. Strategically, it's probably the safest place for me to birth the next heir. First, the boys and I have to make our presence known within dragon society. I watch the palace and see a contingent of dragons fly out toward us. I feel quite anxious. My beast wants us to shift and be ready.

Alaric reaches out to me to try to calm me. *It's normal protocol, love. Please calm down. We mustn't appear hostile. I can't fight with you and the baby on my back. I will not risk you two.* Alaric's voice is pleading. At his urging, I settle down and rest my hand on my stomach. Fuck, it feels like the fucking thing has grown. Maybe it's just the way that I'm sitting. Nope, I'm pretty fucking sure it's bigger. Fuck my life. How the fuck am I supposed to battle like this?

Alaric roars out several times and banks to his left, showing his cargo to the incoming dragons. I raise my arm and show off my brand, the mark of the House of Marelup. I know the dragons have phenomenal vision, so I know they see it. What appears to be the leader roars at us, then turns back to the palace. *Great move, love, showing off your brand.* Apparently, Sebastian sent word ahead that an imposter was going to be here to kill them off. Alaric has a bit of a laugh to his voice. *The dumb fuck is here somewhere in the castle. Apparently, he has an Earl's protection for his visit. This should be interesting,* Alaric says, still laughing mentally. I'm not finding it funny at all. I'm fucking pregnant and getting fucking huge, and now my psycho ex-mate is here. I'm going to use his intestines for garland.

Alaric lands in the central courtyard, and I don't budge till my guys come to get me. Alaric keeps his head held up high and remains standing till our close-knit group gets to us. I'm already on edge knowing Sebastian is here somewhere in this fucking maze of a castle. I'll kill the motherfucker for what he did. After what feels like forever, the guys finally make it over to us. Dimitri and Klaus are the ones to help me down most of the way, and I'm handed off to Dominik and Jayce. Jayce has decided to shift to his Dire Wolf form because he feels he can better protect me that way. I'll be honest, I do feel better with one of the twins as their wolf. Jayce presses his muzzle against my stomach, and he makes me laugh. I run my fingers through his fur and rest my hand on his shoulders as we walk. Alaric and my father flank my left and right side. Dimitri takes point, while Klaus and Dominik bring up the rear protecting our backs.

I have put my crown back on my head, as well as the dress shoes that were given to me before we departed. I pass off the bag of extra riding gear to Klaus's brother to hold for me. We arrive at the palace's double doors, and a fat, balding man with a sash and medals meets us at the door. "Your Highnesses, I am Ulrick, Duke of the southern province. I welcome you to the Ice Dragon castle." He bows quite stiffly. Every move he makes, I analyze the fuck out of it. My estimation is he's hiding something, and he's protecting Sebastian. My resting bitch face is perfect, nothing is betrayed.

Alaric steps forward and introduces us to the Earl. The Earl's eyes widen as he looks at me. He recognizes the crown, and he acknowledges my name and father. I don't bother moving from Jayce's side, nor do I try to extend my hand for the Earl to kiss. On the flight over, my father educated me on how my great-grandmother used to be. I am emulating her the best that I can—the I don't give a fuck game is strong with this one.

Once inside the castle, Jayce growls lowly in the back of his throat. I speak to him through the bond. *What is it, love?* I run my fingers through his fur, trying to calm him down.

I scent Sebastian, he's not far away. I gently pat Jayce's back once he finishes speaking to me.

I know, I smell him too, I reply to him through the bond, allowing Alaric, Dominik, and now Klaus in on the conversation. Klaus looks at me, shocked that he just heard me. Dominik goes on to explain to Klaus about the bond and how it all works.

We continue through the halls and are led to a suite similar to the one we shared at the Chalet. Dominik strips and shifts to his Dire Wolf; he and Jayce search the rooms making sure they are safe and secure. "Is this truly necessary?" the Earl states in a rather uppity tone.

Oh, fuck no, I'm not having this. I motion to my guys, and they move to stand beside me. Jayce and Dominik flank my sides as I stare at the Earl. "Kneel," I say—it's the first word I have spoken since my arrival.

The Earl starts laughing at my request. "Me? Kneel? To you? Ha! You're just a mutt that won't last a day on the throne." The Earl keeps laughing as I slowly remove the flight coat, passing it to Dimitri.

I unbutton the top of my sleeves so that they fall to hang loosely at my side. I smile and wink at Alaric before looking back to the Earl. "You have been weighed and measured." I shake my head at him and shift my arms to my armored gauntlets. Thick, pearl-white scales cover my arms from elbow to fingertips; my nails turning into long, thick, curved, white dragon talons. My eyes shift to my beast's mercury orbs with the black dragon slits; small, pearl-white dragon scales decorate around my eyes and down the bridge of my nose. "You are Earl no more." I unleash the full weight of my Alpha power, making the Earl crash to his knees before me. I hear several people fall and glass shatter.

"I'm not the one who needs to worry about surviving with me on the throne. My mother was Anca. My great-grandmother, the Blood Queen. Who the fuck do you think you're talking to, you insolent whelp? You want to call me a mutt?" My upper lip curls up to expose my canines that have descended. "For a pure-blood, you're too inbred to remain in power. I now strip you and your family of title and lands." With a flourish of my hand, I curl my fingers in so that I can examine my talons before looking back up at the Earl. "If you're not careful, your skull will join my collection." Alaric comes up to my side and kisses my cheek. I slowly release my grip on my power, reining it back in. Ulrick is ghost white as he looks at my partially shifted form. Alaric stands beside me, his arms shifted to look exactly like mine. We present a unified front. Ulrick starts begging for forgiveness: apparently, Sebastian had gotten to him first and fed him lies. Oh yes, I will be hunting Sebastian down real soon.

Dimitri ejects Ulrick from the suite. As soon as the door closes, I shift back to fully human and almost collapse from exertion. The boys grab hold of me and move me to the big bed. Alaric and Nicodeamus leave the room, seeking out food and drink for me.

Jayce and Dominik, in their wolven forms, lie on either side of me, keeping me warm and safe so the others can move about and unpack.

I see the worry on Dimitri's and Klaus's faces as they look at my semi weakened state. I gently rub the small swell of my stomach as I ponder the events of our arrival. There are several things I know that are true. First, my ex is here spreading lies and sowing the seeds of fear among the ranks. Second, he wouldn't be here of his own volition; he's definitely not smart enough to target this place on his own. Third, my strength is directly tied to how well I'm being fed while carrying my baby. It's been about a week and a half since I enjoyed the twins during my heat, and less than a week after it was Alaric. Any of the three of them could be the father; the big difference is the gestation length. The door opens suddenly with Alaric and Nicodeamus carrying trays of food. Katherine and Alaric's sister, Sabine, enter the room behind the guys. It's the first time I've seen Alaric's sister in her human form. She's beautiful and is almost a carbon copy of her mother.

Dominik and Jayce start to growl at Sabine, she's someone new to them, and I'm not feeling well. My father and Alaric set the spread for me to eat at the table in the middle of the room. Jayce and Dominik move their large wolven bodies, assisting me to the chair at the head of the table. They flank my side, watching the room very closely. "What brings you to my chambers, Katherine?" I ask before sniffing the leg of lamb several times before biting into it.

"We wish to check on the child you carry. Rumors have it that it's very powerful," Katherine states with a hopeful look in her eyes. I narrow my eyes as I look at her. A deep, rumbling growl escapes my lips as the tabletop begins to freeze before me.

I look between the guys, shifting my eyes to that of my beast, and really look at Katherine and Sabine. I don't see anything out of the ordinary with them. I reach out through the mate bond to the guys. *Alaric, I know it's your mom and sister, but their interest concerns me greatly; I'm not comfortable with them being here. What are everyone else's thoughts?* I leave it as an open question to the group. Maybe I'm just paranoid, or perhaps I'm onto something?

The twins chime in together almost precisely at the same time. *We trust your instincts: if you say something is wrong, then we believe you.* Both guys' wolves nuzzle me at the same time, emphasizing their stance.

I can tell that Klaus is struggling with trying to use the bond since it is not fully cemented in place. I extend my hand to him—direct contact will allow the connection to flow much easier for him. Gently, Klaus takes my hand in his much larger one. *My grandmother is a very experienced midwife, perhaps we can send for her?* The other guys nod in agreement with Klaus's suggestion.

Alaric, love, please take some guards and Klaus back to his pack. Gather his grandmother and whatever she feels she needs to take care of me. For all intents and purposes, I must not appear weak at any time. My mates nod at me, and I look to Dimitri. "Care to escort me around the castle while Alaric is busy?" I manage to gorge myself on enough food that I feel my strength returning in full. I carefully re-button my sleeves then extend a hand to Dimitri. He places my hand on this thick forearm and allows me to use him to steady myself. "As for my child, Katherine, its power is none of your concern. If you're not careful, you'll find yourself right along with Ulrick."

CHAPTER 58

Aurora

December-

We leisurely stroll through the halls, looking at art and listening to the local gossip. Apparently, the servants are singing my praises for putting Ulrick in his place.

We finally find the throne room, and I move towards it. Dominik and Jayce both start growling immediately, which halts me in my tracks. Sebastian comes strolling out from behind the throne, missing half of his left arm. *Gee, I wonder how that happened?* I should have taken his heart instead.

"Is it mine?" Sebastian asks, looking at my elaborate dress that emphasizes the small curve of my growing belly. He attempts to move closer, Dominik and Jayce immediately move in front of me. My Dire Wolf mate's hackles stand on end as their heads lower into attack mode. I can see the venom dripping from Jayce's canines, I look at Dominik, and I can visibly see the tension in his coiled muscles.

Dimitri is the only one that appears to be completely calm. Dimitri moves to wrap his thick arm around my middle, opening his hand wide, and palms my belly, covering it completely. "It's not your's, you dumb fuck, it's mine," Dimitri growls and bares his teeth. I witness his canines descend while his eyes take on the amber-gold color of his bear. It's the first time he's shown any possession over me; I'm getting wet just thinking about it.

Dimitri's proclamation visibly shakes Sebastian to the core. I can see the white-blue of his wolf's eyes glowing from where he stands on the steps leading up to the throne. *"If he charges, he's mine. I'm going to provoke him a bit more first."* I speak through the bond so that everyone knows what's going on. I rest my hands on Dominik and Jayce simultaneously, silently telling them to move to the side. I turn my head and kiss Dimitri on the lips passionately. Sebastian's growl is unmistakable. At this point, I'm pretty sure I've got him.

Sebastian starts to clap and sarcastically say, "Bravo!" over and over. I break away from Dimitri and look at Sebastian. "All you had to do was give me an heir, then the Lycan throne would have been mine. But no, you had to send Andre to investigate all the elder families. You signed his death-warrant that day." I feel scales emerge along my spine and ripple from my hairline base down to my tailbone. My stomach twists in knots, listening to Sebastian, thinking about Andre and how he died. Shot down like common prey instead of face to face like men. Sebastian drones on, eventually snapping me out of my inner monologue. "It's your fault, really, that he's dead. Poor bastard trusted the wrong people." Sebastian slowly strolls down the stairs, enunciating every word spoken. He's smart enough to remain out of my phys-ical strike zone, that cocky grin I used to find sexy now grates on my nerves. "If you haven't connected the dots, Aurora, I killed Andre."

I shift my eyes to that of my beast. I focus on the area behind the throne while Dominik and Jayce scan the rest of the room. Sebastian has at least four others behind a secret passageway behind the throne. I reach out to my father and inform him as to what's happening. He, in turn, learns from Alaric how to access that area from a different room. "I figured you did. Let's face it, you and your witch of a mother got too comfortable and sloppy." I start to laugh as I lean back against Dimitri's broad chest. Slowly, I close my eyes and open the bond wide so that all of my mates hear everything.

"By some miracle, I ended up being sent, by Vlad's sister,"—I hold up one taloned finger—"to his other sister, who just so happens to have a son." I hold up a second taloned finger, counting off the facts. "Elena purposely spiked my tea then sent three genetic rejects and you to meet me." After raising the third finger, I shake my head and then raise it to look at Sebastian again. My steel-grey eyes lock on him; I'm starting to enjoy this way too much.

"Of course, the first Strigoi attack I experience is with your pack. Coincidence? I think not." A fourth finger is raised. "Then, there was your cousin's attempt on my life and two different females, one of which was probably your true mate." I raise a fifth finger, then lower one, counting now up to six. "Oh, and don't get me started on the Strigoi camp stationed not far from your pack." I lower another finger now up to seven. My eyes move between Jayce and Dominik then back to Sebastian.

"Your greed robbed us both of our Lycan's true mates." Smirking, I look down for a moment then smile broadly as I look back at Sebastian. "Well, actually, just you. I found mine. You've been

reduced to a feather-light ghost in the back of my mind." A maniacal laugh escapes my crimson lips. "Hell, I probably killed your
true mate at your camp." I flex my taloned fingers that I had used
to count with before resting the tip of a talon on my chin. "I
wonder which bitch it was?" I narrow my eyes on him; his grief-
stricken reaction tells me that he's more attached than I am. This
is handy information.

I slightly pull away from Dimitri and rest my hand on his side
where Sebastian had touched the blade to his ribcage. "What's
the one thing I've always said, Sebastian?" I turn to face him and
slowly prowl towards him—my ample breasts struggling to break
free of my heart-shaped gown top. I step more towards his left
side, stopping within my striking distance. Under the sleeves of
my beautiful gown, I calmly flex my hands, itching to sink my
talons into his flesh. I look up to Sebastian adoringly, all the while
plotting his death that's seconds away.

Hesitantly, he raises his hand and rubs the back of his knuckles
along my jaw. His touch repulses me to the point my stomach
starts to turn sour. I keep telling myself, just a few more seconds.
"Care to remind me, beautiful?" He leans in slowly, and just before
his lips touch mine, I lunge forward and drive my talons up into
his stomach, continuing up into his chest. I feel that all too
familiar tearing of flesh and the sliding of scales over intestines.
The muscle that separates the abdomen and rib cage really isn't
that strong and easily grants passage to his vital organs. The
rhythmic beating of his heart in my hand is soothing. Small pulses
of blood run down my inner forearm as I look up into his shocked
eyes. His lungs slowly expand, touching my sharp, bladed scales. I
know every breath he takes is shredding his lungs to pieces. I give
his heart a bit of a squeeze to emphasize the dire situation he's
currently in.

Quite literally, I have his heart in my hand. I quickly take my left hand and cut his right hand off, then grip his throat—the dripping of his blood echoes in the silent throne room. His blood has managed to ruin my pretty gown, and it's sprayed all over the throne room floors. Sebastian is gasping for breath as I slowly apply pressure to his heart. I feel when Alaric and Klaus use the bond to watch through my eyes.

"Sebastian, tsk tsk tsk... My golden rule hasn't ever changed. Never fuck with those under my protection and never threaten what's *mine!*" As I scream the final word, I rip down, pulling his still-beating heart free from his chest. His blood runs slowly between the spaces of my scales. My left-hand moves quickly as I use my talons to sever his head from his body. In a very "300" style move, I kick his chest, sending his body to the floor in a pool of his own blood.

I bend my knees and pick up Sebastian's head with my free hand and turn to Dimitri. Drawing in a deep breath, I stare at Sebastian's head, his admission of killing Andre echoing in my head. My eyes then look at Sebastian's heart in my bloody talons, the quivering mass of smooth muscle still twitching randomly. I'm finally free of his false echo, and I've managed to avenge one of the people I've loved most. Without hesitation, I close the distance between Dimitri and me. Tears are streaming down my cheeks because of what I need to say next. "I want you to have these. Our Andre has been avenged." I swallow hard; I'm all choked up with emotions I can't easily process on my own. I hold Sebastian's head and heart in my now human hands offering them to Dimitri.

Dimitri accepts my gifts then kisses me softly, his lips lingering on mine. "He would be very proud of you right now. He would also be proud that you kept your promise to him when you set him free." Dimitri reluctantly moves over to one of the closest tables and sets down Sebastian's head and heart. He wipes his hands on his pants and then comes over to me, smiling ever so softly. His thick arms slowly band around me, holding me tight and flush to his chest. I feel his lips lightly press against my temple before resting his cheek on top of my head. We stay like this for what seems like hours when in reality, only several minutes pass. We hear the sliding of stone, and the smell of burned flesh hits us. My father emerges from behind the throne, four heads in his hand dangling by their hair. He chucks the heads towards the table where Sebastian's head now rests.

"It's about bloody time that wanker finally got what he deserved," My father says with almost too jovial of a tone for someone who has just finished killing four assassins. He smiles at Dimitri and me and gives us a slight wave before herding the twins out of the room. Dimitri and I can't help but laugh as we watch my father herding two large male Dire Wolves out of the room.

Dimitri gently cups my cheek, and I raise my gaze to look at him. Lightly, he kisses my lips, then smiles. "I have always loved you, Aurora. Regrettably, I'm just not ready yet to take the next step. As much as my bear wants me to, mentally, I'm having a hard time getting over being your guardian all these years. I hope you understand that it has nothing to do with you; it's my own hang-ups. Nico is right, it's all mental with me."

I listen ever so carefully to every word that comes out of Dimitri's mouth. He's speaking honestly and from the heart. I value that. I guess in my heart, I always knew he would end up being mine someday. My wolf isn't a crazy bitch after all. Since the ascension, my instincts are sharper, my emotions run deeper, and to have him be by my side for the rest of my life would be my greatest treasure. Treasure? Now I'm genuinely speaking like a dragon. Maybe my dragon side is much stronger than I initially believed?

"Dimitri. You have always been my rock, my strength, and as frightening as it sounds, my sanity," I say as I take both of his hands in mine and look up to him. "Without you, I probably would have gone on many more bloody rampages. Let's face it, neither one of us knew what we were dealing with when it came to me." Tilting my head to the left, I feel my cheeks flush under his intense gaze. "I'm the first of my kind, a true hybrid of two powerful species. Some days I don't even know what to do with myself." I release my grip on his hands and slide them up my face and into my hair. "The instincts that both creatures have are sometimes at war with each other."

I remove my hands from my hair and snuggle back in close, hugging him around his waistline, resting my head on his chest. "You will always be the one who I come to for comfort, for protection, for shelter." I lift my head up to look into his hazel eyes. "But you also have to understand each of the others have their own qualities that I need to seek out as well. You know I hold none above the other. But you do have an advantage over the others. You've been with me since day one; you've seen me at my best, and well, at my worst."

I smirk and start to laugh ever so softly. "We've cleaned up some real fucked-up messes together over the years. Like the intestine Christmas tree decorations. I'm still not too sure what to make of that, really. I remember Dad said it had something to do with the ascension, the internal wars that my dual natures had amongst themselves, struggling for power." I shrug my shoulders. "But I honestly can't blame either of them for what happened. They were protecting what was theirs. If those two assholes didn't interfere when they did," a soft growl escapes my lips. "We would have been together all this time uninterrupted, and you would have been the first mate." Tears roll down my face as I make the admission to him. I see tears form in the corner of my Great Bear's eyes. The huge softy is feeling how I feel at this moment, that we were both robbed of precious time. I swear to myself and to the others that are with me, I shall seek out my vengeance. Elena is next on my hit list, and trust me, once my child is born she will have limited days left. I have a very good feeling as to where I may find her. For now, though, I will not expose my suspicions. I don't want to panic the others.

In a rather romantic move, even for this Great Bear of mine, he scoops me up in his arms and carries me to the dining hall. The rest of my mates still here in the castle are already sitting at the table waiting for me. Each piece of meat put on the table is closely examined by my father and the twins. No one is taking any chances of anything getting to me that can harm the baby or me. I guess I'm not the only one whose instincts have been kicked up a notch by the impending birth of my heir. Dominik's phone pings with several messages in rapid succession. Silence falls over the dining hall as we look at him, waiting for him to finish reading all the messages.

"According to Alex, there has been a lot of movement at the American Lycan camp. A good number of the Lycans have started to head their way down to our home. They are seeking refuge in case of retaliation by either the Strigoi or Sebastian's family." Dom looks up briefly before returning to the messages. "I told him to vet each individual thoroughly before allowing them into the compound. We need our forces as strong as possible for the next leg of this journey. I don't think the American Lycans will be able to hold up against the Strigoi. Still, at least the extra numbers will bolster our ground defense," Dominik states before he fires back several more messages to his brother and receives two more back just as quickly. "Okay, Alex says that he will look into everything and everyone. He allows them to set up camp in the desert instead of letting them into the heart of the fortress. He doesn't want them in there on the off chance anyone decides to cause a coup."

As I listen carefully to what Dominik is telling me, I look over at my father then to Dimitri, seeing as both of them have more experience when it comes to wartime. They both gave me a slight nod, and I look back to Dominik. "Tell Alex that his plan is solid, and I appreciate him being so cautious with our people. When we reach the German Lycan camp, I will send for them. Keep up the training, and don't let anybody slack off; the war is coming faster than we think." I go back to eating my leg of lamb that I've had sitting in front of me for the last ten minutes. I'm starving, tired, and there's way too much shit to get done. Nobody ever said being a queen would be easy, nor would it be easy to wage and win a war.

My boys are taking excellent care of me, making sure my drink is full, as well as my plate, and that everything I need is within reach. We missed the Krampus celebrations in Germany at the beginning of the month; I'm really disappointed about that. Right now, we are setting up for Christmas that is only three days away. Father receives word that Alaric and Klaus have acquired Klaus's grandmother and are on their way back with a good headwind. I should see them within the next two hours. I watch as the servants move around the room, changing the decorations to get ready for the holiday. I'm kind of upset I didn't get to go shopping for my mates, but I carry the greatest gift of all right now.

CHAPTER 59

Alaric

THE LAST THREE months have been the craziest three months of my existence. For the last almost four hundred years, I had lost faith that I would ever find my mate. Then out of nowhere, a hybrid is born, a beautiful little ray of sunshine to call my own. Fast forward three months, we cemented our bond and she's expecting our first child.

I'm ninety percent sure the child is mine. I felt the shift and change in her energy when the baby was conceived. I don't want to say anything to the others. I don't want them to be disappointed since they technically had gotten there first. Little known fact about dragons: if a dragon is available, the female will always choose the viable dragon over any other species. So when it becomes time for the others to father their children, I'll have to remove myself from the equation. That way they will have a chance to have their own children. I guess good old Nicodeamus forgot to tell them about that fact.

We make good time flying over to Klaus's pack in Germany. The prevailing winds are in our favor for the entire flight. Well, that and my superior wingspan did help speed the journey along. Klaus is an interesting fellow. Aurora's beast claimed him but did not follow through with cementing the bond as of yet. I suspect that it's because Sebastian is still breathing, and there is always a faint echo of him in the back of her mind. Mating bonds are a funny thing, even the ones that are conceived through magic.

We spend as little time as possible with Klaus's birth pack and urge his grandmother to come back with us to help Aurora and the baby coming. As soon as the old crone hears a baby is involved, she moves about as fast as a two-hundred-year-old can. She grabs her bag of goodies, all full of medicinal herbs and supplies. She also brings along an assistant with her, which I advise against. I know my mate. She will not be thrilled that a young, viable female is riding back with Klaus and me or around her other mates. I'm almost afraid to find out if she will go into full-out battle attack mode and have this poor, innocent female die at her talons.

On the return flight, I sense that something is amiss with Aurora, my dragon roars out his agitation. Because Klaus has direct contact with my scales, I help him to use our bond to see through Aurora's eyes. Probably one of the coolest tricks that dragon-kin has: the ability to see what each other sees. Before her, we watch Sebastian, with all of his false swagger, attempt to sway her. Aurora rattles off all the facts and gathered information that she has pieced together herself. Most of it, I was not aware of. She is definitely a female to be afraid of. She's better than half the investigative units I've ever seen.

We watch as the idiot approaches her and attempts to woo her yet again. Our girl is not having it. When the moment is right, she sinks her talons deep into his chest, gripping his still-beating heart. In the back of my mind, I'm cheering her on. That is what makes me so proud of her; she is a no-nonsense, take-no-prisoners type of ruler. Either you're guilty, or you're innocent, very rarely are there shades of grey with her. Her golden rule has always stood firm with her beliefs—you don't fuck with what's hers.

We get to watch Sebastian fall down dead, decapitated, and short of his heart. Nicodeamus comes out bearing the heads of more enemies. I know what my stewards are going to be doing later. They will be cleaning skulls to add to the growing collection.

I see the castle in the distance, its tall spires like homing beacons for me to find my way back. Klaus's grandmother and her assistant sit all safe and snug inside the traveling case that I had brought with me. On the other hand, being the bold motherfucker that he is, Klaus is sitting in front of my wings, enjoying the view. I circle the courtyard several times before finding a place to land. I roar to announce our arrival. Ever so carefully, I lower the carriage. After several more beats of my wings, I land about fifty feet away from them. Klaus immediately jumps off my back and runs to go check on his grandmother. Aurora and the guys come running out as soon as I've settled.

My Aurora, as radiant as ever, is glowing with health and happiness. Her hand rests gently on the small swell of her growing stomach, and she smiles looking up at us. I say *us* because my dragon is sitting here arrogantly proud of what he's done. He's claiming full paternity like I had nothing to do with it. It makes me want to laugh sometimes at how man separates himself from beast and vice versa. Yep, my dragon is sitting here, chest all puffed up, scales raised to make himself look larger, imposing, and proud as a freaking peacock. But then again, I'm proud as fuck too. My child, my heir, is growing before my eyes.

I lower my massive head down so that I am eye level with Aurora. She carefully comes over and caresses the scales on my cheek. Just to be a complete ass, I stick my forked tongue out and wrap it around her waistline ever so gently. Yeah, a little bit of dragon saliva never hurt anybody, especially not that babe in her womb. She's laughing hysterically at me, lightly slapping my face. I know she doesn't mean it; she's just being silly. Dimitri is slightly panicked; he's still worries my dragon will harm her. Nico tries to calm him down, like usual that big old bear is just overly protective of our girl. Can't really blame him. He's been around her for over two hundred years, watching her grow from infancy to the queen that she is now. One more throne to take, and everything will be in place. Though, that last throne will be a tough one to take back.

My steward comes out, bringing yet again, the changing blind and an outfit for me. When will they get over the fact that when we shift we're naked and don't care? It's not like it's nothing my mate and my bond mates haven't seen before. However, there's that sense of propriety—that being a royal—you must maintain. Completely sucks the fun out of everything. I shift back before they have the chance to get them lined up, and I rip the clothes out of the man's hands. I start walking back into the castle with Aurora on my arm.

We make it inside, and I head off into the study to quickly throw on my trousers and shirt before Klaus brings his grandmother and her assistant. Aurora sits on the desk, smirking while watching me get dressed like I am a hunk of chocolate. It's great to be home.

I know what I'm going to be doing later, and it's sitting right in front of me.

Eventually, the boys catch up and enter the study. A cautious knock sounds at the door; Dimitri opens it slowly. Behind the door stands Klaus with the two women with him. I move myself to stand in front of Aurora; she places her hands on my shoulders and tries to peek around me to see who's here.

The grandmother enters first, Aurora just watches her as she lightly strokes my shoulder blade. Next, the younger female enters; Aurora's whole demeanor changes instantly. I quickly send out a warning through the bond to the other guys that she's getting ready to go into attack mode and that I don't know what to expect. Klaus comes forth quickly after my warning and attempts to introduce them so that there wouldn't be any blood on the floor.

"Aurora, my angel, this is my grandmother Elsa and her assistant Lorraine. My grandmother has come to help you through your pregnancy and make sure that we keep you and the baby as healthy as possible. I've already updated only her as to what's been going on. So far, everything that we've already been doing for you has been the correct course of action." Klaus nervously moves aside and lets his grandmother approach Aurora and me. I can feel the waves of energy coming off her: a slight bit of agitation, apprehension, or whatever you want to call it. She's not comfortable right now. Aurora looks around the room rapidly and decides that she is trapped.

"I don't want to be in here. You have to get me out," Aurora states loudly, her eyes the liquid mercury of her beast, those black dragon slits eyeing and sizing everyone up, trying to decide the safest course for her to go to protect herself and her child. I was once warned by my mother that a female dragon with young could be the most dangerous creature on the face of the Earth. Having a front-row seat to this is quite scary. I'm very concerned, and I'm starting to fear for my own life.

The room pretty much parts like the Red Sea did in the Bible. Aurora jumps down off the desk and toddles her happy ass out of the room. We watch her as she heads into the main hallway. There's plenty of escape routes; she's not confined and constantly eyeing everything up, making sure she has options. Elsa tries again to approach Aurora. She has her palms flat and facing up, showing that she is no threat. I still haven't figured out how an almost four-hundred-year-old Lycan female could be a threat to a very young Dragon-Lycan hybrid.

Eventually, Aurora stops pacing and allows Elsa to approach her. I can scent the fear coming from Klaus. He's quite concerned for his grandmother's life as well as her assistant's. I know in my heart that the grandmother's not a threat, nor would she be seen as one. It's the assistant that I'm concerned for.

All of the guys stay away from the assistant, ensuring we keep ample distance between her and us. Aurora's watching our movements and keeping her eyes on the new girl in her castle. Elsa comes over and starts speaking to Aurora in German. I have no fucking clue what that old lady is saying to her. Klaus, on the other hand, is giggling. Aurora surprises me by answering her back in German. Son of a bitch, she's fluent in a language I don't speak.

Out of the corner of my eye, I see Nicodeamus pointing to himself and smiling. Ah, I get it now, she learned from him during one of their dream walks. That sneaky old bastard has tricks up his sleeve that I haven't even thought of yet. I'll have to sit down with my father-in-law at some point and have him teach them to me, it'll be quite useful in the future.

Aurora calls for the twins and me to come up to her suite, along with Elsa. The assistant attempts to follow Elsa, and Aurora instantly spins on her heels, shifting almost completely into that of her beast. She's three-quarters of the way shifted, and that's about as far as she goes. I'm not sure if it's because of how far along she is in her pregnancy that she can't or doesn't feel the need to complete the shift. If it's the pregnancy thing, then I'm starting to get concerned that she will become vulnerable very soon.

We make it up to the suite and Jayce helps Aurora out of her gown, then she slowly lays herself on the bed. I swear to the gods that her stomach has almost doubled in size. She is about the size of a woman who's about three months along, thus further confirming that I am the father. Elsa sits there and goes over Aurora from stem to stern. She listens to her stomach then lays her hands on it. I can see that my mate is quite uncomfortable at the moment. Dominik and I go over and grab her hands. Oh, it's not really for comfort, it's more to protect Elsa if Aurora just reacts on instinct.

CHAPTER 60
Alaric

December -

Once the exam is over, Elsa sits back and smiles, then kisses Aurora on her forehead like a good grandmother would. "Congratulations, my Queen, your child is healthy and growing steadily. I'm guesstimating that within the next two months you'll deliver. Considering that time frame, I'm guessing that the child is King Alaric's. Only a dragon's child grows this quickly, and with you only being a hybrid, it would take a pure-blood to accelerate this process." Elsa smiles and bows her head slightly.

"Congratulations, my Lord, on the birth of your future heir. My lady, I am at your service and wish only to serve and protect this child of yours." Elsa's eyes shine with a hint of tears threatening to break at a moment's notice. "Thank you for allowing my grandson to bring me here to witness this momentous event. It's also brought our family great honor learning he is one of your mates. If there is ever anything I can do for you, please do not hesitate to ask or call me at any point in the night." Elsa lightly bows to Aurora and then to Alaric. She walks over to her grandson and gives him a hug before departing the room with Jayce to find her suite.

Against her better judgment, the assistant remains in the room. As Aurora stares at the assistant, her beast starts that rumbling growl deep in her chest that vibrates the entire bed. I can feel the shift in power, the pull on mine, and by the look of Nicodeamus, the pull on his as well. Dimitri feels the room's shift and quickly ushers the assistant out before we end up with a bloodbath. Almost immediately, Aurora settles back down. She looks over at Dominik then back at me.

Well, I guess that solves that mystery, now, doesn't it? She carefully slides off the bed and goes into her closet. Son of a bitch, I see all different size sweatshirts, and none of them are hers. She rifles through the collection that she apparently swiped from each of us at some point and pulls out my favorite sweatshirt. I've been wondering where the hell that one went. Well, another mystery solved, it's on her now. Aurora finds her fuzzy socks in a drawer, and she has her most comfortable leggings on. Aurora throws her hair up in a messy bun then proceeds to put that ruby crown back on her head. I guess she does love her great-grandmother's crown.

It's kind of concerning that her great-grandmother's nickname was the Blood Queen. Come to think of it, that name would be very fitting for my mate as well. She has bathed in the blood of her enemies for the last four to five months along her journey. Hell, she recently bathed in the blood of a deceptive mate. Now I'm kind of curious. Since Sebastian's dead, I wonder how soon she'll wait to complete her bond with Klaus. I'm almost betting it will be sometime after the baby is born and she has a chance to heal. But who knows, I could be very wrong with that assumption.

Aurora grabs my hand, then Dominik's, and drags us out of the room and back down to the dining hall. Kind of figured this would happen, especially after the display of power that she just put on. We've concluded that if she doesn't eat with that kind of power exertion, it leads to her collapsing. It's safer to keep Aurora fed than to let her health be at risk. Out of the corner of my eye, as we walk through the halls, I catch Klaus running around with a Santa hat on, darting in and out of the throne room. I begin to wonder just what the hell is he up to. I pass Aurora off to Dominik so I can go and investigate.

I tiptoe my way into the throne room. Even as king, sometimes I just enjoy getting the drop on people. Klaus is going through the room singing 'Oh Tannenbaum,' decorating it in very festive Christmas decorations that he must have brought from home. I watch our little elf, yeah total joke there, he's definitely over six foot. He has brought a bit of his home here so that Aurora doesn't miss out on a traditional Christmas. "Hey, Klaus, do you need any help with that?" The poor man practically jumps out of his skin hearing someone behind him, until he realizes it's me.

"If you don't mind? It would be greatly appreciated. I want our mate to experience what Christmas would be like in my home. It's a big deal for my people. Granted, we missed the first part of the celebration which is Krampus, around the seventh of the month. But a little bit is better than nothing at all, don't you think?" Klaus looks so hopeful and exceptionally pleased with all that he's accomplished so far.

I smile and start to laugh. "Yeah, I really don't think having a six foot, demon-looking creature running through the castle would put Aurora at ease at this point. Somebody would end up getting hurt and or killed just because she didn't realize who it was." I tilt my head to the side and raise one eyebrow, looking at Klaus to see if what I'm trying to get at sinks in.

"Oh shit, I didn't think about that! Thanks for saving my ass, man." Klaus had utterly forgotten how defensive our mate can be. Then again, he's known her for less time than I have.

We work together for a few hours setting the room up. My lieutenant returns with the perfect Douglas fir Christmas tree. The blasted thing has to be twelve feet tall and about eight to nine feet wide. I have to admit, he did pick a stunning tree for our first Christmas as a family. I know I still have family living, but my mother and sister are not exactly the warmest people to be around. When he was alive, my father was more concerned about war and treasures that he may acquire from those that he thought he was going to conquer. I now have a mate that's my wife, a child on the way, and bond mates to share the rest of my life with.

Who knows how many children are going to be born in this union. I can guess at least one for each of us. I watch Klaus run around the room, decorating every little thing with ornaments that he has brought from home. I send a couple of the girls who poke their heads in to grab some of the decorations I have in my private chamber. It's stuff that came from my grandmother and my great-grandmother that hasn't seen the light of day since they died.

The girls return quickly with the boxes in tow that I have requested. Most of the ornaments brought down are either made of crystal, glass, blown glass, or rare stones that I have found along in journeys. The ones that are the most special to me are what my grandmother and great-grandmother had made themselves.

We think we're pretty slick being here, with the door closed but nope, not that slick. A few hours must have passed since I came in, and Aurora became curious about where I had gone. I see her poke her head in the door and smile broadly. Through the bond, I reach out to her only. *My love, please don't let Klaus see you. He wants to surprise you by decorating this room with things from his homeland. It means so much for him to be able to do this for all of us. I'm just here helping him so that he doesn't feel like he's doing it all alone.*

Aurora smiles, lightly waves at me, then ducks back out the door again. *This is what I love about you, Alaric, your heart is as big as your dragon. I am truly blessed to have you as my mate.*

I can sense Aurora walking away from the throne room. I see Klaus looking towards the door nervously, almost expecting her to come walking through. I shake my head at him, letting him know that she's gone. He smiles, nods, and goes back to hanging his decorations, then begins to trim the tree. He's back to singing his German Christmas carols, that for the love of the gods, I don't understand a single word that he's saying.

Eventually, the door opens again, and I turn to find his grandmother and her assistant coming through, closing it behind them. "Klaus! I'm quite concerned for my assistant's life. Your mate does not like her and is continuously growling at her. You must speak to her. I don't want my assistant living in fear being under this roof. We have at least another two months before that child is born and to live in fear for that long is never a good thing." For a wrinkled old sprite, that woman has a commanding presence to her. Then again, to be an elder as old as she is, in a pack as large as she lives in, you have to be tough as nails, hard as steel, and take no shit from anyone.

Klaus audibly exhales, and his shoulders lower. I can see the defeated stance he's currently taking. This is not a battle that's going to be easily won by either side. Do you go against your mate? Or do you go against your grandmother? It's a lose-lose situation no matter how you shake it. The old crone stands there tapping her foot as if she believes her word is law under my roof. I look over at her after laying my hand on Klaus's shoulder, trying to comfort him.

"Ma'am, my mother has instructed me that female dragons and dragon-kin tend to get extremely possessive and hostile when they're pregnant. I'm sorry that my mate's temperament is making your assistant uncomfortable." I shake my head from side to side slowly. "But you have to look at it from Aurora's angle. You bring a young, unmated female into her nest, while she's pregnant, around her mates. Actions like this never bode well for the invading female. As long as your assistant stays away from Aurora's mates, she should be perfectly fine." Slowly I steeple my hands in front of me in a power move.

"Let me define staying away for you. It means do not touch, do not be alone in a room with them, and absolutely by no means get your scent anywhere on them." Smirking, my eyes focus their intense gaze on Lorianne. "You can ask Dimitri what happened the last time Aurora scented another female on him. They weren't even mated yet and she shredded that woman into thousands of pieces. It took them several hours to gather up all the remains." A slight chuckle escapes my lips before I continue.

"Her beast's sick sense of humor used the woman's intestines as Christmas garland on Douglas fir trees in the middle of the forest." I cross my arms over my chest, watching the range of emotions flitter over both women's faces. There are moments of horror and fear, understanding, then back to fear again. The assistant looks back to the old crone and then states she will be in her room and will not be coming out until absolutely necessary. While this doesn't please the old crone, she understands that this is the safest bet for her assistant to live. Eventually, the old crone leaves the room, closing the door behind her. I look over at Klaus, and the amount of relief I see on his face is immeasurable. You would think I just waged the greatest battle of all times, won, and saved him by the look on his face.

"Thank you so much, Alaric. I have never in my entire life ever won a battle with my grandmother. That old she-wolf will keep attacking until she wears you down, and you just don't care anymore, you just want her to shut up. To be perfectly honest, I'm more frightened of Aurora being mad at me than her these days." Klaus and I look at each other and then bust out hysterically laughing.

We return to finish decorating the throne room, putting up the candles and lights. Klaus even thought this plan through enough to have table decorations. He wants to be able to put the different cookies out that he was having the pastry chef make for tonight. I know Christmas is two and a half days away now, but according to Klaus, it's never too early to start celebrating.

Out of the five of us, Klaus and Jayce are the most similar in temperament and thoughtfulness. While as Dominik, Dimitri, and I are battle-hardened warriors prepared to fight at a moment's notice. I leave Klaus to finish his decorations, and I head back to my suite. In the middle of the floor, Jayce, Dominik, and Dimitri are all shifted in the central living space, lying curled up with Aurora in the center, sleeping soundly.

Dominik lifts his head, and his golden eyes lock with mine. *Her beast was unsettled after eating. When we started shifting one by one, she calmed down and went to sleep. I have a feeling we will be in for a rough few months.* Dominik turns his head to look at Aurora, who has her head resting on Dimitri's bear's ribs. Dominik and Jayce are curled around Aurora tightly. Jayce has his head laying on Dimitri, right beside Aurora's, and Dominik resting his head on her hip. Shit, I can't shift here and join in. My dragon is way too big to fit. I move to the corner of the room and climb into the recliner so I can watch over my sleeping family.

CHAPTER 61
Klaus

December –

My trip home was super short. Much shorter than I would have liked it to be. So much happened in the short time we were away. Sebastian was killed, which was a freaky bonus. I mean, seriously, I got to watch it through Aurora's eyes. I know I'm not fully bonded to her yet, but still, this gift is creepy as all hell. Creepy, yet super useful. I ponder the last forty-eight hours' events and conclude that my life as I knew it is over. It's not a bad thing really, I'm looking at it as an improvement. Let's face it, all I did before was continuously train and read.

I'm just about done with my decorating and really feel like I accomplished a lot today. I grab ahold of my new book, "Once Upon a Raven" by Serenity Rayne, and head back to the suite I share with my bond mates. It's pretty late at night, so I carefully and quietly open the door to find a giant wolf and bear pile with Aurora sleeping in the middle. Apparently, I'm not the only one watching their little fuzzy snuggle fest. I look up to find Alaric sitting in his favorite recliner, waving at me. "What on Earth did I miss?" I whisper to Alaric, creeping closer to him.

He shakes his head and sits his glass of brandy down next to the decanter. "Apparently, while we were decorating, her animal wouldn't settle down, it is on edge about something. One of the twins shifted first and figured out her animal felt better that way. So everyone that could shift and fit in here did." Alaric looks at the pile-up sadly. I can tell he really wants to be there with our mate.

I grab a glass from the ensuite bar and sit in a chair on the opposite side of the table near Alaric. "If it makes you feel any better, I wouldn't fit into the pile-up either." Slowly I raise the glass to my lips and sip at the brandy. It's an excellent year, super smooth and full-bodied. Alaric and I take turns sleeping in shifts throughout the night. Without Aurora telling us what set her animal off, it is better to be safe than sorry.

The next morning comes way too early. Seriously, way too early. The first rays of the sun, of course, decide to land right in my eyes. I really want to yell "I'm blind!", but I value my life and don't want to wake the hellion, otherwise known as my mate. I motion to Alaric that I'm going for coffee and breakfast food. He writes down quickly no eggs. I make the motion for why and he imitates puking and pointing to Aurora. My eyes widen at the news, and I receive the message loud and clear.

It takes me several minutes, and a few wrong turns to finally make it down to the kitchen. I give the cooks the family's order with the request of no eggs. The chef questions that odd request, and I tell them about Aurora puking. Two of the three chefs turn pale-white and start making waffles and bacon for the group.

The older chef takes the time to tell me about when his mate was with child. He gives me fresh, whole ginger root and several bottles of water. He teaches me how to prepare it with the instructions of drinking half the bottle before eating. I prepare one bottle in front of him to make sure I do it correctly. He smiles and pats me on the back, then points to the supply closet. He tells me where everything is if I ever needed more. He is most helpful and I tell him how much I appreciate what he has done. I leave the kitchen and head back to the suite with my cart of assorted foods and drinks.

Before I enter the suite, I go over everything, making sure nothing harmful was snuck into the buffet. Everything checks out fine, so I slowly open the door, silently closing it behind me. I figure the smell of the food should wake everyone's animals up.

Aurora is the first to pop her eyes open; I see her nose twitch as she sniffs the air. "You brought me bacon?" Aurora begins to try to untangle herself from the guys. Alaric and I move over to her quickly, and each take her under one arm, lifting her out of the pile-up. She heads straight to the bacon and the selection of cheesecake pastries I picked out for her.

I move quickly and offer her the fresh ginger water. "Please, love, drink about half of this before you eat, I don't want you getting sick again." I must have pulled off the sad puppy eyes perfectly because she doesn't fight my suggestion. I help her over to the chair I had been in and bring over a folding table, placing it in front of her, then set up all of her goodies. Aurora drinks the ginger water to the halfway point, looks up to me, then over to Alaric. We both nod at her that she was safe to start eating. Slowly she eats everything that is in front of her. We all wait until she has eaten her fill before we eat what is left.

"Aurora? Do you feel up to seeing what we've set up for you?" I move the tray out of the way and offer her my hand. I assist Aurora in standing up and I swear to the gods, her belly has grown again. I watch the other three guys look puzzled at my question.

Alaric must be filling them in through the bond about my surprise because their expressions change to understanding. The twins and Dimitri raise a fist over their hearts at me. It seems to be our way of showing respect towards each other. Alaric takes Aurora's other hand, and we lead her down the hall. When we get to the throne room, I move behind Aurora and place my hands over her eyes. Alaric and Dimitri open the doors, and I carefully move Aurora into the center of the room. I wait until the guys have a chance to look around before I uncover Aurora's eyes.

Aurora moves in a slow circle, keeping one hand on me as she moves. Her eyes widen with wonder as she takes in all that Alaric and I have accomplished. The chefs start arriving, placing tray after tray of assorted cookies and pastries from my home, as well as something from each country the others came from. Dimitri whispers "it was a very Klaus Christmas" and well, that nickname stuck for our first Christmas. It is the guys' way of giving me full credit for what I have pulled together for everyone. I know back home I'm the Alpha of my pack, but here we are equals and I'm okay with that.

We spend the rest of the day tasting all of the desserts brought in by the chefs. Granted, it isn't a traditional Christmas this year because of everything that's going on. The greatest gift of all is growing within Aurora's womb. We each take turns sitting next to her and bringing her different food trays from our own homelands.

Dimitri seems like the biggest child of all. I found out from Nicodeamus the name of the town that Dimitri was born in. Luckily for me, one of the chefs in the kitchen initially came from a town not far away from there. He helped me pick out desserts from when he was young. The look on Dimitri's face is completely worth the extra effort. I now know the true meaning of what a bear hug is; that big guy practically squishes me. About mid-afternoon, Grandma Elsa decides to show up and pisses in my Cheerios.

"Klaus! Your mate should not be eating all these sweets! She needs a balanced diet, especially with meat; she's a carnivore." Grandma's arms are flailing around as if she was doing a flag routine on top of a destroyer trying to get a plane to land.

Now grandma makes the grievous error of looking at me with her eyes shifted to that of her wolf. It just so happens that Aurora is sitting next to me at the moment. Carefully, she stands up and steps towards my grandmother. We all watch in horror as the scales ripple up and down her forearms. She apparently has had enough of my grandmother's domineering ways.

"Ma'am, I don't know how things are done where you're from, but when you're a guest in someone's house, you do not yell at their mate. I'm trying to control my temper here, but this is the last straw. Klaus is the alpha of your pack, yet you decide to stand here and chastise him like he's a five-year-old pup that stole a cookie out of the cookie jar." Aurora narrows her eyes while looking at my grandmother.

Fear starts to build in the pit of my stomach. "Have some bloody respect for the man. This was a present they have done for me since none of us have been able to get out to do any kind of shopping. Klaus brought me a well-balanced breakfast with meats and cheeses and those horrid vegetables that you want me to eat, for your information." Aurora makes a yuck face after talking about the veggies. "Everything that should have been eaten has been eaten for this morning. I'm going to kindly ask you to back the fuck off, leave the goddamn room and not bother us till this evening's check-up." Aurora's eyes are glowing. We can feel the room's temperature dropping quickly. We can see the frost starting to form and gather on her long, white hair. She is doing everything she can not to shift and not lose her temper on my grandmother.

My grandmother stands there slack-jawed, looking between Aurora and myself. She is in complete shock at the way she was just spoken to. Finally, my grandmother looks around the room to see if anyone will support her and what she is trying to accomplish.

One by one, the guys look away from her and will not maintain any kind of eye contact with her, not showing any semblance of support. A gentle knock is heard at the door. All eyes are on it as it slowly opens. Unfortunately, my grandmother's assistant poking her head where it really doesn't belong, while Aurora is already mad.

Aurora attempts to start going towards the door, Alaric and I end up holding onto her tightly. We yell for the assistant to run quickly. She closes the door and we hear her steps running down the hallway. Dimitri brings over one of the pastries from his country that seems to be one of Aurora's favorites in a move of absolute brilliance. He waves the pastry in front of her face until her appetite overrules her anger. Exertion equals hunger, so the big bear figures based on what we are feeling would cause her to be hungry again.

Eventually, Aurora stops struggling between Alaric and me and grabs the pastry out of Dimitri's hand, gives him a kiss, and then pushes Alaric to sit. Once Alaric situates himself on the bean bag that we brought in for Aurora this morning, she plops down on his lap.

"Grandmother, all the pastries that are here have been made with healthy fruits and berries known to be excellent antioxidants. As well as being high in Vitamin C and other various trace minerals that you suggested she should be eating." I smile at her, being the epitome of calm and serenity. "The flour, eggs, and other ingredients are all organically sourced. Aurora is not eating anything with any kind of preservatives or chemicals in it. If the meat wasn't killed by one of us or hunted by one of us, it's not being served to her." I motion to my bond mates one by one to emphasize my point.

"We are taking the utmost caution to make sure that she's getting the best of everything. Unlike the females in our pack that only have one or two mates, she has five, plus a legion of dragons and a horde of various species of wolves." Ever so slowly, my grandmother bows her head to me and apologizes for the first time in my life.

I officially think hell has frozen over, or this is some sort of alien, and my grandmother's been abducted. We watch the old crone leave, and I close the door silently behind her. I'm congratulated, swept up in hugs and back-pats, high fives, you know, typical guy shit. Aurora is sitting on Alaric's lap, laughing her ass off. Apparently, she thinks the display between myself and the guys is the most hysterical thing she has ever seen in her entire life. I honestly don't believe that Alaric notices that while Aurora has been sitting there, she braided one side of his head. This causes the other three mates and myself to laugh hysterically right along with her.

The big, tough king is sitting there with tons of braids on the left side of his head. Then again, I think Aurora could sit there and draw dicks on his cheek, and he wouldn't care. The celebration continues well into the night, each of us trading out every hour or so, allowing Aurora to use us as her personal chair.

Aurora finally starts yawning around eleven or so, and it is time for all of us to go to bed. I can see the scales rippling along her arms, on her cheeks, and under her eyes. Her beast obviously is worried about sleeping. "I have an idea. Alaric, how big is the grand ballroom?"

Alaric stands there tapping his finger on his chin, looking around the inside of the throne room, then back over to me. "About twice the size of this room, why?"

"If we have the servants clear what furniture is there and push it against the wall, do you think your dragon would fit in there?" Alaric's eyes light up as Nicodeamus's head whips around to look at me, intrigued by my query.

Nicodeamus approaches and places a hand on my shoulder, smiling broadly at me. "Absolutely brilliant, my boy. Two dragons and all of your animals can easily fit in that room. I can turn the doors and windows to ice to make it more secure, so that way my baby girl can rest without worry." Out of the corner of my eye, I see Aurora going from mate to mate, hugging everyone. She announces she needs to go get changed into her pajamas, and she'll join us in a few moments. Jayce and Dominik escort Aurora out of the room and back to our chambers.

The rest of us practically race down the hall heading to the grand ballroom to rearrange it. By the time Aurora comes in, the room is all settled. Alaric and Nico are in their dragon forms. Dimitri and I are waiting in our human forms to assist Aurora with whatever she needs. In typical Aurora fashion, she arrives making a statement. She is riding on the back of Dominik's dire wolf. Jayce is walking alongside her in his human form, making sure she doesn't slide off. If dragons could laugh, the noise that Nicodeamus and Alaric are making would qualify as laughter.

"What?! I'm tired!" Aurora states as she looks between all of us standing there, watching us try not to laugh our asses off. Jayce helps Aurora slide off of his brother's back and onto the ground. Her eyes move between Alaric and her father, and they light up instantly. She walks over to both dragons as they turn and lower their heads to her.

She reaches up and strokes both of their maws, as well as placing a kiss on each of their cheeks. Ever so carefully, she moves between the two great beasts, trying to figure out exactly where she wants to sleep tonight. Alaric and Nicodeamus's heads turn and follow Aurora's movements. Aurora places her hand on Alaric's wing and looks up at him. "Love, can I sleep under your wing tonight?" Aurora tilts her head left then right, looking into Alaric's dragon's eyes.

Alaric's body shifts slightly so that he is leaning back a bit more than before. Ever so carefully, he lifts his wing out of the way to allow Aurora to step under it. Dimitri moves and helps Aurora up onto the top of Alaric's hind leg. The way he is lying creates the perfect area for her to lay safely. Once Dimitri is sure she is safe where she is, he gets out of the way, and Alaric lowers his wing. Aurora is wholly encased in Alaric's thick leather wing. I honestly don't think she could get much safer.

"What's causing Aurora's need to sleep with our animals?" I cautiously ask the others. Nicodeamus shifts back to his human form and pulls on his robe that he had sitting nearby.

"I have several theories about that, Klaus. The first, it's a safety thing. Her beast knows that she can't shift fully anymore. It's concerned for its baby's safety. The second, I think that Ulrick being here, as well as the damage that Sebastian has already caused here, behind the scenes has her on edge." Nicodemus begins to pace the room in front of us, pondering what may be setting his daughter off.

"Another issue is that she has no idea, exactly, where Elena is. I think if we could figure out where she's hiding, Aurora may settle down just a little bit." Nicodeamus taps his chin several times. "I highly doubt it though, because she is who she is. My poor daughter has been hiding since the moment of her birth. Now that she has revealed herself, she's constantly hunted or having to battle to protect herself. It's not the life I wanted for my child, but we couldn't have known the level of dissension in the ranks. We couldn't have predicted that we had enemies living amongst us that would turn on us when they did." He stops pacing and turns to face us.

"Right now, if half my thought process is correct, without knowing exactly who here is, friend or foe, she is not going to settle down. Growing up without her mother, everything from the Ascension to now, she's had to figure out on her own. It's probably a terrifying journey for her, and it's more than likely the reason why she's always quick to shift and jump into a defensive stance." He shakes his head from side to side, looking sad over what his daughter has been through.

"Being a hybrid doesn't make it any easier either. As much as she looks more wolven than dragon, her tendencies are all dragon. I never would have guessed she would have taken after me more than her mother. In one way, she and I are both in the same boat, dragons unable to fly. However, she does have the advantage of a mate with wings, and for that Alaric, I thank you for being by her side." Alaric bows his head to Nicodeamus in thanks, then he curls up tightly, making sure that Aurora is well protected.

I pay attention to everything that's being said by Nicodeamus, and his words bear great wisdom. Being the only Lycan here, I genuinely don't fit in with the others, except for Aurora. I do feel like the odd man out, being the last to join this ragtag bunch. There's been so much betrayal and heartbreak for this poor woman that my chest aches thinking about it. I know it's only a matter of time before she fully claims Dimitri and me. Once that's been accomplished, she will be at full power, and whatever other gifts that she shall gain from Dimitri and I will only help her cause in the future.

We make sure that all the doors to the Great Hall are locked, all the windows are sealed and blocked before we get ready to settle in for the night. I have a feeling, sleeping in here as our animals will soon become routine. Aurora will need us to keep her calm and allow her to feel safe as she rests. There are only two months left until she gives birth, hopefully, less. Even though the actual holiday is still only a few days away, I spend it here with Aurora and my bond mates every day it feels like Christmas.

CHAPTER 62
Klaus

December -

~Christmas morning two days later~

Three nights in a row we've shuffled the sleeping arrangements so that our beasts could sleep near Aurora for her security. Local dignitaries are due to arrive again today for the actual Christmas celebration. I manage to get up before my bond mates, and sneak my way into the kitchen to gather breakfast for everyone. Just when I think I have managed to pull it off, I look over my shoulder to find Jayce watching me load the service cart.

"Morning, Jayce! Mind giving me a hand, so we don't have to drag strangers into Aurora's nesting area?" Learning all these dragon terms for everything is really starting to make my brain hurt. Unfortunately, it's necessary to keep everything in an orderly fashion for Aurora's comfort.

"Sure, man, tell me what you need help with." Jayce comes over, and I point to the various drinks and juices on the counter that the chef has left out for us. We arrange the two trays and the carts as well. We walk back down the hall to the grand ballroom to surprise our bond mates with breakfast.

As we get closer, we notice frost lining the hallway. We pick up our pace, running as we push the carts. The doors are covered in ice, about two inches thick. I shift quickly and begin to claw at the ice. After I finally make it through, Jayce and I burst into the room to find my grandmother's assistant Lorraine being held under Alaric's dragon's foot. Aurora is behind Dimitri's bear and Dominik's wolf. Nicodeamus has shifted back to his human form. He stands there yelling at Lorraine about the poisoned stake she has attempted to kill Aurora with. My grandmother comes rushing in, crying and screaming at Alaric to release Lorraine. I shift back to my human form and grab hold of my grandmother.

"Grandma, she tried to kill Aurora with that stake." I point to the stake on the ground not far from Lorraine's prone form.

Elsa looks between Lorraine and the stake several times, then begins yelling at her in German, questioning her. Apparently, Vladimir had threatened to kill her sister if she didn't kill Aurora. We all share a look, then Aurora moves forward, now riding Dimitri's bear. Her eyes shift to that of her beast as she and Alaric lock eyes. We watch the black slits in both of their eyes pulse, expanding and contracting as she speaks to him through the bond.

"Lorraine, I now sentence you to death for the attempted assassination of your monarch." Aurora looks up to Alaric and nods her head once. Alaric applies his full weight to Lorraine's body, squishing her like a bug. Aurora finds it funny when Lorraine's head shoots off like a cork from a champagne bottle.

My grandmother stands there in shock, crying and staring at the bloody, squished remnants of what used to be her assistant. I really look at my mate now, and that silly woman is in my sleep pants and Jayce's sweatshirt, her hair is up in another messy bun, yet again adorned by her ruby crown. "I smell bacon, Dimitri! Tally ho!" Aurora leans forward and lightly kicks Dimitri like you would a horse to get it moving. Dimitri follows his nose out of the grand ballroom and down the hall.

"When the hell did this happen?" I look between Nicodeamus and the now-human Alaric.

"Apparently, Aurora's gut instincts were correct about Lorraine. She snuck in here shortly after you and Jayce had left. Nicodeamus and I were awake and only had one membrane over our eyes, giving the appearance we were sleeping." Alaric smirks as he motions between himself and Nico. "We left Aurora exposed between us just to bait Lorraine into our trap. Dimitri and Dominik were awakened, using our bond to alert them to what was going on. They pretended to still be asleep until I sprung the trap." Alaric smiles broadly as he motions towards Dominik.

"Dominik grabbed Aurora by the sweatshirt and dragged her out of the way, while Dimitri moved to protect Aurora. It was rather brilliant planning on Nicodeamus's part, really. Being able to speak through the bond makes life a ton easier. Thankfully, not too many people know that we can communicate that way," Alaric says as Dimitri walks closer with his precious cargo.

Aurora has the plate of bacon in her hands and a bottle of orange juice under her arm. "Best morning ever! No puking and I got to see a head go flying like a cork!" Her eyes widen, and her eyebrows raise in elation. "Oh, and bacon. We can't forget the bacon." Aurora nods happily, occasionally leaning forward to wave bacon at Dimitri. His long bear tongue sticks out and wraps around the bacon, taking it from Aurora. Her eyes go wide, and I can see the gears turning.

"I wonder if I can convince Dimitri to put his bear tongue for a better use? Like me?" Aurora wiggles her eyebrows and Dimitri starts choking on his bacon. His bear is coughing so hard that Dominik grabs Aurora off of his back, allowing Dimitri to shift back.

Dimitri stands there, bent over in all his naked glory, hacking up a lung trying to dislodge whatever is stuck in his throat. "Woman, are you trying to kill me!?"

"No?" She attempts to look utterly innocent as she peeks around from behind Dominik. "But seriously, you can't do shit like that and have me not think of your tongue between my legs, for God's sakes. I'm pregnant, not dead, you know." She stands there with her hands on her hips, attempting to look serious. Meanwhile, her eyes drift around the room to all her naked mates, each one sporting a boner, including me. All because she mentioned licking her nether regions.

I just realized my poor grandmother is standing there, slack-jawed, looking around the room. Her cheeks are a brilliant red, but she decides to throw her two cents in. "Nicodeamus, I can see why your daughter is pregnant. Bravo, my girl, bravo!" Grandma does a golf clap then promptly exits the room.

At this moment, I don't know if I should be embarrassed or... well, yeah, embarrassed is the right feeling for this moment. Aurora begins to look at the five of us and starts shuffling us around in a fucked up lineup. "Aurora, what in the world are you doing?" I raise my right eyebrow as she shuffles us into a line. Dimitri is first, then it's Alaric, Jayce, me, then Dominik last.

Dominik looks up and down the line-up, then throws his hands up in the air. "Why the fuck am I last? I'm the first mate." Apparently, Aurora's lineup has him upset.

"Dom, baby, look down. I put you guys in order of peen size. Dimitri's is a world ender. Look at the size of that thing; it's freaking huge, Alaric's isn't as long, but it's just as thick." Aurora moves down the line-up, motioning to our members, describing how they appear to her. "Jayce's is a really nice balance of length and thickness. Klaus's is not as thick as Jayce's, but it's got some good length to it. Dominik, your dick is just right and very comfortable to ride." Aurora managed to make Dimitri blush, Jayce, and Alaric high five in a single move, and Dominik starts to compare his dick to the rest of ours.

From this line-up, I can tell you for sure that Dimitri and Alaric will never get any ass play from Aurora. Jayce has a fifty percent chance, I have a seventy-five percent chance, and Dominik has a one hundred percent chance.

~LATER THAT **day**~

The day proceeds like expected. Aurora is all over the place, ripping into presents that the visiting dignitaries have brought for her. It is quite a comical sight if you ask me. Dimitri is in his Great Bear form, being used as a back support. Dominik and Jayce are in their Dire Wolf forms, investigating every present and person that wishes to get close to Aurora. I am in charge of keeping Aurora fed and her drink full—easy enough. I snap a few pictures of Aurora sitting on her pile of pillows, with Dimitri's bear sitting tall behind her, looming over top of her. His gigantic paws on either side of her body and her back against his bear's chest.

Alaric is going about his kingly duty, greeting everyone as they approach then introducing them to Aurora. Every once in a while, there is a potty break needed and it becomes a procession. Aurora tells Dimitri, he lies down, and she climbs up onto his back. When his bear starts moving, the twins will flank him, escorting them to and from the bathroom. All I can do is shrug my shoulders and clean up after our pregnant mate. Aurora returns, and the gift-receiving line resumes well into the night.

Last to arrive is Alaric's mom and sister. Two guards are assisting, bringing in two large boxes with them. I can visibly see Aurora tense up the minute they start entering her space. Aurora scoots further under Dimitri, and she pulls Jayce closer to her by his tail.

Alaric has notices what Aurora is doing and decides to meet his mother and sister halfway. Both begin to protest about not being allowed closer. Aurora scoots herself backward and out, under Dimitri's arm, and still pulling Jayce with her. Now she's got my attention. Dominik is moving to block the front of Dimitri. I creep around the back, and I catch Aurora climbing onto Jayce's back, getting ready to make a fast getaway.

Being the good mate that I am, I walk casually to the door in the back of the throne room and stand ready to open the door for them. Alaric looks at me briefly and begins to maneuver his mother and sister so that their backs are facing where Aurora once was. When he is in position I nod to Jayce and Aurora, they sneak to the door, and I let them out.

I follow behind them, making sure no one is following us. We make it to her room, and Aurora busts out laughing over her well-executed escape plan. "I can't believe we pulled that off. If I had to sit there and deal with his mother and his sister, I think I was going to make Dimitri eat them," Aurora says with all seriousness.

I just have to ask the burning question. "What is it about those two that you don't like, Aurora?" Jayce steps out of his room, pulling his shirt over his head, indeed, just as interested as I am.

"Gut instinct," Aurora says, sounding quite bored. "They just set my fur and scales on edge. I'm not comfortable around them. If the mother was such a crown supporter, she should have sent her people to guard my father. Instead, she did nothing." Just as Aurora finishes the sentence, Nicodeamus walks in, catching the tail end of the conversation.

He walks over and wraps his arm around his daughter. "Trust your gut, daughter. It's your animal's instincts that will keep you alive." Nicodeamus starts laughing to himself, then looks at the two of us.

"Congratulations on a brilliant escape plan there, boys, excellent teamwork." Nicodeamus looks down at Aurora and gently moves so that he can touch her belly. "Your child is quite strong, I can feel its power already. Stubborn little hatchling won't tell me if it's a boy or a girl, just like someone else I know wouldn't either." He playfully raises an eyebrow at Aurora and smiles at her.

Aurora starts to giggle and rub her belly. "Silly baby, tell Grandpa your secrets. Mommy wants to know." She continued to rub her belly then freezes, she goes so far as to stop breathing. Her eyes become that of her beast, and frost begins to coat her skin.

"Nicodeamus! What's happening? Is she alright?!" I nervously ask him. Jayce is in panic mode and begins to summon the others. The door flies open several seconds later. Aurora takes a deep breath, then freezes yet again.

"I feel the baby through the bond," Alaric says before he goes and lays his hands over Aurora's, on her belly. He, too stands way too still for comfort, Aurora's frost begins to coat him slowly. The rest of us are concerned as fuck, and Nicodeamus is standing there smiling.

"The baby is talking to its parents. I believe we will know its gender shortly." Nicodeamus moves away and begins to pour glasses of brandy, ready to celebrate.

Suddenly, there's a burst of frost. Aurora and Alaric stand there smiling at each other. Slowly, Aurora turns to look at each of us; tears are threatening to roll down her cheeks. "We have a daughter." Aurora starts to cry, resting her forehead on Alaric's chest.

Alaric wraps his thick arms around her, holding her tightly against his chest. "We have decided to name her Tiamat Andrea Kraus. Tiamat was the dragon Goddess of Chaos; Andrea, after Andre and his great sacrifice," Alaric says proudly as he kisses the top of Aurora's head. Nicodeamus moves forward and gently rubs his daughter's back. The look he and Alaric have on their faces says it all. We are witnessing a real miracle. The first daughter of a first daughter that happens to be the daughter of a first daughter herself. Three generations of first daughters is unheard of for any species, especially dragons. Alaric and Aurora make room and bring Nicodeamus into their little hugfest. They are all snuggling in, all nice and tight. The three of them are sobbing happy tears. Let's face it, Nicodeamus went from no family to a daughter, to now having a granddaughter on the way.

I look around the room at the rest of us in turn. Aurora is far enough along that the baby can communicate somewhat with her parents. Each mate is taking the news of a daughter differently. Most of us are weeping tears of joy. Dimitri is trying his best to hold himself together after hearing the name. Jayce and I move to embrace Dimitri and hold onto the big guy as he fights hard to resist crying.

Dominik is standing watch over us all, allowing us to have our moment to process what's happened. We all take turns swapping who is hugging whom. It comes down to Aurora and Dimitri last. The big guy drops down on his knees before her and kisses her stomach. We depart the room, leaving those two alone. They've had the roughest time with their relationship, and it isn't even their fault. Sebastian and his mother screwed them over and damaged their bond. I can tell you one thing: I wouldn't want to be Elena at this point. Aurora is going to gut her when she finds her. I retire to my suite for the evening.

Best Christmas ever.

CHAPTER 63
Dimitri

I HAVE DECIDED that I am not leaving Aurora's side unless she asks me to. I'm concerned for her safety and especially her health while carrying her first child. Ulrich is still stirring up trouble on occasion, causing minor incidents periodically. I have a feeling that fucker is going to try something when we least expect it.

Little does that rat bastard know, I'm constantly expecting it. This morning, I'm escorting Aurora into the throne room for the typical first week of the month meet and greet with the local nobles. Alaric is overseeing the training of the troops for the next leg of our journey. Aurora has been in deep thought, receiving intel from other eagle shifters that she had me hire to work for her.

In the last few months, not only has she managed to locate Elena but she has been tracking her movements. If I know Aurora, she's plotting to attack Elena the minute she's healed from giving birth to her daughter. Two War Dragons have answered Aurora's call to arms. They remain in the corners of the throne room, acting as extra security for her. I've personally vetted these two and remember them from Anca's rule. It's interesting to know the same two War Dragons that used to escort Anca now watch over Aurora. They are loyal to a fault; they have also confirmed my suspicions that Vladimir still lives in the old castle. He's disfigured from Nicodeamus's fire, but alive, sadly.

Ulrich is back in the throne room, starting shit again about having his title stolen by a mutt. Aurora looks at both of the War Dragons and halts them in their progress towards Ulrich. "You still haven't learned, Ulrich? I am of two royal lines and two mighty species. Your ass will never sit upon this throne as long as any of my bloodline or my mates breathe. Stand down and live, proceed and die," Aurora states in a very bored tone. Her hand rests upon the swell of her stomach. She looks to be the size of a woman that's five months along now.

I move slowly around the room, positioning myself not far behind Ulrich, just in case he gets stupid enough to try anything. From somewhere behind me, I hear a rustling and a click. Before I can react, a dart goes whizzing past me, right at Aurora.

Ulrich side steps it shortly after the click, proving he knows about it. Aurora's shifted hand comes up without missing a beat, and the dart bounces off her heavily armored scales. A single nod of her head sends the War Dragons into action.They grab the man behind me and Ulrich.

Son of a bitch, Aurora was aware of the plot to assassinate her. Jayce and Dominik come bursting into the room fully shifted, as well as a fully shifted Klaus. Aurora rolls her eyes at the three of them, then bows her head to me. "Dimitri and his elite guard had me protected." Aurora raises her shifted hand, makes a fist, and holds it over her heart, slightly bowing her head to each of us in turn. "Bring forth the assassin and his boss." Dominik and Jayce take their place on either side of Aurora, Klaus stations himself off to the side, watching in his Lycan form.

"Do either of you have anything useful to say in your defense?" Aurora tilts her head to the left, then to the right, studying both of them. Her beast's faint white glow fills her eyes. Slowly, they bleed liquid mercury with black dragon slits. I'm already signaling for Klaus to leave and get food.

Ulrich starts laughing to the point of tears rolling down his cheeks. "Child, I have lived longer than you and shall continue to outlive you for centuries to come. You can't touch me!" There is his fatal mistake. Aurora's eyes move to Jayce and give him a nod. Jayce lunges forward and bites deeply into Ulrich's calf, injecting his toxin into Ulrich's bloodstream. Jayce moves back and rests his head on Aurora's lap to be petted.

"You know what, Ulrich, you're right. I don't have to touch you to kill you. That tightness you feel in your chest is from my mate's toxin. It's slowly causing your platelets to explode, and it's increasing your clotting factor. So, in a short, ten or so minutes from now, you'll be one huge blood clot. Your body will be deprived of oxygen and your lungs will collapse from increased pressure." A wicked grin graces Aurora's ruby lips as she watches Ulrich starting to look panicked. "The best part? I didn't have to get dirty, and you die a horrible death, just like the horrible person you are." Aurora smiles sweetly at Ulrich as she watches him die slowly with sadistic glee. She is definitely her great-grandmother's descendant. The original Blood Queen would be pleased with her bloodline right now.

Aurora's eyes slowly move to lock with mine, and in my mind I see what she wants me to do. I reach over, taking the assassin away from the War Dragons, then drag him before Aurora. I shift my right hand, allowing my bear's claws to be seen. I press them to the man's throat as he begins to beg for his life. He spills every ounce of information he has within his memory. As he confesses, Aurora has the War Dragons empty out the throne room. The assassin names every aristocrat that has anything to do with the plot against Aurora. I can tell by the way her eyes look, she's letting Nicodeamus and Alaric see through her eyes. They see and hear what she's hearing—scary yet effective for communicating over long distances. Aurora snaps out of her trance and issues a kill order for all those named. The twins rapidly tear out of the room. Alaric is waiting with the Black Dragons for those that try to escape.

Me, I get the pleasure of decapitating the assassin. Slowly, I begin to apply pressure to his soft, thin neck. Second by second, I watch his flesh flex then break under my claws. Rivulets of blood begin to roll down his pale, white flesh.

There's a gleam in Aurora's eyes as I take my time carrying out her orders. I can tell Aurora is pleased as my claws cut first through his windpipe, then his esophagus. The assassin begins to struggle harder in my grip as blood leaks into his lungs. A slight nod is given by Aurora—playtime is over. His head falls free off of his shoulders and rolls across the floor, leaving a bloody trail behind it. Aurora smiles, watching his head roll across the floor like a beach ball. Carefully, she leans over and grabs a drum stick off of the tray that Klaus has left her. "Not bad for a Monday, D. Two dead in the throne room, and another nine to die by any means possible. Eleven really isn't a horrible amount, I honestly was expecting it to be much worse." Aurora smiles as she stands up, stretching carefully.

I have to admit, she's even more beautiful pregnant. Her curves are fuller, and that ass, damn, I just want to bite it and slap it a few times to watch it jiggle. Aurora raises an eyebrow at me, then looks down at my cock. Fucking traitor. I roll my eyes and offer her my hand to help her down. Quickly, she shifts her hand back to human and takes my hand in hers.

Aurora is still smirking at me as we walk. Damn my cock for giving away my thoughts. I lead Aurora back to her part of the private chambers. Her eyes cautiously dart around her room before she enters. I truly wish she didn't have to worry so much right now. Aurora should be just enjoying her pregnancy, not watching for assassins at every turn. "I'm going to draw you a nice hot bath so you can relax some. It'll be good for you and the baby." Slowly, Aurora nods and follows me into her vast bathroom. I swear her tub could be confused for a swimming pool.

I get the bath three-quarters of the way full when Aurora stops me. She's standing next to me, completely naked. "Join me?" she asks softly. I can see the fear of rejection in her eyes. I thank the gods for this chance, to have such a wondrous mate as I do. As I slowly nod my head, agreeing to join her, her face lights up.

Aurora's small hand rests between my pecs as she backs me away from the tub. What is this girl up to? Aurora's nimble fingers make short work of the buttons on my shirt. Her small hands glide up my chest to my shoulders as she slides the shirt off of me. I never would have thought in all these years getting undressed could be so sensual.

Aurora locks eyes with me, then tilts her head to the side, asking permission as her hands rest on my belt. This Alpha female, probably one of the strongest creatures in existence, is asking my permission. Again, I lightly nod my head, granting her permission. I feel like a teenager right now. My palms are sweaty, my heart is racing. Honestly, I'm scared I'm going to fuck this up.

Aurora, sensing my feelings, stops just as she undoes my belt. "You can tell me to stop, D, it's okay. I know I'm being rather forward with you. I need you." Aurora looks up at me with those sad eyes, and it crushes me. I reach down and cup both of her cheeks, kissing her gently. My tongue dances at the seam of her lips, trying to gain access.

Aurora opens her mouth to me. Our tongues dance and glide over one another, causing my cock to pulse with anticipation. As we kiss, I lower my hands to rid myself of my pants and boxers. Quickly, I toe off my shoes and step out of my pants the rest of the way. Aurora starts to giggle at my antics, then her eyes go wide, looking at the size of my shaft. I smirk at her. Yeah, that is definitely a confidence booster.

I help Aurora carefully get into the tub and quickly follow in behind her. My bear is pushing, practically shoving me to claim her right now. I, on the other hand, have different plans. I slowly move her to the far side of the tub, where the stairs are. My hands slide under her arms, and I lift her effortlessly to sit on the top stair. Aurora raises an eyebrow at me, curious to see what I do next. I lean forward over her, the hair on my taunt abs lightly brushing her belly, making her giggle.

"I'll be gentle, I promise." My voice is rough with desire, my Romanian accent heavy, as I speak to her. I watch as she looks me over slowly, a soft smile plays upon her lips as she leans forward briefly. The tips of her fingers ghost over my skin setting my nerve endings on fire. Anticipation builds in the back of my mind. I know what I want to do, what I need to do. Over two hundred years of fighting my instincts and feelings and it all comes down to this moment. The way she's looking at me makes me feel like the only man in the world. I just hope that I can show her how much and how deep my love for her is.

CHAPTER 64
Dimitri

JANUARY -

Lightly, I kiss her lips, then begin to kiss a trail down her body, painfully slow. I descend upon each breast as if I'm starving, sucking and flicking her nipple with my tongue. Aurora's moans fill the air and drive me to do more. Her fingers thread through my thick hair, holding me to her breast. Her powerful thighs come up and attempt to wrap around me. After several moments, I kiss my way over to her other breast. She's writhing beneath me, trying to shove me to where she wants me most.

It's so odd to me to know that right now, she's all mine. I have her full, undivided attention. I release her nipple with a pop. Ever so slowly, I kiss my way down her body, my lips feather-light on the swell of her stomach. I raise Aurora's legs, one by one, and place them on my shoulders. She had admired my bear's tongue earlier, I guess it's time to show her what it can do. My bear and I are in full agreement: please Aurora, and make her scream our name.

I widen and lengthen my tongue to be close to that of my bear. I lower my head between Aurora's legs, her feminine musk is intoxicating to me. My tongue stretches out to its full length, and I lick her ever so slowly. Her sopping wet folds are as sweet as honey. I delve my tongue deep within her heated canal. Aurora gasps, then moans, sinking her fingers into my hair again.

Aurora attempts to grind herself on my face. I pull back just enough to tease the tip of her clit with my tongue. Her muscles jump under my fingers as she strains, trying to get me to apply more pressure. I give Aurora a cheeky grin as she stares at me, panting heavily. My eyes drift down to her weeping lips and I drag my index finger through her sticky, sweet fluids. As my eyes lock with Aurora's, I feel my bear come to the surface. Ever so slowly, my tongue slides free of my parted lips to lick Aurora's essence off my finger. Aurora's mouth drops open, and her canines descend slowly; her nostrils flare, trying to catch more of my scent.

I lower my head again and lap at her wet folds, dining on the sweetness leaking from my mate's hot, welcoming core. Aurora's moans become louder the more I furiously work her clit with the flat of my tongue. Gently, I begin to probe her core with my fingers, stretching her, preparing her for my girth. For several minutes I bring Aurora so close to orgasm, then stop, letting her body calm down some again. Most extended session of foreplay ever, it's been nearly forty minutes and I've yet to allow her a single orgasm. Cruel? Yes, very. When I am truly ready for her to come, it will be glorious.

One more time, I lower my face and allow my tongue to lap at her sweet wet folds. I suck and nip at her sensitive flesh. I drop my right hand to lightly stroke my engorged cock. I ache horribly. As much as I'm prolonging this for Aurora, I am giving myself the worst case of blue balls in the history of the world. I know deep in my heart that the wait is well worth it. Hell, I've waited this long, right?

Aurora's muscles begin to twitch and spasm. Just when I know she's balanced on the precipice, I stop licking again. This time, I carefully slide my cock deep within her. Inch by inch, I take my time, sinking ever so deeply within my mate. Softly she gasps and grabs onto my biceps. I lower my head slowly and capture her lips in a gentle kiss. I feel myself sink to the hilt, my balls resting against her ass. I give Aurora several moments, kissing her passionately to allow her to adjust to my girth and length.

We're not called Great Bears for nothing. Obviously, it's not just the size of our beasts but the size of our cocks as well. When I'm absolutely positive that Aurora is ready for me to move, I slowly withdraw almost all the way to the tip, just leaving the head of my cock within her. Painfully slow, I slide all the way back into the base again and gyrate my hips slightly. I have her full attention now. She's clawing at my arms, wanting me to move faster. I'm more concerned for the babe's well-being within her rather than rushing either of our orgasms.

Just to make her happy, I start to move slightly faster than I did before, keeping a steady rhythm and the perfect angle to hit all the right spots. I feel her muscles tightening around my shaft, beginning those early movements just before her orgasm. I roll Aurora onto her side and throw her left leg over my shoulder and wrap her right one around my hip.

At this angle, I've changed how I'm hitting her g-spot. Her orgasm almost instantaneously hits her with that one slight change. Her muscles crush down rhythmically hard upon my painfully engorged cock. I'm so close to blowing my own load, it's not even funny at this point. I keep thrusting deep within her, mindful of the babe she's carrying, not wanting to cause it harm.

Aurora screams fill her bathroom, echoing off the walls as if she is screaming bloody murder. Water is sloshing everywhere, coating the floor, the walls and anything within reach of us. I hear the doorknob to the bathroom jiggle slightly, barely over the noises that she's making. I look up, the amber-gold glow of my bear's eyes are locked and focused on that door. Whoever is about to enter will know the true meaning of pain if we are disturbed.

Jayce apparently is the poor soul sent to make sure we are okay. I bare my teeth at him and growl deeply, threatening his life at this moment. His eyebrows shoot up in understanding, and he backs out of the room just as quickly as he arrived. At least one of the others was smart enough to send the Omega, who wouldn't be perceived as a threat. Aurora is so lost in her sensations that she doesn't even notice anything is going on around her.

I change the pace of our mating and roll her onto her back again. My arms band around her waist and her upper back; I lift her up as if she weighs nothing. I switch positions with her and sit on the seat, barely in the water, allowing her to straddle my lap and use the rail next to her for support. This new position has me buried so deep in her it takes several moments for her to adjust to it.

The faint glow of her beast's eyes are starting to shine through. I know right now she is defenseless and unable to shift to protect herself. I pull her close to me and begin to nibble at her neck, spurring her on, trying to get her to start moving. My balls are drawn up so tight against my body, aching and begging for release. Aurora adjusts how she's sitting, then begins to bounce as hard as she can, riding my cock for all it's worth.

I'm so close. My large hands grip her ass cheeks, helping set the rhythm that I know will get us both off. Aurora doesn't last long on top. She's already starting to fatigue from the effort of carrying her own weight, plus that of her child. Good thing I'm really fucking strong, now isn't it? I keep the momentum going and lean forward, just as I get to the point of release. I nuzzle her neck and move her hair away from her shoulder before sinking my canines in deeply, marking her as mine.

The minute my canines sink into her flesh, her orgasm hits her like a freight train. Aurora's muscles begin to crush down and milk me for all that I'm worth; my seed pulses out in thick streaming jets, filling her already full womb. Several seconds pass, and I'm in a complete state of bliss, then the burning, stinging sensation of her canines sinking into my flesh hits. I'll be damned. I feel like a ruddy teenager, orgasming quickly for a second time, all because she bit me.

In my heart and soul, I feel the bond snap into place. It's like nothing I've ever felt before in my entire existence. The first bond that Aurora and I shared was nothing like this. Oh, I feel her in my heart and soul. I can feel her emotions, her joy, her elation, and ever so faintly, I can feel the life within her. I lick Aurora's wound ever so gently, making sure that I help speed up the healing process. Aurora carefully withdraws her canines from my shoulder, then begins to lick it clean and kiss where she bit me.

When she's done, she leans forward and places her forehead against my throat, snuggling in to be close to me. I band my thick arms around her and hold her tightly, not wanting to let go. The water in the bath starts to cool, so my next step would be to maneuver us to the shower to clean up after our fun. "Baby? We need to go get cleaned up now," I say softly to Aurora.

"If we must… I'm perfectly happy right here." Aurora kisses my neck, then wraps her arms around it. I slide my arm under her ass and stand up carefully. I slowly head to the walk-in shower and turn on the water, waiting for it to get warm. Gradually, my flaccid cock escapes Aurora's warm canal. She sighs softly and nuzzles in closer to my throat. A thump is felt against my abdomen; I believe it's her baby that moved. Aurora lifts her head and looks at her stomach, then back at me. "Did you feel that too?" she asks softly, almost whispering it to me.

I calmly nod my head at her and smile. "Thank you for that, my love. It's truly a precious gift I've been blessed with." I gently rest my hand on her stomach, about where I felt the baby move. We stand still for several moments. Eventually, the baby moves again. It's a fantastic feeling, the baby's soft bump against my hand, and the look of wonder upon Aurora's face. The accelerated gestational period because of being mostly dragon is intense. Three months is such a short period of time for her body to go through all its changes.

Carefully, I carry Aurora into the shower and set her down. I know her favorite shampoo and conditioner by heart. I proceed to work her thick white hair into a good lather before rinsing it. I wash her hair at least twice how she likes it, then I massage in the conditioner, making sure not to get it up into her roots.

I reach for the washcloth when Aurora slaps my hand away. She looks up at me sternly, then points at the bench in the shower. "Sit!" is all she says.

I comply quickly. After all, I don't want this little hellion angry at me. I watch her go through all of her different scrubs and washes. I swear, I think she bought out the damn store the last time we went shopping. Aurora settles on a Himalayan rock salt scrub, soap thing. I watch Aurora load up her loofa and move towards me. Is she seriously going to bathe me? My eyes widen in shock, and it causes Aurora to pause.

"Did I do something wrong, D? I just want to take care of you." Aurora's tone sounds defeated. Fuck, I don't want her to feel that way.

I rise to my full height and bend down to kiss her lips ever so gently. "Never, Aurora. You haven't done a thing wrong. I'm so used to taking care of you that the thought of you taking care of me shocked me. I'm sorry, love." I lower my forehead to rest against hers, hoping she understands. Just as we are having our moment, Alaric opens the shower door, his dragon eyes glowing as he looks at the two of us.

I lift my head slowly and sigh. "I'll leave you two alone, I guess."

I prepare to leave the shower stall when Aurora's little hand grips my wrist. "You will do no such thing. Go sit on the bench again." Aurora pulls me back then gently shoves me towards the bench. Her head whips around to Alaric, who looks quite embarrassed at the moment.

Aurora takes his hands and places them on her stomach, remaining still for a few moments. I watch Alaric's eyes widen, then look between Aurora and her belly. I have never seen Alaric smile so broadly in all this time. "We need to celebrate. Our daughter is quite active. Um, sorry for the disturbance." Alaric spins to quickly leave when Aurora grabs his wrist and stops him. Her hand comes up and pulls on Alaric's beard, getting him to lower his head. As he does, Aurora kisses him, then sends him on his way.

We take our time washing every single inch of each other. This one-on-one time is very much needed, it allows us to build a solid foundation outside of the guardian figure and child one we have developed over the years. Aurora and I take the time to dry and dress each other. In a sense, I have it easier than the others. But in another sense, I have it much harder. I was her sworn protector for over two hundred years. We return to the dining hall, hand in hand. Apparently, Alaric wants to celebrate his daughter's first movements.

CHAPTER 65

Aurora

JANUARY-

I ARRIVE in the dining hall, right in the middle of a party that the boys apparently decided to throw. The party itself could be for one of a million things. The first reason could be that my daughter has decided to make her presence known. The second reason could be finally completing the bond with Dimitri. The third reason, it's been almost two weeks since the last time that we've had to kill somebody for attempting to try to kill me—doubtful, but it's a nice thought.

I watch the guys as they pass out their bro hugs, back claps, and steins of beer. Silently, I walk into the room and lean against the closest wall, watching them and their funny antics. Wouldn't you know, my father is the one that notices me first. Slowly, I shake my head, trying to signal him not to reveal that I'm here. He gives me a quick wink of his eye, then goes and refills his stein.

The guys are having pep talks with Klaus, trying to reassure him that his time will come. He seems somewhat dejected because I had chosen to take Dimitri before him, even though I had bitten him first. Klaus really doesn't understand the history that Dimitri and I have and how long we have been denied our bond. I'll have to speak with him one-on-one later and let him know that he does matter greatly to me.

Eventually, I feel Alaric reach out through the bond, trying to sense where I am. Dammit, I'm busted. He finds me in a matter of seconds. A smile creeps slowly across his perfectly plump lips as he looks at me. His right-hand raises and he gradually does the come here signal with his index finger.

I roll my eyes at him while shaking my head no. I'm feeling a little defiant at the moment, so I stomp my right foot and use my left hand with my index finger pointing directly at the ground, demanding he comes to me. The other guys all look shocked as their eyes move quickly between myself and Alaric. He's definitely more Alpha than the rest of them, but he's not more Alpha than I am. My father forewarned us that there will be times we would test each other's dominance. Apparently, now is one of those times.

Jayce and Klaus both look panicked as their eyes move between Alaric and me. They huddle up tight, obviously trying to decide what to do to help diffuse the situation. Dimitri starts laughing, almost hysterically, over what's going on. He claps Alaric on the back and tells him good luck, that once I've made up my mind, there's no changing it. I just smile, ever so sweetly, looking at Dimitri, and I lightly bow my head to him for acknowledging the fact that I am one stubborn bitch.

I feel the scale on my chest getting too warm. Alaric is pushing his dominance through it. Smart male, he's not blanketing the entire room with it, just me. I start to laugh that maniacal laugh of mine when I know I can gain the upper hand. I draw in a deep breath, ever so slowly, finding my center. In my mind's eye, I reach out through time and space, feeling my dragon family. I start to draw upon my father, as well as Alaric himself.

The moment the guys catch on, they turn to stare at Nicodeamus and Alaric as to what I'm doing. My eyes begin to take on a very haunting look; frost begins to spread out around me, surrounding me almost in a mini storm. The boys can feel me pulling. Alaric starts to move, not of his own volition but of my desire. My father stares, watching in an almost horrified shock over what I am capable of doing.

Several knocks occur at the double doors that are not far from me. The doors open, and eight more male dragons come in, almost zombified at my call. Apparently, thanks to Alaric, my dragon side has become ten times stronger than it was before. When I realize what I have done, I release my grip on the power that I've tapped into. The eight males who have found their way into the room look around, confused about how they got there. I'm as strong as ever and this time, my use of power did not exhaust me. Perhaps my body is changing along with the growth of my baby. I can't wait until my little angel, Tia, is born. Oh, there are so many things I can't wait to show her.

Alaric comes over to me and drops to his knees before me. He carefully grabs both of my hands and kisses my knuckles. "There has only ever been one dragoness able to pull dragons to her from far and wide. That dragoness just so happens to be your great-grandmother, the Blood Queen."

I pull Alaric to his feet and gently kiss his lips. I take only one of his hands and take him with me back towards the other guys. My eyes land on my father, and I look at him, studying as he is studying me. "By the way you're looking at me, Father, I can only assume that you have never seen this done before."

Nicodeamus begins to stroke his beard as he looks at me. He tilts his head left, then slowly back to the right again, then back left again. He bites his lower lip before speaking. "It's like your mate has said, the last time I have seen anyone summon other dragons like that was the Blood Queen. Apparently, my bloodline was much stronger than your mother's and is obviously the dominant side of you. This would also explain why you carry Alaric's child before the twins. A dragoness will always pick the strongest male to reproduce with. So in the future, if you wish for children with your other mates, before going into heat Alaric must leave."

I watch the twins share looks of confusion between them. Their eyes move over to Dimitri and Klaus next, then over to Alaric last. Alaric slowly nods, acknowledging what my father has said is true.

All I can do is blink because of the information that is given to me. It doesn't matter which of the guys I had sex with during my heat, it was always going to be Alaric's child. Well, isn't that just a curious turn of events? It's quite interesting how genetics plays a huge role in the survival of the species. For example, what we have here today, even though I have spent time with Dominik and Jayce far before Alaric, it's Alaric's child that I now carry. I understand in the wild the need for the strong to survive and the weak to perish; those more diluted bloodlines no longer carry on. But all of these males that I have gathered, each are the strongest of their species, by rights.

Gently, I rub my stomach, feeling my daughter's movements within. *Oh!* I go to Jayce and place his hands on my belly. A slow smile creeps across his face as he feels my child moving. He seems just as enamored with the situation as I am. We smile ever so softly at each other, and he lightly kisses my lips before he moves away. I look over at his brother, Dominik next. I can see the anticipation and excitement in his eyes as he looks at me.

Slowly, I toddle my happy ass over towards Dominik and sit on his lap. I wait until I start to feel my daughter's movements within me before taking Dominik's hand and placing it in the proper place. Several seconds pass before I see his eyes light up and a smile move across his lips. One by one, I moved to each of my mates, making sure that they feel the babe within me. The look of wonder and happiness, the feeling that a miracle has occurred for us warms my heart. This is one of the few days that I can honestly say the entire day has been happy.

We retire to bed this night, exhausted yet happy. I find myself, tonight, between Alaric and Klaus. If you ask me, they're absolute polar opposites in their personalities. Alaric is your typical dominant male, wanting to make sure everything is in its proper place and order. Even though he's an Alpha, Klaus is more concerned about my well-being and the well-being of those around us. I'm guessing it's partially a species difference versus how they both individually were raised. From what Klaus had told me, his father was very hands-on and very affectionate. Alaric's father defined the word rat bastard. He couldn't give two shits less how anybody felt or what their thoughts were if they were outside of what he wanted.

I'm thankful to the gods that Alaric is not his father's son in the sense that other people's feelings matter to him. I think back to the night that my mate ripped his own father's heart out for his transgressions against me. I stood there and tolerated it, his father belittling me and treating me like nothing more than a broodmare and property. It warmed my heart and comforted my soul that Alaric sought vengeance in my name.

I look between Alaric and Klaus while they sleep curled up around me. I definitely think I hit the mate lottery when I ended up with these five guys. I am so thankful that no matter what I've already been through, each man handled it in his own way. Therefore, I can seek out the mate that I feel I need at that time. I know on the schedule somewhere out there, I need to finish and complete the bond with Klaus. My eyes move over to Alaric then back to Klaus as an idea forms in the back of my mind. I wonder if these two will play as nicely together as the twins do.

Carefully, I lean over and kiss Klaus on the lips, then I turn and kiss Alaric on the lips. No mate above the other, no favorites, and most of all, all are equal in my eyes. It doesn't take long for me to drift off to sleep. Tonight, visions of the daughter that I carry in my womb are dancing in my head. That, and of her future.

Sometime in the middle of the night, I'm awakened. My body is drenched in sweat, all because of the dream I just had. In that dream, the daughter that I carry now has long, light blond hair, steel-grey eyes like mine, and her father's stare back at me. A man I've yet to meet, covered in tattoos, hugging her, embracing her like she is the greatest treasure that he has ever found. Whomever this man is, he is pivotal in her future. Unlike my daughter, from what I can sense, he has already been born. I sit here panting from how real the dream had felt to me.

Are these the future dreams that my father warned me about? Is this strictly a dragon thing, and since taking Alaric as a mate, it has become more substantial? I'll speak to my father about this in the morning after I've adequately rested. For now, I wiggle myself between Klaus and Alaric, trying to get comfortable again so I can slip back into a nice deep slumber.

CHAPTER 66

Aurora

Janualry -

Early the next morning, I'm awakened by a pair of hard cocks getting ground into my thighs from either side. I double-blink my eyes, then slowly rub them to free them from sleep. Alaric is wide awake, smiling at me. I turn to look at Klaus, and he's sleep-humping my leg. I raise an eyebrow looking over at Alaric, and he just smirks. Apparently, Klaus's subconscious has taken over. Alaric gives me a nod, so I turn and back my ass up to Alaric. I'm facing Klaus, and I reach forward to grip his hard cock in my hand.

A soft moaning growl escapes Klaus's lips as he begins to thrust into my hand. I feel Alaric move and reach into the side table. I hear him pop the top to the lube, and I know what's coming next. In the middle of him massaging my rosette, he turns on the MP3 player, Ginuwine's "Pony" comes on. Excellent mood music. I move onto all fours and push Klaus onto his back. He rolls over without a fight, still in his dreamlike state. I manage to shift a finger into a talon and cut his boxers free from his body. My eyes travel up his body, and he's still sleeping.

Ever so slowly, I move to kneel beside him. My eyes drift over his body once more before I run my tongue from the base of his cock up to the tip. More pre-cum spills out onto Klaus's lower stomach. Greedily, I lap it up before licking him again. Klaus is somehow still sleeping through all of this. *Wow!* Without warning, I take his cock in my hand and deep throat him in one shot. I hear him gasp awake as I start sucking his cock for all that it's worth. Alaric uses his alpha tone and tells Klaus to lie there and enjoy what I'm doing. I can see where this morning's antics are going to go. Alaric is on a power trip, Klaus is mostly submissive, and here I am in the middle of a man sandwich.

Klaus comes hard, and I devour every single drop his body offers me. I feel my canines descend as I crawl my way up Klaus's body. I look at Klaus through my shifted eyes, and he's just as beautiful as he is when my eyes are human. Klaus's eyes turn to that of his wolf as he stares back at me.

Alaric moves to my side, takes Klaus's hands and places them on my full, heavy breasts. Klaus looks at me shocked, then over to Alaric, then back to me again. "Alaric likes being dominant, and with me being heavily pregnant with his child, he's going to be protective of us. We need to complete our bond Klaus, now seems just as good as any other time." I speak to him softly as I run a hand up his chest. Alaric helps me move to straddle Klaus's abdomen to not injure myself or my baby. Gently, Alaric grips my hips and slides me back till my dripping wet core touches the tip of Klaus's cock. Several careful rocks of my hips and I finally get Klaus's cock to line up the way I need him.

Alaric slowly pulls me back, further impaling me on Klaus's cock. I breathe in deeply, feeling quite full at the moment. I know what Alaric is planning on doing; part of it is for Klaus's comfort. I know I'm very Alpha at times, and Alaric believes that because of it Klaus may be hesitant to finish the bond. Alaric instructs Klaus to start moving, and almost instantly he does. *Hmm, Klaus likes being controlled.* This could get very interesting, indeed. I move Klaus's hands to rest on my hips as we start to move together. Alaric is right behind me, and he grabs ahold of my breasts, stimulating my nipples. My moans begin to mingle with Klaus's as we continue to move. I'm absolutely soaked, drenching Klaus with every single move. Alaric cheats, leaning forward, and bites my shoulder, instantly sending me crashing over the edge. My screams fill the air as a burst of frost coats the room.

Several seconds later, my other mates enter the room, having heard me. I lunge forward, without warning and bite Klaus, sending him over the edge with me. I feel every single pulse of his cock as he fills my womb up with his hot seed. I stay latched onto Klaus as his movements slowly even out. I carefully release his shoulder as I feel the bond fully snap into place. It's only then do I feel Alaric slowly begin to press his cock against my rosette. I slowly roll my neck as I now look to find both twins on the bed with us and Dimitri in a chair nearby with his cock in his hand. *Holy shit, this just got really interesting.*

Dominik and Jayce come forward, and each latch onto a nipple and start to tease it with their tongues. If I weren't already pregnant, I'd swear to the gods it would happen tonight with all these dominant males. Alaric carefully sinks deeply into my ass; I feel overfull, like to the point of bursting. Eventually, Klaus and Alaric begin to move. Every nerve fiber in my body feels like it has been set alight. Every move, every touch feels a thousand times more intense.

Eventually, Dimitri comes over, and I look at him shocked—I didn't think the group play would be his thing. Dimitri's eyes follow the movement of my other mates, then he looks back down at me. Dimitri grips the back of my neck roughly and kisses me deeply. I come almost instantly the minute Dimitri begins to kiss me. He swallows my screams of pleasure and helps to hold me up as I writhe from every powerful contraction of my pussy.

Light bursts explode behind my eyelids as the guys fuck me furiously, their movements beginning to become erratic as they climb the precipice. First Klaus, then Alaric, go over the edge, both of them screaming as they come hard while seated deep within me. I feel their cocks pulsing and throbbing against my very sensitive nerves. I have to admit, pregnancy sex is fucking amazing.

Alaric slowly and carefully withdraws from my ass, then collapses at the foot of the bed. I start to laugh as I look at Alaric lying there dead to the world. The next thing I know, Dimitri has scooped me up and is carrying me around the bed to the other side. The twins look on, puzzled as to what the big guy is doing. Dimitri maneuvers me with an incredible show of strength, then slides me down his body to his waiting cock. My legs rest over the tops of his forearms as his hands cup my ass cheeks. Dimitri moves so that his back rests against the wall for support. Ever so slowly, he begins to rock his hips, thrusting that huge, thick, throbbing cock up and into me. I gasp at every thrust; he's hitting all the right places every single time. My hands are buried deeply into his thick locks, my fingertips applying pressure to help me hold on.

I look over to see Jayce and Dominik stroking their cocks, watching Dimitri slowly torturing me with his precise strokes. Klaus and

Alaric lie on their sides, watching my big bear work me over with his deliberately slow movements. My juices start to drip onto the floor as I feel another orgasm approaching. Every attempt at moving is met by Dimitri stopping his movements and him growling at me, baring his canines. I narrow my eyes and growl back at Dimitri after the third time he decides to stop. Out of nowhere, my ass cheek starts stinging; I look back and see Alaric standing there smiling at me.

"Behave, or no more dick for you," Alaric says in that dominant tone of his.

I bare my canines at Alaric for interrupting my fun, and he smacks my ass yet again. I keep my eyes narrowed on him until Dimitri thrusts up hard into me. I whip my head around to face Dimitri; I'm shocked, to say the least. "I'm the one fucking you, not him. Eyes on me, baby girl." Dimitri says, his voice thick with desire and the growl of his beast.

I barely open my mouth, my canines easily visible. I'm horny and too fucking close to the edge for us to be having an in-depth conversation right now. I decide it's in my best interest to behave. I'm aching in all the right places and want more. Finally, Dimitri starts to move again with a renewed sense of purpose. Holy fuck, can the big guy move when he wants to. I eventually succumb to my orgasm and tilt my head back, screaming as Dimitri picks up the pace, slamming that long, thick cock deep within me. Our soaking wet flesh slaps together as my muscles milk his length rhythmically. Dimitri's eyes glow as his bear comes to the surface; his voice is a mix of man and bear as he screams his orgasm. His grip on my ass tightens as he grinds down, milking himself of every ounce of seed. Eventually, we both rest forehead to forehead, panting, trying to catch our breath from some of the most intense sex I've ever had. Our mixed fluids begin to drip onto the floor as his erection slowly softens.

Dimitri's still impressive flaccid cock falls free from me, taking with it an extensive gushing of fluids. Dimitri kisses me tenderly, then carries me back over to the bed and hands me off to Jayce and Dominik. I giggle as Jayce proceeds to kiss my poor hand-printed ass cheeks. Dominik holds a juice out to me and a cookie. I sit there happily snacking and drinking when I notice that Alaric and Klaus are missing. I look around the room to find Klaus bent over the tabletop and Alaric fucking his ass. I had my suspicions that Klaus may have been bi, but I never would have pegged Alaric for being a switch hitter. I sit there and watch them for several moments. I can see the scales rippling up and down Alaric's spine as he dominates Klaus.

Wow, I knew watching the Jayce sandwich back in the day was hot, but fuck, this is hotter, by far. I push Jayce down on the bed so that his head hangs over the edge so he can watch Klaus and Alaric. I straddle Jayce slightly off-balance for a moment. I look back over my shoulder to find Dominik hypnotized by Alaric and Klaus. "Dominik! Twin sammich. Now!" I practically growl out the now, and he jumps into action. He finds the lube on the bed and makes his cock nice and slick before sliding deep in me. I moan softly, feeling the fullness from the twins within me. We start moving together, perfectly in time with each other.

Dimitri walks past us and grabs a chair and drags it over. Dimitri proceeds to stand on the chair and sticks his cock in my face. Well, alrighty then, I guess I know what I'm doing now, don't I? Dimitri's cock is the largest out of the five, so trying to give him a blowjob is a project all by itself.

Jayce and Dominik slow their motions down so that the four of us can find a suitable rhythm. Several moments pass, and we finally figure it out. I can only take about half of Dimitri's cock into my mouth, so I use a hand to stroke him as I suck. I feel that familiar tightness in my lower stomach starting to build. Jayce's movements have begun to get more erratic in time with Klaus's increased moaning. Dominik adjusts himself to support my ribcage as I move to caress Dimitri's balls while I suck and stroke his cock.

The visual was more than poor Jayce could take. He screams out his orgasm as he suddenly thrusts up into me, knotting himself deep within me. Dominik, I can tell, isn't that far behind his brother. I focus on sucking and licking Dimitri's cock till he spills every ounce of seed down my throat. I gulp it down as fast as I can, being careful not to waste a drop.

My own orgasm rips through me the minute Dimitri roughly grabs both nipples and squeezes hard. I scream loudly, my voice a mix between mine and my beast's. Dominik can't hold out any longer. I feel his cock begin to pulse and throb deep within my ass as he dumps his seed. Klaus and Alaric are standing there watching our little party over here. Both guys pleasantly spent, Klaus with a new bite on his shoulder from Alaric. Hmm, I guess it's a dominance thing in the group.

I yawn softly and cover my mouth. Jayce is still locked deep within me, so he lays us down on our sides so my head can be cradled in his arm. "I'm hungry and tired," I say softly, then yawn again as I close my eyes, listening to Jayce's heartbeat.

Hopefully, tonight will be different than every other night. I miss sleeping with my mates in their human forms. I understand why my animal needs them shifted; we're practically defenseless. I just have to make it through this month and next month, then my daughter will be here. For now, hopefully, I'll sleep well. This little hellion of mine is super active and feels like she's running laps around my stomach most of the time now.

CHAPTER 67
Alaric

January -

Is it wrong that I'm attempting to hide in my own castle? Aurora's sexual appetite has gone through the roof. On a good night, she goes through all five of us in any way she can have us. I'm tired. I honestly don't know how much more I can take. I know the other guys are in the same boat I am.

I move out onto the balcony and look out over the frozen gardens, watching Aurora walk around escorted by Dominik in his Dire Wolf form. She's laughing as she waddles around the different statues looking at some of mine and her father's ancestors. In the distance, I see bodies moving in fast, closing in on Aurora's position. Without a second thought I leap from the balcony, shift to my dragon, and bellow out my warning to my mate. Dominik lowers to the ground, and Aurora climbs onto his back without any prodding. He takes off towards the castle with our precious cargo on his back. My bellows summoned my guards, and we close in quickly on the intruders.

It's more warriors from a rogue Lycan pack that apparently Sebastian and his mother had teamed up with. They are attacking a dragon fortress. *What the actual fuck are they thinking?* We rain fire down upon the assault force, burning them to ash. We circle the castle several times before I feel a burning pain in my shoulder, and fall from the sky. *Fuck! Aurora!*

My body impacts the ground hard, and I send my guards back to the castle to search for my mate. I hear the guys panicking as they try to break into the throne room where Aurora is being held. She's hurt, and we all know it. I scramble to my feet and fly towards my balcony again.

Quickly, I shift and run through the halls, heading towards the throne room. Nicodeamus is attempting to get in through the secret passageway to no avail. Bastards know the castle too fucking well, this seriously isn't good. I feel a faint tug at my dragon's power, and I know it's Aurora. I look to my guards and have them form a chain. I focus on my bond with Aurora and the power she's seeking, she's weak from blood loss.

Through the bond, I reach out to Nicodeamus and tell him what I'm about to do. I begin to draw on all the dragon's power that I am directly connected to. I hold it tight in my chest and begin to send it through the bond to Aurora. Several moments pass, and I feel her strength begin to return. Then it happens, the sudden burst of permafrost that coats the door and probably the entire inside of the throne room. "Dimitri, now, break down the door!" I shout as I strain to maintain the connection with Aurora.

Dimitri shifts instantly and his Great Bear rears up onto his hind paws, and comes forward with the force of almost a ton of angry bear. The door splinters and falls apart from the strength of the impact. Aurora stands there, in the middle of a slaughter. Her right hand is holding her left shoulder; blood has drenched her top, making it stick to her body. Twelve dead bodies are on the floor, two of them I am shocked to see. My mother and sister lay at Aurora's feet.

My mate's eyes look hollow, haunted, and empty as she stares at those who have fallen around her. I sprint over to Aurora and scoop her up into my arms, checking her over. The wound appears to have been healed by the power gifted to her through the connection. "They came to kill me... Your mom and sister, I'm so sorry, love. They gave me no choice." Aurora sobs and sniffles as she explains what has happened.

Klaus removes the barricades from the hidden door and lets Nicodeamus into the throne room. Aurora was so distraught over what she had to do to save herself and our child. I honestly don't think it is the killing that bothers her. I think the fear she felt that she had almost died carrying our child is what's really bothering her. Dimitri's bear comes up alongside of us and nuzzles Aurora's side. Gently, Aurora kisses me, then moves to hug Dimitri's bear's neck. That gentle giant sits down on his rump and wraps a clawed paw carefully around her.

Nicodeamus moves around the room, looking at the destruction that Aurora managed to cause, even unable to shift. "Boys, take Aurora and get her cleaned up and fed. I need to have a discussion with Alaric and Klaus." Nicodeamus's word is final, leaving no room for argument or discussion.

Dominik helps Aurora climb up onto Dimitri's back. Jayce and Dominik walk in silence, each with a hand on her thigh as they leave the room. Nicodeamus turns to look at us. I can see the fear and pain in his eyes. "They came for my granddaughter, my daughter. The cowards strike when she's most vulnerable. No more!" Frost shoots out in several directions at once from where Nicodeamus stands. Klaus and I look at each other and nod slowly.

"What will you have us do, Father?" I figure I may as well ask the question now rather than later. Me, personally I'd like to burn the place to the ground. Nicodeamus strokes his beard, then walks around looking at the bodies.

Nicodeamus looks to me, then back to the bodies and the thick layer of permafrost that Aurora had covered the room in. "Smart move, supplying Aurora with more dragon magic. She's almost become an energy vampire, in a sense. The amount of power I felt you move to her probably saved her and your daughter."

Nicodeamus stops before my mother's and sister's bodies then looks up at me. "You know Aurora never trusted them. I'm surprised they lived this long." Nicodeamus moves around, checking the other bodies. All are dragons from lesser houses, except my mother and sister. A female of any species is rare these days. To lose so many in one night is a crushing blow to dragon kind.

"I know, Father, I just hoped that my mother wouldn't do anything this stupid. I know she didn't love my father. I think it was more because Aurora is the rightful queen and not her." I look down upon my mother's corpse, the remnants of an icicle protruding from her chest.

Apparently, my mate has new skills she's acquired. As long as Aurora can protect herself when she can't shift, I feel a tiny bit better. I move over to my sister and roll her over; I really wish I hadn't. Apparently, Aurora ripped her throat out, froze the blood in her body, making every vessel explode from the pressure. My sister's eyeballs dangle by their nerves from her skull, frozen in place, hanging down. I really need to talk to Dimitri and find out exactly which horror movies my mate has watched, so I'm not so shocked by what I find.

I spend the next two hours supervising the cleanup of the bodies and blood. The skulls are ordered to be harvested from the corpses and prepared. I know being king will never be an easy job, but to know my family is possibly being hunted, that makes my blood boil. Eventually, I leave the throne room, letting Nicodeamus finish overseeing the cleanup.

Carefully, I turn the doorknob entering the room in full stealth mode. The twins are sitting in their wolven forms, guarding the bathroom door. I nod to them, and they let me pass. Aurora is in the massive bathtub, floating around, using Dimitri's lap as a pillow. Klaus is at Aurora's feet, massaging her arches, trying to help her relax. I can see from here our daughter is quite active right now.

Silently, I back out of the room and close the door. I tell the twins I'm going for food, and I'll return soon. I never made such a fast trip to the kitchen and back as I did tonight. After that display of power, I know Aurora is going to be starving. The bonds have been sealed with all five mates, all four species. I know she has received my scales and my magic.

From the twins, I know that she has Jayce's toxic bite; I'm not sure what she received from Dominik. From her false Lycan mate, she received his battle strategy and nothing else. Klaus, I'm not entirely sure what she could receive from him. Dimitri is one scary mother fucker; I'm really concerned about what she could get from him. I mean, seriously, that man is a one-man wrecking crew. My cart from the kitchen is loaded to the brim with all kinds of different foods. The one old chef gave me a live lamb to bring to Aurora. So, here I am with this adorable little furball prancing along behind me.

I enter the suite, and the twins are back in their human form, sitting around the bed where Aurora is resting. I see her nostrils flare, and her eyes take on that ghostly glow of her beast as she stares at the lamb and me. For being pregnant, she crosses the room much faster than any of us expected. Even without being able to shift, her nails became talons, and her canines descend. Faster than I can blink, she has the lamb in her mouth, and her talons sink into its flesh. The poor thing didn't even have time to scream before she ended its life. We watch our mate in horror as she feasts on the young animal's still hot flesh.

Nicodeamus chooses to walk into the room. He pauses, looking at Aurora, and then goes to the bar for a drink. We look from Aurora to her father, then between each other, then back to Nicodeamus. "Is this…" I wave at Aurora, eating the fresh lamb. "Normal? She killed it and just started eating it," I say, exasperated. I've never witnessed a female dragon pregnant nor a female Lycan pregnant. This is probably one of the most fucked up Aurora moments I've seen to date.

"Perfectly normal, boys. The baby needs fresh blood and meat to grow to her potential. We must send out a hunting party for fresh, live meat for her as she comes into the home stretch. Cooked food may make her sick to her stomach." Nicodeamus just shrugs his shoulders and sits down to sip at his brandy. I'm seriously in the middle of a horror movie gone wrong.

Dominik facepalms while his brother leaves the room to get a washcloth and towels to clean Aurora up. "This is normal? In what world is this normal?" I can't help but shout my frustration. I've never witnessed anything remotely close to this in the last several hundred years.

"Aurora is a hybrid, first of her kind. She's showing tendencies of the most primal of us. Her base animal instincts are much stronger than the rest of ours put together. She may not be able to shift, but she was still able to decimate a room without breaking a sweat." Nicodeamus gets up and moves towards Aurora, who now is attacking the dinner cart. "I'll be honest, guys, I'm a bit frightened. Good luck and good night." With that, Nicodeamus leaves quickly, locking the door behind him.

Nicodeamus being frightened is not very comforting to me in the least bit. Aurora finishes eating and moves to sit in front of the fireplace. Jayce cautiously approaches her, offering to help clean her up. Aurora smiles and nods, allowing Jayce to strip the blood-covered garments from her. Klaus approaches next, holding up his fuzzy sleep pants and her favorite shirt that happens to be mine.

Dimitri approaches me, offering a glass of brandy. "Her mother was like this towards the end. I'm just worried we may lose her like we did Anca. I think Aurora shifted because of the stress her mother was under. If we make sure she feels safe and secure, there's no reason for the baby to shift." Dimitri looks down at his brandy. I can tell he is reliving that moment.

"Want to tell me what happened? That way history doesn't repeat itself." I rest a hand on Dimitri's shoulder, and he nods in agreement. Quickly, I text Nicodeamus so he's present for the story. Several minutes later, he unlocks the door and enters the room again. Aurora is curled up in her favorite chair, sleeping in front of the fire. We gather around Dimitri and wait for him to begin.

"It was the Night of the Wolf. The yearly celebration of the wolf moon and the great hunt. Every clan minus the dragon clan was in attendance." Dimitri pauses, taking a sip of his brandy, and draws in a deep breath. You can tell the memory still haunts him to this day.

"Anca went into labor on her dais, so we escorted her to her chamber. We weren't in her chamber for more than an hour before the attack happened. Vlad was with us as we prepared to protect Anca and Aurora at all costs." A single tear rolls down Dimitri's cheek as he attempts to get himself under control. "Anca started to scream and thrash suddenly. The Elder Dame was giving her herbs for pain, but it was too late. Tiny talons broke through the flesh of her stomach. Blood began to flow freely from the wounds. Anca's ear-piercing screams were answered by Nicodeamus's dragon. As fast as it had started, it was over. Aurora had cut herself free of her mother's womb. That little hellion attempted to claw at anyone who came near her. Anca's last words were to protect her baby." Dimitri begins to uncontrollably sob.

His distress wakes Aurora up from her slumber. Silently, she moves towards Dimitri and climbs into his lap. I'm not used to seeing this side of Aurora; perhaps we brought balance to her temperament. Aurora works her fingers through Dimitri's hair, massaging his scalp. "My daughter and I are well. We will go somewhere far from here when I go into labor, so I don't feel threatened. This birth is different; we have both parents' species present. Alaric's dragon can soothe my baby when she's distressed in a way I can't. You won't lose me, too." Aurora's words make all of us cry some. She somehow knew why her mother died. Aurora gently kisses Dimitri, then looks back at us.

"Father, dragons didn't always give birth in buildings. Are there ancient birthing grounds near here that are isolated?"

Nicodeamus begins to pace, then stops suddenly. "Yes, high up in a mountain range not far from here. Alaric can fly there and make sure it's safe. When the time comes, we can take you there." Nicodeamus smiles broadly. I swear he looks like a deranged serial killer at times.

"Let's go under cover of night. I want to make sure that Aurora has a safe place to go when it's time." I move to Aurora's side and kiss her temple. I close my eyes as I breathe in her scent. I will do everything within my power to protect her and provide for her. If it means I have to spend the next few weeks searching the mountain ranges for a cavern for her, I will.

Nicodeamus and I move swiftly through the castle, heading towards the gardens, I motion to four of my closest friends. Two I put on Aurora duty, which they cringe over. Well, there are two reasons for that. First, she hates having guards escort her everywhere. The second, she threatened to hang them by their testicles if they try to get too close. My other two friends leave with Nicodeamus and me.

We fly for about forty-five minutes before Nicodeamus starts telling me where to head towards. On one of the tallest peaks, there is a cavern on a cliff face in the most dangerous mountain range. I bank and fly past it three times before I decide I can fit. On my final approach, I tuck my wings in and land in the mouth of the cavern. I guess it's an advantage not being an overly huge dragon species. Carefully, I lie down and allow Nicodeamus to slide off before I shift back to my human form. Nicodeamus hands me clothing, and I dress before we go exploring.

Talon marks line the walls of the cavern as we move deeper into its depths. Eventually, we come to a large opening where stalactites and stalagmites line the room's outer edge. In the center of the room, a hot spring has created a pool, as well as an island in the middle.

"It's been almost eight hundred years since I was last here," Nicodeamus says as he moves around the room. He bends over slowly and picks up a fragment of an eggshell. Nicodeamus moves the piece of white shell around in his hand before handing it to me. "I was born here; my mother laid my egg instead of carrying me as a human. She felt she could protect me better as her dragoness than a weak human." Nicodeamus sighs and looks to the island, then back over to me.

"I wish Aurora had a dragon form. I'm so scared for my daughter it's not funny. I saw what was left of her mother, and I honestly don't think I can survive that again." Nicodeamus's voice breaks raw with emotion. Tears roll freely down his cheek as he looks to me. I didn't know fear till now. I'm blubbering right along with him.

My heart breaks for Nicodeamus, especially after the story Dimitri told. I'm scared of watching Aurora being ripped apart by my daughter. My chest tightens with fear. I look back over the water, trying to compose myself. I draw in a deep breath, then turn around to Nicodeamus. "I'm sure Aurora will love it here, especially since you were born here." I briefly embrace Nicodeamus, then smile. "Let's head back before she starts to worry. I'll bring a couple of the guys here tomorrow night, and we'll work on setting it up for her." Nicodeamus nods and follows me to the entrance. I strip out of my clothing and put it back in the sack Nicodeamus was carrying for me. Quickly, I shift back to my dragon and lay down for him. He climbs back on and gets settled on my back.

I leap out of the cavern and go into free fall for a few moments before deciding to open my wings. We glide silently, just over the treetops, trying to remain out of sight if anyone is looking for my dragon. As we approach the mountain the castle is on, I decide to do laps around it, changing direction several times before landing. I can't be too cautious these days. The courtyard is vacant and silent. I'm concerned, so I refuse to lower myself to the ground.

One of my guards send a plume of acid towards the corner of the courtyard. Screams erupt as a Lycan comes out of the corner, its flesh melting away from its skeleton. As a precaution, I breathe fire, lighting up the entire courtyard. No other intruders are present, other than the remains of the fifteen that were in the corner. I send out a small force of Black Dragons to scour the mountain and burn anything that moves to a puddle of flesh.

My guards land near me, watching my back during the vulnerable mid-shift time. I lie down and allow Nicodeamus to slide off my back. I shift back to my human form and slip on my clothes that Nicodeamus hands me. Once dressed, Nicodeamus moves off with my guards to investigate the bodies. My concern right now is that Aurora is in danger. I race through the halls and into the joint suites. Jayce meets me at the door and raises his finger to his lips, signaling for silence.

I follow Jayce into the room, and there's Aurora, asleep, cradled in Dimitri's arms. Dimitri looks at me and mouths *help me* and then looks down at Aurora. At least lately, she's been allowing us to sleep as humans with her. I approach slowly and nuzzle Aurora's cheek and let my dragon rumble to her. Almost instantly, she curls towards the sound and rolls right into my arms. Ever so carefully, I stand with my beautiful mate in my arms, I listen carefully, and I hear her beast rumbling back at mine. I walk slowly and carefully, heading to the massive bed we all have been sharing lately.

Ever so gently, I lay Aurora on the bed and tuck her in tightly. I feel like I'm defusing a nuclear bomb with every movement I make as I step away from the bed. Now, it is time for our nightly ritual: the rock, paper, scissors tournament for sleeping position. Dimitri and Dominik are out since last night they won. I look between Jayce and Klaus; we nod that we are ready and Dimitri starts the competition.

"One, two, three, shoot!" Dimitri says, and we each pick an object. My dumbass chose paper, of all freaking things. Klaus and Jayce picked scissors, an automatic win for both of them. They smile and high-five each other. Deep down, I think they ganged up on me. I laugh and motion to the bed, and they assume the positions closest to Aurora. Dimitri chooses the foot of the bed. I lie above where Aurora is, and Dominik takes first watch.

There have been too many attempts to let our guard down now. In four hours, Dominik will switch out with one of us, then the next swap will be four hours after that. The only two to get a full night's sleep are the ones sleeping next to our beautiful mate.

This next month coming up is going to be hell. Between having to sneak out to work on the cavern, pretending to make preparations here, and keeping Aurora fed is becoming a challenge. Oddly, cooked food is making her sick, but raw food she can stomach. I know they say each pregnancy is different. I hope the next four are easier on all of us.

CHAPTER 68

Dominik

February -

We're in the home stretch, and I feel as though we are walking on eggshells lately. Aurora is miserable; her poor body aches, and her breasts have started to leak on occasion. Her sexual appetite has calmed down some to where it's manageable. The days of teaming up with my brother are over for now. Thankfully, we are not fucking to the point of exhaustion anymore. Now, Aurora wants it slow, sweet, and gentle, Honestly, it's because she's afraid the baby will be born with a dick imprint on its forehead.

We all attempted and failed miserably at trying to keep a serious face when she said that to us over dinner. Poor Nicodeamus needed the Heimlich maneuver because he decided to literally inhale his chicken wing. The rest of us have gotten smart. We don't eat or drink when Aurora is talking at the dinner table. I can say, without a doubt, you never know what's going to come out of that girl's mouth.

In theory, today is going to be an easy day. Jayce and I have Aurora floating around in her oversized bathtub to ease some of her discomfort. My brother and I take turns holding her head above water as we walk backward around the tub. Hell, this thing shouldn't be called a tub. It's a fucking small pool. It's gotten quite interesting to watch the odd shapes Aurora's stomach takes on when the baby moves. The freakiest thing to date was the hand. I say the hand because out of nowhere, the baby pressed her hand to Aurora's stomach, and the outline was perfect.

We all stared in wonder as that little hand slid around the one side. Klaus decided to reach out and touch it, and immediately the hand disappeared. The next thing we know, there's a little foot there instead. Nicodeamus and Dimitri sat there telling us stories about what Aurora was like when Anca was pregnant. I'm glad Aurora isn't going through half of what her mother did.

Dimitri regaled us with stories about how constantly nauseous Aurora's mother was during her pregnancy. There were days on end that she couldn't keep any food down, which made her very angry for a she-wolf. Nicodemus told us about how he would hunt for her to bring her back fresh meat, but she wouldn't touch the raw food because of the way she was raised. Aurora sat there rolling her eyes because the raw food doesn't faze her one bit. To be perfectly honest, she prefers to hunt and eat her food as her animal versus as a human.

Aurora comes over and sits on my lap, curls up, and presses her forehead to my throat. She stays snuggled like this for several minutes, and eventually her breathing evens out and she's fast asleep. We've all noticed that she's napping more often and for longer over the course of the day. We know it's getting close to time for her, and we're doing everything within our power to keep her happy and healthy. Klaus's grandmother has been on high alert, preparing everything that she feels she may need to deliver the baby. Little does she know, she's going to be riding a dragon, probably in the middle of the night, to a destination we're not telling her about.

We're keeping everything very quiet about our plans for the swift departure when we know it's time. Just recently, there was another attempt on Aurora's life in the middle of the night. I'm very thankful that my brother, Jayce had decided to remain as his wolf that night. With his heightened senses and not needing to sleep, Jayce was vigilant throughout the entire night. Somewhere around one in the morning, someone entered our quarters through a hidden passageway that we were not aware of. The assassin did not know Aurora would have all of her mates with her. He didn't even make it ten feet out of the passageway before Jayce was on him and ripped his head off instantly.

Jayce was so stealthy that night we didn't even hear the body hit the floor, nor was there any evidence of the attack the next morning. He pulled us aside and told us what happened so that we didn't concern Aurora with it. We've gotten rather sneaky in the last three months, things that would stress her out, she has no clue happened. Alaric, Klaus, and Nicodemus have been running the kingdom for her. We've hosted several dinners with visiting dignitaries. Still, at the slightest notion she was getting tired we would give Aurora an excuse to leave the room. So far, the kingdom is unaware Aurora is unable to shift. We fully intend to keep it that way, especially for her and the baby's safety.

I feel the baby moving within my mate's womb, up against my stomach. The baby does unfortunately seem to prefer her father over the rest of us. I'm guessing it's a dragon thing. Hopefully, it'll work out differently for Aurora than it did for her mother. She has the advantage that her mate will be present for the birth. There's also a lot of things different between Aurora's birth and now her baby's. Firstly, Aurora is half-dragon, so her body is already acclimated to the child she's carrying. It wasn't like her mother, whose body was hosting a tiny alien that literally burst free of her body.

Secondly, we are on her like white on rice; she doesn't sneeze without all of us being alerted to it. From what Dimitri and Nicodemus told us, Anca's other mates had very little to do with her during the pregnancy. They spent very little time interacting with her, and most nights she slept alone. That, by itself would cause undue stress to the mother and child.

We only have maybe a week, possibly two at most before the new little princess is born. I'm kind of frightened right now. Let's face it, I've never witnessed a birth, nor have I ever had the title of father. Genetically we know the child isn't ours, but it's Aurora's and Alaric's. As a group, every child is all of ours; paternity doesn't matter. I motion to Alaric to come over and take our beautiful mate from me.

I feel how restless her child is and I'm guessing it wants its father. Almost instantly, the minute Alaric picks her up, the baby calms and Aurora starts making that odd hybrid noise of hers that's a mix of dragon and wolf. It's definitely a dragon thing. I wonder who will get to father the next child that she's going to carry? It really doesn't matter if you think about it. She said each of us would have our own child; it's just a question of when. I'm kind of excited, mostly scared, but excited all the same. Only time will tell. For now, we do what we have to do. We have to make all of our preparations and wait for Aurora to say to us that she's ready.

Tonight's my brother's and my turn to go out with Alaric to work on the birthing space. We're adding our own little touches, each one of us, so that something of ours is present with her.

Nicodeamus and Alaric suggested that it just be the three of them when it comes time because of the child she's carrying. I don't like the idea, but if we're to maintain any semblance of control here, some of us must stay behind. After all, we don't want anybody looking for Aurora while she's off giving birth.

A little after midnight, Alaric gathers Jayce and me up and takes us out into the courtyard. I'm really not too keen on the idea of flying. The gods gave me four paws for a reason and not wings. Jayce looks so excited. Then again, he likes looking at Alaric naked. Alaric, like most dragons isn't very selective about what gender he takes his liberty with. I was however shocked about Klaus being bi. He didn't seem like the type that would be on the receiving end. Hell, I've caught Jayce and Klaus more than once taking care of each other's needs. Aurora doesn't care, as long as her needs are met and no other female is ever involved.

Alaric finishes his shift and Jayce walks over to me carrying Alaric's clothing bag. I have our bag of stuff for the birthing nest. Wow, a birthing nest for our mate. The weight of the situation hits me harder than any punch ever delivered to my body. I'm amazed and in awe of what Aurora is capable of. Here is one of the strongest females I've ever known, heavily pregnant and defenseless. Aurora isn't the type to like to depend on others, and here she is, trusting us to protect and provide for her. I can tell Alaric is getting impatient when he thumps his tail on the ground near me. Fuck, I'm really not looking forward to this. Aurora once asked me if I'm afraid of anything and I answered with losing her. The truth is, I'm scared of heights too.

Reluctantly, I climb onto Alaric's back where he had instructed us to sit. I have a death grip on the spine before me. I'm terrified. Jayce looks back at me and smiles at me. I force a fake smile at him and draw in a deep breath. I admit it, I scream like a little bitch when Alaric launches himself into the air. We circle the castle once, waiting for his personal guards to join us. Aurora is standing on the balcony with Dimitri right behind her, holding her tightly. I couldn't think of a better male to entrust her care to.

We turn to the north, following the ridge line, staying low to the ground to not attract attention to ourselves. Jayce is ecstatic, looking everywhere, making me a nervous wreck with how he's constantly twisting and turning. Me, personally, I feel like I want to puke my dinner up. The dips and rises on the thermals make my stomach flip and flop with every beat of Alaric's wings. Up, down, up, down…. How much fucking further is this damn place!

Out of nowhere, a mountain rises up out of the fog. The side facing us is almost perfectly vertical, disappearing into the clouds. I'm starting to panic when Alaric reaches out to me through the bond. *Relax, we're almost there now. Just a straight climb up the side of the mountain. I won't fly straight in like I do with the others.* I roll my eyes as if that makes me feel better.

Suddenly, Alaric flair's his wings as if hitting the brakes, and he brings his body up and parallel to the mountain. Yup, experiencing terror in this moment. I can feel his dragon laughing at me, the bastard. Alaric lands, and his talons dig into the stone as he begins his climb. Several minutes later, we reach the opening and he climbs in. I look around cautiously, and my eyes widen. He flies into this opening? Yeah, I'm glad he decided to climb this time. As soon as it's safe, I slide off Alaric's back and begin to look around.

As I step away from Alaric and Jayce, I shift my eyes to the ones Aurora gifted me with. My mercury, wolven orbs look around, taking in the layout of the caverns. You can tell, once upon a time, that a dragon dug the cavern out itself. I run my fingers over the groves that were left behind. I'm genuinely amazed by the strength of the dragons, more than anything. Alaric comes up beside me and lays his hands on the groves as well. "The Blood Queen dug this cavern; it's been in Nicodeamus's family for generations. From what Nicodeamus told me, he was the last hatchling born here. He had fully intended for Aurora to be born here, but the attack happened and well, we know what happened after that." Alaric looks down and moves away. One of his guards lands in the cavern opening and lies down, blocking the entrance.

CHAPTER 69

Dominik

FEBRUARY-

We follow Alaric into the depths of the cavern to this grand opening in the center. It is like a mini oasis hidden within the mountain. I'm guessing the Blood Queen scented the oasis or something then decided to dig towards it. There's a beautiful moss-covered island in the middle of a stunning clear water pool. Small fish swim in the water in circles around the island. I wonder exactly how long they have been here and if they naturally occur.

Jayce and I begin to work in tandem with cleaning and moving rocks and various other items, clearing Aurora's path to arrive. Alaric has shifted back to his dragon and uses his fire to remove mushrooms and various other mold spores from the walls and ceiling. Jayce and I stop to watch Alaric work; it's incredible to think that a living creature can carry and produce fire. His dragon's coloration is quite unique; he's mostly white with gold and blue mixed in. Typically, his species are not large dragons, but he's on the larger side than Nicodeamus. Alaric's guards are Black and

Red Dragons. They have fire and acid weapons at his disposal. My thoughts are sidetracked for several moments watching Alaric work when my brother taps my shoulder.

"Dom, we really ought to hurry up. I don't like being away from Aurora for long." Jayce smiles at me, showing his level of concern because of our absence.

"Yeah, you're right; I think we have everything done that we can possibly do for today anyway. Alaric, when you're ready, we are!" I shout so that hopefully he hears me over his fire's roar. Slowly, his great head turns to look at Jayce and me, and he begins to head towards the entrance. "I guess he's ready to go, Jayce." I lightly nudge my brother and gather what's left of our belongings.

As we head towards the cavern, I notice something shiny sticking up in the black sand. I bend down and grab ahold of it; it's a bracelet made of gold with jewels. Nicodeamus would know who this belonged to, so I stick it in my bag and run to catch up to Jayce. He's already sitting on Alaric's back, waiting to leave. I love him. He's my brother, but at times like this, I just want to smack him. Reluctantly I climb into my spot on Alaric's back and pat his scales so he knows we're all set.

Alaric being the resident wise-ass, goes running towards the mouth and just launches himself out of the opening. We go into free fall. I'm terrified. My fucking brother is hooting and hollering like he's on a fucking roller coaster. If we didn't look so much alike, I'd be questioning if we were related or not. The flight back isn't as horrible as the ride out; I'm guessing the winds are behind us, pushing us home. We glide towards the castle, and Jayce and I shift our eyes, searching for any possible dangers. We don't see anything as we make several passes around before Alaric lands.

His guards take position so that he can return to his human form safely. Once shifted, Jayce and I head in the front door, we split off, Jayce heading straight to Aurora and I head to the kitchen. I don't even wait to look for the cooking staff. The enormous walk-in refrigerator is amply stocked with all kinds of meat. I grab a leg of lamb and a few raw steaks and set them on a platter. I then head out into the central part of the kitchen and find several types of pastries. I grab as many as I can before heading back to our suite.

Once inside the suite, I don't find anyone in the bedroom which is concerning to me. I reach out to sense Aurora; she's resting comfortably, floating in the bathtub of hers. I head to the master bathroom. Dimitri is leaning back on the stairs supporting Aurora's head and shoulders out of the water. "How are you feeling, love?" I ask softly, just in case she's sleeping as she floats.

"Dominik, I'm glad your back. I'm hungry and uncomfortable and fat and hungry. The baby won't sleep because Alaric isn't here." Aurora starts crying, and then the water starts to freeze around her.

"Love, please calm down. The boys are back. I'm sure once you've eaten Alaric will help settle the baby down so you can rest comfortably." Dimitri attempts to soothe Aurora before he's turned into a bear-cicle.

Jayce comes running in and stops dead, seeing the half-frozen tub. Jayce goes to the side of the tub and turns on the hot water and the bubbler. I move to the side of the tub, waving a pastry at Aurora, trying to draw her out of the water.

Unfortunately, Aurora almost instantly looks sick. She immediately hurls herself over the edge of the tub. She promptly vomits her entire stomach contents onto the marble floor. Alaric comes running into the bathroom; his own color matches Aurora's, and he's holding his stomach. Alaric runs to the side of the tub and slips on the vomit and falls on his ass.

I'm trying my best not to laugh at the man that can roast my ass in an instant. Nicodeamus is not as cautious as he proceeds to full belly laugh at Alaric. "Poor guy just puked his guts up out of nowhere, now he falls on his mate's puke. Priceless. Welcome to being mated!" Nicodeamus raises his arm at the last part of his statement before moving to help Alaric stand back up.

Dimitri helps Aurora out of the tub and sets her on her feet. Slowly, Aurora waddles her way over to Alaric, takes his hand and leads him to the shower. I hear Aurora say she's sorry she made him sick too. He kisses her forehead and tells her not to worry about it. Aurora leans into the shower and turns on the water for Alaric. He shakes his head at her and makes her sit on the bench close by.

Jayce removes the pasties from the bathroom and goes to set up the steaks for Aurora. I walk over to the mini fridge in the suite and grab a few bottles of juice and bring them over to offer to Aurora. "I'm so sorry; I didn't know the pastries would make you sick." I feel horrible that my decision had made her ill.

In typical Aurora fashion, she pops the top on two drinks and takes a sip from each before settling on the one she wants. The second bottle she offers to me then returns to watching Alaric's shower. "It's almost over, Dominik. I'm so tired and uncomfortable. I just want my daughter to be happy and healthy," Aurora says as she rubs her stomach. She sighs softly and scoots so she can lean back against me. Slowly she sips at her juice, and I watch her wince.

"Are you ok? Is it time?" I'm anxious and excited about the impending birth. Alaric heard my question and pops his head out of the shower.

"I'm fine. Klaus's grandmother said it's normal to have these fake contractions. As long as my water doesn't break, it's not time. From what she said, a first birth can take up to a day." Aurora shrugs her shoulders like it's no big deal. A day is a long time for something to go wrong.

Gently, I kiss Aurora's temple and nuzzle her cheek. Suddenly she sits up and waves her hand frantically at me. I assist her in standing and move with her quickly. Apparently, Tia moved and is now pressing on Aurora's bladder. I've never seen a woman so happy to make it to the toilet. I stand nearby, not really sure what to do while my mate is peeing her brains out. Dear Lord, how much did that girl have to drink? Alaric eventually joins us just in time for Aurora to finish up. It's times like this I'm thankful I'm not a girl.

Slowly, I raise my eyes to watch Aurora's stomach change into unnatural shapes then settle down. Aurora starts laughing and rubs her stomach. Alaric and I are both concerned, and Aurora is over there laughing. We collectively shake our heads at her and move back into the main suite.

There are several platters of assorted raw meat on the center table for Aurora to choose from. She waddles over and grabs her favorite chair on wheels, and rolls the rest of the way over to the platters. The rest of us are taking turns leaving the room to eat the food that may make her sick. Alaric and I decide to go last since we went first at lunchtime. Aurora is rolling laps around the table, picking at chunks of raw meat.

Klaus's grandmother enters the suite and looks shocked at what Aurora is doing. She makes the ultimate mistake of trying to take the raw meat away from Aurora. Without batting an eye, Aurora freezes Klaus's grandmother to the ground.

"Give me back my supper! I'm hungry!" Aurora's voice is the blended tone of her beasts. Her eyes are liquid mercury with the dragon slits. Aurora is mad and hungry, definitely not a good combination. Klaus runs over, takes the platter from his grandmother then offers it back to Aurora, and softly kisses her lips. It's frightening how fast Aurora can go from demon bitch from hell back to adorable sweetheart. I swear to the gods, there's a faulty switch somewhere that randomly flips.

Klaus remains at Aurora's side, calling her his angel. He gently caresses her stomach and then kisses it. You would think he would learn by now. The minute his lips touch her stomach, the baby decides to kick him. We've almost started placing bets as to how long it takes for Tia to strike. Tia is definitely her mother's daughter. The baby is already very opinionated about what she wants. She's not even here yet.

Tonight we have a surprise for Aurora; we completed the nursery for Tia. We know it's not going to be used long, but it's the thought that counts. Aurora's starting to yawn, so we decide now is the perfect time to show her what we've been working on. Since Jayce gave up his room, he's the one tasked with leading Aurora to the nursery.

We signal Jayce and he moves to Aurora's side. She smiles and takes his offered hand, following him. It now dawns on her that Klaus's grandmother is still stuck. Aurora says "oopsie" and releases her icy grip. The old crone isn't happy but oh well, she'll have to get over it. We move as one towards Jayce's room and

Aurora's eyes light up. I have to believe she thinks she's going to get laid. I come up behind Aurora and cover her eyes before we lead her into the room.

Aurora hates surprises and well, as a group we decided this was one worth taking the risk. The room is painted in a soft blue-grey; the accent colors are rose and silver. We are pretty sure Aurora wouldn't want a really girly room because who knows what gender the next babies may be. We really lucked out with Aurora. She's efficient and doesn't buy too many lavish things. I slowly remove my hands from her eyes and back away. On all the walls there are scenes with each of our animals painted on them. Some would say it look like a horror emporium. I'd say it looks just right.

Slowly Aurora opens her eyes and gasps. Her hands fly up to cover her mouth. Happy tears stream down her cheeks as she slowly walks around, looking at everything. This is definitely one of our better surprises for her. Aurora turns and walks up to each of us, thanking us and kissing each of us repeatedly. Nicodeamus finally joins us and is as moved by the gesture as Aurora is. This is definitely one of the best nights of my life, and it's only going to get better from here.

CHAPTER 70
Aurora

FEBRUARY -

THE POOR GUYS have been going nuts, especially this past month. Jayce and the guys not only built me a nursery, but they are also at an undisclosed location setting up for my birth. Poor Klaus and Dimitri are on Aurora duty today. Klaus has been my designated pillow most of the day. Dimitri is taking care of my every want and need. These stupid Braxton contraction thingies have been happening most of the day today, and are getting rather annoying.

I swear to the gods, if Klaus's grandmother pokes me one more time, she's gonna be a grandma-cicle real soon. "Guys, I need to pee again!" I practically whine out my words because I'm at my wit's end with this. I don't know how other species carry for longer than three months. The baby is upside down, and I keep seeing the occasional ass print pressed against my stomach. The guys help me up; Klaus and Dimitri escort me to the bathroom. A girl can't even pee alone anymore, all because of what happened to my mother. I get it, really. I'm the first of my kind, and no one knows what will happen with Tia and me. We make it to the bathroom, and I kick the boys out as far as they will go.

I know I'm getting closer to time. I mean, if guesses are right, it's any day now. It's been really odd lately; I feel like the baby never sleeps. I bet my baby has a full-blown circus going on in there. Thankfully, my bathroom trips are always uneventful; I wobble and waddle and take care of business. We head back to what has been named my palace of pillows since regular chairs are so freaking uncomfortable right now. Klaus climbs in first, and Dimitri helps lower me back into my epicly soft snuggle area. The guys curl up around me, and I decide to take a nap until my next feeding.

I wake up late in the afternoon and my stomach feels really tight, worse than it did before I laid down for my nap. Klaus and Dimitri are both out cold, I'm actually kind of jealous. I reach out through the bond to sense how far away Alaric and the twins are. From what I can discern, they are on their way back. I'm seriously not feeling good, and I can't block the guys from feeling it anymore. Dimitri and Klaus wake up with a start, holding their stomachs and looking at me. They know it's me; they also know I've been hiding my discomfort from them.

Klaus moves and kneels before me, wrapping his strong arms around my legs. "My angel, what can I do to ease your discomfort? Name it, and if I can do it, I will." Klaus looks up at me, his eyes full of love and concern. I don't know what to say to him at this point. It's a natural occurrence; I can't stop what's already starting. I reach down and rub Klaus's scalp before doubling over, holding my stomach. Fuck, I think labor just got real. I feel my beast surge, scales ripple down my arms and spine. It's time, and now every single one of my mates knows. The power surge I feel is absolutely insane. I start pulling energy from the closest, biggest dragons I can sense.

Nicodeamus comes running into the room and looks at me with my scales rippling across my skin. "Shit! It's time! It's time!" He starts running around the room, grabbing my go bag and several other little things he thinks we need. Dimitri and Klaus come to my side and help support my weight as I almost double over from the contractions.

"Alaric is almost here; we need to go outside now." We start to walk through the hallways; one of the dignitaries attempts to block our forward progress. I feel a power surge unlike any I have felt before. I raise my now-shifted hand at him and a large ice spike shoots up from the ground, impaling him where he stands. We need to leave, and we need to go now. My beast doesn't feel safe here, and she wants to get out quickly. The guys look at me briefly and then proceed to expedite our departure. By the time we make it outside, Alaric has landed with several other dragons. He made arrangements earlier for everyone to fly with me.

"I can't climb." I'm almost crying as I look up to Alaric's dragon for understanding. I double over again, and this time my water breaks. We're running out of time, and now my father and the guys are starting to panic. Alaric opens his dragon's hand, extending it to me. He has his little finger curled so that it would act like a seat for me. Dimitri and Klaus help me get comfortable before Alaric closes his hand gently around me.

I feel safe and protected in Alaric's dragon's hand, but I'm too warm. Through the bond, I reach out to him. *I'm too warm. Please use your frost if you have any; otherwise, I need to—* Alaric's hand slowly becomes cooler until it is a more comfortable temperature for me. I sigh softly and relax against the palm of his hand. I can feel that he is pushing himself to fly faster than he usually would.

It feels like only moments have passed by the time Alaric lands in our secret location. The first face I see when Alaric opens his hand is my father. I carefully step out and almost go to my knees from the next contraction. They seem to be worse without Alaric; I look back to him in tears. "Shift, love, I need you!" I hold tightly to my father's one arm as the other guys run up to assist. Alaric shifts quicker than I have ever seen him do, and he runs over to me. Something about him soothes my beast, and the contractions are not as severe as they were before. I'm having a hard time making the journey to wherever they are taking me. Dominik shifts and lies down, allowing me to climb onto his back. He moves slowly and cautiously through the cavern, making the trip much more pleasant for me.

As we enter this grand opening, I can't help but look around in awe of the beauty around me. Various crystals line the walls, as well as hang down from the ceiling. I feel an odd sense of home here. An instinctual urge calls to me to go to the water.

"Dom, please bring me to the water; my beast wants to be in the water." I look over to my father and he's smiling. I love my dad, but he looks like a happy Hannibal Lecter.

"Something I need to know, Dad?" He's still smiling, and if these freaking contractions didn't hurt so much, I would almost find him comical at the moment.

My father takes my hand and begins to lead me to the water's edge. "Your ancestors, when they chose to carry their babies as humans, used to birth in these same waters. They have healing and soothing properties. All the great queens of our bloodline have swam in this pool. Now it's your turn Aurora. Go forth and deliver the future into this world." He leans forward and kisses my forehead, then moves towards the opening of the cavern. He shifts to his dragon and takes on a blocking position, guarding the only entrance.

Alaric and Klaus decide they will go into the waters with me first. As we wade deeper into the water, a sense of calm washes over me, and the contractions are bearable. The guys take turns switching out, helping support me in the water. The only constant throughout the hours is Alaric holding tightly onto me in some shape or form. I scream, cry, and want to give up at some point. I can easily take out a horde, but this tiny little being, this piece of me, feels like she's trying to rip my insides out. At some point in the last few weeks, the guys have managed to stock juices here for me as well as food—mostly for them.

When I reach hour number ten thousand and eighty-five, I feel like I'm finally progressing somewhere. My beast urges me to climb onto the moss-covered island. "I need to move. I need to climb." I'm panting between words as Alaric and Dimitri help me up onto the moss. I crawl on all fours until I find a spot that my beast and I agree on. The contractions are stronger and closer together now, and I've regained the ability to partially shift. My forearms shift to my armored gauntlets. As I sink my talons into the earth, I bear down through a contraction.

"Alaric, you need to get over here!" Klaus calls as he sits at my feet. For now, he's in charge of watching for the baby. I have my head resting on Dimitri's shoulder, my talons sunk into the earth on either side of him. Jayce and Dominik were on either side of me, pouring cool pool water over my back to keep me comfortable. Alaric is on his way back with my juice when Klaus calls him. The panic in Klaus's voice makes my father turns his great dragon head to look in our direction.

On his way past me, Alaric hands Dimitri my juice, who in turn offers me the straw. I take a nice long drink of the sweet, cool pineapple juice. I feel Alaric's hand on my hip as he bends to see what Klaus is looking at. Here I am on all fours, in labor, and the guys are having a meeting staring at my hoo-ha. "Everything is okay love, we see the baby's head, that's all," Alaric says, then comes forward and kisses my temple. The twins go back to rubbing my lower back, each of the guys keeping some form of contact with me at all times.

"Angel, I'm going to need you to push and hold it real soon, okay?" Klaus's German accent is still sexy, even though I feel fucking gross and tired.

Dimitri nuzzles my cheek then kisses it. "You can do this, baby girl. If you can take out a horde by yourself, you can push out one baby." I smile at Dimitri's encouragement as I hear the other guys back up his statement.

I'm tired, I won't lie. I feel one of the guards enter the cavern, and I start to draw some dragon energy from him. Right now, I need it more than he does. I hear Alaric say the man is down and to release him. I release him quickly and push hard again on the next contraction.

I feel my baby slide free from my body, but I don't hear any noise from it. I turn quickly to see what's wrong, and then I see it. My baby was born as her animal; Tiamat is the cutest little thing. She has almost pure white scales that are edged in fur. Her front legs are typical dragon hands; her hind legs have wolven paws for feet. Tia's tail is mostly dragon in shape, but it has fur along the underside of it. As a matter of fact, her underbelly scales have more fur on them than the scales on her back. I reach down and pick up my daughter, holding her tightly to me. Tia's eyes are like mine and her father's silver orbs with a black slit in the middle.

CHAPTER 71

Aurora

I am in complete awe of this beautiful little girl in my arms. My father's dragon comes ambling over and lowers his large head to look at the baby. Tia attempts to blow fire at her grandfather. She blows a small plume of frost flames that are quickly snuffed out. I can't help but laugh at the tenacity of my daughter.

Alaric moves off the island and shifts to his dragon, lowering his head to Tiamat. My brave little girl slides off my lap and onto the ground. She walks wobbly over to her father. Alaric opens his mouth and without hesitation Tia climbs in to lie down on his tongue. I'm kind of jealous; I will never have that part of the dragon connection with my daughter. I watch Alaric and Nicodeamus with Tia, playing on the ground on the other side of the pool.

Slowly, I move and climb into Jayce's lap to rest and watch my newborn dragoness play with her father and grandfather. I'm in shock when I suddenly feel another contraction out of nowhere.

Dimitri assures me it's normal for my body to expel the placenta from my body. I shrug and look around, over by where I was before is Tia's placenta.

"Guys, Tia isn't an only child!" I scream before doubling over from the force of the contraction. Jayce is in panic mode, Dimitri is white as a sheet, and Klaus is holding another juice for me like it's no big thing. Dominik comes running back in from the cavern that we have deemed the bathroom.

Alaric shifts back to his human form and carries Tiamat back over with him. This baby is coming much faster than the first one, and that scares the shit out of me. I feel like I've barely had time to rest after the first baby, and now surprise, there's a second one in there. Klaus switches out with Dimitri. The twins are on baby watch; Dimitri and Alaric are at my sides, comforting me. The cool water feels freaking fantastic running down my spine as I rock back and forth with each contraction.

I open my eyes to find Tia looking up at my face from underneath me. I can't help but smile through the pain at my baby girl. I shift my arms to my gauntlets, and Tia moves to go investigate my scales. When her nose touches my scales, I feel her frost move over them slowly. That's my girl. She may have grandpa's fire. But she can freeze a fucker like her momma.

Eventually, I feel my second baby slide free, and I hear it cry out. I can just see a small plume of blue flame. Okay, we have a mostly frost dragon hatchling this time. I move so I can see my child and it's beautiful. I make sure to shift my hands back so I can handle my new baby. I'm saying it because one, I wasn't expecting this one. Second, how do you sex a baby dragon? Alaric picks up the baby, flips it back and forth, earning him a blast of blue flames in his face. He smirks as he shifts his eyes to his dragon's, and the baby settles down. "He's going to be a tough one," Alaric says and then tilts his head, looking at me, waiting for me to catch on.

"Aren't all babies hard, though?" I say, not catching his drift in the slightest.

"Aurora, love, I know you're tired, but you have a son to help me name," Alaric says, passing the new baby over to me.

I smile, looking him over and nuzzle his face. *His* face! I look up in shock, from the baby back to Alaric, then to the guys, finally back to my son. He's almost exactly like Tia, except he has more wolven features than she does. His front hands look like my shifted ones: heavily armored gauntlets with long white talons. His hind feet are all wolven. He also has less fur adorning his scales than Tia does.

Like his sister, his stomach and underside of his tail are covered in my white fur, thick armor scales protect his chest and belly underneath the fur. For the most part, his face is all dragon until you get to his eye shape and his ears. I smile softly and grumble at my son; his little tail whips about excitedly.

"Ladon Uther Kraus. Named after the legendary thousand-headed dragon, and after the original Pendragon from King Arthur's court." Ladon blows more blue flames, celebrating being named, and then proceeds to slip from my hands, chasing after his sister. The two babies play-wrestle back and forth. They are just about equal in size and strength; that is until they start blowing fire at each other.

At this point, Alaric intervenes and I just lay back, resting against Klaus. "Well, that explains why I felt like I was going to explode." I motion to my babies and rub my stomach. I notice I'm still bleeding, so does my father.

"Aurora, you need to shift. I think the babies' scales and claws cut you up a little on their way out. I can bathe you in my flames to help heal you faster."

The guys all freeze looking at me, only now noticing the small, steady stream of blood running down my leg. I stand and stretch before walking to the middle of the cavern. I look back at my babies and smile before I begin my shift.

Slowly, I shift my body to that of my beast, making sure everything moves and rearranges in perfect order. My animal has grown in size again. Her frame is more muscular and defined. I'm easily ten foot now. My arms and legs are as thick as tree trunks. I swing my great wolven head around to look at my body, I now have heavily armored scales on my paws up to the bend of my knee. Next, I raise my hand and examine my gauntlets; they have become more aggressive-looking. My scales have sharper edges to them than they had before. My talons are still long, hooked, and razor-sharp. I have the urge to try something new. I reach down deeply as I probe my father's knowledge.

Nicodeamus's eyes light up as he senses what I'm searching for. He shifts quickly and demonstrates how to breathe fire; his flames bathe me and help accelerate my healing process. I tilt my head several times before that familiar sound of the ignitor clicks can be heard.

My mates leap back as my beast breathes fire for the first time; I freeze everything in the flame's path. My babies leap towards me, and I lower myself down onto all fours, greeting them as my animal. We sniff and lick at each other as we get to know each other. My mates are concerned as to what this will mean for me. As far as I'm concerned, today is just another day, and I've acquired another weapon to help me on my journey.

I lock eyes with my children, and as I shift back I force their shift to happen along with mine. Both children's transition to their human is rather effortless. I don't have to use too much Alpha influence to help them assume their other forms. I now have two chunky little cherubs sitting there looking at me. Having been born in their dragon form gives them an advantage. They have the trunk control of an older baby. I am truly amazed looking between them as I move to pick them both up.

I snuggle my babies to my breasts and both latch on, feeding immediately. Softly, I yawn, and immediately Dimitri and Alaric are at my side to guide me over to where Jayce and Dom have set up a place for me to rest. I snuggle in, holding both babies, watching them feed from my breasts. Now I really must work on hunting down those that may bring my children harm. First, I need to make sure the Ice Palace is sorted before moving on to my next target.

The guys all gather around, looking at the twins in my arms. Both babies have platinum blonde hair and grey eyes. Tia has flecks of green in her eyes, like Alaric. Ladon has blue flecks like Nicodeamus and I do. Both babies have my birthmark on their wrists; it's a white crescent moon. The twins finish feeding, and I pass one off to Alaric and the other off to my father after he sits down. I smile softly, looking at my little family that I've made. The rest of the guys gather around the babies, excited to get a closer look at them.

I slowly remove myself from my pillow palace and head to the water surrounding the island. My father said it has regenerative properties. To be brutally honest, I feel like I was just put through a shredder. Slowly, I swim lazy laps around the island, letting the water work its magic. Under the water, I notice movement, so I dive and go after it. It's a large catfish. Apparently, there's a small feeder stream that it must have used to get here. I surface, drawing in a deep breath before hunting the catfish. Two attempts later, I'm finally able to sink my talons into its flesh.

I throw my catch up onto the island and swim to the edge after it. My shift comes quickly, and it just so happens, my baby's shift too. They wiggle out of their father's and grandfather's arms to head over to my catch. I quickly skin the catfish, lower my muzzle, and rip a chunk of flesh off to eat. The babies imitate me, biting and ripping at their food.

My wolven and bear mates look at the scene before them in horror. The twins and I are eating sashimi as our animals. The dragon's side of the family is happy to see my young eating so well. I eat at least half of the catfish, leaving the rest for the babies. Slowly, I shift back to my human form and sit close by, watching over my children. For now, my enemies have been given a reprieve. I'll soon be going over all of the intel I've been given, and I'll formulate a plan of action.

The babies eat their fill and come over to me, ready to go to sleep. "We need to be thinking about heading back. The babies are safer if they remain as their animals for now. At least they can run, hide, and defend themselves if they have to." I lay a hand on each child before looking to my mates. Slowly they nod, agreeing with me. Alaric moves to the end of the cavern and starts making arrangements for our trip back. Klaus helps me stand and dress in my flight clothing.

Now that I'm not pregnant, I have room in my coat for my babies. I haven't bounced back one hundred percent yet; a few more shifts should have me back in top form. I gently pick up my sleeping babies and bundle them in my coat to protect them from the wind. Alaric gives me a look as if to say, "What the fuck are you doing?" I open my coat to show him our babies, and his dragon's head nods slowly. He then gets into position so I can climb on. Once in place, my father joins us, sitting just before Alaric's wings. *Are you ready, love? Are the babies settled?* Alaric asks me through the bond.

I gently rub my cargo and smile. *Our children are asleep. Tomorrow, however, we will rain hell upon those that may stand against us. Then we leave as quickly as possible to Klaus's pack and then summon the others,* I say to Alaric through our bond. I feel Dominik's fear through the bond as his guard goes into free fall out of the mouth of the cavern. Jayce, on the other hand, is elated, enjoying the fall. I swear those two crack me up. They are such opposites. One tough, one soft, one terrified of heights, the other loves it. It's kind of comical if you ask me.

Alaric carefully launches us out the mouth of the cavern. We gently glide upon the thermals until he feels it's safe to start really flying. I feel my babies moving about within my coat, so I pop two buttons in the middle, allowing them to poke their heads out. *Is it too cold for them out here, Alaric? They are quite curious about the flight.* I gently stroke my babies' heads, waiting for Alaric to answer me.

No, love, they are part Ice Dragon after all. Take them out one at a time and let them see over the top of my head as I fly. Make sure to keep a good grip on them, so they don't go into free fall. Alaric's concern for the babies' safety warms my heart.

Carefully, I pull Tiamat out first and rest her little taloned hands on the ridge of her father's dragon's crown. She calls out her excitement, making her little baby dragon noises. We spend the remainder of our flight with the babies taking turns watching the flight over the top of their father's head.

My own father is quite amused watching me with the babies. I guess, in a way, he wishes he could have done this with me. I mean, have my mom hold me while he flew us around. It makes me want to cry over all that we have missed out on, all because of Vladimir. There will be no mercy for him, nor for the rest of his bloodline.

We arrive back at the castle by early morning and apparently, we've attracted the attention of all of our guests. I pull both babies out of my coat, and they perch on my shoulders. They are looking around curiously at all the people. "Do not trust anyone other than whom your fathers, grandfather, and I say it's okay to go to. There are bad people here who would love to see us dead." Both babies move to look at me, and I shift my eyes to that of my beast and begin to teach them the recent history.

Alaric senses what I'm doing, and keeps his head held high, and remains standing. I gently pat his scales, letting him know I'm done, and he slowly lies down when the rest of my mates gather. My father slides off first and moves to back the crowd up. My War Dragon guards assist my father in containing the group. Jayce and Dominik are already shifted to their wolves waiting for me. Dimitri and Klaus are in a position to help me off of Alaric's neck.

Oohs and *Ah's*, and a ton of *oh, they're so cutes* are heard as I'm escorted into the castle, then back to our private chambers. I'm starving, and I have two babies I still have to nurse yet. Everyone gathers in what I call my bedroom, and the babies are let loose to play as they wish. "Any updates while we were gone?" I ask, looking towards my father and Alaric.

My father is the first to respond. "Your personal guards snuffed out several more usurpers in our absence. Having them sleep in your bed was a stroke of genius, daughter. All appears to be settled here. We just need to have a gala to announce the babies' births, and then we can leave. We can plan the christening for some time after we take back the Marelup throne." Nicodeamus smiles, then jumps because it seems that Ladon just tried to freeze his grandfather to the floor. I can't help but laugh at their actions. Alaric, however, is just shaking his head, looking at the twins.

"Oh, relax, grumpy! They are just playing!" I say to Alaric as I try not to continue to laugh at my children's antics. The babies continue to run and play as the guys sit down to do all the planning.

When I say the guys, I mean Jayce and Klaus. Dominik, Alaric, and Dimitri are handling setting up security, and Nicodeamus is on the floor playing with the kids now. My mates are all bonded to me, my babies are happy and healthy, and my father has a perpetual smile on his face. Everything is very good in my world right now.

CHAPTER 72
Alaric

February-

I'm back at my favorite crystalline desk; it feels like forever since I've sat here to conduct business. I still have all the maps and sketches I made when I was first aware of Aurora. I run my fingers over the charts and my doodles I had made of her face. It's hard to believe that almost a year has passed, and here I am a father, her mate, and now king. Slowly, I open the top drawer of my desk, taking out my favorite parchment. I begin to write the birth announcements that shall be personally flown to the different kingdoms around the world.

To my right is the list of godparents that Aurora and I have come up with for our children. Aurora barely trusts any females so there will be no godmothers for our kids. She has however picked out three godfathers, and I agree with her choices wholeheartedly. I have chosen my long-standing friend Austin Skybane as a guardian for my daughter. Austin's Kingdom is on a hidden island off of New Zealand. Aurora has chosen Ellis as a guardian for our son, as well as both War Dragons. She figured since Polar Bears are not long-lived, the War Dragons would be a good backup. I decide to write Austin's letter first.

Dear Austin,

It feels like forever since the last time I have put pen to paper. I have wonderful news to share with you. Remember that unique female I wrote to you about? The hybrid? Well, she's my mate, we married and have birthed twins! Twins! Can you believe it? I hope you would do me the honor and agree to be my daughter, Tiamat Andrea Kraus' Godfather. No pressure or anything. If you have found your mate, I would be honored if she would be Tia's Godmother. I hope all is well with you and your family. As soon as we have a date for the christening and the proper coronation, I will send word.

Respectfully,
King Alaric Kraus

I LAUGH TO MYSELF, thinking about how I have signed the letter to one of my best friends. He's going to shit bricks when he sees I'm now king and not my father. I feel the guys panicking and Aurora's agitation. Something's set my mate off. I need to go defuse the bomb before there's a slaughter on our hands.

I run downstairs and head to the fitting room. Aurora looks like a heavenly vision in her flowing gown. That is until I notice her arms are shifted, and she has a seamstress in an ice prison. "Aurora, baby, what seems to be the matter?" I look at the beautiful dress and then over to the seamstress.

"She said she had a hard time with you and your trousers. She doesn't belong anywhere near your trousers. Where's the usual seamstress that does your clothing?" Aurora is using her talons to accentuate her displeasure over a single female making adjustments to my wardrobe. That's where the problem lies.

"Love, Helline passed on while we were gone. Her granddaughter took over her duties so that we wouldn't be without a head seamstress." I hold my hands up in a placating manner, trying to get my mate to calm down. She's definitely more territorial now that the babies have been born.

Aurora looks between the young seamstress she has trapped and me. "Sorry for your loss." She releases the girl quickly, then her eyes move between her other mates and me. "No one gets fitted alone. *Ever*." Aurora's eyes land on the young girl now, and she looks her over. "You're a wolf, am I correct?" Aurora slowly shifts her hands back to humans as she waits for an answer.

"Yes, my Queen," the girl answers softly with her eyes low, staring at the ground.

"Klaus, Dominik, gather all our single males. This young female shouldn't be without a mate during times like this. If one is her mate, fantastic. If not, she comes with us when we leave to go to Klaus' pack. Hopefully, she will find her mate and my animal will settle." Aurora looks down at the girl and notices her smiling. Slowly, a smile creeps over Aurora's lips. Her eyes raise to me, and she winks. Apparently, she's pleased with her progress.

Dimitri meets me by the door as I go to leave. He motions for us to walk away from the others. We head down the hallway and into the library. "Something on your mind, Dimitri?"

"Da, Alaric. Aurora has located Elena. She's not far from Klaus's pack. There's been minor skirmishes between the packs lately. Thankfully, Klaus's pack is larger and stronger. Aurora is planning on hunting down the old witch and slaughtering her." Dimitri word vomits the information, sounding like it's no big deal.

I raise an eyebrow at him, then start to stroke my beard. "So what you're essentially saying is that Aurora is going to go all homicidal when we arrive at Klaus' pack, but not to worry?" I tilt my head to the side, looking at Dimitri, waiting to see if I have made a fair assessment of what he's told me.

"Sounds about right, Alaric." Dimitri shrugs his shoulders, then goes and pours two glasses of brandy. He returns and hands me one of them. "She's also planning on searching for my people to see if any still live before we attack the castle. Aurora figures that if any Great Bears still live, it would be an asset to have them with us." He downs his glass in one swallow. I can immediately tell the subject bothers him greatly. Dimitri won't meet my eyes as I rest a hand on his shoulder.

"Aurora wants to search so you don't feel alone in the world. She loves you so much, and I have it on good authority she wants to try to have your cub once the war is over." Dimitri's bear surges to the surface and he now looks at me, smiling.

Without warning, the big guy wraps his massive arms around me and literally bear hugs me. I'm almost unable to breathe with the force he's exerting. "This is fantastic news! Thank you, Alaric," Dimitri spins me in circles as he lovingly squeezes the life out of me. Dimitri eventually stops spinning us, and I'm dizzy as fuck. I look up towards the door to find Aurora with the twins latched to her breasts. Her robe is open just enough that I can see both babies' shoulders while keeping herself covered.

Aurora smiles and starts to laugh. "I'm guessing Alaric told you my plans, D?" Aurora's eyes shift to that of her beast as she stares at me. Yup, I prematurely spilled the beans, and now she's not happy with me. Aurora's eyes shift back to human as she turns to look at Dimitri.

"Does this news please you?" I watch Aurora move slowly and rests her forehead on Dimitri's shoulder. I still can't get used to the idea of Aurora looking unsure of herself in regards to anything.

Dimitri lets go of me like I was set on fire, and he carefully turns and takes Aurora and the babies in his arms. I watch Dimitri's hand come up to gently move aside the robe, and he kisses the crown of both babies' heads. His hand moves to cup Aurora's cheek; he lightly kisses her pouting lips. Honestly, I feel like I'm watching one of those Hallmark movies. "Aurora, I am extremely blessed just by being allowed all this time with you. You've gifted us with babies, your undying love, and loyalty. We are blessed every day we get to have you in our lives." He sighs and glances at me briefly before continuing.

This level of emotional honesty from the big guy is definitely a huge change for him. "One day, when the time is right, and you gift me with my own cub, it will be the second greatest day of my life." Dimitri ends his declaration by kissing Aurora. Me, I'm over here blubbering like a fool, having listened to one of the most romantic speeches I've ever heard.

Aurora has her own tears freely flowing down her cheeks. Carefully, Dimitri wipes them away. Being the wiseass that I am, I search my phone and put on November Rain by Guns n Roses. Both of them look at me and smirk. It seems like it's the sound-track of their love story. I leave my phone on the desk and walk out of the room, leaving them to their moment.

Those two I swear I don't know how Dimitri went from guardian to mate. I know our animals have a lot to do with how we process things. Dimitri explained it to me: his bear wanted her from the moment she turned a hundred. As soon as those womanly curves kicked in, it was over. It was the reason he kept going to town to relieve himself. I don't know if it is just because Aurora is a hybrid or something else that kept her from ascending. Aurora should have ascended long before her hundredth birthday. I'll have to ask Nicodeamus about that one. Even to this day, that one little fact still puzzles me. I wonder exactly how far Elena meddled with Aurora and her life?

I find myself wandering into the throne room, looking at all the decorations going up. It's nice to feel the lack of my father's oppressive presence. After Bane's death, it seems like a new life was breathed into the castle and the staff. Random staff approach and congratulate me on the birth of our children.

Not a single soul here knows of Aurora's changes, and we are not about to let anyone know until we absolutely have to. I find Nicodeamus making an ice sculpture in the corner of the room. He absolutely cracks me up with the odd things I see him doing. The statue is of a dragon with hatchlings at its feet. I'm guessing a family portrait in ice? I watch him for several moments more before turning to leave.

I need to seek Klaus out to make sure the arrangements for our trip to his pack are under control. Klaus' twin and grandmother are flying back to Germany this morning. That way they can begin to set up for the Dire Wolves, as well as the American Lycan pack. I reach out through the bond and find Klaus and Jayce are together in the war room.

Good, I get to kill two birds with one stone. On the large mahogany table, they have a map of Klaus' pack lands; the board behind them has Romania's map, the region that Dimitri comes from. On the wall opposite the board, they map the area around the Marelup castle in the Carpathian Mountains. Right now, the boys are focused on Klaus's pack lands and the existing structure.

"Need any help?" The guys aren't expecting to hear my voice, and they jump. Klaus starts to laugh, and Jayce still appears to be slightly shaken. "Sorry about that. How are we making out with the plans for the big move?" I walk over and sit in the leather recliner stationed in the corner, waiting to hear what they have to say.

Klaus moves and hands me a smaller version of the three maps, then moves back to the big one on the table. With Jayce's help, they pin it up on the wall over the map of the castle. "The housing situation has been resolved. The indoor training pit, as well as the storage hanger, have been emptied out. Both are being filled with cots as we speak. We figure we'd keep the two species separate, just because we are not sure if there are any traitors in the American Lycan pack." Klaus moves and points to the large buildings on the map, and I look at the corresponding spot on the map in my hands.

"Klaus, where on here is the Alpha house? Is it in a safe location in relation to the temporary housing? The last thing we need is Aurora going on a murdering spree because someone got too close to her babies." I raise both my eyebrows, looking at my expert planners. I watch them both look at the map, back at each other, then finally settling on me as they smile.

"Yes, it's far enough away," Jayce says enthusiastically, then spins to look over the map one more time. "They have a hot spring on the property, as well as a day spa. Aurora will love it. Oh! And the best part is the chocolate factory is only about two miles away." Jayce is beside himself with excitement. I haven't seen that man this happy since he watched me fuck Klaus.

I shake my head at the two of them and just start laughing. "I'm glad the logistics of the move are left in your capable hands. Just remember the gala is at sunset. You're expected to be in your tuxedos and dress shoes. Aurora has gone into the treasury to retrieve the adornments she wants us all to wear." Jayce and Klaus look at each other with such excitement. Without warning, they both leave the room to go investigate. Actually, come to think of it, I'm quite curious myself about what Aurora has picked out for me to wear.

CHAPTER 73

Alaric

FEBRUARY -

I wander the hallways heading back to the suites, grabbing my bond mates along the way. We make it into the shared living quarters and there's Aurora, standing on a pedestal in all her celestial glory. Her gown makes it look like she has wings hanging down her back. She's currently wearing a crown I've never seen before. The crown is rather ornate; it appears to be made of Elven mithril and adorned with thousands of diamonds. It's as if Aurora is wearing all the stars in the sky upon her head.

In front of her stands a man with long, black hair and pointed ears. I've never seen him before, but apparently, Nicodeamus knows him and Aurora is comfortable with him being in her nest. Aurora's head turns slowly and she smiles. "Hey, guys! I'd like you to meet Oberon, King of the High Elves," Aurora says as she motions to the man before her. "He's come to bless the children and me. I, apparently am a beast of legend." She smiles and looks back down to Oberon.

"Yes, Young Queen, you most certainly are a beast of legend, but the question is, which path will you choose once your mission is complete?" Oberon states in that musical voice of his.

He slowly turns to look at the rest of us; he moves forward to greet each of us in turn. High Elves themselves are beings of legend, and to attract the attention of the king himself is a huge deal. "You have gathered the strongest bloodlines from each of the species of old." Oberon moves and stops before Dimitri and lightly grips his jaw.

"Great Bear, you are not alone. Your original tribe is still alive in the mountains where you were born. My people and I maintain a barrier around their territory to protect them." Oberon hands Dimitri an amulet and smiles. "This will help you find your people when you are ready to go home." Oberon moves away from Dimitri then back over to Aurora.

Oberon offers her his hand, and he assists her down off the pedestal. "You are ready, Young Queen. Remember, hide your true potential until your final battle. You don't want anyone preparing for what you can accomplish." Oberon leans forward and kisses Aurora's forehead, then vanishes into a shimmering mist.

Aurora looks serene. It's quite scary to see her like this. She seems at peace, settled. I'm happy but concerned at the same time. "Aurora, you seem a bit different. Is everything alright?" I tilt my head to the side and look at her, waiting for her to answer me.

With a fluid grace I haven't seen before, Aurora seems to glide over to me. Gently, she lays her hands in mine and looks up at me, her steel-grey eyes focused on me. "Oberon helped settle my dual nature. Unfortunately, unlike the rest of you, I technically shouldn't exist. Well, what I mean is I shouldn't exist as I am, being an almost equal split of both species." She tilts her head to the side smiling softly.

"Oberon said my dragon side is the most dominant. He used some old elvish magic to help my animal sides be more at peace and work together. I know we're not separate beings, but the dual natures and instincts sometimes confuses the hell out of me. Oberon said that's why my temper has such a short fuse. It's because I couldn't handle the mixed signals." Aurora shrugs her shoulders and just smiles up at me like it's that simple. To be honest, it really is. If her dual nature was causing her homicide-switch to flip, and he just fixed it, well, that's the best news ever.

"What did Oberon mean by which path you'll choose?" I lean forward and gently kiss Aurora's full, blood-red lips. Nicodeamus takes Aurora's hand and leads her over to the tall stool for her to sit on.

Aurora draws in a deep breath, then looks back to me. "I'm not the first of my kind; I'm actually the second one to be born like this. The first was a Black Dragon and Lycan hybrid. He went insane from the power of the two bloodlines. It took an entire army of elves and other dragons to take him down." Aurora looks down, then at her own hands, shifting them to her beast's gauntlets.

"Oberon says I'm more deadly than that male was because my beast literally took on the most dangerous traits from each mated species. I have Jayce's venom and can release it in either form. I have Dominik's agility and his night vision. From Klaus, I have his added speed and ability to jump to great heights. Dimitri, oh gods he was a deadly addition. I gained the mass and strength of his bear and its height. Alaric, my love, I gained your immunity to both types of fire. You've also given me the ability to breathe fire, which is unheard of."

Aurora slowly shifts her hands back, looks back up, and smiles. "I gained a lot of good traits as well from Jayce: his soft heart and compassion. Dominik gave me the ability to assess a situation quickly and pick the best course of action. I gained an almost extrasensory perception—Oberon said the older species of Lycans just know things. I got that gift from Klaus."

She smiles then turns slightly to look at Dimitri. "From Dimitri, I gained his infinite patience, and now that my beast is settled, I can use it. From you, Alaric, I gained a stronger will than I had before and a higher value on life." She reaches out and grips my hand and gives it a squeeze." All of these extra gifts were hidden by how unsettled my beast was. Oberon blessed our babies and me so that we all can be at peace." She glances down for a moment before looking up again making eye contact with each of us.

"I choose the path of the benevolent leader, not the bloodthirsty tyrant. Well, that is, I will. After I kill Elena and Vladimir, then take back my family's castle." Aurora takes the offered drink from Jayce and looks at all of us.

I'm honestly floored by all that Aurora has said. To think, all this time, she's been struggling with an internal war, and none of us knew about it. I feel horrible that our mate was possibly in her own private hell and never told any of us. Our servant comes in and alerts us to the fact that the guests are starting to arrive. Aurora rises up ever so gracefully and walks over to where the twins are curled up, sleeping as their dragons.

Aurora shocks me by making dragon sounds at the twins to wake them. I look to the guys, and yup, we're all surprised to watch and listen to what she can do now.

Tiamat and Ladon have almost doubled in size over the last few weeks. We attribute their rapid growth to the fact that they spend more time as their dragons than as babies. Aurora believes they are safer as their dragons, and I hate to admit it but she's right. Aurora bends down and picks up Tiamat, passing her to me. She then reaches down and picks up Ladon holding him close to her breasts. Slowly, he climbs up and wraps himself around her shoulders, preferring to sit up there so he can see better.

Tiamat, having seen what her brother did, also climbs up on my shoulders and lies down. I guess this is how we're presenting the babies to the world: as their animals. Through the bond, Aurora reaches out to all of us. *I want our babies to have a happy childhood. People cannot abduct children whose faces they have never seen. They are the first children born of me; those seeking to snuff out my bloodline will go for the children first, not me.* I hate to say it but Aurora's logic completely makes sense. We each take a turn kissing Aurora, then line up to head out.

Dimitri and Klaus take point, Jayce and Dominik following behind us. Aurora has her hand resting on my forearm as our children happily chatter with each other. We enter the grand ballroom to find Nicodeamus already standing on the platform near all of the thrones.

Not only did Aurora make sure each mate has a crown upon his head, but she also made sure they have a throne. We walk in time with the music that Nicodeamus has chosen for this momentous event. I feel Aurora's hand tighten on my forearm, and she begins to look around the room slowly. Something isn't right and she's on high alert. I look up to see Nicodeamus with his eyes shifted, looking around. Aurora's breathing has slowed as she uses her father's vantage point to look around. At the very last second, she shoves me out of the way and catches a knife in her now-shifted hand.

I feel the room shift, along with Aurora's temper. She's commanding the dragons under her rule to seal the room. Carefully, she hands Ladon off to Dimitri and turns to walk through the crowd. Aurora stops before a female Red Dragon. She is one of the females my father tried to force me to take as a mate. "You threaten my mate? Your king?" Aurora's voice is a mix of her beast, with hints of her human tone. You can see Aurora's canines descend, as well as hear her talons clicking together in agitation.

"Abomination! You do not deserve a dragon like Alaric. He is to be mine!" The female screams at Aurora and shifts her forearms to her gauntlets. I compare the two quickly, trying to assess the situation. The red female has nothing on Aurora in the weapons department. "I challenge you to the pit. Beast on beast for the king's hand."

Aurora just starts to laugh hysterically at the female before her. "You? Wish to fight me? I killed Nexus by myself. Besides, if I die…" Aurora moves her hair aside to reveal my scale upon her chest. "Alaric will follow me into the great beyond, to the land of our ancestors. However, you will be left alone here, in the land of the living, having killed a monarch and sentenced to death. Your soul will never go to Elysium. Oh no, a far worse fate awaits you, my dear." Aurora bows her head lightly to her father. "Prepare the pit! Tonight, I get to stretch my talons and add another head to my throne." Aurora's words have struck fear into Camile, and she comes running over to me, dropping to her knees.

"Please. Spare me! Forgive my trespass!" Camile grovels at my feet, kissing the tops of my shoes. Before I have a chance to answer, Nicodeamus comes up to my side and rests a hand on my shoulder.

"At the stroke of midnight, on the Ides of March, your wish to battle the new Blood Queen shall be granted. Be happy she didn't call for the horde to descend upon you." Nicodeamus speaks like the King of old, like the man he used to be before losing his mate. Tiamat moves and climbs onto her grandfather's shoulder, then breathes fire at Camile, sending her scurrying backward away from us. In typical Nicodeamus fashion, he tells Tiamat how proud he is and she's such a good girl.

All I can do is shake my head at him, then look up at Aurora sitting upon her throne. She's switched crowns to her great-grandmother's, and she's owning the title her father has bestowed upon her. I approach Aurora, and she smiles at me like nothing has happened. Dimitri sits to her left and me to her right; Ladon now sits upon his mother's lap watching the celebration. We have fifteen days until the battle. Camile will sit in a cell waiting for death during that time. Tonight, we celebrate our children and the successful birth of a princess and a prince.

CHAPTER 74

Jayce

March-

It's been fourteen days since the last attempt on anyone's life. Since then, life has been pretty good. The babies are growing quickly. Especially since if we leave our chambers, they return to the forms of their animals. Aurora and the children are in the main landing area today because the babies keep trying to fly. Alaric feels it's time for them to start learning. So, he's lying down, letting the babies climb up him and jump off of his head. Aurora and Nicodeamus are cracking up, catching the babies when they don't quite get the lift they need. Ladon seems to get the longest hang time when he jumps.

Aurora doesn't have a care in the world right now. Well, all she cares about is her mates and babies. Alaric is nervous, but he won't say anything to Aurora. Klaus and I are terrified for Aurora; we don't want her to die. Klaus comes over to join me at the bench, carrying the laptop and drinks for us.

We sit side by side, booking the last of the flights for my people, as well as the American Lycans my brother feels are loyal. This morning, Alex sent word that he had to put almost a dozen Lycan down because they tried to cause an uprising. Without their Alpha, they are more prone to their base urges and for Lycans, it's to battle.

Ten hours until battle time, and my nerves are shot. Klaus, Dimitri, and I spent a good three hours in and out of bed with Aurora this morning, trying to dickmatize her into not wanting to battle. Her answer was that honor dictates she answer the challenge. I get that. I really do, but she's a mom now and they should come before honor and duty. Currently, Dominik and Dimitri are in the pit, making sure it can withstand what will happen tonight.

Several hours pass, and it's dinner time. We decide to dine alone in our private chambers so Aurora can relax. The babies are the size of toddlers, walking around all wobbly. Still babbling since their human vocal cords haven't fully developed yet. Ladon has learned to speak through the bond, mostly through direct contact with the family's non-dragon members. Tiamat doesn't even try since Ladon speaks for both of them most of the time. His parents and grandfather can hear him over a distance through the bond.

In a way, I'm a bit jealous of that level of connection to the children. But I know in time I'll have my own pup to have that special connection with. In a way, it's great that the dragon babies were born first. They'll help protect their younger siblings.

A knock sounds at the door and Dimitri moves to open it. The pit master is at the door. Nicodeamus walks over to him with the list of dignitaries that are allowed to witness the battle tonight. None of us know what Aurora is going to do, or honestly what she's capable of since Oberon's visit. Aurora's power and her beast seem to be more focused and in tune with her. There are no more internal power struggles or wars going on that would lead to her lashing out over nothing. The guys and I are concerned about what's going to happen tonight, especially since she's so deadly calm right now.

Aurora watches the exchange at the door and goes back to eating her almost raw venison. She isn't being snobbish about her power or swinging it around like a big dick in the wind. I feel it's like she's playing a huge poker tournament. She's holding her cards close to her chest, so no one knows what to expect from her.

Here it is, go time. Aurora has Klaus in what looks like a mobile DJ booth, up in one of the standard viewing booths. Aurora has apparently set a playlist for this battle. Dimitri said that Aurora always has a soundtrack for every part of her life. Every big event and challenge, she's pinned a song to it, just to keep her focused.

Camile enters the pit first and goes through her shift, nothing theatrical like Aurora does. She's rather large for a Red Dragon and a female to boot. Camile proves her power and dominance by blowing, and sustaining, a stream of fire for a long time before roaring.

I watch Klaus's eyes bleed to mercury when Aurora reaches out to him. Klaus's eyes meet mine and the other mates before he nods his head. The song Aurora chose to walk into the pit is "Feel Invincible" by Skillet. The first few powerful hits of the bass and guitar trigger the side doors to blow open.

Aurora enters in a cloud of frost-like mist. Aurora is wearing a two-piece bikini with a sheer robe that shimmers in the light like diamonds. The part comes when the singer hits "There's a reason to fight," she points up to us then sends a wave of frost to coat the pit. Aurora cracks her neck, still prowling around the pit, looking

Camile over. Aurora's eyes are that of her beast, and she's searching for weaknesses. I see Alaric's, Nicodeamus's, and Dimitri's eyes are all mercury. They apparently are teaching her about Red Dragons.

There's the smirk I was waiting to see from Aurora. She nods her head slowly then wiggles her finger for Camile to attack. I'm borderline ready to have a heart attack. Aurora is just standing there when Camile opens her dragon's maw and rains fire down upon her. It looks like a river of lava flowing over her, I can't see her and I'm terrified.

Alaric and Dominik come over to hold me, telling me to have faith in our mate. Then it happens, a mass of frost starts to overpower the fire. Aurora is fully shifted, and her beast is mammoth; roaring blue frost flames—like Nicodeamus can do—right back at Camile. Camile's dragon leaps back, not sure what to make of the hybrid beast before it.

Aurora looks like an interesting blending of her Dragon and Lycan bloodlines. Aurora stands bi-pedal like a Lycan—her feet are all Lycan. The shape of Aurora's head is mostly Lycan with some dragon traits. Aurora's taloned gauntlets look even more lethal than they did before. Aurora's body shape is basically Lycan except for the addition of scale armor on her arms, legs, and muzzle. Aurora takes full advantage of Camile's shock and charges at her by launching up into the air. The talons on her hands and the claws on her feet gain purchase on Camile's scales.

Camile attempts to shake Aurora off of her, only causing more damage to herself in the process. Aurora makes several swipes, and Camile's left wing falls to the ground before Aurora leaps off and lands on a column of stone. Her talons sink deeply into the sandstone as she watches Camile writhe and roar in pain.

Camile's blood is spraying everywhere as she spins and thrashes. Aurora picking her moment, leaps off of the column to land on Camile again and starts to rip at her scales. Camile can almost reach Aurora when she slides off Camile's side to slip under her. In a swift decisive move, Aurora goes and disembowels Camile, using her talons to rip along the seam of her soft underbelly. Intestines slither their way out of Camile's abdomen and onto the pit's floor. Aurora is bathed in Camile's blood as she stands back, watching Camile look at her mortal wound.

In an attempt to save herself, Camile shifts back to human and begins to plead with Aurora, begging to be saved. Aurora shifts back to human and slowly saunters over to Camile. A soft smile plays upon Aurora's lips as she goes and embraces Camile. We are all really fucking puzzled by this show of sympathy from Aurora.

Ever so gently, Aurora kisses away Camile's tears then moves and kisses her lips, almost passionately. I am definitely having a what the fuck moment up here. It's hot as fuck that our mate is kissing another woman, but her? Just as Camile is getting lost in it, I hear the ignitor click.

Aurora swiftly becomes covered in frost and shoots her blue flames down Camile's throat. Aurora's flames burn through the back of Camile's neck, leaving the girl's severed head in Aurora's hand. Aurora spins around in the pit, holding up the head high, and our people cheer and chant her name. Every day I'm in awe of my mate and what she can do. Today, *awe* doesn't even come close to what I'm feeling right now.

Collectively we run down to the receiving room, where the fighters go after battle. Aurora is sitting on the back of one of the War Dragons in his shifted form. Thank the gods the room is big enough for him to be here. Aurora's hand is running over his scales, glowing faintly. If I'm correct, she is siphoning power from him to recharge herself to full strength.

When we arrive, Aurora slides down to the ground and walks over to us gracefully. She gives me a wink then mouths *fatality* to me. Apparently, we've been playing a little too much MK in our spare time.

We all take turns hugging and kissing Aurora, checking her over just to make sure she's in one piece. Out of the corner of my eye, I see one of the servants walking out with Camile's head on a silver platter, off to be prepared for the collection. Aurora is perfectly calm and relaxed as she moves between all of us. Tiamat and Ladon both chirp for their mother's attention, and Aurora gladly gives it to them. Aurora quickly moves to sit on the floor, allowing her to hug them both simultaneously.

Nicodeamus makes the motion to get me to follow him, so I do without question. "Yes, Dad?"

He smiles, looking at me, then back towards everyone else in the group. "Aurora's actions shocked us all tonight; you are not alone in feeling that way. Her great-grandmother was the last dragoness able to breathe fire in her human form. I don't know what King Oberon did, but whatever it was has made her more lethal." Nicodeamus shrugs his shoulders and looks at me. "How are you handling it, Jayce? I know you're more sensitive to her changes than the other mates."

I ponder his question for several moments before formulating a response. "It's scary how she goes from chaos to peace. The flaming death kiss was definitely over the top for ways to kill enemies. I love her and will do anything for her. But I'll be honest, that scared me." I motion with my hands back towards the pit and then look lovingly back at my mate before turning to Nicodeamus.

"I know she's better equipped to face what's coming, but that doesn't make me any less afraid for her. We have babies now. They need all of us." I sigh as I realize that I've gotten to the heart of what's really bothering me about all the changes.

Nicodeamus gives me a knowing smile and then kisses my temple. "See, you figured out the problem all by yourself. I'm proud of you, Jayce. Now you just need to talk to your mate and bond mates about your concerns. I'm sure everyone will be happy to listen to you." Nicodeamus just smiles and walks away.

CHAPTER 75

Jayce

We gather up Aurora and the babies. Returning to our suite, Klaus and I set up the bath for her with her favorite scents. The babies have shifted and are toddling along in their human forms, gods those two are adorable. Klaus and I wistfully look at the babies, imagining our own when the time comes. Aurora catches Klaus and me sitting on the floor with the babies playing with them, and she just kisses the tops of our heads before cannon balling into her bathtub.

Ladon and Tiamat shift and run towards the water. They both slide in without fear to swim with their mother. The rest of the guys eventually join us, watching Aurora bathe both babies in the tub. I don't know what's keeping my attention more, Aurora's boobs bobbing in the water or the babies getting their scales scrubbed with a loofa.

Aurora passes each clean baby off to Alaric to dry; he gets each baby to shift back to their human form and dresses them for bed.

Klaus and I are the only two left in the room with Aurora. I guess the guys are giving us some alone time with our mate. I look over at Klaus and motion towards Aurora; he catches my drift and strips and then slips into the water. I turn on the bubbler, then turn on the heater to keep the water hot. Aurora watches me closely; her curiosity is getting the better of her, to the point she's not really paying attention to Klaus.

Klaus slides up behind Aurora and lightly bites her shoulder over his old bite mark. "It's a whole different experience with me completely awake, Angel." Klaus lightly growls near Aurora's ear as I watch his hands grip her breasts to tease her erect nipples. I can tell by his stance he's lining himself up with her entrance, and suddenly he thrusts home. I hop myself up on the edge of the tub, watching Klaus take Aurora from behind.

Slowly, I begin to stroke my cock, watching and listening to them fuck in the tub in front of me. I have positioned myself above a bubbler, and Klaus notices it. Slowly, he maneuvers Aurora so that her breasts are tickled by the bubbles. "Angel, poor Jayce looks like he could use a hand. Why don't you suck his cock so he doesn't feel left out?" I raise an eyebrow looking over at Klaus. Mentally, I am giving him a high five right now.

Aurora's grey eyes look up at me as she braces her hands on either side of my thighs. "Is that what you want, love? Do you want to feel my lips around your cock? Do you want me to swallow every drop?" Aurora raises an eyebrow, knowing full well that I have a hard time verbalizing my desires. I playfully bop her nose with the tip of my leaking cock. All I can do is nod my head at her and offer her my throbbing shaft. Aurora is trying so hard to break me the rest of the way out of my shell. I moan softly as she takes my length deep into her throat. I can't help but move my hips in time with Klaus's thrusts.

Aurora suddenly releases my cock and screams out her orgasm; her hands shift, and her talons dig into the marble on the side of the tub. I look around me at the damage she's causing—at this point, I'm quite thankful she isn't holding my cock. Aurora's eyes are glowing, and she attacks my cock with a new intensity. Her hands shift back, and she starts to caress my balls as she leans on my thighs for support.

I'm close, so fucking close... I wrap her hair around my fist and start to meet her halfway, thrusting up into her mouth. Her animal grumbles its approval, adding vibration to the world's most epic blow job. My moans begin to deepen, and my thrusts become erratic. Klaus screams out his orgasm, thrusting one last time up into Aurora. He slides free of her pussy and comes up alongside of us. He moves me in such a manner so I'm kneeling on the side of the tub now.

Aurora stands up straight and continues to allow me to fuck her mouth. Klaus hops up onto the side of the tub and licks his index and middle finger; slowly, he presses them into my ass and starts finger fucking me. Oh, by the gods, I can't hold out much longer. It feels too fucking good; I don't want to stop. Without warning, Aurora releases my cock and jumps up onto the side of the tub with us; she drops onto all fours in front of me. She keeps wiggling her ass in my face, her puffy pussy dripping, begging me to bury myself deep within her. *Who am I to deny my mate?* I grip her hips tightly and pull her back hard, thrusting my cock deep within her tight, welcoming folds.

I thrust into her as hard as I can; I feel empty at the sudden loss of Klaus's fingers. He reaches around me and gathers some of Aurora's cum on his fingers; within seconds, my once empty ass is full of Klaus's cock. I almost blow my load feeling him penetrate me so deeply. I gasp and lose my rhythm for a moment. Aurora is close; I can feel her muscles twitching around me. I start to thrust into her once again. Klaus for the most part, has found a good distance to stand and allows me to impale myself upon him.

With all the friction and twitching from Aurora, I can't hold off any longer so I bite Aurora's back, instantly causing her to orgasm. Her muscles crush down upon my shaft, sending me crashing over the edge after her. The minute my thrusts slow down, Klaus starts pounding into me like a man possessed. Klaus's hand finds my throat and he grips it, pulling me back towards him. I love being handled like this. I love the dominance of my bond mates.

Aurora slides free of my cock and turns to watch Klaus dominate me. "This is so fucking hot, Jayce. I love watching the guys fuck you. I love watching the pleasure they give you." Aurora moves closer and begins to lick and bite my nipples. My once flaccid cock is hard and dripping again. Her hand moves to grip my shaft roughly as she jerks me off in time with Klaus's thrusts. Klaus's moaning gets louder, and Aurora rises up to look around me. "Don't you dare come yet. Jayce needs time." Aurora growls out her command, and amazingly Klaus obeys.

On the other hand, that just ramped up my arousal, and my cock starts to leak more than before. Aurora's eyes look down as I grip my cock taking it away from her. My one hand cupping my balls, the other gripping my throbbing cock—I'm jerking off as if my life depends on it. Aurora is smiling at me, then her eyes lock on my cock again. She drops to all fours once more and starts to lick at the tip of my dick. Feeling her tongue does me in. I come so hard, and without warning, I shoot my load all over Aurora's face.

Klaus, hearing me scream from my orgasm, comes hard in my ass and thrusts into me twice more before knotting, locking himself deep within me. He lays his head on my shoulder, looking down at a cum covered Aurora.

Klaus and I are scared for our lives, to the point the other mates come running into the bathroom to behold the disaster before us. I hear Alaric say, *"Oh, fuck."*

Then Dimitri is saying, *"Not good"* over and over again.

My fucking brother, Dominik, is taking pictures because he's an asshole. I'm holding onto Klaus for dear life because if I'm going to die, I'm taking the fucker with me. Aurora slowly stands up; my cum starts running and dripping off her face onto her chest. Suddenly, she reaches down between her legs and scoops up a large mass of our combined essence from her pussy. She proceeds to splat the side of mine and Klaus's face with it before heading off to the shower. I hear her in the distance, starting to laugh her ass off, then the shower starting.

I'm not sure if we're in the clear or if she is silently plotting revenge. Dominik walks up and crosses his arms over his chest. He's doing that cocky smirk that I'd love to punch him for. "So, genius, how does it feel to have committed the ultimate fuck up? I mean, seriously, I'd expect that from Alaric or Dimitri, but not you two fuckers." We look back at Dimitri and Alaric, and they are both nodding and laughing.

I can't help it, but I'm quite concerned for my personal well-being. I shot her, not Klaus. Granted, we're both wearing her goo on our faces but still, I'm pretty sure I'm going to be toast. Klaus's knot finally releases, and he withdraws slowly. I walk back to the shower stalls, open the first one and turn the water on. I step in and shower off quickly. If I'm going to die, I'm at least going to die clean.

I walk through the castle and it's silent, like scary silent. I'm absolutely paranoid at this point; I feel like I'm being hunted. More
than likely, I am. Aurora has a sick sense of humor. She'll get me
eventually.

Do you know what it's like to spend your day living in fear? *I do*.
Trust me, it's not fun. Everyone is prepping for the flight over to
Klaus's pack territory. Some of our troops are already en route to
meet up with Klaus's brother. Everyone is busy, and all my jobs
are complete. I head into the den and start a fire in the fireplace.

Carefully, I slide my favorite chair closer to the fire so I can enjoy
its warmth. I'm not sure at what point I dozed off, but boy, do I
feel so much better after my nap. I wake up to find everyone in the
den; the babies playing with toys on the floor. Aurora is
attempting to teach herself how to knit. *Who in their right mind
would give her stabby, pointy objects that she could kill someone with?*

Slowly, I rise and stretch, then reach for my phone on the side
table. My background is still Aurora topless with her arms shifted.
Our messenger app has twelve messages waiting to be opened. I
look around at everyone, and they are busy with entertaining the
twins. I pop the messages open; the first few are from the splat
heard around the world.

Fear rises in my gut and my wolf bristles beneath the surface of
my skin. I go to the next photo, and it's me creeping through the
halls trying to be cautious. I notice now that picture is from
Aurora. Fuck, she was hunting me. The next image is taken from
high above me, looking down as I move my chair into place. My
eyes fly up to the ceiling, and there are claw marks in the wood.

Again, that image also came from Aurora. I feel a distinct chill run
up my spine. Now I'm really getting frightened, there are three
more messages left, all from Aurora. The next is Aurora doing a

selfie with me sleeping in the background. The last picture is of her nipple next to my mouth while I slept. Ok, so it's not bad; she just fucked with me knowing my fear would be far worse than she would ever to me.

I rub my eyes, then look down at the backs of my hands; a brilliant iridescent blue coats my skin. It's that color blue the character Mimi—on that Drew show—used to wear. I open up my photo app on my phone, putting it in selfie mode. What the actual fuck?! I have long, fake eyelashes, peacock blue eyeshadow, and Aurora's signature blood-red lipstick on.

The room clears out, leaving only me and Aurora left. She's standing there with her full, pouty lips smiling at me like the cat that swallowed the canary. I'm feeling ballsy at the moment, so I approach her. I pin Aurora to the wall and kiss her hard. Aurora gasps and runs her fingers through my hair; I just smirk and pull away. "I apparently need to go use your makeup remover. I'll see you later." I turn to leave. I can smell her arousal in the air as I walk away. Score one for me. I lived and left her wanting. You can bet your ass she's going to make me pay for this later, but it will be well worth it.

CHAPTER 76
Aurora

Alaric circles Klaus's pack lands several times, allowing the babies and I to get a good view of the Black Forest. I scent the different game animals on the wind, and to be honest, I can't wait until I can go hunting. We land in a field not far from camp; Alaric shifts back and dresses quickly in the clothing I offer him.

Our children follow us in their dragon forms as we walk toward the main part of the camp. My eyes fall on the American Lycan pack and the Dire Wolves hanging out in a group by themselves. Jayce and Dominik are speaking with their brother Alex, catching up for lost time. Alex is inspecting their mating marks and smiling broadly, proud of his brothers.

Personally, I'm not comfortable in large groups, so this gathering is making me quite anxious. Alaric senses my uneasiness and wraps an arm around me, pulling me tight to his side as we make our way through the camp.

I spot Klaus surrounded by at least eight females, all of them trying to touch him. Nope. I'm not okay with this. It's cold, and there's snow on the ground, so what I have planned next really won't take too much effort on my part. I tilt my head to the side when I spot one of the Black Dragons nearby, I wiggle my fingers at him and he approaches. I push his sleeve up and place my hand on his forearm.

Now the fun begins. The ground rumbles, and an ice spire erupts out of the ground under Klaus, and elevates him ten feet off the ground. Klaus is basically standing on his very own ice pedestal. I know my eyes have that haunting glow to them; the frost I command coats my hair. I release the Black Dragon male I used for a boost, I really didn't take much from him this time. Alaric is trying to soothe me, and I just give him my best death glare. I tilt my head to the side, looking at the females still clamoring up at my mate. I turn my back to the crowd and shift. Thank the gods, I wore an outfit I wasn't fond of this time.

My beast's mass dwarfs all the Lycans present. I gained mass from Dimitri's Great Bear and more dragon characteristics from Alaric. I'm an almost ten foot tall, just about half-ton hybrid, bent on death and destruction. I click my talons together and shake out my armored dragon scale gauntlets. My snow-white fur and scales almost make me invisible against the wintery background. Out of the corner of my eye, I watch the American Lycans, and the dires flee the scene; they know what's coming next. I focus on the females who are still trying to get Klaus to go down. Dumb bitches don't even realize I'm here yet.

Without warning, I focus the full fury of my Alpha powers on the bitches trying to get to my mate. I'm growling, almost foaming at the mouth from rage. I watch him show them his mating bite from me, and still they try. Slowly, one by one, they turn to face me and start crying. I release my grip on that particular power only to howl my summoning howl, ripping the wolf from every single wolf that can hear my voice. The only beings unaffected are my mates and the very old.

The camp is filled with Lycans of all different shapes and sizes; there's a slight variation in color within the pack. I force the pack to remain as their beasts, and I use the pack link to speak to all of them in their minds. *I am Aurora, daughter of Anca Marelup and rightful heir to the Lycan throne. You either stand with me or against me. If you are with me, you have my protection. If you choose to stand against me, you will meet my talons in the pit. Decide now; I will not offer twice.* Wolves and Lycans only understand the old rule of *only the strong survive*. I will battle if I have to; I kind of want to after that long flight. It's been two weeks since my last decapitation. Shit, I sound like I am in a confessional. One by one, the Lycans and other assorted wolves kneel before me. Some hesitate, and I mark their faces in my memory. I will watch those five closely. I share that knowledge with my mates, and they agree to keep a close eye on them.

I release my grip on the pack and return to Alaric's side. Slowly, he removes his fleece and offers it to me. I shift back to my human form and slip on his shirt. I look back at the pack, and here comes Klaus with his mother and grandmother in tow. His mom seems pissed. I guess she wasn't a fan of me forcing the shift to prove who I am. "My Angel, I wish to introduce my mother to you," Klaus says, with so much love and affection.

His mom looks like the type of woman who should be filed under demon-in-law. Damn, that woman makes my resting bitch face look jovial. "Who the fuck do you think you are coming onto my land like this?" Klaus' mother questions without hesitation. My team hears his mom and starts backing away. My own mates start backing away as well. Klaus' grandmother starts cursing at his mother for being disrespectful. Klaus' mother turns quickly and stares down Elsa. "I don't fucking care who this bitch claims to be. She is no Marelup!"

I start that sadistic laugh of mine as I stare at this insolent female before me. I push up the sleeve on Alaric's shirt and shove my family brand in her face. She stares at the brand for several minutes then looks back up at me. By this time, my father is by my side and holds his brand next to mine. It's amazing how quickly someone changes their tune when they realize they are standing before the harbinger of death. Lucky for Klaus's mom, I promised him I wouldn't kill anyone today. I look over to Klaus, and he seems scared of what I may do. "My love, please make with the introductions. I'd like to eat and shower before the festivities." I'm tired and hungry, and trying my best not to lose my shit and kill his mom.

"My angel, this firecracker is my mom, Agnes. Mom, this is my mate, and queen of the Ice Dragons, and future queen of the Lycans, Aurora Marelup." Klaus finishes the introductions and kisses my cheek.

By this time, my remaining three mates flank me. My hatchlings sit at my feet, ready to breathe fire. I extend a hand to Klaus' mother, waiting to see what she does. Slowly, Agnes shows me her brand then grips my forearm. We hold onto each other silently, our grip firm. She attempts to look me in the eyes several times, and she's unable to for more than a few seconds. When she finally gives up and lowers her head, I lunge forward, biting her throat and growl. I wait for complete submission from her. My now extended canines applying pressure, almost to the point of breaking the skin. I hear her wolf whine, and her body goes limp, no sign of struggle or resistance left. I release her then grip her jaw, forcing her to look me in my now-shifted eyes.

"If you ever pull any of that bullshit again, I'll be having your heart for dinner." I let go of her jaw, and she stumbles backward. Promptly, Elsa starts to beat the fuck out of Agnes for her stupidity and disgraceful behavior. I tilt my head several times, watching the entertainment. Softly, I laugh and allow Klaus to lead us to what will be our home, for however long we need.

The Alpha House is impressive with high vaulted ceilings, carved support beams. These people really take pride in their work. I have to admit, it's an impressive sight to see. Fuck, I may recon-sider my decision to live in the castle after this. Klaus leads us to the back of the house to a room, I assume, in the master suite. Quickly, Klaus moves past all of us and locks the door. He moves to the bed and reaches under it, hitting a secret button. The bed raises, and there's a stairway leading down into the bowels of the house. Klaus raises one finger and makes the *shh* motion before heading down the stairs.

Curiosity has definitely gotten the better of me, so I follow. My children race down the stairs into the room below. Ladon starts to breathe fire, lighting up the room for a brief moment. Klaus finally makes it downstairs and turns on the light switch then hits the button to close the hatch above us. "Okay, so sorry about all the spy activity, but I had this constructed for us for when we need time away from everyone. The pack is nosy, very nosy, so I figured this would be awesome for us to have. We have a heated pool, a shower that can comfortably fit three. Oh! The master bed, wait till you see that." Klaus is like a little kid on Christmas morning; he can barely contain his excitement.

Klaus runs over, grabs my hand, and starts dragging me to the back. So I grab Alaric who in turn grabs Jayce, who grabs Dimitri, who finally grabs Dominik. We have literally formed a human chain and are being dragged through the hallways. Finally, we arrive at what Klaus is calling the master bedroom. This room looks like it was built for the sex Olympics. The fucking bed is absolutely mammoth; it can easily sleep all of us no matter what direction we decide to sleep in. There's a fucking massage table in the corner—what he's calling an inversion table. I'm already picturing how I'm going to use these items, and it's not for their intended use. I start rubbing my hands together like one of those cartoon villains.

"Oh shit, that look concerns me, babe. Where has your dirty little mind gotten to already?" Dominik is the first to question me, and I just smirk.

"Wouldn't you like to know? Play your cards right, and you may find out after tonight's celebration." I wink at Dominik, then head towards the showers. "Can someone grab my bags and bring them down here? I don't feel like socializing yet." Truth be told, my beast wants to make sure she has total dominion over all the other wolves, and I just can't allow that to happen yet.

Most of the guys leave except Dominik. I look over my shoulder as I turn on the shower. "Penny for your thoughts, Dom?" I step back under the water, looking at him.

Dominik looks down, and I can tell what he's about to say is really bothering him. "I was so hopeful... I mean... I was happy when we heard you were pregnant. I was happy that either my brother or I had fathered a pup with you." He sighs deeply, then roughly rubs his eyes with his hands and looks up to me. I hate this look; he's in so much pain.

I step out of the water and start to undo the buttons on his shirt, looking at him. I see Alaric is moving to come in to see what was wrong. Through the bond, I reach out to him. *Please leave, my love; Dom needs me. He's hurting because he was sure our babies were going to be his or Jayce's.*

Alaric's eyebrows shoot up, then understanding flitters across his features. *I'll tell the others. Remind him we love him,* Alaric says before leaving silently.

"I'm so sorry, Dom. I was honestly sure myself that the baby was either yours or Jayce's until things progressed the way they did." I rise up on my tippy toes and gently kiss his lips.

Shower sex isn't going to fix this. He needs my love and attention. It kind of explains why he's backed off some. I gently remove his belt and free him of his pants and I start pulling him back into the shower stall with me. I sit him on the bench and use the shower wand to get his hair wet before I start to wash his hair.

"Aurora, you don't have to wash me. I'm a big boy, I promise." Dominik smiles up at me. There's that smile I was hoping to see.

"You're right, Dom, I don't have to. I **want** to. You need my love and attention. You are hurting enough that you told me. I'm sorry I'm a bad mate and didn't see it sooner. The babies are a handful; I can only imagine what your momma went through with you and Jayce." I smile and bop his nose with my finger, leaving bubbles on the tip. I continue to run my nails over his scalp as I work the soap up to a good, thick lather.

Dominik wraps his thick arms around my waist and rests his head against my stomach. "You're not a bad mate; I just handled the news poorly. As for my mother, she's here if you would like to meet her." He looks up at me and I can't help but start to laugh. I am looking down at him between my boobs.

"Hmm, hopefully it's a warmer reception than I got from Klaus's mom. I really wish I didn't promise him I wouldn't kill anyone." I smirk, then grab the shower wand and start to rinse his hair for him. I remove every trace of soap, then I select the conditioner to work into his hair. "I'm just glad we could save your mom from your dad; he was a real douche canoe. I'm sorry, but he really was." After calling his father a name, I wince because that was rather insensitive since we watched my dad killed his.

CHAPTER 77

Aurora

Dominik suddenly stands and rinses his hair out then looks at me, his wolf surfacing. I stare at the golden glow of his wolf's eyes. I'm not using any of my Alpha powers on him. I like seeing the guys' animals in private; it's a trust thing, really. They know I won't use my strength of will against them.

"He deserved to die! He cut off your father's arm and held him hostage for over two hundred years. He raped my mother, as well as two of his other mates. He forced himself on any female he wanted because he could." I watch Dominik's muscles jump and shift under his skin from his wolf's agitation.

"That's not an Alpha; that's a serial rapist. Who knows how many half-siblings Jayce and I have in the pack." Oh boy, this has definitely struck a nerve with Dominik. I lower my eyes, feeling bad that I wrecked his mood. "Aurora, love, I'm sorry. My dad is a very touchy subject. It's mostly because of how he treated my mom,

Jayce, and Alex." Dominik starts to apply shampoo to my hair and work it into a lather.

"Then I don't feel bad for my part in his demise. You're not your dad, Dominik. You're a very kind and gentle mate. That is unless I want it a bit rougher at night." I smile, looking at him.

I want him to see how much love I have for him. "After we take back my mother's castle when my next heat comes, Alaric is going to head to the Ice Dragon castle and will stay there until my heat is over. All four of you will have an equal shot at being a dad. As long as I nurse the babies, I won't go into heat for a while. For now, Klaus's grandmother has herbs to help me sleep through the next heat until we are safe to have more babies." I honestly do look forward to having kids with each of the guys. I raise an eyebrow out of reflex, thinking about delivering Dimitri's baby. Wow, that's going to hurt. I truly hope and pray my hoo-ha survives.

"What thought just crossed your mind, love?" Dominik asks as he begins to rinse my hair.

"Dimitri's cub…" I really don't need to say more; the look on Dominik's face says it all.

"Fuck! I didn't think about that. Oof… Don't worry, I volunteer as tribute to lick your hoo-ha till it's all better." Dominik starts to laugh as he finishes working the conditioner into my hair.

I can't help but laugh along with Dominik as he massages my scalp. "I'm sure there will be another rock, paper, scissors tournament over this honor too."

I look up to Dominik as innocently as I can manage. "Yes, I know all about how you guys fairly decide the nightly sleep order."

I lightly tap my chin. "Maybe I should make it easy and take on a sixth mate, so you guys can rotate out in pairs?" I say it jokingly, but by the look on Dominik's face I know he's already talking to the others.

"Sold! We agree a flight shifter, or a tiger would be cool. Alaric says he knows some nice Siberian Tigers." Dominik says it with such a straight face, I stop breathing from shock.

All I can do is just double blink, looking at him, then I turn my attention to the other assholes in my family. I focus hard on them and force their asses to enter the bathroom. I stand up and rinse my hair out, then turn off the water and grab a nearby robe.

I stare at the five of them, and each one looks more guilty than the next. "What the actual fuck are you assholes thinking? It's not like I can go to the corner store and pull a sixth mate off the fucking shelf!" I wouldn't say I'm angry per se; shocked and taken back is more like it, and it's causing me to lash out.

Alaric gets all suave and gives me his best smile. "Well, a sixth mate solves many problems. Sleeping arrangements are one. All the chores can be equally and fairly divided. No one is left holding his own cock when we all do our thing." I raise an eyebrow and start to laugh.

"You fuckers have been planning this conversation for a long time. I can tell. It's why Alaric is delivering the proposal." I'm practically yelling at them, holy fuck! How long have these assholes been planning this coup?

"How did you know?" Dimitri pipes up, looking like the kid that just got busted with his hand in the cookie jar.

I shake my head and laugh more. "Y'all fucked up! Usually, you send Jayce with the ideas that may piss me off. Alaric, Klaus, or Dominik doing it is a dead giveaway you planned this."

I wrap my robe tightly around myself as I look between the five of them. "*If* there's another suitable mate, I will decide if I accept him." I exit the room and promptly hear high fives being exchanged behind me. Jerks...

I shake my head and head into the master bedroom, then into the walk-in closet. Damn, Klaus went all out; my wall is organized and stocked by color. The boys have racks that pull out of the opposite wall. We have a party tonight with dancing and feasting, so I don't want to wear anything over the top.

I find a blood-red sweater and pair it with some insulated black leggings. Slowly I move over to the shoe rack and search for cute boots to go with what I'm wearing. Hmm... fuck it. I pull out a pair of black Docs and red fuzzy socks. I return to the master bedroom and find my box with my crowns in it. I pull out my great-grandmother's ruby crown and place it upon my head. Perfect!

The guys are all gathered, having what they think is a quiet discussion. Dimitri keeps shooting down everyone else's ideas. I sneak up behind Dimitri and lean on his back, wrapping my arms around his neck. I kiss his cheek then look to the others. "Are we ready to go to the party? Elsa has agreed to watch the twins tonight so we can enjoy ourselves." I smile and arch an eyebrow looking at them.

"Da, let's get going, boys. Our mate wants to have some fun," Dimitri says. He grabs my arms, which are still around his neck, as he stands up, taking me with him. Quickly, he releases my arms and grabs my thighs, hiking me up his back for a piggyback ride. I start laughing hysterically because I can't wrap my legs completely around Dimitri's waist.

"Tally ho, D! There's food to be eaten, drinks to be drunk, and music to be danced to." I reach down and smack his ass, making my hand sting.

"Don't start nothing you can't finish, baby girl." I kiss Dimitri's cheek and nuzzle his beard.

"Have I ever not followed through, D?" I lean forward and try to look him in the eye. My eyes shift to that of my beast. Dimitri smiles then kisses my cheek.

"You do, love," Dimitri tells me. The soft rumbles of his bear can be heard and felt. I can't help but smile, happy that he's finally all mine.

We make our way through the house and out to where the packs have gathered. There are three food stations, two large bars, and a giant dance floor with a DJ. I slide off Dimitri's back and run to the dance floor. I move my body in time with the bass hits, lost in my own world. I close my eyes, feeling all the beings around me. My link with the packs, as well as the dragons, has grown considerably.

I can tell the moment that any of my mates approach me; their bodies' vibrations are different from the others. Their aura vibrates, not only with their life essence but also an echo of mine. I feel Dominik's strong hands grip my hips as he pulls my ass flush with his crotch. I don't bother opening my eyes, reveling in the feeling of the connection that we have at this moment. I feel a second set of hands, also resonating with my essence—it's Klaus. He's in front of me, his hands caressing my face. We move in time with the music, bumping and grinding in a sensual dance just for us.

The guys eventually break off; I'm left all hot and bothered. I watch them head up to what looks like a makeshift stage. Alaric takes Dominik's position behind me, and I open my eyes to see where my other two mates have gone.

The music switches to something more American, "SAIL" from Awolnation comes on. Now, I have to say, I've been to a few male reviews in my time, but holy shit, is this hot. Two of my mates are gyrating in time, exactly to the beat of the song they have chosen. I pull Alaric towards the stage, that way I have a front-row seat to the entertainment. They are lost in the music, moving exactly like the guys did in the movie that used this song. I watch them both intently, occasionally they lock eyes with me, and I know the dance is just for me. I did not know either one of them could move like this—you know who's testing that out later.

The song switches and they slowly remove themselves from the stage. Thunderous applause from the females in the packs greets them. Thankfully, no one now is stupid enough to even attempt to get close to them. My skin hums with anticipation, knowing full well that I will have a private show later. They both approach me and take me from Alaric. Dominik kisses me passionately, pulling me up off my feet and flush to his chest.

When Dominik finally releases me, Klaus picks me up, allowing my legs to wrap around his waist and starts dancing with me, kissing me tenderly. I feel Dimitri press up behind me, only to steal me from Klaus' grip. I can't help but laugh at the guy's antics. Poor Jayce is standing off to the side, kicking at rocks. My heart breaks seeing him so upset. I kiss Dimitri and motion towards Jayce. Dimitri nods and slowly lowers me to the ground.

I blend myself into the crowd and grab two red wine glasses before heading over to Jayce. "What's a sexy wolf like you doing here all alone? I could just eat you up." I playfully snap my teeth at him, and he finally smiles. He really enjoys it when we role-play sometimes.

"Well, I was waiting for my beautiful and lethal mate to want to dance with me. But the others, well, they always get there first." Jayce lowers his eyes, and I want to cry. I rush over and hug him tightly.

"I am so sorry, my love. I love you so very much. I hold none above the other. I'm sorry you're feeling this way." I kiss his lips ever so softly. I hate feeling as if I've wounded my gentle mate. I hate to have favorites, but for my emotional needs, when I feel I need a gentle touch, it's Jayce. It's always Jayce that guards my heart. He reminds me that I am more than just my animal; he reminds me that my life doesn't just have to be about killing.

"Shhh, my love, I'm a lot tougher than most give me credit for. I know Dom talked to you; we were both hurt when we realized the baby wasn't ours. We're twins, so it really didn't matter to either of us who fathered the child. Genetically there's only one or two genomes difference between us. More than likely, when one of us does father a child with you, it will end up in twins again." Jayce smiles, looking at me, happy with the possibility of multiple sets of twins.

Wow, that just knocked my world off-axis; another two sets of twins are possible. Fuck me sideways! Well, I did always want a large family, so I guess this is one way to do it. I smile softly at Jayce, rest my head on his chest, and then press my nose under his chin. In one sense, it can be viewed as a sign of submission. To my family, it's more a sign of trust. I am blessed that my beast is trusted this close to his tender throat.

Lightly, I run my tongue up the artery in Jayce's throat, my beast rumbles in my chest. I nip his jaw then kiss him. "You will be in my bed alone tonight. You need me just as much as I need you." Jayce's eyes light up, and his smile shines brighter than the brightest star.

"Sounds like a wonderful plan, sweetheart. Shall we soak in the bath together before bed? I'll give you a massage?" Jayce truly knows how to spoil a girl. Fuck, how did I get so fucking lucky? I'm lost in the adonis known as Jayce until I hear Klaus trying to whisper yell at a female to leave him alone.

Jayce knows the minute my beast awakens. It's already cold out, but I am making it damn near arctic conditions. I slowly strip off the beautiful red sweater I'm wearing and hand it to Jayce as we approach where Klaus is. The other guys are there, along with an older man trying to reason with Klaus about accepting his daughter. My mates sense my bloodthirsty mood; others feel the temperature drop before they notice me. My eyes have shifted to my beast's, mercury dragonic orbs lock on the female that's attempting to touch my mate.

Klaus is doing his best to keep her at arm's length, but that bitch is slipperier than an eel. Swiftly, I close in; my movements are nothing but a blur to onlookers. I grab the female by her shoulders and throw her a good twenty feet away from Klaus. Quickly, I shift my stance and then my arms to my dragon-scaled gauntlets. I click my talons in agitation, staring the stupid female down.

She shifts and charges, her movements seem off as if she's not moving of her own volition. No matter, I don't budge one inch. Instead, I remain relaxed; the minute she's close enough, I raise my hand and hit the dead center of her chest. She's sent flying backward with her chest partially frozen solid. I just sent icicles through her heart with a single hit. Another female's life wasted; another unnecessary kill on my hands.

I run and jump up on stage and use my Alpha powers to draw everyone's attention to me. Through the pack bond, I decide to speak to everyone at once. *My people. One thing I am not lenient with is someone attempting to poach a bonded mate. I have a feeling she was under the witch Elena's power. I will be hunting that bitch very soon. For now, do not eat or drink anything unless someone you completely trust gives it to you. She has blood magic and the power to create false bonds and loyalties. I will protect us all the best I can, but you need to help me by protecting yourself the best you can. I'm only one being; I can only do so much. If anything concerns you, please speak to me, or one of my mates, or my father.* I watch the pack's response, and one by one they lower their heads slightly to me then go back to the party.

I hop down off the stage and look at my guys. "It's begun. I will hunt Elena soon. Up the training on our fighters, pair each Dire with a Lycan. Give each team a dragon to lead them. If we can find the bears, we'll see if they have the numbers to help." My eyes move to Dimitri and I smile. "I've located your clan; we leave in the morning to go see them. Alaric, Dimitri and I will be riding Dante to get to the bears. I need you and my other mates to keep the camp running as usual and keep the babies safe. Dante will be flanked by Edgar and Marco; I'll have two War Dragons and a Black Dragon with us."

Alaric contemplates the information I've just given him and strokes his beard. Having heard their names, the dragons in question arrive and bow to us before awaiting Alaric's judgment. "I'd prefer you riding Marco and let Dante and Edgar flank him. Size-wise the War Dragons are more maneuverable than Marco's giant Black Dragon."

Alaric crosses his thick arms over his chest then turns to look at the dragon men. "You will be traveling with my heart; protect it with your lives. You will also have my bond mate, protect him like you would your own brother." The three dragon guards nod, bring their fists to their chests, and bow. Oddly, the three dragons and Alaric slice their palms and shake hands. They just gave their oath in blood. Okay then, I feel a fuck ton safer now.

The party rages on well into the night, everyone getting to know each other and bonding wonderfully. Dimitri, Jayce, and I slip off by ourselves sometime around one in the morning. Dimitri and I need sleep, and Jayce needs quality time with me. Jayce was kind enough to share his time with me with Dimitri too. We snuggle and fuck until we are tired, morning is going to get here quickly, and we have a mission to complete.

CHAPTER 78
Dimitri

March-

Morning has come, and Aurora is asleep with her head on my chest. Jayce is curled up behind Aurora so tightly. I honestly hate disturbing both of them, but I'm kind of anxious about seeing my clan's descendants. Gently, I kiss Aurora's lips, and I can feel the rumble from her beast. I still get concerned when I hear it; that thing makes me feel small. Slowly, her eyes open, then she rolls to kiss Jayce awake. He immediately pouts because he knows it's time for us to leave. Sleepily, he extracts himself from the bed and heads out of the room. "Are you ready, Aurora?" I ask her softly, my thick accent rolling off my tongue like silk.

Aurora smiles up at me, then lunges and kisses the tip of my nose. "Yup! Let's go!" Aurora climbs over me to get to the other side of the bed. Apparently, walking around the bed was too much trouble for her.

Aurora disappears into the walk-in closet and comes out fifteen minutes later wearing an all-leather outfit. There's thicker leather on the inside of her thighs and the crotch, like those fancy equestrian pants. Her jacket is perfectly tailored and makes her tits look phenomenal. I watch Aurora struggle with braiding her hair, so I go over to where she is and knock her hands away.

Aurora smiles up to me sweetly and offers me her brush. Fuck, I think I just got played. She runs over and sits in a chair, waiting for me to come over and braid her hair for her. I do two french braids in her hair, parting it right down the middle. "Let's go; the dragons are probably waiting for us to arrive at this point."

Aurora points over by the door. "My go-bag has been packed and ready since yesterday; I even packed yours, D. You're welcome." She sings the last part, like the Hawaiian demigod in that kid's movie she loves so much.

I can't help but start to sing the song in my head. Andre and Aurora drove me absolutely nuts with that fucking movie. *Andre.* I honestly haven't thought about my best friend in a very long time. I've been so focused on revenge and Aurora that I haven't had time to wallow in my grief over his loss. I follow Aurora out where the second biggest dragon I've ever seen is lying in the field. This dragon isn't as big as Nexus was, but fuck, he's damn close to it.

Aurora strides up like it's nothing and rubs his nose gently. Alaric is at her side, giving directions as Dante and Edgar make lazy circles in the air waiting for us. I approach the dragon and look at all the spines along his back. There's one spot before his wings that I'll fit in. "Alaric? Where's Aurora sitting?" I look over the length of the dragon, then back to Alaric.

"She'll be riding up on his head behind his horns, so she can direct him easily. Don't worry, big guy, she'll be safe up there." Alaric smiles, not a single worry in his mind. Me, I'm ready to freak the fuck out thinking about all the danger she'll be in without me.

I turn to watch Aurora's eyes take on that haunting look as she stares up at Marco. His amber eyes glow faintly as he stares back down at her. Fuck, is she talking to him? What the fuck can't she do these days besides fly? Marco lowers his massive head to the ground and moves his wing forward. Aurora steps onto his wingtip and gets lifted up to the crown of horns on his head.

I watch her find a comfortable position and sit down like she's done this a hundred times before. Hesitantly, I move over to his side and look up to where Alaric suggested I sit. "Baby girl? How am I supposed to get my fat ass up there?" I look back to where I'm supposed to sit, then back to Aurora. The next thing I know, I get slapped on the back of my head by Alaric. "What the fuck did you do that for?" I practically growl out at Alaric.

"Brother, Aurora said to do it because she doesn't like you calling yourself fat. She thinks you're perfect just the way you are." Alaric shrugs his shoulders then looks back to Aurora.

"Climb on Marco's wing when he extends it, then walk along the bone to his back. Try not to step on the leather of his wing; that will hurt him," Alaric says, then pats me on the back before backing up.

Marco extends his wing, and I examine the scales along the bone. They could be used as stairs the way they overlap along the bone. I carefully climb along the scales on his wing bone, being very mindful not to step on his wing's leather. I reach his back, and trust me, I'm fucking thankful I made it up here.

Great Bears are not known for being the most graceful creatures. My eyes move along the planes of his massive back and see the area where I was instructed to sit. I finally get myself situated when the dragon starts to stand up. I hold onto the spine for dear life. Aurora, on the other hand, is standing up, leaning back against the spine behind her. I see her hands are shifted, and she has a good grip on the horns in front of her. Aurora lets out a call that's a true mixture of her dual nature; it's a cross between a roar and a howl. The moment her call is done, Marco launches us into the air. I feel my stomach head towards my ass from the sheer power of Marco's take-off.

Aurora is laughing hysterically, enjoying the wind in her face. I can feel through the bond the worry from Jayce and Klaus; Dominik is playing it cool. Alaric is the only one I'm not really sensing.

A few moments later, I see exactly why I'm not sensing him. He has shifted to his dragon and has decided to escort us to the edge of the pack lands. Aurora is smiling and waving at Alaric as he flies beside us. With a dragon Marco's size, we should reach the bear territory's outer edge in about forty-five minutes. Alaric roars his goodbye at the edge of the region. Aurora turns her head and calls back to him; I can see a sadness there. I have to admit, I'm a bit jealous of the bond that they share. Alaric and Klaus have the best understanding of her beast's nature. I have the best under-standing of *whom* she is.

Marco starts making a clicking noise, and I see Aurora nod. Slowly, that crazy female makes her way back towards me. Aurora is walking down Marco's back like she would around the porch on the house. "D, we're getting ready to land. I came back here to help you through the landing. Unlike last time you rode in the carriage box, this is much different. You need to stand up." Slowly, I slide my way up the spine I'm leaning against, then look to Aurora for the next step. "Okay, so here's the easy part, brace yourself between the spine behind you and the one in front of you. Marco will lower his head before he starts the descent, so that will give you a warning to brace. Alaric said that Marco is going to take every precaution to make the landing as soft as possible."

Aurora leans forward and kisses me softly before she turns and runs back up to her position on Marco's head. Aurora raises her arms over her head like we are on a roller coaster, then it happens. I watch Marco's head lower, and I feel like the ground is coming out from under me. I hope I don't embarrass myself by puking. Quickly, the falling feeling lessens, and I'm okay with the speed we are going. I'm guessing Aurora said something to Marco because he changed his approach.

We land softly on one of the higher hillsides overlooking the forest of my youth. I smile, breathing in the air of my homeland. Things have changed since I was last here; there's actually a dirt road leading towards where our camp used to be. I slide off Marco's back and look around at the hill's grass and dirt. The bear prints I find are old, but it's a good sign my people are nearby. I look at my right forearm and roll up my sleeve. I have the brand of my clan and the brand of the house of Marelup as a royal guard. If we find my people, I will have to show them my brands to validate who I am.

Aurora eventually goes and talks to Marco, and he takes off, leaving us till we need him. "Ready to play hide and go seek, D?" Aurora smiles at me as she adjusts the straps on the backpack she's brought with her.

I slowly take my pack off of my back and start to strip. "I'm going to shift so it's easier for me to track my people. Besides, each family covey has specific markings as their bear. I may be the last of my bloodline, or maybe not. Either way, they will accept who I am much faster as my animal than if we both approach as humans." Aurora nods in understanding as I remove the last of my clothing. I feel her eyes roam all over my body. It's times like this I am thankful for all the extra training I do.

Aurora finishes stuffing my clothes into my bag then waits for me to shift. My bones break and realign slowly. Unlike the wolves, unless I'm angry my shift is slow and methodical. When my shift is finally over, I stand on my hind legs and roar, alerting the others to my presence. It's a cultural thing for a dominant boar to announce his presence before entering another boar's territory. I lower myself back down to four legs and listen for any kind of a response. In the distance to the north, I hear an answering roar. For now, we are welcome in his territory. I swing my head back to Aurora and lie down; carefully, Aurora climbs onto my back. She manages to clip the two packs together, arranging them to rest over my shoulders so she doesn't have to support their combined weight.

Slowly, I start to head in the direction of the roar I had heard. The silver fir trees along the main game trail randomly bare the dominant boar's claw marks. Aurora looks at the marks then back down to me. *He's not as large as I am; if anything over time, my people may be no bigger than the common brown bear.* I say to Aurora through the bond.

"Do you think he's smaller than I am, D?" Aurora asks. I'm pretty sure she is just testing me. Her beast rivals mine when I'm on my hind legs.

It's safe to say. I believe he's smaller than both of us, I say to her through the bond again. If my bear were able to smirk, we would definitely be smirking right now. The game trail leads us through some of the most beautiful sections of the forest. Aurora is enjoying our journey; she's looking in all different directions, catching all the new scents. I can tell she's trying to resist the urge to hunt the roe deer, as well as the chamois.

We come up to a water crossing, and I stop then lie down. Aurora takes the hint and slides off my back, taking the bags with her. Slowly, I wade into the water to test its depth. It's not bad at all, and for the most part I'll be able to keep her dry. While I stand in the stream, I notice a good-sized wild trout population swimming in and out of the current.

Quickly, I plunge my head under the water and catch a medium-sized trout. I whip my head to the side to throw the trout towards Aurora on the bank. She starts to laugh hysterically as she catches the fish when it hits her on her chest. "Lunch!" Aurora yells as she moves back a bit, then smashes the trout's head with a rock, ready for me to catch another. I haven't seen her so happy being in the outdoors in such a long time. I throw three more fish to her, and she's having giggle fits over it.

I climb back up onto the bank and shake out my fur, sending water flying everywhere. Aurora is still laughing, now over the water getting to her from way over here. I shift back to my human form and grab my pants from the bag. It felt good to hunt for my mate and to provide for her as my bear. He's so proud of himself right now it's not even funny anymore. Aurora has shifted her hands and started to use her talons to gut the fish.

I pull the fire starter out and make a small fire to cook our fish. I turn around to find Aurora already eating one of the fish raw. I just end up double blinking as I watch her. I was not aware that she can still tolerate raw fish. "What? I was hungry, and cooking would take too long," Aurora states so matter of fact, like it was the most natural thing in the world. I just start laughing and join her in eating my fish raw. I'm just thankful one of her natures just made this trip a fuck-ton easier. We enjoy our meal in relative silence before going and discarding the skeletons far away from where we stopped.

Aurora cleans up quickly, then walks over to me and kisses my lips softly. "Thank you for lunch, D. I haven't had fresh fish since the last time I went hunting. Trust me when I say fishing is not in my wheelhouse. I missed more fish than I came close to catching. My only really successful fishing trip was in the birthing cavern," Aurora says, shrugging her shoulders. "If you want a deer, I'm your girl. Fish, yeah, we'll starve before I catch one." She starts laughing at herself. At least she knows what her strong suit is.

"Let's get going. It's going to get cold when the sun sets. I'm hoping we find the camp before then." Aurora nods, agreeing with me, so I begin to strip so I can shift and carry her. My shift is smooth and comfortable; it feels great to spend so much time as my bear. After I stretch out, I lie down and make it easier for Aurora to load the bags and get back on. Once she's situated, I rise up onto my paws and start walking towards the stream. After having fished the stream, I know where the shallow parts are. I take the higher route to keep Aurora dry.

Serenity Rayne spends most of her time either howling at the moon or creating cheeky crafts in her lair. Since she published the first book in the bestselling Aurora Marelup series, she's released sixteen more books while surviving being a nurse during the COVID-19 pandemic.

Serenity writes strong women who find their way in the world through blood and fire, learning to love and trust the men who adore them. Her books also feature positive LGBTQ representation, loss, and all the emotions that transcend species. Though her catalog has been focused on paranormal why choose and horror, she is now branching out to write contemporary why choose as well. She lives on a farm with dogs, chickens, peacocks,

a one-eyed horse, and her son, who is way more like her than he
wants to admit.

Follow Serenity Everywhere:

Facebook: Serenity Rayne

Readers Group

Twitter: Author Serenity Rayne

Instagram: Author Serenity Rayne

Goodreads: Serenity Rayne

BookBub: Serenity Rayne

Amazon: Serenity Rayne

Website: https://www.serenityrayne.com

WebStore - https://serenityrayneromance.com/

Innate

Balance

Destroyer

Daughters of the Destroyer - Nikita

Stand alones:

Heart Shaped Box

Blood Moon Pack

Once Upon the a Raven